THE NEWS CLOWN
A NOVEL BY THOR GARCIA

EQUUS

© Thor Garcia, 2012

ISBN 978-0-9571213-2-4

Equus Press
Birkbeck College (William Rowe), 43 Gordon Square, London, WC1 H0PD, United Kingdom

Typeset by lazarus
Cover design by Ned Kash
Printed in the Czech Republic by PB Tisk

All rights reserved.

Composed in Aldus, designed by Hermann Zapf (1954), named for the fifteenth-century Venetian printer Aldus Manutius.

AUTHOR'S NOTE: The characters and situations in this work are wholly fictional and imaginary and do not portray, and are not intended to portray, any actual persons or parties. Any similarity to actual persons or events is coincidental, and no reference to the present day is intended or should be inferred.

In Memory

Elizabeth Bennett (1968 - 1993)

Michael J. Gallant (1955 - 2005)

THE NEWS CLOWN

1. **SHOCK CLAIM: Clown Says 'I'm The Greatest!'** *Page 11*
   THOR declares his intention to explode "journalism" at its core, bringing the city to its knees in a rain of shame & indictments. He explains his work at CITIES NEWS SERVICES, covering BAY CITY'S crime & mayhem, his duty to bear witness. Introduction to the NEWS EDITOR KATE UHLI & the founding editor, DICK TRIMBLES. *(10 news articles)*

2. **LOADED: Clown Boards Midnight Train to Oblivion!** *Page 24*
   THOR & JERRY visit CANDACE & HEATHER'S apartment. JERRY tells a story about an affair involving CANDACE & HEATHER'S mother & their family being threatened by the Russian mafia. HUGH arrives, everyone gets loaded & goes to play pool. Back at the apartment, THOR shares an intimacy with HEATHER, after which she tells him to leave. *(1 news article)*

3. **ANIMALS! Young Girl Shot by Vicious Thugs** *Page 34*
   THOR covers the shooting death of a nine-year-old girl, whose cousin spits at him when he tries to ask questions. Introduction to the CHIEF EDITOR ROB SERNATH & fellow reporters RICHIE – who routinely mocks THOR & his pretensions – & TOMMY-G, who seems to be an albino. *(7 news articles)*

4. **CURVEBALL: Gal Pal's Baseball Delight!** *Page 48*
   THOR goes to a Cuban restaurant & a baseball bar with KATE, who talks about stories she covered during her old job in Miami. She invites THOR to her apartment. THOR declines, buys a bottle of vodka & walks home. He is beaten by a security guard outside a transition home. *(1 magazine article)*

5. **ADDLED: Young Men Stupid Enough to Live with Worms!** *Page 58*
   THOR describes life among the winos, junkies & prostitutes in the Silvertown area of Bay City. THOR & JERRY discover WORMS living in the ceiling of their apartment.
   (1 news article, footnote)

6. **FIGHTIN' WORDS! Clowns Talk Love, Get in Brawl** *Page 66*
   TV journalists report warning of "possible terrorists on the loose." THOR & JERRY struggle to achieve their dreams of art & stardom. They discuss love, get in a fist fight.

7. **MNUNG'S WORLD: President to Naughty Dick: Drop Dead!** *Page 74*
   PRESIDENT WOLFGANG G. MNUNG announces launch of Operation: Peace, Freedom, Security, Justice & Liberty in historic address from the Oval Office.

8. **PATRIOTS DEMAND: Stop Smoking Crack!** *Page 83*
   THOR covers son's axe-murder of parents. At a ball game, JERRY tells THOR that HEATHER went to the Alps for special health treatment. THOR observes patriotic display at ball game. He & JERRY join with crowd in chanting at youths to "Stop Smoking Crack!" *(3 news articles)*

9. **WHEN FOOLS RUSH IN: Ivy Leaguer Joins Clown Squad!** *Page 93*
    The Ivy Leaguer SCOTT T. VARICK comes to work at Cities News Services. THOR covers arrest of REVEREND LANGLEY CHOWDERMILK, accused of sexual assaults on children. *(3 news articles)*

10. **LOVEBIRDS: Drunken Romance Flowers at Sad Wedding!** *Page 99*
    THOR attends the wedding of an old college friend, SAMANTHA, whose mother is dying. THOR describes some of his college experiences, the person he was in college. At the wedding, THOR has an intimate encounter with TERRI, drinks too much & vomits. *(1 footnote)*

11. **IN OUR TIME: War is Over, Clowns Drink Free!** *Page 112*
    THOR watches PRESIDENT MNUNG war victory celebration on television. SCOTT VARICK has been promoted after nine weeks on the job, & THOR attends a party in his honor at the 50 Million club. VARICK displays his wit & wisdom, buys drinks for everyone. *(2 news articles)*

12. **HIDE IN 'PLANE' SIGHT: Cannibals on the Loose!** *Page 118*
    THOR has no money & goes to ex-temping colleague GENE KEAKS' house for free booze. They watch *Cannibal Holocaust*, discuss presidential assassination attempts & the 9/11 attacks.

13. **GANG BANG! Clowns Crash Massacre Meltdown** *Page 124*
    THOR recalls his office's reaction to 9/11 attacks. He leaves GENE'S house & goes to a hospital to report on victims of a mass shooting. *(1 news article, 1 footnote)*

14. **BRAIN DRAIN: Cops Claim Man Not Used For Target Practice!** *Page 133*
    THOR covers police shooting of an unarmed man. Also: Transcript of PRESIDENT MNUNG news conference on location at president's Mississippi ranch set. Event features water balloon fight between visiting Saudi & Israeli envoys. *(1 news article)*

15. **LET GOD SORT HIM OUT: Christ Commits Suicide!** *Page 140*
    The ROCK STAR CHRIST SUNBEAM commits suicide. THOR & JERRY drink whisky, THOR remembers the magic & mania of SUNBEAM'S incredible career.
    (2 footnotes, 1 magazine article)

16. **BLOCKBUSTER: Clown Clutches, Touches Rich Babe!** *Page 148*
    THOR & JERRY host party for SUNBEAM'S suicide. HEATHER attends with an older man, CURTIS, a photographer. THOR meets CHRISSY. They smoke drugs & he kisses her. *(1 footnote)*

17. **OPERATION SCUMBAG: Clown, Cops Team Up for Drug War Combat!** *Page 155*
    THOR goes out on a night reporting mission with the Bay City drug detectives WODGERS & BANTING. THOR participates in bust of drug suspects. *(1 news article)*

18. **ENCORE: Clown Hits Sex-Pot with Juicy Babe!** *Page 165*
    CHRISSY calls THOR at office, invites him to her new house. They have sex in CHRISSY'S pool, eat hamburgers & watch a Bruce Willis film.

19. **KILL CITY: Send in the Clowns!** *Page 177*
    THOR & RICHIE attend MAYOR FAVELLA'S press conference after 37 people are killed in 36 hours in an unprecedented Bay City crime wave. RICHIE is thrown out of conference after angrily questioning the police seizure of just four guns in a crackdown. *(10 news articles)*

20. **DIZZY: Babe Leads Love-Drunk Clown by Nose!** *Page 186*
    THOR begins living at CHRISSY'S house. THOR describes their life together, incidents in CHRISSY'S past. They "appeared to live in a state of high intelligence & being, untroubled by daily hassles." THOR meets CHRISSY'S mother, MAXINE, who suffers from Parkinson's, & her boyfriend, GERARD. They attend the Feed World Hunger benefit with Hollywood stars. *(3 news articles, 2 footnotes, one transcript)*

21. **UNGLUED: Paranoia Peaks as Clown Lives Lush Life!** *Page 211*
    THOR & CHRISSY attend Passover celebration in New York. They return to Bay City, where CHRISSY is threatened by a man masturbating in a parking lot. THOR gets paranoid. They have a disagreement over the French film *Hell Is My Body & Other People's*. CHRISSY gets emotional, asks THOR if he loves her. *(4 news articles)*

22. **LUNA-CRAZY: Love Gets Loopy in Mountain Paradise!** *Page 223*
    MAYOR FAVELLA launches "Permanent Crime Amnesty For The City" crackdown. CHRISSY introduces THOR to anal sex. CHRISSY leaves to visit a spiritual guru in the mountains, an experience that leads to her painful confession of a college abortion. CHRISSY & THOR go to the Lunabear new-age convention in Colorado. THOR watches coverage of terrorist attack in Russia on television, gets drunk. CHRISSY locks him out of hotel room. *(5 news articles, one footnote)*

23. **HAIL, HAIL! The Clown King is Dead – Long Live the Clown** *Page 240*
    DICK dies. THOR attends funeral service & staff party, gets drunk. KATE corrals him into a taxi & takes him to her apartment, where he spends the night. *(1 news article)*

24. **HELL HATH NO: Babe Fury at Cad Clown!** *Page 250*
    THOR & CHRISSY have a fight. CHRISSY storms out, drives off somewhere for the night. THOR gets drunk & watches TV news. *(2 news articles, 1 press release)*

25. **MOMMY'S LITTLE HELPER: A Clown's Homecoming** *Page 260*
    THOR goes home for HIS MOTHER'S birthday, watches television with his mother & her husband, HANK. Hank tells dirty jokes, shows THOR inventions he's working on in the garage. THOR goes to a mall to buy gifts for his mother, including a PRESIDENT MNUNG DOLL. *(2 book excerpts, 2 footnotes)*

26. **NO MÁS: Clown Pounded in Fist Frenzy!** *Page 274*
    THOR goes out with his boyhood friend, TOBY, who is married with children & works as a prison guard. They get drunk, clash with high school acquaintances who have become neo-Nazi skinheads. TOBY hits a cat while driving drunk. THOR is beaten when he tries to enter a party without an invitation. THOR, his MOTHER & HANK attend church. CHRISSY calls THOR to say that GERARD has had a heart attack. THOR decides he'll ask CHRISSY to marry him. *(1 footnote)*

27. **DYNAMITE! Clown Left in Dust as Babe Blows Stack** *Page 289*
    THOR goes with CHRISSY & HER MOTHER to see GERARD in the hospital. THOR leaves the hospital, buys a bottle of alcohol. THOR & CHRISSY go to see the film *Mnung Is A Cancer That Is Destroying America*. Afterwards, they have a fight. CHRISSY drives off, leaving THOR in the street. CHRISSY sends THOR'S belongings to him by mail. *(1 news article)*

28. **BAY CITY BOZO: Clown Boozes as Gal Pal Sobs!** *Page 295*
    KATE has been offered a job in Cleveland & suggests THOR move there with her. KATE also would like a BABY. THOR declines, KATE sobs. They have difficult sex.
    (1 footnote)

29. **SPRINGTIME FOR DUNDERHEAD: Nazi Kid Guns Down Schoolmates!** *Page 303*
    TOMMY-G tells THOR he's planning to leave Cities News to take a job at *Lawn Care & Mowing Weekly*. THOR covers a shooting at a high school. *(1 news article)*

30. **DOG DAZE: Clown Called in as Canine Kicks!** *Page 308*
    CHRISSY'S DOG, ANDY, dies. THOR comes to CHRISSY'S house to comfort her. They watch PRESIDENT MNUNG interview on television, during which MNUNG displays the CAPTURED DICTATOR'S artificial leg. THOR helps MAXINE after she falls. CHRISSY asks THOR to bury ANDY in her backyard, but slaps his hand away when he gets in bed with her.

31. **FOR THE BIRDS: Band Beaten at Music Melee!** *Page 316*
    THOR attends JERRY'S performance at a Best New Band contest held by MUSIC MONKEY TELEVISION. JERRY & his band mates are assaulted during a robbery outside the club. THOR attends a post-contest party, meets the DEEJAY DEB FLOWER, who has a cold sore on her mouth. THOR goes to DEB FLOWER'S house, sees a DEAD BIRD in her bathtub.

32. **CLOWNFEST! It's Clown v. Clown in Job Showdown** *Page 326*
    THOR sets up a job interview at the *EXAMINER-MAIL*. However, there's a PROTEST outside the office, & editor BOB NEATH does not have time to meet with him. THOR returns home & receives phone call from NEATH, who regrets to inform him the paper has a "hiring freeze." *(3 news articles, 1 footnote)*

33. **FUNHOUSE: Clown Collapses at Babe's Birthday Bash!** *Page 335*
    CHRISSY takes THOR out for his birthday. They go to the swinger's club BAMBILAND, where THOR gets drunk on vodka & absinthe. He vomits & is escorted out of the club.

34. **EDGE WORLD: Clown Terror on Nightside Nightmare!** *Page 341*
    THOR is promoted to NIGHT SHIFT, working alone through the night. He drinks heavily during his off hours, plagued by visions of CHRISSY & HEATHER, obsessing over crime in the streets, throwing objects at the WORMS sliding down the apartment walls. He goes to a party & sees that as part of her medical treatment, HEATHER has lost her hair & had a chemical pump implanted in her shoulder. HEATHER gets in a fist fight with another woman at the party. THOR receives an anguished voice message from KATE in Cleveland.

35. **BOOBTOWN: Booze-Maddened Bozos Go Berserk!** *Page 350*
    THOR, SCOTT VARICK & TOMMY-G go to a strip club to celebrate TOMMY-G leaving Cities News. THOR talks to several strippers. THOR & VARICK drink heavily, take cocaine, get in a fist fight on the street. VARICK says his mother had an affair with his hockey coach. *(1 news article)*

36. **MEDIA IS MURDER: Clown Cracked at Cop Smackdown!** *Page 355*
    THOR covers PROTESTS at PRESIDENT MNUNG'S "ROLLIN' ON AMERICA" REELECTION TOUR. A protester gives THOR a pamphlet explaining the forces allegedly controlling the MAINSTREAM MASS MEDIA. THOR is beaten by police, taken into custody. *(6 pamphlet excerpts)*

37. **NO BEANS ABOUT IT: Prez Sez: 'America Wins!'** *Page 365*
    THOR, who has been slightly injured, is released from custody after providing police with his media credentials. In his speech, PRESIDENT MNUNG declares: "We have embarked on the march for PEACE, & we will win the WAR, because the war is right for AMERICA." *(2 pamphlet excerpts, 2 footnotes)*

38. **BOATER-GATE: Clown Confounded by Colby Conundrum!** *Page 378*
    THOR researches the career of FORMER CIA DIRECTOR WILLIAM COLBY, who was quoted in the protest pamphlet saying the CIA controls "everyone" of significance in the major media. THOR finds evidence of media manipulation, but no proof the COLBY quote is factual. *(13 footnotes, 2 e-mails)*

39. **RELIGION: Nutjob Insists: America Must Die, Die!** *Page 389*
    ISLAMIC TERRORIST LEADER OOMALAMMAH "NIPSY" VAN GHOUBELIN threatens AMERICA with destruction in a video released days before presidential election. Insta-Poll shows surge in voter support for PRESIDENT MNUNG

40. **SHAME, SHAME! Clown Drowns in Human Waste** *Page 393*
    THOR is promoted to Courts Reporter, a move that submerges him in a world of horrific crimes. He calls the criminal courts THE DUMP, a place where human trash piles up. The suffering & cruelty on display exact a spiritual toll. THOR suggests there's just a "meanness" in the world. *(6 news articles, 2 footnotes)*

41. **QUICKSAND! 'No Sense in This Thing,' Says Clown Confidant** *Page 406*
    RICHIE announces he's leaving Cities News to become a freelance correspondent covering the WAR. RICHIE was recently detained after erupting at the MAYOR over a corruption scandal. *(1 news article)*

42. **TEXECUTION: Clown Confab as Killer Croaked!** *Page 412*
    THOR & fellow legal reporter MARTY ATRAZINE cover the execution of SERIAL KILLER STEPHEN "TEX" WALKER. THOR loses in a lottery with other reporters & must witness the execution by video link. MARTY fails to write his post-execution "think-piece" by deadline, instead passing out drunk as he & THOR watch HARDCORE PORN FILMS in the hotel room.

43. **DADDY KNOWS WORST: Clown Cowers as Father Flounders!** *Page 425*
    THOR receives a phone call from HIS FATHER, who has been arrested for physical violence against his fifth wife. His FATHER calls from the rehabilitation center where he is receiving treatment for alcoholism. His FATHER says "GOD'S WILL" must be operating in their lives. *(1 news article)*

44. **PECULIAR: Drunken Genius Writer Invades Police Party!** *Page 433*
    THOR gets drunk, wanders to the police festival We're Winning The War Against Crime. He makes phone calls to his friends & women he knows, but no one answers. He finally contacts his boss editor, SERNATH, & curses at him drunkenly. After hours more drinking, THOR winds up outside CHRISSY'S house. CHRISSY, who has called the police, warns THOR not to bother her anymore. Police officers take THOR'S PHOTO & escort him to a taxi.

45. **SHE TALKS TO ANGELS: Funeral for All-American Sweetheart** *Page 441*
    THOR attends HEATHER'S FUNERAL, has a brief exchange with CHRISSY. SCOTT VARICK shows up unexpectedly at THOR & JERRY'S apartment with boxes of food & booze. They eat & drink & look at pictures of U.S. SOLDIERS torturing PRISONERS on the internet. *(excerpt from military training manual)*

46. **LIFE'S PEACHY! Clown Gets Raise as Riot Rages** *Page 446*
    SERNATH gives THOR his job evaluation & a 1.87 percent salary increase. A RIOT, meanwhile, is breaking out in the streets over the police killing of an unarmed suspect. THOR gets into a confrontation with a fellow patron at a bar, where he has gone to watch the riot coverage on television. *(1 office document, 1 news article)*

47. **SHE'S THE BOMB: Clown Cuddles With Court Cutie!** *Page 454*
    THOR goes out with CATHY FONG, a clerk he met at the court building. THOR spends the night at CATHY'S house. CATHY wants to set up further dates, but THOR is noncommittal. *(1 news article)*

48. **NEW GAL PAL CLAIMS: Better Living Thru Therapy!** *Page 463*
    JERRY & his new girlfriend, JOYCE, arrive to move out JERRY'S belongings. JERRY has become a Christian & started to attend Narcotics Anonymous meetings. JOYCE says the health authorities should be called due to the high volume of WORMS infesting the apartment. THOR & JOYCE clash at a bar, THOR telling JOYCE of his intention to "continue until VICTORY." *(1 news article)*

49. **VICTORY! Clown Wanders Through Death, Misery** *Page 468*
    THOR is visited by BEARDSLEY, who is troubled by the WORMS covering the ceiling, walls & floor of THOR's apartment. After a concert, BEARDSLEY is injured when he & THOR help capture a suspected thief. THOR & BEARDSLEY go to a donut shop, then see a DEAD MAN in the street after a gang-related shooting. They wait for a bar to open at 6 a.m. THOR bets another bar patron on flips of a coin. BEARDSLEY LEAVES THOR IN THE BAR.

SHOCK CLAIM:
Clown Says "I'm The Greatest!"

★ 1 ★

The plan was simple, basic, a no-brainer. I figured, first, to explode "journalism" at its core, pocketing at least one Pulitzer by the age of 30. I'd rock the city at dawn, I'd crack the dirty, filthy, louse-ridden bitch wide open. I'd sit back and watch, smoke curling around my lips, as the chips of deceit and depravity fell in a rain of shame and indictments. The establishment elites would cower under my onslaught, railing red-eyed and blustering as I brought them under sword.

I would move quickly into books, mainly novels and short stories, as well as plays and poetry. I would storm the arena of the writers, drinking and taking drugs extensively. My material would be big and raw and new – ahead of its time, yet also timeless, cleaving to the classic eternal themes, but leaving out the bullshit. I'd name and master my sorrow, my every sentence would contain a hidden dagger. I would break the neck of the accepted banalities, shatter into disorganized dust the sophistries that formed society's creaking stilts. I would slam into the teeth of the matter, throttle the masses, erupt in a massive, fiery blossom that would burn for the ages.

POLICE: 13 KILLED IN WEEKEND VIOLENCE

BAY CITY (CNS) – Authorities said 13 homicides occurred over the weekend in Bay City, among them five teenagers and three people over 60.

Sgt. Alan Jondh said the first murder was reported at about 12:30 a.m. Saturday, when Miguel Pedernales, 19, was shot and killed as he sat in a car in the 3200 block of 277th St. in Pine Ridges.

Jondh said that at about 3:30 a.m., Benjamin Oates, 23, and Deniro Robinson, 18, were gunned down by unknown assailants near the intersection of Gonis Drive and Clover Ave. in the Silvertown section.

Jondh said that about 10 a.m. Saturday, neighbors found 71-year-old Burma Deros dead inside her Hennessy Ave. apartment in Six Points. Jondh said evidence suggested she may have been beaten to death.

At about 6:10 p.m., Jondh said a 17-year-old youth was shot to death...

People were shooting, hacking and mutilating each other, blasting, strangling, torturing and butchering. They were killing for drugs, for money, for love, for hate, in pursuit of sick joys. They were killing over "disrespect," real and imagined. They were murdering for pure ego thrill. They were gouging and biting and stabbing for no obvious reason at all.

Some of the killings were big news that traveled far and wide, especially mass killings involving three or more victims. Most, though, were just "blips" – killings and murders as real as they come, but unnoticed by anybody except possibly the families, maybe a cop or two, and our desk. It was our duty to bear witness, to cover them all at least once.

The killing of a single white, especially a little girl, could provoke days of wall-to-wall coverage, depending on where it happened and how. On the other hand, the average prostitute found stuffed down a toilet, or single black man cut down in an alley, were not going to trigger a wave of mass coverage – if they got covered by TV or the dailies at all. Somebody's paint job did still matter, and "black-on-black crime," it turned out, had never been a big ratings leader. It would generally take the brutal and tragic killing of a straight-A aspiring black scholar-athlete, or helpless old lady, or a multiple killing of blacks and/or Mexicans, to get the TV and newspapers interested.

I went to the scene of shootings and murders, car crashes, suicides, drug busts. I spent 90 minutes across the street from a burning apartment building, inhaling smoke and knocking away flaming debris, only to hear the screams of a mother being told her three children were dead. On another occasion, I spent six hours standing outside a hotel where Nelson Mandela was staying, in case he happened to die.

> COCAINE, PILLS, MARIJUANA FOUND IN SOFA
>
> BAY CITY (CNS) – Bay City police said more than 50 pounds of cocaine, 100,000 ecstasy pills and 250 pounds of marijuana were found Wednesday stuffed inside a hollowed-out sofa that had been left for trash pick-up in the Commerce Avenue area.
>
> Sgt. Ricardo Del Pena said the street sale value of the drugs was estimated at more than $10 million – one of the city's biggest seizures of illicit drugs ever.
>
> Del Pena said city sanitation workers became suspicious and called police after a quantity of white powder spewed from the sofa as it was being thrown into a sanitation vehicle.
>
> "They made the right decision," said Del Pena. "The war against drugs requires that citizens be alert and notify police of all suspicious activity."

The job involved making upward of 100 phone calls a day – to the police, the County Sheriff, the Fire Department, the Highway Patrol, the District Attorney, the Drugs-Enforcement Agency, the FBI, the Customs Service, the Bureau of Alcohol, Tobacco & Firearms, the hospitals and county coroners, the airports, the Harbor Authority, Environmental Protection Agency, the State Department of Forestry, the National Weather Service – basically every publicly known law enforcement agency in the nine-county area.

Each place had to be called every 15 minutes (Bay City Police Department), half-hour, hour or 90 minutes, depending. You sat at the desk, marking off the places from these colored checklists. All the phones had been programmed with speed-dial codes.

"Cities News Services... Anything to report?"

Mostly, it must be said, the cop or publicity person on the other end would sigh. They might even yawn.

"Nope, sorry fella. Nothing going on since the last time you called."

But 12 or 13 times per day, and sometimes more, the line would pop and hiss, the cop or P.R. man would *give*. Out they'd blurt with one or more of the key words: "shooting," "homicide," "drive-by," "fire," "explosion," "stabbing," "assault," "robbery," "gang," "weapons," "rape," "carjack," "cocaine," "crack," "methamphetamine," "marijuana," "substance," "armed," "multiple," "hate crime," "abduction," "hostage," "homeless," "seizure," "indictment," "felonious," "suspected," "warrant," "raid," "collision"…

We took anything and everything with words like this.

> GANG-RELATED SHOOTING IN SILVERTOWN
> BAY CITY (CNS) – Bay City police said a 20-year-old man was shot to death Thursday in the Silvertown area in a suspected "gang-related" homicide.
> If confirmed as gang-related, it would be the 128th gang-linked murder so far this year in the city, Sgt. Ricardo Del Pena said.
> Del Pena said witnesses reported that the victim, Damon Garey, was walking in the 6700 block of Elmhurst Lane when an individual leaned out a passing sports utility vehicle and fired multiple shots at Garey's back.

The cop flack would spiel it. I'd lick my lips, get a tingly feeling. Sometimes my heart pounded, my head might slightly spin – especially if it looked like I was the first clown to stumble across something really bloody and horrifying, or better yet, something still "in progress," such as a hostage-taking or a "gunman on the loose." That was what you really wanted. The editor stuck a "bell" on top and away we'd go with what they called the "running add."

Gee whiz, it was fun.

> \>NEWSFLASH – URGENT
> BAY CITY – GUNMAN OPENS FIRE AT SIX POINTS
> APARTMENT COMPLEX – POLICE
> MORE

Depending on the nature of the bloodshed and the potential body count, the story was sometimes repeated by the bozos on local TV and radio within minutes. They never bothered to check it themselves. We'd tune in for the headlines:

CLOWN: *There's a report of a multiple shooting in the Six Points area of Bay City. Latest word from the police is that SWAT units have surrounded an apartment complex in the 5600 block of Pryor Avenue. So if your business is taking you in that direction, be on the lookout for the city's finest doing their duty...*

"Great job!" Kate Uhli, the Day Editor, would say, hopping up and down like a cheerleader. "We're leading everywhere right now!"

Kate was the desk pro, responsible for final edits on all dayside breaking. She was somewhere in her 30s and wore flesh-colored braces on both her wrists – the price of too many newsbiz years of too much typing. Her last job had been for a newspaper in the Miami area, where she covered the many Cuban problems. She claimed to love Cuban food, Cuban music, Cuban dancing, Cuban etc. She lived with her boyfriend, Joel, who allegedly made his money "designing computer games."

Kate would call me over to explain some change she had made in a story. She'd look at me, the lines around her light blue eyes crinkling: "Nice work, stud." Or she might walk up behind my chair, briefly massage my shoulders: "Good one, Thor."

"Thanks, Kate."

> BODY OF MISSING 11-YEAR-OLD GIRL FOUND
>
> MT. BURNEY (CNS) – Mt. Burney police said the body of an 11-year-old girl was found Monday, and that an ex-convict has been charged with her murder.
>
> Police Chief Oxley Rice said the suspect, Eric Stanton, 34, led police to Kimberly Nellison's body late Sunday in a wooded area on the Toca Linda-Lakeview county line, about three miles from her home.
>
> The girl had last been seen at her home in Mt. Burney on Thursday.
>
> Rice said Stanton had become acquainted with the girl's family while working with a landscaping crew at their home.

The cop flack would spiel it, or he patched you through to an officer or detective handling the case. You'd bang the info into the computer, sometimes following with a quick call to the hospital or somewhere, depending on the casualty situation. Whether it was "true" or not was of very little concern. We likewise had little time or motivation to bother with "context" or "background." The thing that mattered was that a cop had said it.

A cop would spiel: Some kind of major blood, an apartment on fire. The editors would clear on it and I'd grab a map and recorder and jam out there, piling in with a photographer or jumping a taxi. In most cases the "event" was already over, the guns tossed and the bodies carted, but still you found cops and firefighters standing around, puddles of blood, the stench of burnt flesh, smoldering ash, various smashed remnants of hell that had fallen on somebody's head.

I'd flash my press badge, lurk on the edges of the police yellow tape. I'd poke around, digging up some "color," trying to scrounge an interview – with cops, with "witnesses," with sad crying people who had somehow in a flash lost everything. I'd call it in. Kate would slap in the new details and throw a new version on the wire. Cities News was the reigning champ when it came to marking Bay City's daily outpouring of grief and human wretchedness.

> ARRESTS IN CONNECTION WITH DRUG DEATHS
>
> BAY CITY (CNS) – Bay City police said five people were arrested on suspicion of selling a mixture of cocaine and heroin blamed for the deaths of up to 17 people in the last two weeks.
>
> Capt. Stuart Stennis said the suspects were taken into custody Tuesday and Wednesday in raids at four separate Bay City locations.
>
> Stennis declined to release the identity of the suspects, saying some of them were minors.
>
> Stennis said three of the suspects have admitted to investigators that they delivered drugs to 16-year-old Pamela Gutierrez, who died of suspected drug-related poisoning on Sunday.
>
> Officials said toxicology tests have indicated the deaths were likely caused by a combination of heroin, cocaine and the painkiller fentanyl.

The operation was pure "scientific management," as dreamed up by sadists, designed to minimize thinking and errors while maximizing "story sausage" output. The system relied on a rolling rotation – as soon as you finished the calls on the Bay City North list, for example, you switched to West Bay/Santa Costa. Someone else would ditch 4-County and get the jump on Bay East. The editors watched like hawks, they kept a running tab on how many stories you pulled and how often you rolled into the street for on-the-spot bloody-and-breaking. Under the grand theory, you were supposed to knock off at least one phone call per minute, and the only times you were allowed not to be dialing were if you were typing or had gone street-side for a debacle. Another rule: you always led with the source: "The police said Tuesday..." It was easier that way, for us, but also for the radio and TV subscribers, who preferred it so they could "rip and read."

We made the phone calls and checked off the lists. Kate or one of the others kept an ear cocked on the police scanners, listening through the mud and crackle for Code-3's (lights and sirens blazing) or shout-outs of "Officer Down!" Officer Downs were not uncommon, but they rarely meant a cop had been shot. Mostly they meant that somebody in the ghetto needed help, fast. Ghetto residents had long ago learned that "cop shot" was the one way to guarantee a police/ambulance response. Cities News policy was to wait for official confirmation before rolling to an "Officer Down."

Bay City burned like a smoky red cinder at the tip of the peninsula, the crown jewel megalopolis of the nine-county zone. The zone claimed 17.9 million people, five cities, hundreds of square miles of suburbs, farming hubs and fish towns, two-thirds of a mountain range, 26 lakes, seven rivers and associated tributaries, four pro sports teams, nine universities and junior colleges, 238 high schools, six airports, one U.S. Army base, one Air Force field, two state prisons, one federal penitentiary, two amusement parks, four water slides, three horse race tracks, one dog track and 27 public and private golf courses.

It was lively, there was never a shortage of action. The city was gripped by cross-currents of high tension and malaise, it wobbled between crushing despair and last-ditch optimism. Taxes had been cut, drug prices were down, murders, rapes and food-stamp disbursement were up. Armed bank robberies were averaging 1.8 per week in the greater metropolitan area, while official school district figures said violent attacks on teachers were averaging 3.1 per week. Unemployment officially stood at 12.8 percent (23.9 percent in "minority" zones, i.e. black and Mexican), while the federal stats said one of every 5.4 residents was officially "living in poverty."

> POLICE HIT DISTURBED YOUTH WITH STUN GUN
>
> BAY CITY (CNS) – Bay City police said a 14-year-old boy suffered severe burns to his head and back Thursday after police sprayed him with a flammable

> chemical then shot him with an electrical stun gun, igniting his clothing.
>
> Commander Dennis Honig said Police Chief Nathaniel Nachba had ordered the chemical Oleoresin Capsicum removed from the police arsenal immediately following the incident in the Silvertown section. He said an official investigation has been launched.
>
> Honig said officers had initially responded to a 911 call from the youth's mother. Honig said the youth was acting "irrationally" and carrying "two knives and a hot plate" when officers arrived at the Beck St. address…

Of course, you could always quit, no one forced you to stay. There would never be a shortage of kids who thought news was a fun game, who wanted to come to the big city and get in on the "news gig." Cities News had more applicants than they knew what to do with, young crapheads from across the country came to bang at the gate. Maybe it wasn't always the alleged cream of the crop, but the bosses could take their pick in the slave driver's economy and they knew it. The bosses didn't care if you quit, and many did. I saw ten or twelve go – most within months, a few within weeks – fleeing at the first opportunity for the better-paying shores of public relations and "teaching."

Strange as it seems now, I had to bare my teeth and battle my way in. There had been no response from Cities News (or anybody else in Bay City) after I sent in my resumé and clip package. Several e-mail inquiries and an online application had also failed to elicit a response. That was wrong – that was *clearly wrong*. So one day during my lunch break while temping at the Telephone Tower, I looked up the office on a map, took the bus over and rang at the door.

"Yes?" said a voice over the intercom.

"I'm here, uh, um," I mumbled, "I'm, yes, I'm…"

"You have an appointment?"

"Yes, the editor…"

The door miraculously buzzed. I yanked the handle.

I was *in*.

It smelled like smoke. A blond girl with a small, mouse-like face stared at me quizzically from behind a brown plastic desk.

"Yes, I, you see, I –"

I was reaching into my satchel to remove my folder of clips when… The gods sighed or frowned, I still don't know which.

A short, fat old man in a white-grey beard, smoking a cherry-smoke smelling pipe, walked up. A cheery light burned in his eyes.

"Young man, are you here for *the job?*"

"Yes, sir, of course..."

"Well, that is a convergence indeed. We placed the advertisement for a new reporter just this morning. I looked it over myself not more than two hours ago."

I reached out to shake his hand.

> SANTA COSTA MAN SEVERS THREE BODY PARTS
>
> SANTA COSTA (CNS) – The Santa Costa County Sheriff's Dept. said a 36-year-old man on Monday used a knife to cut off his finger, scrotum and penis in an apparent act of self-mutilation.
>
> Sgt. Dennis Mickleby said the victim's wife indicated Neil Gennert was acting under the influence of drugs when he attacked himself.
>
> Mickleby said Gennert's wife told investigators that during an argument, Gennert chased her from their home to a neighbor's lawn, where he pulled down his pants and cut off his scrotum and penis in front of several bystanders.
>
> Mickleby said it was not immediately clear if doctors would be able to re-attach the severed body parts.

Dick walked me through the office to his glass box and sat down at a desk stacked high with papers and books. He cleared a small space and flipped open the folder of stories I had written for small and tiny papers in the desert and on the coast, for miniscule weekly rags, in the years before the big blind Bay City leap: County funding crises, debate-club champions, bingo games for the elderly, school building repairs, hobos who had fallen asleep on the train tracks and the predictable results that followed...

Those thin strips of fish wrap were my best and only evidence. I had slaved and sweated over each word. Many a night had found me staying alone at the office until nine or ten or even midnight – hammering it down, honing my craft, proving I could stick it out, tightening and hardening myself into condition to play with the big boys...

Dick yawned, puffed his pipe. I sat, breathing heavily.

Dick's walls were crammed with shelves of books and knickknacks, dusty wood carvings of birds and ducks and elephants. A gold-plated plaque behind the desk read: OH LORD, BRING ME A BASTARD WITH TALENT. There were scale models of antique cars, framed political cartoons, an engraving of Benjamin Franklin, water-related landscapes and plenty of photographs – shots of somebody who looked like Dick with Wilt Chamberlain, Dick in a group with Arthur Miller and Mickey Rooney, Dick with Joan Baez and Jacques Cousteau, Dick in oily overalls next to a motorcycle, Dick shaking hands in the Oval Office with Gerald Ford...

"Yes, indeed," said Dick. "Everything seems in order. I notice you used the term 'hands of bananas' in this article on dock workers. That is an interesting locution."

"Pardon, sir?"

He peered at me. "I said that – 'hands of bananas' is quite an interesting locution to see in a newspaper story."

"Oh yes, that's what they call them – 'hands.'"

Dick nodded and shuffled paper. It was hard to believe, and also I couldn't quite hear. Dick had a way of talking like his mouth was full of sawdust.

> SEVEN DETAINED FOR SWALLOWING COCAINE
> BAY CITY (CNS) - Federal drug officials said Tuesday that seven people have been detained at Bay City International Airport on suspicion of swallowing packets containing cocaine.
> Andrew Tischling, spokesman for the U.S. Drugs-Enforcement Agency, said the suspects arrived Monday on two flights originating in Kingston, Jamaica.
> Tischling said cocaine had been found in condoms recovered from two of the suspects so far.
> Tischling said drug-trafficking and conspiracy charges were expected to be filed after authorities obtain all the suspected cocaine packets ingested by the suspects.

Dick Trimbles had founded Cities News 35 years before and was the guy who had sold it off to Capps-Neubold. Under the deal, Dick was bestowed the title "Executive Senior Editor," which apparently gave him clearance to puff his pipe in the office. He also was allowed to interfere in any aspect of the operation that interested him. Dick would putter around in his glass box, thick and blocky like a bag of wet sand, flipping through magazines and newspapers, cutting out articles and putting them in folders. He would pop out and invite you into his office for a chat.

"Young man, have you ever read the speeches of Abraham Lincoln?"

"Some of them, I think, yes."

"I must tell you, Lincoln was the master of mounting a sentence. He could spell out a fine point, and clearer, I think, than any man of his time. Any young journalist would do well to read his speeches. I've been reading them for about 50 years now."

"It must be rewarding."

"Bet your bippy, it is."

Or: "Young man, are you familiar with the Five P's?"

"I'm not sure..."

"It stands for Prior Preparation Prevents Poor Performance. You'd do well to think about that."

Or: "Always be careful with statistics, young man. Just remember, a fellow with his head in the oven and his feet in the freezer is statistically O.K. In reality, he's dead."

> HOMELESS MAN LOSES LEGS IN TRASH TRUCK
>
> BAY CITY (CNS) – Bay City police said a homeless man lost both his legs early Wednesday when the Dumpster he was sleeping in was emptied into a city sanitation truck.
>
> Sgt. Dave Chester said sanitation workers heard the screams of Amos Atterlee and stopped the truck's grinders in time to save his life.
>
> Chester said Atterlee, 56, lost both his legs above the knee in the accident in the Financial District.
>
> Bay Community Hospital spokeswoman Melinda Dowell said Atterlee was in critical but stable condition.
>
> Sanitation Dept. spokesman Reuben Matas said the members of the truck crew – Jaime Acton, Javier Lafianza and Douglas Yates – would receive official commendations for their life-saving action.

Telephones buzzed, workers mumbled, computer keyboards clacked – the wire rolled. Internet technicians with bum-fluff mustaches took our stories and photos and pasted them up for the world to admire. The smell was of paper and dust and electricity-fried copy machines, burnt coffee, Dick's smoke and last night's spaghetti with mushroom sauce that someone had heated up in the microwave.

I wore ties and button-down shirts, polyester slacks, my shoes were a three-dollar pair of maroon Salvation Army wingtips. I often felt bad, generally, but I was never "sick," I never missed a day at the office. I showed up on time, even early, some days I'd be on the phone by 6:55. Looking back, I probably raced around brisk and quite stiff, like a two-dollar firecracker had been lit and stuck in my ass.

I remember, it felt like I'd been punched in the stomach when I saw my first weekly paycheck: $294.19. It was impossible to live on money like this, it was certain to keep me hooked on noodles and trapped in the ghetto. But no way was I going to quit.

I didn't care, the fucking hell – I was slinging blood and guts in the big city at long last. For one thing, it had taken me out of working "temp." For another, and this was the main reason – I was the World's Greatest Journalist And Writer. Cities News was only the necessary first part of my destiny.

For most of my life I had been fodder for sixth-rate dictators. I had come out of a long line of religious nuts and suicides, jailbirds, drunks and pot gobblers, half-wits and half-time whores. They had smacked me around with two-by-fours, unloaded on me with backhands, and when they weren't beating me or lying to me, they had ignored me. They had taken me before priests, preachers and high honchos from three sects, who had all performed their voodoo in an attempt to save me and set me upon the right path.

I had never belonged anywhere. I was always looking out from the dark and tangled forest. The stuttering kid, the kid allergic to cats, the kid with "asthma," the kid coughing phlegm into his pillow, the kid sleeping in a pee-stained sleeping bag. The kid standing off to the side with a red eye swollen from "pollen" and a shirt a size too small. Even the alleged "outsiders" were disgusted – I had been *outside* the outsiders.

It far from mattered now – I had stepped out from the dead grey debris. My fate was to be the Conquering Writer, loved and feared and hated – but mostly loved, it must be said. I'd be constantly in the newspapers and magazines, pictures of me would flash upon the world's television screens. I would be continually drunk, stoned, loaded, blitzed out, nine-and-a-half feet high and getting taller. I saw it as the only possible outcome, the only possible option.

LOADED: Clown Boards Midnight Train to Oblivion!

★ 2 ★

Jerry had a girlfriend, Candace, who was rich. She lived across town on Ocean Way, sharing an apartment with her sister, Heather. Candace was a law student, Heather was in her sophomore year or had failed her freshman, it was never made clear.

In any case, their dad paid for everything. The dad was an old man who had made a fortune in cable television and magazines many years before. Now he "did nothing" while the money "rolled in." The mother was still young and good-looking. The old man had met her when she was nineteen and working as a cocktail waitress at the old Playboy Club in Chicago.

"The old guy's cool," said Jerry. "He bought Candace's mom this little house so she could screw her boyfriend in private. This big Greek guy named Thomas."

"The fuck he did, Jerry."

It went on for like, four years, until one day the Greek guy just dumped the mom. She went into these huge depressions, they spent thousands on psychologists. She went to Beverly Hills and got all this plastic surgery, these injections. She was depressed for like, nine months. They put her on five different pills.

Then, when she was almost through it, the Thomas guy started to go nuts. He started calling all the time – in the middle of the night, at five o'clock in the morning. He would drive by in his car and yell out the window, honk his horn. He got all fat and huge, didn't cut his hair or shave. He would sit in his car down the block, jacking off and giving kids the finger.

Then one day, Thomas says he's gonna put the Russian mafia on them. That's what he says: "Russian mafia." Candace's mom and dad got super scared, they didn't know what the hell. They called the police, but all the police said was nothing could be done until an actual crime had been committed.

They hired all these security guys to guard their house 24 hours. They hired a team of private detective dudes to spy on Thomas, find out what he was up to. The guys followed him around a few weeks, but all they said was he was crazy – that he might kill them, but then again, he might not. They couldn't figure out crap.

Finally, Candace's dad had enough. They set up a meeting at the Black Angus. The father went with one of the detective dudes, who had a gun in his coat and was secretly recording everything. These other detective dudes were secretly filming it from this other table.

Well, said Jerry, so Phil ended up giving him the little fuck house for free. Signed it over to him right there in the Angus. Believe that?

"Now he sells vitamins, nutritional pills, this kind of crap from there by mail."

"Who does?"

"The Thomas guy..."

"*Gave* him the house?"

Jerry nodded. "Gave it to him. I totally kid you not. It was a pretty nice house, too."

I'd known Jerry a couple years. Jerry was a bank clerk, guitarist and songwriter, and fairly decent at all three.

It was the afternoon by the time we got there. We stood at the stop, waiting for the bus. We checked the schedule, but still no bus. Only a gray cracked street, a variety of dried turds. I gandered a stained newspaper against the fence, a cantaloupe rind, a burnt trashcan lid. Cars crawled past stupidly – an old Ford, a lousy Mazda, a rusty Toyota dragging a chain. A pile of wet cardboard sat on the sidewalk, next to a torn sock with a black and green stripe.

A fellow in a reggae-style cap shuffled about in a slouch in front of the PRINCE OF PEACE – A HEARTREACH CENTER, something that might have been a brain sitting in a plastic sack over his arm.

We crossed the street and went into a place for take-out coffee. NO SLEEPING! a sign screamed. DRUG-FREE ZONE – NO GUNS!!!

MUST WEAR SHOES NO SKATEBOARDS NO LOITERING NEIGHBORHOOD WATCH YOU ARE BEING FILMED NEW! TERIYAKI DOUBLE-BACON WISCONSIN CHEDDAR

We came out of the place with the coffees. As we did, a guy in a beard, scarf and yellow rain slicker came hustling down the sidewalk at us. He was sweating terribly and carrying a black dog in his arms.

The guy saw us, stopped and spluttered. I didn't catch all of it. Then he held up the dog by the neck, let him hang a second, and drop-kicked him. He held up the dog by the scruff of the neck, glared at us, spluttered, dropped the dog and let fly with the boot.

The pup let out a shriek then whimpered. He clattered against the sidewalk, pulled himself along, whining. The guy muttered something, spluttered again. I still didn't catch it. Finally he snatched up the pup by the ears and took off.

✪

Candace and Heather lived in a garden-style apartment complex, about a block off the ocean. We rang at the security door, then went up about four flights of stairs. It was a big sunlit place, smelling of cigarette smoke and laundry. Giant varnished wood tables were everywhere in the main room, stacked with computer gear and legal books, piles of discs, stereo equipment. The ocean glinted from the picture window. You could see little sailboats out on the water.

Candace was a short-haired dirty blond. She sat next to us on the floor, wearing a blue flowered skirt and a plastic sunflower on her chest, sucking at her drink from a straw and punching buttons non-stop on her cell phone. She smoked ultra-thin light cigarettes, about one every five minutes. Packs of them, full, empty and half-empty, were scattered around the apartment.

We sat with our drinks and looked at the TV with the sound off, music droning from the stereo system.

Pretty soon Heather came out from the shower, hair piled in a towel on the top of her head.

"This is my sister, Heather," Candace said.

"Nice to meet you, Heather," I said.

I stuck out my hand, but Heather didn't bother taking it. She pulled off the towel and started working on the hair. Possibly she tried to smile, but her mouth just wouldn't obey.

She was wearing yellow slip-on sandals, light blue short-tights, tan thighs tapering into tennis-player calves and the daintiest of ankles. Heather's hair wasn't blond like Candace's, but more of a light brown. She had more freckles, and her lips weren't as big. Also, her nose was smaller. She looked enough like Candace, but prettier and smoother, as if she had been caught under rushing water for several years.

Heather came back wearing a bright green eye shadow. It was really very bright green. Medium-size gold hoops fell from her ears, while on her lips she had put a light purple lipstick. I liked it, I liked the look. She sat back down and used a red ribbon to tie her hair into a stiff little tail sticking up on the top of her head. A few hair strands sprayed out over her forehead.

I took a drink off the vodka-cranberry. On the wide-screen, a raccoon was wearing a cowboy hat and riding a surfboard. Palm trees danced in a conga line. Mice, chipmunks and a zebra suntanned on the beach. Waves crashed, the sun rose, a chipmunk hugged a bunny rabbit. The sun set. FEEL THE FRESH FRUITY FLAVOR. I took another drink, draining the glass.

Heather took a pack off the coffee table and lit a clove cigarette. She got up and started to dance.

"I love this song," she said. "It's so good."

She spun around slowly, holding the drink in front of her, the cigarette tilted between the fingers of her other hand. The disco-hippie music droned, six thousand beats per second, a squeaky door hinge endlessly looping...

...*moovin' groovin' keep on moovin sittin' twistin' always winnin' slammin' rammin' body jammin' spyin' cryin' keep on flyin'...*

Heather turned and twirled, glancing at the ceiling, out the windows, at nothing. She rolled her shoulders, took a sip from her drink, blew smoke. She shook her hips and arms, her earrings twisting. Strands of hair fluttered, the hair tail whipping.

The doorbell rang. Heather ran off to get it. She returned with a little hairy fellow in knee shorts and leather sandals trailing after her. This was Hugh, apparently. Hugh had recently made it all the way to junior big-shot at a law firm, according to Jerry. He had a little crop of dye-blond weeds on the top of his head. The rest of his hair was balled up and pinned into a bun at the back. Long sideburns running down each cheek. We shook hands.

"So what's your business?" said Hugh.

"I'm a reporter, a journalist..."

"Yeah? For who?"
"Cities News Services..."
"Here in town? I've never heard of it."
"Few have..."

Hugh reached into a little zipper pack around his waist, took out a plastic sack and dangled it in the air. Pills.

"Who wants an Archie Bunker?"

Heather and Jerry laughed. We all had at least one. Candace went back into the kitchen and came out with a wine bottle.

"It's a Beaujolais."

"Oh, perfect..."

I didn't care what it was, it hardly mattered. I didn't know wine from fruit punch, except they tasted a little different. She popped it and poured.

"Wow, it's excellent," I said.

"Oh, good," said Candace.

Hugh sat in the corner of the couch and rolled a thick one in a white paper. He and Heather took several long drags. They passed it over to Candace. Finally Jerry got it. He took a hit, then looked over at me. He held it up, the saggy butt end between his thumb and forefinger. It shined wetly in a shaft of sunlight, little curls of smoke wafting off.

We sat there, the music blaring.

On the TV, something had gone down in TV-land. The screen showed women weeping, smoke and flames rising from buildings, a milky blue sky. Ambulances driving off, cops waving their arms. News clown lips flapped with concern.

54 DEAD IN FIRE AT CULT

Jerry smoked the last of the stogie. He tossed the butt in his mouth and swallowed.

Heather and Hugh laid back on the couch, staring at a large hippie-type drug drapery that had been tacked to the ceiling. It had circles and squares, triangles, squiggles and various lines, purple and yellow explosions, orange and green blotchings. Possibly something of an Aztec theory.

I poured another wine. I lit a smoke from my pack. Somebody yawned.

Layers of smoke hung in the air, barely moving. Heather lay against Hugh's shoulder, her eyes closed.

✪

After a while we went down to the pool place, a billiards bar – Shuckum's it was called, a few blocks from the Clifton Fish Market strip. The place stank of boiled clams and chicken wings, "Hard To Handle" blasting on the jukebox. Candace and Jerry went to get pitchers, then they all went off to play pool, leaving me at the table.

It was fine, I enjoyed it. I never had liked pool. Pinball was my game.

I drank down one of the beer pitchers, sitting there alone, exuding aloofness and stoicism. I glanced over. Jerry missed a shot, said something. Everyone laughed. He twisted the ball cap on his head and walked like duck, the pool stick between his knees. Everyone chuckled. Candace took a slug of beer and missed her shot. Everyone guffawed. Heather, wearing white high heels with leather straps winding up the calves, came up and nibbled Hugh's ear. Nobody said a damn thing.

The game ended and they came back. Hugh took out his phone and made a call. Candace took out her wallet and went to get more pitchers.

Heather had a lollipop in her mouth, grape flavor it looked like. She moved the sucker in, took it out, nibbled the nails of her other hand. She leaned back in her chair with the lolly-sucker in her cheek.

Her eyes locked on mine once, but there was nothing much in it. She was lazy-eyed and limp, played out – too much fun. Her thighs streamed out of her short-tights, fanning out over the orange plastic chair. Billiard lights caught dozens of small brown-blond hairs on her thighs, throwing little shadows behind them.

"Enter Sandman" chugged like a chainsaw on the jukebox. At our table, Jerry and Candace had started eating a pizza. A greasy squish of cheese fell to the table. Jerry scooped it up with his fingers and dangled it into his mouth. Candace slapped him.

✪

Everybody came back to the shack. Lights flipped on and off, toilets flushed. Heather immediately disappeared somewhere. Candace turned off the lights and turned on the TV. She and Jerry stood watching it. Squiggly drug things started glowing on the drug carpet stuck to the ceiling.

Words in a nonsense language came out of Hugh's mouth. He knocked around the room a minute, then sank down on the couch. He put his feet up on the coffee table.

A talk-show came on: INVASION OF THE LITTLE PEOPLE. The TV light blew up around the darkened room.

"You gonna crash here, man?" said Jerry.

"Yeah," I said, "if it's all right."

Jerry turned to Candace. "It's cool, isn't it, babe?"

"I guess so," Candace said, shrugging.

"The couch folds into a bed," said Jerry. "Just wake up Hugh. He'll get out of your way and go to Heather's room."

"Great. Thanks a lot."

They walked off.

In the refrigerator I found four cans of Michelob Light. I went back to the living room and sat in the recliner. On the TV, big trouble had broken out between the little people. Midgets were shouting, hopping up and down, giving each other the finger. A stocky little fellow with a red beard made an ugly face, jabbing his finger in the air. Then two of them rushed forward and banged into each other. They fell to the ground. Midgets rushed from both sides, jumping into the pile. A full-size black guy and white guy, huge and muscle-ripped, ran out to separate the combatants. They tossed shrimps to the left and right. Audience members cheered and laughed, giving each other high-fives.

I burped. Liquid, including a quantity of vomit-type material, came up. I sucked everything back down, then took a long swallow off the beer. I wiped my mouth with my hand, then wiped that on the carpet and the side of the recliner.

I finished the beer, set the empty on the floor, opened another.

Hugh let out a snore. Could have been a fart. His chest rose and fell.

Heather appeared in the doorway. The white heels were gone and she was wearing little ankle socks. She gazed around for a moment, moving her head to one side and the other, as if trying to figure something out. She took a glance up at the drug rug, squinting. Finally she started into the room, slowly and jerkily, as if the floor had suddenly turned into mashed potatoes.

I stuck out my leg. She knocked into it with her knee.

"What?" she hissed.

She stepped around me and went out to the kitchen.

The kitchen was dim, just one light rod over the sink. Heather was taking a glass down from the cupboard. She started to fill it from the bottle tank. She lifted the glass and drank, looking at me. Her eyes were large and calm. Her hair had been let out. It fell to the tops of her shoulders, a curtain of wavy brown.

I reached for the glass, took it from her hand. I drained it in a gulp, set it on the counter.

I turned and poked my nose into her hair. It smelled like cigarette smoke and soap. My tongue reached out and grabbed hold of her earring. I sucked on the earring, then began to chew her ear. I reached down and picked up her hand. It was warm and flimsy, weighed hardly anything at all.

"What are you doing?"

She giggled. Her voice was lazy, sloppy.

I hugged her a few moments, then hung a few light kisses on her forehead, on the top of her nose, on both cheeks...

Her lips loosened and gave.

My tongue darted in. Heather tasted a bit like over-ripe plums, but cool from the water.

The refrigerator hummed, shook once, made a series of clicking noises. It made a few more clicks before seeming to sigh and settle. Purple-blue TV glow leaked in from the other room, reflecting and smearing itself across the smooth white fridge front.

Heather's mouth attacked, seizing my tongue, sucking it, pulling it in.

My hand came up, moved her hair over her ear, caressing and petting. Her hair was smooth, buttery, almost melting. My other hand came up and did the hair on the other ear. I moved around her, kissing both ears, her cheeks, her hair, her mouth. I kissed her softly, tenderly, as tenderly as I could make it.

"Ouhhh," Heather moaned.

✪

"Get off me," Heather was saying.

"All right," I croaked.

"I said, Get off me."

I don't know how long we had been laying there. I lifted my arm.

Heather flew up and flicked on the light. She towered above me in her socks, the gym top around her stomach, hands on her hips, white kitchen light burning around her head.

"Get out of here!"

She spotted her short-tights in the sink. She went over and pulled them on.

"Get out!"

"O.K.," I croaked, not moving. "All right."

There was a hard snapping as Heather pulled the straps of her top over her shoulders. She spun and walked off.

My eyes were tearing up. What felt like giant shards of glass slammed repeatedly into my head and face. A blast of stabbing pains hit my right side. I was horribly thirsty.

I crawled over to my shorts and slid them on. I hoisted myself up against the counter, tried to steady. I listened for voices – Heather talking to Hugh, for example. But there was nothing.

Finally I went out there. Heather was nowhere. Hugh was on the couch, curled up in the glow of the TV and the drug shag.

Police sirens flashed on the TV movie. Cops wearing sports coats jumped out and started running, looks of what-the-shit on their handsome faces. One had an Italian greasy look and wavy black hair. The other was balding and taller, classic white man with a blond mustache. The scene cut to dead people, women and children, little girls, smeared with blood here and there. Beautiful people with pink cheeks, blonds and brunettes, wearing pajamas and nightgowns. Paramedics in surfer haircuts started putting them into black zip bags. A sunburned fellow in a priest's collar and a brown and white snowflake sweater walked up, his thumb stroking a silver crucifix. He waved it over the bodies like a wand. He was pained and tearful, tragically mournful, drenched in the juice of his soggy soul. A red emergency light blinked pulse-like against his cheek.

First-class film direction.

ADMINISTRATION: WAR MAY BE 'NECESSARY'
Dictator's Regime Amasses Deadly Weapons, Drugs
President Would Rather Not See 'Mushroom Cloud'

By Gordon Vubbles Jr. and R. Snegg Mitchell
The New York Times Service

WASHINGTON – U.S. President Wolfgang G. Mnung is becoming increasingly concerned that all-out war may be necessary, senior officials say, as the dictator's regime continues to amass aluminum tubing for possible nuclear weapons, traffic in illegal drugs and have potential links to terrorists.

"The president doesn't necessarily want to invade, but he may not have a choice," said one senior Administration official.

The official, who spoke on condition of anonymity, added: "All negotiating options – including the use of force – remain open. But if it came to a conflict, the goal would be to decapitate the dictator's regime, while trying to minimize civilian casualties."

U.S. civilian and military officials from a range of agencies said intelligence operatives had recently discerned indications that the regime may be in the advanced stages of pursuing a "quick-start" nuclear weapons program capable of striking valuable security assets in as little as 45 minutes.

A senior Defense Intelligence Agency official, speaking on condition of anonymity, said there was evidence suggesting the regime may have also purchased as many as 4,000 PlayStation video game units.

The official said intelligence agencies believe the PlayStations, which have the ability to generate up to 75 million 3-D "polygons" per second, could be bundled together into a kind of "crude supercomputer" and used in military applications such as surprise chemical or nuclear attacks.

High-level government defense sources said it appears the regime may also be in the process of developing VX nerve gas in liquid and solid form, as well as botulinim toxin, smallpox, ricin, sarin and deadly anthrax and their delivery systems, including unmanned long-flight robot drones.

The officials added there are increasing concerns that these robot drones could be passed along to terrorist groups for devastating strikes upon the United States and its democratic allies.

"The president's leaning towards a massive military intervention," said a senior White House official. "He'd rather not wake up and see a mushroom cloud over D.C. while having his morning mocha double-fudge."

ANIMALS!
Young Girl Shot by Vicious Thugs

★ 3 ★

Pretty soon I would break internationally, dominate the field commercially. I would take to the lifestyle like a shark in a tank full of baby seals. I would scream and vomit at parties and everyone would be grateful. I would be arrested for threatening behavior on airplanes, but no charges would ever be filed. I would be simultaneously plagued by self-doubts and a flopping, self-flagellating ego.

Women would hurl themselves at me. There would be no more of this grappling in the darkness, this shameful pawing and clutching and grabbing and pleading. The orgy would rocket out of control – drug-addicted supermodels, jaundiced art-adoring society princesses, heiresses from Europe and Brazil, sex-starved ballerinas, cock-crazy ice dancers, tattooed alternative-rock girls. We'd spit in the eye of the so-called civilization, jeering at the gilded meritocracy and its pathetic delusions. We'd binge and ball and suck and sing through the dawn, cocaine straws jutting from our every orifice. We'd probe the outer limits of human endurance in a majestic conflagration of tragic, dusk-colored beauty.

✪

I wiped at the dripping loogie, pulled a page from my pad and wiped. The guy went up the stairs and glared at me from the stoop, chin jutting, hands curled into fists, chest pumping, the corners of his mouth twisting downwards.

Her body was already gone, but some of the family was inside. Cops were wandering around, scratching their heads in the stinking afternoon heat.

"I apologize, sir, I'm only trying to, to... Perhaps if your family will speak out, others will understand what –"

I jiggle-stepped. The loogie flew.

The skinny little guy in bare feet and a tank-top pulled again at my satchel.

"I don't think he want you around, *maaaaan...*" The freak danced and pulled, yanking at the satchel. "I don't think he want you around, *maaaaan...*"

"I heard you..."

"I don't think he want you around, *maaaaan...*"

Who was this guy? My hand was shaking, face burning. It felt like everybody was looking at me. I was the worst kind of geek. What the hell was I doing? I didn't know what to *do*...

A bit more of the loogie from the vic's family member dripped down my eyebrow. I pulled a page, wiped again. I just wished somebody would *do* something...

The little guy danced and pulled. "I don't think he want you around, *maaaaan...*"

"I know. I heard you, man..."

Finally a police captain walked over and shooed the little fuck away. The cop put his hand on my shoulder.

"Hey big guy, why don't you give it a rest? They do got a right to their privacy at some point."

The cousin went inside, the door banged. I wiped loogie off my forehead, pulled another sheet and wiped.

"So what happened?"

The cop shrugged. "What happened? Little girl got shot. That's all. It's stupid. It's crazy."

"I mean... so what *happened?*"

"Pray and spray, guy. Missed their man, popped the girl."

"Catch anybody?"

"Working on it, guy."

"Who you think done it?"

"Who *you* think done it? I'll tell you who done it: Animals done it, beasts of the jungle. That's who done it."

Our staff photog, Deshaun Parker, lowered to a knee and took snaps of latex-gloved Scientific Investigation Division techs digging in the sand. Techs went back and forth, hoofing evidence kits from the back of the van parked across the sidewalk. Police tape surrounded the swing-set and go-round, the graffiti-blackened ball wall. Cops walked beneath the barred and boarded windows of the ground floor, throwing dead leaves, searching for evidence. I stepped over sidewalk weeds and a sea of broken glass, something like fishing line in the gutter. I counted five cop cars with their doors open. Cop radios crackled, cops muttered into shoulder radio rigs.

A helicopter swished up high, the thwapping rotor blades echoing off the street and ring of towers. Kids and old people walked up and stared. They looked tired and beaten, barely curious. A woman put a clump of white flowers next to a candle that was burning in a small glass. By a nearby tree someone had left a dirty panda bear and two dandelions. A few yards off lay a pair of blue children's sandals.

Residents opened windows and poked their heads out. They pulled back in, rattling window frames. Little fires of sunlight bounced off the cement. Bursts of sunlight appeared and died in the dirt and tufts of grass. The trees stank, dry branches bending toward the ground, little yellow petals falling to the cement...

A cop car drove up, followed by a bright orange and black van from the "reality" series *COP PARTY*. Clowns in orange *COP PARTY* t-shirts got out holding mini-cams, walking up to the police tape, shoving cameras into the faces of the crowd.

A bum with plastic wrap on his foot staggered up to a trash can. He took out a paper cup and sucked on the straw. He tossed it back in. He picked up an empty bottle of cola and sucked down a few drops.

"Out of here, soldier," said the captain, grabbing the hobo and hustling him off. The captain turned to me.

"Listen, you can't quote me on that 'animals' stuff. Got that? Can't quote me... Not even without my name... I'll have your ass in a sling... Hear me?"

The cop looked tired. Lines grooved all over his face, white hair sticking out of his ears.

"I wasn't planning on it."

A couple of clowns walked up: Stanley Hough from the AIP and Deidre Flitch-Burghardt of the *Star-Chronicle*.

"Did you get anything from the family?" said Stanley.

"No," I said.

"Oh, poop," said Deidre. She turned to the captain. "Officer, do the police have any suspects?"

That was my cue to exit.

NINE-YEAR-OLD SHOOTING VICTIM BURIED

BAY CITY (CNS) – Hundreds of mourners attended the funeral Tuesday of nine-year-old Veyneisha Blockton, whose life was taken last Friday by an apparent stray bullet fired on the playground at the Louis Armstrong Residential Estates in Bay City's Pine Ridges section.

The memorial service at the Sacred Heart Church of the Ecclesiastical was attended by members of Blockton's family and neighbors as well as Bay City Mayor Ernest Favella, Police Chief Nathaniel Nachba, U.S. Representative Ruth Wallis and Nation of Islamicists leader Rev. Dr. Drew "Noble" Ali.

The Rev. Winniford C. Hawkins, who led the memorial service, urged residents to regain control of their neighborhoods.

"We must not let Veyneisha die in vain," Hawkins said. "It is time to stand up and take back our streets. We must police ourselves first and foremost, and that includes each mother knowing what their baby is doing. I am not speaking about Veyneisha's mother. I am talking about the mothers of those gunmen who took her life."

A small white coffin containing Blockton's body was later laid to rest at Shepton Memorial Park in a ceremony attended by at least 200 people, according to police estimates.

In a brief interview, Police Chief Nachba told CNS that investigators were pursuing "several leads" in connection with Blockton's death, but declined to give details.

"We don't do, quote-unquote, investigations," Sernath had said during the interview. "We don't launch crusades. We don't call for grand jury action. We don't do analysis or write flowery essays about how to make the world a better place. There's no lack of experts and mouthpieces out there – and in all due respect, you're not really qualified for that, are you? Maybe one day, if God is good to you... Your job, should you be accepted, is to be the shock troops of our operation: To provide the information as straight as possible. Nothing more."

"Yes, of course," I had said.

"Just so you understand," Sernath had added.

"Sure, I understand."

Editor-In-Chief Rob Sernath was a come-in-at-7 a.m., leave-at-6 p.m. type. He kept his office clean as a new bird cage – spotless walls and a clutterless desktop. He dashed around the office in creased trousers, a sweater vest and penny-loafers, thin as a water moccasin, neck erect as a plastic fork, face bunched and powdery like a moldy lemon. His hair, mainly greasy, was raked across his forehead, while his eyes sat like grey pebbles in the moldy yellow, endlessly darting behind rimless glasses.

"I'll be frank with you – the basis of our business model is no money for the employees. This is America – no free rides," Sernath had yukked, slapping a pen in his palm. "Because there's no premium on what we do – it isn't, as they say, rocket science. You won't get rich here, but you will gain a wealth of real experience – things you could never learn in 25 years at those so-called journalism schools."

"I never went to a journalism school..."

"Please – please – it doesn't matter. What I'm saying is, if you wanted money, you'd go elsewhere, wouldn't you? You'd go into finance or government or the law, or syndicated television sales... If you were really smart, you'd have started selling dog food or corn futures or something on the internet." He leaned back and yukked, his chair squeaking.

Sernath was a Philosophy Master's out of Princeton, had supposedly been with Capps-Neubold since the age of 22. He was "25 years in Detroit with Capps-Neubold." Now, in the last year, Capps-Neubold had sent him to Bay City to handle the takeover of Cities News. The advertising said he was brilliant, a management whiz, a news chief of the highest caliber. Under no circumstances had he been "forced out of Detroit for sheer stupidity," as Richie liked to claim.

"Do you believe in the concept of the journalist as a revolutionary – as an agent of change in the larger society?"

"Well, could be, in theory..."

"That's right, in theory. Not our line."

"Fair enough."

Sernath had left his wife back in Detroit somewhere. According to Richie, she was either planning to come out to Bay City, or not planning to because they were getting an ugly divorce. It wasn't totally clear. Sernath didn't seem overly concerned. He appeared to be screwing a sallow, hollow-cheeked lady with short brown hair whom he called "my good friend Lynn." Lynn, who had big teeth and liked to show them, was a professional woman of some sort who favored the look of a purple or pink scarf and good, firm calves peeking out from an expensive skirtsuit.

Sernath enjoyed showing Lynn around. He would escort her through the office and they would go into his glass enclosure, carrying plastic containers of sliced fruit and pasta salad, bottles of ice tea for lunch. They'd close the glass behind them. Sernath would sit back with his arms around his neck, flashing his gums.

"My bosses," Sernath continued, "the people I work for, and who you will work for – we view Cities News and our other outlets as a public trust. By that I mean we serve the public interest, broadly defined. We strive to inform, number one, and to mildly entertain, number two. We are not a tool for private agendas. We are not a tool employed to settle the petty rivalries of bureaucrats."

"Of course not."

"So where do you see yourself going in this business – five, ten, twenty years down the line?"

"Well, my ultimate goal is to be Editor of *The New York Times*, if that's what you mean. That's what I'm shooting for."

Sernath yukked.

"Now there's an ambitious young man. Haven't heard that one in a while."

> HOLIDAY DRUNK DRIVING: 32 DIE, 534 ARRESTS
>
> BAY CITY (CNS) – The Highway Patrol said 32 people were killed in accidents and 534 people were arrested on suspicion of driving under the influence of alcohol or drugs during a crackdown in the Bay region over the Memorial Day weekend.
>
> Cmdr. Bert Bemelmans said the Highway Patrol recorded at least 155 alcohol- or drug-related crashes that resulted in deaths or injuries in the nine-county region over the four-day holiday.
>
> Bemelmans said the accidents left 32 people dead and 63 with minor to serious injuries.

> In an interview with CNS, Janet Ayodhya, spokeswoman for the Bay Chapter of Mothers Against Drunk Driving, welcomed the police crackdown but said her group believes it should be a daily police activity, not just during holiday periods.
>
> She described the weekend death toll and arrest figures as a "disgusting atrocity" and a "sad commentary."

The TV and radio subscribers repeated what we put out nearly verbatim, without saying it was we who had done the reporting, not them. It was also true of the newspapers, the smaller papers in the counties but also the two major Bay City papers – the semi-tabloidish *Star-Chronicle*, which took bitterly hardline positions on nearly all subjects, and the more "intellectual"-appearing *Daily Examiner-Mail*. Day after day, stories I had written would appear nearly as they had gone out over the wire, without any credit whatsoever, stuck in the "Briefs" or "From Our Wire Services" sections of the papers. This was the essential reality of the wire-service reporter and I accepted it, for the most part. However, the one thing I could not accept was when whole chunks of stories I had written, including quotes, would appear word for word on the front page of the *Star-Chronicle* or *Examiner-Mail* – under the byline of one their reporters.

What the hell type of deal was this? I remember thinking. THIS WAS MY IMMORTAL SHIT! It rubbed raw, it rubbed wrong. These were supposedly "pro" reporters, making at least twice the money I was!

Richie had been telling me this was the way it was, that nothing could be done, but still it burned, so one morning I barged into the glass cage and demanded an answer from Sernath. He was far from interested. He slowly batted his eyelids and told me that while it was "somewhat frowned upon," they were allowed under "the contract" to do it as much as they pleased.

"Sorry, we don't have an oar in the water on this one."

I came back to the desk.

"HEY, CLOWN!" Richie roared. "I told you, it's all been made legal. Nobody gives nothin' for free, never. It's got to be demanded, backed by a threat, then locked down in legal writing. When are you going to start demanding, kid? Or are you just gonna sit there and take it?"

"That's it, Richie. You're done."

Richie stood up and spun around, waving his arms.

"DON'T ANSWER, KID! Listen to Mr. Richie: IT'S TOO LATE! They've already turned you into their tool. They've made of you a moron. Don't you get it? How you think you got in here?"

"Aw, man..."

"That's right, The Man! The Man pays the bills. The Man makes the rules. The Man keeps the Negroes down! You kill me, kid, you knock me out. They pull your string and you squawk like a chicken. BWAWK, BWA-BWA-BWA-BWAWK!"

> MAN ARRESTED FOR MUTILATED DOGS SCAM
>
> BAY CITY (CNS) – Bay City police said a man was arrested Wednesday on suspicion of mutilating dogs as part of a fraud in which he netted thousands of dollars from people at college campuses including Bay City State University and East Bay City College.
>
> Lt. Michael Cunahill said Edward Knebelt, 43, was charged with 10 counts of animal cruelty with special circumstances, and one count of fraud.
>
> Cunahill said a female Dalmatian puppy, with her right paw missing, was seized when Knebelt was arrested at his home in Verniss, Ortega County.
>
> Cunahill said investigators have spoken to witnesses who alleged that Knebelt would put a dog with one or two missing limbs in his bicycle basket next to a sign saying: "This dog needs to go to the vet. Please donate."

Richie was a big old bag of onions. From day one he thought he had me held down by the scrotum. Richie thought he had a scrotum-lock on everyone. Richie had been at Cities News Services for more than 10 years, making him the "senior" reporter on the staff. A few years ago he had been promoted to City Council & Government Reporter – the highest staff position short of editing and management. Even he knew they weren't going to let him go much higher.

"NEWS CLOWNS," Richie boomed daily, marching around, wringing his hands. "Never trust a News Clown, kid. Look it up: News Clown – a small, mainly brainless specimen. Arrogant yet cowardly, boastful yet unseemly. Collaborating with the authorities for pennies on the dollar to bring you death and destruction, lies and misery, foolishness and humiliation — not to mention unwavering support for the status quo and the powers that be. And worse."

"Yes, good sir..."

"And worse!" he would say, shaking his finger, his black wad of mustache wobbling, purple neck blotches darkening. "Don't forget the worse!"

> WOMAN ARRESTED AFTER PASTOR STABBED
>
> EAST BAY CITY (CNS) - East Bay City police said a 40-year-old woman was arrested on attempted murder charges after she allegedly stabbed a pastor after a Bible study.
>
> Sgt. Barry Leamon said Pastor Lee Jonathan was attacked Monday as he talked with members of his congregation at Trinity Faith Christian Church.
>
> Leamon said witnesses told investigators that the suspect, Linda Yergin, ran up and stabbed Jonathan with a 10-inch knife several times before she was restrained by other study group members.

Richie was originally from Dakota or Carolina somewhere, where he had started out writing up the high school football games and the hog report. Then he and his wife had the idea to move out to Bay City. Richie claimed his wife had left around the time of his City Hall promotion — taking the two kids, moving out of state and studying to become a psychiatrist. Richie stayed at Cities News, and kept staying. He claimed he had promised to quit being a News Clown, to become a "nice guy," get a "real job" and "start whacking my meat to her god." From what I could understand, she was now remarried to a rich chiropractor or something.

Richie would glare at me. "Think you're hot stuff, don't you, kid?"

"Hell no."

"Yeah, you do. I can *smell it* all over. You're the pig, you're the swan. World's greatest journalist, greatest writer of all time. Packed so full of sperm and hot shit, it just *oozes*. Thought I smelled something funny."

"Thanks, Richie."

"That's right, kid, you nailed it! Sunlight is the best disinfectant. Ignorant and free has never, ever. Afflict the comfortable, comfort the clueless. Spice the pork, sell the sizzle. The pen is mightier than the world's second oldest profession. Neither favoritism for friends, nor friends of friends, no, never. A baby cries, a cop dies. Rape, murder – hey hey children, it's just a shout away. When the going gets weird, the weird freak out. Copy and paste, copy and paste, copy and paste..."

"You said it..."

"That's right, kid. Half-truths and non-truths, nothing but... Sworn on a stack of Bibles, over and over, in the Supreme Court of the United States of America."

"Yes, quite possibly."

"TRUTH, HAH!" Richie's eyes popped and he rolled back in his swivel chair, knocking against a file cabinet. "If you want to know the truth, you got to dig up Johnny Booth. Ever hear of Johnny Booth, kid?"

"Sure, he's that guy that did the first heart transplant."

"That's right, kid, he's the guy who invented dynamite. Great American, Johnny Booth. Made our country what it is today."

> TRUCK KILLS GIRL DURING STOP FOR TURTLE
> LAKEVIEW (CNS) – The Lakeview County Sheriff's Dept. said a five-year-old girl was hit and killed by a passing truck after her father stopped their vehicle to help an apparently lost turtle off the road.
>
> Sgt. Dan Lantana said the father and daughter were travelling on Road 174 when they spotted the turtle in the center of the road.
>
> Lantana said the 31-year-old father had told the child to stay in the car as he went to the turtle, but "curiosity apparently got the better of her."
>
> Lantana said the truck driver passed tests for alcohol or drug use, and no charges were expected to be filed.

Sernath was technically the biggest of the crappers, and Dick could not be touched, but the real power belonged to Wayne Brownberger. Wayne had been Dick's right hand man since the start of CNS, the first person Dick hired. Wayne, whose official title had always been Assistant Editor, had, along with many lawyers, negotiated the deal for the Capps-Neubold takeover. Wayne supposedly knew all the "secrets." He cracked the whip, controlled the logistics, implemented the cost-reduction. You went to see Wayne first thing after Dick, Sernath and Kate had cleared on your hire. Wayne set you up with your insurance forms, your building pass, your cell phone account. He helped you file for your official press badge.

"If there's any improper behavior on your part, the police will revoke your press pass. Maybe the courts will exonerate you later, but the police don't care. Also, under the law, you must defer to any instruction given by an officer of the law. Even if you think you are within your rights, you must defer. We will sort it out later."

"Yes."

"Because, if for any reason your accreditation is revoked, we will have to release you. Every journalist in this office must have a valid accreditation."

"I understand."

Wayne had thinning light blond hair and a skin condition which sometimes left him with raw pink patches on his cheeks, neck and hands. He took pills and had many bottles of them laid out on a stand next to his desk. Each day he put a white cream on his lips and face. He would lock his glass cage and turn and face the wall, working at his computer, as the cream worked its way in.

"If you do any amount of illegal drugs and/or alcohol, and we come to believe that it is affecting your on-the-job performance, we can and will take a hair and blood sample and proceed from there. You are not allowed to be intoxicated while working for Cities News Services."

"Of course not."

"You are free to quit at any time without prior notice and without giving a reason. For our part, we retain the legal capability of letting you go without prior notice and without listing a reason. Anything can happen in a courtroom, of course, so it is our unofficial policy not to exercise this right. But we feel you should know it exists."

"Yes."

"If you are a smoker – first, I suggest you quit. There is, I believe, a smoking cessation benefit within our insurance policy, at a nominal cost. If you are a smoker and you absolutely must smoke while on the office premises, you must go to the Lounge on the northeast corner of the first floor. You are entitled to two 15-minute breaks and a half-hour for lunch per nine-hour shift. It is illegal to smoke in the restrooms or stairwells. Security will issue you a citation if you are caught smoking in an unauthorized zone. Two citations and your building pass will be at risk. You must have a building pass to work at Cities News Services."

"Absolutely."

"Under the insurance benefit, it's a $250 deductible every time you visit the doctor, even for emergencies."

"Yes, thank you."

I didn't go to the doctor or dentist for five years.

> CONVICTED MURDERER RELEASED BY MISTAKE
>
> BAY CITY (CNS) – State prison officials said a 17-year-old convicted murderer was released by "mistake" Wednesday after a court hearing in East Bay City.
>
> Prison Service Spokeswoman Allison Wohlstetter said Maurius Billingsley was convicted last November of stabbing to death 13-year-old Jerome Ghawar.
>
> Wohlstetter said Billingsley was "mistakenly" released after he appeared in court for an unrelated case.
>
> Wohlstetter said prison authorities and police believe Billingsley could be dangerous and that his re-capture is a high priority.

My first day at CNS, a guy with short white hair, a thin pink face and an extremely large nose came over and shook my hand.

"I'm Tom," he said. "You can call me Tommy-Gun."

"Serious? All right, Tommy-Gun."

Tommy-Gun may in fact have been some kind of albino. He was one of the sports reporter-editors, in charge of the high school and college games. He worked mainly in the afternoon and evening, taking calls from stringers and getting the scores out. He would go out to cover some of the big games, the college bowl and the high school championships.

Tommy was fixated on Shally, the thin mouselike girl with long hair who sat at the front desk answering phones and typing entries for the Daily Calendar listing. He would pull a chair next to her desk and sweet talk her, staring into her ear and trying to knock knees. I wasn't sure he was getting anywhere.

Tommy-G would corner me in the hall or at my work station.

"You think Shally's hot? Do you? C'mon, man, do you?"

"She's all right, Tommy... Yeah, she's hot, sure."

"She's cool, man. I can talk to her all day."

"So... what? Ask her out. Just fucking go for it."

"Not yet... I'm working on it, it takes time. You got to build up to it..."

"No, man, hell no. Do it now, today. Ask her and get it over with..."

"Nah! She's not ready yet..."

"She'll never be more ready than she is now..."

Tommy-Gun could be good, as long as you didn't let him get going on money. Tommy claimed he kept track of "every penny" he spent, writing down each expense in a notebook he carried around. Everything went into the book – colas and chewing gum, socks and light bulbs, etc. The idea was to "discover" what you were spending your money on, then cut some out to save a few cents. Instead of buying a sandwich at a deli, for example, Tommy made cucumber and cheese sandwiches at home and claimed he saved "a ton" of money. He was highly critical of people who bought things like a bottle of water, when you could get water for free from drinking fountains or bathrooms. This way he was able to save more and "invest" it. He was saving with several bank programs.

"You probably waste $150 a month on cigarettes and coffee. You don't need any of that."

"It's not waste," I said. "I need that stuff. It keeps me alive."

"It'll kill you. It'll turn your lungs all black and mushy."

"I said, it keeps me alive... What kills you? You could walk down the street and get hit on the head with a dictionary. Your brain could explode and start dripping out your nose. Run right down your face and on to your shirt. Then what would you say?"

I had always hated going through this with people.

"But that's a lot of money you could be saving."

"I don't want to save it. It's so little, its not worth saving. I'd rather waste it."

"That can't be true," he said, shaking his head, "but it's your choice, I guess. It's still a free country."

"That's right, Tommy-Gun. And let's not forget it."

> WOMAN HIT BY THROWN SCHOOL DICTIONARY
>
> BAY CITY (CNS) – Bay City police said a woman walking on a sidewalk was seriously injured Wednesday by a dictionary thrown from a fifth-story classroom.
>
> Sgt. Alan Jondh said two 13-year-old male students at Thomas Edison Middle School were being questioned by detectives in connection with the incident.

Jondh said the dictionary that struck the 34-year-old woman weighed about 15 pounds.

Bay Community Hospital spokeswoman Leah Floch said the victim was in critical but stable condition with head and neck injuries.

CURVEBALL:
Gal Pal's Baseball Delight!

★ 4 ★

TIME TO TAKE OFF THE GLOVES
By Robiann Coughan

Next American Century Policy Project Studies Journal Quarterly

Confronted with deadly attacks and challenges to our authority on every front, it's time for America to stop being Mr. Nice Guy. It's time to stop worrying about "collateral damage." It's time to take off the velvet gloves. The so-called "peace-loving" people of the Middle East need to be shown that it doesn't pay to mess with Americans. They need to be shown once and for all that there is no profit in provoking Uncle Sam and our interests. They need to learn that the principle of "blowback" goes both ways.

It's a good sign that President Wolfgang G. Mnung seems to understand that the time for "compromise" and "realpolitik" was over the second the first 9/11 hijacker stood from his seat and slashed the neck of an innocent stewardess.

We should not waste another second trying to gain an "international consensus" for anything we do. We should stop apologizing to the "world community" for defending our country. Since when should terrorist-supporting, human rights-abusing dictatorships such as Sudan, Iran, Saudi Arabia, Syria, Cuba, Myanmar, North Korea, Russia, Zimbabwe, Venezuela and China have a veto over the Land of the Free? France, Germany, Belgium, Luxembourg and the other sponges who run the corrupt United Nations bureaucracy have no right to tell America how to protect itself. It should go without saying that these weak-sister "allies" would all be speaking German with a Nazi accent now if wasn't for America's bravery and determination to defend Freedom during World War II.

If Timothy McVeigh had really wanted to take out America's enemies, he should have blasted his rent-a-truck bomb on Manhattan's 43rd St. – headquarters of *The New York Times*. Better yet, Timothy could have blasted his truck at Dag Hammarskjold Plaza, the seat of the United Nations. Another good target would have been the London headquarters of Amnesty International – otherwise known as the official propaganda arm of Al-Qaeda.

(Sensitive liberals, internationalists, "human rights" activists and other readers of *The New York Times* don't like what I have to say? Then maybe it's time to hold another Third-World teach-in at Harvard Square. You can invite your dear friends, Mumia and Peltier. Oh, I forgot, those harsh critics of American policy are where they belong – in prison for murder.)

America's history is rich in bold strikes against tyranny, and we need to call on that history now. Look at the peace that has reigned in Germany and the rest of Europe since America and its allies laid waste, without qualms or remorse, to the Nazi vermin and their supporters. We don't hear much from the worms of Paris about that one, do we? Look how peaceful and profitable Japan has become since we cast aside doubt and imposed Freedom's will with two nuclear bomb detonations that shattered the hold of the degenerate emperor and his minions.

America outsmarted the Soviet Union move for move in the Cold War, building up our military and threatening nuclear annihilation until the Soviet system collapsed of its own decay and corruption. Now Russia shames and soils itself on a daily basis, drowning in a morass of crime, terrorism and prostitution.

The CIA famously meddled in Iran, ousting the democratically-elected Socialist-Nationalist government in a 1953 coup and bringing the pro-America Shah to power. Later, after Islamic fascists got rid of the Shah and took Americans hostage, we gave Saddam Hussein helicopters and other materiel so Iraq could chemically attack Iran as part of the 1980-88 Iran-Iraq War, which killed an estimated 1.5 million human beings. (And to ensure they kept killing each other, we secretly funneled arms to Iran in what history books now refer to as the Iran-Contra Scandal.)

America courageously held the line against Commie domination in Vietnam, and we supplied Stinger missiles to help the valiant mujahedeen in Afghanistan send the Soviet invaders limping back to Moscow. We supported military coups in Guatemala and Chile, Reagan bombed Libya, and Grenada was freed from Commie clutches in a matter of days thanks to bold U.S. action. American forces stormed into Panama to make sure the loathsome drug kingpin Noriega spends the rest of his days rotting in jail. We put right-wing death squads to work in El Salvador, and funded our own Contra Freedom Army to rescue the Nicaraguans from Commie squalor. We continue to actively support the paramilitary Freedom squads and their allies in the Colombian armed forces in the struggle against Commie guerrilla cocaine-traffickers. America bombed the Serbs back to World War I levels – to defend Muslims, no less – and now the only squeaking we hear from the vile Milosevic is in a war crimes court. And let's not forget that for decades, America has worked to suffocate the despotic Fidel Castro regime, and one day soon the proud Cuban people will again be ringing Freedom's cashbox.

If we want to survive as a country and civilization, we should not restrain our Air Force and artillery batteries from wreaking devastation on Middle Eastern nations who fail to adapt to our policies. In other words, we may need to flatten them. We may need to pulverize their cities and salt their soil, as the Romans did with troublesome enemies. We may need to decorate the Middle East with "daisy cutter" bombs and make the region our stomping ground, with

Freedom's boot prints in the sand of every country.

We need to make clear our message, once and for all: Don't Support Terrorists Who Hate America.

No blood for oil, they say? I say, If not oil and Freedom, then what is worth fighting for?

I hate to break the news to the delicate-hearted, but oil in fact means Freedom. Without oil, our way of life would break down in a few hours. If we don't control the world's oil and guarantee its supply to our friends, somebody else will – Europe and Japan, for example, would start building up their militaries to try to control it. And we definitely don't want that to happen.

Why do they hate us? Because we don't accept the Islamo-fascism they want to impose on the world. Because... who cares why they hate us? Does the cat try to understand the canary? Does the tiger feel sympathy for the travails of the antelope? Hate is a fact of life in this world – Earth is not Heaven. Life on this planet has always been a power struggle between living things battling to sustain themselves, and survival has always favored the strong and ruthless. And the truth remains that when you attack the United States and its people, you must be whacked down. History has shown that America's ability to maintain global supremacy depends on showing those who would challenge us that their action is futile.

They call us the Great Satan? I've got no problem with that. And maybe it's time to show them just what it means.

We need to show our strength. We need to show that we stand for Justice and Freedom. We may need to bomb their vapid desert lands and dusty tent cities into one giant tennis court. We may need to convert them to Christianity and Judaism – the two religions that have demonstrated they can support democracies. Because democracies don't start wars against each other or fund anti-American terrorist killers. And when the dust clears, we may need to train their survivors in the rules and means of the service-sector economy. Because countries with MacBeefy's and Buckfriars don't attack America.

The writer, a blond actress, is professor of International Relations at John H. Hotchkiss Law University and author of The New York Times *bestseller* 1,871 Ways Liberals Hate America.

We were in a baseball bar, The Dugout it was called, most of it in the basement. Kate's idea – one of her "favorite bars." It was Friday night, tables of college geeks and office goofs, woofing it up in baseball heaven. Baseball hats and bats and pennants hung from the rafters, posters and photo shots of baseball players hung everywhere across the varnished dark red wood.

It was after the "Cuban food." The Cuban food appeared to have been something involving bananas, eggplant and eucalyptus leaves, and already I was forgetting it. I was forgetting everything. I had a beer in front of me, along with a tall thin "Triple Play" – Cutty Sark, Scoresby, Tanqueray and cherry coke on ice, a dusting of crushed crackerjack. It was $10.50 per for these drinks, but Kate had insisted. She had demanded. Kate was wearing a light blue sleeveless blouse, a pink rag with yellow and purple flowers in her hair. She had been talking, talking.

She moved her ass snug against mine, rested her hand on my wrist.

"Your right eye is a little smaller than your left. Did you know that?"

"No..."

"It is... Your eyebrow comes down lower on the right. It's cute!"

"It doesn't, Kate."

"It does! Oh, it does!"

The waiter came by. I ordered another beer, along with a "Switch Hitter" – Jack Daniels, Finlandia, Kahlua Mudslide and Sprite, poured over crushed ice and powdered sugar.

I wanted to drink and drink. God, I deserved it. It had been a week. MOTHER CHARGED WITH MURDER AFTER SON DIES IN CLOTHES DRYER. MISSING NIGERIAN STUDENT'S BODY FOUND BURNED. FIRED EMPLOYEE KILLS WORKER AT MENTAL HEALTH CLINIC had been some of the choicest morsels – since Wednesday. I'd been called at 9:30 Thursday night to run my ass out to a fire at the Parchman Baptist Church across the water in East Bay. They hadn't been able to save much of it. And I still had the Saturday afternoon shift to go.

"You're starting to scare me with how much you drink!"

"Kate, relax. I haven't drunk nothing..."

I got up to have another smoke. I was having to go out every ten minutes.

"My gosh, you smoke a cigarette every ten minutes! You'll kill yourself! I've never seen anybody smoke like you."

"Could be, Kate."

I grabbed a handful of popcorn from the barrel on the table and went back up the stairs. We were in Nowell Heights, not far from where Kate lived. She had already told me twice about how the rent was more than half her salary, but it was O.K. because the live-in boyfriend, Joel, kicked in his half, making the rent and utilities "almost one-third" of her total pay.

I stood out front and lit one. College kids and vagrants walked by under a golden dark sky churning with burnt orange clouds. There was a brief buzz and the rows of streetlights flicked on together. In the bookstore window next door, a fellow in striped long sleeves and acid-wash jeans searched for a clue in the section labeled Maps & Atlases. A portly woman in a black sweater walked by with a paper cup of coffee and the new copy of DOLLS & DOLLHOUSES TODAY.

I came back to find Kate on the phone again. She hung up.

"So Kate," I said, "how's Joel doing?"

"Don't worry, I told him I was going out with work people. It's fine…"

"One of those type of deals, huh?"

"What type of deals? We're out having dinner and a drink after work. It's not like we're having sex in some sleazy hotel." She laughed.

I drank some beer, had three or four sips of the "Switch Hitter." It tasted like cold pancake syrup, they all did. On the TV, Jon Bon Jovi was walking through a Hindu temple wearing sunglasses, his hair flowing and rippling. A small Asian child smiled. Somebody in a soldier's costume snapped photos and pointed a gun. Shirtless longhairs from Bon Jovi's band grimaced and stroked guitars. Karate boxers did slow-motion kicks, a Chinese woman smiled. Hindu temple shots rolled in grainy black and white. The Chinese woman appeared in her underwear, sitting next to Bon Jovi on a bed in dim lighting. Bon Jovi looked troubled, pained, majestic. The camera panned across his tangled carpet of chest hair…

Kate started talking about Miami again. At her newspaper, she had worked on a series about refugees who had escaped the war zone in some hellhole, finally making it to America. One woman's husband had gone off to fight the war, leaving everyone behind. Then one day, bad guys from the other team dropped by the village. They were very bad guys. Nobody, somehow, had thought it might happen.

The bad guys killed or chased off the few men who had stayed behind, then beat the woman, beat her sister, beat her daughter, then raped all three repeatedly for four or five days and nights. They tied the 14-year-old son to a chair and made him watch, declining to even let him use the bathroom for several days. Then they chained up the son in the barn, next to the cows they had shot with machine guns.

The bad guys went through the houses and shops, boiling eggs and eating sausages and stealing anything of any possible worth, even door hinges, knobs from the oven, silverware with plastic handles. What they didn't eat or steal, they burned. Finally they left, taking the son to go fight the war for their team. Stupidly, the females continued to stay in the town until a different group of bad guys from the other team came. The lady and her sister and daughter were split up and taken to "rape camps." They were raped several times per day. The soldiers would get drunk, rape them and beat them and rape them again. The soldiers burned them with cigarettes, carved swastikas on their breasts, called them horrible names.

Then one day a peace agreement was announced. The bad guys ran away. American soldiers showed up and gave the women food and medicine and drove them to town. Unfortunately, the soldiers had got the lady's sister pregnant and she had a baby. She killed it. The daughter also got pregnant, but she kept hers. The lady found her son in the hospital. He had lost a leg and a hand and suffered spinal damage in a land mine blast. He couldn't talk, only drool.

Eventually, the whole pack of them applied to the U.S. embassy and got permission to come to America. The U.S. government set them up with an apartment and money. The daughter works at a beauty salon and her rapist offspring son goes to daycare. The lady's son sits in a wheelchair at the YMCA and plays chess. The lady sits and cries to reporters. It was a long story.

"Over what?" Kate said. "That really proved to me there's evil in this world."

"You bet there is, Kate..."

I downed swallows of beer, scarfed popcorn, looked at baseball flags and pictures of baseball players. The waiter came up.

"Want another drink, Kate?"

"Sure, I'll have one more!"

Kate got a "Grand Slam." I got a beer and an "Extra Innings" – Chinaco, E & J Gold and Hypnotiq, mixed with pineapple juice and 7-Up.

"So what's your dad do?" said Kate.

"He's a submarine pilot..."

"Oh, really?"

"No, he's a fry-cook... He used to have his own restaurants, but they failed. He lives in Wisconsin. They have a contest for the worst beard in town and he wins every year. They put him in a little jail and roll him down the street and everybody claps. He's been married five times."

"Five times! Different women? Wow, how fascinating!"

"Yeah, he's a real hero. Never met a woman who'll say no to him."

"Oh, wow," said Kate, laughing. "What about your mom?"

"She works in a lab. She does tests on blood, shit and piss for the hospital."

"Wow, interesting..."

"Not really..."

Kate came forward and touched her nose to mine, ran her fingers through my hair. She turned away, cheeks flushing pink.

"You act so tough," said Kate, "like the toughest guy in the world – like you don't care, like you got it all figured out... But you're not so tough, everyone can see! You've got all this, this – this, I don't know, hope!"

"You're drunk, Kate..."

"I'm not drunk!"

Kate ran her finger down my cheek, traced it around my jaw. Her lips and eyes were moist, she looked tired. She lifted her leg off my thigh, leaned forward and kissed me – not so much a kiss really, as a bumping of her lips against mine.

"There," she said. "I did it."

"That's fine, Kate..."

"You're so strong," she said, her hands massaging my biceps. "Young and strong..."

She kissed me again, harder, and tried to stick her tongue in. I squirmed to the side so she couldn't get it all the way in. She reached down and stroked the inside of my thigh. I turned away, then turned back. Kate punched her tongue into my mouth. The tongue poked around wildly, straining as if to leap down my throat. Without really meaning it to, my hand came up under her blouse. My fingers moved on their own, dancing amongst her braless breasts, rolling them from side to side, pulling at the nipples. Her slippery tongue flipped and twisted inside my mouth.

I leaned back, pulled out my hand, turned away.

"I know, I know." Kate grabbed for her phone. "I'll call a taxi."

"Look, I've got a 10-dollar bill..." I started to reach in my pocket.

"I've got it," said Kate, waving a credit card. "You can get it next time."

"You bet..."

Kate put her arms around my waist as we walked out, pit-a-peppering my neck with kisses. I lit a smoke as we stood in front waiting. Streetlights and neon bounced about, ricocheting against car windshields and storefronts, caroming off reflectors and stop signs. A motorcycle screamed past at about 90, the geek suddenly stomping the brake just as the light went red. He idled at the crosswalk, gunning the motor.

I gushed smoke. I was still thirsty, thirstier than ever.

"We could go to my place," said Kate. "You should see it... It's got a great balcony."

"What about Joel?"

"He's probably asleep. Maybe he'll want to have a few beers... We can get a 12-pack and play the new Johnny Cash album."

She got in the taxi, leaving the door open.

"See you later, Kate."

"You're not coming? We can drop you at your place..."

"Kate, no – it's all right, I'll walk. It's not so far..."

She threw a sad face, blew me a kiss.

"See ya later, Thor." She slammed the door, the taxi tore off.

Silvertown wasn't close at all, it was going to be a 45-minute walk. I saw a liquor store and went in. A bottle of vodka caught my eye first thing. They didn't keep it on shelves behind Plexiglas out here, but under the counter, behind glass. It came to $9.13. The fellow put it in a brown paper sack, and I slipped it into my coat pocket. This would get me into the pad and then some.

I cruised along, feeling better and better. Kate was O.K., but I was better off with the vodka.

The vodka got easier, the gagging stopped, I was taking bigger and bigger slugs. I hit the Silvertown border, the bottle about half gone. I had begun to stagger every so often, toes not quite lifting all the way off the pavement.

Dammit, I thought – I had kissed Kate. I had grabbed her boobs.

I wobbled deeper in. Silvertown guys peered out from doorways. Guys squatted under streetlamps. Guys slammed car hoods. Skinny Silvertown guys flashed hand signals, whistled at windows, licked their fingers, smoothed down mustaches. Drug guys starting rushing me, smacking into me, about four per block. I lipped vodka, pushing forward.

"What you looking for, dude?"

"No... nothing."

"Hey bwoy!"

Smack-smack-smack. I swerved past dudes monitoring pedestrian traffic in front of the Hacienda, swam past grab-ass guys in front of the Pinkeye and Jet Rainbow. I bumped into a large bunch of them doing the smashed potato in the square by the Old Beacon Theater. I weaved and smacked and knocked my way through, swatting away various hands.

Dudes blocked the walk, groaning and playing bongos outside the Poly Vinyl. A siren wailed, a dumpster rattled down the curb. Dudes did hand-claps and jumps, singing ditties. Dudes smoked shit off cola cans and did spin moves. Dudes smashed the potato atop a stretch of spackled marble. An explosion went off somewhere. Dudes in stetson brims drove by in candy-apple cruisemobiles, booming tunes that made the blacktop turn to liquid.

Hey-ho, what do we know,
We from Ida-ho!
Hey-ho, what do we know,
We from Ida-ho!

Prosties in blue feathers splayed their legs beneath a row of palm trees, laughing. Prosties rushed forward, pawed at my crotch, blew in my ear. Peach-colored lights whirled over a guy writhing on the sidewalk, his eyes closed. Dudes in leather caps and chainwear did tap-dances, shaking the potato. An explosion went off. Shadows darted, shapes flew. A German shepherd rose on his hind legs, leaping for something a dude in goggles was dangling.

I leaned back on a bench and sucked vodka...

A guy with a thin black mustache came up and smacked me.

"Wanna buy a nice bitch?"

"Huh?"

He sat down, slapped his thigh. "You know, *man* – a bitch." He pointed his index finger at me, brought down his thumb, blew the top of his finger. "A real clean bitch."

"Uh... uh..."

"Seventy-five, no, sixty, for you... Sixty-five for you."

I leaned forward, drooling.

"Shit, lemme have a drink."

He took a knock and handed it back.

"You ain't with the police are you, man?"

"Oh, no... no..."

"You sure you ain't with the police?"

I sucked drool back into my mouth. "I – I – I'm..."

He stuck out a hand. "'Nother drink."

He had his guzzle and stamped off. I stood and took a guzzle. A prostie bounced into me, cackled, danced off. I took a gurgle and spun out, leaning against a wall, checking my front and back pockets. I took another gulp, stepped, crashed into the wall.

Two foot-patrol cops holding foil-wrapped burritos walked back and forth, guarding an automatic bank machine.

An explosion went off. Cops jerked around. Didn't see nothing.

I threw up in a bush near the Sunny Day Transition Home – "Helping Those Who CHOOSE To Help Themselves NO

SOLICITORS PLEASE." I fell to my knees and let go – it was like I was was spitting up pieces of my throat, my stomach squeezing and knotting. Popcorn and sauce came up, plenty of liquid…

Something hit my ear, the side of my face. I rolled, sports coat elbow slipping in the vomit. A man, apparently some kind of security guard, lifted me by the neck of the coat. He turned me, shoved and kicked me in the ass.

I tumbled a few steps, then was down again. The man roared, something I couldn't make out. He charged at me, a silver flashlight swinging from his fist.

I rolled off the grass, knees tearing into the sidewalk. His boot made the side of my thigh. I rolled again, chin smacking the concrete. His boots bombed the pavement close to my head.

I hit a tire, clawed up the side of a car, started rolling down the block.

I hit The Quarter, 26th Street, 27th… The index and middle fingers of my right hand had got smushed. Blood rolled down my palm… drops falling from my wrist to my shoes and the cement. I pushed the hand into my sports coat pocket and kept going. I was getting closer, almost to the place now.

An explosion went off. Just another ten blocks to go…

I turned the corner. I could see the apartment, a block to the left. I slunk past a group standing around a can fire in the alley.

"Tole the bitch – tole her a tousand times, tole her – I say, getcher goddamn tubes tied! What I says to her. Says to her, getcher goddam tubes tied 'cause I don't want no more goddam rugrunts runnin' 'round here! Them sunbitches drive me crazy. Drown 'em all. What I says to that bitch. DROWN 'EM ALL! Don' wan' no more a them goddam rugrunts! An' that sunbitch, why, she ain't nothin' but a goddam ho, I says to her, GETCHER GODDAM TUBES TIED! I told that ho, GETCHER GODDAM TUBES TIED!"

ADDLED: Young Men Stupid Enough to Live with Worms!

★ 5 ★

I would get bigger and bigger, continually gaining torque. There would be annotated editions, movies, Broadway productions, multi-volume sets, internet sites, annual conventions devoted to my work in Ireland, Shanghai and St. Petersburg. Intense young men in floppy hair would flock up, claiming to belong to my "school." I would send them away, yawningly telling them that idol worship was cheap stuff for chumps. I'd be announced winner of every major prize but famously decline them all, accusing the givers of fraud and rank political hypocrisy.

I'd be drunk in Paris for six days. I would move into a phase of bitterness and high wisdom, somewhat imbecilic, yet at the same time magisterial, immaculate, beyond further stain. I would broadly condemn man's fate, declare pain the source of all beauty, wrap myself in lineaments of false fragility and humility. I'd contemplate man's nature at some length, concluding it was likely incapable of changing. I would denounce "fame" and all that came with it as a hideous, worthless joke. I would become bloated and tawdry, yet still maintain the winning hand. All worry would be over, the fear and threats long gone. I'd give millions to charities, I'd be a soft touch. I'd walk down the street passing out packets of $1,000 cash to any bum or kid who passed. "Waste it," I'd say. "Go ahead, have a party."

I'd grow a beard and dreadlocks, live in a mansion on a cliff, surrounded by wives and children. I'd abandon them to live nude with camels on a remote beach island. I would renounce all writing and move into painting, sculpture. Young girls would come from around the world to surf and study under me. I'd become bored, move to the top of a mountain, refuse to talk to anyone for four years – intent on my work, my struggle...

✪

A major rule in Silvertown was that the liquor stores and markets kept all the booze, cough syrup and infant-formula behind locked security Plexiglas. You could never be too safe anymore, nobody could – a crook or a crackdown, you could never tell which was coming.

Jerry and I would get beers or wine coolers and cruise around the neighborhood in the evening after work, two bwoys on the street. It was illegal to walk the streets with booze, but the liquor store men would put it in a little brown sack for you so no one would know. We'd walk around with the brown sacks, real tough guys, short sleeves rolled to the shoulder, hats at an angle, arms rocking wide, faces a stone scowl. It was all about puffing yourself up and blowing past, you didn't want no one to start messing. We'd head to the park to check up on the basketball games, loop around to Verdugo to look in on the prosties and rappers, the various shoeless freaks.

If you can't beat the bass
Take your crappy ass home!
If you can't beat the bass
Take your dead ass home!

Silvertown shuffled to the groove and rattled to the rumba. It moaned and writhed to the jive and a monstrous croaking sound. Nobody ever bothered to do a damn thing in that place, the steel bars and metal grating, the barbed wire, just kept going up – across shop windows and doors, corn cob stands, junkyards and rubble-strewn vacant lots.

Every so often the schools and social services people would get together to clear a vacant lot so little kids could plant carrots and radishes. They'd immediately padlock a 10-foot iron fence across it. There were just too many goddamn junkies and thieves, wild-ass midnight cocksuckers who could not allow a carrot to grow in peace. A kid would get popped and the world's greatest mural artists would flood out from the woodwork, throwing up vast scapes of sad-faced children and tear-stained mothers, souped-up superbikes, statues of liberty next to tombstone high-rises, giant crucifix steeples next to the eternal sunrise.

The crisis, for the most part, appeared permanent. Uncle was a pimp, mommy had been murdered, daddy was a dope fiend, brother Joe-Joe would be getting out of the pen in seven more months. It was a place where 11-year-old boys were caught with guns at school, 12-

year-old girls got pregnant, and the drug turnover was estimated at $1 million per month – in a roughly 26-block area.

It was hard to take, and most could not take it. Everyone was looking for the easy ride out, for the quick rocket to wealth and notoriety, maybe just something to dull the misery for a minute – anger or insanity, dope or dope-dealing, rap or basketball, prison and gangs and thievery and superstardom.

It could be frightening, the fear was real, the air was thick with threats, real and imagined. Junkies would bop along the street, knocking against buildings and parked cars, until they'd collapse in a blind stupor. Girls in dirty summer dresses and blackened teeth would limp down the block, tears running down their faces, some hell-bent shit-eyes stalking behind. You'd walk across the empty cans and broken glass and couldn't but notice: They'd jabbed the same spot over and over, until their arms and legs had swelled up and the pus ran like rivers out of brown and red dripping sores.

The cops and ambulance boys were always on time when somebody got clipped and didn't get up, but otherwise they tended to be a few minutes late and about a billion dollars short. The cops thrived on "shows of force" and giving pep talks down at the community center, but the reality was like trying to glue together pieces of a popped balloon. No one seemed to have much of a clue, the schools, corporations, government, religion, gangs, "charity" – they had all had decades to show their bungling and uselessness. I would go to the office and catch up on the latest neighborhood developments:

>BOYS HOSPITALIZED AFTER EATING CRACK
>
>BAY CITY (CNS) – Bay City police said three elementary school boys were hospitalized Monday after they "ate" small amounts of crack cocaine in the Silvertown section.
>
>Lt. Al Nouci said a nine-year-old boy found a plastic bag containing the illicit substance near where he was waiting for a bus to Abraham Lincoln Elementary School.
>
>Nouci said the boy "ate" some of the crack cocaine on the bus, apparently thinking it was candy.
>
>Nouci said an 11-year-old boy and a six-year-old boy also consumed some of the substance.

> Nouci said the three boys became sick and were taken to Bay Community Hospital, where they were listed in stable condition.

Dumpsters and trash cans could smoke and burn for days, while around the corner old farts played shell games on boxes and a guy in a cowboy suit did highly evolved dances and bowed to ladies. Freaks whispered to themselves in alleyways and doorways, sat on stairwells continually flicking plastic lighters that would continue not to work. Guys would erupt screaming, stabbing themselves with a screwdriver, lurching down the road, growling and yipping. A woman would be sitting at the bus stop with a checker board on her knees, using her hands to slice and stack invisible ham sandwiches.

Down the block, another rag-man would be on the pay phone, standing there mumbling and gesturing, a large hole in the crotch of his pants. He didn't seem able to afford underwear. He'd be on the line for hours at a time, resting his weight on one leg, then switching to the other. He'd turn nonchalantly and scratch a strange itch. He could be cool and calm, nodding his head sympathetically, or sometimes he might be shouting and arguing with whomever was on the other end. Mr. Goodbar, we called him.

Skinny rag-men would hit the streets, battling the prosties for sidewalk space, hanging out a cardboard shingle: "I HAVE AIDS – Please Give."

You could find the prosties at all hours, fluttering and staggering along the palm-lined boulevards, congregating in small packs along the avenues, dotting the walks around Rockwell Park like boils on a leprosied leg. In the afternoon they'd really start to swing it, pumping their hips, rolling their heads and blowing kisses, as they stuck it on sale and hashed it out with stopped drivers and the never-ending flow of dudes high on beer in a bag and a taste of wicky stick.

"Hey bwoy, looking for a date?"

"Oh, not today, ma'am..."

"What you, faggot?"

"Oh, no..."

The world might have been twisting and boiling out of control, but it was all just a gas in Silvertown, where all that was obvious was consequences. The key fringe benefit was no one cared how much you drank, the noise you made, what you smoked or plugged in. No one cared if you shaved off your eyebrows and ate them. It was the last thing they cared about. The truth was, nobody cared about a damn thing unless you got in the way of whatever scam they were pulling, in which case you might get shot.

Bare-chested toughs with thin little mustaches and india-ink tattoos[*] would swagger around as if they ruled the place, the latest pretenders to the thug throne. If guys could pull it, and many could, they walked around with an angry face. Some could pull a strange glow in the eyes. Guys in sweat suits and hairnets would swagger around like chief chickens, giant gold watches on their wrists, untucked funeral shirts trailing behind. They'd be drinking 40-ounce bottles of beer and Jack from a sack, screaming and hee-hawing into phones, bouncing and squeezing racquetballs. These were "pimps," other times "gang bangers," according to Jerry, sometimes "drug guys," sometimes all of the above – but never the guys Jerry would go to when Candace would order him on a drug run.

Gangs were ever-present, an ill wind that stank up nearly everything. They called themselves the Blood Bounty Hounds, the Original O.G.'s, Mara Salvatrucha, La Colonia de Silvertown, 18th Street Gang, Plug Uglies, Eastside Locos, Eight Trey Brims, Supreme Team, Insane Vice Posse Nation, the Real O.G.'s…

It was hard to keep track, but they were up to something. Most were shrimpy guys whose main job seemed to be scaring people, selling and ripping off drugs, screaming at their bitches, shooting and stabbing each other in revenge for the previous assault, which was retaliation for the earlier attack, which was payback for the attack before that in which the cocksuckers had used a machete to chop off the fingers of the cocksucker who had got his gang symbols tattooed all over each digit…

At the same time, the little wankers seemed deathly frightened of both each other and of the cops. "STOP SNITCHIN'!" they whined, scrawling this pathetic weasel command across the walls and pavements. Absurdly, they combined their pathetic "outlaw" shtick with the worship of "designer" logos and corporate clothing brands, and someone had apparently never told the little runts – it was a lousy style, and they were suckers across the board.

Muthafucka goin' call 911
Sucka gonna spoil alla our fun
Can't trust no sucka

---

[*] Suggests prison time. – ED.

Where da money sucka
Said get ya dick out sucka

Once Jerry and I saw what looked like a dead or wounded animal on the patch of dirt in front of the apartment. Perhaps it seemed a bit like a rabbit, maybe a cat. We came closer to inspect the brown-blond fur. One side was matted with a reddish type of color, still wet.

Jerry took a stick and flipped it. A number of flies and other bugs zoomed out. We saw the manufacturer's tag blowing in the breeze.

"That's a bloody wig!" screamed Jerry.

My last job had been 200 miles down the coast, *The Armadillo Daily News*, crime/county supervisors beat reporter. Brad, the managing editor, refused to believe it when I announced I was quitting. Brad was a bearded, shell-shocked "gunner" from the Vietnam War, or at least he claimed to be. He had an easy time, seven-hour work day, big ranch-style house, decent pay, newspaper job that required little effort. Brad would sit staring out his office window, every so often running his fingers through his beard.

I had walked in on him, blurted it. He had stood up out of his chair, blinking his eyes. He just couldn't believe it.

"You're *taking off?*" he had said. "In *this economy?*"

Brad's beard had started to wobble.

"Got a job?"

"No..."

"Where you going?"

"To the city."

"Got money?"

"About a thousand, I guess..."

"*In this economy?* You're nuts, you'll live in the ghetto..."

Well, nothing had helped, nobody had provided the good information. I lived on cookies and peanut snacks, pretzels and 19-cent bags of noodles, into which sometimes I would mix a can of tuna. We kept the empty tuna cans, washed them out and used them as ashtrays.

It was hard, it took me years to realize the futility and stupidity. It was still unclear to me whether you were supposed to live in constant war with the world, or try to somehow "get along" with it and "cash in" when you could. Therefore, mainly I drank – mainly I WAS TRYING TO KNOCK MYSELF OUT.

Booze was beautiful, you could sort it out at your own pace. Slipping into that weird womb, that half-coma, that warm haze where everything was *still out there* – but at an easy and comfortable distance now, you'd get to it later, maybe. If you could hit the boozing right, it could be like being halfway between living and dying. Some claimed that sex came close, and maybe so, but the odds were better with a bottle. With a little determination, you could nail it every time.

We lived amid torn furniture in a ground-floor unit of the St. Stephen's Apartments, a collapsing wood and graffiti structure on the corner of 27th and Armey St. The unit had cracks on the walls, a stained brown carpet, kitchen sink with rust rings, a toilet green and golden brown with years of untouched crust. Tiles were falling from the bathroom wall at a rate of about one every week. The other residents were furtive, seldom seen – older, obese, red-faced men stumbling along with plastic sacks, a dark-haired woman with a giant Doberman, an old skinny black man who wore a pashmina shawl and a beret, several apartments-full of Filipinos and Vietnamese, possibly Cambodians, who cooked things in pots and smelled up the whole place…

One of the more mysterious residents was a thin white girl with long brown hair. She wore glasses, which seemed to add to the mystery. But the real issue was her breasts – these marvelous, gigantic things that were bursting out in front of her like battleships. Insanely, she would walk around with them riding high in a t-shirt one or two sizes too small, or they might be bundled together in a sweater, creating a shelf upon which one longed to lay one's head. Megan Dierkner said the name on the mailbox. After a period of referring to her as "Megan," Jerry and I soon settled on "Stacks."

"Just saw Stacks…"

"How'd she look?"

"Aw, man. My God! Stacked all to fucking hell…"

Stacks never spoke to us, never even acknowledged us. You'd see her coming in or out the front door, but she always looked away. She seemed in a hurry, there never seemed to be a good moment to attempt an introduction. But it was very odd that she lived in that part of town, she did not seem the type. We tried to figure the reasons why. She was a lonely painter or perhaps an exotic dancer, we theorized. We invented many stories, sitting there as we drank in the apartment – that she was a clarinetist in the symphony, a librarian, some big-boobed white trash slut from Alabama who had come to Bay City to make it as a stripper and porn star. That she worked in a prison, that she was a lesbian prison guard, that she was spying on us for the anti-drug authorities. We made plans to get in her the apartment for a drinking session, during which she would finally spill everything, ask if we wanted to see her tits, and fuck us both. That never happened.

I was sitting there one day when Jerry walked up.

"What the hell?"

It was some kind of little worm on the tip of his finger, about a quarter of an inch long. It was tan in color, shining greasily, a black dot on one end. Head or asshole, it wasn't clear.

"Look," said Jerry.

I looked up. Worms were all over the ceiling.

A few days after the discovery, we had become pretty sure they were busy mating and laying eggs. In the corners of the ceiling you could see these brown lumps – "egg sacs," Jerry deciphered.

You knew they were up there, twisting and moving around. They would surprise you, falling on to your shoulder, into your hair, on to the table, the plate. Sometimes, at the beginning, we went berserk, standing on the kitchen counter with a broom, the kitchen table, thrashing at the worms and the egg sacs. When they fell, the other guy would try to smash them with his foot. There would be less worms for a day or so, but then many more of them would be back.

Once we bought a can of insect killer and hit every every worm and egg sac we could find. We emptied the can, the place stank of the poison for a day. It seemed to have little impact.

FIGHTIN' WORDS!
Clowns Talk Love, Get in Brawl

★ 6 ★

BREAKING: TERRORISTS ON THE LOOSE
The theme music blared, ominous and nerve-wracking, yet also triumphant. The clown logo veered and flipped about before vanishing. Mugs of varying photo-quality flashed on the screen. Five dark-skinned bearded men. The camera zoomed in for close-ups. It zoomed out, zoomed in. Greasy brown skin, beards of varying thickness and length. Dark evil eyes.

CLOWN: *I have just been handed some breaking news from the White House... The word is that American forces have seized videotapes in which these five men you have been looking at threaten the destruction of the United States of America and western targets. According to U.S. counter-terrorism officials, these men may be trained and prepared to commit future suicide terrorist attacks. Officials say the videotapes depict these men delivering what appear to be martyrdom messages from suicide terrorists. U.S. officials appeal to American citizens and citizens worldwide to help track these terrorists down before they detonate a possible nuclear dirty bomb in an American city, God forbid... And that's what it says. We'll go live now to our Pentagon correspondent, Clive Lockwood, for an in-depth report. Clive, how does it look from over there at the Pentagon?*

CLOWN: *Well, Duke, officials here are very concerned indeed. They have no idea where these young men might be, and apparently these fellows have made videotapes in which they threaten the destruction of our nation and way of life. The Pentagon people are calling them 'martyrdom messages from suicide terrorists.' I just finished speaking with one senior official and his words to me were, quote, "Attack-attack.*

Terrorist-terrorist. Dirty-bomb-dirty. Hijack. Jelly bombs fragmentation. Terrorist-attack-bomb." This official continued, again quoting here, *"Bomb-bomb. Attack-attack. Weapons of mass destruction. World Trade Center. Shark attack. Hijack-attack. Freedom. Anthrax. Assassination. Martyr-bomb. Columbine massacre. Central dope intelligence Hussein Nazi news electronic good American condition shark attack young white girl homosexual marriage male homosexual. Terrorist-terrorist."* So as you can see, Duke, they are very concerned indeed. Though they emphasize they have no direct knowledge of a specific attack plan, officials do believe these men may have something spectacular in the works. The official I spoke to added that he hopes the American people will be on the lookout for men who look like these five, and to report anything suspicious to the authorities immediately, so the suspects can be captured and brought to justice before they can carry out a suicide dirty-bomb martyr Islamic weapons of mass destruction anthrax shark attack white terror.

The camera zoomed in, zoomed out. The greasy eyes stared. BREAKING: SUICIDE TERRORISTS ON THE LOOSE. The camera zoomed in, zoomed out.

CLOWN: *Thank you, Clive. That was Clive Lockwood, NNN's own Pentagon correspondent, with breaking developments about threats to our freedom. And you're up to date on the War on Terror and Defense of Freedom. Any-hoo... Coming up next in the program: Cosmetic genital reconstruction. Some say it's not for everyone. Our experts weigh in. And later: Is your teenage daughter secretly working for an escort service? Some surprising results from a new survey. We'll be back after these messages. The terror alert level is blinking orange and you're watching NNN, the News Now Network. Your news peak on media mountain...*

✪

Let you get under my skin
Now I'm tryin' to retrieve it
Playin' my guitar
Buh-neath the vampire stars, yeah

Jerry could be off with Candace three or four nights a week, but sometimes we would sit in the apartment evenings with the candles lit and the television on. We'd drink beer and smoke, or I'd make coffees, boiling water and pouring it through a 59-cent plastic filter I'd bought on the street from Vietnamese.

Jerry would be working out songs on his guitar, scatting and scratching out lyrics in the corner with a notebook. I would be blackening a pad myself, mainly poetry-style ditties with titles such as "Whoremaiden Of Thy Recompense," "Petalas De Culpa," "I Beseech Thee," so on. I also had a pile of used paperbacks I sometimes thumbed through – Tolstoy and Hardy, Scott Fitzgerald, Graham Greene, John O'Hara, Stephen King, John Updike... Most of these involved vaguely unpleasant stories about small towns, as I recall, rather sour tales filled with details about paper factories and shoelaces, baptisms and dead babies, the perceived bleakness and symbolism of decaying buildings, feelings of general dampness... They didn't help at all, I didn't know what they were trying to prove.

"What ya sparkin' up over there?" I would ask Jerry.

"Pipes of peace, bro," he would say, grinning and licking the length of a stogie in the candlelight. "You want in?"

Jerry was trying to write songs, while also scanning the weekly newspaper ads for musicians to start a band. He had a big project in mind, a group he was planning to call Rocketdogg. From what I could gather, it was going to be pop and also punk, with a sort of neo-Springsteen feel and the occasional hip-hop influence. He would meet up with guys now and then, but a band had never come together. He hadn't had a band since he was at the junior college several years before. That band, Moe's Art, had played some pretty big parties, according to Jerry.

"We rocked, but we totally sucked," he would say. "It was punk rock, but we didn't know what we were doing. I've changed everything..." He would scat and croon and strum it out in his style, red beard glinting in the candlelight, earrings rocking back and forth.

No, the odds weren't even

Read 'em and weep

The odds weren't even

Here I am again, crying myself to sleep

Absolutely, nothing was helping, nothing was clicking. My head was soggy, my heart shards. All I had was a constant aching. The aching had changed over the years, worsened or lessened or shifted shape, but I could remember having it since I was about five. It would flit in and out, mixing with completely new feelings of shame and injustice, humiliation and inadequacy, poverty and ambition. I would sit there for hours, staring at my toenails, staring at the wall. There would be a slight buzzing in my ears, a feeling as if my head had been stuffed with cotton. I would meditate on things like the apparent stupidity of nearly all people. I would submerge into lengthy meanderings on earthquakes, nuclear bombs, the depths of the oceans, all the girls who had ever touched my penis, until I was all but paralyzed, half-comatose, dry-mouthed, like my head and balls were going to simultaneously explode.

I would crank "Riders on the Storm" while Jerry would spend hours on the computer, playing "games" or looking at the internet. The internet was a horrifying world, it had always made me ill, physically sick at the sight of it. It had seemed obvious to me from the beginning that the internet would end up doing more harm than help, make everybody even more poor and stupid than we already were, a degrading little tool that enabled people to express new lows of cruelty and spinelessness.

Nobody needed that much madness from human minds. I stayed away as much as possible. I didn't want to belong to anything, certainly not the internet. I yearned to be beyond...

Jerry would wake up and realize it was midnight and he had wasted most of the night looking at the computer. "I HATE THIS!" he would shout.

Once he called me over to the machine to look at a picture. "Look! A dead baby shot by the Palestinians!"

It was a picture of a baby with its eyes closed, blood coming from the top of its nearly hairless head. Dark red blood leaking onto a white towel underneath.

I spun dizzy a second, felt briefly like vomiting.

"Wow, that's what it really looks like," I said.

"NO WAY, MAN!"

"Forget it, Jerry. Let 'em kill each other. They're angry at God. As they should be. What's God ever done for them, after all they've given Him? Zilch, Jerry, zilch. Nothing to be done except stay out of the way."

"NO WAY, MAN! THEY WANT TO THROW ISRAEL INTO THE OCEAN!"

"Some of them probably do."

"NO DEALS WITH BABY-KILLERS!"

"Israel's killed some of their babies."

"THAT WAS AN ACCIDENT!"

"It's always an accident..."

"NOT WITH SUICIDE BOMBERS!"

The talk would ramble on for hours. We'd attack the booze until it was gone, then complain loudly upon seeing the bottom of the box or bottle. It would be 3 a.m., too late for another run. At about the same time, we'd reach the end of the smokes and start digging through the tuna cans for butts. We gather enough and tap the remaining tobacco and ash on to a rolling paper for one more smoke. The sirens and booms would finally ebb, purple-pink slinking in through the window bars.

"No, listen, bro, I'm not trying to say that everything means –"

"Nothing means anything. That's totally the truth –"

If it was a Saturday or Sunday, we'd wake and Jerry would call Candace. "We're dying," he would whine. She'd be over within the hour, delivering hamburgers and burritos, big coffees and bagels, a fresh 12-pack of Heinekin, whatever Jerry had ordered.

Jerry was having problems getting to work on time on a regular basis. He was being pulled apart by the job, his dreams of rock stardom, Candace and the crowd, all of it mixed up with drinking and drugging. The drinking and drugging seemed to be the only areas where his performance had any chance of being consistent. He would be late to the bank branch sometimes as much as a three times a week. Candace kept him running, she would demand his presence immediately, or send him out on a mission to pick up drugs. He would have to run across town to get the cash from Candace, head back to the neighborhood to make the buy.

Sometimes he went to the Cherry Bomb or the Spotlite, but the main locales were Beirut and the Silver Spur. Fat Mike was his main connection. Fat Mike went for the "beach bum" look, shorts and baggy t-shirts, carrying his drugs around in nylon zip-bags that he wrapped around his waist beneath the shirt. He had a huge head and red face, a ponytail and a white beard. Mike's claim to fame was having been a "roadie for James Brown." He would tell stories about James Brown getting false eyelashes, about James Brown gathering everyone around to read the Bible while he was high on PCP, about James Brown impregnating his backup singers, about somebody from Rod Stewart's entourage injecting their penis with cocaine...

The bank people seemed to put up with Jerry's lateness, so long as he was at his teller-station when the branch opened to the public at 9 a.m. He could perform actual miracles in the morning: Visine, deodorant and teeth brushed, a tie on and pumped full of aspirin – no one would have a clue he had been laid out on the couch just 45 minutes before, bombed as a zombie. The bank even put up with his shaved eyebrows, followed by the blond dye-job, and the red.

One night Jerry painted the nails on both of his pinkies black. It was one rock star makeover too far. The branch manager, Craig, told him to get rid of it – but Jerry argued. "Within a minute," according to Jerry, Craig threatened to fire him. Jerry backed down. "Craig backed down." Somebody backed down. The black nails disappeared. But Craig said he was putting a "note" in Jerry's personnel file.

Sometimes Jerry would get down. "I got to clear my head," he would say, grabbing for the whisky bottle. He'd put on Corpse By Day's *Mass Grave* album and we'd sit at the kitchen table. "I got to get straight. Let's drink. I'm tired of all this crap." After a couple swallows, he would bring up Candace. He was starting to wonder about the guys at the law school.

"She's fucking some guy," he would say. "I know she is. I can tell..."

"Oh, *come on*, man..."

"What do you think she's doing when I'm at work all day? Studying? She's only got, like, four classes the whole week."

"Well shit, Jerry."

"Rich fucking mommy boys. You should see those pricks, driving around in their BMWs and Porsches..."

I could see how it might burn. A cheatin' woman was a sure sign you hadn't made the sale. There were two options, really – either she hadn't understood what you were really about, or she was a crazy slut. Either way, it was bad news.

Jerry stomped around the apartment, kicking cans and stacks of old newspapers. He tossed his guitar down on the couch. He took the whisky bottle and guzzled a mouthful. Candace's father had given him the deal, a big brutal thing of Irish whisky, twice as big as any other I'd ever seen. He took in another mouthful. He shifted his head slowly from side to side, cracking the bones in his neck.

"I just think I, that I – I just *love* that girl, man. I think I literally love her."

"I know you do, man. I know you do..."

He took in another sloppy drink. Some of the whisky dribbled down into his little patch of red beard. He picked up the pack and lit a smoke. Worms danced and writhed on the ceiling.

"You don't experience love until you really experience it. Not *real* love... You ever been in love? I mean, *really* in love?"

"Maybe I was in love once, for a few weeks, Jerry. Two weeks, maybe... Then she dumped me, dropped me like a piece of old garbage. Like I didn't even exist. I took it hard, insane and stupid fits, all that. Then it was O.K... I don't think it was love, though, not the real love. Maybe a kind of love. She let me fuck her a few times, that's all. That's all you really need. She was letting a lot of guys fuck her. I never knew what the hell she thought. We all ran around at her feet, trying to fuck her... All the girls I ever loved were sluts. That's the truth. I can't help it."

"Yeah, no, this is the real love with Candace," said Jerry. "I know it is. It really is, it's..."

Jerry threw back the whisky. One of his earrings caught a blade of light from the hallway and glinted.

The tensions would eventually rise to the surface. Jerry was a superb guy, we shared poor-boy dreams of glory and lives of leisure, we claimed to insist on our *own* art on our *own* terms – but on some basic level, our pinwheels were blowing in different parking lots. It didn't take much to get us calling each other on the bullshit, blasting away the star shine we tried to rub over everything.

"Gimme a break, yeah?"

"That's it... I'm taking you down –"

We lurched out of the chairs, Jerry taking some kind of karate-judo position. I surged at him, trying some kind of tackle. One of his hands went up. I rushed forward. The hand caught me on the forehead. I fell to the left, landing and rolling into a bunch of cans. Some of the cans had been used as ashtrays. I tasted ash in my mouth, ash floating into my eyelashes...

Jerry screamed. His knees slammed into my chest, his fists flying. I spasmed viciously, throwing him off. He hit the carpet with a crack and gave off a small whine. I stood up.

He came rolling into my legs. I fell onto the futon. I could feel him crawling up my legs.

My hand found the pillow – a big heavy squishy number, weighing four or five pounds. I kicked him off, rolled and got up. He snarled and lunged at me. I smacked him with the pillow, a quick underhand that caught him on the side of the face. I danced into the middle of the room.

Jerry rose, staggered a step. I swung the pillow wildly. Jerry connected with a looping right to my ear. My head rocked to the side. I felt nothing, then my ear started to burn.

I savaged him with the pillow, a devastating backhand across the nose. He sagged under the blow, then rushed forward again, hurling an open hand shot that caught my chin, his fingernails breaking open the skin.

I bashed him with the pillow. He grunted, fell to his knees. He was far too slow getting up. I came hard with an uppercut. He spun, knocked into the chair, came to a stop in the corner.

I whacked him again, another smack to the side of the head.

The pillow exploded. Hundreds of white feathers floated into the air.

MNUNG'S WORLD
President to Naughty Dick: Drop Dead!

★ 7 ★

My fellow Americans, the president was saying on the TV, *the dictator has failed to repudiate his murderous ways and submit to the peaceful and honorable requirements of the civilized world. He has instead chosen the path of defiance, deceit, propaganda, lies and threats...*

The president was wearing a dark blue suit and yellow tie, an American flag eye patch over his right eye. Ten or eleven American flags were arrayed behind him. White marble busts of Winston Churchill and Henry Kissinger sat to his left and right. In the center of the desk was a large black-leather covered Bible. The president rested his right hand on the tome. His left eye squinted into the camera.

My fellow citizens, the United States of America and our allied nations have respectfully and repeatedly asked the dictator to halt his assault on decency and disarm for the benefit of mankind. But he has ignored our reasoned cries. We, together with our friends and allies in the international community, have solemnly demanded, in the name of security, stability and freedom, that the dictator terminate his transgressions at once. But the dictator has failed to seize his many opportunities. And now, tonight, time for the dictator and his regime has finally run out... History has again called America to action... We must bring the regime to justice before the hour of horror beyond reckoning obliterates civilization's highest hopes of freedom and prosperity...

The president continued: *We did not choose this war, but make no mistake: We start it at a time of our choosing... Every statement I make tonight is backed up evidence and solid sources. These are not assertions –*

they are facts and conclusions based on intelligence. These facts tell us that the dictator and his regime are capable of producing enough dry biological agent to kill thousands of people. The dictator has never accounted for 550 artillery shells with mustard gas, 30,000 empty munitions, nor precursors that could increase his stockpile to as much as 500 tons of chemical agents. Even the low estimate of 100 tons of chemical agent would enable the dictator to cause mass casualties across more than 100 square miles of territory, an area nearly five times the size of the isle of Manhattan... Intelligence indicates the dictator has also recently acquired from Africa a quantity of aluminum tubing that could, in conjunction with yellow cakes and other devices, be used to concoct nuclear weapons.

Fellow Americans, we cannot allow these weapons capabilities to stand. We cannot permit the dictator to hand them out to terrorists, who would most certainly use them against our nation and her allies. Our intelligence agencies estimate it would take only one vial, one crate, one canister, one massive bomb – one tiny bomb – to create a day of savage horror that would be beyond human contemplation... We cannot allow the first warning sign to be a mushroom cloud over an American city.

There is no knowing how many battles will be needed to secure freedom in the homeland, **the president continued reading.** *The war upon which we are tonight embarking is perhaps better called only a battle in a much longer and continuous war, which we will wage in the unconditional interests of peace... Our intelligence agencies have determined that the enemy is composed of a vast network of evil-doers who seek one thing only: The complete destruction and dismemberment of the United States of America and the submission of our people to rule by fundamentalist tyrants. Our intelligence experts inform me that the enemy is not a rational actor, deterrable by conventional death-related means. Rather, this nameless, shapeless enemy has no discernable identity, demands, nor goals other than worldwide enslavement to its twisted whims. Negotiation is therefore impossible... Make no mistake: This enemy is committed to raw hatred and random, vicious violence, which could strike anywhere, at any time, without warning. We cannot, in the name of peace and security, allow this anti-American hatred to persist. We must take the battle to the enemy and confront the threat of violence before it emerges.*

My fellow citizens, as a people, we the American people are now freer, safer and more prosperous than we have ever been, despite the undeniable decline, the many attacks and ever-escalating threats. Make no mistake:

Our people possess skill and ingenuity, we possess wealth and faith. God hath blessed our land... It is thus our sacred task to harness this bounty for the whole of humankind – to secure the harvest of peace, freedom and prosperity – to be a light unto the nations. Because America's vital interests, and our deepest beliefs, are now one. From the day of our founding, we have proclaimed that every man and woman has rights and dignity and matchless value, because they bear the image of the maker of the Heaven and the Earth... As the history of our great nation demonstrates, without liberty, there is oppression; without freedom, there is bondage; without free markets, there is subsidy and state control...

History has further demonstrated that the readiness to employ military force is part and parcel of the peace platform. As God-fearing Americans, we rush to the battlements reluctantly, a peace-loving nation, our hearts swollen with sadness... We thus act in the holy name of peace, in the honorable name of freedom, in the sanctified name of the rule of law. And we intend to be victorious. Make no mistake: We charge into the unpredictable whirlwind of war because of our deep belief that the survival of liberty in our land increasingly depends on the success of liberty in other lands. Our choice, fellow Americans, is stark: Either we change the way we live, or we change the way they live. Changing our way of life is, of course, an unacceptable demand. We therefore choose the latter. Make no mistake: We are resolute...

The president continued: *To the people whose nation we are tonight invading, I say to you that our unrelenting assault is directed against the lawless, power-drunk men who rule your country – not you... As our coalition takes away their power and deposits it in our hands, we will deliver the food and medicine you need. We will tear down the infrastructure of terror and weapons. And we will help you build a new country that is prosperous, peaceful and free. In your new country, there will be no more wars against neighboring countries, no more poison factories, no more nuclear bombs, no more executions of dissidents, no more torture chambers and rooms for rapists...*

President Mnung bowed his head. *I will conclude tonight by reminding you that we, the American people, are strong. We are bold. We are brave. We are resolute. Even when it is hard, when circumstances are difficult, we know that Americans always do what is right, and our word cannot be doubted. We therefore enter tonight into a long, hard slog, in the interests of freedom, security and free markets for America – a long and continuous war that we will wage in the unconditional interests of peace... I tonight declare a victory for the American people, the dawn of a bold new era in this great nation. I say to America: No one loves you like I, your president, does. I promised you I would restore honor and dignity to the White House, and I have solemnly done so...*

Mnung took the Bible from the desk and lifted it to his chest. *Peace, freedom, peace, yes, strength, peace, prosperity, freedom, liberty and peace... I have just given the order for Operation Peace, Freedom, Security, Justice, Democracy and Liberty to commence. Fellow Americans, I am tonight in possession of the faith, confidence and patience that history will prove us correct by our action... Courage, America, and hope for freedom. Love, resolve, patriotism, victory and freedom, support for the troops and America's commander-in-chief. I have ordered our armed forces into battle, and the hour is at hand for our fighting men and women, who will make our hearts swell with pride. The bombs will soon be falling... The liberation has begun...*

The president returned the Bible to the desk, patted it once and saluted the camera. The scene faded out.

CLOWN (WHISPERING): *If you're just joining us, President Wolfgang G. Mnung has just officially announced the new war... and now, as you can see, he is exiting the White House with the First Lady, Sharia Mnung... The president has his beloved dog Nubbles in his arms, while Sharia Mnung is carrying Muffin the cat... Yes, and now, as the White House has informed us, I do believe the president will use his personal sidearm to obliterate a few targets there on the West Lawn... There he is, walking out there now, yes, flanked by the generals and the singing children... The president is quite a marksman, of course... He's got his black stetson, and he's putting his protective eyegear on...*

A flag fluttered behind the president. A red and gold backdrop had been erected, the words PEACE SECURITY N' FREEDOM stamped out over and over.

The president's gun boomed. A row of targets exploded. It boomed again. Target debris fluttered down like confetti. The president emerged, surrounded by great blooms of white and pink smoke.

CLOWN: *YES! THE PRESIDENT HAS HIT THE TARGET! Oh, my, there are no words... Quite a performance. Quite a performance indeed. We'll go to the instant replay.*

They showed it again: Mnung cocking the trigger, pressing, the target exploding. The smoke clearing to reveal the president wreathed in smoke, hat and goggles. Then again in slow motion. And again.

CLOWN: *So there you have it, Mr. and Mrs. America... Another war... Another target obliterated... President Mnung taking the initiative... The man is indeed resolute. Quite a performance from the former spoiled son, the formerly failed vacuum salesman. Tonight, you saw it live – reading a speech in warrior-king fashion, then gunning down the pre-selected target from close range. Quite a night for the president and his handlers... Yes, indeed... There were some, of course, who didn't figure he had it in him – who thought his drug addiction, for example, or his conviction for drunk driving that he tried to cover up, the secret abortion of his teenage girlfriend, his craven draft-dodging for which he was never held to account... his failure to win the most votes in the presidential election... and so on, would have hurt him... In fact, it hasn't. The American people just don't give a darn. They just – apparently, they just like this man... They believe in him, they sense his soul... The president of course hails from an extremely well-connected family, no secret there – his oil baron father used to run this nation's secret police, after all... Indeed, the Mnung family has many powerful friends in and outside of government. Big business, including this network, got behind him in a massive way, pushed his candidacy – rammed it right down the throats of the American people. The powers that be let it be known that this fellow was their front man, and by God, we did our best. And, with the help of the Gang of Five on this nation's highest court, young Governor Mnung was vaulted into the highest office in the land – facts and vote counts be damned. And then, of course... well, we all know the story – America the Beautiful was horribly attacked on a gorgeous, sun-splashed September day... And there was President Mnung, leading the way. A real American comeback – a success story, we called it. We all called it like that. Boy, that seems like a long time ago... In any case, history marches on. As they like to say: Get over it. We've got a new war on, forces of freedom in action... We're furnishing the pictures, and they're furnishing the war... You're in the War Room with NNN, the News Now Network – your news peak atop the media mountain. I'm Flip Puddington, and we'll be back after these messages...*

 Theme music thundered, vaguely military, vaguely disco drums, swelling orchestral strings sending forth a message of victory and resolve mixed with danger and foreboding. A new NNN logo, Operation: Truth, Freedom, Equality, Prosperity & Security, veered across the screen. The News Now Network – YOUR NEWS PEAK – YOUR NEWS SOLUTION.

 Pizza-Size Your Breakfast, America! New at Pizza Highway – the Sicilian Jalapeño breakfast pizza! Get ready to snarf down steaming scrambled egg, pepperoni, jalapeño peppers, reeeeeeeeal cheddar cheese and Siciliano rosemarine and oregano – served piping-hot on a sesame-seed sourdough croissant! Everything you've seen, everything you've heard, is only the beginning! Come in before eight a.m. Monday through Thursday and get a free jelly or chocolate-cream donut and small cappuccino with every order of two egg-pizzas... While supplies last. Only at Pizza Highway!

CLOWN: You're back in the War Room, live from New York City, capital of the free world. I'm Flip Puddington and you're live with Operation Peace, Freedom, Security and Liberty on NNN, your News Now Network. In case you're just joining us, another war has begun, President Mnung has just announced it live from the Oval Office. The armed forces – the mighty military machine of the United States of America – has once again swung into action in defense of freedom... We've got a big show coming up for you tonight, including, we hope, live shots of the first bombs falling. We'll go live now to our correspondent in the battle theater, Billy Hantha, who is embedded with U.S. forces in a location we are not allowed to disclose for troop-safety reasons. Good morning, Billy, can you hear me? Have the bombs started falling yet? Is the liberation underway? Come in, Billy, repeat, Billy come in!

CLOWN: Hey there, I'm hearing you loud and clear, Flip. No, no bombs as of yet. But we have been told, and have been cleared to tell the audience tonight, to look out for some real fireworks. This is what the Pentagon spokespeople have been telling us. But all of it – and I emphasize, all of it – is designed to minimize civilian casualties... As in previous wars, the coalition has the ability to conduct precision-guided strikes on military and regime targets, thereby avoiding collateral damage to civilians and water supplies and electricity and hospitals, things like that. I've been told by military officials that we can expect a success rate of between 95 and 98 percent with these bombs.

CLOWN: I hear you, Billy – boy, oh boy, has the dictator got it coming! Very well, Billy. Stay safe out there with the troops. And give 'em our best. Nice goggles, by the way.

CLOWN: Thanks, Flip. I'm in good hands. Our troops are a tough bunch of good guys. We're doing our best...

CLOWN: That was our correspondent out in the field, Billy Hantha, embedded in a secret location with U.S. troops. Let us turn now to our expert analyst, the Reverend Anthony Samuelly... He is of course a U.S. Department of Defense assistant undersecretary, deputy chairman of the Christian-Holy Land Action Forward Progress Committee and author of

The New York Times *bestseller,* Ending All The Evil: How America Can Bring Peace In Our Times... *Good evening, Reverend...*

CLOWN: *Yes, amen. It is a very good evening... A glorious evening...*

CLOWN: *Dr. Assistant Undersecretary, Reverend Samuelly, sir... if we can, for fairness' sake, talk a little bit about, perhaps – oh, some of the criticisms of this war, particularly from the minority in this country who, well – they say this is the wrong war at the wrong time, for the wrong reasons, for example. That we should not provoking war and invading foreign countries many miles from our shores who do not threaten us. Are they mistaken?*

CLOWN: *I would say so, Flip... If you oppose freedom, you are clearly mistaken. If you oppose hunting down this dictator's deadly weapons and defending civilization from terrorists, you are certainly mistaken...*

CLOWN: *Reverend Samuelly, sir, another potential criticism – that this war is about, say, stealing resources from another country... That, you know, well, these really aren't the same folks that attacked us on September 11, 2001, and they don't really threaten us, but rather – that's it's about, say – oh, I don't know, quantities of oil they may possess, or illegal drugs networks and transport routes that we'd like to control, or the minerals to be found in that particular land, perhaps something about a pipeline or what have you. Is it? I know this is a sensitive topic –*

CLOWN: *Of course not, Flip. These are precisely the type of conspiracy theories that one sees in the left-wing liberal leftist elite mainstream media. You're just doing your job, repeating the nonsense, I understand – but there's no such thing as conspiracies, certainly not at the Pentagon where I work... Whatever this war is about, it is absolutely not about seizing control of vast oil reserves so such reserves can be used as a lever to exert decisive regional and global influence, as we see fit. That's the farthest – my lord, I've heard stories that all U.S. ground troops are carrying a length of pipe and instructions to lay it in the direction of the U.S.A. It's just not true! The United States has never had any interest in oil. President Mnung, though his family has vast fortunes in the oil business – along with many of his cabinet members – it's not about oil, Flip... This is about rights and weapons – mass weapons and human rights and terrorists. The United States has never, to my knowledge, exploited or provoked some conflict for its own oil or commercial interests. We are not about making a profit off somebody else's death. On the contrary, we want to save those lives. And as the president said, we want to protect the peace.*

CLOWN: *Sir, I'm just repeating –*

CLOWN: *I would add, Flip, that if we did not intermittently impose our will on smaller, weaker nations, it would be very damaging to the American nation, psychologically. As I say in my book, repeatedly, we are the indispensible nation. We must keep the world safe for freedom and free markets. Without us, the world descends into war and invasions and savage barbarities, as sure as the night follows day.*

CLOWN: *Yes, and –*

CLOWN: *Nothing to do with oil or interests!*

CLOWN: *Fair enough, sir. Finally, Reverend, what are the chances of America's fine fighting forces delivering a devastating knockout blow to the dictator with our smash 'em-dash 'em smart-weapons? A matter of days – or even hours?*

CLOWN: *The chances are extremely high, Flip. Our great nation has spared no expense in equipping her forces to do freedom's work. The consequences for the dictator and his regime will be swift and severe. It will, I am confident, be shocking and awful – for the dictator and his cronies, that is...*

CLOWN: *Thank you, Reverend Secretary, thank you for joining us and offering some much needed perspective. We'll be back with the war after these messages. You're watching NNN, your News Now Leader...*

Roll on to freedom, America, with new-formula Mediterraneo Musk deodorant and after-shave! Combine stay-fresh power with the sultry, spicy scent of the ancient world and the Riviera. Available in sport, creamy, dusk, lavender, campfire and new green mustard. Roll on, America, to new horizons of freshness with new-formula Mediterraneo Musk! In traditional stick, splash, spray or new time-release capsules for 24-hour protection...

CLOWN: *We're back, and you're live in the War Room on NNN, the News Now Network, with me, Flip Puddington... We're bringing you live prime-time coverage of Operation Peace, Justice, Security and Prosperity, which President Wolfgang G. Mnung has tonight formally announced in an historic speech from the Oval Office... America is at war again, and it looks like a doozy... O.K., I've just been handed something to read here – the first results of our NNN Insta-Poll are in, and it looks this war is a big hit with the American people. Support for President Mnung has jumped to 89 percent. And the American people are backing this war, 74 percent in favor to two percent against... About 24 percent people said they were not aware... So in any event, quite a success for President Wolfgang G. Mnung, even before the first bombs have exploded on the screens of*

America's televisions. Now then, time now for our next guests – two folks on the opposite sides of the spectrum, because we believe in giving you both sides of the story here at NNN... On my left is Robiann Coughan, blond actress, Hotchkiss University professor and author of 1,078 **Ways Liberals Hate America,** *currently holding the Number One position on* The New York Times *Bestseller List. We are also joined in San Francisco by an, er, individual named Santana Rigoberto, uh, Shornwell – am I pronouncing that correctly? – of the American Anti-War Action Solidarity Union... We'll start with you Mr. Shornwell. I take it you are opposed to this liberation of mass destructive weapons, freedom on the march, so forth and so on. Why is that, exactly? Go ahead, Mr. Santana Shornwell, you're on live national TV with Flip Puddington...*

CLOWN: *Thank you for having me. Firstly...* (STATIC)... *brazen hypocrisy... appeal to fear and nationalism... big-lie tactics... at least Hitler was elected... U.S. government accuses others of the same crimes...* (GARBLE)... *guilty of...*

CLOWN: *Uh, we seem to be having some audio transmission difficulties. Apologies to Rigoberto out there in, uh, San Fran...*

CLOWN: *I – I – I'm sorry, did he just compare President Mnung to Hitler? He's lucky he lives in a country where we don't shoot him for saying that! Flip, this is a perfect example of how Americans abuse their freedom...*

CLOWN: *– audio difficulties at our San Francisco affiliate, er...*

CLOWN: (STATIC)... *shameless... nation-states don't have morals... self-interests... cowardly assault... women and children will be...* (GARBLE)... *bombed to the Stone Age, gangsterism... Israel... narco-traffic...*

CLOWN: *Excuse me, so then why aren't you over there as a so-called human shield? I'll pay the plane ticket one-way, first-class, O.K.? You'd rather sit there in your socialist-communist paradise in San Francisco, safe and warm, as real Americans die for your free–*

CLOWN: *– excuse me, Robiann, but – O.K., yes... I'm getting word now that the bombs are going to start falling at any second... You're looking live now at the dictator's palace...*

PATRIOTS DEMAND:
Stop Smoking Crack!

★ 8 ★

The next day it was discovered that a guy had sawed up his parents and distributed their arms and legs, various pieces, around the neighbors' yards. This was in the Sunset Line neighborhood, a place of beachfront mansions and golf courses, shaved lawns and precious shrubbery. The cops had been forced to hunt around for the pieces, adding them up to see if they had found everything. I didn't see them drag "Tony" into the cop car, but O'Mulligan and I got out there in time to see the techs slipping what appeared to be half a calf into an evidence bag. It looked a bit like a piece of raw chicken, a few long pink dangling pieces around the knee. A tech tagged the bag and handed it over to the meat wagon crew.

O'Mulligan started transmitting. I mashed the Kate button. Police dogs whined and pawed the ground.

"Super!" Kate said. *"Police wearing gloves were seen putting at least one leg into a plastic evidence bag... Now go talk to some neighbors!"*

A pack of them were standing around in front of a fountain beneath a palm tree. "I'm sorry, excuse me, so sorry to bother you... Did anyone here know the family?"

"Well, yes," a blue-haired lady volunteered. "I feel so sad for Gay and Ed. They adopted Anthony when he was just a baby. Gay could never have children. They were quite a bit older when they got him, in their fifties, I believe. They tried their best to give him everything, but he was always trouble. Now this."

She shook her head, took a hit from a cigarette.

A skinny man with a salt-and-pepper beard and eyeglasses piped up.

"Tony was crazy in the head, since day one. They got him off the streets, who knows from where? Ed would tell me, 'I'm having problems with my son. I'm concerned about my son.' They took him to every doctor they could find. I just can't believe it... Aw, they were the nicest people you could ever want for parents. Ed used to take Tony out to race model airplanes at Hamzy Field..."

"Did they win?"

"Well, Ed showed me two or three trophies. I honestly don't know if they won."

"Tony used to talk to himself," said an old man with a red face crumpled like a cabbage. "He smashed their windows, smashed their car windshield. The hospital people took him away a bunch of times. I would see Gay crying. I knew something like this was going to happen..."

"They had him on drugs," said a younger blond lady holding a baby. "They took him to church."

She had large full lips, a mole on her chin. I stared at her through the sunglasses. I heard birds tweeting in the trees. She had massive, beautifully shaped breasts hanging braless in a green-and-white striped tank top. Blond hair clipped at the shoulders, a few puddles of baby drool on her arm.

"Yes, what kind of drugs, ma'am?"

She shrugged. "I don't know the names. Ed paid for them all out of his own pocket. But then Tony wouldn't take them anymore, I heard..."

A squat, older guy with large wet cheeks pushed his way through.

"I saw the whole thing!" he exclaimed. "The guy was runnin' around in front of the house. 'I KILLED EVERYONE! I KILLED EVERYONE!' Just like that. 'I KILLED EVERYONE!' I didn't know what it was, you know, until I saw him carrying the hands. That's something I'll never forget. I said, 'He's carrying somebody's hands!' I called the cops, but it was too late."

"What else?"

"Oh, he was like the devil! He would go into the garage and listen to that heavy metal music, you know? He would take off all his clothes and lift weights out there with that racket. We called the cops on him but Ed always said, 'No, I've got my son under control.' Sure, Ed... Now they're all dead."

A van of TV clowns drove up: Channel 4, "Where News Comes First." Fat guys in black T-shirts jumped out the side door. Nick

Noxford, TV star, stepped out of the back and put on his white blazer. A taxi pulled up behind the van. Seth Sillicott of the *Examiner-Mail* hopped out and strolled over.

"You get anything?" said Seth.

"No," I said. "Nobody's talking."

> SON ARRESTED IN SUNSET LINE AXE SPREE
>
> BAY CITY (CNS) – Bay City Police said a 24-year old man was arrested Thursday on suspicion of using an axe to kill his parents and distributing parts of their bodies in the Sunset Line neighborhood.
>
> Sgt. Dave Chester said Anthony Camerlingo, 24, was taken into custody after neighbors called police to report the apparent murder and dismemberment of Edward Camerlingo, 68, and Gay Camerlingo, 66.
>
> Chester said Anthony Camerlingo was arrested inside his parents' house after a brief chase and charged with first-degree murder. No bail was set.
>
> Chester said Anthony Camerlingo had been spotted by neighbors as he allegedly distributed parts of his parents' bodies in hedgerows and under trees along the 5800 block of Dresdall Lane.
>
> Neighbors said Anthony Camerlingo had been adopted by his parents as a young child and that he and his father used to participate in model airplane contests.
>
> Neighbor Andre Escobarge described Anthony Camerlingo as an aficionado of heavy metal rock music who often spent time lifting weights in his parents' garage.
>
> Neighbors told Cities News Services that police were called at least several times due to previous erratic behavior by Anthony Camerlingo, but each time his parents intervened to prevent charges from being filed.

I had said I would go with Jerry to a game. His father or grand-dad or someone had conned the team-allegiance thing into him from an early age, and every so often he'd build up a head of steam and would not be denied.

I eased myself up and sipped at the coffee Jerry had brought to the futon. A few drops fell into the pit of my stomach and exploded.

Something squeezed the back of my head and let go, squeezed and let go. I spun dizzy, bursts of white and popping pink.

"Jerry," I rasped, laying back down. "I don't think I can make it."

"MAN, YOU GOTTA GO!"

Jerry sat next to me, wearing his red and white team cap and rolling a stogie from his sack. He sighed and looked at his watch. He lit the stogie and handed it over. I took a pull and began to cough horribly. Goddamn thing tasted like manure. I coughed, my head feeling like it had cracked open at the top and bottom.

Jerry went in the other room and came back with an inch of whisky in the bottom of a glass. I sat up and drank it down.

"YOU GOTTA GO, MAN!"

"Jerry, *please*," I begged.

"YOU GOTTA GO!"

I had two more of the whisky, another hit from the stogie. Then another whisky, another sip of the coffee. My arms and hands were shaking. I got my shoes on, had one more whisky.

"Dude," said Jerry, "you kissed that fat chick! Remember?"

"The fuck I did! What was her name?"

"Amber. The gross Amber. And you told her you loved her and gave her your number. We all heard it! It was hilarious."

"The fuck I did!"

"Dude, and she had a dyed white stripe of hair on her head, like a skunk, remember? The little zircon diamond pierced over her left nostril? Ha, ha! And cowboy boots?"

"Right, Jerry. And a short skirt with her underwear missing. A troll must have taken them. Hell, just kissing? That's nothing."

"You shoulda seen yourself, man! Did she have a tattoo on her lower back? Ha, ha! Bet you anything she did!"

"Wow, it feels like I'm going to die. Help me up, Jerry. Come over here, help your father..."

We went out into the furnace-like heat. I took out a crushed cigarette from my back pocket and lighted it. I got down about half a throatful. Around the corner a car alarm was going off – beeping and honking, lights and blinkers flashing.

"Oh, pete," I said, collapsing to my knees. "Oh, pete... oh, pete..."

"You'll make it, you'll make it... YOU GOTTA GO, MAN!"

"Oh jeez, Jerry... Oh jeez..."

I bent over and a stream of it shot out of me. A bunch of it came out, pink juice and some brown, the sound of it clapping against the pavement. I stood up and leaned against Jerry, drool mixed with vomit sliding from the corners of my mouth.

"Jerry, Jerry..."

"You'll be all right, man, you'll be O.K...."

Jerry walked us down Verdugo toward the subway. A woman with a scarf around her head was selling cups of pineapple and watermelon sticks for a dollar. A guy was selling loose cigarettes on a card table for 25-cents each. We stopped at a bank machine and I withdrew $40. The receipt said I was down to $32.53.

We went next door to the market. I bought two newspapers, a 40-ounce bottle of malt, a vanilla-flavored coffee in a cardboard cup, a pair of sunglasses. Total bill: $28.71.

"WE'RE GONNA BE LATE!" Jerry screamed.

"Just let me finish," I said, choking down the malt in the alley. "Five more minutes."

We came out of the alley and saw Mr. Goodbar in a booth making a call. He gestured philosophically, leaned back in the booth. He took a step out, looked both ways, and stretched. He nodded his head in apparent concern and mumbled.

"Who's he talking to?"

"Stacks," said Jerry. "He's on the horn with Stacks. That's who."

"Oh pete, oh pete..."

I was laughing so hard drool fell out of my mouth again.

"Oh goddamn pete..."

Soft blue skies stretched out in every direction, criss-crossed in places by puffy white plumes of jet exhaust. It was 20 minutes in line to get scanned by wands for bombs. We didn't have any. We finally made it inside and rushed around the corner, where Jerry threw down $28 for four beers. Candace's father had given him two $100 bills for the big game, and Jerry was planning on spending at least one of them on beer. We sat on a table under a shaded awning and drank.

"They're gonna stomp their balls off, Jerry!"

"Yeah, they are!"

Jerry explained that Candace's mother and Phil had just returned from Fiji, where they had received an exclusive Indian diet/Pakistani enema treatment. In the weeks before that, there had been some concern after Phil discovered "blood in his stool." There had also been several incidents of "cloudy urine." The doctors were still doing tests. In any case, it had been a successful trip to Fiji, they felt "refreshed."

Heather had meanwhile "gone to the Alps" for several weeks. Doctors had ordered her there "for the air." She needed clean air to help "clear her up." Doctors had found a "little nut"-type growth in her uterus, but it wasn't believed to be a problem. They believed it would go away with some drugs and "healthy living."

"Jerry, not a word of what you say is true..."

"No, all true, 100 percent..."

Jerry threw down for four more beers. I unwrapped the *Examiner-Mail* and saw a front-page color picture of the president with a monkey on his shoulders.

> MNUNG HONORS RETIRING RESEARCH CHIMPANZEES
> By Doreen Slaba
> Examiner-Mail Staff Writer
>
> WASHINGTON – President Wolfgang G. Mnung on Friday signed legislation under which the federal government will pay $300 million to help build a rest home in Tennessee for aging chimpanzees once used for scientific and medical research.
>
> "We need to thank these heroic monkeys for what they've done to improve our lives," a visibly delighted Mnung said at the signing ceremony in the White House Rose Garden, which was attended by eight of the chimps that will live in the new home.
>
> "This is a cost-effective program for the humane treatment of chimpanzees that have been used by the federal government for research beneficial to humankind," Mnung said, reading from prepared remarks as he held Tommy, a blind 13-year-old chimp who once participated in the testing of military lasers.

Boots in yer behind
Gotta get ya outta my mind
Down the two towers fell
Look out now we're throwin' holy hell
From the Golden Gate
To the Ol' Euphrate

Down on the field, the singing, dancing mountain of marshmallow known as Darryl "Dookie" Dunphy was rattling off his pre-game performance. Dookie, the recent recipient of a *60 Minutes* profile highlighting his former heroin addiction and current love of meditation, ginseng steam baths, vegetarian chili, and Jesus, was riding hot off his million-selling album *Let The Eagle Soar*, which featured the Number One smash "Boots In Your Behind (God Bless the Red, White & Blue)," as well as the follow-ups "Jimmy Don't Ask How (Don't Ask Where)," "No Worries, No Bother," "Gimme Six Bucks (We're in This Together)," and the gospel-tinged "Wakey-Bakey Cornbread."

Boots in yer behind
Said get ya outta my mind
Now we're ringin' freedom through
From Baton Rouge to Kathmandu
From us to you
God bless the red, white and blue

Dookie was soon joined on stage by contingents of servicemen from the Army, Navy, Air Force, Marines and Coast Guard. "Thank you, brothers and sisters," said the former addict and pipe-fitter, his face appearing 14 stories high on the Jumbotron. He went around, shaking hands with each soldier. "God bless you. God bless you. God bless you..."

Dookie began to sob. "I don't deserve to be up here with people like this. Because I am nothin' but a sinner and recovering addict! I'm not worthy! I'm not worthy! These men and women are so much more than I'll ever be. I just want to thank the Lord Jesus that we have such super people defending this great country. We couldn't do it without 'em! Let's all give 'em a round of applause and tell 'em we love 'em...!"

When Dookie was done, a six-year-old girl in a wheelchair came on to sing the national anthem. Fifty-thousand human beings stood, many dressed in red and white stripes, many with hands over their hearts.

I flipped to the "Local News" section of the *Star-Chron* to search for my stories. I counted four from the last shift: 'ECO-TERRORISTS' SUSPECTED IN HOUSING DEVELOPMENT FIRES. 6 DEAD IN 25-CAR PILEUP ON I-94. WAL-MART CLERK FOUND DEAD. DEAD SQUID INUNDATE SANTA COSTA BEACH.

"Get up!" whispered Jerry, who had taken off his hat. "Don't sit there, get up!"

"Oh, all right..."

As the tape hit the climax, a dozen U.S.A. jets overflew the stadium in formation, spewing red, white and blue smoke behind them. Fireworks exploded over the waterfall and plastic canyon. A Navy Top

Gun dropped out over the ocean and floated in toward a bull's-eye on the grass, a stars-n-stripes parachute trailing in the blue. The audience roared its admiration, thousands of U.S. Armed Forces recruiting fliers floated into the air.

"Flyin' High Again" blasted over the loudspeakers as a montage of legendary athletic feats played on the Jumbotron screens. Leggy bimbos in wet team-logo t-shirts walked along the edges of the field, using air-guns to shoot hats, shirts and water bottles into the stands. Jumbotron pictures showed bimbo boobs heaving, bimbo legs streaming out of bimbo red crotch-huggers, bimbo blond hair in pigtails, brilliant bimbo teeth flashes. Young geeks sniggered, straining unsuccessfully for bimbo-lobbed freebies. Jerry returned with four more beers as the match got underway.

"They're gonna stomp their balls off, Jerry!"

"Yeah, they are!"

A thunder of booing and catcalls ensued as the mountain of acne, tattoos and diamond-encrusted jewelry that was Bilbo "Bomber" Blaines took the field. The Jumbotron showed Blaines barking, snorting and pawing and stamping the ground, eyes fiery with hatred, diamond-encrusted nose-ring glinting wetly in the sun.

"FUCK YOU, BLAINES!" a small beaver-faced man to our left exclaimed.

"YOUR MOM SUCKS COCKS IN HELL, BLAINES!" shouted a baboon-faced man sitting next to a squirrel-faced woman.

I pulled out the Weekly Views & Reviews section. THREE CHEERS, MR. PRESIDENT headlined the lead editorial.

> President Wolfgang G. Mnung has again demonstrated strong resolve in a moment of crisis. Where other leaders might have dithered, at a potentially great cost to the nation, the Mnung Administration has shown bold leadership in working to protect America's security. Rejecting those who have urged caution and common sense in the face of threats to our freedom, the Administration has embraced policies of invasion of sovereign countries that have vast oil reserves, imprisonment without charges or trial, secret executions, surveillance of enemies at home and abroad, so-called "stressful" interrogations to extract the needed confessions, the kidnapping of entire families, and the

organized evacuation of populations in foreign lands to achieve the Administration's political goals. In previous eras, such measures would have been scorned with lip-service about being un-American, but we are living in a qualitatively new time. If America is to succeed in our vitally important new wars, and protect our security and hard-won freedoms, it will require tough, courageous...

I got up and went down for a smoke and a piss. The toilet line was out the door and around the corner. I lighted up and waited. A lengthening stream of fluid oozed out the doorway and across the cement to the stadium's outer ramp. Inside, the fluid was about half an inch deep – piss and water mainly, a few turds. Goofballs splashed around, laughing. Goofballs leaned forward against the wall, groaning and sighing as they drained their weasels. When it was almost my turn, a young boy or girl began wandering through the water, crying. "Daddy! Daddy!" Back and forth the little thing wandered, until finally it slipped. A few weasel-drainers giggled. The little thing screamed and flailed about, completely wet. It pulled itself up and continued to splash through the water. "Daddy! Daddy!" It was still there when I left.

Back in the seats, I watched carefully as a rat-faced boy threw peanut shells at a turtle-faced man. The man turned and looked accusingly at a fish-faced teen who was sitting next to a bird-faced girl. Two or three rows down, a frog-faced man leaned over and kissed a horse-faced woman, then crammed a half-finished cajun-spice rotisserie hoagie into his face.

There still hadn't been a score. The Bay City squad just couldn't get off – it was a constant build up but no explosion. Everything staying bottled. They just couldn't stay hard enough to ram one home.

I pulled out the People & Style section.

FULL LOAD! announced the lead feature piece. *School Backpacks Are Getting Heavier And Parents Are Concerned...*

Inside, I found the Janet Lynn Adams advice column, *Ask Janet*. I stared at the headline for several minutes. At first I didn't understand. It seemed rather hard to believe. It got funnier and funnier, the more I stared at it:

SEEK COUNSELING TO MAINTAIN SANITY

The stadium heaved in a massive cheer. Bay City had got one! The Jumbotron flashed on Bilbo Blaines. He glared, stamped and pawed the ground, his eyes burning with anger, diamond earrings swaying and glittering.

A few minutes later, some kind of commotion broke out in the stands. It was one aisle over and a section or two above us, not far from the outer edge of the stadium. People were shouting, standing and pointing.

We stood and looked. A chicken-faced youth emerged on the staircase and shouted.

"HEY, THESE GUYS ARE SMOKING CRACK!"

He pointed toward two guys standing at the very top, next to the chain-link fence. They were wearing ball caps, jeans and T-shirts with the sleeves hacked off.

The chant built quickly, hundreds of human beings turning and rising and pointing their fingers.

"STOP SMOKING CRACK! STOP SMOKING CRACK!"

"Yeah," said Jerry, "Hey, stop smoking crack, you bastards! STOP SMOKING CRACK!"

The crowd pulled back as three cops in helmets came running up the stairs.

"STOP SMOKING CRACK!" I yelled. "STOP SMOKING CRACK! STOP SMOKING CRACK!"

The two crack-smokers finally tried to move, but the crowd had blocked them in. The flatfoots rushed forward and grabbed the crackheads, twisting their arms around their back and pushing their faces toward the seats. One of the cops stuffed something into a large plastic zip-bag. The cops led the pair down the stairs, through a hail of Army recruiting pamphlets, empty cups and other wadded up trash.

The crowed roared, clapped, gave each other high-fives and threw things.

"STOP SMOKING CRACK! STOP SMOKING CRACK!"

WHEN FOOLS RUSH IN:
Ivy Leaguer Joins Clown Squad!

★ 9 ★

Sernath came around the office one day introducing Scott T. Varick. Sernath had never introduced anybody as long as I'd been there, but here he was, introducing "Scotty" with great fanfare. Scotty was "from Connecticut," had gone to "Penn" and had interned at *The Boston Globe* last summer, right out of college. Now he had landed his first "real job": Legman at Cities News Services.

Sernath walked Scotty up, arm over his shoulder. Scotty stuck out his hand.

"Hey what's up, man? Nice to meetcha."

"Hi, Scotty."

Scotty was of average height but on the beefier side – a combination of beer fat and second-string high school linebacker, it looked like. He had greased-back yellow cornstraw hair, sparkly grey-blue eyes, a series of bumpy red acne splotches on his cheeks. He wore a dark blue suit and starched white shirt, a mint-green tie. New brown leather shoes – about $400 worth, according to the smell.

"Listen," said Sernath. "I want you to show Scotty the ropes, but don't go easy on him." He patted Scotty on the shoulder and grinned. "This guy comes highly recommended. Let's see what he can do."

"Sure, boss."

Sernath led Scotty over to his computer work station. I sat and went on with the phone calls. After a few minutes I heard my name and looked up. Scotty was waving to me. I got up and walked over.

"These computers got any games?"

"I don't think so, Scotty."

"Aw, dude."

The 5-County list was laying on Scotty's desk.

"You got it? Know what you're supposed to do?"
"No problemo," he said.
I went back to the desk.

> WOMAN KILLED, OFFICER HURT IN SHOOTING
> BAY CITY (CNS) – Bay City police said a woman bystander was killed and a police officer injured in a shootout with four suspects Tuesday in the Pine Ridges area.
> Sgt. Jake Tallman said the suspects were captured after the officer who was wounded, Joseph Pilsudski, rammed his car into their vehicle, bringing it to a stop and allowing other officers to move in.
> Tallman said Pilsudski was grazed in the head and was hit with two shots in his protective vest during a shootout in which one of the suspects shot a woman who was walking on the street...

A few minutes later, Scotty was calling me over again. His feet were up on the desk. He had found some game, a card game it looked like, on the computer.

"You wanna play? C'mon, take five. You can do it, dude. You're not doing shit right now."

"I hate card games," I said.

"You hate card games? Aw, dude. It's cool." He leaned back in the chair and kinked his head to the left. "So who's the kitty?"

"The who?"

"You know. The kitty."

He nodded over at Shally, who was talking on the phone at the front desk. Her eyes swept past us once, then looked off. She picked up a pen and tapped it on the desk.

"You mean Shally?"

"Yeah, her. You fuck her?"

"No, I don't think so..."

"Dude, why not?" Scotty grinned at me.

"That's a good question..."

> FIVE ARRESTED IN MERINGUE DRUG PROBE
> MERINGUE (CNS) – The Meringue County Sheriff's Department said a nine-month drug

investigation has resulted in five arrests and the seizure of 119 pounds of marijuana.

Lt. Douglas Haig said officers carried out eight coordinated raids in three areas of northern Meringue County early Tuesday.

Haig estimated the street-sale value of the 119 pounds of marijuana that was seized at about $180,000.

Haig said the raids also resulted in the seizure of trace amounts of methamphetamine, "drug paraphernalia" associated with the manufacturing of methamphetamine, six firearms and $1,200 in cash.

Haig said a 3-year-old child found during the raids has been taken into protective custody.

Next day, Sernath came over first thing in the morning.

"Hey, I told you to help Scotty. He didn't do a single story yesterday. He should have done at least one on his first day."

"What am I supposed to do? I can't make the calls and write it myself."

"You know what to do." Sernath hustled off.

Scotty came in about 15 minutes late. I went over and sat next to him.

"Look," I said, "you got to make these calls. You call the cops and you mark 'em off the list, right? You ask 'em if there's any news. If there's anything, you write it up. If it's something serious, you got to tell Kate or someone to see if they want to roll somebody out."

"I GOT TO CALL *ALL* THESE PLACES?"

He tossed the clipboard on to the desk.

"Dude, you are *kidding*..."

He got out of the chair and walked off.

"Where you going?"

"Gotta pinch a loaf, man..."

A little while later, Kate came rushing up. Her eyes were huge and crazed.

"They're going to arrest Chowdermilk!"

"Who?"

"Father Chowdermilk! They're gonna take him down. GO OUT THERE AND SLAM THE SLEAZER!"

"Huh?"

She came up and took hold of my arm. "What I mean is, Thor, you got ask him if he rapes little boys. You have to."

"I do?"

"Yes. Say it loud and clear so he hears, O.K.?"

"Like, 'Father, did you rape, like, boys?' Like that?"

"No. Listen, I'm telling you. You got to shout it out: DID YOU RAPE LITTLE BOYS, FATHER CHOWDERMILK? Like that."

"Scream it?"

"Maybe not scream it, but loud enough so he hears. That's why they called us, so we can have a crack at him... O.K., let me hear it."

"Father Chowdermilk... did you rape little boys?"

"O.K., but louder. I'm going to be watching on the TV, so go for it! You got to hurry, they're supposed to do it in half an hour."

Richie looked up from an egg-salad bagel.

"Go, kid! The gang-bang cannot commence until your wee willie winkie has made its grand entrance!"

"SHHH!" said Kate.

I grabbed Parker and we sped out to the address, a peach and lemon stucco duplex on the the semi-suburban ocean flat south of Castle Hill.

Sheriff's guys had already gone inside to snatch the high priest. We sprinted over, Parker pulling a lens from his bag as we scrambled. There were a couple satellite trucks, various vans, unmarked sedans, eight or nine police cars parked on the street, sidewalk and front lawn. Various locals wandered about, deputies chasing them down and herding them behind a roadblock. On the clown side, I saw Blaine Podgett of NBS and Bob Hoffwein of Channel Five Live. Also present in full clown gear were Jessica Schneffer from the *Examiner-Mail*, Kenny Ladoga of the *Star-Chronicle* and Orozco Mandelbaum from Smith-Jones, along with their associated film crews and photogs.

Deputy Ernesto Diaz ushered us behind a tape line. "Nobody move," he said.

On the other side was the contingent from the Bay County District Attorney's Office, including the D.A. himself, Michael J. Chernoyski. Chernoyski, a former junior college wrestling coach, was dressed in a charcoal pin-striped suit and glittering chartreuse tie. He appeared closely shaven and freshly showered, his cheeks pink and hair slicked back, a little curl dangling over his forehead.

A cool ocean breeze, mixed faintly with oil fumes, rustled through the area, but Chernoyski was sweating. He wiped his forehead with a hankie and flipped through a handful of crumpled papers, aides and consultants clustered around him. A podium and microphone were set up, awaiting the big speech. They had set it up so Chernoyski would be framed by palms and the clear sky, an endless stretch of ocean behind.

Photogs and cameramen stepped around, finalizing their positions. There was a brief murmuring. A cop opened the gate and stood to the side. Two plainclothes detectives jogged out of the compound. Three seconds, four...

Cameras started popping, there was a whirl of flashes and clicks and outstretched microphones as the Rev. Langley Chowdermilk of St. Horatius-Bartholomew Catholic Church emerged from behind the tan brick wall. He was hunched forward, hands in plastic cuffs in front of him, plainclothes cops on each arm. Chowdermilk was wearing baggy blue shorts, green plastic flip-on sandals, a red plaid short-sleeves button-down. He was frightfully skinny, bald with wisps of white hair above the ears, bony legs the color of day-old spaghetti. His face looked something like an alligator crossed with a frog.

"Father, Father –" one of the clowns started.

"Reverend Chowder –"

"F-Father," I heard my voice, "F-f-father Chowdermilk, did you rape little boys? DID YOU RAPE LITTLE BOYS?"

Chowdermilk turned vaguely towards us, frog-face convulsing. "Ubba-ub-ub, ubba," he seemed to say. "Ub, ubba-ub –"

He was on to the sidewalk. A door opened, cops were pushing him into a maroon Ford Escort. The door slammed, the wheels screeched.

"Was that a no comment?" said Kenny Ladoga. He giggled.

I hit the Kate button.

"They got him. Cuffed and in the car. They're on the way to the station."

"I know, we're watching it on TV. He say anything? We didn't hear a word."

"Ubb-ubb, it sounded like..."

"What?"

"Nothing... He didn't say anything."

"O.K., moving it now."

Cops came flooding out of the house, arms full of boxes and plastic bags. A Sheriff's Department van backed over the curb. Cops opened the rear doors and began sliding the stuff in.

>CNS-BULLETIN
>REV. LANGLEY CHOWDERMILK OF BAY CITY ST. HORATIUS-BARTHOLOMEW ARRESTED ON 64 COUNTS OF SEXUAL ABUSE OF MINORS

Back in the office, Kate came running over.

"Hey stud, great job! Come take a look."

She hit the recorder. Chowdermilk walked out. I heard my voice:

CLOWN: *F-f-father, did you rape little boys? D-did you rape little boys?*

Chowdermilk's head swiveled. The tape caught the frog but little of the "ubb-ubb." He walked under the palms to the cop car. A clown camera flashed on the clown throng. I saw myself, tie and sunglasses, arm outstretched. The video showed the cop car driving away.

"That was *you*, kid!" said Richie. He slapped me on the back. "You hear that – 'Fa-fa-fa, fa-fa-fa-, fa-fa-fa-father, d-d-d-d-did you rape little boys?' Hell, hell... Real star power you got."

"Thanks, Richie."

Chernoyski started reading his speech, the ocean sparkling behind.

We are committed to bringing to justice exploiters and abusers of children, no matter their station in society or position of influence...

Scotty walked up, a toothpick in his teeth and a machine capuccino in his hand. He flattened out his other hand. I smacked him five. He walked off and sat in a chair next to Shally. He took a sip from the plastic cup and put his hand on her knee.

LOVEBIRDS: Drunken Romance Flowers at Sad Wedding!

★ 10 ★

I had known this girl in college and now she was getting married. Wally drove us out. Wally worked two or three cities down, doing something for the school district. He had got his degree in Education, but he was no longer interested in it, if he ever had been. He "loathed" teaching the "little brats" and would not do it. Instead, he had wormed his way into a job in the head office of a small town school district. I believe it had something to do with counting textbooks.

Samantha, when she had been 18 or 19, beginning college, had seemed fresh and lively and I had really wanted to bang her something frightening. She was on the tall end and slender, boobs the size of pomegranates, buck teeth, lips that were always curling back with a smile. What it had meant was that I had spent many hours talking to her, trying to find the right combination of words that would persuade her to get drunk with me. I had been highly unsuccessful.

Several times I found myself bringing a 12-pack over to her dorm room. I would end up drinking them all myself. I would tell many lengthy stories about myself and people I claimed to know during these sessions, downing one can after another, leaning out the fifth floor window to blow smoke from my cigarettes, the ashes spiraling down. Sam would sit there smiling and laughing, seemingly entertained. Her thick and serious roommate, Jeanna, would be in the corner sighing, nose scrunched over a Zoology textbook. Eventually Jeanna would figure out I wasn't leaving and storm off to the Library.

I'd finally come to the end of the beer and try to kiss Sam. I'd sit next to her on the bed, laying kisses on her chin, her cheeks, the corners of her mouth, putting my hands on her hips, massaging her panties elastic, rubbing upwards towards her tits.

"Boy, you're really drunk," she would say good-naturedly.

"No, I hardly drank anything..."

She'd somehow squirm away and lead me to the door.

"I think it's probably time for you to go... Be careful walking home, O.K.?"

"O.K., Sam. See you around, I guess..."

As the college years went by, various shit happened – Sam became leaner and paler, her cheeks more hollow, hair frizzier, the noises from her mouth increasingly clichéd and useless. There really can be a long distance between 18 and 21. I didn't like feeling that way about her, having so much wanted to bang her in the past, but it was unavoidable, it had become a little bit painful to spend time around her. Well, but it was O.K., I would not see her that often anymore, and when it happened, it was usually brief. Sometimes she would ambush me down at the campus "pub," bringing around a few of her friends, mostly chubby girls in knee skirts and flabby male types, whom I would have to talk to for at least a few moments.

"This is Thor, my friend from the dorms!" Sam would tell them. "I met him my first year. Now he's the Editor-In-Chief of *The Daily Nugget*. He's crazy..."

Then I would have to act crazy for them, weaving around, lighting up smokes in the no-smoking zone, denouncing Van Gogh and the president, condemning the student leaders, threatening to take a piss by the table, guzzling down full mugs of beer and so on. They would look at me, saying little. I couldn't tell if they were just purely dull or I was too much of a creep. Yes, a little of both.

I would usually be down in the pub with Fedge McClanahan, one of the English professors. Fedge was a little Irish drunk who was dying of emphysema and walked with a cane. He was about five feet tall, with a belly big and hard as a cannonball, red face and red pointy nose, gold-rim eyeglasses, carroty-grey hair. Whenever he laughed or gnashed his teeth, usually a couple times per minute, he looked something like a chipmunk. He was also always sweating, no matter the temperature. Fedge was different than the other professors, mainly in that he didn't seem to mind the students. He had a good fan base for a professor, literature and film students mainly, who'd sit around the table listening to his routine.

"Yes," he would say, his face purple as a cranberry, hand wrapped around a beer mug, "you're really *on* to something there. Paul *is* to Superman as John *is* to Batman. Ringo is *clearly* The Hulk." He'd cackle and cough – "HACK-HACK-HACK!"

"What about George?" somebody would say.

"George is the Silver Surfer! HACK-HACK-HACK!"

Fedge would order a round of pitchers for the table, cackle and cough, limp off to the bathroom stall where he took his smoke breaks. Fedge would hit the pub right after his last class ended at two or three and stay until his wife picked him up at seven or eight. He would still be shouting as students helped him hobble out.

"Ooh no-no-*nooo!*" he would say. "What you mean is, Hemingway is Luke Skywalker to Twain's Darth Vader... Melville is The Emperor... Steinbeck is Han Solo, yes! Yes! Yes! Mailer is the wookie! HACK-HACK-HACK!!"

It was important for Fedge to be *down* with the students. He would pick your mind, really interested in what you had to say – what was the hot new band, what were the black students thinking, the Mexicans, would we really be renting out part of our brains to the highest bidder in the future? Fedge didn't exclude any of it. He thought it "possible, if not probable," that with the right mix of genetic-manipulation and drugs, people would eventually live for "300 years or more" until they "voluntarily offed" themselves. World peace would then ensue as, liberated from the fear of death, "even the Arabs and Israelis would realize this place isn't so bad." HACK-HACK-HACK!

It was well known that Fedge gave no less than half of the students in his classes A's. I saw him in the pub several times a week, but didn't go more than five times total to the two classes I took with him – "The History of Robots in Science Fiction Film" and "The Poetry and Prose of Alice Cooper" – and got A's both times. It was beautiful. You had to be some kind of real shitbrains to get a B with Fedge. You would have to fail to turn in both required four-page papers and miss one of the two written tests to have a decent chance at getting a C.

McClanahan had published a couple detective novels with a small mystery house. He would mention various big-time parties he had gone to, his New York summits with Norman Mailer and Douglas Adams, Cambridge drinking bouts with Donald Barthelme and Andrea Dworkin, his crazed run-in with R. Crumb, but the books never sold much. A couple months after he died,* I found *Death Rides a Moped* and *The Lady with the Pekinese* at the Salvation Army down the road from the university. Both in hardback, mint condition, 50 cents apiece. Each had the same quote from Mailer on the back: "Fedge McClanahan is the best unknown detective writer in America. *Death Rides a Moped* is a marvelous mystery, fast-paced, funny, full of sting and wit, and I read it straight through!" The books starred McClanahan's private dick hero, Clement "Clem" Vallandisham, an art-history professor with high blood pressure who liked to drink with (and get clues from) his students. I tried to read them, but never made it much past the first chapter.

I hadn't seen Sam in years, but here she was getting married to David Leftwich. I didn't know David, but Wally had met him once. David was allegedly some kind of specialist in the financial services industry.

"He's a millionaire," said Wally, "and he's got a big dick."

"No, he doesn't," I said. "That's a load of crap."

"No, it's true... Annie said so. She talks to Sam all the time."

"No way," I said. "Sam doesn't fuck. She never has. I would be surprised if she even thought about it."

"No, Sam fucks now," said Wally, nodding his head. "Seriously, she likes to fuck now. She's been fucking David all the time. All day and every night. That's what Annie says. You know I wouldn't lie about that."

Wally knew these people more than I did. He hung out with them. He claimed he banged this girl Annie "whenever we get horny." There was a little community of them who hung out together, fucking each other. I liked Wally, but I was glad I didn't have to be a part of it.

"Anyway," I said, "nobody's got a big dick. It's all a myth."

"No no no," said Wally, "I've seen some big dicks. Trust me."

"I never have," I said. "They all look small to me."

The wedding was taking place at Samantha's uncle's ranch, this place set down in a valley about 90 minutes south of Bay City. Wally parked in the gravel lot, we got out and walked past rows of giant

---

* A noted authority on Wordsworth, H.G. Wells and Biblical imagery, McClanahan was voted by students Professor of the Year five times. He was a recipient of the Guggenheim and Fulbright prizes, and served on the Pulitzer Prize Fiction Jury in years where the winners included *The Stories of John Cheever*, *Rabbit at Rest*, and *A Good Scent from a Strange Mountain*. He was 56 when he collapsed died of a heart attack while waiting for a campus bus. – ED.

eucalyptus, down a path studded with bushes that had flowers with little white puffs getting blown around by the breeze. The smell was warm and flower-fragrant, with a tinge of horse shit. We walked around to the rear of the house. Patches of people were standing around – blacks and whites, kids and old people, including at least two men wearing Air Force uniforms. Behind them were vast green fields that ran up to an encirclement of low blond hills. Out in the fields I saw horses, as well as what appeared to be a number of peacocks and ostriches.

Sam's mother was in a wheelchair, surrounded by a throng of well-wishers. Dorothy had come down with a brain seizure or cancer of the spine, possibly some combination of the two, about a year earlier. She was supposed to die within months, according to Wally. Dorothy had worked as a high school guidance counselor for more than 30 years. Already she couldn't talk any more, and her eyesight was supposed to go next. Wally said Samantha and Dave had pushed forward the wedding so Dorothy could see it.

Dorothy was laying back in the wheelchair, head cocked at an angle, frown on her face, eyes staring off into the deep far distance. She was wearing a long light blue gown, a purple knit sweater, a floppy red sunhat on her head. Apparently, there had been several operations.

I went over to see Samantha's father. I had met Gary once at the dorms. He worked, or used to work, as a civilian aircraft maintenance executive at Othutt Air Force base. He was dressed in a charcoal suit and dark blue tie, a thin leaf of hair over his bald spot. He looked a lot older than I remembered. His face was grey and lumpy, ill-fitting, as if it might fall off his skull with a little knock. I came up and shook his hand.

"Hello, Gary."

"Oh, hey there..."

"Must be a big day for you," I said. "Congratulations. Best hopes with everything."

"Well, thank you for being here," he said. "Yes, we're hoping and praying... David's a wonderful man. We're extremely lucky to be getting him in the family. I think Sam will be happy..."

"Yes..."

Gary didn't seem to remember me.

The ceremony was held outside under a giant sycamore tree, everyone sitting in rows of white plastic chairs – black half on one side, whites on the other. The crowd hushed and finally the lucky couple emerged. Sam didn't seem to have changed much. She was still thin and pale with pomegranate boobs, but maybe her skin had cleared up a little. She wore a sparkling white lace dress and had a bunch of daisies woven into a type of crown on her head. Dave appeared nearly bulletproof in a dark gray tux – hair short and tight, a little mustache, along with what looked like a diamond stud in his left ear.

Samantha's father walked her down. Dorothy had been wheeled up to the front.

A white preacher, white-haired and wearing glasses, opened with a prayer. "Dear Lord, we thank you for permitting us to share this day of great joy with Samantha and David. May your blessings and eternal light shine upon this special couple as they set out together on this treasure we have been granted, called Life. Guided by your wisdom and the gift of your mercy, may Samantha and David..."

Eventually he finished. A little black boy walked up with the ring on a pillow. Dave put it on her finger and they had a kiss. It was over at last. Everyone stood and cheered as Sam and Dave walked up the aisle through a rain of confetti. A pack of young girls walked around with bouquets of flowers.

Under a nearby tree, three lesbians in green and purple cheesecloth dresses took out a guitar, flute and a stand-up bass. "We're the Soul Vitamins," one of them announced. "Blessings be to Samantha and Dave, and everyone!" They jangled and tooted away as the crowd milled about. Their repertoire included "Give Peace a Chance," "Tie a Yellow Ribbon" and "Puff the Magic Dragon."

Wally and I waited to congratulate Samantha and Dave. I shook hands with Dave first, then Sam turned to me.

"Hey, I haven't seen this guy in years! Thanks for coming!"

"Wouldn't have missed it, Sam."

I leaned forward and gave her a hug and a kiss. She smelled like daffodils and cinnamon.

"So how's it feel to be the big city reporter? We always knew you would do it!"

"It's great," I said. "It feels incredible..."

"Drink all you want, dude. We got tons of beer and wine, we knew you were coming..."

"Thanks, Sam, you're the greatest. I'm sorry about your mom..."

"Oh, don't worry. There's nothing anybody can do..."

I left Wally and drifted around for a while, having a few keg beers and smoking under the trees, until it was time to eat. I waited in line and got a large slice of ham, a clump of fruit salad, a pile of celery and skinned cucumbers with bleu cheese. I snatched an open bottle of white from the wine table and sat down at the end of a table by myself. I poured a glassful and looked around – it was a table of blacks here, a table of whites over there, everybody chattering in their little group. Oh, well. Some things would never really change. The blacks generally looked good, at ease, laughing loudly and slurping at cocktails. Ambitious, professional black types. The whites were dressed dreadfully for the most part. Nervous, eyes darting around, chomping at the food like horses. Only the bride and groom's table, under a massive oak, had much mixing – Sam's father talking to Dave's.

I was about halfway through the food and wine when Uncle Ivan, the owner of the farm, got up to talk. He wanted to congratulate Samantha and David and thank everyone for coming. Then he wanted to say a "quick prayer," if no one minded.

Another prayer, why not. I looked around. People had stopped everything and closed their eyes. I saw Dorothy frowning under a giant umbrella, staring off, a slice of watermelon on a plate on her lap. I poured myself another wine.

Uncle Ivan had started sobbing. "… And Lord… Lord, please help my sister, Dorothy. We really need a miracle…"

Finally he was done. Everyone stood and applauded. A few were patting tears from their cheeks. I stood and emptied the bottle. Everyone sat back down. I walked and dumped my plate, then went to get another bottle – red this time. I took the bottle and glass and walked around near the fields, staring at the ostriches. I wasn't sure what they were up to. They looked at me, sometimes blinking, otherwise just standing. Damn odd things. I looped back around.

The traditional cake-slicing and eating came and went, then a black deejay wearing a visor started spinning turntables under the tent. Champagne corks flew and everybody gathered round as Samantha and Dave went for their first dance as a married couple: "I Will Always Love You," Whitney Houston. People cheered and clinked glasses and started lining up to dance. Ladies pinned money on David's coat, while Sam stuck out her skinny leg and various males ran up and put bills in her garter. The deejay put on "Word Up" and then "Love Me Do." "Word Up" was always pretty good, but I hated the Beatles. I grabbed another bottle of red.

People stood around clapping as Dave, squatting down, held Sam's mother's hands and twisted his hips. Sam, gripping the wheelchair from behind, moved her mother back and forth. Dorothy frowned.

I found Wally sitting at one of the tables, surrounded by three or four women and a couple guys. All whites. I sat down next to a peroxide blond who said her name was Teri. I had been noticing her here and there – silver eyeliner, heavy pink lipstick, leopard skin miniskirt. Black hose and heels, turquoise earrings. Black blouse, bigger than your average boobs in a black brassiere. Acne-flavored cheeks, well powdered. She was somewhat puffy, face on the wide side – yet not "fat," really, so much as rather grabbable. The peroxide locks swept down past her shoulders, flowing back over her ears. Parted in the center, a stripe of dark brown where it had grown out.

"Jesus, you need more wine, Teri," I said. "Here."

I filled her to the top with red.

"Whoa, not so much!"

"I love your skirt, by the way..."

"You do? I wasn't sure if I should have worn it."

"I'm glad you did. I like leopards..."

She opened her mouth and laughed, her tongue appearing like a pink flame.

"I also like hippopotamuses, anteaters and hedgehogs..."

Teri laughed. Late afternoon sunlight poured in from behind the trees, making them brilliant green and yellow. A Cat Stevens song blared on the sound system: *Oooooh, baby baby it's a wild world, doo-doo-doo-doo-doo...*

It turned out Teri was part of David's group. David had been her boss or had hired her, or had known someone where she worked, something like this, I didn't really pay attention. Teri now worked for the worldwide financial services firm Dewey James-Houghnaught, Santa Costa office, doing something with "accounts," possibly "account maintenance." Teri was intrigued by my work in the news biz.

"There's a lot of bad people in Santa Costa County," I told her. "Please, I hope you'll be careful."

"Really?"

"Of course, Teri. I couldn't make this up. I talk to the Santa Costa cops every day. They are honestly appalled."

I lit up another smoke, ashed nonchalantly. "You wouldn't believe it, but a pregnant woman got a six-inch blade in her gut the other day in Santa Costa. Lost the baby, she's in intensive care. Guy got away... Crazy guys will steal anything for drug money, totally off their nuts. Cops told me about this one guy, they had to cut off his feet. He had shot so much into his toes, the feet just died..."

I belched smoke, leaned back, tossed ashes onto the grass.

"Boy," said Teri, "you really smoke a lot."

"Not really," I said. "Only when I drink. Only at parties."

Teri laughed, sipped her wine. I put my hand on hers, leaned over and gave her a peck on the check.

"I love your perfume, Teri."

"Oh, thank you..."

The strains of "Up Where We Belong" filtered over from the deejay tent. Down the table, somebody's cell phone buzzed.

"My God," said a guy. "More than 47,000 people have been killed in an earthquake in India!"

"Really?"

"Oh, so what," said somebody else. "How's the war going?"

"'So what?' What do you mean, 'So what?'"

"The war? Let me check." The guy started punching buttons. "Here it is... helicopter crash kills nine Americans."

"Was it shot down?"

"Doesn't say..."

I leaned forward, keeping the one hand on Teri's and resting my other on her knee. The sun was falling fast now, shadows stretching out. The sky was marvelously blue, traces of pink and purple and white visible above the tree line. The deejay spun "Sugar Pie Honey Bunch." Out in the field, a peacock screamed, fanning out his feathers. Geeks turned and watched, oohing and ahhing...

I put my hand on the back of Teri's head and brought her to me. I smashed my lips against hers. Her tongue came into my mouth, thick and warm, a bit salty, tasting lightly of wine, Roquefort and lipstick.

I heard Wally snickering.

"You guys gonna get a hotel?"

He snickered again.

I pulled out and looked at him. Teri hiccupped.

Wally was sitting there, tie loosened, a plastic cup of beer in his hand. Next to him was a bull-faced guy who appeared stuffed full of yogurt and tomato paste. He was smiling too.

"No," I said. "Are you guys?"

I turned to Teri. "Maybe we should go somewhere, yeah?"

"O.K..."

"See you later, Wally."

"It was just a joke, man..."

"You're a funny guy."

I took Teri by the hand, we walked vaguely toward the ostriches. I moved my hand to her hip, concentrating on the movement of the hip in the socket. "Dancing on the Ceiling" echoed off the blond hills.

We didn't get very far, however, before three or four of Teri's friends rushed up. I shook hands with Janice, Heidi and Jennifer. Heidi was wearing a yellow headband and a dress of green car upholstery. Janice had on a dress of patched corduroy, little silver chains dangling from her ears. Tiny pink-cheeked Jennifer was in a black velour sheath with neon green arm stripes.

"C'mon, Sam's going to throw her garter!" said the one called Jennifer.

We went over. All the young women had gathered in front of Sam. An Air Force general was squatting down next to Sam's mother, hat in his hand. Dorothy's lips had a light covering of cake icing and drool; someone hadn't wiped very well. The Air Force chief acted like he didn't notice.

The deejay blasted "Hot Blooded" as Sam took off her garter and held it up. She shrieked, blushed, then turned around and threw it over her shoulder. The young women jumped and leaped. It hit somebody's hand, knocked around, then fell to the ground. Teri half-heartedly lunged forward in the scramble. Somebody else got it. Everybody cheered.

Packs of them rushed the dance floor as the deejay began spinning "1999." It was nearly dark now, the sky smudgy with purple and cobalt. Pinpricks of stars were becoming visible, pinpricks scattered everywhere...

"DON'T YOU GET IT?" I heard a guy screaming off in the shadows. "THERE'S A WAR ON, MAN! THOUSANDS OF PEOPLE HAVE BEEN KILLED!"

"Mwah, mwah," a muffled voice seemed to say.

"DON'T YOU CARE ABOUT THIS COUNTRY? WHY DO YOU HAVE TO HATE EVERYTHING? MY GOD, DO YOU WANT THEM TO WIN?"

"I don't hate this country!" went the muffled voice.

"THEY KILLED BABIES! THEY BOMBED THEIR OWN PEOPLE!"

"Damn white people," I said. "Can't they at least keep this crap out of a wedding? People are dying right here. Why isn't he screaming about that? There's nothing worse than a drunk screaming about the war."

"It must be really hard to have your parent dying at your wedding," said Teri. "I feel so sad for Samantha and her mom and dad."

"It's sad, but what can you do? Everybody dies – that's what they keep saying. I don't feel like I'll ever die…"

I jumped away from her, set the wine bottle in the grass and shadow-boxed the air.

"Maybe I'm the exception…"

Teri giggled.

I thrust myself forward and kissed her, grabbing and squeezing her ass. I lifted up the skirt and stroked her crevice, scraping at the hose and making brief cunt contact. We withdrew, sighing. I grabbed the bottle and threw my other arm around her waist. We crunched through tall grass.

I leaned Teri against a picnic bench that suddenly appeared under a stand of trees, "Jive Talkin'" throbbing faintly in the background. My hands went under her blouse, lifted the bra up over her boobs. I tweaked each nipple, twirled my tongue around inside her mouth. My eyes caught party lights down the ridge, criss-crossing white and yellow bulbs around the deejay tent.

We grappled, nipping and pulling. I withdrew after a few seconds, winded, took a lengthy lip of the wine. I knocked the bottle back down to the table. Swathes of moon-shine lazed atop the fields, bathing the wavy yellow strands in green-blue.

A goat bleated deep in the valley. A star shot two inches across the sky and exploded. A zenith hit its apogee.

The trees appeared purple and vine-encumbered, twisting branches angling upward, their progress blunted by dense hanging shrouds of leaves…

"TERI! TERI!"

A car raced forward in the lot, turned, beeped. Somebody banged against the car door.

"TERI, COME ON! WE'RE LEAVING!"

Teri pulled back. "I got to go. I really…"

"O.K. I'll… see you. I'll call you."

"You don't have the number…"

"TERI, COME ON!"

She ran off, never to be seen again.

I drained the last of the wine, threw the bottle in the weeds, lit a smoke. I stumbled down the hill and walked under the tent, "Private Dancer" booming from the speaker cabinets. I found an open bottle of red, splashed some into a glass, stood at the table looking around for girls.

A small, skinny black man in an avocado and burgundy tuxedo moved by extremely slowly. He was mainly bald, but with bushy grey sideburns. He paused to examine me.

"Young fella," he said, putting a hand on my shoulder, "you smell like a right old skunk." He giggled. "Red eyes. Like a rat, we used to say."

He giggled again and went over to the food table, where the caterers had laid out the scraps. I watched him use a gold fork to very slowly slide a piece of ham and a wedge of cantaloupe on to a foam plate. He trudged back past me, the plate shaking in his hand.

"This is good ham…"

He giggled and walked off. I heard somebody yelling.

"THOR, HEY THOR!"

It was Wally, on the grass on the other side of the tent.

"HEY THOR, COME HERE!" Wally appeared to be playing hacky-sack in the darkness with a 14-year-old boy. "COME PLAY WITH US!"

"I don't think so, Wally…"

I walked around to the side of the house and vomited on a patch of stones beneath a window. I sagged to my knees, the bottle knocking against the cement walk and finally falling over, the precious wine gurgling out. Several thin gushes sprayed out of me, my stomach squeezing into a tiny ball each time, then it was over. I rested on my hands and knees, spitting every so often and breathing heavily. I heard voices and crickets, cars crawling across the gravel, Wally grunting and laughing. I farted several times, then got up, wiped my mouth on my coat sleeve and went back to the tent.

A tall hairy guy with a red feather in a porkpie hat was standing behind Sam's mother, rubbing her shoulders. Big wide-faced guy with his hair in a ponytail. Dorothy frowned.

Sam stood to the side, still in full wedding gear.

"What's… going on, Sam?"

"Oh, hi... Daral's going to give my mom a massage, then we're going to put her under hot blankets. Do you want to come do it with us? We're supposed to all hold hands, because the more energy the better. If it's working she'll feel either hot or cold, or a breeze, on her feet. But we don't know if she'll be able to tell us."

"Cool," I said. "I don't think I can go, Sam..."

"It's all right."

I slugged from a bottle of white, fumbled in my pocket for smokes, dropped my lighter. Wine splashed the bricks as I bent to pick it up. Wine darkened my pants, landed on my shoes. I stiffened back up, lit the smoke, exhaled, sucked wine.

Sam stared. Daral looked off. Dorothy frowned.

Eventually, everyone died. Samantha and David moved to North Carolina, where Dave started a computer company and made a million.

IN OUR TIME: War is Over, Clowns Drink Free!

★ 11 ★

The camera zoomed in. The film showed a shirtless Mnung standing on a tank, a red bandanna tied around his head, curl of hair dangling between the eyes. A sheet of early evening sunlight fell across his right side, draping him in golds and amber, his profile outlined against the pink-orange sky. The president beat his chest with his fists and yowled. He stamped his booted feet against the tank armor. A giant banner hung, lights blinking in the virgin dusk: COONSKIN ACCOMPLISHED. The film showed fighter jets screeching overhead, tanks rolling over sand dunes, the dictator's statue crashing down. The film cut to pictures of thousands of troops waving flags and shouting: "HOO-HAAAA! HOO-HAAAA!"

I was in a mellow mood down at the Maxi-Dogs stall. Various seekers shuffled about behind me, muttering and arguing in the neon haze. A couple decked out in plastic and rags started throwing punches over a milk carton they'd pulled from a dumpster.

"That milk's bad, Manny!" the female one slurred.

"Arghgh! Urgggh…"

"Manny – you gimme!"

"Erghh, uggghah!"

Manny swung around, chopped her on the shoulder. She fell and he kicked her. Manny, whose pants were cinched at the waist by an extension cord, drank down the milk. A few of us looked over, but no one moved.

Another Tuesday night in Silvertown, the television fizzing upon Maxi's shelf. Well, but at least I'd be drinking soon. Maxi brought it and I paid the $3.55. I tore a hunk from the bacon, pastrami and pickle, long drips of grease-soaked melted cheese falling on to the *Star-Chron*. They had picked up three of mine from the previous day, all "Local News In Brief": MAN, 4 CHILDREN DIE IN MOTOR HOME FIRE POLICE SEIZE 25 LBS. OF COCAINE SEWAGE SPILL FOULS ORTEGA POND SYSTEM. I reached over and grabbed the *Examiner-Mail*. They had picked up the cocaine job, as well as MAN CHARGED WITH AXING DOG AS KIDS WATCH. In the section labeled "The Nation," the *Examiner* had placed this mystery story:

>DRUG TUNNEL FOUND UNDER U.S. CUSTOMS LOT
>*From Our Wire Services*
>
>PHOENIX – U.S. federal agents say they are trying to figure out who dug a 148-foot long "drug tunnel" from Mexican territory to a hilly, rocky area on the edge of a U.S. Customs Service employee parking lot in Nogales, Arizona.
>
>Customs Service spokesman Barry Ament said the tunnel was found Monday by a security guard who noticed a depression in the parking lot asphalt. He said the guard discovered that a small hole in the asphalt opened to a larger area underground.
>
>The tunnel was built with wood bracing and even had electricity illegally tapped from the Customs parking lot, Ament said.
>
>Ament said officials were "puzzled" over how the tunnel builders could have escaped detection amid the high security measures along the U.S.-Mexico border zone.

CLOWN: *The soldiers have released the little furry buggers, and the president is preparing to enter the free-fire zone... For those of you just joining us, you're watching the President's War Victory Celebration live on NNN, the News Now Network, news peak on media mountain... I'm Flip Puddington, and with me is NNN's own national security analyst, Jamie Hamentire, standing by at the Pentagon. We have been told by the president's staff people to expect quite a performance from the commander-in-chief this evening. So grab your popcorn, Mr. and Mrs. America, and get ready for a loopin' doozy... The president is a man, of course, who as a child placed lit firecrackers in the mouths of frogs that he captured. And that young man, according to his biographers, went ahead* and executed those frogs, no looking back, consequences be damned. And as governor, of course, Wolfgang Mnung executed an American-record 68 people – er, convicts, rather, people convicted of terrifying crimes – and never did he once show a hint of doubt or remorse... Of course, the American people know him now as a resolute and compassionate leader, with a refreshing commonman-ness and directness... But according to all accounts, the president can also be a cruel, vicious man when brought to anger, and that appears to be the case tonight as he celebrates his stunning war triumph over the enemy who had threatened to destroy our way of life with mass destruction weapons... Any thoughts, Jamie?

CLOWN: *You're quite right, Flip. I think the president is trying to send a dual-message here. First, he's telling the American people that he is their triumphant warrior-king, and that they can trust him to secure victory over those who would harm us... And secondly, he's giving fair warning to all the terrorists and non-allied regimes out there – he's saying, Look out, Buster Brown, because I'm coming after you with my bare hands, in the grand American tradition. The strong, tough, American nation that I lead is not in a mood to compromise with anybody, whether you be Islamic fascist terrorist or wine-guzzling, tolerance-spouting European UN waffler... And I think 'COONSKIN ACCOMPLISHED' really declares his resolve, his steel, if you will, and it's a message the American people are anxious to hear, and the community of foreign nations will want to hear as well...*

The president opened fire, mowing down scores of furry objects, the concussion of his weapon booming across the red-pink canyon walls. He yowled, bits of fur and blood raining down upon his hair and shoulders as the sunset daubed him with rich ambers, golds and silver. The film cut to troops jumping up and down, whipping their shirts over their heads: "HOO-HAAAA! HOO-HAAAA!" The president swerved and stalked toward the camera. He climbed a rock and began to beat his chest, his weapon slung over his shoulder. The camera froze on the president's blood and sand-smeared face, his wet lips locked in snarl, unblinking eyes fixed on a position on the far horizon.

CLOWN: *Oh my, what a night for America! What an historic performance from America's commander in chief. Words fail to... to achieve the necessary... We'll go to the instant-replay in a just a jiffy, folks... As I was saying, this fellow, America's warrior-king, has just notched another triumph for freedom – and by golly, now he's gone and told the whole world about it. That's what we've just witnessed here tonight. And I think those words say it all: 'COONSKIN*

ACCOMPLISHED.' Nothing to add there... And Jamie, either the president's packing an extra pair of socks in those long shorts, or female voters are really going to have something extra to think about come the next election, if you don't mind me saying so. Something like that will really stick in the mind, make no mistake about that, Jamie...

CLOWN: *You're quite right, Flip. What an awesome vision of authority and command he is projecting...*

I got up to go. I was due at the 50 Million, where Scott T. Varick had scheduled a press conference for 8 p.m. Scotty had been promoted after nine weeks on the job to Assistant Deputy News Editor, a position which technically elevated him above Kate, but happened to remove him from all daily news-gathering and/or writing and editing activities. Mainly, it seemed, he sat in meetings with Sernath to talk over and organize "long-term projects," which seemed mainly to involve the internet.

At the end of the block, a guy was laid out in front of a doorway. I stepped over him, then turned back and looked down. In the lamplight I could see the guy's face was swollen, dark purple bruises twisting across his face and neck. Something like dried blood under his nostrils. I stood there staring.

Was he dead?

I don't how long I stood watching. Then he moved.

He moved, let out a groan, and fell silent once more.

Scotty arrived with Shally on his arm. He shook hands with everyone before taking his seat at the head of the table.

Tommy-Gun burned, whispering: "How could she?" I could only shrug.

CLOWN: *Gentlemen, thank you for coming. . . . Drink up, it's on my father...*

CLOWN: *Who's your dad?*

CLOWN: *He exploits the weak and indigestible, in order to hire my mother. He beats his dog when he gets drunk, which is every Sunday, Monday, Tuesday, Thursday, Friday and Saturday, or whenever there's a game on TV.* (CLOWN LAUGHTER)

CLOWN: *What kind of dog?*

CLOWN: *English springer spaniel. How the fuck do you get service around here?* (WHISTLES TO SIGNAL THE WAITRESS) *Here kitty kitty, here kitty kitty... Well, hello. You've got a beautiful pair of... hands.* (CLOWN LAUGHTER)

Scotty announced he had determined that Dick was gay. Wayne was also gay. Dick and Wayne "probably have a gay thing going on." Richie, meanwhile, was only possibly gay. Scotty knew Bay City was full of fruits. Snowberg, one of the Internet Team clowns, was "gay as a hummingbird." Scotty would "rip the fruitbird" if Snowie came on to him again. Scotty didn't have anything against gays, he was just saying – he didn't want fruitbirds coming on to him.

Sernath wasn't gay, but he dyed his hair. "The Nath" loved hair dye like "terrorists love virgin pussy." On the other hand, The Nath hated deodorant "the way Nazis hate Jews." The Nath smelled like "clam chowder."

Scotty thought *Apocalypse Now* was the greatest movie of all time – "How could it not be?" Scotty was pretty sure you shouldn't do meth, because it was toxic shit and changed the inside of your brain and you'd never be the same, you'd be horrible and a fucking mess, he'd seen it happen to some people he knew in high school.

Scotty wasn't sure if Kate was a lez, but she sure could "use a shave." Actually, he was only joking, because Kate was "really great." Scotty was glad Parker had come, because it was cool, Scotty was "down with the bloods." Scotty had started at inside linebacker in high school, but he had hurt his knee on a ladder and couldn't play his senior season. A quarterback Scotty's team had once played against had lost his scholarship to Virginia Tech and was now "the biggest drug dealer in Florida."

Shally got up to go to the bathroom.

CLOWN: *No woman is ugly when she's got your dick in her mouth.* (CLOWN LAUGHTER) *You guys heard that one? Ha, yeah. This is cool, we're hanging out... Here kitty kitty, here kitty kitty...*

Tommy-Gun said goodbye and left. He'd really had enough. I got up for another smoke. I came back to find Parker and Scotty getting into it.

CLOWN: *You see me, you just see black. King Kong and all that, hide all the white women. Look out, he's gonna steal somethin'...*

CLOWN: *Not even, man. You're high...*

CLOWN: *You can't get around me being black.*

CLOWN: *You can't get around me being white.*

CLOWN: *You is white.*

CLOWN: *You is black.*

CLOWN: *See, you can't get around it.*

CLOWN: *Nothin' to get around. I told you, I don't got a problem with you or no bloods.*

CLOWN: *I got lots of problems with some white man calling me 'blood.' Don't call me blood, white man.*

CLOWN: *What's wrong with sayin' 'blood'? You say it, why can't I?*

CLOWN: *I got a problem with it, that's all. You ask too many questions. You should try being quiet. Don't call me 'blood,' white man.*

CLOWN: *You don't got a problem drinking my booze.*

CLOWN: *Fuck your booze, white man.*

CLOWN: *You sure do like it.*

CLOWN: *Watch it, white boy. One day there'll be a black president. We'll throw all crackers like you in jail.*

CLOWN: *Black president my ass. When an elephant flies out of my ass.*

CLOWN: *That's right. It'll be like that.*

CLOWN: *They'd shoot a black president. I mean, I hate to say it, but...*

CLOWN: *You the first one in jail, white boy.*

CLOWN: *No, seriously, though, I'd love to see a black president. Seriously. It'd be the American dream come true...*

They were still at it when I left 20 minutes later.

CHILD BODY PARTS FOUND AT BAY PIER

BAY CITY (CNS) – Bay City police said body parts apparently belonging to at least one small child were found Tuesday in several pieces of luggage that had been left at Bay Pier Mall.

Lt. Joel Vasquez said a shop-owner called police after a homeless person opened one of the pieces of luggage and a found a child's foot.

Vasquez said investigators found other human remains in several suitcases and bags in the outdoor shopping area.

Vasquez said the condition of the body parts indicated the child or children had been killed within the past week. He said the identity of the victim or victims was unknown.

Vasquez said surveillance video in the mall area was being analyzed by investigators in an effort to determine who had deposited the luggage.

HIDE IN 'PLANE' SIGHT:
Cannibals on the Loose!

★ 12 ★

I was broke again and had gone over to Eugene Keaks'. Gene had opened the bottle and poured the drinks and started showing the film. It was my day off – bright and warm outside, birds could be heard, but Gene had pulled the blinds and shut off the lights. He insisted. He didn't want anybody "spying" – this thing was "illegal in 36 states." On the TV screen, a woman dressed in a pink bikini was smashing a succession of cockroaches with black high heels.

"OH, THE POOR THINGS!" Gene screeched. He giggled and sipped from his glass.

The blond beauty snuffed out beetles and grasshoppers, twisting her toe, grinding her heel, flicking her tongue at the camera. Slow-motion shots showed her ass quivering in slow motion as she squished. An underneath shot through the glass caught bugs as they exploded and ripped.

"OH, NO! OH, NO!" Gene shrieked.

The film cut to a different girl, a redhead in a blue and yellow cheerleader's uniform. She blew a few kisses at the camera, then stomped on a lizard with her Reeboks. A salamander wandered out, and then a very small green snake appeared. It slithered along, its little head just off the glass. The cheerleader did a striptease, throwing off her skirt and sweater. Finally she was wearing only white panties, a bra and the sneakers.

"I HATE SNAKES!" squealed Gene.

I had met Gene while temp-working at Lisberger-Knox BioPrep, a company that sold and distributed medical supplies – stocks of rubber gloves and cotton balls and syringes, but also parts for heart pacemakers and stents, defibrillators, machine insulators, so forth. Gene's job was to organize the shipping forms, to figure out what was being shipped and to print out the right address labels for the boxes. It was my job to stick and tape the labels on the boxes, then move the boxes to the loading platform. Gene must have looked into my torn and ragged soul and detected another victim, because from the first day I worked at the place, he was inviting me over to his apartment to "watch movies." I said no for about the first two weeks, but the next Friday I found myself without any money.

"O.K., Gene, look, I'll come over but I'm going to want something to drink. A lot to drink. You got anything or am I going to have to bring it myself?"

"Oh sure, I can buy it. What do you want?"

"A bottle of vodka should be fine."

"Oh, no problem."

"A big bottle, Gene, not one of the little ones. I like to get drunk. Really drunk."

"Oh that's fine, you can drink all you want at my place. I live alone..."

Gene had a long skinny neck and was severely slump shouldered, as if the weight of his head was going to collapse his chest in on itself. He had sharp elbows, bony wrists, fingernails which he would eat off until the sides of his fingertips were raw and red. His teeth were grey, his hair a pile of brown mud. He was a member of the group of guys who never seem to notice that a layer of dust and food particles has settled upon their eyeglass lenses.

The second time I was there he started telling a story about how he had been "unjustly" fired as a stock boy at a Rosemary West clothing outlet. It had been "the best job in the whole world," up at the Bay City Oaks Mall. But one day they had fired him, just let him go "without warning." They had claimed reasons of economy, but Gene wasn't buying. He mentioned a conflict with a certain woman supervisor.

"She hated me! She hates everybody!"

"It's possible, Gene..."

Gene had one-bedroom place near Koreatown whose walls were covered with posters for movies like *House of Whipcord* and *They Call Her One Eye*, *Galaxina* and *The Possession of Nurse Sherri*, *The Toxic Avenger*, *Frankenstein Created Woman*, *The Girl Slaves of Morgana Le Fay*, *Creepozoids*, *SLUGS: The Movie*, *Vampyres*, *The Stepfather*, *Malibu*

High, Revenge of the Cheerleader Nurses, Naked Massacre, Zombiegeddon, The Lone Gunmen... He also had several ring binders in which he kept autographed portraits of stars such as Jessica Hahn and Beckie Monroe, Chandra Huss, Julie Strain, Barbara Crampton, Milky Blandot and so forth. He would go to conventions where geeks would pay to meet these women.

"Doesn't she have long nipples?" Gene would say, grinning. "Beautiful long nipples. I've seen them in person, as close as I am to you right now..."

"Nice, Gene, super cool..."

"She's even better looking in real life, if you can believe it..."

"I can believe it."

Gene had another sideline in the field of presidential assassinations and assassination attempts.

"Mnung could be a pretty good president... unless he gets *shot*."

"What do you mean, Gene?"

"Well... Presidents have a tendency to get shot, don't they?"

"Well... Yes and no. You make a good point, I guess."

Gene proceeded to tell, in considerable detail, about the 1835 assassination attempt on Andrew Jackson. It turned out that Jackson was saved because the two guns carried by the assassin misfired. *Both guns.* I remembered hearing something about this at some stage of school, but Gene had the extra details, he assured me that both guns were derringers...

Gene was also absolutely certain that John Wilkes Booth, after shooting Lincoln, had caught his foot on an American flag while jumping from the balcony to the Ford Theatre stage, thus breaking his leg.

Gene would say: "Everything's connected." For example, he said John Hinckley had known the Bush family, and wasn't it "strange" that no one talked about how George H.W. Bush took over as president after Reagan was shot by Hinckley?[*]

"Now, Gene..."

---

[*] Ronald Wilson Reagan, the 40th president of the United States, was shot in the chest by John Hinckley, Jr., on March 30, 1981, shortly after Reagan assumed office. Vice President George Bush served as president while Reagan recovered in the hospital. Reagan went on two serve two full terms in the White House. Hinckley was reported to have been motivated by an "obsession with the actress Jodie Foster," who had played the role of a teenage prostitute in *Taxi Driver*, a 1976 Hollywood film about a taxi driver who seems to plot the assassination of a politician, but fails to carry it out. – ED.

"Everything's connected. *Everything.* Or it just *happens* that way, right?" He grinned hideously. "Just a *coincidence?*"

"Come on now, Gene."

"There's no such thing as coincidence!" he screamed.

Later, I took the time and looked it up. There seemed to be some truth to it. It seemed the Bushes and the Hinckleys *had* known each other, had some connection. I really wasn't sure what to think.

The first time I was over, Gene had thought I should see *Cannibal Holocaust*. "This was banned in at least 50 countries!" he said.

We poured the drinks and he rolled the film. It sort of dragged along for awhile, until somebody suddenly hacked off a monkey's face so they could eat the brain. It looked real.

"It *is* real!" said Gene.

A short time later, they pulled a giant turtle out of the Amazon and a guy hacked off one of its claws. The three other feet flapped. That couldn't have been special effects, but I wasn't sure if it was real till the guy cut off the underneath half of the shell and you could see the turtle's heart and guts laying there, shaking. I was 100 percent sure they couldn't have faked that.

It had been altogether too much vodka and turtle guts. I was ready to vomit and I got up to do so.

"Wait, they're going to eat it!" said Gene.

I didn't wait. I barfed and came back out in time to see a snake bite the guy who had chopped up the turtle. Everybody freaked out. They chopped the snake in half, then quickly chopped off the guy's leg. It didn't help. The guy died and they covered him with leaves.

I sat down and guzzled more vodka. Little did I know, things were just getting started. The smug Americans shot a pig while cannibal villagers cowered. It looked real. The Americans burnt down the cannibals' hut to fake a tribal massacre for a documentary they were filming. Weird hippie flute music rolled. The American men gang-raped a young cannibal girl, while the lone American woman protested weakly and ineffectually. The girl somehow wound up with a wooden pole shoved through her cunt and out her mouth. The Americans called it a "punishment ritual," giggled and made smart-aleck comments and got it down on film for their documentary.

Finally, the cannibals started picking them off. They stripped the clothes off the blond American hippie, snipped off his penis, hacked him into red chunks with their stone knives. Little cannibal devils in Beatle haircuts stripped the woman and raped her, then the cannibal women carried her away and cut off her head. Crazy hippie flute music rolled. I sucked vodka. The callow American film director got his head lopped. Gene grinned. I sucked more vodka. I was going to finish that bottle.

A turtle image flashed, the vodka exploded inside me. I ran back to the toilet.

I came back out and picked up the video cover. Crazy Italian communist devils had made this movie. I sat there, my head spinning. Goddamn devils had trashed life, trashed death, trashed hope. They had cruelly kicked people in the head, and for that I supposed they deserved big medals.

"Gene," I said Monday at work, "you can't show people that when they're drunk! That movie's a dangerous weapon. I've almost gone insane..."

Gene put his hand over his mouth and giggled. "That was my 19th time!"

After I joined Cities News, Gene took it as an excuse to start yanking my chain even harder.

"You claim to be a reporter – or are you one of *them?*" he would egg me on. "You're one of *them!* You probably believe what they say. You probably think *I'm* crazy..."

"The hell," I said. "I don't believe a word they say."

Once, during the break between *Golden Ninja Warrior* and *Bride of Chucky*, I asked him, "So what about the Boeing, Gene. Did it hit the Pentagon on 9/11 or not?"

"THERE WERE NO PLANES!"

"*What?*"

"EVERY PLANE SEEN ON TV ON 9/11 WAS FAKE! THEY WERE CARTOONS!"

"Goddamn it, Gene. Come on, man. I'm seriously asking you about the Boeing here."

"Do you believe everything you see on TV? As long as it looks sort of real and it's on the news, you believe it?"

"Gene, Gene – that's crazy. No planes? Cartoon planes? What the hell are you talking about? I mean, nobody could... it's too... it's *too-too* much. It's way on the other side of too-too much."

Gene giggled, sipped vodka, bugged out his eyes. He cackled.

"Don't think they can't do it? Anything can be faked on TV. Who do you think's running the TV signal? How do you know the TV wasn't on tape-delay?"

"My God, no planes. That would be the biggest fake-out of all time. The absolute biggest. Kennedy assassination and Bay of Pigs and Oswald be damned."

Gene sipped, cackled.

"You're one of *them*. YOU ARE! You're one of *them!* You believe whatever they say…"

"The hell I do."

"It was easy," said Gene. "They exploded the buildings and then pasted the planes on to the videos. It would only take a few seconds to do that. Then they showed it to the world, and everybody instantly became convinced that aluminum airplanes can knock down steel and concrete towers! JUST LIKE THEY TOLD YOU ON TV! The World Trade Center!"

"Goddamn it, Gene. I tell you, that's monstrous. It's sinful to even think about."

Gene cackled.

"Don't you know that the only way to beat them is to think as crazy they do? They call it The Big Lie. Ever hear of the Big Lie?"

"Goddamn it, Gene."

Gene giggled.

"They also call it Hide In Plain Sight. Everything there is to know is right in front of us, right in front of our eyes. They just control us so much we don't even believe our own eyes."

GANG BANG! Clowns Crash Massacre Meltdown

★ 13 ★

We had just come in to start the workday. The towers were already smoking on the TV screens.

The first one fell, sending up bigger clouds of dust and smoke than anybody had ever hoped to see.

Richie had said, *"No no no no no no no no no no no no no..."*

Everyone rushed to the TVs to see the first of the many replays of this amazing thing that had apparently happened. The news swept around the room: The towers had earlier been hit by "hijacked planes." Some of the staff furiously slapped at keyboards, trying to get on the internet. We called the airports, and they were shutting down.

The second tower wobbled... burst into a cloud of powder... disappeared into dust.

Dick walked out and sank into a chair, sweating, a red towel in his mouth. He got up, took a step, sat back down. He gnawed at the towel.

We stared at the TVs, gulping down the replays: The shot, from a great distance, of the smudgy black aircraft shooting across the sky.

The impact obscured by the first tower.

The orange and black explosion out the other side.

The towers smoking, smoke pouring out, billowing into the brilliant blue...

Then the thing so unexpected and shocking there still seems no adequate response: More than 100 stories of steel and concrete coming down in seconds...

The towers *disappearing* in geysers of thick grey powder...

Office people sat around and made phone calls. Some cried softly. Most seemed mainly groggy – shock, combined with a kind of strangling fear that seemed to grow and grow in intensity. A few started wondering out loud whether they knew anyone in the towers, or even anyone who might be living in or visiting New York that day.

Sernath paced back and forth, going from the phone in his office, out to the desk and back.

"Get back to work!" he barked. "No crying allowed here! Get on the phone! Nobody's going to bomb this place. Get going, call the police! You're big people, don't be afraid... This is why you're a reporter. Get back to work! Take a deep breath, now toughen up! We're not going to hide... This is why we're in this business..."

Most made a good show of it, but there was no avoiding the increasingly uncontrollable feelings of claustrophobia and panic that were coming down – feelings of weakness and shame and anger all mixed together – along with a vague awareness of a problem so vast and vicious a mind was not really prepared to handle it. Was this how the world ended, and was this the day?

One problem was, there was no other news. Even the crooks were staying at home to watch the replays of this most amazing thing that had ever been seen on TV. We kept writing the same stories about airports closing and flights cancelled, beefed up security patrols, extra police deployments...

We issued and kept reissuing the same simultaneously threatening and reassuring statements from the authorities, who truly did not seem to have a clue: *Things are continuing as normal, though we are at the highest level of alert... All airports have been closed, extra security forces have been deployed... Please continue with your business as usual, call 911 immediately if you observe anything suspicious or out of the ordinary...*

"The fucking-fucks," Richie kept muttering. "The fucking-fuck, fuck-fucking-fuck-fucks... How'd they get the bombs in?[*] The fucking fuck-fuck fucky-fucks..."

By the time the day was over, we seemed to have survived. No one was sure what the whole thing meant, other than that it had been a super-huge defeat for the United States of America. Somebody appeared to have succeeded in driving airplanes into some of our biggest and most famous buildings. And the buildings had somehow fallen down, crumbling to dust in a matter of seconds, as though made of tissue paper and sand. We'd proven ourselves helpless against the

---

[*] No evidence of "bombs" was found in the World Trade Center wreckage, according to the official investigations. – ED.

attack, our defense systems totally ineffective, and we were bleeding from every hole.

Sernath added an extra reporter for the evening and overnight shifts, but nothing much was asked of anybody else. Go home, come back tomorrow, get some rest, *keep working*. And everybody did.

Richie said, "They cut off the tip of our penis, kid. What do you do when they cut off the tip of your penis? You start pissing all over the place."

The early evening streets were warm and breezy. Cop cars and various official-appearing vehicles whipped down the nearly-deserted boulevards, lights blinking but no sirens. Small groups of people wandered about, cop cars sat at some of the main intersections, doing something or other. American flags had been taped up over a few windows and doors. I felt nauseated, without hunger. I just wanted to lay down on the couch.

I took a phone call from my mother and Hank.

"This is *Clinton's* fault!" said Hank. "He was busy getting his ding-dong tickled while these ayatollah-terrorists were planning this thing... He could have taken care of it a long time ago, but all he cared about was his ding-dong!"

"Sure, Hank..."

"I want to see the bodies of these Islamics stacked up... It's time to stop fooling around. Somebody's gonna pay for this..."

Jerry never came home. I lay on the couch, feeling sick and light-headed, television clowns droning. The TV endlessly showing replays of the dream: The jet hurtling toward the tower... the tower *swallowing* the jet... The terrible explosion, the orange fireball, the rain of glass and paper... The towers giving up and crumbling, disappearing in gigantic sprays of dust, collapsing into nothingness in about 10 seconds... The camera jerking about... then miraculously steadying and capturing the jet as it made its crazy power-dive into the tower... The jet *completely disappearing* into the tower... The astounding, stupefying explosion, the fireball rising above the green trees. The massive streams of black smoke, the whirlwind of shattered glass and confetti... People leaping from the towers, their bodies being tossed and blown in the breeze... The towers smoking like volcanoes. The towers disappearing, the floors exploding one after the other, bursting into *powder*, vanishing in the air...

CLOWN: *America has been attacked by hijacked airliners, the World Trade Center towers have fallen, Manhattan has been turned into a mass grave, the Pentagon has been hit, thousands are dead, the country's airports* are under lockdown. The nation tonight is in shock. Courage and bravery have been shown in equal measure. The nation mourns...

CLOWN: *Suspected Islamic terrorists have hijacked planes and flown them into some of America's most famous landmarks... The World Trade Center is no more. The twin towers have collapsed – falling straight to the ground as if brought down by a demolition team, after being struck by hijacked airliners...*

CLOWN: *The Pentagon, the nerve center of America's military might, has suffered a debilitating blow. A fourth plane, meanwhile, has crashed in a field in Pennsylvania in circumstances that are not yet clear... And yes, the world suddenly seems to be staring face-to-face at a new future, Jack, a new future that no one could have possibly imagined...*

The plane in slow-motion. The plane in a power dive. The plane slicing into the tower. The building absorbing the jet. The gigantic explosion. The towers smoking like volcanoes. The towers disappearing into plumes of dust and confetti. Crowds of frightened people running through the streets of New York, immense clouds of destruction crashing behind them...

CLOWN: *The rescuers have shown immense courage. The authorities are urging everyone to remain calm but vigilant. The president has triumphantly reappeared and vowed to bring the perpetrators to justice. Congress members have returned to their chambers and sung a rousing, patriotic version of 'America the Beautiful.' The nation mourns...*

CLOWN: *The British prime minister has condemned, the French have sent condolences, the NATO Council has been activated. Afghanistan's fundamentalist extremist Islamic rulers have denied any involvement...*

CLOWN: *The nation mourns, the courage has been profound. The World Trade Center in New York City has been destroyed in a vicious surprise attack by suspected Islamic terrorists in a day of terror and infamy comparable to Pearl Harbor. The president has vowed to bring the perpetrators to justice... And Jack, the globe tonight seems to be suddenly staring face-to-face at a new future that no one seems to have imagined...*

The next morning, a sheet had been painted and hung in an apartment window at Omaha and Dewblesbury: GOD HELP BLESS AMERICA. The artist had added scratchings of smiley faces and Old Glory. A shrine of flowers, candles, balloons and crucifixes had come to life in front of the Temple Christchurch. A hippie guitarist stood in front as I walked toward the office, singing "knock-knock-knockin' on heaven's door," a little flag in his hatband. A car from a private security company was parked in front of Condor Business Plaza. It looked like one or two security guards had been added.

We did more stories about security, reactions to the crime against humanity. Finally somebody snagged something normal: POLICE:

MAN SHOOTS WIFE, DAUGHTER. There, the same old future, Jack. I caught another just before lunch:

> BABYSITTER ARRESTED FOR INFANT VIDEO ATTACK
> WESTFIELD (CNS) - Westfield police said a woman was arrested on suspicion of child abuse Wednesday after she was seen on a surveillance video hitting a four-month-old child.
>
> Sgt. Peter Gambetta said the suspect, Colleen Liles, 28, was taken into custody as she arrived to babysit the child at the family's home in Westfield.

On Friday, the Condor Business Plaza staged a memorial meeting in the Atrium. About 100 people showed. Dick was among the dignitaries who read from prepared remarks. He spoke haltingly, with many pauses, fighting back tears that he seemed to wish would publicly flow.

"Ladies and gentlemen... the terrorists have attacked our nation but they have failed to destroy their real target: the American spirit... Instead, their murderous attacks have had the unintended effect of calling us back to our first principles... With their mass murder in New York, Washington and Pennsylvania, the terrorists have succeeded in shocking a good and generous people, who have always assumed that such things can't happen to them in their homeland... We are shocked, yes, but not humbled nor defeated. Because what is already evident is that the efforts of the terrorists have backfired... In the words of the old hymn, they have done the most foolish thing anyone can ever do: They have trampled on the vintage where the grapes of wrath are stored... In other words, they have made us *angry*... I have seen it in the streets, I have sensed it in the stores and corner cafes: Our nation is afoot... I am a journalist at the core of my being, but sometimes the lessons of objective journalism fail us, and we must respond with honest feeling. So allow me to drop that journalistic pretense for just a moment. Our opponents should beware: An angry, purposeful America is not something that anyone can withstand over time."

Tears welled in Dick's eyes.

"At your service, Mr. President!" he at last blurted.

✪

On the television, a girl in a nurse uniform was holding a gray mouse. The nurse was wearing knee-high combat boots. She held the mouse next to her face and gave it little kisses. She looked into the camera, smiling and winking.

"Oh, what a sweet little thing," said Gene. "Oh, I hope she doesn't hurt the little poor thing..."

The movie showed the mouse on the floor, a close-up on its face, its whiskers. It was sniffing and snuffing about. The shot pulled back.

"OH, NO!" Gene shrieked. "NOT THE LITTLE MOUSIE!"

"Jesus, Gene!"

The phone throbbed. I picked it up and looked – Kate.

"Thor – are you drunk?"

"No."

"O.K., there's been a shooting, a bombing. Somebody shot up an office, or bombed it. I need you to go down to County Main to handle things from there."

I shut off the phone and stood. "Let me know how this movie ends, Gene. I got to go."

"What? Already? I rented *Attack of the 60-Ft. Centerfold* and *The Flying Guillotine* especially for today. I don't think you've ever seen them. They're classics."

"Next time, Gene."

The television showed a brunette in silver lipstick and six-inch black heels. The heels seemed unusually long and sharp. She was petting a young guinea pig. She kissed the thing on the cheek.

I saw a helicopter hovering low over the city center as I walked down the stairs of Gene's complex. Then a second helicopter buzzed over. This helicopter seemed angry. It hovered a few seconds, zoomed off and started circling. Smoke was coming up from somewhere – not a lot of smoke, but some, wispy and black.

The rumble and whap of the choppers bounced off the buildings. I heard sirens in the distance. I went out to the boulevard and caught a taxi.

The TV trucks were already at County Main when I showed. I flashed my badge and went down the hall to the Emergency Center. Clown crews had set up their cameras in the parking lot and waiting room. Clowns prowled around like wolverines, woofing and growling questions and failing to get answers. I saw Paul Fratellini from KACH TV-9, Marie Devolites of the *Star-Chron*, Roy Brown from JABN-Satellite Radio, Glenn Little of the *Examiner-Mail*, Poodles Hanneford of the Channel Five Live "News Squad," gangs of photo goons. Shaggy-haired clowns from a *COP PARTY* crew were interviewing a clown-team from Japan. Another bozo squad seemed to be speaking German or Dutch.

Clowns jabbered into phones. Clown eyes darted, seeking out clown info. Clown rumors flitted about: *There were two gunmen, maybe three... It was a terrorist attack, but they didn't want to announce it yet... The governor's brother had been shot...* Every so often, the deputy hospital communications director, Paula Grober, would emerge to get clown-pounded.

"PAULA! PAULA! PAULA-PAULA!"

"HOW MANY?"

"WAS IT A TERROR – !"

I phoned the count into Kate: four dead so far, nine injured, six critical. Other vics had been taken to St. Vincent's, I had no information on that. Cops threw up a body-line as another ambulance arrived. The emergency crew rushed them in on stretchers, clown nuts jumping over railings and screaming after them.

The relatives of victims got mercilessly banged. Cops and members of the hospital PR team were forced to set up flying wedges as they rushed the relatives in, jackets and blankets covering their heads.

In between the vic action, we were able to catch live shots and replays on the Waiting Room TV. BREAKING: GUNMAN BOMBS, ATTACKS LAW OFFICE. Footage of shattered glass and smoke pouring out a window. Firefighters administering mouth-to-mouth. A police officer carrying a limp woman. BREAKING: 7 DEAD, 15 INJURED IN OFFICE BLOODBATH. The TV had phone-cam shots of a man in a business suit holding a bloodied bandage over his eye. A woman with a bloodied face, talking into a cell phone.

BREAKING: COP DEAD IN LAW OFFICE SHOOTOUT

A new crew of about a dozen clown techs arrived and began setting up a generator, cables and arc lights. The word rippled through: The mayor was on his way to deliver an official statement and meet with the relatives of victims.

I went over to get a sip from the water fountain. Down the dimly lit hall, I saw an old woman with a shriveled face looking at me quizzically. She was wearing a pale pink robe and her white hair was tied at the top with a white ribbon. Using a walker, she began slowly moving toward me.

"I'm thirsty," she rasped. "I'm thirsty!"

"O.K., it's all right," I said. "Come on, there's water right here..."

"I'm thirsty... I'm so thirsty..."

I stood there waiting. When she had almost reached the threshold, two nurses rushed up and took her by each arm. They began to turn her around.

"I'm thirsty... I'm so thirsty..."

"It's going to be O.K. Mrs. Kreedler," one of the nurses said.

I turned back in time to see a convoy of nine or ten cop cars and SUVs screeching to a stop outside the glass doors, sirens wailing and lights flashing. A fresh phalanx of aides and clowns rushed in.

"OUT OF THE WAY, OUT OF THE WAY FOR HIZZONER!" screamed a bodyguard dressed in a dark purple and white suit.

There was a brief bugle fanfare from a portable sound rig. Finally it ended. The sliding glass doorway was flooded with another burst of cops and bodyguards as Mayor Ernest "Ernie" Favella made his entrance. Clowns shouted, cameras rolled, flashes exploded. The mayor brought his hands together and bowed his head.

"MR. MAYOR...!"

"HOW MANY...!"

A former U.S. Army sniper who held doctorates in economics and chemical engineering, Favella was about five-two and wore his hair in a severe grey flat-top. He had famously made millions as the chief salesman and TV spokesman for a device that allowed car owners to track the whereabouts of their car, a device that remained popular with the parents of suburban teenage children and other paranoid control types. Favella had spent a record $28 million on his election campaign, more than half from his own savings.

"MR. MAYOR...!"

"WERE THEY TERRORISTS...!"

"Ladies and gentlemen, I wish to express my sincere condolences to the victims of this heinous tragedy today at the Bank of Finance & Chemicals Consolidated. We will find out who did this, and we will bring them to justice. I wish to commend the police and fire department for their heroic efforts in responding in a timely and professional manner. At the current time, there is no evidence suggesting it was a foreign terrorist attack, although the investigation continues..."

I phoned it in to Kate. My head had started to hurt, my stomach rumbled. More than anything, I wanted to get home and stick a frozen burrito in the oven. I wanted to stare up at those worms on the ceiling and guzzle about 14 cold beers...

I walked along, passing a woman selling used purses. She had them laid out on an old blanket on the sidewalk – shiny orange and blue and black and olive-green purses, striped purses, plastic and suede and imitation leather. I'd seen her out there before. I never understood where she had got all the purses. She cackled and grimaced at me, smoking a small wet cigar.

"Hey," she croaked, "hey, Mr. Handsome, whyn't ya buy somethin' for yer girlfriend?"

"Maybe later," I said.

"Cheap azz son of a bitch!"

"Yes, ma'am."

"OH, BULLSHIT!"

A tan, tired-looking old guy came up in a tweed coat and stained beige pants. A strong smell of sweat and turpentine hung around him.

"It's the *Street Scene*, mister," he said in a gentle, tender voice. He looked at me hopefully. "Just a buck. Whatcha say, mister?"

He was holding out a stack of the allegedly homeless-produced newspaper. There was a double-banner headline: HOMELESS QUEER YOUTH SHELTER NEEDS YOUR HELP.

"Oh, sure," I said.

I pulled out a five dollar bill and handed it to him.

The guy bent forward and rattled out a cough. I caught a glimpse of dried blood and a little hole up behind his ear. Some of it was matted over with hair. A trail of dark gooey stuff was visible, running from the hole down to his jaw. An attempt had been made to smear some of it away.

He gave me the paper. I started to turn away, but he tapped my shoulder.

"Spare a smoke, mister," he said, "for an old man?"

I reached and pulled two. "Sure..."

"Thanks a lot, mister!"

"Oh, don't mention it..."

BRAIN DRAIN: Cops Claim Man Not Used For Target Practice!

★ 14 ★

"That's where his brains piece was."

The guy was pointing across the police tape, at a creamy pink-orange smudge four or five inches long. Cops had thrown down a tarp to cover most of the blood, but the smudge remained.

"Looked like chewed-up hot dogs comin' out from the top of his head, you know? This one part of it, like, jumped out, like, two feet. His eye was filled with all this blood. This part of his stomach was flopped out, you know, to the side? The blood shoot up in this, like, *spray*, you know? And you could see this one part of his inside stomach, you know what I mean, pink, was all tore up?"

"Sir, again, how many times did they shoot?"

"Like I say, I don't know, a bunch. Maybe –"

Seven or eight of us clowns were mobbing him. O'Mulligan and the other photo hogs snapped shots as cop techs dusted the vehicle, a Monte Carlo with gold windshield spangles and red and white antenna streamers. More clowns were on the way, I could feel them coming – slamming doors, lugging cameras, clicking heels, twitching noses, flashing badges. At least three helicopters whapped above. Karen Ryan from the *Star-Chron* shuffled up next to me.

"– Thirty? Forty?" The guy shrugged. "The cops yelled, 'HALT, FUCKER! HALT!' Like that. Then they just went, BA-BOOM-BOOM-BOOM-BOOM! BA-OOM-BOOM-BOOM-BOOM-BOOM-BOOM-BOOM-BOOM-BOOM! Like was in Vietnam, was the first thing I thought of."

"He have a gun? A knife?"

"Nothin'… I'm just sayin'. Nothin' that I saw."

"What'd he do?"

"He was standing there. He, like, had, one hand up in the air, like this, and his other arm was, like, reaching into the car... Then they just fired up on him."

"You were in Vietnam?"

"Uh-huh. Maintenance personnel for the United States of America Army. Linens washer, specifically."

"What happened to the brains?"

"One of them ambulance guys scooped it up."

"Scooped up *what*?" Karen Ryan whispered.

"Nothing," I said.

The clown gang rushed back over to the cop truck. The loogie crowd swelled, old guys, groups of teenage girls and buck-toothed boys. Some looked sucker-punched, others had come to camera-hog and bozo with the clowns. My head swiveled, I caught signs through the blinking coplight glare: AAA PAWN SHOP, CASH CHECKS HERE, Reggie W. McKinley Memorial Blood Bank, Cliffie's Auto Fix-It, WinZone Off-Track Palace. A pair of pants fluttered from a fire escape. Helicopters cracked overhead.

"Sir, the witness over there says he was shot forty or fifty times... Says he was unarmed."

"I have no information," said the cop.

"What's the statement, then?"

"In due time, media representative."

"I mean, *come on!*" said Bretton Barber, the baldheaded, bow-tied reporter for Channel 7 ("Your News Solution"). He shook his microphone semi-threateningly. "Don't you guys have *anything*? I'm going on the air in eight and a half minutes!"

About a minute later, Deputy Assistant Chief Harley Hempher exited the Crisis Team van and walked up to the throng. Clowns pushed forward and jostled. Clown noses quivered, clown mouths hung wide. Clown cameras took it live.

"I can confirm the following information," Hempher began, reading off a sheet. "A black male adult was fatally injured. There was a multiple discharge of Police Department weapons. The deceased individual has not yet been positively identified. Initial interviews with the officers involved indicate they believed the suspect was in possession of a weapon. A comprehensive ongoing investigation was undertaken immediately following the incident. The officers involved have been suspended with full pay, in accordance with Police

Department policy. The officers involved were searching for a suspect believed responsible for 16 rapes over a 15-month period. A local resident provided information to Police Department personnel indicating that the rape investigation suspect may have been located in this area. Further information will be made public as the Police Department warrants…"

"Did he have a weapon, chief? Was he armed?"

"Deputy Chief Hempher, sir, was he the rape-o?"

"Further information will be made public as the Police Department warrants. The investigation is continuing."

"Sir, was the victim a gang member?"

"The investigation is continuing."

Hempher walked off. Clowns jawed on phones, clowns went live to the studio with stand-ups. Loogies jostled for position on clown camera fringes. I called Kate.

>MAN KILLED IN BAY CITY POLICE SHOOTING
>
>BAY CITY (CNS) – Bay City police said officers fired multiple shots and killed a man Friday in the Six Points neighborhood.
>
>Deputy Asst. Chief Harley Hempher said the two officers involved, who were not immediately identified, had been suspended with full pay, in accordance with Police Department policy.
>
>Hempher declined to say if the victim, who has not yet been identified, had been armed.
>
>Hempher said the shooting occurred as the officers were searching in the area around 96th Ave. and Staley Lane for a suspect believed responsible for 25 rapes over a 15-month period. He declined to say if the victim was a suspect in the rape case.
>
>Hempher pledged a full Police Department investigation of the incident.
>
>Michael Kittredge, 52, who said he witnessed the shooting, told reporters that officers opened fire as the victim was reaching into his car, a tan Monte Carlo. Kittredge said officers had ordered the victim not to move.
>
>Kittredge described officers firing at least 30 rounds.

The TV camera performed a slow pan across the Mnung ranch stage set, which had been hastily constructed on vacant scrubland in Lucknow, Mississippi, late in the president's failed campaign for election. Mnung, wearing a white cowboy hat, red bandanna and gold star badge, ran across the carefully tended windswept prairie plain, the Saudi ambassador, Prince Ibn-Fuad Bin Ibn Aziz-Abdullah, hanging on his back. The film showed the Israeli Foreign Minister, Omri-Ben Amos Ben-Menasche, who had been hiding behind a large boulder, rising up and tossing a flurry of water balloons.

The Saudi ambassador, surprised by the bombardment, lost his grip on the president's back and fell to the dusty hardtack, his beard and shoulder soaked. He looked around fearfully, then scrambled up, pawing at his mud-spattered robe. The presidential communications aide Ralph Barbigny sprinted after Mnung's hat, which had been knocked off in the commotion and rolled now across the tawny chickweed.

Mnung stopped and grinned, breathing heavily in the midday sun. He removed his bandanna and wiped where he had been lightly sprayed. The Israeli foreign minister walked up, smiling bashfully. The president gave him a soft knock on the shoulder, then laughed and shook his hand. Mnung waved the Saudi ambassador over. Prince Ibn-Fuad limped forward, his robes dragging a clump of brush. Mnung took a few seconds to squeeze out the ambassador's beard, then grinned and put his arms over the shoulders of the two senior officials.

Four high school cheerleaders appeared, taking positions on each side of the president and his guests. Each cheerleader had a different word printed on the front of sandwich boards hanging from their necks:

SECURITY   PEACE   RESOLVE   ALLIES

CLOWN: *Good afternoon, ladies and gentlemen of the media. I have been holding talks here at the ranch today with our good friends from the Middle East, Israel and Saudi Arabia. These are two strong allies in the war on terrorism... My Saudi and Israeli friends won't themselves talk to each other, of course, because of their religious handicaps, though both of these religions – Jewish and Islamic – are of course fine religions of peace, as is our own fine religion of peace... These two Middle Eastern gentlemen will, however, take time to talk to me, the war president commander-in-chief of the U.S.A., when I ask them to – that's because* we're America. We're the ones who buy the gas, America, we fork over the big guns and the big bucks. We're the ones who keep Israel's ass out of the fryer, America is – and of course, we always like to help out our friends and allies of freedom... O.K., I'll take a few questions, as long as you're nice to me. (CLOWN LAUGHTER) Go ahead, Minnie...

CLOWN: How's the war going, Mr. President?

CLOWN: It's going well, I think. We're engaging the enemy on his turf. We're eatin' 'em out and spittin' 'em up... With us or without us, fighting the battle of freedom... Our soliders are making the sacrifices needed to protect freedom, for those who love freedom. They're being attacked by the terrorist enemy, so America won't be. They're protecting the peace. They're looking for the weapons... Yeah, Woodward?

CLOWN: As the war progresses, Mr. President, how has your faith been guiding you?

CLOWN: It guides me, no doubt about that. We were all created by the one single ever-present Creator, as even my Israeli and Saudi friends would agree, God bless them... Our God that we worship over here in America says we are all sinners, and the truth will set us free...

CLOWN: Could you be more specific?

CLOWN: Well... I mean, well, it was God above, after all, that told me to launch the invasions, to set those foreign people free... I bowed down humbly and prayed to the Lord, and the Lord answered and said, 'Bomb and set those people free, in order for the freedom.' And so I did – have done that, doing that, God's will... We're America, let's not forget that – God-fearing nation, God-loving nation, nation of peace. Everyone's free to worship their single deity who is the source of all life. Without God's grace... you know the rest. Freedom and free markets. Freedom of the unborn, freedom from terror, cut the taxes... Go ahead, Curly.

CLOWN: Sir, how long must the killing go on? What can we tell the ordinary American people?

The cheerleaders turned around, their sandwich board signs now reading:

VICTORY   PROSPERITY   TERRORISM   JOBS

MNUNG: Well, I mean... We don't want to kill anybody, Curly. America don't. (CLOWN LAUGHTER). Never have. Never will. That's the last thing we want to do. It's them that wants to do the killing – the terrorists and the freedom-haters... So in answer to your question, we will wage the wars as long as necessary to maintain the freedoms and to protect the peace. That's the official policy: Kill until the peace is achieved, along with our diplomatic and humanitarian angle... Yeah, over here – go ahead, Lois...

CLOWN: Sir, the soldiers...

CLOWN: Yes, well, you know my position – God bless the troops. And God bless America. This is freedom's army you're talking about, let me remind you. And the good news is – many of the troops is being fitted with new limbs and body parts as we speak. We've been producing thousands of new limbs for them – working overtime on it, 24/7. I have asked my staff to make sure of that. Finest artificial limb technology in the world here in America... New arms and legs, hands, ears and eyeballs – why, just the other day, the doctor told me about how they put a new jawbone in some young fella who took a bullet in the head for freedom. Amazing things they can do in hospitals these days with spinal and brain injuries... So yes, the American people can rest assured that their troops are having many surgeries, and successful surgeries at that. Fine young men and women of the armed forces... O.K., over there, you, Macaca...

CLOWN: There has been some concern expressed, sir, about the prisoner camps. We've taken hundreds of prisoners, yet no charges have been filed...

CLOWN: Now, now, you listen to me, Mac. Everyone is being treated with the respect and dignity they deserve. There's no testing going on, no experimenting, nothing like that. Certainly no torture (CLOWN LAUGHTER)... The White House staff – which is a very fine staff, by the way – informs me that these terrorists are being treated, well... well, they're being treated better than they'd be treated in their own terrorist countries, I can tell you that. They are getting three square meals per day. They are getting top-quality dental care. (CLOWN LAUGHTER). Message: This country does not believe in torture... We do, however, believe in protecting ourselves. Repeat, message: We don't believe in torture. Protection – what they call in the office 'harsh interrogation' – that's for sure, for darn sure... but no, no torture. Never have, never will. This is America. And when the president does it, whatever it is, that means it's not illegal. So no one's going to indict me, I can assure you. We indict people for war crimes – America does, we do – and not the other way around. (CLOWN LAUGHTER) Yeah, Slim?

CLOWN: Sir, the Sunni and the Shiites...

CLOWN: What's that? One more time... Who? Can't hear you so well. (CLOWN LAUGHTER)

CLOWN: *The Sunnis and Shiites, you know, I mean, they are, uh, they...*

CLOWN: *Look, Slim... I mean – who? Look, it's awfully late in the afternoon for something like that.* (CLOWN LAUGHTER) *What I do know is, what my advisers have assured me, is that they're all Muslims over there – a people of peace.* (LAUGHTER) *Any questions for the Mr. Foreign Minister, the Mr. Ambassador? Our Middle Eastern friends?*

The Saudi ambassador and the Israeli foreign minister shook their fists at each other. They ran off in opposite directions. (CLOWN LAUGHTER)

CLOWN (SHRUGGING): *Well... I guess that's all, then. O.K., I'll do a few autographs now...*

CLOWNS: *Mr. President, here, here! Please, me! Mr. President!*

(CLOWNS RUSH FORWARD, HOLDING PIECES OF PAPER IN OUTSTRETCHED ARMS...)

CLOWN: *And that was U.S. President Wolfgang G. Mnung, America's commander-in-chief, giving an update from the Western White House on the progress in the War On Terror and the Fight For Freedom... Coming up later in the program: Can oral sex give you cancer? An in-depth report on a surprising new study... Stand by, Mr. and Mrs. America, the terror alert level is blinking orange and you're watching NNN, the News Now Network – your news peak on the media mountain...*

LET GOD SORT HIM OUT:
Christ Commits Suicide!

★ 15 ★

Jerry was lighting candles at the kitchen table. He had them spread across the table, 15 or 16 candles.

"What the hell?"

"CHRIST SUNBEAM BLEW HIS HEAD OFF!"

"The fuck he did."

"It's *true!* It's on the news."

I guessed it probably was true. I'd seen the TV flash from the corner of my eye, just as I was leaving the office: ROCK STAR CHRIST SUNBEAM FOUND DEAD. Helicopter shots of his mansion, dozens of cop cars in the driveway. The footage spliced with the famous crucifix-of-toilet-seats video for "lovesexpainconfusionsuffering," one of Sunbeam's 16 official Number One hits.

"Fuck, Jerry. I'm sorry, man."

"HE BLEW HIS FUCKIN' HEAD OFF!"

I put down my satchel. I sat in the chair.

"That's it, we're screwed," I said. "Christ'll be up there with Shab London and Himi Jankowski now... Jam Jonestowne and Syd Coma... Another legend of our times."

Jerry sobbed and shoved against the table, making the candlelight wobble.

"How could he do it, man? He was the greatest... He had everything."

"Of course he would do it," I said. "It was his whole thing – Christ Sunbeam, out in a blaze of glory. The final fuck you. He didn't need this place any more. He never needed it."

Jerry propped up a picture of Sunbeam on the table, carefully placing candles around it. It was the new issue of *Music Monkey* magazine: CHRIST SUNBEAM IS GOD. Sunbeam was standing in a gas station parking lot, pink guitar over a shoulder, leaning against a rust-pocked sign: FREE AIR. Oversize glittering blue sunglasses, classic half-sneer/smile, a long yellow ribbon tied in the famous greasy mane. Words on his torn T-shirt said: BE THE CHANGE YOU WANT TO SEE.

Jerry looked over at me, his eyes tearing over.

"You think it's real? You think he faked it? Think there's a chance he'll come back?"

"I doubt it... He'll never get bigger than he is now. They'd never forgive him."

The latest mega-smash album, *Entertainus,* was spinning on Jerry's stereo. Sunbeam moaned away in his instantly recognizable sandpaper whine, the music like a thunderstorm mixed with a freight train mixed with a weed-whacker. Hard then soft, fast then slow, mumble-mumble, shrieks and whispers. The impenetrable sludge, the jungle-drum, the jackhammer machine buzz, the pure-luck, too-good-to-be-true sing-along harmonies. Sunbeam's guitar screamed like a siren at the top of Mount Everest before suddenly descending to rough and acoustic, like riverbank reeds rustling in the breeze.

Lick it, I'm not gonna smack, Christ rattle-rasped. *Walking on a sea of incest... see insects... don't you believe me, baby?*

I believe you, Christ baby, I thought. They called you a sell-out and a fake, but I always believed. They kept setting you up to take the fall, but you didn't do half bad trying to save the world. Now the clowns'll make it something different than it was. They'll lie and say they always loved you.

"Let's drink to Christ," Jerry said. "Let's drink this whole bottle right now."

"O.K., man..."

Jerry unpeeled a fifth of Jim Beam Blue. It was going to be a long night, and I was looking forward to it: Christ Harold Sunbeam, dead at the age of 27.

"To Christ Sunbeam," Jerry said. "R.I.P., good friend."

I gulped the whisky down. It hit like a sledgehammer, the magic juice rippling down my spine.

People turn to waste... disappear like minty-fresh toothpaste... if you need a new face... let's destroy this place...

Sunbeam sang like he was walking through a burning building. His noise was the sound of the plunge down the endless edifice. Now he was gone, apparently.

It was, in a way, hard to believe, but now that it had happened, it was not such a surprise. Just a different interpretation of everything. Christ had always kept the option in front, it had always been part of his "package." Yet everyone had lived in denial. Christ had been the greatest show on earth. Yet now that the end was here, the taste was bitter, combined with something like awe that he had actually done it.

It was all right. Everything would be O.K. with more whisky. With enough, I would probably even enjoy it.

"Gimme another," I told Jerry.

Huffy huff huff, I'm contagious... big wheel's turning turning, big rooster's burning burning... huffy huff huff, I'm contagious...

Jerry had placed among the candles the tickets Candace had purchased – fifth row, $200 each. Christ Sunbeam and the Vital Friends had been due at Kerr-McGee/Fajita Palace Stadium in three weeks – the LET YOUR GOD SORT THEM OUT World Tour. Special Guests: Yarl, the Buckyballs and Texas Meat Purveyors.

"I'm never gonna sell these back," Jerry said. "I don't care what Candace says. Probably be worth thousands in five years..."

"Could be, Jerry..."

I downed another whisky. Sunbeam's life and times passed before me in a rush, a blur, a montage – the drug-hazed teen years, the drug-fueled early career, the drug-soaked superstar phase...

Sunbeam had broken on to the scene with his early "punk" bands, the Cummy Yunts and the Jellyroll Abortions, which had yielded the underground classic albums *Strangulate the Dessicated* and *Far Beyond Broken* on the then-famously unknown Crapout Records label. Then had come the official formation of the Vital Friends, the legendary *Weather Wax* album, followed by the notorious tour with Seven Inch Heels and the Stern Gang.

The Vital Friends had hit the cover of *Billboard* to mark their 500,000th sale, and the juggernaut had inexorably led to the controversial $10.8 million Shanft-Micro signing, the poorly-received "Me Love You Short Time"/ "Kill Yer Sons" double single, and finally the consecutive groundbreaking albums *My Junky is a Strumpet* and *THANATOXIS: The Oxygen Thieves* (which had featured the brooding masterpiece "Blood Honey," as well as the acoustic radio hit "Friend Named Lisa"). Specialist technicians had legendarily taken two days to mic the drums for the next album, *Overthrow Vol. 66*, which, helped along by cover stories in *Time*, *Spin* and *The New York Times Magazine*, had stayed Number One for 26 weeks and yielded the consecutive chart-topping smashes "Hairer," "Love in Vein," "What The Hell (Am I Trying To Say)," "Homopolitan," and the driving, lyricless anthem "Feudal Futility."

Then, of course, after most of the hip and hardcore had already written him off as a sell-out and has-been, had come the shattering event, the song that had led to a paradigm shift in pop culture – the *We Came to Expel the Darkness* album and the "WASTE ME" single (hailed by *Shamrock Express* as the "single most important song since 'Crocodile Rock'"). As *Music Monkey* noted at the time, "These are strange sounds, singularly mind-blowing in their searing freshness and brutally intense rock and roll audacity, yet somehow familiar, as if they had existed for all time, but had no architect to give them form – until now. With 'WASTE ME,' Christ Sunbeam has forever modified rock's DNA... and where it will evolve next is anybody's guess."

Sunbeam's behavior, from then on, had in due course become increasingly "erratic" – the run of "bizarre" incidents that had started to alienate even the "original intentists" and "die-hards" but had, in fact, only further inflated sales and corporate cash flow: The rumored prune juice diet... The seemingly endless "maybe I'm gay" public handwringing... The seemingly never-ending feud in the press with Jeremy from Weasel Spit... The apparent disappearance of Christ's allegedly homeless father, Randy, a former F-16 pilot who had flown missions in the first Gulf War...

The *U.S. News & World Report* investigation which revealed that despite Sunbeam's wealth, his mother Nikita was living alone in squalor with 109 cats... The subsequent national TV "repent" interview with Ed Bradley... The widely-panned book of original poetry, *The Principles of Life are Paramount*... The bearded phase, which was followed quickly by the shaved head era (painted red for the *Saturday Night Live* appearance)... The bizarre appearance in pancake makeup and purple priest robes for the National Americans Against Illegal Drugs Action Council TV special... The long-rumored *Sasquatch Plutarch* double concept-album that had never surfaced...

Through it all, Sunbeam somehow kept producing the hits: "Loneliness (Is A Big Part Of Humanity)," "Ego Is A Too Much Thing," "(Life Was Better) With Hutchence," "Naked Movie Star," and of course "Faceless Wind," which had been simultaneously Number One in 47 countries...

After two years of relentless media sunburn, Sunbeam had finally gained his entrance into the celebrity-reality world – a world where the more weak and vulnerable and absurd he seemed, the more invincible he actually became: Showing up in a wheelchair for the Tokyo release party for the *Grey Bloo Belgian Goo* EP*... Claiming he wasn't a junkie, but just had "knee pains" that the doctors were unable to treat... The famous "Today I quit rock and roll" declaration following the stampede that killed nine fans at the Dusseldorf festival... The sudden firing of band members Pea and Kermit, followed by the live reunion on *60 Minutes* one week later... The surprise quasi-legal Mexican death-wedding to feminist-bondage cabaret superstar Pammie Bungen, photographed nearly always with her trademark red ball-gagger... His controversial appearance in a loincloth and the "crucifixion" of his guitar during the Super Bowl Halftime Show*... His furious condemnation as "wastes of ham and eggs" of the Gainesville high school students who claimed the Vital Friends song "Human Grocery Store" contained "secret messages" telling them to execute 14 students and three teachers during a volleyball game rampage...

"Right now I'm probably bigger than Mohammed," Sunbeam had told MSNBC on the eve of the new tour. "I'm a nobody... I'm just a guy who sings songs. People get all confused about what it means." The clowns had run wild in a crazy shit-fit, there had been weeks of coverage and expert commentary. CHRIST SEZ: I'M BIGGER THAN MOHAMMED. Pure, unfiltered genius.

"He was the greatest rock star," Jerry said. "He was more punk rock... He was more pop."

"Could be, Jerry..."

I snatched at the copy of *Music Monkey*.

---

* Which, in yet another brilliantly savvy and controversial publicity stunt, had been recorded at the Sharon Tate house in Los Angeles. For more on Tate, see Manson, Charles, murders of. – ED.

* Which led to three separate FCC investigations and fines of more than $30 millon. – ED.

'EARTH IS PRETTIER THAN HEAVEN'
Christ Sunbeam Says He's Not a Junkie
By Bill Hearns Puing

Christ Sunbeam is sitting in the living room of his Hollywood Hills home, his five-week-old daughter Krishna on his lap. The space is littered with Sunbeam's latest batch of paintings. The works are bruised, child-like masterpieces, some completed, most only half-done, executed with oil and acrylic upon old game boards bought by his assistant at the Salvation Army. Sunbeam's wife, the ex-porn star Pammie Bungen, is sitting sullenly in the kitchen in her pajamas, watching a DVD of *Sanford & Son* on a television as a Schnittke concerto performs convolutions in the background. Bungen has ignored me since I entered the residence, concentrating instead on the antics of Red Foxx and pouring honey-nut Cheerios into a jar of peanut butter, which she mixes and eats with a spoon. Despite her evident hostility, she looks the polar opposite of the hellion dominatrix who allegedly pelted Sunbeam with a flashlight, tonic bottle and microphone stand during a spat in Kuala Lumpur last April.

The occasion is Sunbeam's first official interview in almost a year, coinciding with the release of the Vital Friends new album, *Entertainus*, and the upcoming Let Your God Sort Them Out World Tour. As a listen to the new album confirms, Sunbeam remains the true Original New Master Genius, the one authentic anti-anti-anti-establishment corporate rock star with a lock-grip on artistic credibility and rock-hero posturing.

And the word from his handlers is that Christ Sunbeam has finally gone drug-free at last. This could be hard for many to digest, and predictably, some naysayers have already accused Sunbeam of yet another publicity stunt that seems certain to boost confirmed unit-sales in an era defined by illegal Internet downloads and bootleg trading.

Sunbeam holds Krishna throughout our interview, sometimes setting her down to hand-roll a cigarette. He lights up, carefully making sure to blow the smoke away from the infant. The artist looks tan, rested and ecstatic, a far cry from rumors of AIDS infections or overdoses in grungy Moroccan hotel rooms. He is lively and relaxed throughout our talk, periodically munching from a bag of Kennel-Q Cool Ranch Dog Biscuits or sipping from a milky potion he declines to identify.

MM: *Christ, your people are telling everyone you're off the drugs. Is it true this time?*

CS: It's my life, but if people are curious – I guess you could say my attitude has changed. I don't want my daughter to be hassled by kids at school. I don't want people telling her that her parents were junkies. I know some will doubt me, but I don't want to have anything to do with inciting drug use. People who promote drug use are assholes. I chose to do drugs, and I don't regret a single bong hit, line, nod or trip. But it's a total waste of time. I don't want to tell anyone what to do, because I've always hated being talked down to. But you can get a lot higher a zillion other ways.

MM: *What's it like having a child?*

CS: There's nothing better than having a baby. Period. A child is God's greatest gift. Period. Producing babies, and making the world a better place for them – that's what life's really about. I fully respect and admire homosexuality and people who hate children, who hate family. It's understandable, in many ways, and we need to listen to what they have to say. But holding my baby – to me, it's the best drug in the world.

MM: Newsweek *and some of the major critic-blogs recently accused you of "repressive rockism." Mainly, they say you're responsible for the glut of all these so-called anti-establishment bands who nevertheless make themselves available for corporate advertising campaigns. Any response?*

CS: Guilty as charged by the Central Committee.

MM: *Any thoughts on the political situation?*

CS: Die for your government – why not? A shadow has fallen across our land. Satire has become the reality. The hate cycle continues to mutate. What you thought was freedom was only greed. It seems that while we were sleeping, they started a worldwide religious war. Hell on earth for heaven in the afterlife... That being said, it must be admitted – the world has always been ending. America has always been dying. Rock has always been dead.

MM: *Care to expand?*

CS: Not really... Maybe it helps to understand that all we see are refractions, distortions and manufactured illusions that combine to keep us in a waking sleep. They simply ask that we keep quiet and keep shuffling the credit cards. Cruelty, combined with the willful flight from truth – that's the form of evil that dominates our world. Look around you, man. The enemies of beauty are everywhere. If we have a duty in this world, it's to identify and oppose them.

 MM: *Tell me about the recording process for* Entertainus. *There's a lot of rumors swirling out there.*

 CS: Well, Pammy had just gotten pregnant and we had been like, 10 days in a gondola over Macchu Pichu…

I set the magazine down, poured another whisky. Jerry got up and started to scrape worms from the ceiling. The music chugged along – scratching guitars, drumsticks against a cardboard box. A strangled voice gasping.

BLOCKBUSTER: Clown Clutches, Touches Rich Babe!

★ 16 ★

We rustled up some bucks and went down to the corner for three cases of beer and four jugs of four-dollar wine, red and white flavors. Jerry's pal Noah, who was supposed to be the bass player in Jerry's new band,* was the first to arrive. Noah was packing a few 'shrooms and we all had a sprinkle.

I didn't know more than a few of the rest. Everyone sat around in the candlelight, smoking and drinking. Or we stood around in the kitchen with the light on.

Candace raced around the room with a giant bottle of tequila, handing out lime chunks and pouring salt, shrieking.

Heather appeared robust and well-tanned, a diamond stud in her nose, an orange and blue scarf tied around her head, gypsy-style. She wore a long skirt that seemed to suggest an Indian motif. She saw me, stuck her tongue out, flipped me twin middle fingers.

"Hey, Heather..."

Curtis the photographer trailed after her, a thick stench of patchouli heralding his arrival. Curtis appeared to be around 45, maybe 50, tall and skinny, wearing a beret and sunglasses that had one lens blue, the other red. He sported a hawk nose, many deep lines on his face, rings and studs on both ears. He had on black leather pants, cowboy boots, a white T-shirt with rainbow glitters spelling out DAY BY DAY.

Curtis was allegedly a semi-famous photographer, had scored pictures from the Bosnia, Chechnya and Kosovo wars in *Life* magazine, according to Jerry. But lately he had retired from conflict photography

---

* Noah's previous bands included the Dingoes, Grapnel and Strawberry Grenade. – ED.

and was trying his hand at "fashion." He had allegedly done a series of "test snaps" of Heather. After rejecting her as "not ready for Paris," he had apparently asked her out.

"Love your place," Curtis gushed, looking around and flashing jagged yellow teeth.

I noticed a little grey metal coffin hanging from a chain around his neck.

"Thanks," I said, "and that's a super groovy coffin."

Curtis grinned. He took a little silver camera from a pouch on his waist and snapped a picture of me.

"All right, keep it up, fuzzball," he said. "Bullshit wins the marathon, yes indeed."

He made wavy motions with his arms, laughed again, followed after Heather. The patchouli stench lingered.

In the corner of the kitchen ceiling I saw worms. Jerry had knocked a bunch of them down earlier, but they were already back. Worms were squirming, twisting, rolling around…

At that point I saw Chrissy, the attorney. She was wearing light blue jeans, copper leather boots, bright yellow tank top, transparent bra strap showing. A wave of chestnut hair swept across her shoulders as she turned her head to look and laugh. Her forehead was high – dark thick eyebrows. Her lips were loose and relaxed and the color of raspberries, bubbling out over a firm, determined chin. She appeared to have five or six different Central American-style bracelets on her wrists.

She was standing, talking to a little group in the kitchen. I grabbed a beer, went up and stood there indifferently.

Chrissy was nicely tall, the top of her head well past my shoulder. She took a sip from a beer can, paused and suddenly hit me with blueberry-colored eyes. A brief electrical shock seemed to zap through my midsection. The eyes burned at me, clear and unblinking.

She flicked the eyes away, laughed at the nothing that somebody had said.

I caught patches of light freckles on her cheeks, a gently upturning nose. She had on a little too much dark eyeliner, which meant just the right amount. Circular gold earrings – they had always driven me wild. Around her neck was a puffy red heart on a silver chain. It looked plastic.

Chrissy was an attorney at a big-time law firm – I remembered Jerry having said that. Chrissy "annoyed" Candace, but Heather didn't mind her. Chrissy liked to party with Hugh and the gang and the rest of the party people...

I preened against the counter, throwing off couldn't-care-less vibes. I ran my fingers through my hair, throwing off vibes, as I tried to tune in on the conversation. They were discussing some nonsense.

My mouth seemed to fill with a greater amount of saliva than usual. I paused, trying to choose the key moment...

"I don't give a damn what you believe," I finally interrupted.

Chrissy looked at me and froze, her tongue poising itself amidst perfect white teeth. Marvelous pink gums.

"So look at the big two-fisted drinker," she said.

I raised my beer and styrofoam cup of wine. She nicked them both with her can.

"So *you're* Thor – the reporter guy who lives with Jerry?"

"Yeah, sort of..."

"*Sort of!* That's so hot! So you're that guy. Man, Candace has talked all about you..."

My mind was being scrambled, in ways I would never understand, but it was hard to care much right then. It was the last thing on my mind. I felt a hot rush, a trembling over the entire surface of my skin.

I felt my testicles rise, my buttocks involuntarily clenching...

I slugged from the beer, drained the wine. I lit another smoke, drained the beer.

"Chrissy," I said, "another beer for you? A wine? A shot?"

Jerry had foolishly left the half-full whisky bottle on the counter. Chrissy and I had a shot and two fresh beers from the fridge. I had another shot. She had one. I had another. I poured myself a white wine from a jug, and when I spilled, she laughed. We leaned against opposing counter corners in the kitchen.

"I actually looked you up on the internet," she said. "I was so curious! I hope you don't mind..."

"No, no – it's totally cool... What did you find?"

"Not much really. Just a bunch of articles with your name..."

My heartbeat slammed, the echo crashing in my ears. I downed drinks, lit smokes, ashed into half-empty cans. I looked deep into Chrissy's boysenberry eyes and spun crime and news-clown tales. She was aware of the crisis, she thought it was horrible, but wasn't up to date on the statistics and details I could wield. She had an interest, she led me on, I ran wild at the mouth with crime tales. The babies were being born blind because their mothers were hooked on dope...

Remember the guy who hacked his parents? Yeah, I was there... Goddamn freaks shot six at a laundromat. Some dope damn thing. Mowed them down at point-blank range. I went to the scene. The cops didn't know shit, they never did... This one prostitute got beaten with her own high heels. The psycho tied her up, slashed her, left her in the shower to die. She lived. I had talked to the front desk man at the hotel where it happened. He didn't know much, but he had talked to the psycho...

Chrissy seemed to find it engrossing. She found it curious and a thrill. Chrissy was ready to engage and spar...

Chrissy had style and poise. She didn't ruffle, she didn't self-deprecate. She rolled straight, she rolled head-on. She seemed *hungry*...

"I'm an Aries," she said, "and you are – ?"

As Chrissy spoke, a tall heavy guy in a beard came up and his put his arm over her shoulder. He smelled vaguely of limburger cheese, was wearing baggy brown shorts and hiking boots with green wool socks.

The gorilla stood there. He stared at me like I was some bug.

I looked at Chrissy and cocked my head. "So, well... what's up with the gorilla?"

She giggled. "Oh, I'm sorry. This is Justin. Justin, Thor..."

I was having to shake the gorilla's hand when a girl screamed.

"IT'S A WORM! It fell on my hand!" She looked up. "THEY'RE ON THE CEILING!"

People moved, people ran. Chrissy disappeared somewhere with Justin.

Jerry rushed in. "It's O.K., it's O.K.," he said, holding up his hands. He climbed on to the counter and started shooting poison spray.

"That is truly sick," somebody said.

"It's disgusting..."

Jerry strained with the poison can, blasting worms which fell to the counter.

I went out to the main room. A bunch of them were crowded around the TV. Curtis was on a knee, taking snaps of Heather, who had passed out on the futon.

On the TV, tens of thousands of fans had gathered outside Christ Sunbeam's mansion. Pammie Bungen was in high heels, fishnet leggings and a negligee on the terrace, ball-gagger loose around her neck, throwing Sunbeam's T-shirts, paintings and shoes into the crowd.

"FUCK YOU, CHRIST!" she screamed into a microphone. "WHY DID YOU DO THIS? FUCK YOU, MAN!"

The clown camera zoomed in on her silicone-pumped lips, runny mascara, tits poking out of the negligee.

"C'MON, EVERYBODY, LET'S TELL HIM: FUCK YOU, CHRIST! FUCK YOU, MAN!"

"FUCK YOU, CHRIST," the TV crowd chanted. "FUCK YOU, MAN... FUCK YOU, MAN... FUCK YOU, MAN..."

I went back into the kitchen, mixed myself a Bacardi and coke. Where was Chrissy? I walked back out, weaving through the crowd.

Then I saw them, Justin standing over Chrissy in the corner by the lamp. I walked in that direction, hoping for a Chrissy glance.

"Oh, *come on*, babe..." I heard Chrissy say.

She didn't seem to see me.

Things were starting to get out of control. A bunch of others had also come in, "friends" of somebody. Or maybe not friends, maybe just a couple of Mexican teenagers from down the block. Guys started somersaulting and flipping around, yelling. Jerry staggered after them, shouting.

I saw one of the guys go into the kitchen and come out with the last cardboard case of beer. He dished off five or six cans to his buddies, then threw the case into the middle of the room. A guy dropped his can, then picked it up and opened it, spraying foam all over.

That was no good at all. I bolted over and grabbed the case, sprinting it into the kitchen, where I hid about eight cans on the top shelf of the closet, under some rags and old newspapers. I brought the case back out to the living room and opened a new one. Three or four cans were left.

I stood and had a long pull. Just then, there was a small popping sound and the place went dark. The power had apparently gone out. There were flashes of multiple lighters, laughter, a few moans. I went into the kitchen and grabbed a new can from the stash.

As I was coming out, I bumped into Chrissy in the doorway.

"Oh, there you are," she said. "I was wondering where you went..."

"Oh, wow..."

She waved a thick cigarette in front of my face. "I just bought this. C'mon, let's have it..."

"Yeah, great..."

We went down the hall and sat in the dark on the little bench by the front door. I took out my lighter and lit the stogie in her mouth, her head outlined by the greenish-white light coming in from the window pane. She handed the thing to me.

Chrissy giggled and grabbed on to my arm. I took in about half a hit, held it in my mouth like I was still pulling, then let go. I went dizzy, felt a warm ooze in the space below my heart. A portion of my spine, around the middle, seemed to briefly collapse.

I handed the cigarette back to Chrissy. As she took her drag, I leaned over and kissed her cheek. She was warm and smelled like watermelon.

I put my arm around her waist. We traded a few more drags, sighing gently and resting. She put her hand on my thigh.

"Let's go somewhere," I said.

"O.K..."

We went into the bathroom and locked the door.

"We're safe in here," I whispered. "They won't get us."

Chrissy giggled. We took hits from the stogie, after which I put my arms around and held her, squeezed her. She giggled and puffed a few times more, than leaned over and tossed the smoke into the toilet bowl, *pfffttt!*

I sucked along her neck, moved up to her cheeks, finally back to her mouth. She tasted like watermelon, with a slight after-kick of booze and stogie.

My brain was being scrambled, doing scrambling things. I pushed her back against the sink and began massaging her between the legs, my hand grabbing and pulling at the jean fabric.

I groaned. Chrissy made little squeaking noises. She yanked loose the buttons on my fly, the bracelets on her wrist clinking.

There was a knock on the door.

"Chrissy?" came a voice. "Are you there, Chrissy?"

It sounded like the gorilla. More knocking on the door.

"Christina? Are you in here?"

"Darn!" I whispered. "It's the gorilla."

Chrissy held her hand over my mouth.

"Yeah, Justin, babe... Hold on a minute, hon..."

Chrissy gestured to me. Quietly as I could, I climbed into the tub and hid behind the shower curtain.

Chrissy flushed the toilet, unlocked the door and opened it. Clanging, thumping and screaming could be heard down the hall.

"Is everything O.K?" the gorilla grunted. "I've been looking for you all over... The lights went out, I couldn't find you. Are you O.K.? Is everything all right?"

"Shhh," said Chrissy. "It's so dark, I couldn't see..."

The door closed. I got out of the tub, re-locked the door... I was trembling, thoroughly scrambled, my heart bouncing around in its bag.

I felt myself hurtling to Earth. I couldn't take it. I wanted Chrissy. I wanted booze. I wanted both in my hands now. I was just too thirsty.

A car alarm started going off down the street. I unlocked the door and went down the hall. Dark clumps of them were clotting up the place everywhere. I bumped and bumped, but no Chrissy. I fetched a beer from the stash and wandered around.

"THIS IS A HORRIBLE PLACE!" I heard Candace screaming out in front. "I HATE THIS PLACE! I HATE IT!"

I poked my head out the front door. Rain smacked the against the concrete, coming down like long pencil leads in front of the headlights of Candace's Acura. A little crowd was gathered around the car. I saw Jerry sticking his head through the hole in the smashed side window.

There was a clank and the lights went back on. The Sunbeam song "Hat on the Bed" began to blare.

I wandered through the place, checking each room. No Chrissy.

I cracked another beer. Chrissy was nowhere.

Curtis sat next to Heather on the futon, sunglasses on, flicking a lighter under a piece of aluminum foil. Something brown burned on the sheet, Curtis inhaled. He saw me and nodded sleepily, pushed the foil toward me like a slice of pizza. I took it from him, lowered my head and inhaled.

Guys I didn't know were playing a game on Jerry's computer. They drove a silver car and smashed into a brick wall. They laughed. The car started again and crashed. They thought it was hilarious. The car started again and smashed into a brick wall.

OPERATION SCUMBAG: Cops, Clown Team Up for Drug War Combat!

★ 17 ★

I met up with the two cops at the Bun Boy Burrito stand, at the corner of Ramplegate and Sturgeon. It was Thursday, about 10:50 p.m. Wodgers and Banting were attached to the Street Narcotics Enforcement Unit (SNEU). The idea was to go around with them as they made their nightly drug busts. Sernath had personally assigned it, calling it a "big chance" for me. It had taken a couple weeks to set up through the police Public Relations Office, and I had been forced to wait three more weeks while they did a fresh background check. According to a waiver I signed, revealing any "Classified Police Information" I might learn during the excursion could result in my prosecution. I was supposed to write it up as a human interest feature, focusing on the "human side" of the War Against Drugs. My first full byline piece.

They were sitting outside, coffees and a half-eaten plate of nachos and refried beans on the orange plastic table. Bugs hit the overhead light, bounced off, hit again. I walked up and introduced myself.

"How you doing, guy?" said Wodgers, extending a hand. He looked me over with bloodshot eyes, blew smoke out his nose, spat on the concrete. I caught mustache wax and hair grease, smoke breath and coffee fumes. "Bring your vest?"

Lt. Riley Wodgers exuded semi-entertained White Male Cop, self-impressed with making the undercover detail and intent on keeping his sense of humor intact. He was wearing a dark polyester green suit and black tie, a substantial pot-belly resting leisurely atop his knees.

"Vest?"

Banting, taller and thinner, laughed. "Bullet-proof vest, guy. This ain't a visit to grandma."

Sgt. Andre Banting sported cherry walnut-scented aftershave, a clean buzz fade-cut. He had on a blue Hawaiian shirt with green flowers, black jeans, brown penny loafers. Banting exuded Responsible Black Man, working hard to keep it hip.

Wodgers laughed, dipped a chip in gooey cheese, applied jalapeño, snapped it in his mouth.

"No, I didn't bring anything..."

"It's all right," said Wodgers. He blew smoke, chewed nacho, coughed into his fist. "We'll look out for your behind."

"Let's get going, gentlemen," said Banting. "There's bad guys out there selling drugs to kids."

Banting crushed a nacho, mashed out his smoke, threw his Styrofoam coffee cup into the trash. We walked out to the parking lot. Wodgers clicked the doors of a tan Lexus Caprice.

"Listen, guy," said Wodgers, "we got to frisk you, just to make sure you don't got no listening devices or weapons. Not that we don't trust you. We respect members of the media, but we got to protect ourselves, understand? Trust – but squeeze every muthafucka's balls to see if he's wearing a wire. That's our motto." He looked over at Banting, who laughed.

"Sure," I said.

Wodgers patted me down.

"He's cleaner than my first girlfriend's behind."

"Sweet," said Banting, lighting a smoke. "Right on, Mr. Thor. You're riding with us. Get in. Let's go catch bad dudes."

I got in the back seat and we drove off in the direction of Six Points. Wodgers lighted a smoke, coughed and stomped the gas, hitting 60, 70. The streets got dimmer and dimmer as we drove in, bouncing over the potholes.

"It always seems so much darker out here," I said.

"It's 'cause the suckas shoot out the lights," said Banting. "They think we can't see 'em, but we can."

He dangled a pair of goggles.

"Night-vision?"

"Bet your behind," Wodgers said. "U.S. Army's finest."

We sped past chain-link fences and old industrial lots, liquor stores and warehouses, wood-shack neighborhoods. We blasted past too-dark parks and playgrounds, paper scraps whirling in our wake. Clumps of figures huddled on street corners, guys shuffled solo down empty boulevards. Lights blared yellowly in acres of decaying apartment blocks.

"Here's the deal, guy," said Wodgers. He looked over his shoulder at me as he drove, smoke spewing from his nostrils. "We got people and dogs on-location already. We got aircraft, what we call the 'Eyes in the Sky,' providing data streams in real-time. Sgt. Banting is in contact via the radio. People are sourcing us right now, so when something bing-bings, we move in, get it? We swoop, nail the perps, secure the evidence. What they call evidence is the A-number one primo. Gotta secure the evidence or the district attorney beefs."

"How many you got out there?"

"Can't tell you that," said Banting. "What we can tell you is, say, more than ten and less than fifty. You can write, say, about twenty... And call 'em operatives, O.K.? Some of these jamfs work with us, but they're not police. But you can call them 'police operatives.' That way no one will know for sure."

I scribbled in my notebook. Wodgers, one hand on the wheel, flipped the top off a white plastic bottle and inhaled a mouthful of pills.

Banting mumbled into a handset: "... that's a ten-four, oh-six-one niner... three-niner-oh-two on a double-dutch oh-twenty. Check, sixteen-five, pee-pee-gee on the oh-niner. That's a pee-pee-gee on the oh-niner. Do you copy? Double me..."

Wodgers drummed his fingers on the steering wheel as we sat at a red light. "Ah, numb-nuts," he said. "I got nacho juice on my pants. My wife's gonna think I got a blowjob."

"I'll vouch for you, boss," said Banting.

Wodgers laughed, whirred down the window and spat. He pressed down one nostril and sneezed, then did the other nostril. He whirred the window up. His lighter clicked and he fired up a smoke.

Shapes darted in front of the car, flashed briefly in the headlights, disappeared on the other side. Wodgers turned down an alley. Shapes darted, scrambling behind dumpsters and cardboard boxes.

"Hey lookee lookee there," said Banting. "Watcha think of that. It's our good friend Toothless Jenny... Pull over, Riles. Maybe Walter Cronkite here wants the exclusive interview."

"Well lookee there," said Wodgers.

"Hey there, Jenny-Jenny," said Banting, whirring down the window. "Spare a minute of your time, sweetheart?"

Banting jumped out and slammed the door. He grabbed Jenny by the arm, led her around the back of the car and opened the other passenger door. Jenny climbed in next to me, a stench of urine and methane coming in with her. Under the car light, I saw brown and yellow splotches, three or four open, runny sores. A creased blue ribbon had been knotted into the stiff, scraggled hair. I saw flashes of a pink lace top, black plastic sheeting, dirty white boots with soggy fluff balls on the toes. Jenny moaned. She hit me with cloudy black eyes, opened a swollen, cracked blue cave in greeting. A number of brown stumps were sticking up from places where her teeth should have been. Some kind of thick, milky fluid was dripping out her nose.

Wodgers coughed, lit a smoke. "Ever see something like this, guy? Buyer beware, eh?"

"Mr. Thor, meet Jenny, our favorite neighborhood crack whore," said Banting.

"Nice to meet you, Jenny," I said.

The swollen blue cave opened slowly. "Yeth, yeeth," Jenny seemed to say.

Banting grinned, blew smoke.

"How many dicks you suck tonight so far, Jenny? You high as the sky right now? You high as the space shuttle?"

"Yuth, yeeth…"

Wodgers tapped the gas, easing the car down the alley.

Banting rubbed a 20-dollar between his fingers.

"Where Ricardo at, Jenny? We lookin' for Ricardo…"

"Yeeth…"

We rocked forward suddenly as Wodgers stomped the brake.

"Jenny," Wodgers said sternly, looking at her in the rearview mirror, "you tell Ricardo we lookin' for him. O.K., girl?"

Jenny moaned. "Yeth, yuth-yeeth…"

Wodgers tapped the car forward. Banting pushed his face an inch or so from Jenny's, raising the 20 dollars over her head.

"We gonna rack you up 'less you tell Ricardo. You hear? Rack your bony butt up good. Now, I know you don't want that. You tell Ricardo, hear?"

"Yuth, yeeth…"

"It's every good American's Constitutional duty to rat on his friends and family to save they own ass," said Banting. "Ain't that right, Mr. Thor?"

"Yes," I said.

"You hear Mr. Thor, Jenny? Mr. Thor knows that of which he be talkin'. You tell Ricardo we lookin' for him tomorrow. Tomorrow, you hear?"

Sores on Jenny's face shined. Her tongue came out and licked the the fluid oozing from her nose.

"Yuth-yuth..."

Wodgers drove to the end of the alley and stopped. Banting pulled Jenny out of the car, gave her a shove down the sidewalk. He went around the front of the car and got back in.

"You do drugs, Thor?" said Wodgers. "Little pot on the weekend? Your girlfriend digs it, yeah?"

"Hell, no."

"That's the answer, little buddy." He coughed, rolled down the window and spat. "Goddamn, I hate that drug shit. That shit makes me sick."

Banting lit a smoke and mumbled. "That's a copy... We are seven-two-four on sixty-four Joe thirty-five... nineteen-Ralph-five-oh-niner. Ten-four six-oh-seventeen. We are ten-seven, outward bound. Double me. Ten-three-five-niner... Do you copy?"

✪

"Some things, you will not forget," Banting was saying.

We had retreated back to the Financial District and were smoking outside the Duckback Coffee Shop on Stanwyck.

"You still don't know how you feel, you just don't know... Mother's screaming outside, her hands are red. You come in. You see the first one... She's naked, her head is on the pillow next to her. You think, is that her *head*? She's about, say, four years. You see brown stuff all over. You realize it's blood. You go to the next room. Brown stuff all over. You see two more. Little boy, girl, laying there. You go up. Necks are cut almost all the way, but not cut off. The fuck couldn't even cut off their heads. He fucking gave up."

"Who did it?"

"Psycho scumbag did it... AKA filth of the earth."

"You caught him?"

"Murder dicks run him down about a week later. He was on trial for what was it, Riles – three years?"

Wodgers nodded. "Thing you got to understand, little buddy, the whole goddamn system favors the scumbag... And no, you can't quote me… They shoulda busted a cap on that fuck-butt when they caught him. End all our misery."

He put his hand on my shoulder. "Want to know how we solve the problem?"

He pointed his index finger, blew the tip.

"Shouldn't take more than three or four per day, at the beginning. Then, before you'd even know, it'd be all over. Crime-free streets like we got wet dreams of… And that's another non-quote for you."

We mashed out our smokes, went in to get the coffees.

"Shit," said Wodgers, dumping six sugars into his latte. "We should invade Mexico."

"Yeah?"

"Why the hell not? You ain't with them anti-war people, are ya?"

"Hell no," I said.

"God, I hate them crappy little shits. Everybody's got to drop everything and deal with it whenever they have one of their mealy-mouth protests. The real scumbags get away so we can drag some commie to jail… Where you live, little buddy?"

"Silvertown."

"Ain't that the shit," said Banting as we walked back out. "Damn, you a real man, jamf. You couldn't get me living in Silvertown if you gave me a million in salary every month. I got babies, man. I ain't crazy… I'll let you in on a secret, Mr. Thor. Wanna know how you get out of the ghetto? You get in the car and you drive out. Don't got a car? You get on the bus and go. You don't look back… Goddamn suckas act like they never heard such a thing."

Wodgers lit a smoke, spat, shrugged.

"Hell if I know a better way. They don't pay me enough. That's one part of the problem."

"Get the trunk, Riles," said Banting.

Wodgers popped it. Banting took out a Tampa Bay Lightning cap and put it on his head backward. He bent down briefly. When he came back up he had inserted a grille of gold over his teeth. He completed the look with a pair of sunglasses.

"Hey, homebwoy muh-fuh," he said, slugging me in the shoulder. He laughed and slapped me five.

"Is that real gold?"

He posed with his shoulders humped forward, his hands flung up.

"You know it, homebwoy. We got to keep it real with the police."

Wodgers unscrewed a bottle and tossed pills.

"For my heart, guy" he said, chewing. "I got to watch my ticker."
Banting jumped up in front of me.
"*Said dance, sucka! Move, sucka!*"
He waved his hands in my face, rotated his hips, flashed the grille.
"*Said dance, sucka! Move, sucka!*"
I did a little clippety-clop.

We were parked out somewhere in the darkness. Banting got back in the car, took off the cap and ejected the grille.
"It's on, gentlemen. They out there, and they is carrying."
"You ready, little buddy?" said Wodgers.
"I guess so," I said. "But isn't this breaking some law?"
"Not if you're working on behalf of the police," said Wodgers. "We've given you the official authorization. It's a law-enforcement matter."
"What do I say?"
"O.K.," said Banting, "Well, if I'm the scumbag, I'm looking at your clothes, your hair, the look on your face… Here's what you do: You go up and say, 'Hey yo, man, gimme summa dat yabba-doo stuff you got.'"
"Yabba-doo?"
"Yeah, yabba-doo. Just like that. Hey man, gimme summa dat yabba-yabba-doo stuff you got… He'll know what it means."
"Hey man, gimme summa that yabba-doo stuff you got. Like that?"
"Perfecto," said Wodgers. "Don't change nothin'."
"What if they attack me or something?"
"They won't attack you, guy," said Wodgers. "They're pussies. They want your money, that's what they care about. But if they do jump you, we got you covered on all sides. We'll send 'em home to mommy in a pizza box."
Wodgers gave me six 50-dollar bills from a leather pouch. Banting turned his cap inside out, leaned over the seat and set it backwards on my head. Then he twisted it, so the bill was jutting from my head at a right angle.
"There," he said, "you're set. You look like a right superfreak, Mr. Thor."
Banting slipped the night-goggles over his head.
"Go get 'em, little buddy," said Wodgers.

I was 95 percent sure I was going to die. I got out of the car and walked to the end of the alley, taking one step about every five seconds. I looked both ways, then crossed the road.

The two guys were standing by a dumpster, their backs to me. I took another slow step. I took a sideways step.

A light breeze shushed, twirling torn newspaper and plastic wrappers down the alley. An aluminum can tinkled, rolling along the asphalt.

They both turned.

"Ain't nobody here," said one.

Me: "Gimme summa that yabba-doo stuff you got."

"Said ain't nobody here, bwoy…"

"Gimme summa that yabba-doo, man…"

"You with the police, man."

I opened my arms, waved the cash. "Shoot, no… Come on, gimme summa that yabba-doo you got…"

"Yeah, you is. You with the police."

"No way, man… Come on, you crazy, man. The police? No way…"

They shuffled over. The one wearing a white Dallas Cowboys cap removed the money from my hand. The second, whose hair was in short braids, took my other hand in both of his. He had very warm hands.

When he moved away, I was holding a small package that felt like a plastic ball.

They took several backward steps, turned and jogged off into the darkness.

I walked back across the street. A helicopter whapped into view overhead, shining down a spotlight. Two unmarked cars whipped past.

Wodgers and Banting were standing in front of the Caprice.

"That's a good little buddy," said Wodgers, clapping me on the back.

"Right on, Mr. Thor."

Banting slapped me five and took the package. He pulled off several rubber bands and began to unwrap the ball. Wodgers shined a flashlight. Banting took off several layers of plastic, throwing them on to the car hood.

Finally it was unwrapped. Wodgers shined the light. We saw a number of broken rubber bands, some used paper matches, a cigarette butt.

"Suckas!" said Banting.

Wodgers slammed his hands on the car hood.

Banting held up a hand as he listened to his earpiece.

"All right, they're rolled... Excellent work, Mr. Thor," he said, shaking my hand. "You've done a service to society. Your city thanks you very much."

"Let's go see the handiwork," said Wodgers.

We got back in the car, drove about four blocks to the south. Cop vans and SUVs had driven over the curb, sirens and headlights burning. A helicopter rotated in the sky, shooting down white beams, sending dust and trash swirling. Flatfoots holding shotguns had eight or nine skinny guys lined up against a chain-link fence. Three or four other guys were on the ground, coppers standing on their backs.

UNDERCOVER POLICE NETWORK BUSTS DRUG GANGS
By Thor Garcia
CNS Staff Reporter

BAY CITY (CNS) – That drug addict you see down the block? He or she might not be what you think.

Each night in Bay City, undercover police operatives pose as drug addicts, loitering on street corners and pretending to look for a fix, as part of a campaign to smash the drug gangs that prey upon the metropolis.

No one will ever know their names.

The unknown operatives, working with Bay City's Street Narcotics Enforcement Unit (SNEU), scored big one recent weeknight.

An investigation in the Six Points area led to a series of operations in which 12 suspects, aged between 16 and 33, were arrested.

Officials said an estimated $200,000 worth of heroin and powdered and crack cocaine were seized, along with more than $10,000 in cash and three weapons, including an AK-47 automatic assault rifle.

Inspector Sgt. Riley Wodgers, who has been assigned to SNEU for the past two years, noted that the raids occurred not far from where seven people were found shot to death execution-style in a suspected drug-related massacre last March.

"These drug guys are smart and sophisticated, and we've got to be even smarter if we're going to catch them," said

Wodgers, who pointed out that the suspects and their family members now face the seizure of their property, bank accounts, automobiles and other goods and artifacts under laws aimed at disabling drug networks.

Fellow Inspector Lt. Andre Banting said that in addition to undercover operatives, SNEU relies on a variety of listening devices and other surveillance tools to keep investigators one step ahead of the gangs.

Banting added that the impact of the undercover operatives could not be underestimated.

"These raids have changed the quality of life in these neighborhoods," he said. "Slowly but surely, we are making a difference."

ENCORE: Clown Hits Sex-Pot with Juicy Babe!

★ 18 ★

Chrissy called me at the office a few days after the Christ Sunbeam party.

"Hey, Thor... What are you doing?"

"Not much. I'm at work."

"Oh, is that where I called?" She laughed, a deep belly giggle. "Why don't you come over? I just bought a house. I'm still moving in."

"Yeah, O.K. Where is it?"

She gave the address, some place up in Sunset Hills. The buses didn't run there, I would have to fork out for a taxi. I probably couldn't keep the receipt and list it on my expenses. Brownberger would sniff that one out. But hell, I figured. There might another kind of payback.

I got out about six and went over. I took the bus eleven or twelve stops to the end of the line, then called a taxi for the ride up the hill. There it was, 3802 Princk Street, the number tiled into a high brick wall. I rang at the gate. It buzzed and I went through. Out the other side was a large two-story brick house with ivy running up the sides – spotless white trim, fronted by a manicured green lawn with built-in sprinkler heads. Two cars were parked in the roundabout drive: maroon BMW BandWagen, and seagreen ragtop Nissan Lysteria, four-door. I went up the brick walk, stepped under the portico and slapped the knocker.

Chrissy's long tan legs flooded out of dark blue running shorts. She wore a yellow wrist-band and an old white T-shirt with the sleeves cut off. PROPERTY OF U. MASS. MEN'S ATHLETICS DEPT., the shirt said. Her hair was tied up in a ponytail. There was a powerful smell of paint.

"Hi, come on in!"

I shook her hand and went into the front room. A clutter of paint cans and sheets of plastic, brushes, rollers and plastic gloves, covered the wood floor. A ladder was leaned against the wall, while in the corner, cardboard boxes were stacked to the ceiling.

"Well, this is my place. They're still finishing the painting. No duh." She laughed.

"Wow, it's nice. It must've cost a fortune."

"I guess so... But it's just money, right? Hey, I'm a lawyer."

"That's right," I said. "Money isn't everything – it's only right up there with oxygen."

Chrissy laughed.

A small old dog shuffled up and sniffed my shoe. He was one of the long-type of small dogs with short legs. He was brown with white splotches, a face that was nearly totally white. He seemed very tired.

"This is Andy," said Chrissy.

"Hi, Andy!"

I reached down and scratched his ear. A purple tongue came out slowly and delivered a weak lick to my hand. He then sat down and began licking his penis.

We walked through an arched doorway, through a small hallway, and into a much larger room with giant arched windows and French Revolution-style wainscoting. Boxes were strewn about, flaps opened. The sliding glass was half-open along the west wall, transparent white drapes blowing slightly in the breeze. Out the glass I could see dying rays of sunshine hitting against a swimming pool set in brick and turquoise tile. Inside, to the left, flames danced in an elaborate brick fireplace.

"Nice fireplace," I said.

"Thanks, Thor."

A six-foot flat screen television with three-foot stand-alone speakers flickered in the corner. An inner tube rolled and rolled, down a green grassy hill beneath indigo skies. The camera panned across the hill, lingering on a few puff-patch clouds. A Pink Floyd song was coming over the speakers, just loud enough to interfere: "Wish You Were Here."

I sat down on a low-slung white corduroy couch which took up most of one wall. There wasn't much other furniture – a bookshelf, a table with a lamp, a translucent yellow computer, a bank of electronic gear, racks with dozens of CDs and DVDs.

Andy walked in, his claws clattering against the wood. He slowly laid himself down under a glossy black baby grand piano and began licking his testicles.

Chrissy sat next to me on the arm of the couch.

"So what's new?" Chrissy bashed me with burning green eyes, reached over and stroked my shoulder. "Hard day? Tired?"

"Yeah," I said, "a little."

"What's the news? Anything new?"

"Not really," I said. "Death and destruction, the usual. Bit of sadness here and there. Bad guys got away again."

She smiled. "Want a beer?"

"That'd be great, Chrissy."

She went in to the kitchen. I heard her open the refrigerator and lift the cap. She came back with a Tsingtao Light in a bottle. I took a sip, then a long pull.

"Thanks," I said. "Wow, Tsingtao. Haven't had one in a while."

Chrissy laughed. "You say it, Ching-Dow."

"Maybe you do," I said. "I call it China's best brew."

She laughed and sat down on a Persian carpet in front of the couch.

"I was just doing my exercises. I'll be finished in a minute."

"Sure, go ahead."

Chrissy spread her legs and leaned forward, touching one bare foot and the other with the tips of her fingers. She stared at me, counting off the exercises: "... twenty-four... twenty-five..."

She flipped on to a side and started doing leg rises. Her ass wasn't facing directly at me, but at an angle pointing toward the sliding glass. She wasn't wearing panties, and every time the leg came up, I realized I was getting a pretty good look at her cunt. The leg would go up. The shorts would pull away. There would be a flash of whiteness at the tan line, then I would flash on her pussy – the sides of it stretching apart, but the lips staying closed.

Spurts of fear and horniness rushed through me, I could feel my cheeks starting to burn. Heat was suddenly everywhere. I was suddenly trapped in a box of heat and raw energy.

Nothing, clearly, had been overlooked – it was all part of a negotiation that Chrissy had already settled. I mean, hell – I could be slow to catch on, but I wasn't a total fool.

Chrissy would expect me to perform, and very soon.

I sat there paralyzed, not sure how to react.

Chrissy had played a very nice hand. She had made an offer, and a demand, in a brilliant single move. She had out-maneuvered me, stampeded me into a corner, made of me quick two-dollar change. The pressure was coming down in waves, each more intense than the last. My options were few. I would have to deliver, and soon – or Chrissy would send me home a poor broken boy, one who couldn't hope to play in the big leagues.

I took long swallows off the beer. I took a few more. The beer would help me. I knew it would. I needed just the right amount.

Chrissy stopped, exhaled. She rolled on to her stomach, legs splaying open behind her, ass bubbling up on the Persian. She smiled and looked at me, her face tan and pink, breathing heavily.

"So how's the law firm stuff going?" I said.

She raised herself on an elbow, resting her head in her hand. "Oh, I don't know... Yeah, it's pretty good, I guess."

"That's good to hear."

I finished the beer and set it down on the wood floor. I could have used another, but didn't say anything.

"Yeah, there's a lot of work right now," Chrissy said. "They're keeping me busy."

She launched into a story about the firm. Her work apparently had to do with lawsuits involving the government, something about environmental regulations and liability, toxic disposal, jurisdictional questions, etc. I was finding it hard to concentrate. At the end of the story, I still wasn't sure whether the firm was working for the government or had sued it. Quite possibly both.

"Everybody always says lawyers suck," she said, "and they totally do. I work with them, I mean – I *know* they're assholes. Except when you really need one, right? When you really need to go into court with somebody who knows what's happening. Then they're your best and greatest friend. I've heard it a zillion times."

"It's the same with cops," I said. "No one really likes them, until they really need help for some reason... I spend half the day talking to cops."

"I'll bet they can be real assholes."

"They can, but most of them are pretty good guys, to be honest. You just got to hope you don't run into the wrong one at the wrong time. So how's the Justin guy thing doing?"

"Justin? Oh, sorry about him being such a jerk... He's a good friend, but sometimes he gets confused and thinks he controls me. He's a control-type... The funny thing about control-types is they can never control themselves."

I laughed. "How long have you guys been going out?"

"We've never gone out. We're just friends."

She rolled over and stood up. The nipple of one of her breasts stuck out the corner of the cut-off shirt.

"Whoops, my boob fell out."

"My God, it did..."

Chrissy lifted the top over her head and threw it on the ground. Her breasts swung briefly – medium-size, well-rounded on the underside. Dark pink nipples.

"Wow, I need to cool off," she said, releasing her hair from a rubber band. "Want to go for a swim?"

"Sure," I said.

I saw wide shoulders, wide hips, a flat stomach. Chrissy stepped out of the running shorts and jogged through the curtain to the pool, her ass shaking and firming, jiggling and tightening.

My penis twitched, there was a sudden boiling, itching sensation in my testicles. I noticed Chrissy had some kind of tattoo on her lower back – looked like a dolphin or something.

She splashed into the pool. I got up and walked after her. Andy lifted his head and looked over.

"Hey there, little buddy," I said.

I came out to the deck and kicked off my shoes. Chrissy swam up to the side, water cascading over the tiles, streams rolling down her face.

"Sorry, the pool's a mess. I haven't had time to hire a cleaning man yet... It's a little cold, but it's nice and refreshing."

"Great..."

I took off my socks. Various blue-violet bits, leaves and grass were floating on the pool surface, swirling on the bottom. I started taking of my pants.

Chrissy popped up again, treading water in the middle.

"Wow, you've got great thighs... I like big muscular thighs."

"Thanks... They're from all the walking..."

"You like these jacaranda trees? Don't they smell great?"

"Yeah, they do..."

"I would have bought this place just for the trees."

"Is that a dolphin on your back?"

"It's a seahorse."

"Is it?"

Chrissy laughed and splashed back under.

I dove in. I went up and back freestyle twice, then up and back underwater, paying Chrissy no mind. Then, in the middle of the third underwater lap, I went after her like a shark. She put up a brief struggle, but I had her in my arms within five seconds, my stiffened cock knocking against her back. I probably could have stuck it right in, but I didn't want to just yet. Chrissy was different, I wanted to drag this one out. I wanted to please her. I wanted to get her off. Not only did I want to, I felt I *had* to. I already understood Chrissy was faster and smarter than I was. My task now was to render services, and hope for the best.

She wiggled in my arms, throwing her head back, as I carried her to the stone stairs. I got her up on the second step, laid her down on her back. Our mouths came together, she slid her tongue in. I reached down and began stroking her soaked pussy. Goosebumps erupted on my skin, explosions went off in my head. Chrissy's mouth quivered and thrashed, I caught whiffs of her hair, her skin, the chlorine.

I worked my way across her body, kissing her breasts and nipples, tonguing her navel, until eventually I was between her legs, my face just inches away from her pussy. I paused a few seconds to gaze at the marvelous thing, its swollen folds and creases, its fabulous rosy hue – it was hard to believe I was again this close to the miracle. It had been a long time since I had done something like this, maybe a year or more. Even so, I had not totally forgotten. Pacing would be everything, that was for sure. I kissed the inside of one thigh, the other thigh, then went into a series of long slow licks on each side, gradually moving closer and closer to the hole.

"Auh, auh..." I heard her.

Her back flexed, her hips buckled as she tried to maneuver the button to my tongue. I ignored it. I danced around the button, hitting everywhere but there. I tongued in a circle, reversed, jumped from side to side, narrowly avoiding dipping into the chasm. I massaged her thighs with both hands, squeezed her hips. I went high and fingered her nipples.

My cock strained and bulled, crashing into one of the lower steps. I slowed the tempo, seeking to drag it out even longer. I lavished long, lingering licks in the space between her cunt and bunghole. Finally I darted into the cunt with a sharp, precise downstroke, then followed with a flurry of quick upward flicks. After a moment or two I detected a slight difference in taste and consistency, and it was exactly at this point that I sprang to the button.

I attacked it softly, gently, as if it was a princess, the most precious, valuable thing on earth. As I flicked and carefully nibbled, I stuck a finger in the hole, began moving it in and out. I put the entirety of the button in my mouth and sucked with tender, worshipful humility. Chrissy shook and trembled, her thighs opened and closed, brushing against the sides of my face.

"Auh... auh..."

Chrissy shoved her cunt toward me, straining, insisting. Her legs jumped up over my shoulders and yanked me in.

✪

I was finishing putting on my clothes in the living room, I could hear Chrissy flushing the toilet and brushing her teeth. The fireplace crackled. On the television a fleet of rainbow-colored hot-air balloons sailed over Tibet, "Comfortably Numb" wafting around the room at a moderate volume.

I saw a photo of a bicep sticking out from a stack of boxes. I went over and pulled it out. It was a calendar, French writing – oiled French rugby players, cocks hanging to their socks. Nice.

I stood there and looked at book spines in Chrissy's boxes. She had *One Hundred Years of Solitude, Women Who Run with Wolves, The One L, Madame Bovary.* There was a row of *Guides Michelin, Querelle de Brest, The Firm, The Runaway Jury, Loving Relationships, Inner Communion, Les Particules elementaires, A Jury of Her Peers, Enemies: A Love Story, The Secret Life of Dogs, Bridget Jones' Diary.* Another box held hardback volumes of Cezanne and Gauguin, Basquiat and Rothko, *The Tao of Pooh, Life Doesn't Frighten Me, The Stand, The Shining, How to Be Chic, Fabulous and Live Forever,* Madonna's *Sex* book, *The Complete Prose of Woody Allen...*

Chrissy emerged in black slacks and silver taffeta, transparent bra straps flashing on both shoulders. She was bright-eyed and relaxed, face rosy. I went over and gave her a kiss on both cheeks and the forehead. I hugged her.

"Hey, wow – you look fantastic."

"Thanks, Thor."

"So you play the piano?"

"No... well, I guess a little. I've been trying for the last couple years, but it's really hard. I even took lessons for 75 bucks an hour, but I don't have the time to practice. I wished I had learned as a kid. My mom put me in ballet. Do you play?"

"I can play 'Shortbread.'"

I pulled out the bench, sat down and played it.

"Mama's little baby loves shortnin', shortnin', mama's little baby..."

Chrissy sang and spun around, doing a little tap-dance. "That's great!" she said, laughing. "You've got to teach me... What else do you know?"

"Not much," I said. "There's this one... I think it's a Mozart..." I plinked out a few seconds' worth.

"Oh, that's great!" said Chrissy. "How did you learn?"

"Well, no, I don't really know how to play, I can just plonk these out like a monkey. My mom took me to this babysitter who had a piano. She showed me, and then we stopped going there. This is all I remember..."

"Oh, that's neat," said Chrissy. "I'm gonna make my kids learn. I'll start 'em at like, age two."

"Want to have kids, huh?"

"Sure – don't you?"

"Yes, of course..."

"C'mon," she said, "let's go eat. I'm famished."

Chrissy picked up the remote control. Pink Floyd blinked off first, then the fireplace, the flames snapping off like a light. She threw the remote on the couch.

It was nearly dark but warm, a warm fragrant night. We pulled the top flap off the BMW and she drove us down the hill. We hit Granite Beach Blvd., drove four or five blocks, then pulled in to Kenny's Gourmet Greaseburgers. We got out, locked the flap back on, and went into the bar. I didn't like the look of the menu – $8.50 for a Lowenbrau, $21.50 for a greaseburger and cottage fries...

"Jesus, Chrissy..."

"Forget it, Thor. I'm taking you out." She smiled and kissed me on the neck.

"What are you having?"

"I think I'll get a Tanqueray."

"Me too. And a Heinekin."

We sat in the booth, holding hands under the table, speaking softly, while inside my chest my heart jerked crazily. How could this be happening? It was hard to believe. I knew there would be a down side, somewhere along the line, there *had* to be – but Chrissy seemed satisfied. I felt no static or paranoid vibes, no insane comedown fear, no thirst for negotiations or demands from her for anything more than for me to sit next to her. Excitement and relief thumped through me. Maybe – *maybe* I had pulled it off. Maybe I had pulled off *something* out there by the pool. Maybe...

I was suddenly violently excited about the idea of being able to see Chrissy on a regular basis. Was it possible? She was a loose woman, that was for sure, that couldn't be brushed aside – but it was also different somehow, totally different – *she* was different. It wasn't so simple. It was the society, the propaganda – that was the cause of the madness, I told myself. It was the fact that there were such few good men, and she had never been lucky enough to find one.

I leaned over and kissed her – her lips, her nose, her forehead, her chin. She giggled, fondled my neck. I grabbed her around the waist and kissed, inhaling the fullness of her scent.

✪

Kenny's specialized in greasing it up, but apparently with "all low-fat ingredients." I had a cheddar and jalapeño, Chrissy a Monterey and peach. We shared a teriyaki chicken salad with red onions, pineapple and cilantro dressing. Not bad for $21 burgers.

Chrissy explained between bites that she was rich not only because of her lawyer job, but also because of her father, who had "invented" some important part of voice-mail. Then, when Chrissy was 17, her father had a stroke – he was nine years in a coma so far. Her mother and father were still married, but the mom had found another man four or five years ago. Everybody felt "guilty" about it, but – "people have to live," didn't they? Her mother was a curator at the Museum of Natural History. The other man, Gerard, was an executive at the company that ran concessions at Westinghouse-Taco Station Arena, Bechtel-Bay International Horse Track and other venues.

"I used to date Hugh," she said. "Do you know Hugh?"

"I'm not sure," I said. "Maybe. How long did you guys go out?"

"I've never gone out with anybody. But about two years, if that's what you mean."

"Oh, no kidding..."

It burned, somehow it burned. I sat there silently, burning. Well, but somebody always had to come from somewhere. That was the goddamn truth, if there was such a thing. Chrissy laughed and pulled my earlobe into her mouth, rubbed her cheek against mine. Reflections of candlelight and beer signs flickered in her eyes. We ordered a pair of cream-topped Viennese coffees.

Chrissy wasn't really close with Candace and Heather. They were just "party friends." Did I know Heather was sick? I did know, but not how serious.

Chrissy sighed. "Heather's tragic... Candace is a disaster."

"Hey, they're good friends of mine."

"Sure. They're everybody's good friends."

★

... live now to President Wolfgang Mnung at the White House, he has a breaking announcement...

We were back at Chrissy's shack, television and fireplace on. The president appeared in a Cincinnati Bengals uniform, shoulder pads and wristbands, stripes of black wax under his eyes, a headset with two antenna sticking from the top of his head. He was holding up a plastic bag full of a white substance. Hundreds of news clown photo flashes exploded.

CLOWN: *My fellow Americans, Secret Service agents today bought this 16-pound bag of death in the park outside the White House from terrorists. Furthermore, the terrorists were selling this powdered death in tandem with counterfeit Prada and Gucci handbags and Baumeister contact lenses... Our agents arrested more than 20 terrorists, and more than 400 counterfeit handbags and 8,000 pair of contact lenses were captured during the search and seizure operation in cities across the nation and overseas... We have reason to believe these terrorists were planning a spectacular attack on America, and further evidence indicates we may have prevented such an occurrence. I have declared the captured terrorists non-legal combatants, ineligible for protection or recourse to America's legal system, the best and most judicious legal system in the world...*

"Want a Curvoisier?" said Chrissy.

"Sure. What's that?"

"Cognac."

"Absolutely I want that. Look, I'm gonna go have another..."

"Oh, you can smoke in here," Chrissy said. "I don't mind. You sure smoke a lot."

"Well, I'm nervous. It seems to help. The doctors have admitted it can help, really..."

Chrissy patted my hair, looked into my eyes.

"Why are you so nervous, Thor?"

"I've felt nervous since I was about five years old..."

"They don't help. They'll kill you one day..."

"Everything kills you. Being alive kills you. Believe me, these smokes help a whole lot..."

"Smoking and drinking decrease your sperm count. They've done studies on it."

"I doubt every word of that..."

Chrissy handed me a lopsided orange bowl that had green stripes and gray triangles. It looked like it was made from some type of clay.

"What's this thing?"

"I got it from the Nicaraguan cancer children. They made it. I give them money a couple times a year. Last year they invited me down to see them. I stayed for a couple days. It was beautiful, in the middle of this jungle. It's sad, they're such cute kids..."

I didn't like ashing into the cancer-kids bowl, but I lit up anyway.

Chrissy came back a few minutes later, wearing a light blue silk negligee that fell to mid-thigh. She wheeled over a little cart with the drinks on top. We had a toast "to today." She went over to her boxes and came back with a DVD, *Fifth Element*, and put it in the machine. The film started to roll. From another slot on the cart she took out what she called her "drug bag," a Salvadoran-style pouch with various sacks and bundles inside. She took a stogie out of a plastic sack and lit it. I had a few puffs. It may very well have been high-quality material. Chrissy lay down with her head in my lap. I took sips from the Curvoisier. I yawned.

We looked at the movie, saying little. I couldn't see what they were trying to prove with this film, and I wasn't interested. It seemed nearly completely fatuous and half-ass, gaudy yet lackluster, some French guy's wet dream. One genius move had to be admitted – the twig-skinny girl with the big lips, long legs and tiny titties. But that was her, not them. She had been worth the two bucks.

I finished my cognac and took sips off Chrissy's. I petted her around her neck and collarbone, eventually working down to her breasts. Chrissy stretched her legs out on the couch, brought a hand up to stroke my chest and chin. Bruce Willis flew a taxi through the air. Chrissy pulled my head down and kissed me. I reached further down and started rubbing the insides of her thighs.

The film was a goddamn waste of Bruce Willis. They just didn't care anymore.

KILL CITY: Send in the Clowns!

★ 19 ★

MAN STABBED TO DEATH ON BAY METRO
BAY CITY (CNS) - Bay City police said a man on a Bay Metro subway car was attacked and cut to death Wednesday by an assailant armed with a boxcutter.

STUDENT SHOT TO DEATH AT BEACH
BAY CITY (CNS) - Bay City police said a female Bay State University student was shot to death Wednesday night near the pier at Pine Shoals State Beach.

THREE KILLED IN SUSPECTED GANG SHOOTING
BAY CITY (CNS) – Bay City police said three males were shot to death and two other people were injured Wednesday in what's being treated by investigators as a gang-related incident.

WOMAN FOUND DEAD NEAR COLOSIO PARK
BAY CITY (CNS) - Bay City police said a 25-year-old woman was found dead early Wednesday under an overpass at Donaldo Colosio park, the suspected victim of a homicide.

FOUR KILLED IN SHOOTING AT BAY CITY BAR
BAY CITY (CNS) - Bay City Police said four people were shot to death late Wednesday during a suspected robbery at the Fernwood Lounge bar in the Pine Ridges section.

BASKETBALL COACH SHOT DEAD AT PARK GAME

BAY CITY (CNS) – Bay City police said a youth basketball coach was shot dead after a game Thursday night at Rosewood Park.

Police said coach Arkim Parder, 28, was not believed to have been the intended victim of the shooting, but was caught in the crossfire of a suspected "gang turf battle."

MAN KILLS THREE IN STABBING RAMPAGE

BAY CITY (CNS) – Police said a man stabbed three people to death and seriously injured two others Thursday at a Bay City shopping mall.

Inspector Thomas Pritt said those killed in the rampage at Bay Oaks Mall included a 1-year-old girl, a 26-year-old man and a 69-year-old woman.

Pritt said the suspected attacker was detained after a bystander hit him in the head with a fire extinguisher and restrained him until police arrived.

TEACHER DIES AFTER SCHOOL SHOOTING

BAY CITY (CNS) – Hospital officials said Bay City teacher Franklin Smicer died Thursday from injuries sustained when he was shot by a student.

St. Vincent Medical Center spokesman Lyman Lymnitzer said Smicer died shortly after 8 a.m. from head injuries he received in the shooting Wednesday at Boukman High School in the Pine Ridges section.

GIRL, 8, SHOT THROUGH APARTMENT DOOR

BAY CITY (CNS) – Bay City police said an eight-year-old girl was killed Thursday evening by a bullet that smashed through a door at her family's apartment in the Silvertown section.

Lt. Andrea Childer said Rohanda Plunkett was pronounced dead at her home at the Du Bois Residential Estates after efforts at resuscitation by paramedics failed.

The spree had gone national, a mind-bending 37 kills in 36 hours, and top-ranking clowns had flown in from far and wide for the Monday morning press-bang: Abelardo Guerth from CBN; Roth Stothel from NBJ; Justianne Hamandpour of NNN's *Sunday Night With Justiannne Hamandpour*; Wes Durranty from the *Examiner-Mail*, whose mustache was a bit like Stalin's; Sidney Glass from the *Amercian Business-Advertiser*, who had a little Lenin beard; the incomparable Blair Cooke of the *Beltway Post-Times*, who favored something like a Marx shag; Heanus Williams of *It's Tough-Tough Questions Time With Heanus Williams*; the nationally-syndicated columnist James B. Hogland; Matthew Saffliar of the *Palm Beach Telegraph-Press*, a professional chat-show guest who was nationally famous for his purple beret; Ratzleff Lopauer of the *Washington Daily Standard-Dispatch*; the half-senile "old political pro" Larry T. Freidman of the *Baltimore National-State*; Andrew Blovian of the *Catholic National-Republican Express*; Bob Upshur of the *Washington Citizen-Patriot*; Cookie Boggs of American Business-Interests Radio Corp.; Mario Barnuckle of the *Los Angeles Standard-Retailer*; Venal Rusnert of the *Philadelphia Periodical-American*; along with the usual crew of 10-12 local dingbats.

A few Mayoral press aides stood behind tables on which had been placed urns of sweetly stinking coffee, cheese slices, Danish pastry, bagels and croissants. On another table, four guns had been laid out on green felt, cops standing guard at the ends. Each gun was tagged with a police number on a large yellow card. There were two small revolvers, one a scuffed black, the other a dusty silver with a mother-of-pearl handle; something that looked like a rusting machine gun; and an old-looking rifle whose brown lacquer was peeling off the stock. Top-shelf clowns stood around, staring at the guns and chewing their rolls, every so often mumbling something that was difficult to decipher.

Richie nudged me. "Look at them guns, kid... Takin' a real bite out of crime." He wolfed a mouthful of bagel.

"This is pretty good cream cheese," I heard Sidney Glass whine. He spread a little more on his croissant and giggled.

The hour had nearly arrived. Champion press clowns cleared their throats and unfolded notebooks. Big-time TV clowns straightened ties and yanked last-minute nose-hair in front of mirrors held by clown crews.

A pair from the Mayor's Porter Service, wearing maroon and white striped uniforms and black buckle-boots, walked in pushing trolleys.

"Gift bags heah, getcha gift bags heah!" they hollered. "Free official Bay City Gift Bags for all credentialed media representatives at the joint Mayoral/Police Chief Press Conference! Gift bags heah! Gift bags! Getcha free Bay City gift bags heah!"

The clown gang scrambled forward, the bozo pack lunging in unsion toward the silver Versace cloth bags bearing the official gold and blue Bay City seal. Cooke, Blovian, Saffliar and Duranty made it there first and quickly tore open their bulging goodie sacks. Inside were items including certificates for free music downloads from musictunesdotcom.com; Spring Foam Shampoo and Shave-Buddy razors; Anacapa Cherry Tea; Dewy Spirit body butter; a box of Speruzzi's low-carb wheat pasta; an Interdesk hand-held paper shredder; a box of Bingo Bravo golf tees; a packet of Albanese pet snacks; a Mahjong-To-Go game set; a 10-pack of Skyy Vodka minis; certificates for a Rose Fleming cream cheese poundcake and two free laser pedicures courtesy of Rogers-Stuhlbarg Cosmetic-Dental. Other items included an official Bay City stick pin and an information packet which contained autographed color stills of the mayor and his cabinet.

Mario Barnuckle tore open a bag of Stranger's Almanac apple chips and flipped one into his mouth, then grabbed a handful and tossed them in the direction of Guerth. Blair Cooke popped the flask of Amarula Creme Liquer and had a gulp. I saw that Venal Rusnert was already on his third vodka mini, while Saffliar had begun shaving Blovian in a corner.

"Yay! Body butter!" exclaimed James B. Hogland.

Freidman, a cross-eyed look on his face, removed the paper shredder from its box and began to operate it upon the glossy portrait of the mayor. The journalist stamped his feet repeatedly upon the curly paper shavings as they landed on the floor.

"Two-minute warning!" shouted Trent Ghassanid, the deputy Mayoral press aide.

The bugle fanfare rolled, one of the porters stepped forward.

"All ye rise! Ye ladies and gentlemen, representing the Esteemed Municipality of Bay City, Ye Honorable Mayor Ernest Favella and Ye Honorable Police Chief Nathan Nachba!"

The clown crew stood in unison, many nodding, some bowing. Dozens of photo flashes bounced across the room, TV camera batteries closed in for the zoom. Mayor Favella and Police Chief Nathan "Nate" Nachba walked in, followed closely by Deputy Chief Howard "Howie" Broward, who took a flanking position behind the gun table.

Nachba grimaced, Favella blinked. They took their chairs, grimacing and blinking.

Mayor Favella began: "Ladies and gentlemen, welcome to today's official press conference. We are here today because our city has suffered a series of horrendous tragedies. My message is this: We are putting criminals and gang members on notice. Your time has come. Crime is not, and never has been, accepted in Bay City. I call on all criminals to surrender to the appropriate authorities now, or we will hunt you down and bring you to justice against your will. I call on all criminals to surrender their unlawfully obtained firearms, knives and weapons of mass destruction. The sewage of crime must be eradicated from wherever it squats in our city. We intend to exercise our powers to the fullest extent of the law. I have this morning officially declared a citywide crime emergency which provides for increased police patrols, a 9 p.m. to 6 a.m. curfew for youths under 18 years of age, and the installation of hundreds of the latest in high-technology surveillance cameras in our most troubled neighborhoods..."

Favella blinked, gestured toward the row of four firearms.

"What you see before you, ladies and gentlemen, are some of the vicious tools of death that have brought tears and shame to our city. These weapons were seized over the last 48 hours through the diligent efforts of our..."

Heanus Williams jumped to his feet, waving a microphone.

"Time's up, Mr. Mayor! It's Tough-Tough Questions Time With Heanus Williams, Mr. Mayor, and America's got you on the spot! Mayor Favella, are the police chief and the men and women of the police force up to the job? This unprecedented crime wave has shaken the nation, and the people want to know: Can anything be done in Bay City? What are you planning to do to restore confidence? Time's up, Chief Nachba – you're on the spot with Heanus Williams! It's Tough-Tough Questions Time with Heanus Williams! You're the target and America's got you on the spot!"

Favella blinked, rubbed his temple with both hands.

"Well, I, I... yes, I have full confidence in Police Chief Nachba and his staff. Mark my words: We will be unrelenting in our pursuit to stomp down criminals, these hideous wrong-doers who have brought disgrace to our common humanity..."

Justianne Hamandpour rose, tears flowing down her cheeks.

"Mr. Mayor, what do you have to say to the family of poor little 8-year-old Rohanda Plunkett, who was gunned down by murderous thugs while your officers did nothing to stop them? This is a story that has captured America's heart... Mr. Police Chief, what about the people, the people, the parents, the little boys and girls, the children..."

Chief Nachba: "We deeply regret the loss of all innocent lives, including that darling little girl –"

"But the children," sobbed Hamandpour, "what of the children, the children, but what of the children, the babies, the babies and the children –"

"What I would say," said Nachba, "is that we need information from the community to catch those responsible for these vicious crimes. We need ordinary people and witnesses to call in and report what they have seen. This is how crimes get solved and how we reduce incidents of law-breaking, with the cooperation of the local community and witnesses coming forward to report what they have seen and heard. I would tell residents that if they are worried about retaliation from the thugs and criminals who prey on their community, we can offer the strictest confidentiality and –"

"But what of the children, the babies, Mr. Mayor, Mr. Chief of Police – the children and the babies? Those littlest of ones who ask only for a chance to hope, to dream, to feel safe in America... The children, the babies, a time to hope and to dream and feel safe in America at a time when they should be learning and dreaming and running and playing and dancing and running –"

Nachba: "Excuse me, I'm sorry... Bear with me, please, Ms. Hamandpour, Justianne, I'm sorry for interrupting you, I apologize, please... well, for starters, the mayor has ordered a freeze on budget cuts, and promised additional funding for 1,300 more police officers, as well as 60 new surveillance vans and seven helicopters..."

Cookie Boggs leaped forward: "But what about the rights of the innocent suspects? Surely you have an obligation to defend civil rights?"

Favella: "Yes, of course, Cookie, I guarantee it. The police are the last line of defense between civilization and the rule of the jungle. Police officers have the noble task of holding the line – and we must hold that line. Without decent police officers of the highest caliber, our society risks collapse into savage brutality and anarchy, in which each and every one of us is at risk. We must therefore have the highest caliber, most upstanding officers. I won't tolerate anything less..."

Richie tossed his pen, ground his knuckles against the table.

Roth Stothel jumped to the seat of his chair and smashed his Rose Fleming poundcake into Blair Cooke.

"Oh, come off it!" Stothel shouted, pointing his finger. "I'm Ross Stothel, chief investigations reporter for KNBJ, your ratings leader. I've seen all the documents, mister, and *you've* been wasting America's tax dollars! *You've* been! This is the product of a waffling liberal socialist welfare society gone berserk! Bay City is notorious for coddling criminals and letting perverts run free and wasting tax dollars. And America is demanding a refund! So what's your answer, Mr. Mayor? And what do you say, Chief Nachba? *Blooh! Blooh!*"

Richie's hand shot up.

"Yes?" said Nachba.

"Nope! Not so easy!" shouted Stothel.

He leapfrogged two chairs, stood and pointed both hands at the mayor and police chief. His camera crew hustled down the aisle, moving in for the key close up.

"*That's it, now you've done it, mister!* I'm going to expose you on national TV, and there's nothing you can do! *Blooh! Blooh!* I'm charging you with being a liberal tax-and-spend crime coddler! And America won't stand for it any longer! We're fed up! Tax-and-spender! Tax-and-spender! *Blooh! Blooh!*"

The mayor nodded toward Richie. "Go ahead, sir..."

Richie: "Let me understand: With a police force of over 20,000 cops, you were able to seize four guns?"

"As I said," said Chief Nachba, "the crackdown is continuing. We continue to pursue wrong-doers to the four corners, to the utmost extent allowable under law. Severe punishment is in store for all those who fail to surrender illegal firearms and submit to arrest by officers of the law..."

Richie stood.

"FOUR GUNS? IS THAT WHAT YOU HAVE TO TELL US? THAT YOU SEIZED FOUR GUNS?"

"THAT'S ENOUGH, ZENGER!" the mayor screamed. He pounded the table with his fist, rose to his feet. "YOU SIT DOWN NOW! WE'RE PUTTING ON THIS NEWS CONFERENCE!"

"FOUR GUNS!?"

Bob Upshur hissed. "C'mon, man, don't screw it up..."

"Yeah, take it somewhere else," said Ratzleff Lopauer, sneering. "Go write it on your blog or something... if you must..." He snickered.

"FOUR GUNS? FOUR GUNS? FOUR GUNS?"

Richie's voice trailed off. The room had fallen silent. At last Chief Nachba spoke.

"To you, sir," he said, his voice shaking, his eyes locked on Richie, "this is difficult work here, and I don't mind saying so. It's easy, I would imagine, for someone who's never taken a risk, who's never been responsible for a large work force doing complicated work, to tell me how to g.d. suck eggs... And I don't accept it. We're doing the g.d. best we can here. And if you've got better ideas, you are more than welcome to put your application in down the hall."

Richie staggered across clowns, crawled down the row.

"FOUR GUNS? FOUR GUNS?"

Gift bags fell to the floor, Richie crunched through boxes of pasta, kicked past jars of jam and tins of tea. Golf tees rolled across the carpet as Richie reeled to the end of the row.

"FOUR GUNS?"

Richie hit the aisle and started walking toward the table.

Nachba signalled and a squad of six cops rushed forward. They seized Richie, throwing him against the wall and dragging him toward the hall.

"FOUR GUNS! FOUR GUNS! FOUR GUNS!"

>POLICE SEIZE 4 GUNS IN CRIME CRACKDOWN
>
>BAY CITY (CNS) – Police Chief Nathan Nachba on Monday announced that Bay City's new anti-crime effort had seized four of the many thousands of illegal guns on the city streets.
>
>"These are the tools of violence that are bringing misery to the citizens of our city," Nachba said at a joint news conference at Police Headquarters with Bay City Mayor Ernest Favella.
>
>Nachba said the four weapons were seized in raids carried out as part of the new Operation: Take-Back Streets, which was launched following last week's record-setting 37 murders in 36 hours.
>
>The four weapons included a 9-mm. machine pistol, a 12-gauge shotgun, an AR-15 assault rifle and a gatling-style .45-cal. pistol.

Mayor Favella told reporters at the news conference: "I have full confidence in the ability of our highly skilled police force to restore order and bring criminals to justice."

DIZZY: Babe Leads Love-Drunk Clown by Nose!

★ 20 ★

I was sitting around, having a few beers with Jerry. It was about 10:30. I was having a hard time finding interest in *Harlot's Ghost*. I felt jumpy, unsettled, but not because of the suffocating dullness.

The moment of truth had already passed or was still coming. I was terrified either way. I kept looking at the clock, waiting for 15 minutes to go by so I could light another smoke. The *Head on the Door* album flapped along gently as Jerry worked with a number of papers and plastic bags on the coffee table. TV helicopter footage showed a crowd of cops and ambulances at a gas station.

BREAKING: SNIPER STRIKES AGAIN?

I snatched at the ringing mobile.

"Hey, Thor!" said Chrissy. "What are you doing? I just got home from work."

"I'm just sitting here…"

"Why don't you come over? I worked my ass off today."

"All right."

"Great! I'm making margaritas…"

I tossed the tome, gulped a last swallow and crumpled the can. I threw it down the hallway and stood up.

"Jerry, you got any bucks?"

"For what?"

"I'll pay you back next week. I got to take a taxi."

"For what?"

"I gotta go see this chick. Emergency."

"Dude, *come on*. I'm not that stupid. I know that was Chrissy. Man, don't do this, bro. Justin's my friend. It's not your place."

"Who's Justin? Justin's everybody's friend. I've never had a place. You got the bucks or what? A ten should do it."

"All right, I will for you – but I don't approve. I just don't approve..."

Jerry set down his materials, sighed and opened his wallet, which was connected to a chain around his belt loop. "You guys are just friends, is that it?" He handed over the cash.

"Thanks, Jerry. Me and *you* are friends."

I made the taxi call, then went into the bathroom and took a shower to freshen up. I toweled off, hitting myself heavily with a Cool Air stick. I found a clean pair of Jerry's socks and a yellow t-shirt. I donned the baby blue sports coat.

"I'll check you later, Jerry," I said. "Keep the faith."

POLICE: SNIPER KILLS 8th VICTIM

Chrissy opened the door wearing purple jogging tights, a brassiere of salmon and black silk. She opened her arms and thrust herself into me, pressing her face against my chest. Gentle gusts of booze, garlic and sweat wafted off her. I put my hands on her hips, kissed her forehead. A warm night breeze blew up from behind, tossing the nearby tree branches and bushes. My penis squirmed in my jeans, growing in length. Chrissy felt warm, wet, soft...

"I'm glad you could make it, Thor..."

"I couldn't imagine missing it, Chrissy..."

We came into the kitchen, holding hands. Andy was laying on a gold and green mat in the corner. He looked up briefly, then sank back down. A half-empty pitcher of orange-colored margaritas stood on the kitchen counter, next to Styrofoam containers of prawns, pasta salad and French fries. Chrissy explained they had thrown a party at work – she had made junior partner, and they had given her shares – but she had left early. She had called *me*.

The fireplace roared in the living room. I could see *Lenny Kravitz Live at Stonehenge* playing on the wide-screen.

"Is that Lenny Kravitz?" I said.

"Oh, *fuck* Lenny Kravitz!"

Chrissy grabbed my wrists and pressed me against the counter, grinding her hips against mine. She pushed her tongue into my mouth. She twirled it around.

SEVEN KILLED IN MUIR COUNTY COLLISION

PLATTS (CNS) - The Highway Patrol said seven people were killed late Sunday in the head-on collision of a refrigerator truck and a sport utility vehicle on a two-lane highway outside Platts in rural Muir County.

Officer Samuel Chamzik said all passengers traveling aboard the sport utility vehicle were killed. He said they have not yet been identified.

Chamzik said the driver of the truck, who was not injured, had passed a breath test for intoxication.

I started staying over at Chrissy's a couple times a week. It was different out there. Quieter mainly, and richer. A steady stream of Audis and Volvos, Porsches and Mercedes, the not so random Jaguar or Lamborghini, swept soundlessly up and down the hilly passes. On a certain day, I believe it was a Thursday, several dozen Mexican males of varying ages would arrive in a pack of pick-up trucks to mow the lawns and clip the shrubbery of the neighborhood houses. In the early evenings, if we weren't out, I might stroll out back sipping a Ballantine's, enjoying a moment of solitude and contentment, the grass freshly cut and the sprinklers on. I would gaze out over the smog-domed city and think glancingly of the ones down below, frantically toiling in fear and futility. I used to be one of those, of course – but now, it seemed, I visited the city only to make money, and to author objective reports relating to the sociological development of the metropolis.

It was a drain on my finances to continually be taking a taxi up the hill, but there were plenty of fringe benefits, and sometimes Chrissy would pick me up or provide me with a 50-dollar bill for my trouble. We appeared to live in a state of high intelligence and being, untroubled by daily hassles, focused on the care, feeding and entertainment of each other. We smuggled sangria into the observatory, dined on toasted roast beef and Irish cheddar sandwiches in the nature reserve. We attended beach barbecues, midnight movies, jazz benefits at Chrissy's temple, performances of bunraku. We went to Elektra-Max and Riki's Tiki Bar, the 9th Annual Tofu Festival, to Delfina, Bar Tartine and the Bistro Moderne. We went to Cafe Neu-Neu, Cafe Sadu, Xantypa, Escalier and many others. We made appearances at concerts and museum openings, at comedy clubs and creperies, at flower festivals and wine tastings. We took off our shoes and ran through the park in the rain.

Chrissy owned a set of his-n-her mountain bikes, and every so often we'd use them to cruise the southern beach towns. Early one morning, she even got me puffing in a 5-K run-swim out at Vasconcellos Island. We had steaks and scallops delivered for breakfast, chocolate cake for lunch, champagne whenever we felt like it. We went to garage sales, because Chrissy knew where to go. Sometimes you could pick up real bargains after some unfortunate fellow had died of AIDS: Sequined red cowboy boots, fabulous lamps and floral needlepoints, blue china tea sets, double-walled glasses, vintage Billie Holliday and Stravinsky vinyl, limited-edition Judas Priest box sets... Some of it went into my pile of junk, and some of it went into Chrissy's closet or garage. Chrissy would pay in cash and we'd load the stuff into the BandWagen and jet off to the next place, a full Saturday night ahead.

Chrissy knew what was happening, she knew where it *sat*. She was cool, she was hot, she called Madonna "Madge." She had grasped me by the nose and was leading me on a trip to soaring peaks and desolate valleys, on a journey into dark wet caverns and crevices that I never before imagined existed.

Chrissy loved sex, food and movies, art, music and drugs, in approximately that order. She loved France and hiking and fucking, in no particular order. Laughter and a kind of heat was draped over everything we did – we shared a love of booze and moderate drug intake, and we sometimes seemed to actually enjoy each other's company. Sometimes we'd make love, lay there for five minutes, then do it all over again. I methodically honed my technique to a high, rich polish. I would find myself licking the ocean salt from Chrissy's neck, from between her breasts, from the small of her back and the soft, quivering sides of her cunt. I fell deeply, hopelessly in love with her cunt, with the cunt itself – the way it looked, smelled and moved, the day to day evolution of its colors and consistency, its curves and ridges...

Chrissy wasn't ashamed of her body and what it did, or of mine. She was fearless and creative – she believed sex was not merely a task, but something that could, and should, be a daily dive into pleasure. She gave out blowjobs in parking lots, in the front and back seats of her cars, in the toilet of a Chinese restaurant, in the backyard beneath the satellite dish. Her hunger for it was jaw-dropping, and she did it like she did everything, with flair and ambition. Because Chrissy needed stimulation, action, *movement* – and when she didn't have it, she would go find it. I knew a fatal flaw was likely wrapped in there somewhere, but the incentive was to ignore it.

I did believe, at one time, there was a chance Chrissy and I could get to know each other both as people and *as individuals*. On some basic level, I understood that this was only additional foolishness, I knew some other boot would inevitably come crashing down, at some point – but maybe, I told myself, *maybe it wouldn't*. At the same time, I was well aware that Chrissy had a strong attraction to fakes and fools, and there is never really any getting off that carousel. I knew she had fucked frightful numbers of guys before I had come on to the scene, and I could never quite elude the fear that I was but another name on the lengthening list. It was understandable, in its way – but a thought like that can positively freeze a man. We didn't belong together, not entirely, that was obvious – but hell, I kept telling myself, who did? Where was the evidence that such a thing even existed? And besides, who really knew – *maybe we did*. Maybe there was a chance. Maybe she was *the one*.

Well, but it didn't seem to matter – we let the subject linger unspoken, we kept things cool and easy, at least at the start. Even if it does come crashing down, I told myself – I'm not going to get hurt. It's a crazy ride, that's all, win or lose – a once in a lifetime ride on the Chrissy Express. I was ready for whatever and whenever, and then some – but I wasn't going to go too far, and I wasn't going to let myself get hurt.

"You're cool," Chrissy would tell me. "You're out there doing stuff. You don't sit in front of the computer all day, like Justin or those guys. I'm so tired of that shit."

"But you know, I actually do sit in front of a computer all day. I talk on the phone, then type something on the computer. Only sometimes I get to leave to go see where someone died."

"That's what I mean! You're out there *doing* something. You see what really goes on."

"Sure, I've seen some nasty stuff..."

"Half the lawyers at my work are on Propac," said Chrissy. "They're afraid. They can't take this place..."

"Maybe it helps. It's a hard world..."

"It's Biagra for the mind. Either you can get it up, or you can't, you know? This guy fucked me for four hours straight once on Biagra.

Later, when I found out, I told him he was a weirdo. We never went out again…"

"I would never use that stuff," I said, licking her ear. "It's the last thing I need."

It hurt tremendously when Chrissy said things like that, it was hard to think of her fucking some other guy for four hours. To think of her with some other guy's cock in her mouth – it was *infuriating*. But it pumped me up, too, it was jealousy with a hopeful kick – because for now, at least, *I was the guy*. Chrissy dug *me*.

I felt powerful, just by being around her. In her presence my swagger gained an extra flourish, it seemed I was suddenly several inches taller, my biceps more swollen with muscle fiber, my eyes slightly more piercing, my hair softer and more luxuriant, my penis just a tiny bit longer and thicker…

We'd spend the afternoon walking around downtown and the Diamond District, holding hands and spending Chrissy's money. Chrissy would be wearing light blue jeans, a pink tank top, spiked white heels, a tan wool beret, a little purse of green neon. We'd walk along the avenues, black guys and truck drivers periodically pausing to woof and stare at Chrissy. Sorry fellas, I would think – and I'd squeeze her hand just a bit tighter, lean over and pepper her ear and neck once more with kisses.

We went to places like Scandal and O.H. Lee, to Mania-Mania and the Pink Shoat. I spent hours dressing and undressing in front of mirrors as Chrissy outfitted me to her liking – a J. Junior buckled leather jacket, several Glans dress shirts, olive green thinwhale cords, a selection of pastel briefs from Pineapple Connection. Other key Chrissy recommendations included a grey and green striped Loopwheeler sweatshirt, a cinnamon Zegna tie, Panerai gloves, maroon Cole Haans, Vilebrequin swimming shorts and two pair of Machine sunglasses. Travel was on our horizon, Chrissy indicated, and so my takings also included a couple nice bags – an Orobianco leather wheely, and a tote from Ichizawa Hanpu.

For her part, Chrissy would treat herself generously to offerings from Parique Lobasas, Sonia Rykiel, Yves St. Laurent, Nicole Farhi and many others. She often sought out my advice, and I helped in the selection of several items, among them a burnt orange linen skirt, a cream short sleeve blouse, wooden-sole sandals, a velvet cord jacket and several pair of pleated trousers.

Exhausted from her purchasing, we'd unwind with afternoon cocktails at the Hot Cha Club, or a cruise across the harbor on the Bay Lady.

Once, in the little park in front of City Hall, we walked over to where a crowd had gathered. It was a dog and a cat – they had been placed together in a basket that had been made into a little bed. The animals sat there as if their brains had been plucked out, blinking from time to time, a red-checked blanket tucked in under their front paws. A handwritten sign on the basket said: "PEACE & LOVE. No War." A grey-bearded fat man wearing boots and a yellow apron was running the show. He had set out a little bucket: "Please Give."

"Oh, that's so cute," said Chrissy. She ran over and threw in $10.

Off to the side, a derelict wearing a greasy overcoat and a set of pink rabbit ears on his head sat on a crate, scratching out a tune in very slow time on a cracked blond guitar.

One day when I was lost
One day when I was lost
They hung him on a cross
They hung him on a cross for me

"Shit," some guy suddenly said, "he's got them on drugs. ... This is *bullshit!*"

The fat man stood from his lawn chair. "Sir, I will not have you slandering me nor my friends –"

A French fry hit the fat man in the cheek. Another flew into his eye. He whirled around, clawing at his face. A third fry became tangled in his beard, triggering whoops of laughter. A half-filled cola can arced through the sky and crashed into the cement, breaking open and spraying the fat man and a few others.

The dog and cat sat there, unfazed. The crowd whistled and whooped.

Chrissy stepped back. A look of anguish had overtaken her face. She appeared very upset.

Dozens of french fries flew through the air, followed by a chunk of hot dog bun sopping with ketchup, a soda cup full of ice.

Cops stood on the steps of City Hall, chatting and drinking coffee. The guitarist rattled on. The dog and cat sat under the blanket, sometimes blinking.

They whupped him up the hill
They whupped him up the hill
One day when I was lost

They hung him on a cross
He hung his head and died for me

○

We dined at the world-famous Paschal's, sitting out over the water as a pink moon burned, the candles blazed, the bugs glowed and the fish jumped.

"*Je voudrais une douzaine creuses,*" Chrissy told the waiter. We added mucho foie gras *en torchon.*

We were well into our second wine bottle, a Claude Papin Loire Chenin, when Chrissy leaned back, sighed and stretched her arms.

"Look at the moon and stars, Thor. It's all ours."

"Yeah, it is..."

"Everything's going great, don't you think? I really feel it... It feels great with you. It's like we're, you know, somehow, supposed to be together. You know? I thought so, from the first time I ever even heard your name... Something like, clicked inside me. Then I was just looking to find you..."

To the left, the ocean rolled, shimmering under the moon like a carpet of spilled jewels. A spray of stars vibrated in the misty sky.

"Yeah, it feels good, Chrissy. Really nice."

> TEENS CHARGED IN HOMELESS KILLING SPREE
>
> BAY CITY (CNS) – Bay City Police said Wednesday that four teenagers have been charged with homicide and other offenses in connection with the murders of three homeless men and the serious beatings of five others.
>
> Sgt. Alan Jondh said the eight attacks occurred in the period from March to June.
>
> Jondh said suspects Vincente Marzabotto Jr., 17, and Damon Restavek, 16, who lived in the same Santa Costa foster home, were arrested late last month. He said William Doyle, 17, was arrested Tuesday at his home in Santa Costa. The fourth suspect, Michael Jaynes, 17, was arrested Monday.
>
> All four have been charged as adults.

Jondh identified the men who died as a result of the attacks as Harry Williams, Melvin O'Lasky, and Joe Paracas. He said they were all "middle-aged."

Jondh said the victims were known to frequent a squatter's camp beneath Interstate 490.

Jondh said the arrests occurred after police launched a task force aimed at winning the confidence of homeless witnesses. His said the campaign included undercover officers bringing food and clothes to encampments and funding a weekly barbecue.

Around the middle of October, Chrissy forked out $2,500 for tickets and we went to the Feed World Hunger Benefit. She lent me her credit card for the tuxedo rental, and we shared a white limousine with Chrissy's mother, Maxine, and Gerard Tavistock, her boyfriend, for the ride to Wainwright Seagram's Towers.

Maxine was low-lidded and warm, she had a very rosy face. In her heels, she loomed over Gerard, who was about five feet tall and had a puffy red face and a full head of bushy white hair. Double-checking himself in the mirror, Gerard went to some effort to demonstrate that his teal socks in fact matched the cummerbund and lining of his white tux, as well as the tint of the diamond stud in his left ear.

"I don't know if Christina told you," said Gerard as we sat in the back of the limo, "but a few years ago I had the opportunity to go to David Brinkley's funeral."

"No, she didn't say."

"Yes, um, yes," Chrissy's mother said. "Umm, umm, umm..."

"As you know," said Gerard. "David Brinkley was on NBC for many years... I remember watching him from the time I was a teenager. A great newsman, a real legend. Thor, you know who he is, right? Gosh, he was a real newshound, always chasing the big story..."

"Sure, Gerard..."

"Peter Jennings was there at the funeral, of course... and Tom Brokaw, Henry Kissinger, the Bush family, the Clintons, Jacques Chirac and Margaret Thatcher, Nancy and Michael Reagan. I even had a chance to speak to Dan Rather for a few minutes. He had just bought an antique wine cabinet. He was quite proud of it. He's also quite a horse-lover. He quizzed me on some of the things we do at the track. He was quite the avid questioner."

"Hm, yes, hmm, hmmm..." said Maxine.

"Did you know him?" I said.

"Who?"

"Brinkley."

"Well, not exactly, but it felt like I did... I mean, gosh, you see a man on TV like that, year after year... I know people who knew him."

"Hemm, herm, hmmm..." said Maxine.

"You know, Thor," Gerard continued, "there's real money in television. To be frank, I don't see much of a future in what you're doing – the written word. People want to see pictures these days. They don't care much about what it shows, they just want to watch something entertaining, it could be anything, really... Maxine has told me that the scholars believe the world is returning to a visual culture, for better or worse. People just don't want to read anymore... And I'll tell you one thing: The TV screens just keep getting bigger and bigger."

"It's not *about* money," said Chrissy. "Thor's a real reporter. They pay him nothing for doing something that everyone depends on. You wouldn't see it on TV without Thor doing it first."

Maxine batted her eyelids and stared forward, but not quite at us. "Yes, umm-umm," she said. "Yes umm, ummm, ummm..."

"Say, Thor?" said Gerard. "Would you be interested in an assistant producer's job for a new show they're starting up at the race track? It's for cable – *At the Races*, they want to call it. I do believe they're hiring as we speak. It'll be for a special horse racing channel. I could make sure they see your resumé. I don't know what you make for salary, but I'm sure this would offer more. And it would get your foot into the TV business."

"Umm, umm, yes," said Maxine, her eyes glittering. "Uh-umm, umm..."

"But I don't know anything about TV," I said.

Chrissy took hold of my hand and passed me the Mickey Rourke.[*] I cupped it in my hand and swallowed it down with the complimentary Krug Grande Reserve.

"What's that got to do with it?" said Gerard. "That's how I learned the condiments business. You get in there and you learn fast! Here's a story. I bet you didn't know that most people, the great majority, like their mustard just one color. But the trick is, when you add a second color, your so-called spice, then you have your light and your dark

---

[*] Methylenedioxymethamphetamine that Chrissy had obtained from Hugh. – ED.

colors in one mustard. So then you make up a fancy name, put on new label, you can charge more. People will pay more just for that extra color..."

"Yes, yes, umm-umm, yummm..." said Maxine.

"Chrissy," I whispered, "is your mom O.K.?"

"She's got Parkinson's, if that's what you mean."

"Gambling is the future," said Gerard, "mark my words. That is a demand that won't be going away."

We pulled into the roundabout, blue, orange and yellow fountains erupting from the center of the world-famous stone and crystal garden. The driver popped the doors. As we started to exit, a little white rat scuttled up. Several cameras veered in, bulbs flashed. I saw the flushed, rat-fanged mug of Dickie Dunn from *Entertainment Pronto!*

"Well, *hello*..." he said expectantly. Then his face abruptly saddened. "Oh, you're... you're not, I'm sorry, I mean, I'm..." He struggled, waving a microphone, "I'm sorry, I'm just looking for Brooke Shields!" He groaned. "She said she'd be here at 7:05!"

Dickie and his camera clowns rushed back round the roundabout as a cherry red Hummer limo pulled in and Rob Reiner, Naomi Watts, Kris Kristofferson and Whoopi Goldberg started to get out.

I tucked Chrissy under my right arm and we hit the red carpet, fighting a brief skirmish with Brigitte Vanboch from *EEE! Entertainment Television*, Ned Buntline from *Page Five* and a battalion of other clowns who had set up a mini-ambush near the high-security cordon. We next had to clear a line of armed men dressed in grey jackets and black pants before being allowed to enter the chandeliered splendor that was the Wainwright Seagram's. I flashed immediately on Meg Ryan and Billy Baldwin, Elizabeth Shue, Monica Bellucci, Ruth Buzzi, Lee Sin-Je, Arthur Miller, Kewi Nochschilds, Ghavni Gilbert, Mitt Romney, Luke Ford and Joaquin Phoenix. Uma Thurman sashayed across the parquet and threw me a crazy look.

We went over to a small table where a beautiful blond woman in a sparkling silver dress was handing out champagne. She checked our tickets and, looking each of us in the eye, said, "You've just saved 107.5 lives. The people of the sub-Saharan thank you."

I downed my champagne and headed for another, while Chrissy stopped to write out a $500 check at a booth sponsored by the Society of Threatened People (STP), and another at STOP AFRICA AIDS NOW (SAAN). I returned to find her talking to an eyeglasses-wearing Val Kilmer.

I didn't feel like getting involved – what the hell do you say to somebody like Val Kilmer?

I changed my trajectory and took another swing around the room, sighting Dennis Leary, Michelle Williams, Nawal al-Saadawi, Dakota Fanning, Shilpa Shetty, Larry Gund, Anna Paquin, Cindy Sheehan, Roger Federer, Marilyn McCoo, Denver Pyle and Ruby LaRocca along the way. By the time I made my way back, the star of *Batman Forever* had finally stopped messing with my girl.

"What'd Val say?"

"He asked how you were doing. He was surprised you didn't come over."

"He did?"

Chrissy laughed. She looked fantastically gorgeous, luminous even, in her Manolo Blahnik high heels, strapless Prada dress and goldfire Hermes scarf. She laughed again, snatched the champagne from my hand and drank half.

In the main ballroom, Gwen Stefani and Robbie Williams had started to perform a duet to the accompaniment of DJ Sloppy. Multi-colored lights flashed around, while on the screen behind the stage was projected a solitary apple tree, pristine against a field of amber and spotless blue sky. To the left was a constantly increasing counter and the words: DIED SO FAR TODAY. The number was well above 22,000.

I don't mind stealing bread
From the mouths of decadents
But I can't feed on the powerless
When my cup's already overfilled

Gwen was dressed in a yellow hardhat and pink cat suit, white boots up to mid-thigh, while Robbie had gone with a short mohawk, green halter top and Scottish kilt combo. The duo belted it out, eyes closed and necks taut, to ensure that no one missed the extreme gravity of the situation.

And they're farming babies
While slaves are working
Blood is on the table and the mouths are choking
But I'm goin' hungry... I'm goin' hungry
Hungry... yeah

As the performance drew to a close, a series of explosions occurred at the top of the winding staircase at the east end of the ballroom. Everyone turned, somewhat alarmed – only to see Danny Glover,

Claudia Schiffer and Emmanuel Lewis taking flight aboard a balsa wood plane that had red, black and green Africa logos on each wing.

The plane, apparently remote-controlled, did a slow loop around the ballroom before descending for a perfect stage landing. Once the applause ended, Danny, Claudia and Emmanuel each gave short speeches about the lack of food in Africa, as well as the severe problem of AIDS on that continent. Annie Lennox and Bob Geldof then appeared on the screen via satellite from London, explaining the "enormity" of the task at hand and the shameful failures that would forever spoil the reputation of our generation.

"We don't die of drought in Nebraska," said Annie Lennox, who began to weep. "They die of drought in Africa. Why? Because... *they're poor*. We need to move from charity to political and economic justice. To finally end the pain of poverty, hunger, disease and conflict, one must focus not on the symptoms of poverty but on its structures..."

Geldof looked as if a muskrat had scratched his face and begun living in his hair. He spun around wearing pajama bottoms and a plaid burgundy coat, pointing his fingers at the camera. "It is a terrible thing to know what is happening, to know what needs to be done – and to *know* that it is not being done. Yet every country pretends that it is doing a lot... Your country is not, my country is not, their country is not... So let me now name the guilty parties – us, you, me, the planet, all assembled here and there. Who do I name? Who do I shame? The shame is ours, the name is the world..."

"We're guilty!" someone shouted, and the room erupted in more applause.

Next, everyone had to stand in a line to draw a lottery ticket to determine where they would be eating. We lucked in to the rice and beans tier – representing the daily diet of 25 percent of humanity – alongside such leading lights as Bastienne Schmidt, Michael Minutoli, Monika von Hardenberg, Gavin Rossdale, Bunnatine Hayes, Teruki Norishita, Dolly Kyle Browning, Katerina Konec, David Spade, Diane Selwyn, David Morse and Mena Suvari. Maxine and Gerard got stuck in the cold rice ball and tiny glass of water zone – representing 70 percent of the world – but their celebrity contingent appeared to include Kevin Dillon, Aneta Langerova, Bodie Miller, Kirsten Dunst, Ryan Seacrest, Jennifer Connelly, Frank Bruno, Luis Guzman, Scatman Crothers, Ray Manzarek and Brittany Murphy. The lucky winners of the shark fin soup, poached veal and sauvignon, truffles and

Dom Perignon sorbet dinner – representing the globe's "golden five percent" – appeared to include Neve Campbell, Zach de La Rocha, Atoosa Rubenstein, Tyler Brule, Jean-Philippe Smet, Shirley Manson, Jeff Koons, Dave LaChapelle, Hildegard Knef, Freddy Rodriguez and John Leguizamo.

The eating accomplished and the coffee consumed, everyone was soon herded back into the ballroom for another presentation. The magnificent-looking pair of Jamie Foxx and Kareena Kapoor came on stage to perform the introduction.

It was an exclusive new film from director Julius Mingir showing doctors going around some place in Africa where the people, for some reason that was never clearly explained, didn't have enough food. The music soared dramatically, the film moved into slow motion. Doctors began shoving some kind of white substance into these small black things who were laying on tables. These things did not have hands and arms, but rather stick-like things that could not move. Also, their skin was coming off.

The film showed a close-up of skin falling away from these bone-type things. Doctors shoved the white substance into the mouths of the things. They had to shove, because the small things were not strong enough to move their mouths.

They shoved and shoved, succeeding in getting just the smallest amount of the white stuff in. It seemed hopeless to think they could chew or digest. The end seemed very near indeed.

> HUNDREDS ATTEND FUNERAL FOR FIREFIGHTER
>
> BAY CITY (CNS) – More than 400 mourners attended the funeral Monday of Paul Andel, a Bay City firefighter who was killed after rescuing a mother and two daughters in a blaze last week.
>
> On-duty Bay City firefighters, firefighters in ceremonial dress from neighboring counties, and friends and family of Andel were among those who gathered at Stanley Simmons Memorial Home to pay their last respects to the 29-year-old Andel.
>
> Scores of firefighters offered their respects to Andel's parents and siblings, his wife, Dana, and their three children.

More than any man, drug or trip to France, Chrissy was devoted to the law firm. She could work 14-hour days as many as two or three times per week, and there were occasions, not infrequently, when she would lock herself away in the study until well past midnight, surrounded by stacks of documents she had carted home in cartons. This generally happened if somebody had "fucked up" the case, or if there was a "deadline" to meet. Only rarely did she ever make court appearances, it seemed, instead plotting things out in dozens of meetings, lunches and phone calls. A great deal of her work appeared to involve phone calls and the holding of "negotiations," followed by strategy sessions and consultations with the interested players, in preparation for the next round of negotiations...

Often – too often, for my tastes – she would be off somewhere getting a "raindrop-technique" massage, or there would be a "dinner meeting" she absolutely could not miss, or she would meet up with a "girlfriend" for a "facial," "pedicure," or other cosmetic work. She also took periodic "business" trips to places like Washington and Baltimore, San Diego and Seattle, San Antonio and Atlanta. These would be harrowing times for me, alone with Andy in a house full of booze, marijuana and other materials.

"Don't die!" I would scream at the dog, who seemed to be growing increasingly hard of hearing, and whose nose was frequently runny.

Some days Chrissy would come home as late as nine, collapse on to the couch, and be out for the rest of the night, too tired even to change out of her clothes. I would hold her head in my lap, petting her hair, the sides of her face, as she dreamt in a sweaty sleep, sometimes trembling and mouthing indecipherable words. I'd get up and feed Andy in the quiet of the midnight, put the dirty dishes in the dishwasher, open a new bottle of Anjou Blanc Sec to drink out by the pool. Eventually I'd grab a blanket and curl up next to her on the long, wide couch.

Over time, of course, certain annoying characteristics began to crop up: Her obsession with teeth-whitening (mine and hers); her tendency to change her eye color from green to blue to amber and back with each visit to the eye doctor; her unquestioning worship of Woody Allen; her obsession with TV shows like *Darryl & Carole*, *Chicago Crime Crew* and *Swifty's Place*. She also developed a tendency to ride my ass, often harshly, for things like not brushing my teeth or cutting my toenails, or for chewing my fingernails and "smelling like a human cigarette."

But "things" will show up with anybody, and this was a small-time list. There was real consolation in returning to find a hungry and horny Chrissy after having, say, spent the afternoon trying to interview the sobbing wife and children of a dead firefighter. I looked forward to settling into her warmth and companionship, craving its refuge and relief. Chrissy made having to suffer through the mess of this world, day after day, almost possible. She could be tender and affectionate – touching and analyzing the minute scars on my face, for example, or the map of burn scars on my arm, offering seemingly genuine and sympathetic remarks in response to my tales of hurt, abandonment and fear. From time to time, she would take special care to wash and iron certain of my work clothes, or would surprise me with a new shirt or other item she had purchased during a shopping break.

In long conversations, she opened up about her past – traumas involving her years of braces and dental retainers, fears that her breasts would never grow, and the very scary crisis that had occurred when her appendix ruptured and she was rushed nearly unconscious to the hospital. She also had a complicated relationship with her father – she remembered idolizing him as a little girl, yet he had been increasingly absent as she grew older, busy with his work and the demands of business success.[*] As she moved into puberty, they had begun to clash regularly, and there apparently were several major screaming matches. Chrissy claimed she had hardly spoken to him since she turned fourteen.

Her father, in fact, had suffered his stroke during her "crazy period" at the end of high school, when she ran away and lived in a car for a few months with a "drug addict" named Denny. It was during this period, she explained, that she first experienced "true love" – and also got the tattoo on her lower back (there had been several other tattoos as well, but she later thought them "uncool" and went through the removal procedure.)

Denny, who was somewhere in his mid-20s, had claimed to be both an "anarchist" and an "environmental radical." When Chrissy's credit card was cancelled and the money ran out, they had taken to eating from trash dumpsters outside supermarkets and junior high schools, and turning in bottles and aluminum cans to get gas and drug money. She had found the experience "romantic" for a while, but eventually

---

[*] Her father also had short-term sexual affairs with three women who were not Chrissy's mother. – ED.

she got tired of pissing in bushes and washing herself in mini-market restrooms. She worried she was starting to "lose respect" for herself. When Denny began to turn to petty crimes to feed the drug urge – stealing mail, as well as certain valuable trees, plants, lawn ornaments and lawnmowers from open garages (which they pawned or sold to specialty shops) – she realized it wasn't so much of a good thing and returned home.

Her father had already been three weeks in the hospital when she came back home. She continued to "feel guilty" about it, but it was complicated. On the one hand, she wondered if her running away had somehow contributed to the stroke. On the other hand, life had become easier, even "better," with her father knocked out of action. He was there, but not there, you know? She knew it was "wrong" to feel that way, it hurt her to even think it, but – well, she had to be honest, it could not be denied.

Denny was found dead in the year after she left for college.

✪

We went to a yoga convention at the Beau Montaigne, hit tennis balls for an hour on the court on top of the Hilton. We sipped oolong tea with tapioca black pearls at Kanopos, went to the charcuterie bar at the Roth & Anthony Steak House, drank late with friends and acquaintances of Chrissy at Arbus. We dined on sphihas with soujouk, zaatar and akawi at Ali Amiri's Bake Shop.

I grew accustomed to the smell of garlic and wine on Chrissy's breath, of hot chocolate and crème brulee on her lips. We'd lay together sweaty in the moonlight, hands entwined, my semen drying on Chrissy's stomach and legs. We stayed out late and got up early. We took our morning ibuprofen and paracetamol and headed into the office. We popped Prialts and felt no pain.

"Here, take some acid, you silly man," she said once, before driving us out to the Ortega County Savannah, where we rode an elephant's hairy back as the sun plunged past the hills in slow-motion and sank into the sea.

Chrissy was the definition of *juicy* – for a time, a long time, I nearly believed I would never need another pussy. I was ready to curl up and die in hers. Fucking well was important, of course, but "showmanship" in bed was overrated. Women didn't want a bunch of flips and twists, the half-formed sex-tricks and "ideas" that popped into the average male's mind – it was just so much distraction.

What women wanted was genuine *feeling*. They wanted hugs. They wanted a few things, done with intensity and a modicum of control. They wanted a steady hand – someone who knew when to go hard, and who knew when too hard was too much. They wanted you to touch their thing, and they wanted to touch yours, but above all, they wanted a *soul* to cavort with. The best thing the male could do was lay back and let the female do her work. The sad truth was, most males were simply not up to it.

Chrissy ordered it over the internet, and a few weeks later a guy brought it in a van. It took me three and a half hours to unpack the boxes, stake it to the lawn and finally use a pump to blow it up next to the pool – a 14-foot wide, 8-foot tall inflatable movie screen. Chrissy microwaved the popcorn and brought out the blankets. We flipped on the Jacuzzi, turned up the volume, got naked and watched. It did look wild, spectacular even – the movie image hovering over the pool, airliners angling through the sundown, the snowcapped mountains disappearing in the dusk. We went out there whenever we could. During the first week alone, we made it halfway through *The Color of Money*, *The Pianist*, *I Am Trying To Break Your Heart*, *Blind Horizon*, *The Incredibles* and *Jacob's Ladder*. We didn't miss much.

I would lean down and lap at her pussy, while she jacked me off from the side. Gradually, she'd slide over underneath me, sucking my testicles into her mouth, rolling them from side to side with her tongue. She'd release, let the ball sac rise, pull it down again. She'd let them rise, yank them down. She worked delicately, unrushed, unworried. Her intelligence was highly evolved.

My pelvis would burn as she slammed against me, straining for the final trigger that would deliver her fragmentary slice of paradise. I would slide in and out, slowly letting the tip of my penis nearly exit before crashing it back in. The heat and slipperiness factor would magnify, the tempo would accelerate until I could not be sure where I was anymore. It was like skating on air.

Chrissy's breath caught. My penis swelled just a bit more. She moaned. It seemed to take forever. I took it out and gushed on to her stomach in a series of spurts.

✪

COALITION PROVISIONAL HEADQUARTERS, PRESS ROOM
BRIEFING BY BRIGADIER GENERAL CHIP R. DEMMITT
PARTIAL VERBATIM TRANSCRIPT

CLOWN: Hello, good day, I hope you all are well. We'll start today with an update on the Progress of Operation: Permanent Peace, Security, Justice & Freedom over the last 36 hours, ending 1300 GMT. In the Capital Sector, a terrorist gunman in a Mercedes opened fire on a police checkpoint and killed two U.S. Marines. Marines responded in self-defense and killed the gunman and four other occupants of the vehicle. Two roadside bombs exploded next to a van and a Volvo in separate areas of the Capital Sector, killing an unknown number of local civilians. A mosque in the east of the Capital Sector was blown up by suspected pre-planted explosive charges, killing an unknown number of worshippers. In the west of the Capital Sector, U.S. troops and their local allies killed 13 terrorists and arrested a total of five on charges of attempted murder. Elsewhere, terrorists attacked and killed two contractors from a Western Country who were driving a gravel truck en route to Camp Yellowtail. Six local civilians and two U.S. soldiers were killed in the apparent collision of a U.S. military vehicle and a civilian vehicle outside the Camp Cherokee Air Base Facility. A sniper killed a member of the U.S. Military Police. And finally, terrorists assassinated a dentist outside a hospital in the north of the Capital Sector. In the Western Sector, a U.S. civilian vehicle hit a landmine, killing three occupants and wounding two others. Five U.S. personnel were injured in three roadside bombings and a rocket attack near Camp Beaver. Terrorists used a remote control device to detonate a car bomb in a marketplace near an airport, wounding three U.S. soldiers and killing an unknown number of local police and civilians.

In the Southern Sector, an unidentified headless body was found in a river. A Bulgarian, two Comorese, three Latvians and a Salvadoran, all members of the U.S.-led Coalition, were killed in a mortar attack near Camp Kemosabe. Unknown gunmen shot dead the head of the local University Teachers' Association. A U.S. State Department employee, two members of nongovernmental organizations and two translators were killed when an improvised explosive device detonated beneath their car. In the Northern Sector, more than 20 unidentified bodies of suspected local residents were found bearing signs of severe torture, including acid-related burns, missing patches of skin, missing eyes and teeth, as well as wounds suspected of being caused by electrical power drills or nail guns. Elsewhere in the Northern Sector, a total of 17 roadside bomb explosions targeted U.S. vehicles, resulting in the deaths of six U.S. Marines and injuries to 13 others. A local police chief was abducted by unknown gunmen. And finally, a terrorist suicide attacker blew himself up inside a local police headquarters, killing three local police and a four-year-old girl and wounding 21 other people. In the Eastern Sector, U.S. Military Police killed 14 detainees during a disturbance at the Camp Junipero Prison Facility. Stability at the facility was restored a short time later. Four roadside bomb explosions targeted U.S. vehicles, leaving two American soldiers dead and 12 injured. Mortar rounds hit an electricity power unit in the west of the Eastern Sector, killing two local people and wounding three. And finally, U.S. troops and their local police allies raided 18 terrorist strongholds, killing a total of 32 terrorists and arresting 57 others. Three U.S. forces and nine local police were injured in those operations.

CLOWN: Sir –

CLOWN: The message, I think, is clear: It shows the extent to which things are getting better here. The terrorists and anti-Coalition forces are creating so much violence because, clearly, they are on the run. Democracy is gaining a foothold in this land, and our vastly superior fighting forces are systematically eliminating the ability of the terrorists to operate, and so they are lashing out in increasingly desperate death throes. In other words, the better things get for the pro-Democratic Coalition - and I think you'll agree, they are steadily improving - the worse they will get, in terms of general violence, until the terrorists and their allies realize they cannot defeat the United States Military and our local allies. And that inescapable realization is, we believe, not too far way.

CLOWN: Sir, Brigadier General Demmitt - we've heard something about a bombing of a wedding party overnight in the Northern Sector. You didn't specifically mention it in the summary. There have been reports of some 45 people killed at this wedding party. What can you tell us?

CLOWN: We are checking that report. There is no evidence of a wedding, according to the United States Military's information. There may - I repeat, may - have been some kind of celebration that occurred. But it could have been the terrorist enemy - enemies, if I may remind you, sometimes have celebrations, too.

CLOWN: Sir -

CLOWN: To recap: We have sealed certain problematic zones in the Northwest Sector with sand berms and barbed wire. At the entry points, everyone who wants to come in will be searched, photographed, fingerprinted and have iris scans taken, and they will then be issued official identification cards, which must be worn in plain sight at all times, at risk of being fired upon.

No private automobiles or cellular telephones are allowed. All males above the age of 14 are being reorganized into Work Brigades to rebuild what has been destroyed in the fighting between the terrorists and Coalition Forces.

CLOWN: Sir, the oil -

CLOWN: American troops were detailed to secure the oil facilities, and those facilities and their records are secure. Guards are standing by, and the Oil Ministry location remains secure. I will remind you of President Mnung's statement of last June - that this conflict is not about securing the valuable strategic asset of oil. As the President's statement said: "This is not about oil. Repeat: Not about oil. Never has been. Oil: Not about." I will reiterate that the massive oil reserves of this nation, amounting to nearly one-fourth of the world's total, is to be held in an escrow account for the local populace, until such a time as they can raise proper security and administrative forces to administer that oil on foreign markets for the benefit of the local people, with the investment of capable foreign partners in production-sharing agreements extending over the next 30 or more years. I repeat: The oil wealth of this nation belongs to the local people, no one else.

CLOWN: Sir -

CLOWN: I repeat: America will not be run out of here by a bunch of thugs and killers and terrorists. Second, we will complete the mission. It is important to remember that the vast majority of those who are doing the dying are the terrorists. You will often hear a terrorist saying they want to die for their god. We are more than happy to oblige. In fact, let's go to some pictures of terrorists right now. Lt. Conrad, if you can dim the lights and throw up those slides…

(LARGE PICTURES OF TWO SWARTHY, BEARDED MEN APPEAR ON THE SCREEN)

CLOWN: These two are some of the most vicious terrorist insurgent killer leaders out there. They are out there killing innocent women and children on a daily basis, as we speak. Our forces have recently acquired, through battlefield operations, several DVD-ROMs in which these men state their intention to destroy America, destroy Coalition forces, foment civil war and prevent democracy from gaining root. Get a good look… These are some of the faces of the enemy. They will be defeated. We are working to capture or kill them and their allies… After the presentation, you can pick up copies of these slides from Lieutenant Conrad for use in your newspapers and television broadcasts. O.K., you can get the lights now, Lieutenant Conrad.

CLOWN: Brigadier General Demmitt, there's a report that some U.S. troops have been bringing back to base fragments of the skulls of those they have killed, to prove that the job has been accomplished. Can you -

CLOWN: I have no information.

CLOWN: There's a tape of U.S. Army soldiers laughing after they shot a pregnant woman.

CLOWN: No information.

CLOWN: Sir, what can you say to the children? How long before things get back to normal and they can get their schools rebuilt and return to class?

CLOWN: I would tell them first: Be patient. What we would tell the kids is, when they hear explosions and helicopters, the planes zooming overhead, what they hear is the sound of freedom - the chimes of freedom, if you will. If you study history at all, one of the first things that jumps out at you is that it takes blood and iron to build a free nation. History is a slaughterhouse - look at our own country, the

U.S.A. There was the Civil War, the Revolution, various struggles and internecine conflicts up to the present day - and there is a cost, no doubt about that, you must employ assets and critical enablers, men and materiel, to get the job done, and that's what we are - and them - what they are doing in their own country, with our support… That's what I would tell these young children.

    CLOWN: Sir, critical enablers… ?
    CLOWN: Bombs. Any further questions?
    CLOWNS:
    DEMMITT: O.K., I want to conclude then with two bits of rather good news, actually. First of all, the Department of Defense proudly announces that 31 young men from Latin American nations who were killed in combat while serving with American Forces in Operation: Justice, Peace, Liberty & Freedom have been posthumously granted U.S. citizenship. This was passed along to us this morning by the Department of Homeland Security. Eighteen of these young men were from Mexico, four from Nicaragua, three from the Dominican Republic, two from Cuba, two from El Salvador, one from Guatemala and one from Peru… Lieutenant Conrad, if you can dim the lights again… Thank you. O.K., a few weeks ago, as you may remember, Coalition Forces carried out air and ground operations against terrorists in the Southeast Sector. In the rubble of one building, U.S. Marines found a survivor - a young boy, who, not knowing his proper name, they called "Danny Boy." There he is, right there on the screen - the brown-skinned one, without arms or legs. Left ear missing… What we determined was that terrorists had overtaken little Danny Boy's home, and all of his known relatives were either killed or fled as U.S.-led forces moved in as part of Operation: Permanent Peace, Liberty, Equality, Democracy & Freedom. We believe he is nine or ten years old. Well, this morning, after weeks of intensive

surgeries and skin grafts, Danny Boy was evacuated aboard a U.S. Air Force C-130 to undergo further treatment in the U.S.A., at the Baltimore Clinic, courtesy of the U.S. taxpayer… There he is right there, being wheeled up into the aircraft, wearing a complimentary official U.S. Marine Corps baseball hat. Resting there on his chest, you'll notice, is a picture of President Wolfgang G. Mnung in a vintage Cleveland Spiders baseball uniform, signed and with best wishes from the president himself…

UNGLUED: Paranoia Peaks as Clown Lives Lush Life!

★ 21 ★

Chrissy bought the tickets and we flew out to New York for a Passover party with some of her closest friends from college and law school.

Chrissy was excited, it had been years since she had seen some of these people. I didn't understand much of the singing or the Jewish routine, but there was no pressure, no one seemed to take it too seriously, and the friends, while mostly dull, seemed to like having me around.

I was fed a steady diet of beer, mixed drinks and little food items that all rather tasted like onion dip. I had well more than the required four cups of wine and crunchy crackers, and when I'd had enough of the chatter, I was able to walk out to the terrace for smokes, standing at the rail over Fifth Ave. – Central Park obscured by trees and shadows to the right, the lights of Carnegie Hall and related environs down a ways to the left.

Chrissy did some bragging about me, about my job, about what a great reporter I was. I fielded a few of the standard questions, preened under the track lighting, made myself seem extra good and interesting. Most of the friends had never met a real reporter, had only read about them or seen them on television. In response, the friends threw names at me – law firms and commercial editing studios, financial services outfits, antiques and art galleries, "internet dating services" they claimed to have launched, so on. It was hard to raise much interest, it was hard to do much except go *oooh oooh*, and move on to the next thing.

One intense fellow with a mop of floppy black hair cornered me for some minutes and insisted I read a book called *Ape and Essence*, which was apparently written by one of the Huxleys. I said I would try to find it (never did do that). The fellow went on to say a few other interesting things, for example how the government and corporations, despite all the claims of the public relations blitzes, were actually creating a world that would, before too long, be fit "only for pigeons."

"It'll be hot and watery, nothing but sand and wind everywhere. The pigeons will pick our bones out of the sand..."

It seemed logical, and I appreciated his concern.

"I'll tell you what the *real crime* is," he went on. "They can call you an unlawful enemy combatant and throw you in prison, secretly and without trial, even though you're an American and never even left this country or fought anybody. They can just *call* you it, and their reason can stay *secret*. They don't have to give a reason. That's the *real crime*..."

"You're jobbing me..."

"No, it's real. Everything's legal now, and if it's not, they just say it is. They could spy on you or arrest you just because some cop or bureaucrat *feels* like it. That's the law: No reason needed. They could put you in jail and execute you and no one would ever have to know. It could stay *secret*. They could hire private companies to do it. They've got all the e-mails you've ever sent stored some place. All the internet pages you ever looked at. They could dig 'em up and use 'em against if they don't like you. It's all legal now. Just because they don't *like* you..."

"Well, you heard what Mnung said," I said. "If the terrorists are calling, Uncle Sam wants to know."

He shook his head in agitation.

"They don't care *who's* calling. They just want to know. They just want to be able to dump you in prison if they don't *like* you..."

"Well... so what's to be done?"

He shrugged, looked off. Maybe he didn't have an answer, or was afraid of saying. In any case, he soon dropped the subject, regressing instead into banalities about the "styles" of various movie directors and how he had made a "killing" editing a commercial for United Airlines, and what "dolts" their executives had been.

I moved around, making sure to maintain a steady flow of booze, trying to dodge all the *New Yorking* that was going on – the New York Zoo this, the New York mayor that, groovy things in New York and New York friends, aren't they great... Several times I found myself laughing loudly at things that were not funny, or saying cute things to babies I had no interest in, and petting several small dogs, but, well – I wanted Chrissy to feel I was enjoying it. To an extent, I was.

Overall, though, I hadn't been persuaded of much – I was still pretty sure that if you could make it New York, you had mainly proven you could toe the line and jump through hoops with the finest of suck-ups and cattle anywhere.

Pretty soon, it was already after midnight and people were clearing out. I wandered through the kitchen, dumping the dregs from several bottles into a large glass, then went out for another quick smoke. Over the railing I saw a few late-night New Yorkers walking in an orderly fashion down the boulevard. Taxis and cars scrolled by calmly, one after the other, endlessly.

What a great town. Manhattan was tame, tame.

I finished the tall glass during the 30 minutes Chrissy took to say her goodbyes, and we finally got out of there. By now it was nearly 3 a.m. During the taxi ride back to the hotel, Chrissy clued me in on what was really going on with the friends – for example, that Cynthia the cellist, who was married to David the derivatives man, was screwing Nathan on the side. That Darlene used to go out with Steven until she married Andrew the arthroscopic surgeon, who was now playing around with Ariane, who was married to Jeffrey, who couldn't make it to the party because he was volunteering as a medic in Darfur... That her friend Stella, who had got deeply into so-and-so guru, used to be married to Teddy, before she hooked up with Michael, who used to go out with Myrna, who had just moved to Atlanta with her new boyfriend, Timothy, who had gone out with Callista for six years before Callista ran off with a married mechanic. And a few others, more dry. Well, I thought, if they enjoyed it...

She asked what I thought about Allen and Daniel. I said I had felt nothing in particular about them. In fact, I couldn't really remember them, there had been so many names and faces. She explained that they were her ex-boyfriends, or lovers, or whatever they had been. She had felt that somehow I would find this information "interesting."

I knew something like that was coming. Well, so it had come – and now it was over. I was sure there were a couple of heavy stories she would have liked to have told about these fellows, but I didn't delve deeper. I didn't feel like feigning interest, and I didn't feel like getting angry. Such tales never really helped anything, they just played into the hands of jealousy and nostalgia. I got Chrissy into the hotel room and fucked her fairly well, I thought. Not a bad day, really. We were asleep minutes later.

We had 10 a.m. coffee in bed, then another fuck session, this one longer. We dressed and took a taxi a few blocks to Hiroshima. This was a place where you took off your shoes and got into a bed and they served you food as you lay there. We ordered plates of sashimi and crudo, ceviche and Carpaccio, sake-marinated black cod with shrimp dumplings. I wasn't sure, it all rather tasted like onions and charbroiled steak. There were 20 or 30 beds in the place, most filled with saggy New York people I didn't feel much like seeing in bed. The entertainment consisted of a grown man and woman, both wearing cloth diapers and baby clothes. They crawled on the floor and pulled themselves up and down ropes, sucking on pacifiers. Every so often they would crawl over and serve the customers wine from these giant glass baby bottles.

Between bites, we took glances at a copy of *The New York Times* – PRESIDENT LISTENS TO VAN MORRISON, TOM PETTY ON iPOD read a front page headline. It seemed hard to believe. In the Arts & Life section, the editors had decided a nearly full page spread was needed to explore the phenomenon of NATION'S TELL-ALL SOCIAL NETWORKERS CRAFTING NEW NOTIONS OF PRIVACY?

As a piano player nibbled and licked at his keys in the corner, I had a look at *The New York Post*, which had always seemed a bit more honest about its dishonesty. THUG RAPES BLIND GIRL IN SUBWAY read the front page spread. The heartless thug had stuck a sharp object against her neck, pulled down her panties and assaulted the 19-year-old inside a darkened elevator at a Brooklyn subway station. Inside, on page 4, I found: DUPED JOHN KILLS AFTER 'PROSTITUTE' REVEALED AS MAN. A column on the *Post*'s opinion page had the headline: LIBERAL UNGRATES ATTACK MNUNG FOR PROTECTING OUR COUNTRY.

Well, who needed this crap anymore. I threw the paper by the side of the bed and kissed Chrissy. She laughed. The female baby finally brought our bottle of ice cold champagne. I drank three glasses in rapid succession, and a feeling of slight numbness came over my face.

Next it was time for a walk down Madison Avenue. We zipped in and out of probably 10 or more shops, Chrissy seemed almost in a rush to spend money. My takings included a $139 V-neck Smedley merino, a set of silk Incotex boxers ($64.99), and a limited-edition Cliffs & Fire eau de toilette, moisturizer and shaving set ($73). For herself, Chrissy collected a $300 pair of Ludwig Reiter desert boots, a purse made entirely out of intricately folded Japanese candy wrappers ($124), a dark violet and pink babydoll catsuit ($89.95), and a Piombo flower-patterned pastel travel bag, into which we shoved all the other items. Chrissy also picked out $850 worth of sheets and pillow covers, for which she paid another $110 to have shipped home. We hit Chelsea for a final round of cocktails in the greenhouse at Pasolini, then caught a taxi back to the airport.

"This was so much fun!" Chrissy said, throwing her arms around my neck.

I picked her up and carried both her and our bags about 20 yards to our seat in the airport lounge. We had more champagne during the flight and arrived back in Bay City, less than 30 hours after we had left.

> 'INTERSEX' FISH FOUND OFF CALIFORNIA COAST
>
> MINNEAPOLIS (Smith-Jones) – Scientists say they have discovered sexually-altered fish off the California coast, raising concerns that pollutants and sewage released into the ocean could be affecting animals' reproductive systems.
>
> The scientists, in a paper presented at the annual U.S. Collegiums of Environment and Toxicology conference in Minneapolis, said they had found that 14 male sole and turbot caught off Los Angeles and Orange counties possessed ovarian tissues in their testes.

Two or three days later, Chrissy came home pink-faced and flustered.

"When I came out of the store, this guy had his door open and was jacking himself off."

"What?"

My blood whooshed. I felt a sudden leaping fear. I rushed forward and hugged her.

"Yeah... He sat looking at me and doing it the whole time I was putting the bags in."

"God, that's sick... I hate that shit."

"That's not even the worst part. He followed me when I drove out."

"What?"

"Yeah, he *followed* me... I started speeding and lost him on the freeway."

"Did you get his plate numbers?"

"Are you kidding? I didn't have time to write anything down."

"Aw, Chris! He probably copied *your* plates. He's probably looking up where we live right now. Shit! He's probably a serial killer. Did you call the police? Come on, we should call the police. Let's be smart about this."

"Thor," said Chrissy, *"relax."*

"Relax? How can I relax where there's some serial killer guy following you? What if he comes over here? What if he goes and kills somebody, molests some kid? A guy like that shouldn't be on the streets. We gotta call the cops." I ran to the window and looked at the wall. "What did he look like? What kind of car?"

"Not until you calm down!" she said. "You're way too paranoid…"

"Paranoid? There's bad stuff out there, Chris, I'm not makin' it up…"

"I still think you're paranoid…"

I did finally calm down, after two beers, but the incident still left me feeling not quite right. We ended up going out to Tamarind, which was known for its fire jugglers, dancers and musicians. We crawled into the tent and shared bountiful platters of king prawns marinated in ginger, paprika and dried cherry, lamb with creamed black lentils, tandoor-smoked aubergine pulp and braised saffron rice. Dessert was a milk dumpling with pistachio glaze. There was much laughter and giggling, they had pulled some nice tricks with the food, and eventually I felt nearly fully relaxed. Back at the house, Chrissy slipped into a lavender silk nightie, leaving off the bottoms. I popped a bottle of Healdsburg merlot, poured two and brought them out. Well, all right, I thought. I inhaled deeply. It seemed the night was heading toward another blissful conclusion.

Unfortunately, Chrissy had recently bought a new French film, *Hell is My Body and Other Peoples'*, and she insisted on playing it. It was rare that these movies ever worked out well, and I felt both claustrophobia and disappointment starting to cascade over me as she slipped the DVD into the player and we cuddled up under a blanket on the couch.

Almost predictably, the movie's opening scene featured some guy sucking off another guy outside a sports stadium. Next, a bunch of gay types are seen dancing and kissing in a club. The main star, a 45-year-old Arab woman, looks bored. She immediately goes into a bathroom and slices her wrist with a razor blade. One of the gay guys comes in to comfort her. They go to a doctor, and as she's leaving the office, she looks into a mirror and "sees" herself slashing open her neck and the blood gushing out. Outside, the gay guy, who looks not a little like a monkey, savagely slaps her face. The lady then proceeds to suck him off under a tree. A drop of semen is seen falling poignantly from her lip.

"Chrissy, what *is* this?" I said, massaging her knees and thighs.

"Shhhh…"

The next night, the gay guy takes a taxi to the lady's house. The first thing she does is go into the bathroom to take a dump. She then gets undressed, an icon of Christ hanging on the cross on the wall behind her. She gives a speech about how men are always trying to lock up and control women, something along these lines. She shows off scars on her back. She shows off her unshaven underarms. The gay guy is horribly unshaven himself, looks hungover.

There is then a flashback sequence in which a boy takes a baby bird from a nest and puts it in his pocket. The bird suffocates and dies, and the boy steps on it. Back at the house, the woman fingers her pussy, while the gay pours himself a whisky. He walks over and takes a close look at her cunt.

At that point there is another flashback, in which some boys make a little girl take off her underwear. She crawls under a bush and the boys look at her pussy while laughing. Back at the house, the guy touches the woman's pussy and gets some clear stuff on his finger. The woman laughs. The gay walks out and smokes a soulful cigarette while staring at the ocean waves. He walks back in to find that the woman has passed out naked. He uses a red lipstick to make a circle around her asshole, then puts the lipstick on her mouth. Suddenly he is naked. He appears to sodomize her. When he is finished, he starts weeping, snot dripping out of his nose.

"Chrissy, *come on*," I said.

"Oh, just watch it!"

Next thing, the woman is seen smoking while sitting on the toilet in a short black dress. The doorbell rings. It is the gay guy again, wearing the same cream-colored suit as the last time. She gets naked again, takes off her red slippers and lays on the bed. He drinks whisky, then falls asleep next to her asshole. He wakes up and stares at the asshole. The film cuts to the icon of Christ on the cross. The gay sticks his fingers in her pussy and finds that she is menstruating. He walks outside, gets a pitchfork from the barn, and sticks the handle end of the pitchfork into her vagina. He leaves the pitchfork sticking out. The woman wakes up and looks at it. The film shows crashing waves at dawn.

The next night, the gay pulls out her bloody tampon and holds it up in the light like a Christmas ornament. He looks very, very unshaven and hungover. The lady puts the tampon in a glass of water, swishes it around, and gives it to him. He drinks the bloody water. Then she drinks some. The blood color seems wrong, too bright, like fruit punch. In any case, the woman drains the glass. The next night, the gay is again looking at her pussy and an avocado slides out. He slides it back in and she appears to have an orgasm. He then appears to sodomize her. He pulls out his bloody dick and there is blood all over the bed. She stands there with blood dripping down.

The gay goes down to a bar, his nose looking very red. A drunk buys him a drink and they talk about pussy. The gay starts crying and leaves a wad of cash. The gay is then seen waking up in an alley. He gets up and goes back to the lady's house. But she is gone, everything is gone, the house is empty except for a bloody sheet on the bed frame. He picks up the sheet and sniffs it.

Then suddenly it is night. The woman is walking backwards through a field, the gay is coming toward her. They get to a fence. He pushes her through. She falls from the cliff on to the beach rocks. Her body lays motionless on the rocks, getting pounded by the surf. He stands on the cliff in the moonlight. The credits roll...

Chrissy was tearful, she had found the movie both "spiritual" and "powerful." She explained it had been a big sensation in France, very famous. I explained, gently as I could, that it had left me with a bitter, stupid feeling. For starters, it had created its own closed system – its own feedback loop, if you will – and there hadn't been enough oxygen to sustain it beyond the tension of its own orthodoxy.

Above all, it had been painful to watch and not entertaining, despite, or possibly because of, all the pussy and cock show. Which was probably one of their points. Therefore, mainly, they had wanted to torture people, that's what they really wanted – to torture people into seeing their point of view, and that was a technique that was always bound to lead to banality and suffocation...

"But there was an honesty there," said Chrissy. "It was... like... a man and a woman, facing each other as real human beings..."

"Yes," I said, "and the ocean was like her vagina engulfing him. But in the end her vagina engulfed her... Because she had only been a thing to men, and had been nothing to herself but her vagina..."

"Oh, don't make fun! That's all you do. You never like anything!"

"That's not true, babe…"

"You're always putting everything down!"

Chrissy grabbed the blanket and stomped off to bed, leaving me there. Andy walked over, rubbed his back against my leg, against the couch, then laid down with a snort.

"Hey there, Andy."

I reached down and scratched him between the ears. He looked up at me, dark little turds around his watery eyes.

> CITY WORKER SUCKED INTO PIPE, DROWNS
>
> BAY CITY (CNS) – The Bay City Fire Dept. said a city worker drowned Thursday after he was sucked more than 200 feet down a drainage pipe at the Bleyer Reservoir basin.
>
> Lt. Jeremy Closkey identified the victim as Erdogan Mejian, 45.
>
> Closkey said that according to other workers, Mejian was standing in between three and four feet of water as he tried to unclog a drain.
>
> After he succeeded in removing the debris, Closkey said, a "powerful vortex" was created, causing Mejian to lose his footing and get sucked into the 22-inch wide drainage pipe.

The Saturday morning sun splashed spectacularly. Chrissy squeezed the tube of Anthelios XL and slapped it across my back and shoulders. I rolled over on the towel and she smeared some across my thighs. She rubbed all around, a smile blooming beneath her sunglasses. She slipped her hand under my shorts and applied some of the suntan grease to my cock and testicles, achieving the desired effect. Then she pulled out – it was my turn, the rest of it would have to wait.

I knew Chrissy was worried about skin cancer, and so it made good sense. I started with her calves and lower thighs, then leaped up to her breasts. I worked in the grease, idly wondering how many others might have grabbed and sucked upon those plentiful, alert orbs. Finally it was time for her back.

I maneuvered her up on her hands and knees and squeezed several blasts on to her shoulders. I slowly massaged my way down, got in maybe a minute's worth on her buttocks before I could resist no longer. I pulled back her mauve lycra bikini bottoms and quickly stuck my tip in, my knees grinding into the stiff green grass. High morning heat bounced into my thighs, sun battered the back of my neck...

Andy walked up and licked Chrissy's face. She laughed and groaned at the same time.

"Andy," I said, "bad boy!" He limped off.

We finished and it wasn't even 11 a.m. yet. I sat back down under the umbrella by the pool, sweating and breathing somewhat heavily. Chrissy came back out with a tray of coffee and tumblers of Metaxa. We sat quietly, looking over the newspapers, sometimes glancing at the television. A story at the bottom of the front page of the *Star-Chron* informed: APRIL IS DEADLIEST MONTH FOR U.S. TROOPS. I flipped to the inside and found three I had written: TWO SECOND-GRADE GIRLS STABBED IN PARK, SNACK SHOP EMPLOYEE SLAIN IN ROBBERY, COLLISION KILLS FIVE. The *Examiner-Mail* had picked up the girls, as well as TWO SHOT DEAD IN PINE RIDGES APARTMENT and ESCAPED PIT BULLS INJURE SIX IN ORTEGA.

Chrissy got up and began spraying with the garden hose, knocking leaves and other debris from the cement on to the grass. Her body was trim and golden, her tits swaying in unison, as she squatted or bent down to fire the water. Andy lumbered around after her, collar jangling, until he stopped to scratch. He got up and lumbered once more, wet pink tongue dangling. Chrissy shut off the water and went in. She came back out with two cosmopolitans, *Space Oddity* booming from the roof-mounted speakers. I gulped down about half of the cosmo and pulled out the Sports section of the *Star-Chron*.

> BASEBALL HERO 'JUG' HACKETT DEAD AT 48
>
> SANTA FE, New Mexico (AIP) – Baseball pitcher Joseph "Jug" Hackett died of a brain tumor Thursday. He was 48 years old and passed away at his home in Santa Fe, New Mexico, his family said.
>
> The lanky right-hander, who won five World Series during a 19-year career with 12 teams in the major leagues, had been diagnosed with the tumor two months ago.

Chrissy was just sitting there.

"What's wrong, babe?"

She took a while to answer. She started several times, stopped, then said, "Thor, are you happy?"

I reached over and stroked her shoulder. "I wouldn't complain if it stayed like this forever. I mean, just like this…"

I gulped down the second half of the cosmo.

"But things always change…"

"Do they? That's ridiculous… Don't say that."

"See, you're not serious… You never say what you really think… I never know who the *real you* is…"

"I'm completely serious…"

Chrissy was quiet a long time. After a few seconds more, I knew she had started crying under her sunglasses.

"Hey babe… babe… everything's great. No crying, huh?"

"Do… do…" she choked out, her face wrenching up, "do you *love* me?"

"Chrissy, come on. What's the, I mean, come on, why –"

"No, I mean it. Do you?"

"I mean… Of course I love you. More than I've ever loved any woman…"

I glanced at the TV. A ticker was rolling at the bottom of the screen: SOLDIER: NO WEAPONS FOUND, BUT WAR STILL WORTH IT.

Chrissy sobbed. "I just want to have a real life. I don't want to turn into some 35-year-old hag going to French Tuesday."

French Tuesday was a dance party-type thing where hard-up French people who were living over here went to try to bang each other, or to bang American people who had fixations on the French. Chrissy had said she liked to go to "practice my French." Plus, "you can really meet some neat people."

She had conned me into going with her once, in the first few weeks of our relationship. I didn't meet any neat people at all. It was pathetic all around, overdressed French people cranking up the coolness factor, bad hair colorings, American loser-type women trying to bag a French guy and escape their hellish existence in the U.S.A. Not much more than that. At the same time, you couldn't feel too good about feeling bad about it. They were trying hard. Some of them were probably bad people, but not all of them. At least French Tuesday gave them some hope, however faint.

I held Chrissy's hand, squeezed it.

"You won't have to, babe… I'm here for you… I'm not going anywhere."

She looked at me, snuffling her nose. She didn't say anything. I moved my chair closer. She laid her head on my shoulder.

I glanced at the TV. The president pulled a hatchet out of his head and got back to chopping lumber. He took a couple swings, not more than three or four, then went and petted some nearby black children. He lifted one of the youngsters on to his shoulders and began reading a book.

Mnung was apparently making his yearly appearance with poor people. With the boy still on his shoulders, the president returned to chopping the timber, wood chips flying, his eyes guarded by goggles. The words SECURING THE AMERICAN DREAM were shown dozens of times on a red screen behind him.

> OREGON TO APOLOGIZE FOR STERILIZATIONS
>
> SALEM, Oregon (AIP) – The state of Oregon plans to officially apologize for the forced sterilization of more than 2,600 people over 60 years, state officials said.
>
> Oregon was one of 33 states that employed eugenic sterilization, a practice that was upheld by the Supreme Court in 1927. Oregon's law was on the books until 1983.
>
> State archives showed that those sterilized included homosexuals and unwed mothers and girls at a state reform school, including some for alleged misbehavior.

LUNA-CRAZY: Love Gets Loopy in Mountain Paradise!

★ 22 ★

Within weeks, the mayor had launched the PERMANENT CRIME AMNESTY FOR THE CITY crackdown.

"Today we initiate this great crusade," Favella announced to the clown throng that had been rustled up to Colosio Park, where three people had been murdered – stabbed, shot, and shot – in the previous four days. The mayor, standing on a stage decked out with balloons and several dozen young children, declared: "I pledge a war without mercy. We must rebalance the system emphatically in favor of the victims of crime. Offenders have gotten away too easily, and the old rules must be swept away. I today vow zero tolerance for violent thugs, panhandlers, illegal street vendors, windshield washermen and shopping cart thieves. The heroic, ordinary people of this great city deserve an amnesty from crime and degradation."

> 22 ARRESTED IN BAY CITY CRIME CRACKDOWN
>
> BAY CITY (CNS) – More than 900 Bay City police officers took part in raids on more than 200 locations Wednesday in what officials described as a "crackdown on gun crime."
>
> Lt. Andrea Childers said at least 22 people were arrested for illegal firearms possession, as well as drugs, theft, and child support-related offenses.
>
> Childers said the initiative, codenamed OPERATION: GUNWAVE, was expected to continue at least until Friday. She urged all persons in possession of

illegal firearms to turn their weapons over to authorities.

On Tuesday, Mayor Ernest J. Favella vowed a "war without mercy" against criminals...

The mayor announced the next week that a "youth curfew" would be enforced during the annual Bay City International Yacht and Catamaran Show. The curfew required that everyone younger than 18 be accompanied by an adult if they went on the streets between 5 p.m. and 5 a.m., starting from the Friday opening of the convention until its end Monday. "We want our guests to be able to enjoy the event without feeling discomforted by swarms of unsupervised teenagers hanging about," the mayor told a press conference on the steps of City Hall. "This international yacht show represents the economic revitalization that our economically-diverse metropolis* badly needs and that my administration has been working vigorously to achieve."

During the subsequent week, Favella saw his "personal approval" poll numbers rise from 24 to 34 percent. With his advisers sensing momentum, the mayor announced the launch of OPERATION: COLD SNAP, aimed at taking the homeless off the streets during "cold weather" to "protect their safety." Civil liberties activists and friends of the homeless declared their outrage and issued several press releases, but the mayor's cause appeared to have been boosted when the police announced that the crackdown on "illegal camping" had resulted in the arrests of more than 670 people on suspicion of "drug crimes."

"Police have taken at least 2,920 homeless people to shelters, hospitals or prisons over the past week under my emergency initiative aimed at removing the homeless from the city's streets during cold weather," the mayor told clowns during a visit to the non-profit Humanity Rising shelter. "It's not against the law to be homeless, but in this kind of cold weather, the rules change. When my health chief tells me it's cold enough to impact the health of a human being, then I am going to take action. If they don't come along, if they insist on staying in the street, we will escort them to a shelter for their own safety. Everyone has a right to safety in this city, especially our homeless fellow citizens. I might add that this program has had the added benefit of removing from the streets hundreds of drug peddlers, gang members and sexual deviants who would threaten our children."

*Means having poor people. – ED.

It hadn't been "cold" at all, but that hardly mattered. The mayor was starting to like the taste, and so were some others. THANK YOU, MAYOR, FOR CRIME CRACKDOWN headlined the lead editorial in the *Examiner-Mail*, while the *Star-Chron* settled at praising the genius of OUR MAYOR McCRIME-STOPPER.

At the end of the month, Favella announced his formal support for police-backed measures to ban private ownership and sales of AK-47 assault rifles and all other automatic or semi-automatic weapons. He also announced that $55 million had been secured, through a combination of federal, state and local funding sources, to install at least 450 Check-All Surveillance Systems on "problem" street corners, buses, subways and public parks. According to the Halford, Connecticut-based manufacturer, the Check-All systems used a series of super-sensitive microphones and cameras to monitor an area of up to 200 yards in any direction. According to the salesmen, the systems were capable of detecting the location of a gunshot, turning a camera in that direction, and automatically making a 911 emergency call so officers could be dispatched. The systems were allegedly so sensitive they could, if programmed properly, recognize and respond to "events" including breaking glass or a backfiring vehicle. Installation of a loudspeaker component could even allow police to "issue warnings and crowd-control orders from miles away."

"They will be used to safeguard the security of the courageous people of this city," the mayor told clowns after a closed meeting with the City Council to discuss the purchase. "There will be no spying or recording the conversations of people engaged in ordinary, lawful behavior. I have been assured by the experts that these microphones can't be used for listening to private conversations, because they haven't been programmed that way. And they won't be, so long as I am mayor. I remain deeply committed to civil liberties and the defense of privacy for all law-abiding citizens. These are tools to assist our law enforcement personnel in the battle against thugs and miscreants who, through their criminal behavior, are using fear to lock people inside their homes and impugn the good reputation of our town. They will also be used in the fight against terrorists who would seek to harm innocent citizens..."

2 POLICE, 3 OTHERS SLAIN IN BAY SHOOTINGS

BAY CITY (CNS) – Two police officers and three other people were shot dead Thursday in three separate incidents as a crime wave continued to plague Bay City.

Lt. Al Nouci said a suspected gang member turned around and shot the two officers during a pursuit in the Pine Ridges section.

He said 250 police were deployed into the area to block roads and conduct a door-to-door search for the suspect. There had been no arrest by early evening.

In the other incidents, police killed two men in a shootout in the Commerce Avenue area, while a 21-year-old man was shot and killed as he sat in a car in the Silvertown section.

GIRL, 4, KILLED IN BAY CITY SHOOTING

BAY CITY (CNS) – Bay City police said a 4-year-old girl was killed and her father was seriously injured when they were shot in a suspected gang-related shooting Tuesday outside their apartment in the Six Points section.

MOTHER KILLED IN SUSPECTED GANG INCIDENT

BAY CITY (CNS) – Bay City police said a mother of five was shot and killed as she walked on the street with two of her children Wednesday in a suspected gang-related incident in the Silvertown section.

Sgt. Dave Chester said investigators are probing whether the murder of Ebonie Willes, 29, was a case of mistaken identity.

I guess we hadn't seen each other for a few days. Chrissy had been out of town for some meeting, and I had returned to Silvertown for the monthly pit-stop. We met up on Saturday. Chrissy seemed happy to see me, and we had driven over to her friend Gretchen's loft. Gretchen worked as a translator of Chinese at the John C. Stennis Military Institute, south of Bay City. Her boyfriend, Erik, had a job "stringing guitars," and also apparently led guitar sing-alongs at a kindergarten.

I didn't mind this pair so much. They were soft, vaguely interesting under certain conditions – though Erik, in my opinion, was always trying too hard to show how clever he could be. He had a cobweb tattoo on his neck, tattoos of flowers and daggers on his fingers, and had grown his sideburns into these gigantic fluffy mutton-chops. His beard, meanwhile, was this goatee-within-a-goatee thing – one strip of hair hanging off the lower lip, a bigger strip hanging from the chin, with stripes of beard going around the mouth. He liked to say things like: "When you cut into the present, the future leaks out. Shouldn't it?" And: "Garlic shakes – that's the future. Really, I've tasted them." Gretchen was not bad, she was actually pretty good, especially if you were able to get her alone, which I was never really able to do. She had wispy light brown hair and was similar to Chrissy in some respects, even a bit taller and more athletic-seeming, though with smaller boobs.

Erik had made "bang" and we all drank some. He explained how he had "worked for four hours" to crush the marijuana leaves and seeds. He had then mixed the stuff with milk and honey and so forth, and it was apparently a thing from India called "bang" and you drank it. He liked to include almonds, he explained, otherwise it could be "too buttery." It was all right – I began to feel a slight wooze during the second cup.

Midway through the third cup, Erik remembered they had to feed the boa constrictor, Courtney. He got up and made a show of dangling a mouse into the tank. At last he dropped it in. The mouse scampered and hid beneath a piece of driftwood.

"You can see his heart beating," Erik said.

We had all gone over to look. It was true.

We left before Courtney performed her natural function, somewhat to Erik's disappointment. Chrissy hadn't wanted to see it, and that was fine by me. We got in the car and went to some place where we ate baby shrimp tempura rolls. I had several beers, several cocktails.

About 8:30, we got back in the cars and drove over to a party in Landpark Shores. Erik knew the people, knew the band. It was going to be "really great." The band, Blacque Mummy, was performing on the lip of a swimming pool, a zombie film projected onto the wall behind them. The water had been drained from the pool, and Christmas tree lights had been hung from the edges. Dozens of people were dancing on the sides of the pool and at the bottom. The band members, wearing lab coats and green hospital outfits with red crosses, writhed and hopped back and forth, crashing out their jungle juju. The singer waggled out his tongue from behind a silver and red mask.

I still felt mostly sober. I waited in a long line for a keg beer, then saw there were several cases of Blue Moose "energy drinks" sitting on a table. I drank six or eight of these cans in rapid succession, adding another a beer and once wandering into the kitchen to pour myself a plastic cup of vodka from a gigantic jug.

I came back to find Chrissy dancing with her arms in the air, bracelets jangling, ass going up and down, left knee pumping to the boom-thump-bang-thump. I went up to wriggle next to her. She was wearing a black choke collar, purple eye shadow, dark pink lipstick, maroon cowboy boots with silver stars. Her eyes seemed unusually radiant, a slightly glowing blue.

The guitarists from Blacque Mummy began French-kissing each other while a Jon Voight film about an attack by a 60-foot snake rolled on the wall. At the climax, one by one, the band members were lined up and executed by the singer, who shot them with a long rifle. The drummer added cymbal smashes after each pop, until it was his turn. On the wall, the monstrous snake pursued frightened numbskulls through oily water.

I put both arms around Chrissy and watched the spectacle. Blood exploded in the light, flying into to the crowd, and after they had each taken their shot, the band members fell on to the party people in the pool bottom.

The singer at last put the gun to his own head. The show was over.

It was time to get out of there. Chrissy drove at high speed through the hills, the new Anastacia album blasting on the BandWagen surround-sound. She rested her right hand on my thigh while I sucked down the last of a Blue Moose-vodka cocktail I had mixed on our way out. Chrissy drove like a pro, whipping the vehicle into the tight turns, tapping the brake then whacking the gas to rocket into the next uphill straightaway. She pulled us into the drive at Princk, jumped out and ran around to the back of the house.

I stumbled after her. She was already half-undressed. By the time I finally jumped into the water, she was scrambling back out and running into the house.

"Hey Chris, wait..."

A few minutes later, I was nuzzling up against her in the bed, her back still damp from the pool. I pushed my hand between her legs.

"No, no, no..." she whispered. "Try that other hole back there..."

"Your butt... ?"

She rolled more on to her stomach, repositioning her hips and widening her legs.

"Yeah..."

There was a bit of resistance, a bit of blind poking about... then I hit an opening. It slid right in with a solid push. I wasn't sure at first, so I used my hand to check. Sure enough, her pussy was empty... I was *in* somewhere.

I stroked away slowly for 10 or 20 seconds, getting more and more excited. In truth, I really couldn't feel much. Then somehow it slipped out. Chrissy groaned. I poked around, trying to get back in. I got in, but to her pussy. I pulled out. She grabbed hold of me, repositioned. I jumped back in and began stroking.

It was different than a pussy – a superb tightness of grip, but seemingly with nothing at the bottom of it.

We started to go at it faster and faster. *I'll pound the bitch!* I thought. The hell, if the lady wanted to get cornholed – I'd give her something she'd never forget!

I lasted two or three more minutes, until about the time she reached around and began playing with my testicles. I kissed her neck, her ears, jammed my tongue in her mouth and erupted inside.

I lay there gasping, my face burning, my head feeling as light as a piece of tissue paper whirling in the breeze. Jesus. Whoever had invented it, it was a remarkable way to love a woman.

Well, I thought, new and important information can arrive at any time. This perfectly proves it. The way I saw the world had changed again... In a way, I was seeing things for the first time.

"I wasn't sure you'd be into it," she said as we lay there in the morning.

"Sure, I'm good for it... It felt darn good, Chris. I never imagined it would."

"It was your first time?"

"Yeah... I always thought, you know, there'd be a lot of trouble and mess, creams and sauces, lotions and so forth. It seemed like a question best left to the gay guys..."

"Some people need that, but it's really just a question of the muscles being relaxed..."

"I guess so..."

Chrissy laughed. "My friend Angie has this saying: 'The way to a man's heart is through your anus.' I think it's mostly true..."

"Sure, that's got a real ring."

CHURCH, CIVIC LEADERS CALL FOR WEEKEND PEACE

BAY CITY (CNS) – The Rev. Winniford Clyde Hawkins and a coalition of religious leaders on Friday pleaded for peace over the weekend after a surge of violence in Bay City this week left at least 14 people dead.

Hawkins and other leaders, speaking at an inter-faith communal service, noted with concern that the deaths included 10 people under the age of 25, including a basketball referee who was shot dead during a youth league game Tuesday in the Six Points section.

Hawkins said a joint letter from the coalition was being distributed to the Mayor's Office and to churches, synagogues and mosques for presentation at upcoming services.

The letter reads in part: "It is intolerable that playgrounds and parks have become places of horrific violence which threatens the livelihoods of our city's invaluable families and young people. All people of faith, and non-believers as well, must come together to halt these episodes of bloodshed."

Other killings this week included two 15-year-old boys who were gunned down in a suspected gang-related incident outside C.L.R. James Middle School, and a 23-year-old woman who was decapitated in what police described as a domestic dispute.

"You were trapped in some repressive organizational structure, like as a monk or somebody in the Catholic Church, in your previous lives."

Chrissy had gone to see the fortune teller for $400.

"That sounds a lot like this life..."

"You're on an upward arc now, but you could still fall back down. You're walking the line."

"She can tell that from talking to *you*?"

"Because you are reflected in me... She said it would really help you if you took the time to resolve your previous lives. You need to clear yourself out."

"What about you?"

"I haven't lived that many lives. I'm young in terms of my lives on this world. I'm compiling experiences..."

Chrissy had begun to study up. She said I was born in the Year of the Monkey, Earth element. She said my Moon was in Capricorn, my Sun and Mercury in Cancer. My tarot card was "the Caesar."

"You're a water sign. I'm a fire sign…"

"Sure, that sounds about right…"

Two weeks later, she took off to Mount Yondo for a one-on-one session with a Buddhist guru who was "originally from Italy" but now lived alone in the mountains. One of her friends had given her the tip. She wouldn't say how much it was costing her.

It was a bad time for me. I tried to be sympathetic, to give her space to work it out – yet I couldn't escape the feeling that things were sliding out of my control, into areas I didn't enjoy. I tried to appreciate her desire for transformation, but things are never that easy. It wasn't clear how her process was fitting in with my personal evolutionary struggle.

Maybe I cared too much – yes, that was it, I had begun to care too much.

Alone in her house, I drank heavily the two nights she was gone, beer and wine mainly, because that way you could stretch out a session to 10 or 12 hours. I spent the hours with bottles in my hands and news shows on the flat screen, CDs on the stereo, the fireplace blazing… When that got old, which it did quickly, I rolled the tray outside to the Jacuzzi to watch films on the projector screen. *Clerks, Kill Bill, Adaptation, American Beauty, Ken Park, Fight Club, Casino, The Virgin Suicides, Eternal Sunshine of a Brainless Mind…*

I couldn't keep any of them going for more than 20 minutes. They were all useless junk, bar none – apparently, turds that had fallen out of someone's head and on to the screen. I couldn't sit still to pay attention, and I didn't care. It was hard to believe they were letting people make movies like these – littering the world with more confusion and nonsense. It seemed nobody understood a single thing about the world.

The desolation caused by Chrissy's absence was near total. I was overcome by overlapping feelings of claustrophobia, panic and defeat. I didn't know anything, except that I wanted her back by my side. No matter how much I drank, I couldn't shake visions of her bending down to fondle the small, nub-like genitals of what I imagined to be a very short, hairy man.

"Yes, my sweet one…" the guru would be muttering, resting his hand on the top of her head. "You must achieve oneness within yourself and your environment through the sharing and onenesses of our essences..."

Awaking hung-over on the Sunday of her return, I was wracked with doom, certain that she would kick me out at first sight.

"You drank the whole time," was what she said.

"Not the whole time..."

Her enthusiasm about the guru, however, seemed to outweigh any disappointment with me. She described the weekend as "intense," "powerful" and "spiritual." It was worse than I ever could have imagined. The guru had bragged to her that he had "completely cured" two schizophrenics and was now working on a "cure for autistic children." He was also apparently working to establish "scientific proof" that reincarnation existed.

Chrissy talked about how he had laid her out on a table and touched her body. He had measured her feet and found the left one "just a bit" longer than the right. He had pressed along her spine and found something slightly off – her "throat chakra." He had turned her over and pressed along her chest and abdominal cavity. He had worked carefully to detect her "aura," and thankfully it was still "whole" – meaning there was no serious disease problem. She explained this was important because all physical illnesses are rooted in an emotional and/or psychological problem, and that all "real healing" and "balancing" must be done on the "soul level" first.

"It doesn't thrill me," I said. "What do you say to the 1-year-old kid with cancer?"

She made some answer, not much of a very good one.

It got worse and worse. The guru had instructed her that she must speak to the baby she had aborted in her senior year of college. She started to cry. I hugged her. She sobbed on my shoulder for several minutes. It was the first I had ever heard about Chrissy having an abortion. I hugged her, her tears slid and dropped – she turned into a sticky puddle as I held her.

The guru had said the fetus was still "following" her around. It was waiting for her to "release" him, so he could be "born again." Chrissy had gone ahead and spoken to the fetus. She said she had cried for hours on that table. I didn't have the guts to ask what she said to the fetus. I did, after some time, ask who had been the father. That was part of the problem – she had narrowed it down to three guys, or two, but she couldn't resolve it and it had created a madness. She had felt so guilty and hadn't dealt with it. She had been living so recklessly at that time, lots of drinking and cocaine and not in shape to bother taking birth control pills regularly. But now that she had spoken to the fetus, she now believed that she and it could "heal" and move on. She couldn't believe that a "stranger," the guru, had been able to do that to her.

Chrissy sobbed. "I feel so bad that I killed that little thing! I should have kept it! Of course I should have kept it!"

"I don't know, babe. You can never know for sure, but... what I know is, you voted for the future when you made that choice. I mean, you were betting that your future was going to be better than what you were going through then...And you know, maybe... Well, I don't know."

"There's no excuse!"

I sat back on the couch, my head throbbing. The four aspirin hadn't totally done the trick. I lit a smoke, ashed into the cancer kids bowl. Chrissy showered and came out clean and moist, wearing a fluffy orange robe that fell down to mid-thigh. Her mood seemed to have improved.

"Don't worry," she said, snuggling in next to me. "I love you, Thor. Even though you smell like a cigarette butt in an empty beer bottle..."

✪

The course of events led, seemingly inevitably, to us taking the flight out to Colorado for the Lunabear Mind, Spirit & Body Expo in Whitehorse Springs. I wasn't so sure it was a good idea, but Chrissy had asked very politely if I wanted to go. Bad as it sounded, another weekend in the house without her sounded worse.

"I just don't want to sit around with a bunch of freaks. I might not be able to sit through everything. I'll go crazy..."

"They're not freaks! They're just people who are trying to help. This world needs a new start. Isn't it obvious? We need to start trying..."

There was some unexplained tie-up at the airport and the flight was delayed. It had taken us 35 minutes to clear the security gate, by the time we had waited in the line, taken off our shoes and put them back on (no bombs found), and I needed a smoke pretty bad. About a quarter-mile down the terminal corridor I found the Smoking Lounge. It was full of soldiers.

"Hey," I said, "how do you get a light around here? The cops took all my lighters and didn't give them back."

The guy laughed and stuck out his burning butt. I leaned forward and puffed.

I sat in the plastic chair and wolfed the smoke in four or five inhales, then lit a fresh one off my own butt. It was like the waiting room to Hell in there – a small, cramped space completely filled with smoke, windows unable to be opened due to "security concerns," nearly everybody coming or going from war...

"You going to the Big Sandbox?" said a white soldier to a black. The white had tattoos visible on his neck, forearms and hands.

That's what he called it: *The Big Sandbox*.

"Going *back*. I just had 15 days."

"Good luck, bro..."

The talk went on and on like that, with little variation and hardly any laughter. As I was getting ready to leave after a third smoke, several women arrived outside the room. The soldiers went out to greet and hug them. The women wore baseball caps advertising military installations and t-shirts that said OFFICIAL HUGGER. The women were crying, tears sliding down in thick shiny streams. The soldiers comforted them, told them everything was going to be O.K. The women gave each of the soldiers a cellophane-wrapped pack of brownies with American flags stuck in the top. I didn't get one.

We stayed at the Overlook Hotel, a fancy place ($350 per night) that featured cris-crossing wooden beams and Navajo-style rugs stuck on the walls. The flight was smooth but several hours late, and we didn't arrive at the hotel until past 10 p.m. We woke early, however, and took our coffee on the deck, gazing out as hawks soared through the cloudless blue crispness, searching below for rodents to swoop on. Chrissy took a new bottle of Olmeca out of her bag and we each downed a couple. I donned the new forest-green parka and water-resistant boots that Chrissy had picked out for me. The snow crunched, the snow crystals caught sunlight and sparkled. The trees were marvelously snow-frosted, and the poor town seemed to be in the process of being overrun with gurus and healers of all kinds.

We joined the crowds wandering through the convention hall, looking at the products for sale in the stalls or checking out the "workshops" on offer from bearded gurus and glazed-faced smiling ladies in the meeting rooms. The convention-goers were mainly from two groups, it seemed: Those either too fat, or those too sickly thin.

They were pasty and pudgy and seemed to have problems walking, or they were too tan and twiggy and seemed to have problems walking. Whatever their situation, there was no doubt they had come with more than a few bucks to spend.

From what I could gather, they were, among other things, investigating ways to integrate multiple levels of experience for energy healing. They were learning how to identify the presence of intrusive energy, and how to see and work with the luminous energy field. They were employing angel mediums so that they might see their guardian angels revealed. On top of that, they were trying to heal their relationship with money – because, in case you weren't sure, money had spiritual aspects – specifically, *money was energy*.

They were pounding on crystal bowls to benefit from vibrational sound. They were listening to experts speak to stones to discover the hidden messages of gems, minerals and crystals. They were studying how to access their Akashic Records in order to learn their soul's intention and discover all thoughts, words and deeds from their past and future lives. For those so inclined, they were examining the potential of Shamanic shape-shifting to heal their animal companions. They were learning about finding balance in an unbalanced world. They were looking at taking Three Peaceful Easy Steps To Change The World, because by connecting with the light and healing each other, we could heal the whole world. They were exploring whether a giant crystal turning upside-down could have led to the sinking of Atlantis. They were teaming up with Toltec Naguals to embrace the Four Agreements, and they were seeking to shine a light on the shadows in their mind to start on the path to real self-actualization.

Most of all, a great many wanted to *lose weight*. Specifically, they wanted safe and effective weight loss and rejuvenation. They wanted to cleanse their livers and redress pH imbalances that had led to the storage of unwanted fat. They wanted to finally, at long last, embrace *authentic health* – mind, body and soul-wise. This could involve looking for solutions to electropollution. It would necessarily involve wholebody solutions, because what was happening in our heads was also happening in our colons. It would definitely involve non-medical ways to achieve a healthy back… There was also the problem of *aging*. They were against it, nearly 100 percent, because the proper way forward was to incorporate natural anti-aging technologies and non-invasive regeneration.

Water sculptures danced and shimmied in the air – watery Grand Canyons and Mount Everests, watery butterflies and orchids that bobbed, burbled and sprayed. There were stalls selling Amazon herbs and tangerine quartzes, stalls promoting holistic prostate massage, stalls plugging potions that provided advanced nutrition for dreams by employing galantamine extract from Red Spider Lily. They were sucking water from the mountain air to make AirWater, and they were turning on orgone radionics machines for the benefits this might achieve. I witnessed a testimonial: During a channeling session, a pretty dark-haired woman had received a vision of a skin-care product that would transform her wallet and the skin of thousands of people forever. Only $79.95.

Everyone appeared eager to receive their free promotional Psychic-in-a-Bag, which included a five-minute prepaid card for telephone psychic readings, a Divination Tools card set, and a non-toxic soy candle.

It was hard to disagree. There had been so much damage and decay – just plain *rot*, really – it was obvious everybody needed a little healing. There was clearly a glitch in our construction and neural wiring that had left us exposed to so much pain and isolation. There was little use in denying that.

Maybe, I thought, yes – maybe it was time to finally get rid of all the old failed religions, the old foolishness, the old crap. The same old tricks, the same old comical-tragical dance, had really left us with nothing, when you looked at it. War, misery and thievery had won out, and decent people had proven themselves helpless against it. It was just a fact now. And so yes, maybe the time had finally come. Maybe this was the thing to try.

It was hard to be totally sure, though, and I preferred not to be totally sure of anything. I just didn't want to be bothered. I wanted to drink. I knew what would instantly treat my pain.

"You want to do a brain painting?" asked Chrissy. "That could be interesting."

We had a look. It appeared to involve them sticking these suck-things on your forehead in order to pick up your brain's electric signals. A colorful squiggle would appear on the screen, and they said it was your brain that had done it. They would print it on a poster or t-shirt for you for $49.95.

"I think I'll pass, Chris…"

I cut out around 11 a.m., just as Chrissy was tucking into a Gupta Juniho workshop on Astro-Palmistry and Facing the Dweller on the Threshold. She was already carrying around an armful of hand painted personal healing mandalas and a box of Vedic aroma therapies she had purchased for her mother. I told her I'd catch up with her afterwards, around 12:30 or so. We made plans for an early evening hike.

I trudged through the snow for about 10 minutes until I found a deserted bar. The Annex, it was called. I ordered a beer, then a beer and a shot. The bartender was bald and wore black pants, a pressed white shirt. He read a newspaper the entire time, saying little, sometimes looking up at the television. I was almost sorry to disturb him with another request. The TV was tuned to news footage of Russian children running naked, fires in a school building, charred corpses, men with guns. I felt nauseated. It seemed as if something beyond horrible had happened in Russia.

I came back to Lunabear around one. There was no sign of Chrissy. Groups of people walked about, some of them eating flat crackers that had a bright green paste spread on top. I looked around the stalls, checked my phone for a Chrissy message. Nothing.

I opened a door and poked my head into a workshop entitled "The Love Power Is YOU." A woman turned around and tried to shoo me away, but I shook my head and walked quickly to the left, coming to a stop in the corner. The room was drenched in a wavering, silvery-purple soft light. A crystal in the center rotated about, shooting patterns of blue and white diamonds over the walls and ceiling. Dozens of women wearing white robes were sitting in rows, legs crossed in front of them, their eyes closed. I didn't see Chrissy among them. The women seemed to be humming – but low, low, the humming was at a very low octave. The room smelled something like slowly baking flowers, mixed with oregano.

The women began to repeat words that were chanted by a frizzy-haired lady who was perched on a small cot behind the crystal. A video screen at the back of the room showed a close-up of her relaxed and shiny face. Her lips upcurled in a joyous smile as she released the words in a gentle, silky voice.

"Since I am divine, I have choice and take responsibility for my decisions… When I share the people I love, the more love there is to go around… and the more love I get… I feel loving… I am responsible for my own orgasm, for learning how to get one and for telling my partner how I get one… My life will not change if I have orgasms… My early painful sexual experiences do not make me a failure in sex... My bedroom is no longer a place of punishment... My bedroom is a safe and pleasurable place to be and I feel loving... I feel loving... I feel loving... Any position in sex is fine... I can be the dominant partner or the submissive one, they are both loving... . I feel loving... Jealousy is not love... Since I do not need my partner for survival, it is O.K. if he or she has other partners... . I am no longer interested in arranging other men to imitate my father... Love has nothing to do with pain, because love is loving... I feel loving... There is nothing shameful about my body, my secretions are acceptable to me... I understand the natural smell of my genital area is designed to be attractive... It is unnecessary to hide it with douches and deodorants... I feel loving..."

I went out and couldn't find Chrissy anywhere.

I still had about $60 of the $100 Chrissy had given me. I picked up a bottle of Tempranillo, a quart of Remy Martin, a six-pack of Beck's in bottles and two packs of smokes at a market on my way back to the hotel. I called Chrissy's number three or four times, but there was no answer. I took the smokes and drinks out to the deck table, watching a rainbow of hang-gliders float over the Rockies as the sun went down. When it got too cold, I went into the room to warm up. Warmed up, I went back out to smoke.

The TV continued the blitz of naked and dying Russian children – children laying unconscious, children getting mouth-to-mouth, farmers with guns peering nervously over hedges.

BREAKING: 300 KILLED IN RUSSIAN TERRORIST BLOOD-BATH

I drank as fast as I could. I had visions of Chrissy giving out blowjobs, or getting fucked by a bearded guru in the bathroom. The wait was excruciating. I wanted Chrissy in the hotel, in the room now. I longed to sodomize her and hold her against me, warm and wet. I masturbated, spilled the bottle of Remy on the carpet. I took a towel and soap from the bathroom and tried to clean it. I turned on the lights. The hang-gliders were gone. It had gotten dark.

I was on the deck having a smoke when the sliding glass slammed shut behind me. I tried to open it, but Chrissy had locked it. The wind howled, swords of freezing wind flew under my shirt, slashing at my chest and ribs. After a moment of confusion, I realized my jacket and boots were securely inside with her.

The freezing gusts made my eyes water. Tears slid from the corners of my eyes, only to be blown away by the wind seconds later. Lights in the rooms above and below went on and off. Teeth chattering, I tapped against the glass. I had never been so cold – my feet through my socks were like stumps of stone against the wood. I tapped and pleaded, all my initial anger having now given way to the slender hope that she might show mercy.

"Chrissy, please... hey, Chrissy... I'm sorry, please..."

I went to the deck railing and looked over. It seemed about a 40-foot drop to the purple snow of the hillside. Well, if I could survive the fall, and didn't slide down too far – maybe I could walk around to the front and get inside. It began to not really matter. If I could just get *inside* somewhere, it did not matter where...

She finally opened it. I remember a beautiful burst of warmth, and quickly collapsing on the couch.

I woke up the next day around noon. Chrissy had emptied all my booze bottles, had in fact left the Tempranillo shattered in the bathroom sink. I tossed some of the glass pieces into the trash, showered, dressed and went down to the restaurant for coffee. I came back, showered again, combed my hair, tried to call Chrissy.

"You've ruined everything with your drinking," she said when she came back that evening. "I'm starting to think you really have a problem..."

"Let's not exaggerate, babe..."

I had to be back at work in a day. Chrissy phoned her office and took another three days. I hugged her goodbye and took the bus to the airport and the flight home. She caught a flight to Boulder, and from there went skiing.

HAIL, HAIL! The Clown King is Dead – Long Live the Clown

★ 23 ★

Sernath walked into the newsroom.

"Listen up a moment, please. Dick has died. Wayne called a few moments ago and informed me. He passed away last night in his sleep."

Sernath turned and walked off.

"Bald-headed Christ goddamn!" said Richie. "That little faggot was like a father to me. Bet your bippy, kid. Made me what I am today."

"Long live Dick," I said.

Wayne came in that afternoon and began setting up a shrine in the Reception Area. He put a vase of flowers on the table, surrounding it with framed Dick action-shots – pictures of Dick with William Holden, Ralph Lifschitz and Walter Mondale, Dick with Warren Hinckle, Dick with Bedford Wynne, Norwin Meneses and Justice Warren Tighe. A shot of Dick shaking hands with Adkins "Spike" Bouregarde, the legendary four-term mayor of Bay City, was placed in a prominent position. Under a large color portrait of Dick, Wayne had printed out a card with Dick's dates of birth and death and the inscription: *A Faithful Servant of Truth*.

Wayne looked at me, his eyes watering.

"Dick thought very highly of you, Thor. He was glad to have you on board. He mentioned it several times. He thought you had a bright future."

"Dick was a great man," I said.

RICHARD TRIMBLES, 78, FOUNDED CITIES NEWS

BAY CITY (CNS) – Richard "Dick" Trimbles, the founder of Cities News Services and a Bay City journalistic institution for nearly 50 years, passed away Wednesday at the age of 78.

Trimbles' longtime partner, Wayne Brownberger, said Trimbles died in his sleep at his residence in Bay City's Citrus Lanes neighborhood, where he had lived for the past 22 years.

Using $560 he inherited from an uncle in Ohio, Trimbles established Cities News Services 47 years ago in a one-room bungalow in Bay Cities' Commerce Avenue neighborhood.

Three years ago, Trimbles sold all Cities News assets to Capps-Neubold Corp. for an estimated $10.3 million. After the deal was finalized, Trimbles continued his involvement in the company's news operations as Executive Senior Editor.

Trimbles hailed the sale, calling it "proof you can still become rich in America through hard work and commonsense thinking."

Capps-Neubold Vice President Stephen J. Griles said in a written statement: "Dick Trimbles will be remembered as a tough and insightful journalist who founded Cities News Services in line with the highest standards of American journalism. Capps-Neubold highly values its relationship with CNS, and we intend to grow the relationship in the traditions of Richard 'Dick' Trimbles."

Dick protégés came from far and wide to attend the memorial service. They included Libby, a staff writer at the *Greensville Observer-Guard*, as well as Gary from the *West Branch Times-Union*, Diane from the *McAllen Register-Leader*, Eddie from the *Everglades City Daily News*, Abigail from the *Lake Charles Post-Advertiser*, Patty from the *Pineburg Press-Telegram*, Kirby from the *Kelowna Weekly Dispatch*, Mary Ellen Sue from the *Owensboro News-Times*...

Dick protégés spieled Dick stories to Dick fans and current employees. Dick, they said, had considered reporting an "art form." Dick was from the "old school." Dick believed in doing it the "old-fashioned way." Dick had a "real hunger for the story." Dick believed it was important to hold the authorities "to account." Dick believed reporting the news could actually help improve society through its revelation of "the truth." Dick believed in truth and justice, in the American way.

Dick could pull the long hours. He was in the office for 20 hours straight during the great oil spill of '79. Dick was very concerned about the future of the environment.

Dick loved the Beach Boys, particularly the song "Da Doo Ron Ron." Dick counted every penny at the beginning, and also at the end, but always had a "personal touch." Dick, it turned out, was an early supporter of full rights for Negroes. Dick had very much admired Janis Joplin and Miles Davis. Dick had been to four Frank Sinatra concerts over four decades. Dick had sent flowers to somebody on some occasion. Dick had given great advice to somebody, when they really needed it. Because Dick cared about people as persons, not numbers. Dick had told the exact same joke to the same guy on three different occasions, years apart...

Dick would have been happy to hear all the laughter during his memorial service, because Dick considered laughter to be a "form of music." Dick had given so many reporters their "first chance." Dick had believed in them. The nation's newspapers were now full of people who had gotten their start under Dick. Dick liked to repair old motorcycles. Dick had stood strong when hippies and Black Panthers had barged into the office making insane demands...

Dick had the great idea for the story. Dick figured out how the lead should go when somebody was having problems. Dick sought out "fresh writing." Dick would always tell this one guy, "Don't be a Dismal Jimmy." Dick was personally opposed to the various wars, but had never viewed Cities News as a platform for his personal views. Dick had been a smart businessman, "sharp as a tack."

Wayne sobbed. Dick had been Wayne's best friend. Wayne talked about how in the early days, he wasn't sure if the company was going to make it to the next week. But Dick never gave up. Dick had a vision. Dick had seen the need. Dick had formulated the formula that made it work. Dick had been generous to Wayne. Dick had been a sweet and super guy. Wayne sobbed.

I sat in the back and didn't speak. I walked out when everyone began passing by the open coffin to have a last look at Dick, who had given me my first real chance in the big city.

Afterwards, it was somehow agreed that everyone would meet up at the Triple-C Bar, a dank dark place near the Fish Market which had a "Yo-ho-ho, he's a jolly good sailor" motif. The rafters were filthy with torn fishing nets, oars and rigging, sets of fish heads and shark jaws stuck on the walls. Dick people sat around tables, eating fried fish. I loosened my tie and sat in a booth with Richie and Tommy-Gun, several beer pitchers between us.

Pretty soon, a bottle of whisky arrived. Richie, who had lightened his hair and was wearing a bright orange sweater, was quickly drunk.

"Everything before the *but* is bullshit!" Richie said, clinking our glasses. "Ah-ha, ah-ha, just tell THAT to the people in North Korea!"

He laughed loudly, downed his mug, poured more.

"Yes, sir," I said.

Richie grinned, clinked glasses. "Said the fat girl to the cupcake. Said the archbishop to the actress. Said the soldier to the watchmaker. Said the pizza-face to the cheerleader. Said the politician to the pregnant girl. Said the bicycle to the cripple. Said the matchstick to the mansion. Said the drowned to the saved. Said the skinhead to God. The Dick is dead! Long live Dick!"

"Long live Dick!" cheered Tommy-G and I.

During a piss break, a drunk lady in a blue dress bumped into me in the hall. She appeared to be somewhere near 40 – large bosoms, washed-out blond hair in ruffles, chapped lips, face lined and splotchy red. She grabbed my hand.

"I'm Bobbi... and you are?"

Bobbi had worked at CNS "years and years ago," or about twelve. Now she was a features writer on the *Altoona Express-Sun*. I stood talking to her for some time, not really finding much interest in it, but wondering about the breasts. She led me by the hand to the bar.

"I just loved Dick... He helped me so much... He was the nicest man."

"Yes, he was..."

"So Thor, do you have a girlfriend?"

"Oh, no... not really."

Bobbi talked about the big stories she had done in Altoona. Some had even won awards. They included a series about kids with some type of incurable disease, a car wash run by homeless people, and an old lady who was famous in the town for making needle points of Cadillac cars. They apparently called her the "Cadillac Lady." Now she was taking requests and selling her stuff on the internet, getting all famous in a down-home way. Bobbi said none of it would have happened without her article.

I sat and drank, sometimes adding a comment. Bobbi was staying at the Commodore Hotel. She had to fly back to Pittsburgh tomorrow. She was glad she had come out, she had loved Dick so much. She couldn't believe he had sold out to Capps-Neubold. She had thought he would never do something like that, Capps-Neubold was a horrible company, but they had offered so much money, hadn't they... She would have loved to have stayed in Bay City forever, despite the crime, but Cities News just didn't pay enough. She got more cash in Altoona, plus it was *a lot* cheaper to live there. She also hated the trash in Bay City, people left it everywhere. Her children were missing her, she had telephoned them earlier that day. She had two children, four and nine years old. She was divorced. Husband run off with another woman after the second baby, sad as it was to say... But he had always been a "real jerk." She could see it now, looking back, but she had been "too young and stupid" to see it when it might have mattered. She couldn't believe how stupid she had been.

The problem now was, there were too many women and not enough "good guys" in Altoona to go around. The "good ones" were either married or dating somebody 25. Some had even gone gay! Most of the available choices, Bobbi explained, were "weirdoes and losers," strange middle-aged men who'd never married or were divorced.

"This one guy told me, 'We might get married, but I'll never let you rip me off.' I was like, '*Married?* No thanks, buddy. I wouldn't want your worthless stuff anyway.'" She shrugged.

"Men are jerks," I said. "Of that there can be no doubt."

Bobbi laughed. "You're one to talk, huh!"

"Have you considered lesbianism? There's always that..."

"Oh, I've heard that one before... That's *your* fantasy! All you men!"

I departed her, saying I had to go for a piss. I came back and joined a crowd that had gathered around Sernath. He appeared pleasantly relaxed, resting on an elbow at the bar, his other arm around Lynn.

"When she was about 16, she would walk 30 yards behind us where ever we went." Sernath laughed. "She acted like she didn't even know us. My own daughter!"

He laughed again, tossed down a shot.

"I didn't know you had a daughter," I said.

"Yes, I did, Thor – she died in a car accident five years ago."

"I'm sorry... Damn it, I'm sorry... "

Sernath patted me on the shoulder. "Yeah... Hey, let me buy you a shot. It's got to be my turn."

That helped, that really helped.

Everyone talked and laughed long and hard for a while, about five or six of us. Scotty showed up in the middle of it with Shally. Scotty, who was wearing a white tuxedo, bought some kind of large flaming drink for Sernath and Lynn. A few minutes later, he ordered several bottles of champagne.

At some point during a wandering, Bobbi ambushed me and dragged me into an alcove beneath a giant rusting anchor. She slid her hand down my pants, and I seemed to succeed in getting a hand around one of those breasts. In any case, we rubbed against each other sweatily, flipping our tongues around in each other's mouths. Bobbi tasted like white wine, lipstick and sauerkraut, but she was warm, warm, steaming. It wasn't long before most of my tongue was in her mouth. She sucked on it like a vacuum, releasing only to draw breaths, and when that happened, an excess of her saliva flooded out and poured down the sides of my mouth.

Bobbi eventually forced me down on a little bench. She pulled back the dress, got her breasts out of the bra and bounced them in my face. The breasts flopped low, and I had to twist my neck in an uncomfortable position to get them in my mouth. I sucked at the boobs while simultaneously working her dress up and massaging her thighs. She had a big ass, plenty of ass. There was much material to work with, soft and spongy. She dry-humped my erection for a minute or two, then suddenly got up, kissed me on the lips and walked off.

I wandered around, my head slightly throbbing. Scotty found me and bought a few drinks, Shally standing on the side. Shally's face had the character of perfect porcelain, and when Scotty went off somewhere, I tried to talk her up. The idea formed in my mind that she would go off with me that night, and we would start a new life together.

I blabbered away, looking intensely at Shally. She nodded her head, backed way a step, looked over her shoulder for Scotty, who did not appear.

I continued with the blabbing. Pretty soon, Shally walked off.

I saw Kate, went up and asked her if she had any aspirin. She gave me a pair from her purse, then took me by the hand.

"What *is* that on your face? It looks like lipstick!"

She took out a tissue, began wiping my mouth and forehead.

"My gosh! It looks like you've been attacked!"

I really had been trying to avoid her, but I had needed the aspirin. Kate led me past the bar and sat me down at a table with a bunch of other people. Everyone laughed at what was being said, but I couldn't seem to. I tried to focus on drinking a large glass of beer that had been set before me. I got a gulp or two down, then began to hiccup. I held my breath, trying to get rid of the hiccups. I counted to 100 while holding my breath, but the hiccups kept returning. I never did finish that glass of beer.

"Don't fall asleep!" Kate said, hustling me into a taxi.

I hiccupped. Kate rubbed my chest, unbuttoned my shirt, slipped her hand in. City lights flashed through the taxi. I felt something like a melting stick of butter.

"Don't fall asleep!"

✪

I awoke around 10 to find my clothes folded in a neat stack next to me on the bed. Kate had left a note.

Make yourself at home! There's English muffins!

Love, Kate

The bedroom had potted plants in the corners, a metal-framed black and white poster advertising the city of VENEZIA on one wall. A gigantic statue of Snoopy wearing a blue hat and raincoat stood by the door. Some kind of hat rack, I guessed. In the bathroom I found a bottle of painkiller, tossed down four and laid back down.

After a while, I felt better and got up and made coffee. I sipped from the cup while sitting at the kitchen table and flipping through Kate's copy of the *Star-Chron*, looking for my stories. Staff Reporter Tracyann Winston had, it seemed, committed a very bad sin – she had, without attribution, used my police quotes for the page B-1 splash SUSPECTS SOUGHT AFTER HOMELESS MAN SET ON FIRE IN PARK. "Local Briefs," meanwhile, had used my 94 LBS. OF METH FOUND IN CAR and PARENTS ARRESTED IN BEATING DEATH OF 7-YEAR OLD.

I sipped coffee, unfolded the *Examiner-Mail*. They had picked up the meth piece, as well as POLICE: PIT BULL GNAWS OFF BABY'S TOES and SECURITY GUARD SHOT OUTSIDE RESTAURANT.

I had a few smokes on the balcony, a few more cups of coffee. Kate's place had mostly fruits and vegetables, nothing much to eat.

On a table by the window Kate had stacks of photographs and a couple draft print-outs of her upcoming series: FOCUS ON THE FALLEN. It would go on to be a big Sunday splash in five or six mid- and small-market dailies. Tributes to local soldiers who had wound up on the wrong end of bullets and bombs while on the hunt for America-hating "hajis" and "terrorists" out in the sand hell.

- ★ Spc. Mark Mohl, 20. Killed by roadside bomb. Hobbies: Windsurfing, weightlifting, clarinet.
- ★ Sgt. Raul Menendez, 25. Killed during enemy combat. Hobbies: Ford GTs, football, baby daughter.
- ★ Spc. Keith Langhorne, 21. Killed by sniper fire. Hobbies: Computer games, chess, cats.
- ★ Sgt. Wesley Schweinsteiger, 28. Killed by roadside bomb. Hobbies: Mountain-climbing, guitar, Comedy Channel. Married, two children.
- ★ Spec. James Chillingham, 19. Killed during enemy combat. Hobbies: Bicycle-riding, soccer, punk rock.

On it went, 30-40 guys worth. Kate had really worked hard, the families would be proud, I supposed. Or maybe they wouldn't be. Why would they be *proud* of something like this?

Well, who knew, people were liable to think almost anything and it rarely made much sense. I re-straightened the stacks, had another smoke on the balcony, then went back to the bedroom and carried out a brief search of Kate's things, sniffing her underwear and so forth. Nothing too interesting. I flipped on the TV.

CLOWN:... *and officials are telling us, Sandy, that this plot may have been just days away from being carried out, killing an unimaginable number of Americans, before they rounded up these suspects. What officials are telling us is indeed chilling – that these young men were planning to explode sports drinks containers and bottles of hair gel to bring down more than 10 airliners in a series of spectacular suicide hijacking terrorist explosions... And appropriately, authorities have fired up the terror-alert level to Code-Red. That's the maximum, folks, it can't go any higher... The terror light is now blinking red-hot, Mr. and Mrs. America, so be on the lookout.*

CLOWN: *You're exactly right, Bill. This terror plot has been in the works for months, officials say, and its goal was truly horrific. One counterterrorism official just told me that this plot may have in fact been 'The Big One' that each and every one of us has been fearing...*

CLOWN: *And Sandy, the impact on air-travelers is going to be profound. From now on, we're being told, mothers will have to taste baby food and infant formula in front of security guards before boarding a plane, and sports drinks, regular drink drinks, all hair gels and ointments, lipstick, makeup, suntan lotion, all electronic items, are now banned from flights. You just can't take it on board anymore, folks – unless, presumably, you are already wearing it in your hair or on your face, or it's already in your bladder... Sandy, will you just imagine the huge impact this will have on the profits of airport gift shops? My Lord... O.K., I'm getting word that President Wolfgang G. Mnung is preparing to make a statement as he steps off an airplane in Butte, Montana. We'll go live now to the leader of the free world...*

CLOWN: *My fellow Americans, the thwarting of this diabolical plot shows that we remain at war with Islamic fascists who will use any means to destroy those of us who love freedom, to hurt our nation's freedom way of life by detonating liquids aboard innocent civilian aircraft. We must remain vigilant and at war until we can exterminate this threat posed by those who would cause death to our people on such a massive scale. This plot is further evidence that the terrorists we face are sophisticated and constantly changing. These killers need to know that America, Great Britain and our allies are determined to defend ourselves and advance the cause of liberty...*

Later in the office, Richie spun from side to side in his chair, gritting his teeth.

"From one clown to another, kid – Kate likes to do the flop, no? She even likes to do the flip-flop. That same Kate Klown of Clown News Services, Bay City's finest, she likes to do the boogaloo..."

"I don't know what you're talking about."

"HEY CLOWN!" Richie roared.

After Richie had gone for the day, Kate rolled over a chair.

"Hey, stud... How *are* you?"

"I'm O.K., I guess..."

She smiled, touched my forearm. Her face looked pink, her nose a strange shape.

"I tried to call, but you didn't pick up..."

"I know, I know... So how're you?"

"Good! Real good! Want to get a coffee or something tonight?"

"I don't know. Maybe not tonight, you know? It'll be late by the time I get out of here. Look at this stuff I got to do... I mean, look..."

She made a sad face. "O.K. Maybe later, huh?"

"Yeah, maybe later."

HELL HATH NO:
Babe Fury at Cad Clown!

★ 24 ★

SEVERED HANDS FOUND DURING TRAFFIC STOP

SAN MARTINO (CNS) – San Martino police said three pairs of severed hands and one ear were found in the car of two men who were stopped for a traffic safety check.

Commander Frank Bristol said Steven Collins, 33, and Felipe Sanchez, 45, were arrested on suspicion of murder and were being held without bail.

Bristol said the six adult hands and the ear were found in a plastic bag in the backseat foot space of a Land Rover that was stopped at about 10:40 a.m. Tuesday on Somerset Road.

Bristol said patrol officers stopped the car because they thought the driver's vision might have been impaired by a large quantity of air fresheners and beads hanging from the rear view mirror.

"Why don't you ever come in me?"

We were laying in the bed, under the plum satin sheets. The windows were open, a breeze fluffling through the curtains. A small blaze crackled in the small fireplace. A crocodile appeared on the television, swishing low through the brown water. A congo-drum rhythm rolled on the soundtrack. The gator suddenly jumped and tore at some deer, grabbing the sucker and dragging him into the mud. Poor clueless deer – what was he thinking? Another croc surged out of nowhere, grabbing and tearing at the deer leg. Rushes of blood appeared, seeping into the white and brown fur, floating onto the oily mud. Where had this second fucker been hiding? I had not seen him. They hide in the swampy mud.

A gator tore at the deer neck. The deer blinked slowly, feebly, tried to raise a hoof, neck bending at a perverted angle. Not a chance, couldn't do shit. What kind of show was this? Why the hell didn't he scream? "The Animal Channel." A third gator jumped, grabbing and tearing at a foreleg. Dirty fuckers.

"Jesus, would you look at that," I said.

I took the Corona from the nightstand and had an easy pull. I put it down and burped softly. Something vaguely Pakistani came up. I took another pull to ease it back down.

"Hey, c'mon." Chrissy raised her head from my chest. Her greens, murky in the TV light, glared unblinkingly. "Answer the question."

I petted her hair, leaned over and kissed her. "I came in your ass, didn't I?"

"Come on! You know what I mean."

I leaned back, reached over, took a sip. A blue cartoon man. Click. A skier with dreadlocks and goggles flew down a hill, zoomed up the ramp and did several flips. Click. Mnung in a Baltimore Ravens football helmet. Click. A brunette mixing a pitcher of glowing ice tea in a flower-filled back yard. Click. Two bloody men in a cage, punching and kicking each other. Click. A geek fishing and smoking a pipe.

Click. Serena Williams modeling leather leggings and combat boots. Click. Bruce Willis winking. Bruce Willis jumping from a helicopter. Bruce Willis with grease and a sneer on his face. Click. A group of old men sitting in a circle, spinning clay. Click. Mnung wearing a sombrero, shooting off a rifle with one arm. Click. A babe fingering herself and writhing in a soapy bathtub: 1-900-978-BABE. Click. Chopped lettuce and tomatoes flying in slow motion, water droplets suspended in air. Something meat-like bubbling above flames. HOT JUICY BURGER.

Click. Monkeys getting out of bed. Monkeys wearing overalls. Monkeys sitting in chairs at a table.

"Hey, check this out..."

Chrissy pulled away. "C'mon, why don't you? You know I'm on the pill... What are you afraid of?"

"Afraid?" I said. "You know I don't *get* afraid, Chris. It's cool... It's not about coming some place or some other place, is it? I just..."

I leaned over to kiss her. Monkeys held spoons. Monkeys spooned from bowls. Monkeys spread jam on bread slices. Monkeys spread jam on their faces. Monkeys spilled on the table.

"I'm serious." Chrissy pulled away and rolled over.

Click. A silver German car slashing across a wet black mountain road. Click. Yellow cartoon people dancing. Click. A man in an orange sweater cutting into a roast with an electric knife. Click. A pack of children running off somewhere. Click. A woman in a pearl necklace sniffing coffee in a small white cup. Click. The Chinese army digging flood berms. Click. Does Your Man Have Stability/Endurance Issues? Try MALE ENHANCEMENT. Click. One hundred spoons flying into 100 yogurts. Click. Mnung wearing a Davy Crockett cap and slicing into a stack of pancakes on top of Mount Rushmore...

"I mean, what's the big deal? You know? I mean, how big of a deal is it? It's just semen, isn't it?"

"You're crazy!" Chrissy said. "Don't you trust me?"

"Sure, I trust you..."

"You don't trust me. You don't trust anyone."

She threw the covers, got out of the bed.

"You're crazy! Like I would want to have a kid with you! You're sick! Like I would want have kids with some drunk, some drug addict! Some guy with a crappy job who can't even afford to buy his own cigarettes!"

She walked out.

"I'm not a drug addict, Chrissy."

Click. Madonna in white, smashing glass cases full of black dildos. Click. A woman with a yellow cream and sliced cucumbers on her face. Click. Bono hugging a picture of a Chinese woman. Click. Overjoyed blacks and whites and Mexicans in a park, digging into bags of potato chips in slow-motion. Click. A Mini Cooper being parked in a cardboard box. Click. Oil-covered birds crawling out of black water. Click. Mnung in his early Robert Smith phase – dyed black hair, silver lipstick, boa constrictor sunglasses. Click. Soldiers in surgical masks and gloves, throwing dead Asians into a muddy hole.

The toilet flushed. Chrissy walked back in, boobs bouncing. She snatched underwear from the drawer, walked to her closet for a skirt and blouse.

"Where are you going?"

"YOU'RE CRAZY!"

"*You're* crazy."

"OH, FUCK OFF!"

She went to the wall and flicked off the fireplace. She walked out. Her keys jingled. The front door slammed.

The door opened. Keys jingled. Chrissy came back in.

"You know, the first night we were together, you said you didn't give a damn what I thought... And that was the truth!"

"Hey, come here..."

The door slammed. I heard the BandWagen start up. She backed it out. She drove it off.

Motorbikes speeding across the desert. Click. Oprah stuffing a turkey. Click. Orioles v. Blue Jays. Click. The pope bowing down as break dancers spun on their heads in the Vatican. Click. A small-titted blond wearing a red polka-dot shirt doing jumping jacks. Click. Marlon Brando tossing snacks to a dog as Larry King leaned forward with interest. Click. Men in wheelchairs tossing three-pointers. A guy with a plastic leg pole-vaulting. The Amputee Olympics.

I got up and went to the kitchen. The clock said 11:29. The hell, I didn't have to be at work until seven. I opened the fridge, got a fresh Corona. I counted another eight left. I went to the wine shack and selected a Willamette County pinot noir. I went back to the kitchen, popped it, poured and had a gulp. Strictly average. I took the Grey Goose out of the freezer, poured some into a shot glass. I knocked it down. Not bad, really. I took out the Glenlivet, the Maker's Mark, the Tullamore Dew, the Beefeater's, the Bushmills, an unopened Veuve Clicquot and another of Perrier Jouet Fleur. I put the bottles on the little cart and wheeled it out.

I clicked on the fireplace, flipped on the Panasonic and went over to Chrissy's DVD racks. *Cat People, The Black Dahlia, Dogville, Trainspotting, Rain Man, Who's Been Eating Gilbert Grape?, Picabo Street, Erin Brockovich, Matador, Sophie's Choice, Swept Away, Chasing Amy, La haine, Mata-Hari, Annie Hall, Talk to Her, The Big Lebowski, Belle de jour, Ghost World, Bellissima, The Truman Show, Legally Blonde, Wicker Park, The Full Monty, Magnolia, Brothers of the Head, La grande illusion, 8½ Weeks, Twelve Monkeys, Sideways, Vivement dimanche!, La cage aux folles, Wasabi, Vanilla Sky, Munich, Le bon plaisir, Coffee and Cigarettes, Donnie Darko, Mother of the Mirrors, Welcome To Collinwood, The Flower of My Secret, Radiohead: Meeting People is Greasy, Donnie Brasco, Unreversible, Law of Desire, Eyes Wide Shut, Buffalo '66, The Draughtsman's Contract, Brokeback Mountain,*

The Whales of August, Sixteen Candles, Le dejuner sur l'herbe, Land of Plenty, Curse of the Jade Scorpion...

Crap, it was all crap.

The Crying Game, A Bout de Souffle, Madonna: Truth or Dare, Breathless, 8 1/2 Women, Le carosse d'or, Meet Joe Black, Tristana, La regle de jeu, Zoolander, Last Tango in Paris, The Nomi Song, The Cement Garden, The Brown Bunny, The Good Thief, The Dreamers, A Perfect World, Les carabiniers, Parapluies de Cherbourg, The End of Violence, Punch-Drunk Love, Dancer in the Dark, Jules et Jim, Being John Malkovich, Amelie, Meet the Fockers, Indigenes, Una giornata particolare, Ani DiFranco: Trust, Match Point, Quiet Days in Clichy, Bridget Jones' Diary, Shortbus, The Informers, Tirez sur le pianiste, Le bon et les mechants, L'amour en fuite, Coastlines, Bad Education, Lost in Translation, Trouble Every Day, Jesus is Magic, Dogma, Zabriskie Point, Les quatre cent coups, Hitch, Requiem for a Dream, Broken Flowers, Zentropa, Les Triplettes de Belleville, Chocolat, Hidden, Mr. Deeds, The Sylvia North Story, Man on the Moon, My Cousin Vinnie, Copper's Gold, Jerry Maguire, Mighty Aphrodite...

Trouble Every Day? Oh, you bet. I clicked to NNN, the News Now Network. I leaned back on the couch, downed a full glass of pinot.

... jump right in to tangy jalapeño, melted Swiss cheese and Kentucky-fixins-style barbecue sauce on a freshly toasted pita bun! And don't forget – free plastic toys for grandma and the kids! Today at Beef Barn, your beef central!... Hey, America – who's the Most Popular Celebrity in the U.S.A.? The most loved... the sexiest... funniest... and most out-n-outrageous celebrities in the red, white and blue? Tune in tomorrow night and cast your vote! Presenting the Greatest Celebrity in America Contest, live from Pompano Beach! Hosted by Diane Sawyer and Peter Jennings, this one-time only extravaganza will feature guest appearances by your favorite stars including George Clooney! Madonna! P. Diddy! Regis Philbin! Lindsay Lohan! Bono and U2! Katie Couric! Allegra Coleman! America's Mayor – Rudolf Giuliani! Hillary Swank! Celine Dion! Kid Rock! Bill and Chelsea Clinton! America's Sweetheart – Jon Bon Jovi! John Elway! Gwyneth Paltrow and Coldplay! Jennifer Aniston! Senator John McCain and the Straight Talk Express! America's Own Fudge Brownie – Sandra Bullock! George Stephanopoulos! Kobe Bryant! Kate Hudson! Borat! Steven Spielberg! The Milton Twins! Ted Koeppel! Pink! America's Preacher – the Reverend James Dobson! Paris Hilton! Ooooprah Winfrey! Arnold 'The Gropenator' Schwarzenegger! Snoop Dogg! Kylie Minogue! Beyonce! Lance Armstrong! Scarlett Johanssen! Gus

Hanspaugh! Halle Berry! Mike Wallace! Mike Myers! America's Slugger – Alex 'Stray-Rod' Rodriguez! Jodie Foster! Donald Trump! Pammie Bungen! Samuel L. Jackson! Colonel Oliver North! Hannah Montana! Anderson Cooper! Nicole Kidman! Martin Sheen and the Sheen family! Bret Michaels! Amy Winehouse! Joe Namath! Bob Woodward! Janet Jackson! Ali G! Kiefer Sutherland! Annabel Chong! America's Coolest and Richest Nerds – Steve Jobs and Bill Gates! Tonya Harding! 50 Cent! Barbra Streisand! Geraldo! Shania Twain! Tom Brokaw! Plus... Live from the Eiffel Tower: Lady Gaga, in a one-time-only appearance with America's Favorite Punk Rockers – Green Day!... and a very special appearance from the Oval Office by the leader of the free world, President Wolfgang G. Mnung!

Andy shuffled over, coughed four or five times, lay down at my feet.

"Atsaboy, Andy..."

I scratched him between the ears, brushed away some of the sticky turds that had gathered around his eyes. I took a pull off the Corona, poured a jigger of Glenlivet, had a sip off the wine, cracked the Perrier.

"Who's a good boy huh, Andy? That's right, that's right..."

CLOWN: *U.S. F-16 Warhawk fighter jets today dropped eight 500-pound bombs on insurgent targets as American-led coalition forces carried out the second day of Operation: Smear, the fifth major offensive in the last three weeks targeting insurgents in the Northwest Sector... U.S. military officials said American forces used napalm-style MK77 incendiary phosphorus bombs in an assault that destroyed at least three insurgent strongholds. No casualties were reported among American or coalition forces. Major-General Tom Midge, commander of the Marine Second Brigades, briefed reporters from an undisclosed battlefront location...*

CLOWN: *We've got confirmed kills of at least 188 knuckleheads, and we found at least two car-bomb factories, which we liquidated... Our guys found and destroyed six arms depots containing RPG launchers, small arms, explosives, blaster caps and in excess of 17,000 rounds of bullets, and we arrested 55 additional knuckleheads... We know there are more knuckleheads out there, and we are amidst operations aimed at disabling them from continuing their knucklehead activity... My message to these knuckleheads is: Surrender now and therefore avoid the certainty that we will kill you later...*

CLOWN: *That was Major-General Tom Midge reporting from the front line of the war for freedom... Elsewhere, nine American Marines* were killed when terrorist insurgents attacked their base with small arms and rockets south of the Capital Sector. A search for the terrorists is ongoing... Coming up after the break: He came illegally to America from Honduras and viciously raped seven American women and girls. He was arrested for being at a construction site without the proper work permits, but the courts blocked his deportation and ordered him back on to the streets, where he raped and raped again... Can anything be done to stop criminals from setting up shop in the land of the free? A special report on America's immigration crisis... And later: What to do about hair color? It's the question on everyone's lips – and we've got the answers. Our experts will be coming to you live from our exclusive NNN Fashion Studio here in New York City, the magical capital of the free world...

I lipped from the Grey Goose, cracked open the Veuve. Andy sighed and put his head on his paws.

✪

"Look," said Sernath. He handed me a print-out. "The feds just released a statement. Write it up."

"O.K., boss."

★ ★ ★ ★   UNITED STATES NEWS RELEASE   ★ ★ ★ ★

U.S.A. DRUGS-ENFORCEMENT ADMINISTRATION
STATEMENT ON 'SHADOWY COALITION' SERIES

The recent stories in the Santa Ortega Press-Express Dispatch about Central Intelligence Agency (CIA) and United States federal drugs-control agents working with anti-government insurgents and illegal drugs traffickers in foreign countries to sell cocaine and crack cocaine in American cities for alleged personal profit and to clandestinely fund rebel forces in foreign countries are riddled with errors and 100 percent false.

The U.S.A. Federal Drugs-Enforcement Administration (FDEA) rejects these spurious allegations utterly. Evidence provided through testimony, documentation and other materials to the United States Congress has demonstrably proven the falsity of the allegations. U.S.A. Federal Drugs-Enforcement personnel and/or persons affiliated with them in a professional capacity would not, under any circumstances, be involved in any illegal operations whatsoever to devastate American inner cities with illegal cocaine and its cheaper, deadlier variant, crack cocaine. The proposition is palpably absurd on its face and the Drugs-Enforcement Administration rejects it absolutely and with vehemence.

Drug abuse and drugs-trafficking are poisons which threaten the social fabric of the United States of America, and the FDEA is committed to working with local law enforcement and other federal agencies to eliminate this scourge from our nation's homes, office places, schools and streets. The FDEA recognizes the Constitutionally protected right of free speech in the United States of America, but emphasizes there is no evidence to support this newspaper series, which is rejected as wholly untrue.

I picked up the phone and called Gordon Nebb at the *Press-Express Dispatch*.

"Hi Gordon, Cities News Services... The Drugs-Enforcement Administration just denounced you and the whole series."

"Oh, darn," said Nebb, laughing.

"I got the statement right here. One hundred percent false, it says. You seen it?"

"I've seen it, but I can't comment. I'm sorry. The paper's doing what they call an 'internal audit.' I'm not allowed to say anything right now."

"O.K. How you doing?"

"On the record, no comment. Off the record, I'm O.K. I just wonder what they're going to do to me. It feels like the whole world is jumping on me. I've made some very serious people very seriously angry."

"Hang in there, Gordon. Great series. Took real balls."

"Thanks... Yeah, it's strange, you know. The editors and lawyers were behind it all the way. I answered every question, everything checked out to their satisfaction – and now this. I'm getting hung out. Nobody's found an error yet. It's just denials – '100 percent false.' But everything's connected, as they say."

"I mean, I can't believe it actually came out. That's great."

"I don't know, to be honest. At this point, I just hope I can survive. It's not looking too good. *The Washington Post* has assigned four reporters to go over every word with a fine-tooth comb. *Four*. They're coming after me with guns blazing. They've already called seven or eight people here so far, that I know of, looking for dirt on me... There's *New York Times* people. At least they had the guts to call me – they asked me to give them my sources. I told them, 'Go get your own sources. You're the *New York Fucking Times*, go do some work.' The *L.A. Times* has supposedly got five or six people on it. Instead of trying to confirm the story, everybody's trying to shoot it down. Somehow I'm the suspect..."

"Be strong, Gordon. You'll make it. You'll be all right."

"Thanks. I hope so."

FEDS DENY 'SHADOWY COALITION' SERIES

BAY CITY (CNS) – The U.S. Federal Drugs-Enforcement Administration (FDEA) said Wednesday it "vehemently" denied allegations contained in the "Shadowy Coalition" series that recently appeared in the Santa Ortega Press-Express Dispatch.

The newspaper series described the alleged collaboration of U.S. federal agents, foreign drugs producers and rebel movements in distributing cocaine and its cheaper variant, crack cocaine, in American cities, including Bay City.

A written statement released by the FDEA said the series was "riddled with errors and 100 percent false." It said the falsity of the allegations had been shown in evidence provided through "testimony, documentation and other materials" to the U.S. Congress.

In a written statement, Press-Express Dispatch Editor In Chief James M. Cheffos said the newspaper was conducting a "review" of the series in light of the denial by the FDEA and an earlier denial issued by the

Central Intelligence Agency (CIA). Cheffos pledged to make the results of the review public when it is completed.

Contacted by telephone, the author of the series, Gordon Nebb, declined comment, citing the newspaper's internal review.

"Nice story, kid," said Richie. "Look at you, a real hit-man for the establishment, official stenographer of the police state... That'll show 'em! They'll say anything and you say, 'Yes, sir.'"

"They got a right to their statement."

"Fair and balanced, that's right... Sure, kid. You nailed it. Message: Don't rock the boat. Stay on side. Watch what you say, and especially what you write. Be a good puppy. Don't do nothin' that'll getcha on the wrong list."

"Yeah, you —"

"That's right, amigo: I am... I don't deny it. Don't say I didn't 'fess up. Shaddup and shooby doo... I know my orders: One mind, brute force, and full of money... Gee whiz, kid. Let me take another stupid pill and I'll get back to you."

Gordon Nebb, of course, didn't make it. The "internal audit" happened to reveal "shortcomings" in the Shadowy Coalition series, and Nebb was removed from the investigations team and transferred to the Meringue County office of the *Press-Express Dispatch* — a two-hour drive from his home. There, he covered the Planning Commission, a school district bond issue, and efforts to rescue lost mountain climbers. The hubbub over the series died away and eventually, Nebb's wife left him. Nebb quit the *Press-Express Dispatch* and moved to East Bay County, where he quietly resumed his drug investigations for obscure internet publications, supplementing his income with work as a substitute teacher.

Then one day, news came that Gordon had been "found dead from self-inflicted gunshot wounds to the head." The police found that, somehow, two shots had been fired in the "incident."[*]

Within hours, the gun was traced back to Nebb and his death was officially ruled a suicide. The investigation was closed.

---

[*] If a first shot fails to get the job done, it is "not totally unknown" for two or more shots to be fired in some "self-inflicted head wound events," according to experts. – ED.

MOMMY'S LITTLE HELPER:
A Clown's Homecoming

★ 25 ★

"What," Hank leaned over, whispering, "what – hey, what do you call a buncha lesbians in a closet?"

"I don't know, Hank. What do you call it?"

He leaned forward and whisper-rasped: "A licker cabinet."

Hank slapped his knees, wheezed out a laugh. His face pinkened a slight bit more. The wheeze turned into a cough.

We were sitting in front of the television. I had come in on the bus the night before, gotten up early and was having my first morning instant. My mother was in the other room, laying on the carpet doing her breathing exercises. Hank tossed another lemon drop into his mouth, rested his hands atop his belly.

CLOWN: *Coming right up: Daddy went to war to serve his country and keep America safe and free. While he was gone, mommy had a breakdown and drowned their three children, aged six months to four years. An American tragedy in Pennsylvania, after these messages... You're watching NNN, the News Now leader...*

Hank leaned forward and rasped. "Hey, listen – so why is eating pussy like being in the mafia?"

"Eating a cat? I'm not sure I understand, Hank..."

"Aw, hell! You know what pussy is, dontcha?" He glanced in my mother's direction, then whispered again. "You're a grown man, ain't ya? I know you are. C'mon, don't pull my leg..."

"O.K... so why is it?"

Hank grinned. "One slip of the tongue and you're deep in the shit!"

Hank wheezed. His belly bulged, his shoulders shook, the captain's hat nearly fell off his head.

Have another taco, America! You deserve it! Are you looking for creamy refried beans, Tex-Mexicali style charbroiled beef, spicy pork, slabs of chewy chicken, reeeee-al cheddar cheese chunks and tangy sour cream? Well, book your ticket down at Taco Station, home of the new three-quarter-pound Taco Burger! Have another taco, America, because you deserve it! TAC-O! TAC-O! TAC-TAC-TAC-O! Free 64-ounce Mini-Mite with the purchase of any 64-ounce drink. While supplies last...

Hank and my mother lived not far from where the airport met the freeway. Hank had worked 35 years at the old Lapp-Spraun plant, 40 or so miles and two freeways to the southeast. Hank would often remind you that at one point, the company had made the special glue for the heat tiles on the space shuttles. Hank had been in the technical-manufacturing hierarchy and had traveled to see several space program launches, as well as a number of landings, and at least one explosion. Then the company had moved most of the glue-plant operations to Taiwan and Slovakia, after getting laws passed in these places assuring that no taxes would be necessary. Hank had taken the retirement buyout and gone on lemon drops and beef jerky immediately after the doctors had threatened him with death – either the 44 years of smoking or the special glue was to blame.

"C'mere, Pepper!"

A little black rat-dog ran over and jumped on Hank's knees. Hank kissed and petted the small animal. Pepper jumped back to the ground and began licking Hank's feet. Hank giggled, snorted.

"Listen," said Hank, "so what did the one lesbian vampire say to the other?"

"Hank, now..."

"See you next month!"

Hank grabbed the flyswatter sitting on the coffee table and swiped at the air.

"Goddamn flies!"

My mother walked past, her face lined and blotchy after four marriages. She lugged a bag out the back door and went to feed the geese.

"Say," said Hank, "you want some freedom toast?"

"Some what?"

"Freedom toast..."

"I'll pass, Hank..."

"Nope, you're getting it. Love it or leave it." Hank laughed. "Freedom toast coming up. Otherwise known as waffles."

I went to the bathroom, then wandered back into the kitchen for another cup of instant. Hank was a examining a bunch of pill bottles in a cabinet.

"It's drug time... Got to take my Procardia, otherwise I might get a headache... Zantac, Flomax, Avandia..." He chuckled. "Hey, look," he said, waving a bottle of Biagra. "Don't tell your mother, huh?"

"Don't worry, Hank..."

The waffles popped out of the toaster and Hank plopped them on a plate. He put in two more. My mother came in and began slicing ham from a plastic package. She threw the ham in a bowl, added a can of tuna fish, then mashed it all together.

"Breakfast, Pepper," she said.

We sat down at the coffee table in front of the television. I picked up a waffle and took a bite. My mother carried over her plastic rack and began lining up sets of vitamins. She counted off 12 tablets, then popped more lids – potassium, so forth. She had worries about kidney stones, concerns about acidity, issues with triglycerides...

CLOWN: *O.K., it looks like we're getting an Amber Alert in Minnesota... Police are reporting that a five-year old girl may have been abducted from in front of her family's condominium in Kwasauchee, Minnesota... The little girl's name is Rebecca Manderson, and she has gone missing... Reports say a man driving a blue Honda Voltaire was seen in the area when Rebecca disappeared... Again, ladies and gentlemen, an Amber Alert has been issued for 5-year-old Rebecca Manderson in Kwasauchee, Minnesota...*

My mother talked a bit about the problems she was having with the "black bitch" at her work. I had been hearing about this problem for years. The woman was incompetent, according to my mother, but kept the job because she was black.

"They don't want to get sued!" said my mother.

She glared. There had, apparently, been another confrontation. The boss had had to take them aside for a chat to sort things out.

"Now, go easy, Pride & Joy," said Hank, using his nickname for my mother. He turned to me. "I always tell her just to ignore it... There's no winning in something like that."

"Sounds like a good idea, Hank..."

It wasn't long before my mother brought up Webster. This was her second husband, who had been fond of whacking us on the ass with a two-by-four if, for example, we didn't finish our fish sticks or had left water on the bathroom floor, among many other things. Webster would make us stand with our pants down as he delivered a lecture of several minutes and prepared to use the two-by-four, which he called The Board.

A teacher and school administrator by profession, Webster whacked hard enough to you make you cry and feel like vomiting, your ass stinging and burning through the rest of the night. In the morning, your ass might be a little sore, but Webster had the touch – only rarely had he hit hard enough to leave a welt or bruise.

Webster claimed to have been "born again" and had ordered us to be baptized as born-agains as well – taken into a tank and held completely under water by a man with an angry red face, bright blue eyes and a thick mustache. And we had been. My mother had gotten deeply sucked in – "Get thee behind me, Satan!" she would tell us to say whenever we had a bad dream.

Once, she had laid her hands on my elbow and we had prayed, and the next day – *voila*, a cluster of warts had magically disappeared...

Hank didn't like Webster either. I was just glad he was gone. I had been glad since the first minute he was no longer around, and had stayed glad, without interruption.

Webster had made my mother quit her job and stay home to bake muffins. He had given her bruises from squeezing her wrists. He had declined to give my mother any money at all when we finally left. Instead, he had hired a private dick to follow her around, accusing her of "having a boyfriend."

Webster claimed the problem was that my mother might have become "possessed by a demon" and needed to be taken back to the church so the preacher could cast out the little bugger. But far from scaring my mother off from Christianity, the trouble only led her to switch brands of it when Hank came along.

Webster had resumed drinking, ballooned up to 300 pounds, had a heart attack two years later.[*] My mother enjoyed mentioning this and she never failed to do so, unable to prevent a little smile from popping out as the tale escaped her lips. It was also good lead-in to saying something about my father.

I shrugged. "I didn't marry him. You did."

"Hey, now," said Hank. "We all make mistakes..."

"Your father *gained weight* eating apples," my mother snapped.

"I know he did," I said. "It's a real legend around here."

---

[*] Webster, a Canadian by birth, also hated baseball. – ED.

My mother looked off, working to get down her vitamins and pills. Each vitamin or pill she swallowed with half a glass of water. She kept getting up to refill her glass. When she was done, she went back to the carpet for another round of breathing exercises.

"So listen," Hank whispered, "this guy can't get a date and he finally decides to get one of those blow-up dolls. He goes into the sex shop and the owner says, 'O.K., we got two models here – one for $25, the other $350.' 'Show me the cheap one first,' says the guy. The owner opens the box. 'O.K., her name is Hot Sally and you blow her up right here at the ankle. Takes about 15 minutes.' 'All right,' says the guy. 'Let's see the other one. Why is it so expensive?' 'Well…' The owner reaches under the counter and takes out the box. 'Have a look. She's a Palestinian and she blows herself up.'"

Hank giggled.

Pretty soon, Hank's daughter Viveca and her daughter Coco came out in their pajamas. Things hadn't much worked out, they had been shacking with Hank and my mother for more than a year. Viveca was apparently studying to get an acupuncturist license. Several years before, she had been married to a Puerto Rican, but he had run off back to Puerto Rico with a young Puerto Rican girl, according to my mother, leaving Viveca and Coco behind.

In previous discussions, Viveca had revealed her belief that human beings had "wiped out" the dinosaurs in a series of epic wars many thousands of years ago.

"It's not backed up by the fossil record," I had said.

"What do *you* know about *fossil records?*" she had responded. "It would change everything if the truth came out…"

"Yes, it would."

Viveca's face was creased and still puffy from sleep. She was barefoot and wearing a long yellow T-shirt advertising HUSSONG'S Bar & Cantina Grill. She went into the kitchen and came back out with a pack of saltine crackers and a tub of Country Crock. She knifed some of the crock onto a cracker and gave it to Coco.

"Be a good girl, Coco," said Hank, "and say hello to your Uncle Thor."

The black-haired child looked at me with curious brown eyes but said nothing. Instead, she threw the saltine cracker on the carpet. She stepped on it.

"COCO!" screamed Viveca. "YOU PICK THAT UP RIGHT NOW!"

"Oh, dear!" said Hank.

Viveca swung out with an open hand, missing her daughter by several feet. Coco ran out of the room.

"FUCK YOU, YOU LITTLE BITCH!"

Viveca sprang from the couch and chased after her offspring. In a room down the hall could be heard several slaps, a number of thuds against the wall, followed by the sound of Coco bawling.

Hank brought a hand to his face. He shook his head, gestured with his hands. He leaned forward on the couch.

"Aw, cripes," he said. "Chicken today, feathers tomorrow..."

My mother walked in with a hand broom and dust pan. She smiled.

"You were the perfect baby, the perfect little boy. When I said 'Sit,' you sat. When I said, 'Get up,' you got up. Both you and your brother. It was wonderful..."

"Thanks, mom."

"Yes, your mother loves you very much," said Hank.

✪

A little while later I joined Viveca outside for a smoke. We walked past geese feathers and droppings and sat on the bench.

"So how's it going, Viveca? Haven't seen you in a while..."

She shrugged, blew smoke, kicked at a few geese droppings. Then she turned and grabbed my arm. Her eyes widened.

"There's a ghost in this house. Did you know that? It comes every night at 11."

"Jesus, I had no idea..."

"If you listen, you can hear it on the kitchen floor. I think it lives in the cabinet under the sink. I tell Coco not to go in there because the ghost might get her..."

"Goddamn, that's really crazy..."

"You got any pot?"

"No, sorry..."

"You got anything?"

"Sorry, Viveca."

"I thought so..."

We finished our smokes and went back in.

✪

Ah, I love the food they serve down at the ballpark. Peanuts and crackerjack, crunchy, cheesy nachos with jalapeño chiles... Why, at most ballparks these days you can even get a slice of pizza. And a hot dog, heck – you've got to have a hot dog at the ball game, or it just wouldn't be American. One of them big ballpark franks, slathered in mustard and ketchup, with lots of onions and relish. Mmmmm, good. Why, sometimes you can even get chili and cheese on 'em... But as I've gotten older, I must admit, sometimes now I get heartburn. That's why I use new Burn-B-Gone. Drink a little before the game... and a little after... and it's noooo problem. You can eat all the good baseball food you want, and you feel just fine. Say, there – are you going to finish those nachos...? Leave the burn behind... With new Burn-B-Gone.

The obese professional clown and pro-football analyst Gus Hanspaugh appeared on the screen. A former chocolate factory worker, Vietnam War draft-dodger and unsuccessful stand-up comedian, Hanspaugh was now universally recognized as the leading talk-jock in the land. In less than a decade, he had succeeded in transforming his little-known radio show on KSLG in Tuskegee, Alabama, into a nationally-syndicated empire. This was due in no small part to his consistently controversial "Two-Minute Offense" segment, in which he was prone to point the finger of blame for America's failures at targets such as "femi-fascists," "enviro-nazis," "immigrant lovers" and "black quarterbacks." Homeless people, prostitutes and drug addicts had also been repeatedly targeted by Hanspaugh for "failing to take personal responsibility and bringing America to the brink of ruin..."

Critics were continually declaring themselves "outraged" by each Hanspaugh provocation, but their unimaginative bellowing had little, if any, impact, and Hanspaugh's market-share only kept increasing, with at least 3.6 stations around the country adding his show each week, according the most recent industry figures. And Hanspaugh had taken good advantage of his opportunities, spinning off books, CDs, DVDs and a special internet-only subscription service that had netted him an estimated $250 million so far. Well, the American people liked success – and who was to disagree with the American people?

"Pride & Joy!" shouted Hank. "Gus is on!"

Gus quickly launched into a denunciation of Eileen Lomax, an obscure columnist who had recently described Wolfgang G. Mnung as "the worst president of all time."

My mother walked in slowly, holding Pepper in her arms. She sat on the arm of the couch and began watching with a glazed look. Pepper's small tongue came out, feebly licking her ring finger.

CLOWN: *How dare Eileen Lomax! She should be arrested for treason in this time of war. Mnung is clearly one of our greatest presidents. He doesn't flinch, he doesn't waver, he doesn't back down. He has phenomenal inner strength. Lomax is soooo old, why, she was getting her first divorce during the Coolidge administration. Heh-heh... She's no different than those Doo-Dah Dixies, who had the nerve to say Mnung was wrong while touring in France! The radio stations are right not to play these Dixies and their style of so-called 'country music,' which might be better described as 'talent-free yodeling.' That's capitalism, folks, that's freedom, that's free choice, and America's airwaves are better for it. It's sure as heck not some government diktat, like you hear these liberals complaining. The truth is, Chowderheads, our country is being made weaker because of the obsession of Lomax and other attack-America-firsters, who are trying to bring down our commander-in-chief... I hate to say it, friends, but they are guilty of dividing the country in a time of war. Eileen Lomax, along with her friends at the arrogant, elitist, left-wing* New York Times, *would apparently sell our nation's security to the U.N. and France for a pittance! My friends, how long would this glorious land be free with them in charge? No, sir. I want Mnung to decide... He believes America is God's land.*

"He sounds like he's high on dope," I said.

"Aw, you're crazy!" said Hank. "Ain't you got nothin' nice to say? Gus is a good man. Everybody thinks so."

CLOWN: *Ladies and gentlemen, if and when we are attacked again, it will be the fault of Eileen Lomax and her like. It will be the fault of Amnesty International, Human Rights Watch, Jefferson Rockton and Senators Johnson, Eibelhams, Moltko, Babbings, Hippering, Bairdley, and good ol' Raquel Roddington, the liberal-left-socialist from Massachusetts by way of Berkeley and the University of Wisconsin, which is famous, need I remind you, Chowderheads, for its all-lesbian dormitories... These groups and individuals do not seem to understand that we are fighting a war for the survival of our way of life... If Mnung is voted out, God forbid, it will be a victory for the terrorists and it will be the fault of people like these. They believe in coddling jihadis and putting them on trial in court, and those trials will still be going on, if indeed they ever start, when – not if, ladies and gentlemen, but* **when** *– when we are hit again by terrorists. It's as if they really do want* **them** *to win...*

Later in the morning, Hank took me out the garage to show me the solar car he had finally started to build. The engine was set up on a table, with a number of wires and test-cables stretching across the concrete to several machines and gizmos that were lined up on a shelf against the wall.

Deep in his engineering heart, Hank was a utopian and he wanted the whole hog: A vehicle that didn't use gas, water *or* batteries... He had explained the principle to me a number of times, but it wouldn't take long before I was left floundering. It would use an aluminum solar cell such-and-such, you see...You would put your direct current into the inverter...

"It'll only go about 20 miles per hour, but think about it – it'll use *nothing*..."

"Nice, Hank, nice..."

Years earlier, Hank had built a battery-less radio using just a matchbox, wires and headset. It was powered by the electricity from a person's body. He loved to show it off, and to mourn that there still wasn't much of a market for it. Somehow, remarkably, it did work, though channel selection and reception tended to be most minimal. He placed it on my head. Hanspaugh's voice came through:... *this is not a resistance, not an insurgency, and the media is getting it wrong when they call it that. It's a bunch of terrorists and thugs who hate America and hate freedom. What the American military should do is bomb the living daylights out them. Level the whole place. Put everything that flies on anything that moves. Set a curfew, and everyone, and I mean anyone, who breaks it – start shootin'. Serve Arab-burger and Pepsi-Cola for breakfast, lunch and dinner... I guarantee, this so-called insurgency will disappear in a matter of days. That would be the final solution for these ingrates who dare attack the same valiant U.S. military that liberated them from the dictator...*

"So listen," said Hank. "Mnung and Jicks are sitting in this bar. And this guy walks in and says, 'Wow, what an honor to meet you guys! What are you guys doing here?' And Mnung looks up and says, in all seriousness, 'Well, we're planning World War III.' 'Really?' says the guy. 'What's gonna happen?' And Jicks says, 'We're gonna kill 200 million Muslims and one blond woman with huge tits.' And the guy says, 'A blond with big tits? Why? Who is she?' And Jicks turns to Mnung and says, 'See, I told you no one cares about 200 million Muslims.'"

My mother walked in. "Thor, please, don't blow your nose and throw the kleenex in the toilet. It's bad for the pipes."

"I'm sorry, Mom, I forgot. I'll remember next time."

She smiled. "I know you will, honey."

I drove Hank's Kia Kolero past miles of car dealerships, supermarkets and coin laundrymats to Willowglen Centre. I parked, went in and bought a cinnamon roll and a cup of coffee for $10.

The BookBarn was nearly deserted, just a few people poking about bashfully, except for one Chinese youth who stood alone in the magazines section, boldly flipping through a copy of *Hustler*. The long wooden tables were filled with a big sales blowout for all kinds of tomes: *How To Build Cabinets, How To Water Plants, 537 Ways To Make a Baby Smile, How to Fix Your Car, How To Cook Italian, 996 Great Quilts, How To Make Love Like A Porn Goddess, 17 Successful Secrets to Becoming a Billionaire by Waldo Stoughmeier Ph.D., The Girls' Guide To Roping and Steering (A Guy!), The Globe Is Flat! Poor Brown People in Foreign Countries Are Speaking English and They Want Your Good American Job...*

A circular carpet and bean bags had been set up in the Fiction Section, where it appeared that a big promotion had been launched for the paperback version of *Flying Cats & Shipwrecked Dogs*,[*] by the acclaimed young author William Derloth Fauffgogg. A graduate of Choate, the New England College of Literary Design and the Iowa Writer's Workshop, Fauffgogg had famously been the favored student of the esteemed novelist and Yale lit professor Carolyne Oonest Eldors, who was herself the winner of three American Book Prizes. Eldors' husband, the *New Yorker* short-story luminary Nathaniel "Jay" Ulker, had written the blurb for Fauffgogg's book cover: "Displaying an incredible ability to pack more substance into one sentence than most writers can convey in ten, young Fauffgogg's debut is dazzling, smart, heartfelt, economical, sleek and overflowing... One is reminded of the early Edwin Pouplans, and one waits with anticipation for whatever comes next..."

Fauffgogg's father was of course none other than Jones Henshaw R. Ford Fauffgogg II, the noted *New York Times* architecture scribe. His

---

[*] Film rights sold to Hollywood before the manuscript was even completed. – ED.

mother, Annadine Plegg Ortiz-Fauffgogg, the celebrated painter of seaweed, had committed suicide several years ago, shortly after the publication of her critically-lauded memoir *Kissy Kiss Kiss*, which had graphically detailed her four-year consensual affair with her father, the Rev. Bournes A. Plegg of LeBecquelle, Ontario, Canada. Fauffgogg's older brother, Coleman "Cole" Fauffgogg, was of course the executive editor of *The National Panorama*, who had recently authored an article, praised in the pages of *The New York Times* and *Washington Post*, on the urgent need for America to nuclear-bomb Iran and several other countries...

The Fauffgogg blurb bonanza continued on the back cover: "A most touching and heart-rending piece of work. Rarely has such genius seemed so mysterious, so great a gift, so desperately welcomed. Fauffgogg writes with the simple but absolute authority of the first voyager to return from unmapped lands." – Kiyaki Hockerham, *The New York Times*. "Engagingly modest, ennui and ecstasy together in perfect entropy, with an alluring power-to-weight ratio. Fauffgogg is clearly a born stylist, a remarkable discovery... A saucy spaghetti of ideas... (that) goes down like spumento ice cream. Think of it as a *Crying of Lot 49* for the reality-TV set!" Brick Pomeroy, *Chicago Times Book World*.

I flipped to page 67:

> She saw now that it was a glow-worm. 10-year old Lily. Ran. Past the apricorn groves and into the drippy-drip drooping cavern of know/be/see.com.
> "Please don't make me do it," she said. "I'm chicken."
> Fauffgogg, with a wither-glum stare, lifted his knees off the window ledge.
> Then. Lily. Masturbated. To an extremely accurate description.
> Lily. Ran. Down Tumescent Avenue, the signs proclaiming "Dymaxion Lives!" The organizers had agreed to accept $50 donations to the Dymaxion Local Improvement Association...

I set it back down.

I finally found what I needed at a display by the cash registers: *Things That Are Right*, by Gus Hanspaugh. Freedom Edition Nice Price: $12.99. I flipped to Page 49.

While America's (for now) majority continues to not reproduce itself, the Third World increases by approximately 100 million people – or the entire population of Mexico! – every 14-15 months. At this rate, there will be nearly 40 new Mexicos by 2045, while Europe will have lost the equivalent of the entire populations of the Netherlands, Belgium, Slovakia, Holland, Hungary, Norway, Bulgaria and Germany. Unless European women return to breeding like their great-grandmothers, people of white European heritage are destined to vanish from the earth, and our freedoms, faith and democracy with them.

Today's young women of European origin like the sex-charged lifestyle, the careers and random sex with strangers without responsibilities. But it is no liberation for womankind – indeed, it is a kind of slavery. The selfishness of these ladies, and of what I call "dinky couples" – double incomes, no kids – is certain to lead to the death of people of European heritage.

Mexican immigrants to America are not only from another culture, they are of another race, and most of them have no desire to learn English. They have established their own television and radio stations, newspapers and magazines, as if they are a separate country within our nation. We must shut the door on these Mexicans before they turn America into one gigantic Tijuana, with all that city's attendant filth, prostitution and drug warfare, but on an even more massive scale...

At a kiosk near the bathrooms I saw the display for President Wolfgang G. Mnung Limited Edition Freedom Platoon Ranger Warrior action figures. *Includes kung-fu grip, authentically detailed cloth flight suit, helmet with oxygen mask, life vest, G-pants and harness, die-cast metal 240-mm blast-cannon and ammunition belt... Made in Republic of South Korea.*

I picked up the sample. It truly was remarkably life-like. The $24.99 price tag intimidated, but – I pulled the little cord.

Bring it on, the voice said. *Hunt 'em down, smoke 'em out... Scratch out their eyeballs with rusty spoons... With us or without us... War on terror, bring it on...*

I pulled out of the mall, drove several miles. I saw a place called The Filling Pump and parked. I bought a small bottle of Jim Beam, two packs of smokes, then drove around the corner into a residential neighborhood, coming to a stop under some trees. I sat in the car and sweated, sucking down a smoke and a couple slugs.

✪

CLOWN:... *in a country of our wealth, it is wrong that we have 40 to 45 million people living in poverty. It is wrong for children to go hungry, for children not to have the clothes to keep them warm.* (CROWD CHEERS) *It is wrong to have folks who are working full time every day, playing by the rules and trying to provide for their families, working for the minimum wage – and still living in poverty. For too long, Congress has behaved as if the only problem in America is that rich people don't have enough money.* (CROWD CHEERS) *This is not the country we want to live in. Why is it that the wealthiest nation finds it so hard to keep faith with its weakest citizens? Why can we not see beyond the veil of race? How can we remain strong in difficult times without destroying what we value most?*

My mother snarled. "I hate Jefferson Rockton! HATE HIM!"

Hank grinned, wheezed. "Really gets her goin,' don't he?"

CLOWN: *We must remain true to our nation's highest ideals of economic justice and a decent life for every citizen, civil rights and a humane foreign policy.* (CROWD CHEERS) *We must renew our characteristic American fairness, curiosity, openness, humility and concern for the basic humanity, courage and faith of others. It is time to move forward, for the country we carry in our hearts is waiting.* (CROWD CHEERS) *We must end our shameful enslavement to oil and the fundamental damage it does to our nation. We need to direct the prodigious scientific talents of this country toward creating, once and for all, renewable non-polluting energy resources...*

"Is that what you tell all your girlfriends?" hissed my mother at the politician on the screen.

She got up and walked into the kitchen. Pepper ambled after her.

"You know," whispered Hank, "they say he's got a bent pecker. Bends down to the left..." He giggled.

CLOWN: *President Mnung has failed the fundamental test of leadership... He has failed to tell the truth, and the American people deserve better. He has gone to war in foreign lands and offered up the lives our young men and women under circumstances that are now discredited.* (CROWD CHEERS) *He has failed to tell you that with each passing day, we are seeing more violence, more chaos, more indiscriminate killings. He has neglected to inform you about what his own intelligence officials have said in confidential reports – that the war mission is failing and has made our country less safe.* (CROWD CHEERS) *The war has damaged our reputation around the world. It has helped the cause of the terrorists. It has cost our nation well more than one trillion dollars – money we need desperately here at home. We must accept that it is time to start bringing the troops home and admit that no amount of American lives can settle the political problems that are at the center of someone else's civil war. You deserve a president who will not misstate the facts about national security, who will not live in a fantasy world of spin and costumes and false pronouncements...*

"I don't believe a word," said Hank. He picked up the remote and clicked to a golf match. "That guy never met a hairspray he didn't fall in love with."

NO MÁS:
Clown Pounded in Fist Frenzy!

★ 26 ★

Toby drove over in the early evening. Toby was still shacked up with Synthia, whom he had started dating when we were 15. They'd had a second kid in the two years since I'd seen him last. Toby still had the thick cop mustache and was still hoping to become a sheriff, but apparently it wasn't so easy. As Toby had explained it, they gave you a bunch of tests then made you work as an Apprentice Prison Guard. If you did well enough in the jails, you might get a chance to move up to real sheriff.

The whole thing seemed difficult. Toby had been in the Apprentice Prison Guard system for four years so far.

Toby had added two sets of shiny "breaking chains" decals to the front and each side of his Ford Focus, as well as a number of decals depicting bullet holes. We drove around the block and Toby pulled out a new bottle of Jagermeister. He cracked it and we each had a slug.

"So how's Synthia doing?"

"Fat as a hog," said Toby. "Her legs are turning like cottage cheese. God, it sucks. You'll see."

"Shit, Toby."

Toby pulled out a tin and we each threw a snuff dip in our lower lips. We spat the juice out the window, had a few more slugs of the Jager. The Focus backfired, chugged, and we drove off across town toward Toby's shack.

Toby said he had bought the Jager after winning $60 in bets from a recent series of fights between rival prisoners. According to Toby, the guards would give the two prison fucks drugs, then let them go at it, sometimes with weapons like metal bars or shivs. It was generally somebody from the Aryan Brotherhood against one of the "nig-nogs," though Mexicans often were involved as well. The jails were apparently strictly racial factionalized territory – white-trash types who used dopey names like Aryan Brotherhood and the Nazi Lowriders, fighting it out against the DC Blacks and the Rollin' 50s, the Mexican Mafia and "the Muslims," each with shifting loyalties and murder on the mind... At the same time, according to Toby, members of all factions were busy "pimping" each other and "going homo" all over the place – yet would kill in a second anybody who dared call them a "fag." In any case, if you got in this jail and didn't join up with one of the factions to protect your ass, you probably wouldn't make it...

Toby had seen one bad white dude bite off the fuckin' finger of a Mexican. Then the jail guards had pulled a lockdown, rushed in and bopped each guy on the head.

"It was nutty," said Toby.

Toby lived in the part of town adjacent to the port container yard, a place of mini-markets and gas stations, auto parts stores and carpet emporiums, places that specialized in Armenian and Mexican wedding supplies. Sixty or 70 percent of the residents were immigrants, mainly Mexicans and some ex-Soviets, the rest being poor whites. Plenty of Mexicans were out and about, on their lawns or in the streets working with their shirts off, fixing cars and fiddling with refrigerators. Many of the men had mustaches and serious faces, they seemed very concerned. The women seemed less concerned. They frequently smiled, often with bad teeth. Their children ran barefoot up and down the sidewalks, shrieking.

Toby and the family lived on the third floor of a washed-out beige and white apartment complex. We walked up, maneuvering around debris that the residents had piled along the walkway railings – cardboard boxes and busted chairs, crates full of old bottles, plants. The sun burned down upon the place with little sympathy, there was next to no breeze, I had always felt hot and claustrophobic there. Little Devyn and Destyny were watching cartoons on television with the lights off, an air conditioner blasting away in the corner. There was the vague smell of old french fries from the oven. Several flies buzzed between the window screen and blinds. In another corner, not far from the TV, was a bench and set of barbells. Toby claimed he pumped iron every morning and evening, if he wasn't too tired or hung over.

Synthia came out from the kitchen, drying her hands with a towel. I thought of what a beautiful girl she had been in high school – a fresh smile and soft milky skin, the girl who would force me to wait outside her parents' house as she and Toby did whatever they did inside. Toby and I would show up. Toby would go in. Synthia's girlfriends would walk out. I would smile and greet them, but they tended to ignore me. I would sit on the curb in agony, watching a string of ants on the walk, the trees glowing green, sunset the color of peaches, having no clue, vowing something like this would never happen to me again...

"Oh hi, Thor. Nice to see you again. Gosh, it's really been a long time."

"Wow, Synthia, you look great... Toby been takin' good care of you, hunh?"

Synthia laughed. I walked forward and gave her kiss. She had added some pounds and a few wrinkles around her eyes, but her smile was sweet, her smell light and flowery.

It wasn't long before Toby brought up money. He apparently thought I was printing it for myself up in Bay City.

"So where's all your bucks, man? I know you got 'em..."

"I don't got no bucks. You make more than I do..."

"Oh fuck, come off it!" said Toby.

"Come on, you guys," whined Synthia.

Toby wanted to go through it again, in front of Synthia. We exchanged the sums. As a couple, they were pulling in nearly $180 more per month than me, if you added in Synthia's part-time shift at Kopie Kings. But they had no health benefits, neither for them nor the kids, while technically I did have that benefit (also, they explained, most of Synthia's check went for child care). An Apprentice Prison Guard apparently made a lot less than a full prison guard or cop. But Toby was still hopeful.

"We got to get out of this place," he said. "Damn, you can get $50,000 just to sign up for the Army. The Army will give you that, just to *sign up*. Shit, I'd go kill me some A-rabs, if that's what they want. But Synthia said no..."

Synthia nodded.

"Shit," said Toby, laughing, "I'm whipped. I'm fuck-whipped!"

"Yeah you are, you fuck!" I said.

Toby talked about how he had been hitting the shooting range with Synthia's father, Bud. They were going to teach Synthia how to shoot. Because you never knew anymore what was going to happen, that was for sure.

Toby scooped up a chair and led me down the hall. He stood on the chair, stepped up to a shelf. He pulled away a plywood board near the ceiling and took out his piece – a Ruger P-94.

He climbed down and handed it to me. It smelled strongly of oil, seemed heavier than I would have thought. I handed it back.

Toby whirled around in a cop pose, kneeled and pointed it me.

"The nig-nog comes sneakin' in – BOOM! POW!"

"Hey, watch it!"

"Don't worry, man," he said, grinning. "I'm a pro."

"That thing loaded?"

"Of course it is," he said. "What good is it unloaded?"

Toby had four more months to pay on the piece. He talked about a few other guns he wanted to get, then climbed back up and put the thing away.

Toby grabbed a basketball and we went down the stairs and around to the alley. We threw in more long-cut snuff and shot baskets on the bent hoop for a while. Toby was still in pretty good shape, still at least quarter-step faster than I was. He burned me bad on several drives, but I was finding it hard to care much. The sun and the Jager and the snuff were having an impact. My heart was flapping around, I just wanted to sit. After the game, which I lost 15-11, we squatted under a garage overhang and I had a smoke.

Pretty soon, a dirty yellow van came rocking down the alley. It was our old pal Yaddy, bearing an 18-pack box of Natural Light. Toby had put the word out that I was in town. We slapped hands and Yaddy opened the back doors of the van. We sat on the end and drank them down, talking about old times.

Yaddy wasn't looking so good. He had always been short. Now he had gained a lot of weight and grown a goatee. The tendency had always been there. Yaddy had been second-string running back and punt-returner on our football team.

"Hey dog, remember Irwin Jowes? He had that thing swinging to his knee! Shit, I ain't gay, I'm just sayin'..."

"Shit, how could I forget? How could anyone forget that thing?"

"Shit, but Irvie could *run*, though. He could *cut*, smooth as ice... But not so much on the hands. That's why he didn't get no scholarship..."

"Shit, Antonucci signed up for the Marines. He's over there, killin' A-rabs..."

"Is he? Shit, that guy was always tough. I never got hit so hard. I was always glad he was on our team."

We laughed.

"Shit, remember when Anto knocked that guy's block off from La Habra? Remember that game? That was fuckin-A great. Left that fucker sprawlin' in the middle of the field. Fuckin' coaches ran out there, didn't know what to do. But was a fuckin' legal hit, totally fair and square..."

Yaddy tried to interest me in his new gig – he was selling "sheepskin" seat covers and cabinet stereo speakers from the back of the van. He was willing to give me a full set of four seat covers and floor mats for $40, while a set of the "pro speakers" would set me back $175. But he was ready to give them to me for $160.

He pulled a sheet off some boxes in the back and we had a look. I said I didn't even have a car, let alone money for speakers. I tried to explain that I had been dumped by my girlfriend, had worms on my ceiling...

Yaddy seemed disappointed. He, too, apparently believed I was flush with big Bay City bucks. These guys were having way too many fantasies. We stood out in the alley, drinking from the cans. Then Yaddy jumped back in the van and removed a side panel.

"Check it out... Rock River AR-15. Semi-auto. Got it for $140 off the internet. New, out of the box."

"Sweet, Yaddy..."

"What the hell," I said.

Yaddy reached into a dirty white duffel and removed a box of bullets.

"Check it out, Thor. Ranger SXT."

"What the hell..."

"Hot," said Toby.

"Meat-cutters, dog," said Yaddy.

Pretty soon Toby and I got in the Focus and followed Yaddy over to Boonie Bryan's. It was nearly dark now, fiery orange-pink sunset swirls visible over the tops of the light purple palms. On the way, we stopped at a Rite-Aid and got jugs of Canadian Club and Borski for $8.99 each. I took lips from both as Toby drove, spitting long-cut juice in between pulls.

Boonie and Benny MacKenzie, Paul Preuss, Robby Gonzalez and Wayne O'Heegan were all in the garage, sitting under the fluorescent tubes. A Cypress Hill album was playing on the stereo, while the TV was showing a "bum fights" video. The hand-held camera jerked around wildly as the derelicts went at it.

A bum hit the concrete. Blood poured out over his lips and beard.

"Oh, dude!" squealed Paul Preuss, who had piercings in both lips, silver rings in his ears and nose, and a tattoo of Elmer Fudd on his neck.

I had heard from Toby that Robby and Wayne had gone "skinhead," and that appeared to be true. Toby also claimed that they now "sold speed." I couldn't tell about that.

They sat in lawn chairs around the ping-pong table, heads shaven tight, white t-shirts and jeans, black boots. They had bottles of Corona in one hand, smokes in the other. On his middle finger, Wayne wore a ring in the shape of a handcuff, while Robby had a three-leaf clover tattoo, inside of which was the number "311," on his right forearm. Big boys both, Robby a good deal shorter, they had been the starting tackles on the offensive line – they seemed to have gained 40 or 50 pounds since then. I remembered them as complainers, always blaming our quarterback, Ricky Fritsch, or running backs Jerome and Demetrius, every time there was a sack, which happened about every fifth or sixth play.

"Hey, guys!" I said.

They nodded at me, mumbled. Then Wayne farted. They both laughed.

I pulled out the Canadian Club and took a swig.

"Want some?"

Robby yawned. "No thanks, man..."

Wayne farted again. Robby laughed.

"White power," I said. "Fear of a black planet, ooga booga..."

"Oh, *fuck you*, man," said Wayne.

"No thanks," I said, taking a slurp off the Canadian. "Come on, your fuckin' name is Gonzalez. What with the white shit?"

"Well, his mom's white..." said Wayne of Robby.

"More power to you, man..."

"Buncha fags up there in Bay City, ain't there?" said Robby.

"You bet. Nothin' but, so to speak..."

"You go fag?"

"Not really..."

"*Not really?*"

"Yeah, not really."

"Yeah, you did. Get the fuck away from me, fucking homo."

Wayne said, "You like livin' with all them niggers up there?"

"Negroes? *Negroes?* Well, we do call 'em nig-nogs, you know... Of course I like it. They are some funny guys. Good dancers, pretty good at basketball..."

"Aw, fuck you..."

"Better watch it, man. One day soon we're gonna have a black president. This black guy told me. Then what? He's gonna throw your ass in jail for even thinking like you. Guys like you, they're gonna love your stinky white ass in jail. You won't get a second to rest."

"Black president? In this country? Ha, ha, ha."

"You *have* gone fag," said Robby.

"Fag? Shit, no. I been goin' out with this Jew woman up there. You should see her. She's so hot. Super hot. Rich, too, likes to suck dick... I think you'd really like her, she could give you some sweet dick-suck tips. She likes to take real good care of a dick..."

Wayne jumped up from his chair and slammed both his fists into my chest. I flew across the garage, tripping against the leg of the ping-pong table and knocking into the wall. I held on tight to the bottle. A little spillage, but nothing broken.

Toby, Boonie and Yaddy moved in between us, everyone shouting. I pulled myself up and stood. Wayne was shouting about how much he was going to kick my ass. Robby rushed in from the side. I saw him coming and was able to get an open hand on his forehead before Toby pulled him back.

I took several slugs off the bottle, reached into my pocket and lit a smoke.

✪

Hank was saying, "Some son of a bitch threw up all over Viveca's car last night! It cost me $18 this morning for a wash and wax."

"Gee whiz," I said.

My mother said, "What happened to your face?"

"I fell down, Mom."

"You're so swollen. Both eyes..."

Hank grinned, knocked my shoulder. "Shoulda seen the other guy, huh?"

"For sure, Hank, for sure..."

Somewhere in there, I remembered, we hit a cat. There was a light clunk, Toby had swerved, skidded, drove one wheel on to a curb before wrestling the Focus back on the street. The car rocked back and forth, tires screeching. Toby had come to a stop just inches from a Nissan Camora.

It was a miracle. Hitting the Camora would have been the end for us.

"Let's go, man, forget it. Fuck the fuckin' cat. He's all right..."

"No, we've got to look!"

Toby had jumped out, slammed the door.

I walked over slowly, the last of the Borski swinging in my hand. Toby was bent down over the animal...

Hank brought out the donuts on a plate. He stuck a candle in one and lit it for my mother. Hank and I sang "Happy Birthday." My mother blew out the candle. She smiled.

Hank came out with his gifts first – flowers, a sweater and earrings, $50 worth of lottery tickets.

I took the birthday bag out from the under the table and kissed my mother on the cheek. Her face lit up as she pulled out *Things That Are Right*.

"Oh, thank you, I've been dying for it!"

"No problem, Mom..."

She seemed less impressed with the Mnung doll. Hank grabbed for it eagerly, though, took it out of the box and yanked the cord.

Scratch out their eyeballs... freedom way of life... Bring it on...

"Well, I'll be golly gosh-darned," Hank wheezed. "Sounds just like him..."

My mother lined up her lottery tickets in stacks and began scratching.

"Is it still alive?" I had asked Toby.

"Yeah, a little... Damn, it's black!"

Toby had stood up, stumbled back a step.

"Aw, man! We are so fucked!"

I got down and looked. The cat raised his head and made a barely audible moan, scratched one of his front paws against the street. He couldn't seem to move his back legs. He tried to raise his head again, but it only weaved about uncertainly.

He lay back down on the street, his chest rising and falling. He looked at me. I wasn't sure what could be done. A hospital? A vet? I lifted up the critter's left foreleg.

"Hey Toby, it's not black, I see some white right here. C'mon, let's get him out of the street..."

My mother, Hank and I climbed into the Kia and drove 40 miles across the county to the Crystal House Cathedral, world-famous headquarters of the Rev. Jeremiah "Saint Jim" Ludovico. This was a place that had been constructed using nearly 10,000 panes of rectangular glass, which allowed the sun to shine through and decorate the marble floors with rainbows of colliding color.

Packs of Jesus-lovers walked along the St. Peter's Shopping Concourse, buying God-books and Jesus t-shirts, sipping decaf lattes and chewing scrambled egg croissants, standing in groups to offer Lord-greetings to each other. This was the same concourse where, several months before, the church's orchestral conductor, Carl Johnnie, had fired several rounds at ushers (missing all) before taking himself out with a bull's-eye temple shot.* It had been a very somber service the next Sunday, according to Hank.

Parishioners glanced at me and averted their eyes. My nose and face were red where they were still swollen, dark yellow circles beginning to turn purple under my eyes. I had done my best in the shower to reposition the nose cartilage, but it still felt seriously mushy. I reached into my pocket and threw down three more aspirin.

On the wall adjacent to the sanctuary, I stood looking up at a 20-foot tall blond wooden cross. There hung the Man – nearly nude, thickly muscled version. Bastards had got him good, that was for sure – *that* was how you punished a man. You pinned him down like a bug on a board, let him bleed everywhere, then put it display for everyone to see... They had carved the Savior's warning into the marble:

He that is not with me is against me; and he that gathereth not with me scattereth abroad. – Thus Saith The Lord, Matthew 12:30

Toby had let me out at the corner. A party seemed to be going on a few houses down from my mother and Hank's – people standing around outside, music.

I walked up the lawn. It was the pink skirt seen through the front door that done it – some girl wearing a hot pink skirt and black heels. She was standing with her back to me – black hair up in a tangle on the top of her head, strands of it twirling around her ears. An exposed back, a marvelous and soft-looking neck...

As I made for the doorway, a giant Samoan stepped in.

"Sorry... invitation only."

---

* Later reports revealed poor Carl Johnnie to be both secretly gay and a boozer, like many belongers to the Christian faith. – ED.

"Thanks," I had said, stepping around him to the right, "I just – I need to – it's all right, totally fine, thank you..."

I sat in a pew, sipping a mocha, listening to the choir. My mother and Hank went up to the front and got on their knees for a few private prayers. About 15 minutes later Rev. Jeremiah finally appeared, his bright red face, nostrils and snowy white hair gigantic on massive twin video screens.

"It's time to take your seat at God's dining table," the reverend announced. "God wants you to be a winner, not a whiner. Because God wants us to prosper. Wealth is God's way of rewarding you. God is with us... God is with us... Amen..."

The Samoan had stepped exactly with me. His hands, which he had been holding in front of him, exploded into my chest. I spun back, rebounded on to the lawn. I was suddenly dancing, swinging my arms in front of me.

The Samoan walked out towards me – a huge, dark blocky thing, porch lights blazing behind him.

I remember thinking, *I'll kick this joker's ass!*

I felt a surge of anger – he couldn't be *serious* about wanting a piece of *me*. I'll knock this fat pig out!

Jesus-worshippers stared at the screens as Jeremiah delivered the good news. As he spoke, the pastor appeared to gradually become more and more agitated. He waved his arms about, royal purple robes twisting and swaying to his exertions, his face becoming ever more red.

"I saw last week in my newspaper about how they are building Islamic mosques here in our fine town. Nice interview with the Muslim preacher man, pictures of their nice new mosque. And I kept going through that newspaper, went through the whole thing – and there was not a word, ladies and gentlemen, about the good news of Jesus Christ... Not a word in the so-called newspaper! All Islam in the newspaper, about how they are trying to build these Islamic mosques, and how they are planning new terrorist attacks and bombings against what they call 'infidels'... Do you know, my friends, what they mean when they say 'infidels'? An infidel, according to my dictionary, is an 'unbeliever.' This what they say *we* are – me and *you* and *you* and *you*... Infidels, because we do not believe in their Islam... But our faith is a force greater than Islam... So yes, I do have news for those reporters: A holy war is a-comin'! The army of Christ will not stay silent!"

My hands had come up in fists, I charged forward. The Samoan's forearm knocked away my incoming right like it was a bag of potato chips. His own right screamed onward through the night.

I spun back again, stumbled, but did not fall. Eruptions of white and yellow went off in my eyes. I could hear people gathering around, murmurs, a few shouts.

"Take this trash out, Nicky," somebody said.

"My friends, Iran is the sex-change capital of the world. Did you *hear* me – they are having a runaway success with sex-change – *in Iran*. The Islamic Republic, which is what they call themselves in Iran, is a place where a man can become a woman – and a woman can become a man. This is due to the fact that, according to my research, the late Ayatollah Khomeini – you may have heard of him – issued what is known as a *fatwa* that permits a man or a woman to change their sex. This is against nature. Why does our news media not report this unholy practice? Why are they covering up for this so-called ayatollah?"

I had been amazed to find myself still standing. Maybe I *had it* tonight, I remember thinking. Maybe he can hit me all he wants, *and it doesn't matter…* All I got to do is land one or two shots and he's a goner…

"Scholars inform us that this Muhammad fellow was in fact a pedophile, ladies and gentlemen. Islamic scholars themselves will admit that this man had nine wives – including one he married at age *six*. Six! And they say that marriage was consummated when that young girl was just nine… So no, if you are asked, my friends – all religions are not the same. All religions are not equally true. Allah and Jehovah are not the same God. There is no other name under Heaven in which we can be saved except the name of Jesus… We must ask – why did the tsunami hit Indonesia worst of all? Indonesia, the biggest Muslim nation and a leading exporter of terrorism? Did it just *happen* that way? I don't think so. That's God's ocean… it's His! And do not think for a moment that God does not know what happens in His ocean…"

I rushed forward again. My fingernails caught bits of Nicky's arm skin, but not much. Nicky dealt me a fresh round of chin music. I caught another in the face. Then a quick Nicky left crashed into my right ear. A Nicky right tossed me back the other way. I caught two more on the nose. Nicky dealt fresh chin music.

"Oh, God!" a guy said.

I heard a girl scream…

As we waited for my mother outside the Biblical Pastures Gift Shoppe, Hank whispered, "Hey, so what's your dream woman?"

"My mother," I said.

"No, no," chortled Hank, "it's, it's... a nymphomaniac who's deaf, dumb and blind – and owns a liquor store!"

"All right, Hank..."

Hank wheezed. "But what, what – if a man, if a man got half his wishes – he'd double his troubles!"

"Yes, indeed. So saith the Lord."

We finally got out of there. Hank splurged for Pasta Factory. As we were playing with the plastic, my phone rang.

The screen said: CHRISSY.

Her voice hit me like a warm mist. She was calling from the airplane. She had gone to Tampa or somewhere for a convention.

"I'm flying back early. Gerard had a heart attack."

"Oh, wow..."

"I miss you, Thor..."

"I really miss you, too..."

I stood outside and puffed another two cigarettes. My insides squirmed and stretched. I was jolted, felt a slight dizziness. I stood there and admitted it: I wanted to get back to Chrissy more than anything. I wanted to taste her mouth, I wanted to see her smile. I wanted to back her up against the wall and inhale her hair.

The hell – enough fooling around. Time was wasting. Hell with it, I would ask her to get married.

Two guys had appeared and led me down to the curb. I collapsed on to the hood of a car, then vomited, several heaves worth. One of the guys pulled me up, held me up by the shoulder. Blood poured from my face, mixing with several strings of vomit. The blood and vomit formed a pool on the car hood, then began to slide down the side.

"Do your eyes work? Can you see anything?"

One of the guys went in and came back with napkins. He unfolded a few and spread them on the car hood to soak up the blood.

"Throw it in the street, man..."

I picked up the sopping napkins and dropped them into the gutter.

✪

"So Clinton is at this dinner," Hank was saying, "sitting next to this beautiful blond. He leans over and he says, 'Missus, have you seen my clock?' She laughs and says, 'Your clock, Mr. President?' 'Yes, my clock,' says Clinton. He gets up and he says, 'Come over here, sweetie.' They walk down the hall and into a cleaning closet. And sure enough, Clinton unzips and takes out his pecker... And the lady says, 'Why, my gosh, that's not a clock, President Clinton, that's your cock!' And Clinton says, 'Well, if you put two hands and your face on it, it – it – it surely will be a clock!'"

Tears started to stream down Hank's face. "And he says... Clinton says, 'It – it – it takes a licking and... and... uh, uh, uh – keeps on ticking!'"

"Nice one, Hank..."

CLOWN: *We're joined now by Vice President Palmer Jicks, who is speaking with us by phone from a secret location beneath a mountain of solid rock in a state we cannot name... Thank you for joining us, Mr. Vice President.*

CLOWN: *Good to be with you, Gus.*

CLOWN: *Mr. Vice President, first off – there are reports that you told Senator Moltko of West Virginia to go eff himself on the floor of the Senate last week. Are these reports correct?*

CLOWN: *Gus, listen... This guy, this Moltko, had just accused me, the vice president of the United States of America, of crimes, corruption and thuggery. And he did so on the floor of the Senate of the United States of America. He accused the president of mendacity and a long list of crimes. He accused us of war-mongering and lying, and spilling the blood of foreign peoples and sacrificing American troops, for no reason. He did this on the sacred floor of the United States Senate, Gus... And then he has the gall to come running up in the Senate to shake my hand. I told him to his face, 'Go fuck yourself. Go fuck yourself over.'* (BLEEPING) *I just won't stand for that, Gus – that mealy-mouthed liberal stuff. You can only take so much of the bullpucky and criticism before you've got to slam people down so they get the message: People need to watch what they say in a time of war. The terrorists are listening to every word. They're looking for our weakness.*

CLOWN: *I've often said on my show that remarks like Moltko's are tantamount to treason.*

CLOWN: *Big-time.*

CLOWN: *In fairness though – some, Mr. Vice President, have said an apology might be in order, given the example it sets for our children. Are you going to apologize?*

CLOWN: No, I'm not going to apologize. The Mnung administration doesn't apologize. We never have, and we won't now. Why should we? I won't apologize for defending America. I won't apologize for knocking back guys who think they can get away with criticizing us. Well, they can't. Concerning children, I mean – like they've never heard the word 'Fuck,' or heard adults say it? (BLEEPING) Look, children talk like that all the time. They shouldn't be shocked and they won't be. That's naive.

CLOWN: Spoken like a true patriot... Vice President Palmer, some have called you the real power behind the throne.

CLOWN: It's not true, Gus. I am not pulling anybody's strings, certainly not the president's. He's free to do as he pleases. I'm hiding in a secret location, out of sight, out of mind. I admit, it's a nice way to operate. But what I really want to tell your listeners, Gus, is that Americans need to make the right choice in November's election. If we make the wrong choice – that is, if President Mnung and myself aren't returned to office – there is the real danger that we will be hit again, big-time, by terrorists.

CLOWN: It certainly doesn't get any clearer than that... Mr. Vice President, before we go, I must – I must ask – what of your lesbian daughter? My listeners would never forgive me if I didn't mention your beautiful lesbian daughter. Reports say she's currently with child thanks to the miracle of artificial insemination...

CLOWN: It's true, Gus. We love her dearly, with all our hearts. It looks like we're gonna be grandparents.

CLOWN: Isn't that special... Thank you, Mr. Vice President, for taking part of your busy day to speak with us. Call us again any time.

CLOWN: You're quite welcome, Gus. I'll do that.

CLOWN: That was the vice president of the United States of America, ladies and gentlemen, Mr. Palmer Jicks... Coming up in the next segment: I'd like to talk a little bit about the controversial subject of aborting black babies. As a God-believer, I of course oppose any and all abortions. But I do know that if you wanted to reduce crime, you could – if that were your sole purpose, to reduce crime – you could abort every black baby in this country, and your crime rate would go down. Now, this not something I support, let me make clear – but it's an interesting thought-experiment about public policy, isn't it? It would be an impossibly ridiculous and morally reprehensible thing to do, abort all the black babies in this nation... but scientists say it's indisputable that our violent crime rate would go down – if that's what you really wanted... Chowderheads on the line! I'll take your calls when we return...

Hank and my mother dropped me at the bus station.

"Hey there," said Hank, "you ever think about getting into television?"

"No, not really…"

"You should. I hear there's a whole lot of moolah in it…"

"Oh, do that!" said my mother.

DYNAMITE! Clown Left in Dust as Babe Blows Stack

★ 27 ★

"Oh, you look horrible!"

"No, it's not so bad..."

The hug was brief, no kiss. Chrissy looked tall and super-cool: Above-the-knee glittering crimson skirt, mauve silk blouse, cream hose, two-inch black heels. Pearl necklace, bracelets, white and orange-striped vinyl purse. Smelling like the day's perspiration, combined with perfume that brought to mind brown sugar mixed with honey and lilacs.

I gave her a version of the story. She stood there impatiently.

"You forgot to say you were drunk."

"Sure, there was that..."

She didn't laugh or smile, or even wince.

"Humm, hmm," said Maxine.

I followed them down the hospital hall. Gerard was laid out in a dim white room, fat arms laying lifeless over a blue blanket. They had shaved his head, there was a tube coming out his nose, another out his mouth. A sucking sound could be heard coming from somewhere. The room, overly warm, smelled vaguely of shit, disinfectant and flower bouquets.

"I think I'll wait outside," I said.

I wandered down to a waiting area and got a machine coffee. I sat on a bench and waited with a few others, watching the doctors wheel by various of the poor and tormented. A succession of old sickly bastards, some laid out cold, others appearing to groan and fart in misery.

A young girl, about ten years old, was wheeled past. She had on a white hospital gown, yellow plastic booties on her feet. She looked at me. Her face was probably the saddest I'd ever seen any face.

A nurse walked by and peered at me, wiping her hands on her apron. "Do you need help, hon? Are you O.K.?"

"No, just waiting," I mumbled.

I got up for another coffee. Another 20 minutes and Chrissy and her mother came out. The doctors weren't sure of the prognosis, apparently. It looked like Gerard was going to stay like that for at least a few more weeks.

Chrissy announced they were now going to visit her father in the Long-Term Care Facility. We got into the Lysteria and Chrissy drove us to the other side of the hospital.

"You want to come in, Thor?"

"Well... I think I'll just wait outside, if it's O.K."

I spent a few minutes walking around the parking lot, watching the late sunset, whiffing the car exhaust from down on the boulevard. Then it hit me: I needed a drink. Just a small one. Four blocks down from the hospital I found a Safeway. I got a bottle of Southern Comfort, one of the tiny ones, along with a $3.99 bouquet of chrysanthemums for Chrissy.

I came back and saw Chrissy and her mother waiting behind the glass doors. It was a bad sign. I tossed the nearly empty bottle into a bush.

I came in, walked up with the flowers. Chrissy turned away, arms crossed in front of her.

"How's your dad?"

"He looks yellow. You drank."

"Not too much... How's your mom holding up?"

"She's probably going to move in with me."

We drove back to Chrissy's, dropped off her mom, then drove back down the hill in silence to the Monarch Theatre. Chrissy had booked tickets for the hit new Morris Morckton film, *Mnung is a Cancer that is Destroying America*. Millions in every state had been flocking to see this heart-warming attack on the president of the U.S.A. by the world-famous pizza-and-fried-chicken addict known as Morckton.

The movie played up scenes of amputated soldiers and crying mothers, all of whom demonstrated their gullibility, stupidity and patriotism by saying they never – *never!* – would have imagined that the U.S.A. president would actually *lie* to the American people. According to the film, the president was venal, corrupt and very bad to his core, a man who had told lies, started wars, and done many other bad things. Soldiers were dying for reasons no one could really explain, and Mnung had only accelerated the country's spiral of rot, hypocrisy, ignorance, greed and manipulation. Such could not reasonably be doubted, but apparently, vast swathes of the American people were either not aware of such developments, or approved of them, and hence a jelly donut-sucking goo-bag such as Morckton had arrived on the scene to clue everyone in.

We endured the Morckton clowning from the Monarch's Balcony Salon, where you were allowed to drink. You could also get eggs Benedict or a crab-meat salad if that was your desire. I stuck mainly to double-Jims, mixing things up with a few Bloody Marys.

The clowning seemed to cheer Chrissy (who cared little for Mnung, to the extent she ever thought of him), and when the film was over we decided to take a detour down the hill at Lake Xenia. It actually did look supreme: A pink half-moon wrapped with misty yellow clouds reflecting upon the smooth lake surface, the southern edge disappearing in a jumble of dark purples and blue. We held hands as we walked along the winding dirt path.

More than anything, I wanted to spend about six hours between Chrissy's legs, and do it again the next night and the next, and the one after that. I wanted to lay in that big warm bed, horribly hung-over and with a morning erection. I wanted to wake up at 5:30 a.m., make love to Chrissy, hung-over and with a morning hard-on. I wanted to get out of that bed, sweaty and with my head throbbing, make some of that Italian coffee, have several shots of schnapps, and jump into the swimming pool for about 20 laps. And do it again.

"Isn't it beautiful?" she said.

"Yeah, but... I don't know, Chris. They say that thing's full of guns and needles. A cop told me once that there's evidence of 100 murders in that lake."

"See what I mean! You just want to criticize everything. You're too dark! You're always finding something wrong. I'm so tired of it!"

"That's not true, Chris. Come on, I'm just pointing out a fact..."

Chrissy released my hand and pushed forward without me. I had to jog to catch up. We looped out of the park, got back into the Lysteria. Chrissy sped over to Kanopos, where we took a table outside on the terrace. She ordered a bottle of El Marco Gewurtztraminer and a plate of garlic-fried frog legs for $35.99. I had a glass of the wine, then went for a Ladybank malt and a Butterscotch Ding Dang Doo.

We gave talking another try. Chrissy had "really liked" the film. I felt it had been a little less than standard. Chrissy had felt Morckton had been funny and "really trying to make a difference." I felt he had been something of a condescending, sentimental goo-bag, and that the film would make no real difference. They'd make sure Mnung stayed in the White House, no matter how many films were made or elections were held.

Chrissy stated she felt I had nothing "positive" to say. I said I felt that I did. I felt that actually, I was all about positivity. I was only trying to "be honest." If we couldn't say what we really felt about a film, then what was the use of anything?

"Why can't you be happy? You always want the music all bluesy and sad. Everything's got to be ugly and dark with you... People are always doing things wrong..."

"Well, they are..."

"See? You can't stop!"

I tried to change the subject. I tossed back the last of the malt, which had not been worth the $11.

"Chrissy, are we gonna make it? C'mon, let's go for this thing, me and you..." I tried to grasp her hand across the table. "Let's do it, babe!"

She pulled the hand away. "You're drunk..."

She leaned back, spooned from a cup of rosewater saffron ice cream. Her mouth was tight, unsmiling, eyes like dull stones. Her hair swayed in the terrace breeze.

"You're drunk and you look awful. You've got black eyes, your hair stinks... When was the last time you washed it? You need a haircut."

"I need a smoke," I said, getting up. "And you're wrong. Way wrong, about everything..."

I went out and stood on the sidewalk and puffed on one, thinking of not very much.

"Hey, Thor..."

I turned around. Chrissy was holding one of her heels. It came down on my shoulder. I caught a second whack on my collarbone.

"*Fuck you, man!*" Chrissy was saying. "*Fuck you!*"

I spun to the left, dropped the smoke and tried to grab her. She was strong and got away. She gouged my ear and neck with another heel blow. I finally grabbed her wrist and squeezed, forcing her to let go of the shoe. Her other hand, though, had somehow got inside my shirt. Seams popped, the shirt began to rip. She clawed at me, ripping the shirt down my shoulder.

Her fingernails tore into my cheek. I tried to grab her. Suddenly she was biting my forearm.

"Ow! Ow! Hey, babe!"

I finally got her off. She ran down the street.

Her heel was laying on the sidewalk. I picked it up, flicked it across the grass.

"Young lady," a concerned citizen called after Chrissy. "Shall I call the police?"

The guy reached for his phone. I stood there like a villain and lit another smoke, heart pumping madly, little tears in the corners of my eyes. There was blood on my arm, where two teeth had broken the skin, scratches on my neck and chest. My ear throbbed painfully. I flopped the shreds of what remained of my shirt over my shoulder.

The Lysteria screeched out of the parking lot, stopped in front of me. She whirred down the window.

"Gimme my shoe."

"All right."

I walked and got it, came back to the car. I handed it to her through the window, then tried to open the door. It was locked.

"FUCK YOU!"

The bouquet of chrysanthemums plopped on to the street. The window zoomed up. The Lysteria squealed off.

I checked my pockets, finding $5.62. Probably not enough for a pack of smokes and a bus ticket. I went back into the restaurant to get my jacket, then walked two blocks until I found a bus stop. According to the schedule, I was going to have to wait another 25 minutes.

A police car drove up. I sat there calmly. The officers looked at me. They rolled on by.

Chrissy sent my stuff to Silvertown in two boxes. She held on to the J. Junior leather jacket.

> MAN 'SERIOUSLY INJURED' IN CHIMP ATTACK
>
> BAY CITY (CNS) – Bay City police said a man suffered serious injuries Tuesday when he was attacked by two chimpanzees at the Critter Haven Ranch animal sanctuary.
>
> Commander Denis Honig said the chimps apparently escaped their cage and attacked Walter O'Dell, 58, for several minutes before sanctuary staff were able to shoot the animals to death.

Alice Liddell, spokeswoman for St. Vincent Medical Center, said most of O'Dell's face had been chewed off, and that the chimpanzees had also torn off his testicles, left foot and at least four fingers.

Liddell said O'Dell had undergone surgery, but declined to give further details about his condition.

Several phone calls from CNS to Critter Haven Ranch went unanswered.

Honig said sanctuary staff members told investigators that O'Dell and his wife were frequent visitors to the sanctuary. He said the couple were believed to have previously owned one or both of the chimps before giving them to the sanctuary.

BAY CITY BOZO:
Clown Boozes as Gal Pal Sobs!

★ 28 ★

Kate was cooking a vegetarian pasta thing, squash, carrots and cabbage mainly, along with an orange-pink cream sauce. I had already popped the second and last wine bottle.

"I was grinding up my father in a meat grinder," she said. Putting his body parts into this big silver grinder, like in a factory... My mother was in the other room, ironing clothes."

"The ironing's delicious..."

"It's not a joke!"

"Had you killed him?"

"It felt like somebody else had killed him. You know how, like, you can feel things in a dream? That's what it was like – I don't know who killed him. My mother? My sister? It was my job to put him in the grinder. It was coming out like hamburger. I was super scared when I woke up." She laughed. "Isn't that strange? I still don't know what to think."

"Don't think about it..."

"I know. I liked my dad. We fought sometimes, but I loved him..."

"He's dead?"

"Three years ago – almost four years."

"It was sad?"

"It was more like... a shock? He keeled over and was dead in five minutes. He wasn't even that old. Sixty-one."

Kate shook her head, blinked, smiled. "Enough of this sad stuff! C'mon, this is supposed to be fun, let's have fun!"

She sneezed, took out a tissue, wiped her eyes, blew her nose.

"So what are *your* dreams like?"

"I don't dream, Kate..."

"Of course you do! It's impossible not to dream!"

"I don't remember them."

"Oh, yes you do! Think! You must remember something."

"Listen, Kate. I'll be right back..."

"Where are you going? We're ready to eat in like, 10 minutes."

"I'm just going to get a couple bottles..."

Kate made a sad face. I stood up out of the chair, gave her a kiss on the chin.

"It's my fault... I should have brought something."

"You want some money?"

"Well... O.K."

Kate took out a $20 bill and told me to hurry.

A sale was on at the market, I wound up getting two more bottles of red for $5.99 each, a six-pack of Coors Light bottles, a medium-size flask of E & J, two packs of smokes, for a little more than $32.

I stood on the street for a while, 15 minutes maybe, having a couple smokes and some bottle slugs. Nothing much happening.

Kate had explained it was "officially over" with Joel, he had gone back to live with his parents in Virginia. His blog site had apparently failed to attract much outside interest, and the video-game design career hadn't really worked out so well, and now his parents were going to pay for him to go back to school to get a Master's Degree in Vocational Counseling or something.

Kate had the TV on when I came back in.

"You were gone almost a half hour!"

"The hell I was..."

I brought the stuff into the kitchen, then went out and sat next to Kate on the couch. Kate nibbled her nails, staring at the screen.

A clown yapped: *Military officials said eight U.S. Marines were killed in clashes that left up to 800 insurgents dead in the Central and Southern Sectors. In another incident, 17 American personnel were killed in the crash of a Hercules transport helicopter north of the Capital Zone. Officials said the cause of the downing was unknown, but there are no indications it was shot down... U.S. officials have meanwhile denied allegations, broadcast on Arab television, that U.S. troops attacked a hospital in the northwest, cutting the electricity and plumbing and leaving an unknown number of dead and dying, as part of the hunt for terrorist-insurgents... Coming up later in the program: She's had sex with more than 80 different men in the last two months. She's a sex-addict, and she knows it's dangerous, but she says she can't stop. We'll talk to a real-life sex-addict and her struggle to change... But first, back to the war. We'll go live now to our military expert-analyst, former three-star General Douglas Colvin, who is standing by in Washington... General, can any of this be right? The president said this war was over. The administration has maintained that for some time now...*

CLOWN: *Well, Kathleen, it – it doesn't mean that the war* isn't *over... What it means is, these insurgents, these terrorists, what have you – they know the game is in fact over, that the war is actually over, and so this is sort of their last gasp to prevent democracy from gaining root, which is their real fear, because they won't stand a chance in a democratic democracy, where we make decisions at the ballot box...*

"Let's turn this crap off," I said, smiling. "I'm hungry. It smells good, Kate."

"I'll have to warm it..."

"Go ahead and do that. I'll pop one of these bottles of red."

We sat and ate the rubberized pasta and salty vegetable chunks. Kate brought up how she had her first boyfriend when she was 14. "Lucas" was 17 and had a car. He worked at a gas station. Kate had kept a diary of their sexual activities – what they did, where they did it. Her dad would have "killed" her if he had found out. They had already "done it 57 times" by the time her mother and father sat her down to explain the birds and the bees. Kate faked like she didn't know anything. Both she *and* her mom faked it, since her mom was the one who had been giving her birth control! Then, in her senior year, Luke dropped out of city college and moved to China to become a missionary. His dad was a preacher of some kind. She had thought they would get married, she was ready to spend her whole life with him, but suddenly he had taken off to China. Now, every few years, Luke sends a postcard saying, 'Hi, Kate! How's my first and best girlfriend doing?' Kate wondered if his wife knew. He had married a Chinese.

Kate thought it the right time to ask about my romantic life. Wasn't I seeing someone?

"Not really," I said. "I've never had a serious girlfriend..."

"Oh, why not?"

"I've never met the right girl. It's hard, you know, the right person is so, well, you know..."

It seemed like a good time to switch to a story about Candace's abortion.

"My friend's girl just had an abortion," I said. "He was against it."

"Oh, my gosh! It's usually the other way around..."

"Sure, he took it pretty hard..."

I went on to explain Jerry's ultimately mixed emotions. "It's the death of life!" he had wailed at one point, only later reasoning that perhaps the child "wasn't really" his. He just couldn't be sure, when it came down to it. Two days, a couple dozen pills and several bottles later, he had decided Candace should have it, no matter whose it was. He was ready to be the father, so long as Candace said it was really his.

"He was sort of half-hoping it would be born black," I said. "That would make almost everything clear. But then she had the abortion. He cried for awhile, then brought her flowers at the clinic."

"Oh, that's sweet," said Kate, "I guess."

I found a brown-blond hair in the food. I tried to quietly slip it off to the side, but Kate noticed.

"I'm sorry!" She jumped up, flushing pink. "Here, let me get it..."

"Please, Kate, sit down. It's nothing..."

I poured another glass for myself as we moved into the inevitable work talk. Kate happened to think I was the "most talented writer" in the office. I was certain to go far, if I kept at it. She rolled her eyes over Scotty. He was a "real travesty."

I was not really too interested in her bitter Richie story. No, I told her, I did not know he had been accused of sexual harassment by "Lulu," a woman who used to work at Cities News several years ago and was now somewhere in New Mexico. No formal charges were ever filed, but it had dragged on for months after Lulu filled out an official complaint form and gave it to Wayne. Something about "brushing up" against her breasts.

"I personally don't think he was guilty," she said.

"No, he probably was," I said.

Kate laughed. I cleaned the last of my plate. I told her it had been a great dinner.

"Want some more? There's plenty left."

"Thanks, but I think I'm all right..."

We went out to the couch and I poured us brandy in special crystal glasses that Kate kept in a cabinet. We had the first sips, and then Kate, after putting on a Coldplay album, revealed she had been offered a job in Cleveland. The music mewled along in the background, whiny and unoriginal.

"That's great, Kate, congratulations. You going to take it?"

She nodded, she was leaning toward taking it, Deputy Assistant Managing Editor at the *Cleveland Post-Telegram*. There were a lot of good things about it, really. She had flown to Cleveland for the interview two weeks ago. It had gone well. Cleveland was a cute town, really. The newspaper staff seemed nice, and it was a lot more money. They were offering her a chance to lead a staff of six people, covering suburban zones. She would be able to do things her way. She had looked at a couple nice townhouses down by the water, really cute things, and not so expensive. Cleveland was a lot cheaper than Bay City...

"Why don't you come with me?" she said, her eyes starting to glisten. "It'll be fun. You can get some good new job. Maybe I could help you get on with the *Post-Telegram*. They'd love you!"

"I don't think I can, Kate."

"Why not?"

"I just... can't. I don't want to move to Cleveland. What would I do there? I'd drink too much, I'd make your life hell..."

"At least you could think about it."

"Yeah... Hey, I need a smoke break."

I knocked down the rest of the brandy, polished off the beer bottle. I briefly touched Kate's hand, smiled, went out to the balcony and lit one. I ashed in one of her flower pots, looking at a selection of Nowell Heights parking garages. I flicked the butt down to the street.

I came back in to find that Kate had started crying.

"I knew you wouldn't go for it! I shouldn't have said anything!"

"Kate, come on, really..."

"You don't want me! I'm too old!"

"Hey, come on. Who said anything about anything like that? Aw, man..."

I leaned over, hugged her.

"Cleveland, I just... Please, let's try not to make everyone feel bad, you know? We can only try to be as honest and good to each other as we can..."

She sat there, sobbing.

"Look, let's crack that last red. Let's sit here and relax. We don't need to solve the fate of the world."

"O.K., O.K.," she said, fumbling with her pack of tissues.

I cracked the red and brought it out. As I started to pour, Kate said, "I'm sorry, I can't drink any more tonight. I'm already pretty drunk, and I've been taking this medication..."

"Oh, sure..."

I drank two glasses down quickly. We sat there, saying little. Eventually Kate said, "I can't believe your friend's girlfriend had an abortion! What a waste! I don't know if I'll ever have a baby."

"Don't say that, Kate. Of course you will."

"Do you think so?"

"Yes, if you really want it. There's all kinds of ways to get a baby..."

She began crying again. "But I want to have it with *someone!*"

"I'm sorry, Kate..."

She got up and went to the bathroom. I went into the kitchen and returned with a beer. I cracked it and had a pull, then poured another glass of the red and had a gulp.

Kate came back out. Her eyes were pink.

"Whew! I'm sorry for crying on you all night."

"It's all right... C'mon, sit down."

She sat next to me on the couch and flicked on the TV. An episode of *Dr. Stan* was on. A couple, Jack and Sherri, were having problems. It seemed they were always arguing. Sherri would get upset because Jack, an "accountant," said things like, "Why are you so goddamn stupid all the goddamn time?" How come, for example, she didn't keep the house clean and change the baby's diapers on time? The baby would apparently walk around in a dirty diaper. Sherri would get upset over the comments and withhold sex, making Jack even angrier. "I just can't have sex after something like that," she told Dr. Stan, who nodded sympathetically. Jack didn't disagree, but said Sherri was always saying horrible things herself. She would call him a "bald fat guy who thinks his poop don't stink." Jack said the comments hurt him, especially in combination with the sex boycott.

Dr. Stan rolled a videotape. For some reason, Jack and Sherri had permitted Dr. Stan to install a video camera in their home to record their fighting to show on national television. The tape showed the couple fighting. "You haven't done *shit* around here!" Jack said, the "shit" being bleeped out by the programmers. "Get off the couch, you bald fat-ass!" countered Sherri. Through it all, the five-year-old son Tyler walked around until he began crying. The child was heard saying, "Please... stop... fighting..."

The show cut to Dr. Stan making a disapproving face.

CLOWN: *See... do you see what you're doing to your most valuable possession in the whole world?*

The audience booed. Jack and Sherri sighed, flushed red, made embarrassed faces.

"We'll be right back," said Dr. Stan, cutting to a commercial break.

"That's exactly how 95 percent of people live," I said.

Kate gave a weak laugh. "Oh, that's not true..."

I got up, went into the kitchen, took two beers out of the fridge. I downed one in four gulps, standing by the sink. I burped, then took the second one out to the couch. Kate had switched the channel.

"Oh look," she said, "it's *The Aviator!* Let's watch it."

We sat there. I finished the wine glass, poured another, took several gulps off the fresh beer. *The Aviator* seemed rather dull, not nearly as rotten as *Gangs of New York*, but the acting undynamic and uninspiring, despite the obvious high production values. People of talent had clearly worked hard to make it look pretty, but something was badly missing, it seemed like just more commercial pap. I didn't for a second believe it had anything to do with the alleged real person who had been called Howard Hughes.[*]

I got up, went into the kitchen and guzzled down half a beer. I walked down the hall, took a piss, came back and finished the other half. I took another bottle back out to the couch with me. In the time I had been gone, Kate had taken out a squeeze-bottle and began rubbing cream into her hands, every so often glancing at the film.

"Here," I said after a few moments, "let me do your hands..."

"Oh, that's nice. You don't have to..."

"I want to, Kate..."

She moved next to me on the couch and I began massaging the cream into her hands. From there, it was another 10 minutes before I unbuttoned her blouse and released her breasts from their tan silk bra. I took a bit more of the cream and rubbed it into her breasts.

Kate stretched out, sighing. Her breasts, as before, were large and wobbly, a bit slack, with wrinkles swirling out from the nipples in uneven patterns. The thought flashed of breasts as being little more than strange sacks of fat and veins.

I undressed her slowly, occasionally sucking on her nipples, kissing her mouth, massaging between the legs. When we were nearly naked, she took me by the hand and led me into the bedroom. I sat on the edge of the bed and she knelt down and sucked me for a while, uninspiringly, until we both seemed to grow a little bored.

---

[*] Hughes, at one time the richest man in America, was famously constipated. – ED.

I helped her on to the bed, then slipped over to one side and lay with my left arm under her, my right hand moving between her cunt and breasts. I worked it slowly, massaging the sides of the cunt lips, the pinnacle of the ridge, then moving back up to work each of the breasts. It was best to first get them wanting more between the legs. Chrissy had taught me that. Kate became very slippery.

"Don't put it in my butt this time. Please. It's just, I…"

"Don't worry… I wasn't planning on it."

We worked at it for a good while, gradually losing intensity. Her pussy had become very loose, sloshy, at the same time declining in heat. She groaned and sighed loudly several times, but I didn't think she had an orgasm. I worked and worked away, sweating and straining. I glanced at the digital clock. It was 1:41 a.m.

I worked away, sweating. I had become very thirsty, my mouth was dry, sticky like paste… I focused on the fact there was one more bottle beer in the fridge. I imagined its coldness in my hand. Also, it felt like I had to piss… I hammered away at Kate's cunt, hiking her legs up so her ankles were at my ears, reaching my hands around and squeezing the flesh near her bunghole… I looked at the clock: 1:42. I worked away…

"I think I got too wet," Kate whispered.

"Yeah," I said, rolling off.

SPRINGTIME FOR DUNDERHEAD: Nazi Kid Guns Down Schoolmates!

★ 29 ★

I popped out of the tower with Tommy-Gun. He had announced he was quitting Cities News after four years to take a Staff Writer position at *Lawn Care & Mowing Weekly*.

"It's pretty interesting," said Tommy-G. "No, really! It is! There's all kinds of different grass, hundreds of types. They got a different special kind for golf courses and baseball fields, cemeteries, tennis courts, the front lawn... It's a huge, huge industry, you have no idea. I mean, I'm gonna have to study up! I've got to read up about all the mowers and machinery, computerized sprinkler systems, planters, the whole economics of it..."

"How much they giving you?"

"Almost twice as much... There's tons of travel, too, it's even in the job description. There's a convention every couple months on something – seeds and shrubbery, hydration, furniture and fountains, everything. All over the country – Florida, Michigan, Utah, places like that... It's a real chance for me. I've never been to some place like Utah."

"You'll miss the sports, Tommy, the soccer babes. You'll be sitting there looking at seeds."

"Screw the sports! I can watch 'em on TV. I'll have enough money to get a huge wall TV... Maybe there's hot grass babes, you never know."

"No, it's all guys," I said.

Tommy laughed. "We got to go out, man. We got to party."

"You know we will…"

We shook hands. Tommy departed to cover the State Women's Volleyball Championship, while I headed up to the cop shop for a clown conference.

> POLICE FORM MUTILATED CAT TASK FORCE
>
> BAY CITY (CNS) – Bay City police announced Thursday the creation of a special task force following the discovery of the 35° mutilated cat in the city in the past 14 weeks.
>
> Sgt. Ralph Prater said the task force includes police detectives, city animal control officers, as well as a number of volunteer animal protection groups and neighborhood watch associations.
>
> Prater told a news conference at Police Headquarters that the latest mutilated cat was found Tuesday in the 4400 block of Gleason St., near Beacon Hill.
>
> "We have seen a pattern in these cat cases," Prater said. "It is serious and we need to find who is responsible."
>
> Giving more details about the cases than police have previously, Prater said most of the dead cats had been "sliced open and many of their organs removed."
>
> Prater said police had made catching the perpetrator a priority because animal mutilation is one of three symptoms that criminologists say are "possible" signs that someone could become a serial killer.
>
> Prater said the other two signs are childhood bed-wetting and fire-starting.

O'Mulligan and I had raced out the minute Kate had deciphered the words through the scanner mud: "Gunshots at Rancho Buena Vista High School." Another Nazi kid, high on prescription pills and the internet.

The police had set up a perimeter, but there was no getting near the school. I was prowling around in the park where they had evacuated the kids, trying to get any drip of information from students or school staff. The school administrators were trying to stop me from doing either.

"I'm telling you to leave now," said Mr. Straczynski, the vice principal. "Please, go talk to the police."

"You can't tell me to leave," I said. "I can go in or around any public school or park, at any time. Only the police can keep me out. That's the law."

"Which law is this, young man?"

He made me tired. He didn't even know the law for his own school. They never did. He never even had a clue that a jackass Nazi killer had been enrolled in his school. I took out the copy of the state code I always carried in my pocket. The geek studied it, the page flapping in the breeze.

"What's your name?" the pockmarked, mustachioed school chieftain snapped. "Who do you work for? We've just had an immense tragedy and you're interfering with my duties."

"Go ahead, call my bosses," I said. "Call the cops. The cops know who I am. I'm not interfering. You're interfering with me."

"My job is to administer this quadrant," he said. "This is according to the emergency protocol. I don't know any more than that."

"You said it..."

"Everything changes in an emergency, young man..."

"No, it doesn't."

"You're wrong, son..."

"No, you are..."

It hardly mattered. It was already all over. Six killed – two teachers, four kids – plus sixteen injured. But nobody would know the official tally for many more hours yet. The cops had locked the whole place in a vise, searching for an alleged "second gunman," whom they would never find and whom they later said didn't exist.

The Nazi kid had been a coward of the worst kind, offing himself as the SWAT force moved in after about 20 minutes of using nine guns to shoot and spray blood on to hallway lockers.

The punk had got busted a few weeks before for wearing a little Nazi hat to school, but nobody thought it was a big deal. His dad was a retired Air Force general, mom a big fan of pills and hysteria. It later came out the Nazi kid had been on one type of pills or another since the age of four. The cops found guns and gun cabinets everywhere in the house, and the young man had apparently been drawing Nazi signs on every paper he could find since about the age of 12. He had sat in the garage with a tattoo gun, blistering his arms and hands with his favorite symbol and other thumbs-up for Adolf. He had wound up age

16, 6-foot-3 and 240 pounds, shaved head except for a little dumb tuft of hair above his forehead, like a horn.

Everyone had carried along, merrily and hellishly, until the day of doom. They said later that little Jimmy "seemed" to have been "acting strangely," but they swore it up and down afterwards, family members and teachers – O.K., he had really dug the Nazis, but so did a lot of kids these days, they thought it was "just a phase he was going through." No one had "imagined" he'd really try to kill them. He was a B-student, after all...

"I'm a rebel from the waiste down," the geek had clowned on an internet chat room. "You had a hundred billon chances to avoid whats coming but you spit in my face. Da time has come 4 da 4th Reich, I will make your own grave. Evilution is the only solution 4 da true Beleiferz." The shit-whine also included a number of interesting algebra equations such as EVE + ADAM = TRUE ISREALITE (WHITEMAN). EVE + SNAKE = JEW. ADAM + STEVE = HOMO. 666 = SATAN. NIGGER'S + BEANER'S = DA MUD PEOPLE. STEPHANIE = WHORE.

The wisdom of the internet, distilled to its purest form. These guys were always Top Ten, top of the heap, bar none.

The morning sun burned the skin, a light breeze whipped through the glowing green trees. A third helicopter joined the whapping overhead fray, beaming the "latest American developments" live to places including Minnetonka, Macedonia, and Madagascar. Sure, another chance to spotlight the rigor and integrity of the American way of family, school and learning. Nobody could resist.

SWAT Team members in black battle gear milled around outside their black trucks, polishing their rifles and dripping sweat, drinking sports drinks, playing with their pointers and German shepherds. Parents began arriving, driving up on to the sidewalk or pulling into a nearby supermarket parking lot and rushing across the damp grass. Some of the mothers were still in their robes and pajamas.

Teens ran and skipped within the park perimeter, chased ineffectually by a few administrators and cops. Fat kids squished through the sand a few yards before collapsing from the effort, wiped out. High-schoolers went around the merry-go-round, climbed the rusting metal tower and tossed handfuls of sand. Kids in the tippy-top of the tower lit cigarettes, throwing down the butts on classmates. A few picked their noses. O'Mulligan went tight-focus on a couple kids sitting under the trees, sobbing.

I went over to get a quote. A skinny kid with a thick stripe of bright dyed-blond running through the middle of his hair, sort of like a skunk, was leaning against a light pole. I came up and introduced myself.

"The teachers started shouting, 'Get in the gym, get in the gym!'" said Jody Slovnik, 15, a sophomore. "Sounded like firecrackers going off."

"Did you go to the gym?"

"No, I just ran. Everyone ran for themselves."

"Did you see anybody get shot?"

"Not shot, but... I saw one guy. He was laying on the ground, like he was... you know, like frozen... There was a big puddle of blood under his back."

"Did you know him?"

"No..."

"Did you know anybody who got shot?"

He shrugged. "I dunno..."

"Thanks for your help, Jody."

"Hey, man, you got a cigarette?"

"Sorry... they'd throw me in jail for that."

There were too many goddamn Nazi kids out there. If you saw one, it might be best to shoot him first.

DOG DAZE: Clown Called In as Canine Kicks!

★ 30 ★

...and our policy, as you know, is to take the pie higher for everyone. That's the America I believe in. And higher responsibilities, as you know, come with that. That's what I believe for America. That's what I would tell everyone.

CLOWN: *Thank you for that, Mr. President. And now it's time for a short break. We'll be right back with Part Two of AT HOME WITH THE MNUNGS: America's First Family – A Very Special White House Celebration. After these messages. You're watching NNN, the News Now Network – your news peak on media mountain...*

Chrissy had called. Andy had died.

I finally got out about seven, taking the bus and then the taxi. Chrissy was wearing a dark blue T-shirt that fell halfway down her thighs – BARCELONA, it said. Her cheeks and the front of the shirt were wet. I gave her a hug.

"Chrissy, damn it. I'm sorry."

"Ewwww," she wailed, throwing her arms around me.

Andy was laying on a green and yellow-striped Guatemalan blanket, under the big bay window in the front room. His eyes were closed, one paw curled under his chest.

"Are you just gonna let him lay here?"

Chrissy nodded, sobbed. "For tonight. I still want to look at him. I thought you could bury him in the backyard in the morning. In that spot at the end of the pool, by the fence... Thor, can you?"

Ah, hell, hell. It sounded hellish. I could already feel the brutal hangover as I stood out there in the pre-dawn, trying to cut into the grass with a shovel.

"You bet I will, Chris."

She took hold of my hand. "I want to go buy a juniper tree and plant it on his grave after work tomorrow..."

"That's a really good idea."

CLOWN: *We'll take you right back to AT HOME WITH THE MNUNGS: America's First Family – A Very Special White House Celebration, but first some news headlines on NNN, your news leader... In the war on terror, it was a busy day for terrorists and homicide bombers, and another American was beheaded in a video posted on the internet... U.S. officials said seven American soldiers were killed and 11 others were injured in a series of terrorist homicide bombings and attacks. America's military later carried out airstrikes targeting terrorist bases, killing an estimated 56 terrorists... In Israel, 36 people, including 29 children, were killed in a triple homicide bombing at a pizza restaurant in Haifa. Israel responded with missile strikes on terrorist command centers in the West Bank, Gaza, Lebanon and Syria, killing at least 67 people, including 48 children... And the U.N. World Health Program said 700 million people could die unless urgent steps are taken to combat lethal bird flu... Back home here in America: Is that oatmeal you're eating safe? The full report after the Mnungs.*

HEY THERE, AMERICAN MEN! Life and old age got ya down – you know, really down? Are you missing that ol' twitchy feeling when in the vicinity of a certain loved or admired one? Then pick up new Biagra Grecian Formula... to give you that ol' jumpin' for joy feeling again! Salute your commander-in-chief today. Because life's too short to just hang around... if you get our meaning...

We walked into the kitchen. I poured us each a tumbler of Maker's Mark, added ice cubes. Chrissy started crying again.

"Andy was my best friend!"

"I know he was. He was a great dog."

I pulled her close, hugged. I kissed her on the forehead, the neck. My hand swept under the shirt. She was naked. I caressed her back, the top of her buttocks. A sprinkle of warm tears fell from her eyelashes, landing and rolling down her hot cheek.

...because, as you know, I'm a believer in God, and what we call God's plan, and it's obviously part of God's plan that I'm the president. And part of my plan is tax cuts. So it makes sense that God would support the tax cut. Cuts of all kinds, really, shrink the government. At the same time, it's extremely important that Americans get their drug benefit. I very much support that...

CLOWN: *A bit on the lighter side here – what's your favorite food, Mr. President? I'm sure there's a lot of curiosity out there among the American people.*

CLOWN: *Well, that's an easy one. My favorite meal is meatloaf with macaroni and cheese. And Dr. Pepper to drink, lots of Dr. Pepper. Real good American food. Food from the heartland of this great country. We have it three or four times a week around here. Plus chips. Lots of chips. I especially like what they call kettle chips, but any kind of chips is good. Tortilla chips, potato chips, cheez-o's, ripple style, salted...*

(SHARIA MNUNG WALKS IN CARRYING A BOWL)

CLOWN: *Well, if it isn't Sharia Mnung, the First Lady!*

CLOWN: *Whatcha got there, honeybun?*

CLOWN: *Thought I'd bring y'all a bowl of Crunchy Goritos brand!*

I poured us a couple more and we sat down on the couch, Chrissy snuggling up next to me under the comforter. I flicked on the fireplace.

"You can get another dog, baby. There's plenty of 'em out there."

She nodded, but the tears started to roll again. "But I want Andy!"

CLOWN: *Sure, we've had some tough times over the years. There was that incident when Sharia ran over her ex-boyfriend with a car. She probably should have gone to prison for that, but the good judge just slapped her wrist... And my father made sure I made that young girl get an unlawful abortion. That was in my mid-30s, during the period when I was years and years on cocaine and heavy booze. Then, of course, the light of the Lord Jesus Christ shone down upon me...*

CLOWN: *Yes, precious, Mr. President...*

CLOWN: *And what I learned was, what I would say to the American people is, especially to those suffering from addiction, is: Help is just around the corner. You know, it is, it's – well, what we like to say is: If there's a barn full of poop, well, dang it, there's got to be a horse around, so maybe we can go for a ride* (GRINS). *You know, we can make it, there's a way out. It helps with life, I think.*

CLOWN: *Yes...*

CLOWN: *And Sharia – why, she's still as pretty as the day I met her. Good woman, the First Lady, Sharia Mnung.*

CLOWN: *Don't know if you know, but the very first day I met Wolfie, he asked me if I had ever milked a male horse!*

CLOWN: *Oh, did he, now? Choff-choff! Choff!*

CLOWN: *Yes, he did! And I thought, well, his father runs the world. Maybe he doesn't look like it, but he must have something going for him.*

CLOWN: *Choff-choff! Oh, choff-choff!*

CLOWN: *But, hey listen, you know, I gotta be careful around here – 'cause, remember, like as I told you, when Sharia did that trick when she was younger, where she killed her ex-boyfriend with her car? Ran him right over? And they called it an accident, and she got off with a little wrist slap? You got to watch it around here, lemme tell ya!*

CLOWN: *Choff-choff! Oh, choff-choff!*

Chrissy got up to go to the bathroom. When she didn't come back after about five minutes, I went and had a look. I found her in the front room on her knees, next to Andy. She petted his ear, his front leg, held one of his paws in her hand. Tears were running down.

"Chris, babe, come on…"

"I know, I know…"

She stood up. We hugged.

"I was just saying goodbye again… Thor, I don't want to see him in the morning. Get up and bury him, O.K.? Set your phone clock."

"I sure will."

CLOWN: *Sir, if we, if we may touch on something of a somewhat, uh, sensitive topic, the, uh, as you know, uh… Some, uh, concern has been expressed in some quarters about the failure to, to – uh, find the dictator's weapons… That the stated reason for this war has, uh, apparently turned out not to be, uh, based on real facts, and real men and women have died, and, uh…*

CLOWN (GRINNING): *Weapons?* (GETS UP AND LOOKS UNDER CHAIR) *What weapons?* (LAUGHING) *Did someone say weapons? We've been goshdarn looking for those weapons everywhere…* (THE PRESIDENT LOOKS BEHIND CURTAIN. PICKS UP BOOK, LOOKS INSIDE, LAUGHS. LOOKS UNDER MARBLE BUST OF ULYSSES S. GRANT. LAUGHS.)

CLOWN: *Oh, choff! Choff-choff-choff!*

CLOWN: *Who got da weapons?* (LAUGHTER) *They've got to be here somewhere. Weapons? Well, you know the whole world thought that dictator had weapons somewhere.* (ANOTHER BURST OF LAUGHTER) *Did you bring some? Weapons, anyone? You mean I – where all them weapons? Who got dem weapons?*

CLOWN: *Choff! Oh, lordy! Choff-Choff! Oh, lord almighty!*

CLOWN: *Chip for you?* (PICKS UP BOWL) *Chip, anyone? They're mighty delicious, these chips, lemme tell ya…*

CLOWN: *Oh choff, Mr. President, choff-choff…*

CLOWN: *Let me show you something – let me show what our troops have found over in that desert land.* (GOES OVER TO DESK, OPENS

DRAWER, TAKES OUT SOILED AND SCRATCHED PROSTHESIS.) *This is the dictator's peg leg, you know, the one that he used to walk around on? Well, it was seized by our brave troops when the dictator was captured, when we rounded him up and snatched him out of his rabbit hole. The dictator is in a jail cell tonight, and the world is a safer place. This is the dictator that tried to kill my daddy, a great man who used to rule this country. And now I've got his peg leg...*

CLOWN: *Mr. President...*

CLOWN: *So in answer to your question, yes, I think the war is going well. We've captured the dictator. The troops have brought me his leg. We have given him a good shave. He is not harming anybody any longer, and he won't be...*

Chrissy sat up and looked at me. "I know Andy will come back. He'll come back as a person. I treated him well. I loved him, and he loved me. He was full of love."

"Yeah, he really was."

"He'll come back. Maybe when I'm old, I'll meet him. He'll be some young boy or girl. We'll know each other... We'll share, you know, a kind of feeling..."

"Sure, could happen..."

She started sobbing again, her face twisting up. "Ewww, I miss him!"

...drain the swamp. We will raze the terrorist and weapons infrastructure to the ground. We're making progress. It's hard work, no doubt. It's a long war, no one knows when it might end... Sometimes, you see, freedom turns out to actually be the greatest threat to freedom. But it's what we believe in, freedom... We will raze the terrorist infrastructure. We're making progress. We'll drain the terrorist swamp. It's hard work, no doubt. It's a long war. We're making progress. Sometimes freedom turns out to be the greatest threat to freedom. It's what we believe in. We will raze the terrorist infrastructure...

CLOWN: *Mr. President, not to interrupt but...*

CLOWN: *See, everything that happens is predestined by Jesus, I believe... I sort of see myself as America's pastor-in-chief, as well as commander-in-chief of the American people, leading us through this time of war, spiritual war and spiritual challenge. We are a Christian nation, God-fearing, Jesus faith-having... Um, as well as a Jewish nation – all the other religions, I mean, as well, you know, they're in there too somewhere, religious freedoms we call it. We all have faith, and faith is believing what you can't know, and we've got plenty of that. Because you just can't know anything, can't know how it's going to turn out. Because remember, at one time, long ago, we fought our friends the British. Now they're the allies. We battled our Indian friends, the Comanches, the kemosabes. Now we've got a helicopter called the Apache, and a football team called the Redskins... We fought against the Confederacy, the Union, the union organizers. We fought the Nazis and the Soviets. We fought the Vietnam Communists and the sympathizers. We fought the Iranians and the Iraqis, the Serbians, the contras... Now we fight the evil, the evil-doers, not Islam, but the terrorist leaders, the evil leaders...*

Chrissy had fallen asleep, her head against my shoulder. I carefully got up, laid her down lengthwise on the couch. I brushed her hair over her ear, leaned down and gave her kisses on the cheek and side of the mouth. I went into the kitchen and had several shots from a bottle of Absolut Spearmint, then spied a Bourgueil cabernet franc. I popped and poured it. I brought both bottle and glass back out to the couch.

CLOWN: *It's really hard to be president. As I like to say in my down-home manner, being president is like being a junebug in a hailstorm, I mean, it's always coming down* (LAUGHTER)... *Well, what happens is, every morning I get a piece of the Oval Office. This paper tells me what I'm going to do all day paper on my desk. I look at as I have my toast, mocha and Froot Loops in long. Where I'm supposed to go, things I'm supposed to say. 'Message of the Day,' we call it. I'm not supposed to go, as they call it, 'off the message.' My adviser Rudy Bloaves is always saying, 'We've got to feed it to the American people one tidbit at a time, so they can understand.' And so that's what we do...*

CLOWN: Mr. President, your father...

CLOWN: *My father was a famous ruler of this country. Now I'm up here. I guess it runs in our blood. The American people seem to respect it. We believe politics is a noble calling, you know, leading the country to freedom and safety and so forth, controlling the oil and the concessions, the important things of this land... The Americans have been trained to think our clan are heartland people, people of the land, good folks to perhaps drink a beer with or shoot a gun – though of course I no longer drink... But yes, we have made it clear that we enjoy tortilla chips and baseball, soccer, tennis, TV dinners, all the good American stuff. We are the real Americans. We say it over and over, all the time: We are in charge. We're the Americans. We have been in charge...*

CLOWN: Mr. President...

CLOWN: *...but I hate football. Yuck, all that rough stuff. Big fellas sweating around like that, bending over, hands between their legs...*

Never understood it. That's what we tell our daughters: No tackle football. No touch football, for that matter. No drugs, no boozing. No cocaine and uppers. No Satanic rock, the devil's music. No sex of any kind, of course. Wear the promise rings, so everyone knows the hymen is still intact.

CLOWN: *Yes...*

I went back to the kitchen to check in with a bottle of Pernod. I had a taste, and while there, also poured myself a jigger glass of Royal Oporto. While drinking, I observed in the corner a Tannahill pinot noir I had not seemed to have noticed before. I removed it from its hiding place, popped it and was ready to head back to the TV when I heard a clattering noise, followed by a kind of grunting.

"Hello?"

I poked my head into the corridor. The bathroom light was on. I went down. It was Maxine. She had fallen or something. A patch of fresh blood bloomed above her eye, around her eyebrow. Her robe had fallen open. I saw hanging, shrunken breasts, a mesh of lines and stretch marks. A roll of veined fat fell over her panties. It seemed everyone started to look more and more like a frog as they got older.

"Hmm, hemmm, heemmm..."

"It's O.K., Maxine. I'm here. Let's have a look at this..."

"Hurmm, humm, heeem..."

I found the sash ends and retied her robe, then sat her down on the edge of the bathtub. I wet a washcloth with warm water.

"Lift your head up, Maxine..."

I gently patted down the wound with the cloth. Inside the cabinet was a box of bandages. I pasted two on to the spot.

"Are you O.K.? Want some water?"

"Hermm, hummm..." She brushed a hand across my face. "Justin? Is it you, Justin?"

"No, it's Thor..."

"Hugh?"

"No, Thor..."

"Hugh?"

"Yes, Maxine... It's Hugh. Come on, let's get you back in bed."

I led her back down the hall to her room.

CLOWN: *President Mnung, how do you see your chances for re-election? Do you think they'll count the votes this time?*

CLOWN (SHRUGGING): *They may. It'll depend on who's winning, of course. I wouldn't want to have my chances harmed, like last time,* when we had to call up the Supreme Court and tell 'em to rule that my chances could be harmed if they counted all the votes. Remember all that mess? But yes, we expect to win. We can't give up now, when victory is in sight. Freedom and democracy is at stake. I'll just quote Vice President Jicks: A vote against me is a vote for the terrorists and drug-pushers. Vice President Jicks is a great vice president... In America, either we win or we don't play the game. Isn't that right? I think that's always been true.

CLOWN: *Yes, Mr. President. Some have said...*

CLOWN: *All I'm going to say is, I do not enjoy killing. I am not a sociopathic killer, without empathy for those I have killed and sent into battle. That's a false thing. Everything I've done is as American as peanut butter fudge and beach volleyball, as American as Las Vegas and the light bulb, chess, checkers and parcheesi, onion rings and chicken-fried steak, King Kong and Godzilla... Know what I mean? And so to those who maintain that I am a fascist twit who is destroying this nation, I say, well, we'll see you at the ballot box.* (POINTS INDEX FINGER AT CAMERA.) *Because I've heard all that stuff, and I know who said it... And what I know is, is that this is America, and I believe we are a great country.*

CLOWN: *And you're watching AT HOME WITH THE MNUNGS: America's First Family – A Very Special White House Celebration. We'll be back after these messages...*

Coming up on Tuesday: Pammie Bungen lost her husband when rock star Christ Sunbeam committed suicide. But now, Pammie is out of rehab and back with a never-before-seen collection of official Christ Sunbeam diaries, paintings and a new four-CD box set of previously unreleased songs. She's also got a new album, book and movie of her own – as well as a scorching nude spread in the new issue of Skanky Queens... Naughty-naughty, golden girl! Is Pammie profiting off the ghost of Christ – or making him live again? Pammie Bungen, exclusively on NNN's The Big Interview, this Tuesday!

I drank till about three, then set my phone clock. I lifted Chrissy's hand, kissed her cheek.

"C'mon, babe, let's go to bed..."

She leaned against me as we stumbled in. I got undressed, climbed onto the bed next to her. She turned over, her back to me.

I kissed her ear, her neck, began massaging around her waist and thigh...

Her hand flew back and knocked me away.

"Don't," she mumbled.

FOR THE BIRDS:
Band Beaten at Music Melee!

★ 31 ★

Jellybean girl ya can't fool me
  I know ya been hangin' out
  Wit' a phony deejay

Jerry jumped about in the stage darkness, waving and twanging his guitar. He whipped himself back and forth, swerving his head to one side and the other like a robotic duck. "9ine," his new co-member in Jerry & The Wastemakers, whacked his hands furiously against the tops of a set of bongo drums.

Now ya shiny red clothes don't fit
  Butcha know I'm too legit to quit... said rock it!

The sound system made several gigantic scraping and squawking noises, Jerry's voice was drowned in a feedback buzz not unsimilar to a jet engine roar. The volume went down to nearly nothing then rushed back up, excruciatingly loud, as a technician sought the fix. One of the clowns from Music Monkey-TV's We're Finding America's Big New Band Contest scrambled forward for a close-up, little red light burning at the top of his rig.

Several more got up and walked out to the Plutoland Ballroom bar. Others sat there, attempting to talk over the din.

I held hands with Candace's friend Ginny, leaned over, kissed her. I rubbed my hand against her waist, the top of her creamy yellow satin skirt. We had been in the bathroom earlier, smoking Candace's cigars, while Jerry and 9ine had stood waiting for their appearance. Ginny was medium height, medium boobs, medium everything except for large bags under her eyes.

"Let's go, Jerry!" I said, then gulped from a Alpine Gold Ale pint, bought by Candace for $8 at the bar. "Yeah, Wastemakers!"

Jerry gave his voice a falsetto boost. Several more got up and walked out.

Ya lied, now ya brain's french-fried
Peppermint candy-girl, doncha hide
In the cool-cool-cool of the mornin'
That's when I'm comin' home

Jerry's mug weaved into view on the overhead video screens. The MM-TV camera clown performed a slow pan, starting from the tip of Jerry's new pink mohawk and lingering for some seconds on his face drenched in eyeliner, his two-inch earring chains, devil's point goatee, cut-off CRADLE OF FILTH t-shirt. His black-painted fingernails flashed menacingly against the microphone stand.

A second camera went close-up on 9ine, who was in his fourth or fifth year at Bay Community College. 9ine, who was also called Larry Cudgemore, had a large silver ring dangling from his nose. The screens showed the metal spoke coming out of his bottom lip, the rows of gold and silver rings in his eyebrows, the writing on his purple shirt which inquired: IS IT FASCISM YET?

As the song approached its surging climax, Jerry hit the switch on the smoke machine. I took out the bottle of Southern Comfort, had a slug, slipped it back in my pocket. White smoke plumes swirled out of the black box, snaking up and around the flailing Jerry.

Tattooed and dreadlocked rockstar hopefuls wearing leather and pancake makeup stood around impatiently, tapping their feet out of time. Fiddle-heavy hopefuls in cowboy boots and neon vests stared at the Wastemakers with hostility. A few more onlookers got up to leave, others stood talking.

The song had ended, but the smoke remained. Jerry swam in it, his arm lashing out to locate the mic stand.

"O.K., this is a new one called 'Tomorrow's Yesterdays.' And it goes like this: A-one, and a-two, and a..."

9ine whacked the bongo, Jerry's guitar twanged boldly two or three seconds then faded out, again becoming unintelligible in the jet-engine buzz. Jerry squawked above the squeaking whine, only the top of the pink 'hawk visible above the smoke.

We went back into the Ladies'.

I heard Candace say, "This is so Loserville, I can't even believe it... What are we doing here?"

She and Ginny laughed. I had a puff from the cigar, then took Ginny into another stall and sucked on her neck for a while. I slipped both my hands down into her underwear and squeezed her buttocks. Ginny seemed to enjoy it.

Candace poked her head in and made a face. Well, what? Ginny and I released and stumbled out. It seemed possible, yet somehow incredibly complicated, to get Ginny to some different place...

Jerry and 9ine were still going at it. The smoke seemed to have cleared somewhat. I picked up the beer pint from the table and finished it, had another gulp of the Comfort. Then somebody cut the sound.

"Thank you, Wastemakers, thank you," said a voice over the speakers. "Thanks for participating... We'll let you know if you make it to the next round. Next we have... Torchcandy... Torchcandy, are you ready?"

Jerry jumped down from the stage and went flying to Candace.

"You did great!" she said.

I slapped him five. "It was awesome, bro..."

"Nah, we sucked..."

"No, it was incredible... It was the sound-man who screwed you!"

He shook his head, tears in his eyes. "We sucked..."

We went around to the rear of the stage and I helped them carry several bongos to the back doors. Jerry and Candace and 9ine walked off somewhere. I went back to the front, found Ginny and took her by the hand to a booth at the back. We sat close together deep in the booth, watching Torchcandy set up and begin. I sucked on Ginny's neck, got one hand up her sweater top. Torchcandy seemed very angry. Though well-practiced, they seemed to be taking most of their clues from famous records five to eight years old.

I sucked on Ginny's neck, every so often taking a gulp of the Comfort. It was dark back there in the booth, no one seemed notice us. Ginny was very grabbable. She put one of her legs over my thigh. I slipped my hand under the skirt and stroked her underwear. It wasn't long before I had pulled aside the panty and got a finger in.

Torchcandy seemed very angry, even angrier than when they had started. The singer, a short fellow with a bandanna tied around his head, glared out from the overhead screens, daring society to challenge him on... on... on something that didn't seem quite clear at that moment. His beard appeared to have been braided into several long strands. He glared out at the small Plutoland world, angry, defiant. I doubted anything would make him happy.

Ginny had moistened up nicely. I fingered away at her, a second finger gently massaging her butthole, and sucked her neck. My penis struggled painfully against the bottom of her thigh, straining unsuccessfully for a hint of relief. Ginny moaned softly, her mouth sopping with saliva...

A few more minutes went by and things had started to become very soupy. My vision blurred, I began to have problems breathing. It came on quick, I didn't totally understand. I didn't know what the hell was happening. A dizzy spell came next, it felt like I might throw up. I leaned to the side and wheezed, my head leaning against the booth cushion... My head pounded, the dizziness came in waves...

A little vomit popped out of my mouth, landing on the back of the booth. I coughed and spluttered, my stomach clenching. I heaved. Another small vomit shot popped out. Some of the juice began to slide down the cushion...

Ginny pushed me off violently, smashing the heel of her palm into my shoulder.

"You're sick!" she said. "You're disgusting!"

She got out of the booth and walked off.

I sat for five or ten minutes, until my head began to clear. I felt a little better. I got up slowly, went to the bar and got a bottle Bud for $3. I sat back down on the edge of the booth.

Torchcandy had finally finished. I drained the bottle in four gulps. Good, cold beer. I went and got another. I only had five dollars left, but Jerry had promised several parties following the gig.

I sat there and watched, taking sucks off the beer, as a chick wearing a rainbow headband, purple corduroys, sandals and a shiny salmon and orange tube top walked on the stage. She had wide hips, a low hanging butt, ample bosoms snug inside the tube.

"Ladies and gentlemen, please welcome... Deb Flower!"

Deb checked her reflection in her turntable screen, made her final adjustments. The music began to chug out. Deb squirmed around behind her turntables, doing little wiggly, or wavy motions, sometimes spinning around in a circle. Video screen shots showed what appeared to be a small, glittering black diamond glued to the center of her forehead.

Deb's music was basically disco, but with a warm, chugging aspect to the rhythm, along with touches of light guitar strumming, traces of bagpipes and piano arpeggios, an indistinct voice wailing in the background. Visions of orangutans and owls, fields of dandelions, appeared on the overhead screens, one glowing image mutating into the next. There were blasts of color, orange and yellow and lime, followed by a series of new pictures – a heaping plate of chicken and mashed potatoes, several bulldog puppies, a child wearing an Indian costume with his face stripe-painted... grey old people smiling and holding hands, a shot of children splashing in a pool, beads of water frozen around their heads... The music wafted about pleasantly and soothingly, not making any obnoxious demands.

Eventually, I wandered out into the early evening. The sky was a gorgeous light purple. It seemed strange to see Jerry bleeding from the mouth, holding a towel and a roll of gauze, blood on his neck and the front of his CRADLE OF FILTH shirt. Candace was crying. They were talking to a cop on the corner. Down the block a ways, ambulance lights whirled beneath the palm trees. Someone was laid out on the cement, a paramedic team working on him – 9ine, it would turn out.

Various furry-feet came down for a look, then walked off. Jerry explained that they had gone around the corner, looking for 9ine's van, when they had been ambushed by thugs. It was apparently a case of black-on-white crime, from what I could gather. The thugs had smashed Jerry in the back, then dispatched him with a few kicks to the face. Candace had been knocked to the ground, her purse and everybody's drugs taken.

✪

9ine was eventually driven off in the ambulance. He would live, apparently. Candace got in a cab. Jerry really wanted to get loaded.

We went up to the second floor of Plutoland, where MMTV was throwing an "invite-only party" for the contestants. Jerry's mohawk was slightly bent, though still bravely pink. His face had several knots, various swellings and scrapes, red splotches. He smiled with some difficulty, his hands still shaking as he again recounted the battle. We had several beers and Long Island ice teas from the bar in rapid succession.

It had been so close, Jerry explained, they "could all be dead right now."

Fresh tears appeared in his eyes, he shook his head. It was just luck, pure luck, that he was here now...

"Jesus, they kicked your ass, Jerry... You have to admit..."

"We were way outnumbered, they were ready to kill, man! I wish you would have been there..."

"Yeah... Jerry, shouldn't you be with Candace? Or 9ine?"

"What else can I do? They're cool, they're all right... I need to get loaded, bro. I'm way too stressed."

"I hear you..."

"We stank it up, huh? We don't have a chance to win this thing..."

"Shit, I don't know, Jerry. Somebody's got to win..."

A few minutes later, he did call Candace. He was on the phone for about 15 minutes, then left.

Deb Flower was a bit shorter and plumper than I had imagined, and talked very slowly. Her voice was sing-songy and slightly hoarse. Her main obvious blemish appeared to be some kind of sore on the corner of her mouth. It was pink-purple in color, oozing slightly. She appeared to have covered it with a type of clear ointment, but it didn't bother me so much.

I had seemingly rebounded. I gulped from one then other of the drinks that filled my hands, gazing at glowing Deb, at her sparkling black forehead diamond. I had spent a few minutes in the bathroom, throwing water in my face and wiping away a few specks of vomit from my shirt. I had also decided to wear the sunglasses. I talked to Deb at some length about the Jerry assault, and how much I had enjoyed her show.

"Are they all your own songs?"

"Well, mostly... I mean, yeah, they're other people's records, but I mix it..."

"Oh, that's great..."

Deb and I exchanged information, gradually seeming to develop a consensus. It turned out she was studying part-time to be a geologist, while working full-time as a kindergarten aide in Sunset Heights. The kids were "so sweet." The deejay career had grown out gradually from her twelve years of playing the cello, from the time she was a girl. She hadn't been dedicated enough to make it as a big-time cellist, it was simply too much time, but the deejay thing still allowed her to pursue her interest in music.

Our talk also touched, seemingly inevitably, on the subject of global warming. Deb was concerned, very. Deb explained she had a great love for animals and insects, big and small. It was her position that it was wrong to kill any living thing. One should avoid killing, if at all possible.

"I know, Deb... People are just... so *stupid* sometimes. Aren't they?"

Deb smiled.

I explained how my favorite animals were aardvarks and anteaters, as well as the little mini-monkeys that jump around, you know, the tiny ones with heads like lions...

"Yeah!" said Deb.

I reached out and took hold of one of her hands. She didn't seem to mind. Every so often I'd lean down and give her a kiss on the neck or behind the ear. She didn't seem to mind.

Several rockstar hopefuls made attempts to interfere with Deb, walking up to babble about types of equipment or to present offers regarding future "gig" possibilities, so forth. I thought it was over for me, as it should have been, but I kept standing there making comments and Deb kept coming back. It helped that the rockstar hopefuls were, for the most part, mushy and boy-like, unthreatening. One by one, they made their meager effort and shuffled off...

Deb told me about a dream she had the other night. She was supposed to go to an ABBA concert with her father. The trouble was, she couldn't decide whether to wear a short jean skirt, or a long one made of "a thousand colors." Her lack of decision resulted in her missing the concert.

"Sometimes I have this dream that I am walking through one dark cave after another," I told her. "Inside each cave is a black horrible thing that I can only see the outline of, but I know it's horrible... Or sometimes it seems like there's these huge knives sticking out from the walls, which will slice me up if I make the slightest wrong move... It's very, very frightening, Deb, do you know what I mean? Then sometimes I come to the edge and I see little things down in this valley. It's a valley with like, these red rocks, yet it's *inside* a huge cave. Do you know what I mean? Like this valley *inside* the cave. And at the very bottom of the valley are like these strange gold and silver rocks... and there are these little living things down there, small ones, but they have big sharp beaks and like, scissors for hands, or wings, but they can't fly... They make strange noises, little squeaks, that I can't understand..."

Deb squeezed my hand sympathetically.

✪

We took a taxi to a house in Sunset Lakes. Some rockstar's idea. Most of the people in this place were passed out – laying across the couches, curled up on the floor. A kind of heavy metal-jazz was going at maximum volume on the stereo.

In the kitchen, a group of them stood around watching a guy wrestle a chair. He got the chair down, but it threw him off. The crowd cheered... He rolled and crouched like a leopard... then leaped and charged the chair again. The chair angrily tossed him away, sending him rolling backward into the cabinet. The crowd roared... He stood, steadying himself and breathing heavily, eying the chair warily... at last he launched himself furiously across the linoleum, flying through the air and delivering a vicious slam to the back of the chair. The crowd booed...

The chair skidded across the lino, smacking loudly into the doorway. The chair was finally down. The end was near. The guy hopped to his feet and charged again...

I went back out to the main room, carefully stepping around a red and black basketball which sat in the center of the carpet, casting off immense shadows. People criss-crossed the floor, but nobody was touching this basketball.

I went down the hall, looking for a bathroom. Through an open door, I saw a guy sitting in front of a computer in a darkened room. He motioned me in.

"Look, man... C'mere, look... Check it out..."

I went in, knocking through piles of paper and bags, food cartons and cardboard boxes strewn across the floor.

"So where's the iguana?" I said.

The guy giggled, took a water bong off the desk and took a hit. He offered it to me. I took in a lungful, set it down. The guy reached over and stuck a piece of beef jerky in a can of chocolate sauce. He removed the jerky, strings of chocolate dripping on to his pants, chewed off a chunk and handed it to me. I dunked the jerky, dripping the chocolate on to the carpet, and chewed off a piece. Not bad. Not bad at all.

On the computer screen was a picture of a guy's body on the floor, his head cut off. The head was lying on the back of the headless body. A bloody knife was leaning against the side of the head.

Sons of the Faithful will arise to destroy the Crusader, plucking out the eyeballs from the Crusader serpents, said a text scrolling along the bottom of the screen. *Freedom in this land is not ours. It is the freedom of the occupying soldiers in doing what they like, abusing women, children, men, old men and women whom they arrested randomly and without any guilt. No one can ask them what they are doing, because they are protected by their so-called freedom. They express only the freedom of rape, the freedom of nudity and the freedom of humiliation. The U.S.A. is attacking our nations like a plate of food. O Great Allah, America came with its horses and knights to invade, slay and humiliate. O Great Allah, destroy the kingdom of Mnung as you destroyed the kingdom of Caesar. Death to the fascist insect pig that preys on the life of the people...*

"Look what they did to this guy!"

The fellow tapped buttons, finally arriving at a movie. It showed a fat white guy with sandy brown hair. He was blindfolded and wearing earmuffs and an orange jumpsuit, his hands tied behind. A guy wearing a hood took a large knife and began sawing at his neck. Blood ran down into the jumpsuit, pooling up and finally rolling over, the stain spreading across the cloth.

"Goddamn weird stuff," I said, reaching for the bong.

When I came out, Deb was sitting on a stool, playing a guitar. Five or six people were gathered around her, looks of delight and incredulity on their faces. A lava lamp blew purple and green bubbles on a shelf in the background.

Deb played with simplicity, unrushed, unstrained. She did "London Bridge," then "Teensy Weensy Spider." Her voice was sweet and melodic, sweeping high and suddenly low, sometimes wavering and cracking on the extended parts. She smiled at the end of each number, nodding her head and reaching up to tune. She did "Mulberry Bush" before concluding with:

Be kind to your web-footed friends, everyone!
For a duck may be somebody's mother
Be kind to your friends in the swamp
Where the weather is always damp
You may think this is the end... and it is!

✪

Deb's apartment was bright and stiflingly warm. There was a cage containing her guinea pig, Richard, while a clear plastic box next to it seemed to have a slightly curling turd inside. "Commemorative Panda Poop," said the gold lettering, from when the Bay Zoo & Aquarium had hosted the Chinese pandas a few years ago. Yes, interesting. A large tank along the wall had a dozen or so red and yellow fish swishing around. On the wall above the tank was a gigantic poster featuring waterfalls, rainbows and sunsets. THE WHOLE WORLD WANTS PEACE! it said.

A collection of stuffed animals was arrayed on her futon-bed – elephants and giraffes, a number of toucans, an alligator, a pig and several tigers. Deb began talking, with some difficulty, about a trip she had taken to Cambodia or Thailand, somewhere like that.

I sat on the corner of the bed, nodding my head. She sat down next to me with a little buddha pipe. We used my lighter to smoke something dark brown. It didn't taste like much of anything. We both yawned. It had been a very lengthy day.

My face had begun to feel super hot. I went into the bathroom and ran the tap, taking in several mouthfuls. Then, as I was taking a piss, I noticed a dead bird in bathtub. It was black, perhaps a crow. It was laying on a section of newspaper, its feathers dried and razzed, its feet waxy and grey, sticking out at different angles.

I shouted out, "Hey, did you know there's a dead bird in your bathtub?"

She came in. "Yeah... I found him on the street... yesterday... Isn't he... beautiful?"

"Yeah... yeah... What are you going to do with it?"

"I... don't... know... It just seemed... wrong... to leave him... on the street."

"Sure, Deb."

I turned and kissed her. She helped me carefully remove her top. Deb's tits flopped out, swinging to the sides. Each nipple was pierced with a small metallic butterfly.

CLOWNFEST! It's Clown v. Clown in Job Showdown

★ 32 ★

Through a combination of letters and phone calls over about a six-week period, I was able to trick my way into an appointment with Bob Neath, Assistant Managing Editor for News at the *Examiner-Mail*.

I prepared for the moment meticulously, wiping down my maroon wing-tips, installing a pair of new shoelaces. I wore a white shirt Jerry had recently dry-cleaned, a red tie with white daggers, dark blue slacks, the grey-green sportscoat. It was my big Schanft-Micro opening – the gateway to book conglomerates and Hollywood, to television and the glossy big-name magazines.

The bus pulled in a block from the historic, blond-marble colonnaded *Examiner-Mail* building, which had been famously acquired in 1889 by J. Quinlan Buerst as payment for an alleged gambling debt. Buerst had legendarily emblazoned "Mothership of the Dailies" across the building facade, thereby setting in motion one of the greatest stories in the history of American journalism.

The highlights included several decades worth of sensational agitation for any and all foreign wars decreed by Washington, followed by scandal-mongering and finger-wagging on a grand scale during the economic collapse at the end of the 1920s and the start of the Great Depression. The paper (then known as the *Examiner-Tribune Mail*) had been heroic in its subsequent full-throttle support for the New Deal and the struggle of the working man, as well as in its promotion of comic strips, celebrities and little blue men from Mars.

This era had of course been followed by a vicious run of strike-breaking, praise for Hitler, demonization of Hitler, and hard-hitting war coverage as our boys took out Hitler and the Yellow Jap Hordes. The post-World War II scene had, appropriately, witnessed the paper's rapid retreat to reactionary politics, as dictated by economic conditions – angry hostility to civil rights for Negroes; angry support for civil rights for Negroes; wild denunciations of the Drug Culture; wild celebrations of the Drug Culture. Then, in due course: Gross fiscal mismanagement, the closure of most foreign bureaux, liquidation of assets, and, finally – death, sale to Schanft-Micro, and full-throated support for all things Mnung and War Against Terror. All in all, a chronicle of our times.

I crossed the street to find 15 or 20 geeks parading in front, holding signs and shouting. "THE LIBERAL MEDIA'S GOT TO GO! HEY-HO, THE LIBERAL MEDIA'S GOT TO GO!" The geeks held signs as they tramped around in a small circle: SAY NO TO THE LIBERAL MEDIA! MEDIA LIES ARE KILLING OUR TROOPS! KNOW YOURE PLACE – SHUT YOURE FACE!

Cars honked on the boulevard, bike messengers swerved. Pedestrians walked through and past, dodging the screamers. Two rows of cops were lined up, five yards apart, one row against the street, the other against the building's smoked glass. Several cop vans were parked at the end of the block.

A geek ran up waving a petition. "Please, sir, please sign. It's so important, I – it's – I – it's…"

WE WANT OUR MEDIA BACK! the page read. There were 20 or 30 signatures.

"Oh, sure," I said, scribbling down the first name that popped into my head: *Rutherford B. Hayes*.

"SAY NO! NO! NO! TO THE LIBERAL MEDIA! SAY NO! NO! NO…"

I saw an opening and slipped past, through the smoked glass and in.

The Reception Desk sat below a sparkling white-stone bust of J. Quinlan and an elaborate color mural that included a golden molehill, faun's head and flaming morning sun over a vague and glistening cityscape. I produced my documents and the security supervisor dialed up to the office for clearance. I signed the waiver and security form, donned the Visitor's badge, set my satchel on the conveyor. I cleared the machines, collected the satchel and boarded the elevator to the 14th floor.

The secretary, Angela, was waiting when the doors pulled open. She ushered me into her quadrant, smiling and offering a hand.

"Mr. Neath's in a meeting right now," she said. "Please have a seat."

"Yes, of course."

I sat and began once more to rehearse my lines: The important events and factors in my rise thus far. The jobs and important articles, my visions, philosphies and theories about hard, discriminating yet fair and responsive news journalism, and how to apply them in our world today... I reached into my satchel and rearranged my resumé, the lists of recommendations and awards, the xeroxes of my key articles...

Every so often someone, usually a younger man, would shuffle by nervously, head down, obviously amidst some pressing task. His eyes would dart out to examine me, before he would shuffle past and disappear into the bowels of the office. A few times a small group passed by phlegmatically, talking softly and carrying cups of gourmet coffee from the ground-level café. The coffee aroma lingered long after they were gone.

I picked up a copy of that day's *Examiner-Mail* that was sitting on a little table. The front page had a giant color picture of the president wearing a tangerine Speedo and sunglasses. He was holding a black dog on his lap.

> MNUNG GIVES MEDAL TO DRUG-SNIFFING DOG
> By Katherine Ann Conners
> *Of The Examiner-Mail Staff*
>
> WASHINGTON – President Wolfgang G. Mnung on Wednesday presented a Presidential Merit Medal to Jim-Joe, a Labrador credited for discovering more than one ton of hidden cocaine, heroin and other drugs.
>
> "This is a superdog that has brought honor to our country," Mnung said as he presented the 8-year-old canine with the Presidential Police Merit Star at a ceremony in the White House Map Room.
>
> "This is a fine American dog," the president added. "Our country is proud."

I flipped to Local News In Brief, in the B Section, to check for stories I had written. It had been a decent day: MAN ACCUSED OF HACKING WIFE TO DEATH FOUR KILLED IN BASEMENT SHOOTING YOUTH, 8, SUFFERS HEAD INJURIES IN SCHOOL LUNCH BOX ATTACK SANTA COSTA PARENTS ATTACK SOCCER REFEREE...

I took out a pen and circled the headers, then pulled the page and nestled it into my stack. Neath, I imagined, might find it interesting.

I went back to the front section, finding the following curious item in National News In Brief:

> COL. ADMITS CONCEALING MONEY-LAUNDERING
> *From Our Wire Services*
>
> NEW YORK – A U.S. Army officer who headed American anti-drug efforts in Colombia pleaded guilty Wednesday to concealing knowledge that his wife was laundering money from illegal cocaine and heroin transactions while they lived in Bogota.

At least twenty minutes had passed by now.

"Excuse me," I said to Angela, getting up and walking toward her. "Is now not a good time? I can come back later, if, you know…"

"One moment, please…"

She picked up the phone, dialed and began speaking softly. She hung up.

"I'm sorry, sir," said Angela. "Is another 15 minutes too long?"

I nodded. "Yes, that should be fine."

"Oh, good."

I sat back down, flipped more pages, scanned World News In Brief.

> REPORT: PRIESTS SEXUALLY ABUSED NUNS
>
> VATICAN CITY (AIP) – The Vatican has acknowledged a report saying some Roman Catholic priests and missionaries have been forcing nuns to have sex, and were in some cases committing rape and forcing the victims to have abortions.
>
> The confidential report, written by a U.S. nun and physician, details cases of sexual abuse in 23 countries, including India, Ireland, Italy, Brazil, Nigeria, Poland, the Philippines and the United States.
>
> In at least one case, according to the report, a priest forced a nun to have an abortion, after which she died from loss of blood and complications. The same priest officiated at her requiem mass, according to the report.
>
> In another instance, 19 nuns in one religious community were pregnant at the same time.

"I'm sorry, Angela – is there a restroom?"

"Oh, certainly," she said, smiling cheerfully. "Down the hall and to the left."

I went down and re-checked the hair and tie. I made a few adjustments, then punched a metal button for cold water. A guy walked in as I was looking in the mirror and slapping cold water my face. He was about forty, nearly bald, in a dark blue suit.

"Oh harder, harder!" he said in a high, yipping voice. "Harder! Oh, I can't take it! I can't take it!"

He laughed, shaking his head. He arrived at the urinal row and unzipped. The water clicked off and I walked out.

Angela was standing to meet me when I came back.

"I'm sorry... Something's come up and Mr. Neath can't see you today. He said to tell you that he will telephone you at 3 p.m. sharp. Again, he apologizes."

"Oh, sure," I said. "I understand..."

I left her my package of clips and resumé, and walked out.

✪

I went into the apartment and took my second shower in two hours. I dried off, got dressed in shorts and a t-shirt, and walked down to the store. I bought two twelve-packs of Iron Lion beer, two packs of smokes, a little flask of Dublin's Imperial Whisky. All the cheapest money could buy.

I set the stuff on the table, flicked on the TV and started to clean up a bit. I threw all the empty cans and bottles into the trash, emptied the ashtrays, threw away the stacks of newspapers and junk mail...

It's showdown time, America... the TV voice boomed ominously. *Tomorrow night at 9 p.m. Eastern... live from Chicago, eating capital of the U.S.A... Who will be crowned America's greatest eater... Man... or beast? It's man against dog in the first-ever eating clash of the species... Watch as America's champion human lawnmowers – the Bratwurst King... the Pizza Inhaler... the Fried Chicken Fanatic... the Pancake Pounder... take on man's best friend in the world's greatest eat-off of all time. The target: 50 ½-pound hamburgers. The prize: a half-million cold clams... Tune in and find out who's really got the chops – man... or man's best friend? It's the eat-off of the century, live, tomorrow night, right here...*

It wasn't long before Mnung appeared with British Prime Minister Douglas "Dougie" Sepoy at the president's television ranch set in Lucknow, Alabama. The two allies walked along, Bibles in their hands, followed by several dozen advisers from both nations, many also holding Bibles. A contingent of cheerleaders moved in from the sides, holding signs reading FREEDOM, PEACE, DETERMINATION, MISSION. The president stopped before a bank of microphones.

CLOWN: *Ladies and gentlemen, our good ally Dougie Sepoy and I have just held a very important strategy session. We have seen the way forward in the war, the blueprint for freedom. We will continue until victory and democracy is established... I would like to add that Dougie has definitely got, as we like to say in America, real* cojones *for having his army join us in the attack and bombing of the target country. British troops have been very important to the war-peace process, and that should not be forgotten. Dougie believes in freedom, and the kingdom of England of course shares our freedom and democratic way of life, and that is why they are amongst our most esteemed co-patriots...*

CLOWN: *Yes indeed, ahem... Thank you, President Mnung... I, ahem, would just like to begin by acknowledging that indeed there have been certain criticisms of this war-peace process, as the president called it, and justifiably so – but I daresay the entire world is better off now that the dictator is gone. I daresay so. Not to say there aren't problems, most certainly there are, any objective analysis would indicate that that is the case. But I would daresay, with all due respect, to the critics out there, those who have questioned our policy, that sometimes the best chance for peace is war... Tough on war... and tough on the causes of war... Because, I daresay, we will stand up for human rights, and we will oppose these terrorist groups and insurgents that are fomenting the multi-pronged sectarian conflict that threatens to tear apart that young and important democracy that we are helping to implant in the Middle East. Because violence to bring about political change, from the point of a gun, is always wrong. Always. I'll repeat: Always wrong. The terrorists need to understand this. Our decency demands it. We are decent people and we demand it. At the same time, we must urgently seek a solution to the Israeli-Palestinian crisis...*

BREAKING: BLUNGEFORD BUSTED

CLOWN: *Ladies and gentlemen, we're pulling away now from President Mnung and the prime minister of Great Britain, Dougie Sepoy, to bring you some breaking news... We are just getting word now that Rusty Blungeford, star of the new blockbuster film* Dr. Destructo, *has* been arrested after throwing a telephone at a concierge at a New York City hotel... Repeat, Dr. Destructo heartthrob Rusty Blungeford has been arrested for throwing a telephone in a midnight rage at a New York City luxury hotel... Repeat: Rusty Blungeford, star of the new blockbuster action-romance Dr. Destructo, has been arrested by New York police after flying into a rage and throwing a telephone at a luxury hotel concierge in New York... We'll go live now to our Hollywood correspondent, Pepe Cameron, who is standing by with the latest developments in this breaking developing story...

I snapped it off and had a few drinks. The phone rang at 4:05.

"Gosh, guy, I'm sorry," Neath said. "I got tied up – I've been having to deal with those wackos in front of the building. Did you see them? I don't know what the heck they want. I mean, what more can we do? We've supported all the wars, Jesus, we've called for more wars, if necessary... We supported Guantanamo and Abu Ghraib to the hilt, before we condemned them. But we had to condemn *that*. We're a newspaper, I mean, we had to do *that*. Gosh, we've printed so many articles hailing the president as a strong leader, I just, I don't know...We've always supported Israel to the max, while expressing caution about the West Bank settlements. Bingo, can't fault us there. Bingo, we've repeatedly demanded school vouchers. *Repeatedly*. We've supported a referendum, heck, we've *demanded* referendums for *everything*... Bingo, we've demanded the building of fences along the *entire* Mexican border. The whole goshdarn thing, guy. What else can we do? Our head corporation has given hundreds of thousands of dollars to the Mnung-Jicks campaign. I don't get it. What else can we do?"

"Jeez, I don't know... Sounds like a tough situation..."

"Listen, first I got to tell you – I can't take you on right now, not a chance. We got a hiring freeze in the News Division.[*] It would be different if it was up to me, but so would a lot of things. And that's on top of the whole buyout-package thing the company's been running. They've been cleaning house by offering some pretty snazzy buyout packages, depending on your level of seniority. Around 140 people from all departments have taken it so far..."

"Oh, wow..."

---

[*] In fact, the *Examiner-Mail* would within six months complete cuts of 35 percent of its News Division staff, reducing the number of full-time reporters covering the city to seven. At the same time, circulation would continue to plunge, falling 22 percent during the 18 months ending at the next quarterly reporting period. – ED.

"Wow is right, guy."

We briefly discussed my career hopes. Neath suggested it might be a good idea for me to try to get on with a newspaper in a "mid-size local market" and start working my way up.

"I'm looking at your paperwork right now, guy. To be honest, it looks a little thin for elite media... I'm not seeing Harvard, I'm not seeing Yale, I'm not seeing woman. Are you an expert on anything?" He laughed. "The truth is, guy, unless you're a Chinese lesbian single mother from Harvard in a wheelchair with a degree in nuclear physics who can write a punchy feature lead, you need to be an expert on something. You aren't recording this are you?"

"No," I said, "But –"

"What I mean is, it helps, guy," Neath said. "These days it really helps to be an expert on something. Everything's specialized now, it's the name of the game. It's a specialized world and becoming more so..."

"Yes..."

"You wouldn't happen to have any intelligence background, security or terrorism? Military, missile systems, something like that? It could be helpful, it's very hot right now. That's the kind of person we're looking for – intelligence background, military, with the insider's perspective and contacts..."

"No, I –"

"It's like – well, here's an example for you. One of our last hires was our Health & Wellness reporter, Jane Martense. Smart young girl. She's an expert on cancer, studied it at Cal Tech. Got a doctorate in it, I believe, something like that, from MIT. Super reporter, and a hell of a nice gal, by the way... We've got another guy, been with us a couple years now in the Washington Bureau, Ed Hichmann. He's an authority on the aviation industry, actually used to work in radar at John F. Kennedy Airport before he got into reporting. This guy knows things you and I couldn't even dream about knowing about planes and airports and ticket prices, security screening, plane engines, fuel prices, the whole economics of it. So that's what he covers for us – aviation. And that's a hot, hot world right now. You see what I'm saying?"

"I guess so..."

"O.K., guy?"

"I was just hoping to get on as a general reporter, you know. Covering crime and the sanitation district, City Hall and the drought, things like that."

"I hear you, guy. We all love that stuff. That's where we all come from. I'm just giving you the view from here, all right? Just something to keep in mind if you want to move up in this line of work..."

"Yeah..."

"I mean, gosh, guy – I don't even know if we're going to have an actual paper printed on newsprint in five or ten years. They tell me everything, and I mean everything, is going to the internets and blogs. The blogs and internets is the new winners and losers, that's what they tell me. Be new and be cool, or be a loser, you know? Hard facts. Because it's a go-go, now-now kind of world these days. Gosh, you've got to have heard that..."

"Yeah, for sure..."

"But the main thing is, guy, the internets or blogs is a lot cheaper. There's none of the trouble with printing plants and truck drivers and plastic bags, strikers, everything like that... It's something to think about."

"Wow, no kidding..."

"Do you, by the way, know how to put up the internets or blogs? We can always use guys who can put up the internets blogs..."

"Well, I – you know, I was sort of hoping –"

"Keep it in mind, guy, putting up the internets and blogs is a very useful skill in this day and age. We got to get our hits, that's what we keep hearing from Advertising. It's all about the hits, the unique visitors to the internets and blogs. They measure what they call 'the internets traffic' on a quarterly-hour basis, I'm told. They are keeping tabs on all the hits in real-time, guy. That's the reality in this day and age. They want to know who's getting the hits and when. And don't ask me why, guy – I haven't the foggiest."

"Yeah... Well, thanks for taking the time to call."

"No problem. Look, you want to come down and see the office? Maybe we can fit you in on a tour sometime. It's quite an operation, all told. Quite a little hive of energy over here. I always give a little speech when a group comes through, if I got the time."

"Sure, sounds good..."

"Call in advance to the secretary. Her name's Angela. How's that sound? Cool?"

"O.K., yeah... Well, thanks again for calling."

"No problem, guy. Good luck to you. Sincerely. I mean it."

"Thanks a lot. I appreciate your concern."

FUNHOUSE: Clown Collapses at Babe's Birthday Bash!

★ 33 ★

Chrissy was wearing bright orange tights with double white racing-stripes down the sides. She wore a frilly long sleeve pink top, a black choke collar with silver studs. Swirly silver triple-rings swung from her ears. Black heels, silver anklets on each leg.

She began by catching me up on the latest office scandal. One of the boss lawyers, she explained, had for several years been fucking some "coordinator" woman, whose job was mostly like a secretary's, but they called it "coordinator." The lady did things like arrange catering for meetings and designing the firm's calendar, i.e. picking out the teddy bear photos or Monet paintings for each month's spread.

Her husband wasn't having much luck on the job market, apparently, they had two kids and money was tight, so the wife had helped set up for him a "consultant" gig down at the office – advising the firm on its "information strategy," something to do with collating and otherwise restructuring their "systems." The husband claimed to have expertise in this sector, though Chrissy wasn't totally persuaded. In any case, the guy would go into a meeting room for a consulting session with the lawyer boss, the coordinating wife, various others on the Information Taskforce. The wife would take the notes.

"Everyone" in the office knew what was going on, and even Chrissy admitted, it was kind of "gross." The scuttlebutt in the office was that the lady's latest child, a daughter, looked "a lot" like the boss. Chrissy had seen a few pictures, and she couldn't disagree.

Then, during the final session of the consulting contract, the husband had thanked everyone and said, "Now, which one of you has been fucking my wife?"

Chrissy laughed.

"So what happened?"

"They all laughed like it was a joke. Then he walked out."

"What a guy," I said. "I guess people will do nearly anything for food."

We were in a cafe, Lokarno, famous for its white-on-white decor. There was candlelight, we were having Dubonnet on ice. A few thin bearded fellows were playing guitars in the corner. Chrissy got up and went to the restroom. In the minute after she returned, the waiter hustled up. He set down a small cake and a bottle of champagne.

"Happy birthday, Thor!"

"Oh, wow..."

The guy lighted the single candle. The guy poured. I blew the candle.

Chrissy beamed. She leaned across the table. We touched lips and clinked glasses.

"I brought you some presents..."

"Oh, great..."

She handed over, first, a bottle of imported Squinky's Emerald Inferno absinthe. Then came another bottle, something that was labeled Zelator's Cannabis Vodka. Finally came a little box. Inside was an expensive watch with a red-brown leather band – a silvered gold dial, according to the tag, sapphire case back, automatic time zone sensor, second time-zone indicator, water resistant, self-winding...

"I don't know what to say, Chris... Wow, it's just so... nice... You really didn't have to..."

"C'mon, you don't have to say anything..."

She reached across the table, squeezed my shoulder.

"You don't have to say anything... I know what you mean... *You're my Thor guy.*"

To fill out the birthday celebration, she had decided to take us to "closing night" at Bambiland, which had apparently hit its six-month expiration date. We had several more bites of the carrot cake and I finished the champagne. Chrissy removed two Barney Rubbles from her wallet and we popped them during the taxi ride.

We got out at Camp and Kyle. Chrissy said the password and forked a few bills. We crossed the threshold and went down three or four flights of stairs.

The first hideous vision was of a dyed-blond short guy wearing a too-tight yellow t-shirt that said HOSEBAG. Disco music pumped along at a low volume, nothing too obvious. People stood at a bar and sat on couches. They were dressed casually, some in pajamas, some in tight-shorts or multi-strap leather get-ups, some of the women in lingerie. The decor was mainly brickwork and black metal, curtains across cave-like openings, a smell of burning wax and flowers. Around three-quarters guys, unfortunately – about 95 percent white, it looked like, five percent "other."

"We don't have to do anything," said Chrissy. "We can just sit and watch. Or there's a lot of girls around... And you're looking pretty good, I must say..."

"Yeah?"

"Yeah! Go ahead, drink, meet some people... Have fun, do what you want... Explore... Hey, it's your birthday."

"Thanks, Chris."

I leaned over and kissed her on the neck.

I got a beer at the bar, Chrissy got a Semtex mixed with red wine. Holding hands, we walked down a corridor.

We pulled back the first curtain and looked in. A woman was leaning back on a couch. A guy was on his knees in front of her, her legs over his shoulders, his head under her skirt. A bunch of guys sat around watching – young guys, a few old guys with hairy bellies, some wearing masks. It seemed hard to believe at first, but most of the guys were stroking their cocks. Two guys on either side of the lady came up and began massaging her tits and nipples. They flopped the sagging tits around, lifting them up and away from her body to lick and nibble. The woman, who appeared somewhere past 40, made a series of gurgling sounds.

"Ohhhh... that's *f-a-a-a-a-bulous!*" someone said.

Chrissy turned and kissed me. She reached down and grabbed my balls. She undid my fly, put in her hand. We stood like that, watching the guy with his head under the lady's skirt and the guys jacking off. About the time I got nearly hard, a guy came up next to Chrissy, smiled at her, and kissed her on the cheek. Guy in his mid-40s or so, brown mustache. She kissed him back.

I walked down the hall and unlocked the absinthe, set the fucker free. A wave of alcohol and chemicals swirled into my face. I had a gulp, and another. Shockingly harsh, horrible stuff. I gagged, forced down another mouthful. A couple walked past me holding hands, the male and female each wearing kneepads.

As I was heading toward the bar, Chrissy ran up and grabbed my arm. One side of her top was pulled down her shoulder.

"Come on, man, don't be like this! It's just *fun*, that's all! Everyone's nice, they won't hurt you. It's just fooling around..."

"Yeah... Maybe I'll just watch..."

I took the vodka out of my other pocket and unscrewed the cap. I stood at the bar and ordered a beer. I took a beer sip, followed by an absinthe slug, a beer sip, and then a vodka gulp, until the beer was gone. I got another.

I felt my hair being stroked. A tall redhead had come up next to me. She was nearly as tall as I was, her nipples visible through a lace pink robe. She had a large nose, long eyelashes, light amber eyes...

She came closer. Our lips met. It was so very casual and easy. My tongue entered her mouth. She sucked on it gently. I withdrew my tongue and licked her lips. She tasted light and bouncy, like vanilla soda and lipstick. I set the bottle and beer glass on the table. I brought one hand to her hip. I brought the other to her left breast.

My eyes flashed on the wall mirror behind the bar. Several guys had shuffled forward, cocks in hand, jacking themselves off. The purple-faced bartender gooped some cream into his hand from a plastic dispenser.

A guy came up and put his hand on my back. He kissed the redhead, turned and kissed me on the cheek. I stumbled away, turning toward the jackoffs.

"Oh, pucker up, for heaven's sake!" some guy said.

I pulled the absinthe and took a slug. I moved back in the direction of the hall, a few jackers following after me. Music pumped in the background, a lazy disco beat overlaid with a banjo:

People like you and people like me
Need someone to lean on if we want to stay free
If you're lonely or dissatisfied
Give a hand to the man who is standing by your side

Somebody bumped into me. I turned. It was a guy with black masking tape completely covering his head. Tiny nostril and eye slits. He was wearing a shirt unbuttoned to reveal a thickly haired chest. He stood there with a bottle of Cristal in his hand.

A blast of woozy hit me, a wave of dizzy. A burst of white fireworks exploded in my eyes.

"Yeah... ?"

"Go ahead, touch it," he said. "I seen you looking..."

I touched his forehead.

"Yeah... ?"

"Touch my chest... Come on, I know you want to... You don't have any idea who I am. Live out your fantasy... Come on, touch me..."

"No, thanks."

"Why not?"

"I don't feel like it. It doesn't turn me on."

"Come on, man... Come on, you don't even know who I am..."

"I like it that way. I don't want to know who you are."

"You're in denial!"

"No, you are..."

"Aw, go to hell..."

I walked around, trying to find Chrissy. I saw one guy rubbing a clear cream on another guy's lips.

"It's hot," he moaned, "oh, it's hot..."

In another room, a brunette wearing jeans and a navy blue bra walked around shooting whipped cream on to the naked chests of people lined up along the wall. A skinny woman with ridiculously big boobs trailed after her, giggling and licking the cream. A fat guy with a beard and shaggy head of hair stood in a corner on the opposite side, naked except for a towel around his waist. Somebody wearing a fur coat had their head under the towel, apparently swoggling his horn.

I took out a smoke, lit it, had a pull from the absinthe.

A guy who had been putting lipstick on another guy hissed at me: "No smoking in here! Only in the courtyard!"

I walked out and down the hall.

A guy wearing a Richard Nixon mask knocked into me. I spun dizzy, felt little critters scratching around inside my stomach. The guy lifted the mask, revealing a swollen and oily red face.

"Hey, man... you got any B-6?"

"Sorry..."

I turned and staggered down the hall. The disco music thumped, my eyes began to close. I forced myself to keep them open.

Tomcat, you know where it's at
Come on let's go to my flat
Lay down and groove on the mat
Well you can be my coo-ca-choo

I ran out of air going up the stairs and vomited, holding myself against the railing as my head banged against the wall. The stuff gushed on to my shoes, ran like a goopy yellow river down the stairs.

The absinthe bottle fell, exploding in fizzing green. Several great sheets of blackness waved in front of my face. I lost power in my arms and collapsed, my forehead smacking against one of the stairs. I heard voices flying around.

"AW, GODDAMN!"

"NOT COOL! NOT COOL!"

Two muscley men lifted me up roughly and dragged me out to the front, the tops of my shoes slapping against the steps. They pulled me around the corner and let me fall to the sidewalk.

A kind voice: "You want a doctor? A taxi?"

Somebody kicked my shoulder.

"Faggot ass bullshit!"

A nasty voice: "Just don't die out here, asshole! Go somewhere else!"

A different nasty voice: "I'm gonna call this shithead a taxi. This isn't cool…"

I couldn't seem to move my mouth.

After a minute or two, I rolled on to my stomach and somehow stood. I began trudging away from them, the air cool on my face.

I lurched around the corner and made it halfway up the hill. I saw a patch of grass in front of an office building and laid down.

Cars whirred by. The sound of the tires against the street was comforting. I farted several times in rapid succession, and that seemed to bring great relief.

EDGE WORLD: Clown Terror on Nightside Nightmare!

★ 34 ★

I had been doing so well they gave me the "promotion" to night shift.

"It's a real chance for you, Thor," said Sernath. "It means we trust you. You'll be the captain on our night ship, flying solo. Welcome aboard."

What it meant was I sat alone in the empty office from 11 p.m. to six in the morning, Monday night through Friday, dialing cop numbers from a special night call sheet.

I'd locate and secure a sausage, type it up, and send it out on the wire. Then, a few minutes later, I'd plug a copy of the thing into the internet site. Copy, paste, kill the codes. Copy, paste. Format, synch. No one looking over the shoulder. If something really big happened, like a nuclear bomb explosion or the assassination of the mayor, I was supposed to get on the horn to call in the clowns.

Nothing like that occurred. It was nearly all an unvarying diet of poor folk shooting and stabbing each other, structure fires in the ghettos, multi-vehicle car wrecks on state highways, a preview of the morning traffic difficulties. MAN KILLED AS TRACTOR-TRAILER HITS PICKUP. TWO DEAD AFTER CAR HITS RAILROAD UNDERPASS BRIDGE. POLICE: BAR PATRONS DETAIN SUSPECT AFTER SHOOTING. CONSTRUCTION: I-67 RAMPS CLOSED FOR 2.5 MILES...

The nights and days passed in general agony. I was playing my small role in the service sector economy, nothing more. I finally realized that this was what I had become – a service worker, Information Sphere. Instead of burgers, I was flipping names and numbers. Instead of fat and poison, I was serving up second-hand midnight sketches of death and destruction.

I believe the spree began on the Thursday morning of the first week. I stopped at a liquor store on my way home and picked up a six-pack. I sat at the kitchen table and slowly unwound from the night's cruel visions, sucking at the beverage, listening to the stereo, looking at the funny people shuffling by outside the window. The booze made me feel so relieved that when the six had been drained, by about 10 a.m., I wandered back out and picked up six more in tall cans. After finishing them, I finally fell asleep.

From that day forward, I would stop in for a case of 12 to 18 beers on my way home nearly every morning, sometimes adding a bottle of something a bit harder. (On a few occasions I got red wine, but it tended to taste sour, and I came to believe it was filled with many chemicals). With Jerry off to work or somewhere, I'd sit at the kitchen table and drink through the morning. The worms would wriggle and churn on the ceiling, and when they fell to the table, I knocked them to the floor with my index finger and stepped on them.

I believe this routine may, in fact, have kept me alive – kept me from going "insane." The injection of booze, sitting there alone, lent me a feeling of peace and calm like no other. I found that the beer started tasting rather good at about can number seven, and I soon came to the conclusion that, all things considered, it was better to drink alone. I began to wonder how and why one ever bothered drink with "others." Alone, there was no confusion of "others" to navigate – no mess, no foolishness and sales-pitches, to complicate one's thought-process.

And I came to understand that, with little ado, I had become a member of what might be called the Edge World – a blankish, blackish place on the fringes of whatever the hell was going on out there during the daytime. Sometimes the hours passed swiftly… other times it was a slow crawl to my oblivion.

I would look out the window, the stereo music pounding and sawing. The people would stagger along on the other side of the glass, many of them with their flesh covered in scabs, and I would think of Chrissy. Some of these denizens would pass by repeatedly throughout the morning, performing their mysterious tasks. I came to believe that most were criminals. Others would make an appearance just once, never to be seen again. Maybe the cretins just died.

I witnessed things I never noticed before, such as the individuals who would appear at the STOP sign at the appointed hour each Tuesday and Thursday to pick up a white envelope that had been placed exactly *there*, amid the trash and cans (never did see who did the placing)... Or the skinny, bedraggled punks in their twos and threes, who would amble down the road, pulling at car door handles, sometimes sticking pointed tools in the locks, not caring at all that it was broad daylight... I would feel a brief surge of outrage and consider calling the police – but such a step seemed complicated and troublesome, and the chances of the police arriving soon enough to catch them seemed minimal. Instead, I would watch them go around the corner. I'd gulp a couple long pulls and think about Chrissy.

I wanted Chrissy more than anything. No, I didn't want Chrissy at all, I would tell myself – I was through with the nightmare, I needed to rebuild. A few times I punched in her number, but never did raise the courage to actually try to reach her. Sometimes I threw things at the wall, trying to knock down worms.

I'd aim for passing out no later than 2 p.m., becoming somewhat alarmed if I was still awake by 3. Sometimes the session could really drag out, as I might spend 20 or 30 minutes staring at the wall, or chewing my fingernails, or grinding my lip between my teeth until it bled. More than once I managed to stay awake beyond 4 p.m., wondering half-heartedly if I would be able to make to the office that night (I never missed a shift, was never even late). There was the additional issue of occasional kitchen emergencies – a can of baked beans on the burner, or a frozen pizza in the oven, that I would forget about or fall asleep in the midst of – resulting in the occasional smoke-filled apartment or ruined piece of metal pottery.

Eventually, though, without fail, I'd succeed in putting myself down. I'd awake to find only night. Every so often I was capable of a shower and bag of noodles upon waking, but sometimes it was just a slice of cheese, and many times nothing. Frequently I'd return to the office still wearing the clothes from the night before, possibly stopping at a market beforehand to collect a bag of chips or sack of peanuts, a package of cookies.

I inhaled this junk throughout the night, mixing it with coffee until my eyes bulged and my heart stuttered. I'd log the cop calls and suck in the TV – witless movies and game shows, endless news shots of dead bodies lying in the sand of some hellhole half the world away, carefully clipped and censored pictures of bodies dead and chewed up from bombs and stampedes, floods, hurricanes and earthquakes. It was all I could do to booze up so I could come down.

"I think there was actually something *there* with Chrissy," I would tell the worms. "Yeah, yeah, oh yeah, man... and that's what makes it so... *insane*..."

"No no no no," I would tell the worms, "you only were the latest in Chrissy's entertainment, that's all. A little trophy she carried around to prove she was interesting. You serviced her, but you didn't meet her standards. She burned through you the way she burns through $1,000. Toughen up, that's all. She popped you like a plastic bag."

"No, I made it *real* for her. She'll never have it so *real*..."

"Hey, listen up: Adversity is the mainspring of self-realism, Thor... Beauty is the result of struggle... Adapt or die..."

"No way, man... See, there is no *real* beauty. It's all a prejudice, a myth, a trick of the eyes..."

One morning, I watched as a cop car raced around the block several times, chasing after a dirty red car. Next thing, two cops ran up the block and went into a building. I hadn't seen anybody run in there, but maybe I had missed it. Within the next two minutes, six more cop vehicles arrived in front of the place. Cops swarmed around, going in and out of the building.

As they did so, two females appeared in the second floor windows. They tossed to the curb several balled-up sweaters, along with a few things that looked like hats. The police seemed slow in noticing. A woman and three or four children darted over, gathered the thrown items and ran toward a dark, squat car on the other side of the street. Two cops chased after them and managed to grab some of the items, but at least one kid scrambled away and was able to push a couple hats into the vehicle. As the cops stood unfurling the sweaters, the car sped away.

I'd noticed this bunch in this house before, and I hadn't liked them. I disliked them so much that I felt a burst of happiness, just then, to see the police going in and out their door. They'd been threatening at all times, even the children, always strutting past and giving you the eye – like, who was *I* to be on *their* street? I had felt a queasy, general revulsion whenever I had been forced to look at them. Winos seemed so much nicer and kinder, civilized and noble, than these... These who dressed in such bad drug style – stupid hats and baggy sweat suits, hoods and foolish mirrored sunglasses, bracelets and rings, horrible piercings. They helped nothing, they were takers and polluters only, offering nothing but misery and confusion and bad style. Scumbags, in a word.

My spirit slumped as, eventually, the officers emerged with only two of them in cuffs – a buzz-cut punk with jail-muscles, and a crazy-face girl with a bad blond dye-job. The muscled punk played tough-boy, throwing himself around and trying to run off, even with his hands plastic-cuffed behind him. Big tall cops with bulging biceps smashed him against the hood of their car, then tossed him against the building. He tried to roll and scuttle away. Another cop came up and zapped him with a zip-gun. He lay there motionless, face pressed against the sidewalk. The girl sobbed. Crowds gathered around, older women wailing, old men walking down the block, raising their hands at the "injustice." A crowd of young boys milled about bewildered, pushing each other. Finally an ambulance came and carted away the rough-boy.

The cop cars drove off, the street was suddenly empty.

I checked that night, and didn't see a mention of any such raid in our news file. I didn't ask about it when I made my calls. I didn't know what it was about, and I didn't care. I didn't want to know, it would have been only more pointless information. All I knew was there was a very serious scumbag problem outside my door... This was the same old future, the same old scumbag future.

Scumbags, scumbags, scumbags everywhere. The only thing to do with scumbags was to survive them, and hope they got smashed. I'd shed no tears for a scumbag. One less scumbag on the block could only be a reason for a small celebration – though I realized, of course, that it would make no difference whatsoever to the general level of criminality. My only question, asked with all appropriate pointlessness, was why the cops did not bother to smash them harder.

Not long after this, I remember, at a party, a guy came up and said, "I just got finished greasing up this Japanese girl."

I really wasn't in the mood. I had gone to this party at Jerry's urging, it was a bash I "could not miss." The guy was walking around in a blue suit and black tie, white basketball shoes, a cardboard box under an arm. Bald on top, but long black hair running down the sides of his head. He had looked over the crowd and picked me out. Was something wrong with my face?

"I just greased up this Jap, man... Greased her up good. They love getting greased up... They like it 'cause I got lotsa money. They love money, Japs. I took her out for cocaine and quiche, then I took off her clothes and greased her up and tied her up. She's in my trunk now. I'll take you, but no touching! God, she loves to be greased up. You can't grease her, though, just me. She loves it when I'm greasing her..."

"Yes, I'm sure she does..."

"I always say: Drive Jap. The Japanese get the good mileage. Know what I mean, yeah? Always drive Jap. Good mileage. Very good mileage. Easy on the wear and tear. Drive Jap, I always say. Keep 'em greased and drive 'em like crazy..."

"What's in the box?"

"What box? Huh? What box?" he said, swinging around and looking to each side.

"The one under your arm."

"Oh... *this* box!" he said, tapping the top of it with his fingers and giggling. "Well... it's, uh... it's your head, my little friend... I've got your *head* in my little box... It's true, true! Oh, it's true! I just love your little head!"

He laughed and ran off.

A little while later I saw him opening the box and showing the inside of it to a group of people sitting on a couch. They laughed.

Heather was there, and she was goddamn drunk. She kept running up to some guy, putting her wig on their head, and touching their cock. It was a big dumb blond wig to cover the surgery scar. GIMME A CALL said wavy words on her pink tank top.

She hadn't bothered with a bra, and when she sat down, the top would move away from her body, giving you a side view, through the flashing lights, of her nice little breasts. The lack of cloth also provided for a good display of the tiny black and silver drug-pump machine that had been installed at the top of her right shoulder, not far from the neck. The doctors had stitched it into her. The doctors claimed the machine automatically pumped out the correct doses of the various chemicals that were supposed to be keeping her alive.

Heather ran up to me, threw her arm around my neck, made me take a swallow from her Bacardi bottle.

"Thor!" she shrieked. "Thor! I love you, Thor!"

"I love you too, Heather... Take care, O.K.?"

She had staggered off, gone off and touched some guy's cock.

The place belonged to somebody who had made a million through "movie sound," Jerry had claimed. It was half a full floor of remodeled downtown skyscraper – massive concrete columns, clear plastic sheeting dividing the rooms. Trampolines had been set up in a row down the middle, and there were several black rubber couches, a stainless steel kitchen, a mini-bar in the corner.

The movie-sound mogul was a fat longhair guy with tattoos, piercings and a bum-fluff mustache. He skipped around from group to group, giggling and shooting out coke from the mouth of a plastic frog hanging around his neck.

People set things on fire and threw them out the gigantic skyscraper windows. I saw a hunchback skinhead sitting in a chair under a bright light, licking a girl's fingers. Party people jumped from trampoline to trampoline. Party people toyed on four computers, each screen projected onto the bare walls. On one machine, they were playing a game in which you shot flamingoes. You shot at the neck and the flamingo head flew off in a spray of red. Another screen was showing a film of a rat chasing after a chopped off penis. Every time the rat came close, the penis jumped a bit ahead, just out of reach. The rat would sniff, wiggle its snout and whiskers, continue the chase. On and on it went, the rat chasing the penis down a hall.

"SHOW IT AGAIN!" a guy screamed.

I imagine I tried to get drunk, tried to take myself out. I went from serving station to serving station, ingesting various potions from Korea and Europe, Cuba and Japan and so on, each tasting like floor-cleaning solution. I spoke briefly to Jerry, to Candace. At one point Hugh tried to speak to me, but I really couldn't hear a word he said. The music was just too loud. On the side of his head he wore a silver earphone, little microphone jutting out. I couldn't make sense of a damn thing. It seemed like just a lot of smoke coming out of his mouth.

It got late, and some of the girls started walking around with their tops off, rubbing a kind of glittery paste on each other, screaming and tossing various liquids. They cavorted around, shimmying and flaunting, jumping on the couches and trampolines. Guys sat glued to their seats, watching with half-smiles. They didn't seem capable of offering much more. They were like rocks on the bottom of a tide pool, looking up at the jellyfish waving in the current above. I went to get a refill...

There was a brief excitement when Heather got in a fight with some bitch. It looked like Heather had the upper hand early, due to her quickness, but the whore, bigger and brawnier, fought back courageously. They slapped, punched and pulled, and it wasn't long before Heather lost her wig. Finally they were separated. It appeared that the bitch had left several red splotches on Heather's face and neck.

The whore grinned triumphantly, flecks of blood on her teeth from where Heather had bashed her lip. A minute later, she fell to her knees to search for an earring Heather had ripped off.

Heather was led away somewhere, holding her shoulder, and I didn't see her again until I was leaving. Somebody had draped a jacket over her shoulders, and she was sitting on the ledge of one of the open windows, the street 15 or 16 floors below. A number of females and males were grouped around her in the shadow, laughing hysterically. I moved closer, trying to see what was going on. They were covering Heather's bald head with lipstick, glue and glitter. Heather emitted a series of guttural noises, made a strange face, a strange, monkey-like face...

Sernath caught me early one morning and asked, "How are you holding up, Thor? You're doing a real fine job."

"Oh, I'm good, thanks..."

"You want a break? Few weeks on day-side? We can arrange it. Sometimes the night shift makes people crazy. I've seen it happen to the best."

"No, I'm good. I like it, really, like the time alone, to think..."

The pictures would mix and mutate. Chrissy with her legs open, Heather with a needle taped into her arm... Chrissy tan and grinning, on her hands and knees on the white sheets... Heather with her shorts at her ankles, Chrissy with her tits poking out of a pale green bra... Heather saying, 'FUCK YOU!'... Chrissy rolling tan stockings down her legs, a red ribbon in her hair. Heather in white high heels... Chrissy in a black vinyl coat, Heather in an oxygen tent...

Round and around I would go, my insides turning watery then hard, watery then hard. I carried around a feeling of weight, the air was like sandpaper against my skin, I was plagued by periodic flashes of cold and hot. Sometimes it felt as if a bag of boulders had been tied around a knob that was connected to the middle of my chest.

I rarely talked to Jerry, or to anyone, aside from the usual crew of cops and clown-flacks. My social life, such as I once seemed to have it, had disappeared. There were no "romantic interests," no "quick fucks," let alone "fuck buddies," and little desire to search them out.

I could easily get rid of any desire by simply thinking of *bodies* – bodies sweating and stinking, fluids leaking from their holes. *Bodies*, and all the demands and madness that emanated from the injured minds and injured souls that occupied them. The idea was tiring, sex itself seemed uninteresting and even a little revolting – there was nothing original or inspiring about it, it was little more than a series of chemical reactions and automatic responses kick-started by a particularly moist monkey-part of our brains. We really had very little to do with it.

The greasy ceiling worms would come to mind, worms fucking and laying egg sacs, and all I wanted was another five beers. I'd let my phone ring, never bothering to pick up unless it was the office, and especially never returning a call from someone who might want to do something "social." There were very few of these, and in any case, I didn't want to go much of anywhere. If I went out, somebody was sure to see me, and who knew what might happen. The threat seemed very real – that somebody would come up out of the blue and decide to punch or stab me and grab my bag... or walk up behind me with a gun and blow my brains out, simply because I had that *look* on my face.

Every so often I'd check my "voice-mail," and after a while I stopped that as well.

Hi, Thor, this is Kate... I'm sorry O.K.? I'm sorry if I upset you. I don't even know if you're really upset... I'm just having one of those nights here... maybe you know how I feel. One of those really, really, really (COUGHING) *devastating nights.* (COUGHING, COUGHING, COUGHING) *And...* (MORE COUGHING) *I don't know. I need you as a friend. 'Cause life's just... difficult sometimes, honey.* (COUGHING) *I know that's hard, but, sometimes... Cleveland's O.K... I hope you're doing good, sweetheart. I have a urinary tract infection* (COUGHING)... *You mean the world to me, you're a very special person. I love you to death, and I really need you as a friend... I'd really like to talk to you now... I miss you so much... I'll talk to you later* (COUGHING). *Goodbye.*

BOOBTOWN: Booze-Maddened Bozos Go Berserk!

★ 35 ★

I told the first stripper I was a reporter from *The Las Vegas Journal-News*.

She wore a little cop hat, shiny pink negligee, peroxide hair falling past the shoulders. Maybe I just seemed like a nice guy, in the darkness, flashing lights and mirrors. Maybe the hapless, more than slightly drunk look on my face, made me look like soft prey, an easy touch, or at least someone who wouldn't try to rip her tits off. Maybe she really had to rustle up some bucks.

I pulled the bourbon from my inside coat pocket, had a slug, sloshed the bottle at her, grinned.

"You know you can't have alcohol in here." She brought a finger to her lips and smiled. "Shhhh... Don't worry, I won't tell... So how 'bout a private dance? Thirty bucks for a full half-hour-plus."

"What's a private dance?"

She winked and leaned forward slowly, eventually resting her hand heavily on the inside of my thigh. She breathed several times in my ear, then whispered, warm and wet: *"You can get as close as you want to every part of me... without touching."*

That seemed more like torture, for all concerned. I didn't tell her that. I had a bourbon suck.

She pulled back, waiting for the "go" move. She wrinkled her nose, her tongue posed playfully, half out of her mouth. I really didn't have the money. Just about $10, as always. Bottomless Scotty T. had been taking care of all our needs, and quite a bit more. I pulled from the bourbon.

"I'd love to, but... Maybe later... ?"

She was gone before I noticed.

I told the next one I was employed at the *Milwaukee Sun Sentinel-Times*, Legal Affairs Reporter. She didn't seem very impressed.

I explained to the third that I was the twice-weekly windsurfing columnist for the *Chattanooga News Gazette-Courier*. Yes, visiting Bay City for a convention. It was really quite interesting, I said, windsurfing and column-writing. She smiled good-naturedly, an overweight blond wearing lacy white leggings. She really had been the nicest. She, at least, was willing to go down to $25 for a half-hour.

For the fourth, I took out the biggest gun and waved it crazily: Keep it low, I told her, but I was an Investigative Reporter for *The New York Times*, visiting Bay City as part of my work on a "massive story" that would soon "be all over the place." I hoped she understood, but I just couldn't provide her with any more information than that. It was too crazy-insane, this thing, the ramifications too big, and I still had a lot – a *lot* – to confirm, but if even a fraction of it checked out, the country was sure to blow its top, and things would likely never be the same...

She shrugged. "I don't watch the news. I like to be happy."

She got up and walked off. "Nothin' Can Keep Me From You" cascaded in gigantic, crashing waves from the sound system. I sucked bourbon.

Five or ten minutes later, this same one was on the Cheetah Teaszer's stage – on her ass, spreading her legs, while "Cradle of Love" blasted. So happy she was, not a thing to hide. It truly was the greatest miracle of the world – the tunnel of love, these jaws of life. The roomful of sweaty guys sat with mouths open, as if ready for pie. They rubbed their chins, shook their heads.

Scotty threw down another 20-dollar bill, we were treated to another special close-up. Scotty swooped forward to within an inch of the waffle and whooped. Tommy-G blinked his eyes and kept blinking them. I reached in and took another bottle suck.

Scotty T. tapped my shoulder. Why not, I followed him back into the bathroom stall for another round of salt off our fists.

Scotty growled like a tiger, punched the cheap metal stall, punched it again. He posed with his hands curled in fists, teeth clenched, making a noise like "ARR-ARRRGH!" over and over. His faced shined, a length of hair limp across his forehead, like a rag. He tapped out more of the white stuff from his little blue-metal box.

"FIRE UP! FIRE UP!" Scotty shouted. "FIRE UP! FIRE UP!"

The first couple times it had hit me like a mule-kick in the face, but now I couldn't feel much of anything except the rollercoasters thundering and doing loops around my heart.

We were pigs, pigs, hogs. Scotty slapped my hand away from the toilet paper.

"Don't blow your nose, don't blow your nose! Suck it in, suck it in..."

I sucked, sucked, sucked it right back in. I gulped, down the hatch it went. All right, yes, all right... I felt my heart bouncing around, pounding and prancing about in its pouch. Rollercoasters racing, knives carving and hacking at the root of my brain. It was nothing, nothing but six cups of coffee, two or three times...

Scotty cursed, banged his fists against the side of his head.

"FIRE UP! FIRE UP! FIRE UP!"

We each had another bottle-slug.

"I've seen enough poontang," said Scotty, "let's go get drunk... We gotta drink or we'll have a heart attack..."

"Sure, Scotty, you bet..."

A clock-check showed it was just past 10, plenty of time for something. We gathered up Tommy and took the Cheetah Teaszer stairs two at a time to the street. We went several blocks, turned the corner and started taking pisses under a tree in the semi-darkness.

Scotty punched me in the shoulder.

"You don't like me, man. Why not? What you got against me? C'mon, spell it out."

"You kidding? I love you, man. You're the greatest..."

He smacked me again. "You tryin' to start a rumble?"

I tackled him to the grass. Scotty was a big boy, but I had power and speed. I was seasoned and battle-scarred. At this point, I feared only Samoans.

I got him by the waist and pile-drove him backward across the grass. He hit me with a flurry of rabbit-punches in the gut and upper groin. It felt like a hamster pawing ineffectually at a cardboard box. I heard Tommy start screaming, but I had things well under control. The only moment of concern was when Scotty finally kicked me off and I went rolling, landing hard on my side. It was one of the bigger bourbon bottles, banged against my ribs pretty hard.

Folks and furry-feet streamed by on the street, but no one dared interfere, it wasn't their place. We were just more freaks on the boulevard, displaying our sleaze in public. A couple of guys even stopped to watch for a few seconds.

We finally stopped when Tommy yelled, "COPS! THE COPS ARE COMING!"

We jumped up and stood there, breathing heavily.

Scotty had his shirt ripped in three places, blood bubbling from a split lip. The collar of my jacket was torn, I had scratches on my neck, a long one on my cheek. We didn't see any cops.

Tommy grinned. "I knew that would get you guys to stop!"

"You shithead!" said Scotty, bringing up his shirt to wipe his lip. "I *had* him!"

"Dude, don't lie..."

Tommy-G shrugged. "O.K., it was a tie..."

We each had bottle slugs, limped a few more blocks to a place and sat at the bar. Scotty kept the barman running. We had beer with scotch, beer with tequila, beer with vodka. Finally Scotty gave the guy $30 for half a bottle of El Tesoro de Don Felipe. It sat on the counter in front of us.

"I'm a believer in Dogism," Scotty said.

"What's that?"

"It's a religion that says, 'If you can't eat it or fuck it, piss on it.'"

"HA-HA," went Tommy. "HA-HA-HA!"

Scotty had begun to perspire heavily. He seemed still in a somewhat painful spot over the dumping by Shally – though he admitted only that "everything's cool," and "it was time, it was time." Also, Shally's mom was crazy. Her dad was crazy. Her sister was crazy. Her "little shit dog" was crazy. Shally herself was of course seriously, seriously crazy.

They were all crazy. Shally liked to eat cottage cheese mixed with onions and ketchup. It was all crazy. Jesus, though – she was such a "hot little dick-sucking machine."

That would be missed. Scotty hung his head.

Round and round went the talk, naturally retreating back to harder terrain when the ground got too soft and squishy. Scotty soon announced the words it seemed we had been waiting for: "Shit... My *mom* fucked my hockey coach."

I wasn't sure what time it was when we walked out. Scotty began spitting on parked cars, hitting nine in a row at one point.

"MY MOM FUCKED MY HOCKEY COACH," he yelled into the night. "MY MOM FUCKED MY HOCKEY COACH!"

Scotty grabbed a parking ticket off the windshield of a Subaru Cezanne and threw it into the air in several pieces. We ran through the streets, kicking down two potted trees in front of Scarabelli's Old Time Italian Eatery. We pissed on trash cans, on several parked cars...

A car alarm started going *whoo-whoo-whoo*...

We ran and ran, making several turns, until Tommy said, "Wait, wait!"

He bent over and it began pouring out of him. He fell to his knees, stuff pouring out his mouth and nose. We gathered around, helped him back to his feet.

"I love you guys... I'll miss you guys. We got to hang out, man, always!"

"Sure, Tommy..."

"It's not that far. Plane tickets are cheap..."

"You know it, Tommy..."

We held him by each arm as he bent over and let go again.

Tommy-G was off to the Carson, California, headquarters of *Mowing & Lawncare Weekly*. It must have been all right. I never saw him after that night. He never got in touch. And I never tried to contact him, either.

> 42 PERCENT IN U.S. WOULD 'NUKE' TERRORISTS
>
> NEW YORK (AIP) – Results of a new survey say more than four of every ten Americans would go so far as to use nuclear bombs in the fight against terrorists.
>
> The Hopps-DeGoey Organization asked a sampling of Americans whether they would be "willing" or "not willing" to support the U.S. government taking a range of options against terrorism.
>
> "Assassinate known terrorists" won the highest support, with about 82 percent of adults being in favor. "Torture known terrorists if they know details about possible future attacks inside the U.S." drew the support of more than 57 percent.
>
> The option of using "nuclear weapons to attack terrorist facilities" won the support of 42 percent of adults, with nearly 35 percent opposing. About 23 percent of poll respondents had "no opinion."

MEDIA IS MURDER: Clown Cracked at Cop Smackdown!

★ 36 ★

The four-eyed woman had a pile of gray hair and a terribly wrinkled face. She was holding a two-foot cardboard sign: DROP MNUNG NOT BOMBS. She fingered through the load of security-clearance badges and official passes chained around my neck, finally finding my city press card. She tossed it to the side and laughed.

"Cities News? What's that?"

"It's, ah..."

"Oh, heavens! Are you with the media, honey?"

"I guess so."

"You guess so?" She laughed, shook her head. "Can't you do better than that, honey? Who owns you, Cities News?"

"Capps-Neubold."

"Capps-Neubold? Oh, heavens, you're one of *them!*"

I had counted no less than 49 folks milling around inside the FSZ – the official "Free Speech Zone" between Asquith and Widgery. The FSZ was nearly a mile-and-a-quarter from Arbuckle-Burger McMasters Memorial Arena, but there was no other option. If you wanted to protest at Mnung's Rollin' On America/Family Faith & Freedom Tour fundraiser/political event – and some seemed to – it was the FSZ or nothing. All "unsanctioned protesters" were to be arrested immediately and charged with trespassing, the police had announced the previous day at a joint news conference with the mayor, FBI and Secret Service.

The downtown streets were locked down, blocked off and frothing with cops – the city had sprung for 9,400 uniformed extras to guard the event, double-time and overtime. Thousands more cops, from 16 separate state, federal and local agencies, were staffing emergency command centers, conducting surveillance, patrolling the streets, conducting random i.d. checks. They didn't say how many cops, as this was "officially classified."

I had hit three checkpoints since I had entered the two-mile square "sterile zone" around the arena. At each checkpoint, bomb-sniffing dogs and cops with hand-held metal detectors did full body scans on anybody who tried to go through. Cop sedans and trucks hurtled through the intersections, lights and sirens blazing as they blasted off to who knew where.

The entrance to the FSZ itself was protected by twin cordons of cops with machine guns, goggles, gas masks and black armor. I had also spotted sharpshooters on the roofs of the nearby Citgo station, Security Savings Bank, Taco Station and Food Warehouse.

"What are you doing here?" the lady said. "Honey, did you come to spy? Where's your camera person? We need pictures out in media-land, not the half-facts and manipulation that you specialize in..."

"He was around here somewhere," I said, looking around for O'Mulligan, but not finding him.

"Did you come to spy? Honey, did you come to get us in trouble? Are you going to start a riot so you can get us all in trouble? So you can film it and show it on your propaganda news?"

"I, ah..."

"No, no, honey... oh no, I'm not saying a word!" She turned toward a group and pointed at me. "Watch out for this one! He's with Capps-Neubold!"

Faces turned. "UGH!" said a pack of three or four men in goatees. "OH, BOO!" said a woman in a MNUNG'S DUNG T-shirt. "SHAME! SHAME! SHAME!" several began chanting.

"Honey, here." The lady handed me a folded yellow Xerox from a sheaf in her waist-pack and walked off.

WHAT'S WRONG WITH THE MAINSTREAM MEDIA? The picture was of a TV news clown, but with $ signs in each eye and bandages crisscrossing his mouth.

> The mainstream American media is run by a small oligarchy of rich men and some women. Less than 10 companies control the production and distribution of over 90 percent of all television, movies, newspapers, magazines and books consumed by the American population. On a worldwide

level, the situation is even more severe, with just six massive corporations controlling the distribution of news across the globe – AOL/Time Warner, News Corp., Viacom, Disney, General Electric and Bertelsmann.

Any study of the news industry should begin with the understanding that "news" is only a small component of what is a gigantic and profitable commercial enterprise: The Entertainment Industry. The main concern of the owners of the Entertainment Industry is making sure that their business is not threatened. Stirring up "political trouble," i.e. challenging the authorities about their criminal and immoral behavior – or what used to be called "covering the news" – is therefore NOT a priority. The first loyalty of the Entertainment Industry is to the state apparatus which defends the ruling elite, of which they are prominent members.

Often, the mainstream news media's sole purpose seems to be to sow confusion and paralysis among the masses, i.e. proposing contradictory and illogical assumptions and promoting red herrings. For example, the mainstream media frequently fund and present surrogates who absurdly promote the myth of a "Liberal Media," when nothing could be farther from the truth. In reality, the "keyboard commandos" of the U.S. media reliably and systematically fall in line behind the dictates of Wall Street, the White House, and the shadowy "security bureaucrats" who control the long-term policy of this nation.

A group of them started clapping their hands and stamping their feet: "HEY-HO! MNUNG HAS GOT TO GO! HEY-HO! MNUNG HAS GOT TO GO!" A helicopter whapped invisibly in the murky grayness above, more or less drowning out their voices. O'Mulligan stood off to the left, bulb flashing, his face hidden behind his rig. Ten or twelve circled around, some carrying American flags, others with signs: MNUNG = WAR CRIMINAL / NO BLOOD FOR OIL / MNUNG LIED PEOPLE DIED / GLOBAL WARMING IS THE REAL THREAT / WHO WOULD JESUS TORTURE? / FREEDOM FOR PALESTINE. Three or four were dressed in Halloween skeleton costumes and holding black flags, their faces painted white with red running down the sides of their mouths. WE'VE BECOME THE MONSTER / WAR ON TERROR IS A HOAX / MNUNG IS A TRAITOR / RECREATE

1776 / BOMBING 4 PEACE IS LIKE FUCKING 4 VIRGINITY / 9/11 – SEEK THE TRUTH! The ANSWER, said one sign, was to ACT NOW TO STOP WAR AND END RACISM.

Pretty soon, a large bunch formed a circle and began to clap. "WOLFGANG MNUNG, YOU CAN'T HIDE! WE'RE CHARGING YOU WITH GENOCIDE! WOLFGANG MNUNG, YOU CAN'T HIDE! WE'RE CHARGING YOU…"

> The U.S. media has manifestly failed to hold this president and Congress to account, turning its back on the tradition of media independence and oversight and achieving a new nadir of obeisance to the powers that be. The media has thoroughly failed to do its job of informing about real events and fostering a discussion of past and current American foreign policy. It has permitted patently Orwellian phrases such as "war on terror" and "defense of freedom" to dominate what passes for discussion about the state of the world. With its wholesale adoption and backing for government spin and talking points, it can fairly be said that the U.S. media functions as little more than a semi-official propaganda agency of the government.
>
> It must be understood that the members of the mainstream media are chosen and elevated precisely because they understand that their role is to promote the consensus view of the wealthy elites. Whether or not they admit it or are even aware of it, the truth is that the members of the mainstream media hold their positions because they can be trusted to reflect the interests and worldview of their billionaire oligarch masters.

On the legal documents and police permit papers, the FSZ was actually called the FAREZ – the First Amendment Rights Exclusion Zone. The city had taken several months to design and construct the cage (at a cost of some $229,000) – 1,840 square feet of empty parking lot with two entrances/exits. The fence itself was covered in bulletproof sheeting, blocking out all outside views, and topped with barbed wire. I had so far counted eight security cameras positioned at the corners and top of the fence.

The American media has, with nary a word of protest, permitted the negation of our Constitution and the dictatorial consolidation of power in the hands of the president. Repeatedly, the mainstream media has stood by, either helplessly or in full support, as the unelected Mnung Administration has executed its finely-honed war hoax strategy: Making dictatorial demands on small weak states, refusing to negotiate with anyone, spreading accusations and lies in the media, suggesting "evidence" that no one gets to see (and which later proves false), and inciting Americans to hate another country of human beings.

The regime's war-making method further involves socializing the costs and risks of the war (i.e. making ordinary, vulnerable young people fight it) but privatizing the "profits" of it (i.e. giving oil concessions and "rebuilding" contracts to crony companies, who complete the circle by funneling millions of dollars back to the politicians' political machines). One obvious example is NBC Universal and its outlets NBC, Telemundo, MSNBC, CNBC and Universal Pictures, all of which are owned by General Electric – a gigantic company which makes billions fulfilling contracts with the military and for the government's "War on Terror."

No protester was allowed to have a "mask," such things had been absolutely ruled out by the authorities. Following what had become known as the West Bay Riots in April, the city and state governments had also passed ordinances banning the wearing of bandanas or facial coverings during anything that could be construed as a "political event." Drums and drumsticks, imitation coffins and other props or "objects" that a police officer might find "threatening" had also been banned, as had all wooden, plastic or metal flagpoles. All flags and signs had to be hand held, and they had to be printed on "unreinforced" paper or cardboard no thicker than an eighth of an inch and no bigger than three feet long and two feet wide. The details were listed over eight pages in the City Code, and copies of these pages, covered in plastic, were tacked up at the entrance to the FAREZ.

> America has already become the "leading" war crimes and torture nation of the 21st Century – but you will not hear about

it in the U.S. media. Turn on any mainstream channel and you will hear reporters and pundits incessantly chattering about bringing "democracy" and a "free press" and "American-style values" to foreign lands with oil and pipelines under their sand.

What you will NOT hear is that these American values now include torture, kidnapping, incarcerating people without charges, razing entire cities to the ground, massacring residents who get in the way, and running illegal gulags in various parts of the world. It is obvious by now that "humanitarian intervention" and "weapons of mass destruction" have turned out to be just propaganda cover for American imperialism, the "war on terror" mere camoflauge for schemes to steal oil, kill Muslims and fight the enemies of Israel.

When Wolfgang Mnung, after executing 76 inmates as governor, said Jesus Christ was his "favorite philosopher," where was the media to point out the decadent hypocrisy of the man who would lead our nation? The media was nowhere – Mnung was instead hailed as a "born-again" and "man of resolve" who would never be "soft on crime." By failing to shine a light on Mnung's idiocy and/or cynical contempt for the intelligence of ordinary Americans and ignorance of Christ's essential teachings, the media demonstrated that in today's America, Jesus and mass murder go hand-in-hand.

It is obvious that U.S. Imperialism does not intend to allow anything to stand in the way of its goal of establishing global hegemony, in the process dragging the American working class and the rest of the world into catastrophe. The so-called War On Terror has never been about taking out real jihadists – rather, the War On Terror is the cover excuse that's given as the regime seizes more power at home and imposes domination abroad.

The U.S. ruling elite has found no other solution to the inherent contradictions of capitalism and the late-capitalist crisis of profitability than to impose greater restrictions and poverty on the U.S. middle and working class, and increased barbarism and wars of plunder abroad. The ultimate goal of its invasions of the Middle East and Central Asia is to establish a permanent U.S. protectorate and military bases in the region, thereby giving American capitalism a stranglehold on world oil reserves, and setting up forward military positions for future wars of aggression against other Middle Eastern states, and eventually China and Russia.

The protesters began to chant, stamping around in a circle, waving their signs and flags. "THE PEOPLE! UNITED! WILL NEVER BE DEFEATED! EL PUEBLO! UNIDO! JAMAS SERA VENCIDO!" Phalanxes of cops hung on every word, arrayed in position, hiding behind each other, hands and arms sheathed in bulletproof gloves, holding black shields.

> As Aldous Huxley wrote, "Used in one way, the press, radio and cinema are indispensible to the survival of democracy. Used in another way, they are among the most powerful weapons in the dictator's armory." In Huxley's book Brave New World, non-stop distractions such as "feelies," "orgy-porgy," and "centrifugal bumblepuppy" are deliberately employed as instruments of policy for the purpose of preventing the people from paying too much attention to the realities of the social and political situation.
>
> Look at the American media today: an endless diet of celebrity intrigues and sports; gladiator and war films that promote mass killing and the solution of problems through violence; sex scandals and tabloid murders; right-wing hate radio; perversity-sodden lowest common denominator "reality" television programming – while in Washington, dictatorial powers are amassed and war-mongers run amok, planning and carrying out perpetual "pre-emptive" wars against countries too weak to defend themselves.
>
> The U.S. media is indeed "free" to report on all the sex scandals, stock market news, sports rivalries and health fads. But when it comes to what really matters, such as the livelihood of the American people and the abuse and slaughter of their sons and daughters in the armed forces, it is rarely discussed and only in a token fashion, clouded by rhetoric and distortions from Mnung regime spin doctors on channels claiming to show "both sides" as part of a "fair and balanced" program. As Hitler and other historical examples

have shown, fascism and dictatorship require either direct media control, indirect control through regulation, and/or sympathetic media spokespeople and executives. America is clearly the victim of all three techniques.

A ruckus of chanting and stomping could be heard vaguely outside the FSZ. Then a few of them began slipping through the entrance – middle-aged women in American flag sweaters, men in U.S.A. hats. They began lining up against the northeast fence, collecting themselves into a tight formation.

"ISLAM IS A LIE!" they boomed, "HOMOSEXUALITY IS A SIN, ABORTION IS MURDER! ISLAM IS A LIE, HOMOSEXUALITY..."

Having achieved mass, they began to march, shield-wielding cops flanking them on both sides. "U.S.A.! U.S.A.! U.S.A.!" they shouted, clapping, "FOUR MORE YEARS! FOUR MORE YEARS!"

A counter-counter shout-out arose, the anti-Mnungists joining together to meet the challenge. "NO MORE TROOPS IN THE SOIL! NO MORE BLOOD FOR OIL! NO MORE TROOPS..."

American democracy and media are an embarrassing farce. The U.S. media is part and parcel of the same system that permitted the September 11, 2001 attacks to occur, and that has failed to investigate the real perpetrators and causes of the events of that terrible day. The attacks, combined with ready-made media fear-mongering and cheerleading, unleashed a wave of bloodlust for Americans to kill who they told them to kill – who just happened to be the people they wanted to steal oil from. After all, what has corporate America been instructing Americans for all these years: "JUST DO IT."

"A newspaper is not just for reporting news, it's to get people mad enough to do something about it." – Mark Twain

"Think of the press as a great keyboard on which the government can play." – Nazi propaganda chief Josef Goebbels

"The Central Intelligence Agency owns everyone of any major significance in the major media." – Former CIA Director William Colby

According to the CIA's own documents, the key precept of psychological warfare operations as practiced by the CIA

involves creating the "psychological conditions" among the targeted population that guarantee majority compliance with the demands of U.S. capital and its political representatives – to literally "manufacture consent." Have the American people been victims of such "Psy-Ops," as implemented by their own CIA and allied media corporations? Is the criminal Mnung administration "playing" its own tune across America's newspapers and airwaves? It's long past time for Americans to start asking themselves some difficult questions, for the future of the republic is at stake.
   U.S. CITIZENS FOR MEDIA TRUTH www.uscfmtruth.org

A woman who looked to be in her late 40s, wearing a red sweater with large white letters saying PRESIDENT MNUNG YOU KILLED MY SON, suddenly broke away from the anti-Mnungists and charged toward the newcomers. She bared her teeth, a kind of guttural whine seeming to exit her mouth. She got about 10 yards before she was swarmed by cops – I counted at least six. She gave off several screams, which quickly turned to muffled cries and then silence, as the flatfoots succeeded in neutralizing her.

The flatfoots lifted her up by the arms and legs and frog-marched her out of the FAREZ. She would be taken to the Pier 31 Holding Facility, set up (at a cost to taxpayers of $157,000) specifically to handle Mnung-related arrests, of which there would be 139 over two days.

Several phalanxes of flatfoots surged into the FAREZ, weapons raised. They rushed to the four corners of the cage, some dropping to combat position on one knee, others bracing themselves against the fence. Several of the most daring deployed into forward probe formation, weaving back and forth as they scanned the cage for lawbreakers.

O'Mulligan crouched on both kneepads, getting off shots that would appear on the back pages of several newspapers in the nine-county zone.

"U.S.A! U.S.A.! U.S.A!" the Mnungists bellowed.

A siren wailed, a helicopter whapped overhead.

"HEY-HO, MNUNG HAS GOT TO GO! HEY-HO! HEY-HO!"

Flatfoots pointed weapons, staring through telescopic sights. Flatfoots rocked back and forth on the balls of their feet, heads swiveling as they searched for any suggestion of rule-breaking.

I reached into my coat pocket. As my fingers searched amidst the fabric, I was knocked to the ground by an overwhelming force from behind. Pain exploded across my back and ribs as I slammed to the concrete, landing on my side on top of my computer bag.

I rolled over and smelled oil – the snout of a long pistol sweeping across the tip of my nose. I looked up at the black glove, the black mask.

A noise like "Ooooof!" came out of me as the cop mashed his armored knee down on my chest.

To the left, the Mnungists had begun to sing:
We shall overcome, we shall overcome
We shall overcome some day
Oh, deep in my heart
I do believe we shall overcome some day...

The flatfoot holstered the gun. Black gloves seized my wrists. The black mask and goggles looked down as a second flatfoot worked to lace my arms together with plastic.

"It was just... my phone," I said, tears sliding out the sides of my eyes.

"Says *you*," said the voice.

I heard a series of pops, smelled a chemical stink as the flatfoots began unleashing sprays at the anti-Mnungists. Sirens starting going off, smashing the place with an ear-ringing *whee-ooo, whee-ooo...*

I heard the pounding of boots as a small army of flatfoots surged into the center of the pen, grabbing protesters and running them out of the FAREZ. They would take them into the streets and load them onto buses. After a day of detention, they would each be charged with Resisting Arrest and Obstructing the Work of a Peace Officer.

Whee-ooo, whee-ooo...

I heard somebody scream, "I'M BURNING! I'M BURNING!"

NO BEANS ABOUT IT: Prez Sez 'America Wins!'

★ 37 ★

"Yo mister, off the sidewalk!" the flatfoot shouted.
"Huh...?"
"Yo, into the street, yo..."
I limped toward an opening in the cattle gates, crossed through. I hopped off the curb and limped into the street.
I made it about 20 yards before another flatfoot shouted.
"Hey, bozo – off the street!"
I nodded, waved a hand.
I limped back toward the cattle gates, hopped the curb and got back on the sidewalk.
It was about 90 minutes later. Things had worked out O.K. My ribs and left hip seemed to have been deeply bruised, and there was a pulsing pain on some bone that seemed to be just behind my heart – but there had been no loss of blood. Just a few scrapes and a bit of swelling around my wrists from the 30 or so minutes I had spent laying on the ground, with the plastic handcuffs on, after two flatfoots had carried me out of the FAREZ and dumped me on the sidewalk. My press identification badges had, thankfully, cleared me before they were able to get me on the bus, and I had again cleared all weapon-checks.
The cops even apologized. No hard feelings.
"You want to file a complaint?" one of them asked, and we all laughed.
They had taken me into the fenced-off trailer Command Center, pasted some bandages on my scrapes and offered me a full medical check, which I declined. They gave me a cup of coffee, which tasted

rather good, and half of a ham sandwich. I signed another legal form, this one apparently saying I couldn't and wouldn't sue the police, city, federal government or Mnung Administration, and they sent me on my way.

I limped the 200 or so more yards to the arena complex, went down the stairs, through the glass, past several more gates and down a long white hallway toward the entry booths. I was one of the Official Embeds, and as such I had, about a month before, signed a release saying I wouldn't "impugn the Office of The President of The United States" with my behavior during the event. I didn't bother to ask what it might mean – you just didn't bother anymore, because that would just be causing "trouble" and was likely to get you permanently banned from something or other. More than 1,500 reporters had officially registered to cover the H. Murray Glattman Production,[*] and the signing of the oath was a no-exemptions requirement.

After another 60 yards or so the hallway divided into two lanes – one red-lettered sign read PRESS, the other said DELEGATES. The security huts were staffed with less cops but more thick, intense, pink-faced men wearing suits and earpieces, a few with tiny microphones tucked snug against their jaws.

WARNING: You Will Pass Through A Bio-Watch Pathogen Detector

I passed that, then was ushered into a Holding Area, where I had to wait about 10 minutes while a new fingerprint scan was checked against the database. Following that, I had to take off my shoes while a very polite fellow wearing white gloves checked my bag, phone, computer and unscrewed my ballpoint pens to check for bombs and/or contraband. Found not-guilty of potential wrongdoing, I then had to spend another 10 minutes putting the stuff back together.

"Thank you," clowns and delegates said, one after the other, "thank you very much."

Finally inside, I looped around the lower tier to take my first look at the arena set. Blue-, white- and red-lit panels raced around the upper and lower decks, blipping on and off in combination with bursts of exploding electric stars. Dookie Dunphy and his band were on the stage performing "Sunday Morning Coming Down," while members of the Pine Ridges Dance Ecstasy Gospel Choir did flips and the hustle-dance off to the sides. Several dozen mainly white people stood up front, clapping and raising their hands to heaven.

---

[*] Emmy- and Tony-winning producer of *I Did It for Lilly, Last of the Wagoneers, R.O.W.F.* and *Faces of Sadie.* – ED.

As Dookie launched into his new cover version of "Wonderwall," I limped back out and went down the northeast corridor. This was "Freedom Central," according to a twinkling stars-n-bars sign. I stumbled past rows of promotional stalls and "open party rooms" hosted by "Official Contributors and Mission Helpers" including Pfizer Inc. and Bank of America Corp., the Ford Motor Co., Wachovia Corp., United Parcel Service...

I ducked into the Bristol-Myers Squibb Freedom Forum and helped myself to a plate of king prawns and a beer from the bar. I sat on the couch and nibbled, watching Dookie perform "Early Morning Rain" and his new hit, "Sword and Shield (Bone and Steel)," on the giant plasma monitor. I limped out after about 15 minutes, passing party suites hosted by Lockheed Martin (prime rib), Goldman Sachs (poached lamb knee) and Occidental Petroleum (Mexican Fiesta!). A long promenade against the arena windows included pit-stops promoting Microsoft Corp., Blackwater Security, the New Energy Corporation of South Bend, Indiana, and Northrop Grumman.

Delegates walked by dressed in American flag costumes, in red, white and blue hats, leggings and sweaters, waving U.S.A. flags. Several had come dressed as Pilgrims in knee-boots and floppy brown hats, or as the Statue of Liberty, faces painted white and with tinfoil crowns. Other groups walked around in flowing robes and holding hands, their heads bowed as they mumbled out prayers. SOUTH-CENTRAL MISSOURI PRAYER TEAM, said a sign hanging around one skinny old fellow's neck. FLORIDA CHRIST-MNUNG PARTNERSHIP said the gold and maroon banner hoisted by another prayer squad.

Men in suits walked around brandishing smiles and shaking hands, while young men and women dressed in tuxedos came up offering drinks and snacks on trays. Every so often, a group of men with shaved heads and wearing military uniforms would pass. They carried open bottles of champagne, and some seemed very drunk, red-faced and weaving about and laughing, shouting something or other. They had apparently been in attendance at the FIRST LADY'S MILITARY TRIBUTE BALL, an ultra-exclusive event located in the Celebrity Lounge on the third deck.

I wandered off, before long arriving at the Freedom Marketplace that had been erected between the ChevronTexaco Liberty Lounge and the ExxonMobil "Forward to the Future Celebration." Stalls had been set up where you could purchase items such as framed pictures of

Mnung down on his knees praying, ghostly images of George Washington, Martin Luther King, Jr. and Abraham Lincoln kneeling beside him, their hands resting on the back of the president's gold and silver robe. MEN OF GOD SPECIAL EDITION, $58.95. You could buy books and coffee-table picture albums, die-cast metal Mnung and Jesus figurines, video sets of child Bible training and "Classic President Mnung Freedom Speeches," not to mention Reverend Robertson's Prayer Power Protein Diet Shake Mix and *Pastor Ted's Guide to Weight Loss and Bodybuilding The Christian Values Way*...

The merchandise was moving, the stalls were alive with the blur of credit cards and cash rolls unfurling. People's eyes spun crazily as they held large "W" crystal sculptures and "W" key chains up to the light. Sculptures of the middle three fingers of a hand, thrusting up from the ground, were going for $94.95.

Delegates gazed approvingly at paintings of nearly nude muscular black men, some of whom were depicted bound in chains or lugging a cross and wearing a crown of thorns. One painting depicted a group of naked female angels with bountiful white breasts. The angels were pouring a golden fluid on to the bald head of a well-muscled black man. The man appeared to be trapped in a pit of some kind, surrounded by cobra heads and demon faces, thick tangled vines wrapped around his biceps. The golden fluid dripped over his head, down his nose, on to his chest. The look on his face was strangely peaceful. Just $189.95.

A huge crowd was blocking most of the corridor at the end of the row. I went down, pushed through the throng and beheld the bony blond frame of Robiann Coughans. She was sitting behind a table signing copies of her new *New York Times* bestseller: *GODLESS TRAITORS – How Liberals Are Making Us Lose The War on Terror and Promoting Homosexuality.*

"Robiann! Robiann! Here! Here!"

Robiann, wearing a sequined V-necked rainbow-striped dress, appeared to be laughing as she scratched out her autograph with a black felt-tip. Over her left breast had been pinned a large red, white and blue button: I'M NOT BIASED – JUST NEVER MET A MUSLIM I LIKED.

I turned down the southwest corridor, passing the Oracle-NNN TV "A More Hopeful America" room and hospitality suites operated by Home Depot (Bill's Buffalo Burgers), DynCorp Inc. (Texalicious BBQ!), Marriott International (Thai Chicken Delight), the Quickboat Brigades for Facts (Bloody Marys). I decided to pop in for a complimentary beer and chili-cheese dog hosted by the Family Christian Network & Indian Gambling Lobby Tribe.

A man wearing a dark brown uniform, Stetson hat and a button that said JESUS CHANGED MY HEART walked over.

"Hello, young man."

"Hi. I..."

"I'm Jesse Lefebure, sheriff of Wildmon County," he said. He handed me a glossy brochure.

WE WANT OUR COUNTRY BACK! the brochure cover said. The cover image was of the Statue of Liberty, tears falling from her eyes and her face covered with graffiti. RECLAIM THE GODLY HERITAGE it said at the bottom.

"Thank you, sir, that's very nice of you."

He laughed and coughed. "Well, I wouldn't say I'm nice, young feller. Just have a read of the good news."

"Thank you, I will."

I flipped to the first page.

AMERICA THE BEAUTIFUL IS BEING PUNISHED FOR TURNING AWAY FROM GOD!
THE CRISIS IS WORSENING EVERY MINUTE!

★ Atheists abolished school prayer and replaced it with the yellow crime scene tape that is so familiar in our streets and cities

★ Supreme Court decisions made in the 1960s led directly to the AIDS and hepatitis scourge

★ Rabid feminists, bondage deviates and other satanic pestilence have caused the epidemic of homosexuality and mass killings we see in our schools, day-care centers and places of worship

★ They refuse to teach in our public schools the fact that homosexuals average 500 sexual partners in their short lifetime, and because of their deviant and unsanitary sexual practices, homosexuals harbor the great bulk of all bowel disease in America

I glanced at the plasma. Dookie was doing a mournful acoustic version of "We're In This Together (Gimme Six Bucks)."

The sheriff came back over. "You want a chili dog?"

"God bless you..."

"With cheese?"

"Double me up, sheriff."

Jesse grinned. "You got it, brother."

- ★ When our schools teach things like "tolerance and diversity," they mean shut up! to Truth in Christ!
- ★ You can say "Allah Akbar" with impunity in America, but if you say the Judeo-Christian God is on America's side, you are condemned as a "divisive bigot"
- ★ So-called separation of church and state is what got us into this mess, not the other way around!
- ★ Embryonic stem-cell research is just another name for state-funded cannibalism

Jesse brought the dog over a minute later, saying "There's a lot more where these came from…"

"Hey, that's great. Thank you so much."

On the plasma, Dookie launched into his version of "Crazy" – "this one's dedicated to Jefferson Rockton," he said.

PRIORITY STRATEGIES FOR THE NEXT CONGRESSIONAL SESSION

- ★ Continued support for abolition of government-mandated minimum wage
- ★ Legal and financial support for landlords who refuse to rent to cohabiting homosexuals and lesbians
- ★ Termination of parental rights for those convicted of second drug offenses
- ★ Continued opposition to socialistic national health care system – because health care is a privilege for the lawful and working, not a Right!
- ★ Continued support for U.S. withdrawal from United Nations and removal of U.N. headquarters from American soil
- ★ Support for Constitutional Amendment denying U.S. citizenship to children of illegal immigrants born in America
- ★ Support for rebuilding of Third Temple in Jerusalem as integral part of fulfillment of Prophecy

The sheriff came back over with another something in his hand.

"This DVD here is $19.95. All the money goes to the Freedom of Unborn Life Foundation. Tax-deductible, of course…"

"Well, I…"

"Aw hell, just take it!" he said, shoving it at me. "Here!"

"Thank you for the chili dog," I said, moving toward the exit.

"Jesus be with you…"

I walked out, had to hustle – the corridors were nearly empty, it was almost time for the main presentation.

Somebody handed me a pair of purple plastic flip-flops as I shuffled into the TV & Press Pavilion and took my seat at the end of a roped-off section of 12 or 13 *New York Times*, *Wall Street Journal* and *Washington Post* reporters. A few of the clowns were typing into laptops, while most of the others were busy slapping each other with the flip-flops and tossing sushi rolls.

A lone spotlight shone on the Reverend Bobby "Joe" Long as he strode to the podium to perform the Invocation.

"Whereth he goeth, he carrieth a messageth ofeth hopeth – a messageth that ith both ancienteth and evereth-neweth," spake the reverend. "Foreth Presidenth Mnungeth hath saith: 'To the captiveseth, cometh outeth, andeth to those in darknesseth, beith freeith.' The Spiriteth of the Lordeth Godeth ith uponeth him, becauth the Lord hath anointedeth himeth to preacheth good tidingseth unto the meeketh, hath senteth him to bindeth up the brokeneth heartedeth, to proclaimeth libertyeth to the capitveseth and the openingeth of the prisoneth to themeth thateth are boundeth. He ith greatly rejoicedeth in Our Lord, and his soul ith joyfuleth in Oureth Godeth: for the Lordeth hatheth clothedeth oureth presidenteth witheth the garmentseth of salvationeth, with the robeseth of righteousnesseth; as a bridegroometh decketh himselfeth with ornamentseth, andeth aseth a brideth adorneth herselfeth with jewelryeth. Presidenth Mnungeth hath setteth the watchmeneth uponeth the wallseth of Jerusalemeth, tilleth he maketh Jerusalemeth a praiseth uponeth the eartheth. Weeth hatheth awaiteth, andeth preciouseth watereth hatheth floweth frometh hiseth bucketseth, o holieth, to seedeth the fertile valleyeth. Outeth hith mouth goeth a sharpeth swordeth, andeth with ith he striketh nationseth. He treadeth the wineth presseth of the fiercetheneth and wrath ofth the Almightieth Godeth. O'ereth oureth nationeth hith headshipeth reigneth, andeth the Blessedeth Dominioneth he worketh to secureth… Ineth the nameth ofth the Holieth Father, the Soneth and the Holieth Ghosteth, Amenetha… Andeth ameneth…"

"Andeth ameneth," said the audience in unison.

The spotlight vanished, drenching the auditorium in absolute darkness.

There was a sharp, echoing crack, followed by several long white flashes. A hologram of an eagle with a golden sword in its beak soared around the expanse before rising and disappearing into the roof.

A series of shrieks and shouts erupted from audience members as the room was once more plunged into darkness. "Won't Get Fooled Again" began building over the sound system, the rock track growing louder and louder until the floor and chairs began to vibrate. Film began to roll on the dozen or more screens – sunrises and flowing fields of wheat at first, then action clips of U.S. tanks speeding over sand dunes, ships rocking over foaming seas, soldiers and sailors manning radar stations... a series of explosions over palm-shrouded cityscapes... then army troops being greeted by smiling brown natives waving American flags.

Crowd screams reached deafening proportions as the screens filled with clips of the president – Mnung in slow-motion... Mnung in classic black and white... Mnung in high-definition freeze-frame... Mnung in a George Washington costume striding across the ruins of the World Trade Center...

A smoke bomb went off and the president, roses in his hair, appeared at the back of the stage, striding between two gigantic American flags and a pair of white Corinthian columns. The Jumbotrons froze on the image of an immense golden seal declaring: "The United States of America."

Mnung walked up several terraced steps to the podium, which suddenly rose about six feet into the air.

"I'm President Mnung, and I'm reporting for duty..."

Audience members roared, waved three fingers, stamped their feet and clasped their hands together in prayer. There was a flurry of fireworks behind the president, then pictures once more filled the Jumbotron screens: a shot of the Washington monument at dawn, a dove with an olive branch in its beak, a picture of a small girl in a yellow dress holding a sunflower... and at last, the single word FREEDOM.

"FOUR MORE YEARS!" the crowd thundered. "FOUR MORE YEARS! FOUR MORE YEARS!"

"My fellow Americans," the president began. "I have a simple message for you tonight: The state of our nation is excellent... And freedom is once again on the march..."

The crowd erupted. Pictures of Mount Rushmore and Disneyland flashed on the screen, followed by the words PRESIDENT

WOLFGANG G. MNUNG – COMMANDER IN CHIEF OF THE UNITED STATES OF AMERICA.

"U.S.A.! U.S.A.! U.S.A.! U.S.A.! U.S.A.! U.S.A.!"

"I want to thank everyone who's here tonight," said the president, after the crowd had quieted somewhat. "The fine members of the National Rifleperson's Association, and the Holy American Heritage Foundation... The Christian Families Research Council is here, as is the National Right of Life Organization, Operation: Save America and the Royal Rangers Fellowship. The National Association of Televangelists has come in force, as has the Confederation of Mountain Peoples, the Rushdoony Institute for American Justice, and the He Who Holds the Stars in His Hand Foundation. And of course, no meeting of our party would be complete without the participation of the Traditional Family Values Coalition, the Friends of Stonewall Jackson Action Network, and the America for Americans Solidarity Association..."

The audience roared, hands waved in the air, three fingers upraised. Pictures of Babe Ruth, Benjamin Franklin, Jimi Hendrix and the Alamo blinked across the screens, followed by the words AMERICA – HOME OF THE BRAVE.

"FOUR MORE YEARS! FOUR MORE YEARS! FOUR MORE YEARS!"

"I also wish to extend heartfelt thanks to your fine Governor Edwin 'Astro' Wattle, who has organized such a fabulous meeting here in Bay City. We, together, have proven we are stronger than the criminal or dictator or terrorist cell. I am proud to have Governor Astro on our side. He is with us, not against us. I want to thank you, Governor Wattle, for implementing electronic voting machines across your great state. These machines have cut government waste by reducing the amount of paper generated by the bureaucracy. These modern vote-counting machines leave no paper trail, taking full advantage of the digital revolution. This is a step for progress, and Governor Wattle is a true visionary. I know that together, with these voting machines now operating in key electoral states, we are headed for victory when the citizens of this great country cast their ballots next November 6. We will continue our historic mission to restore honor and dignity across this fabulous land..."

The crowd rose, clapping and stamping their feet. Pictures of Steve McQueen, Geronimo, Mean Joe Greene, Lucille Ball and Abraham

Lincoln flashed on the Jumbotrons. AMERICA – HOME OF THE FREE.

"For too long," continued the president, "some in this country have preached defeatism and surrender to the criminals and lawbreakers, the murderers and drug dealers, the dictators and terrorists, who would enslave us under their tyranny. At one time, elite opinion held that law enforcement and good citizens could do nothing – that we were doomed to live in the midst of evil. These elites have argued that criminals and drug traffickers and terrorists and baby-killers were driven by circumstances and root causes beyond the control of decent human beings. Ladies and gentlemen, they have been proven wrong..."

The crowd screamed, a flip-flop flew through the air. Pictures of the Grand Canyon, Vice President Palmer Jicks, Mickey Mantle, Michael Jackson, Ronald McDonald and Ronald Reagan flashed on the screens, followed by the words LIBERTY and SECURITY.

"U.S.A.! U.S.A.! FOUR MORE YEARS! FOUR MORE YEARS!"

"To the brave American troops listening tonight," continued the president, "rest assured – we are defeating the terrorists were they live and plan, and through your sacrifices in rock-strewn desert wastelands far from our shores, you truly are making America safer. Because the appropriate role of the military is to fight and make war, and therefore prevent war from happening in the first place. America has always been called to lead the cause of liberty and security, and freedom has always had a price – and that price, my friends, is blood. We are living in an iron time, and we must therefore sweep with iron brooms. The terrorists are fighting freedom with all their cunning and cruelty because freedom is their greatest fear – and they should be afraid, because freedom is on the march. I will never surrender America's right to protect itself to the United Nations or the foreign ministries of Paris, Beijing and Moscow..."

"BOO! BOO! BOO! BOO! BOO!"

The screens flashed mug shots of Stalin, Pol Pot, Lenin, Hitler, Darth Vader and Jerry Lewis, followed by close-ups of audience members waving flip-flops and giving thumbs-down.

"Fellow Americans, any glance at history demonstrates that the military is the foundation of American democracy. It is the soldier, not the reporter, who has given us the freedom of the press. It is the soldier, not the poet, who has given us freedom of speech. It is the soldier, not the unhappy agitator or jihadist fellow-traveler, who has given us the freedom to protest. My friends – every man, woman and child on this earth has a choice to make: Either you are with us, or you are with the terrorists. Because protecting freedom inside America depends on promoting freedom outside America. Because only the fire of liberty can purge the ideologies of murder by offering hope to those who yearn to live free. It is a noble mission, and it is critical to our world that it succeeds. We shall yet master fate..."

The crowd wailed. The screens flashed: AMERICA THE FREE, interspersed with pictures of the Beatles, General Douglas MacArthur, Popeye the Sailor, Al Capone, Gregory Peck and Charlie Chaplin. Flags rippled, there was another small burst of fireworks. A NATION OF STRENGTH & HONOR. The crowd roared.

"My friends," said the president, "some have said that our nation's two-party political system represents merely a propaganda contest between two stripes of the same flavor, each controlled by powerful business interests and elites. But they are wrong. Let me, if you'll allow me, to explain the difference: The other side believes America's best days are behind her. We manifestly don't... The other side believes America's defenses should be surrendered into the hands of terrorist-coddlers and the humanitarian do-gooders of the United Nations. We resoundingly don't... The other side believes the best way to support our military is to gut it and strip it of all resources. We, my friends, do not... The other side believes the best way forward is through fair multi-lateral negotiation, touchy-feely summits and adhering to rules and treaties to which our nation has agreed. We, obviously, do not... The other side believes that the best way to defend ourselves is to obey our own laws and international prohibitions against torture and holding suspects in detention indefinitely without charge or legal recourse. We, absolutely, do not... The other side believes the best way to keep America strong is through government handouts and set-asides to redress historical injustice and continuing deficits of opportunity. Simply put, we do not... The other side offers more lectures, more legalisms, carefully worded denials and phrases of reassurance. Goodness gracious, they want to know what the meaning of *is* is![*] We, clearly, do not... My good friends, they will lose, and we will win – because THIS IS THE REAL AMERICA!"

The audience screamed, dozens of flip-flops soared through the air. Pictures of Albert Einstein, Thomas Jefferson, Frank Zappa, Spider-

---

[*] See sex-crimes trial of Bill Clinton, 42nd president of the United States. – ED.

Man and Frank Sinatra jumped across the screens, followed by the words COMPASSION and DUTY. Rainbows of lasers blasted from the corners, filling the auditorium with colorful webs of infinite complexity.

"My friends, we support a Constitutional Amendment to ban all forms of homosexual marriage and civil union. We are a free nation, and that freedom includes marriage between one man and one woman only – not between a man and manatee, or a woman and a Doberman. In the same vein, we oppose all measures that contribute to the wanton killing of unborn babies. Our opponents call this process 'abortion,' but we know this child sacrifice by its true name: Murder... Because we believe life is intelligently designed. We believe life is not a commodity to accept or reject or be bought and sold to the highest bidder. Life is the precious gift of the Almighty Lord... We furthermore support the repealment of any and all mechanisms to process, license, record, register or monitor the ownership of guns. We will fight to restore the legal right to own fully automatic handguns... And we will fight to ensure that all Americans receive their drug benefit, because it is that right thing to do and the American people have demanded it!"

The screen flashed on a live shot of a vivacious-looking Sharia Mnung holding the dog. Crowd members wagged three fingers and leaped up and down screaming: "U.S.A.! U.S.A.! U.S.A.! U.S.A.! U.S.A.! U.S.A.! U.S.A.! U.S.A.!" Lasers zoomed, pictures flashed: Smokey the Bear, Bill Gates, Superman, Tina Turner, Elvis and Betty Boop.

"And it is no secret, my friends, that we oppose punishing through taxation those in our society who have been successful. We seek the abolition of all income tax, inheritance tax, capital gains tax and corporation tax. We are the party that believes in an America in which people can still get rich. America must be the best place in the world to do business. Let there be no doubt that each and every regulation covering employment, wages and workplace safety must be dismantled. All restrictions on the right of large businesses to extract profit from labor must be abolished. This is part and parcel of creating a vibrant ownership society, in which all Americans may battle each other in the marketplace in a competition without end, nor any hope of security. It is America's money, not the government's, and we're giving it back!"

Audience members squealed, jumped up and down and stood on their seats and raised their hands. Words flashed: PEACE, JUSTICE,

HONOR, followed by pictures of Winston Churchill, The Brady Bunch, Michael Jordan, Bruce Jenner, Sly Stone and Marilyn Monroe.

"So let us therefore continue to do our best for the forgotten Americans, the non-shouters, the non-demonstrators, for the good people who work and save and pay their taxes and hope for a more peaceful world where Americans can be free. My friends, I tonight pledge to you to be the peace president. We have embarked on the march to peace, and we will win the war, because the war is right for America. We will win the war against the terrorists. We will win the war against drugs. We will win the war against criminals. We will win the war against child sacrifice... Because I believe in the heart of my soul that Almighty God is not indifferent to America's fate. America tonight is where it has always belonged: Against the tyrants of this world, and on the side of all souls who yearn to live in freedom and free markets. Fellow Americans, we are the last best hope for mankind – and I believe mankind's best days lie ahead. We are climbing the mighty mountain, and I see the valley below, and it is a valley of peace and prosperity and immutable truths..."

Words bounced on to the screens: PROSPERITY, FAITH, ENDEAVOR. Flashes vibrated across the stage, there were several deafening bangs, smoke swirled. Images flashed of flowing American flags and Statues of Liberty. The audience shrieked, lasers criss-crossed, the theme from *Indiana Jones* swelled.

The smoke cleared. Mnung was gone. All that remained was a gigantic glowing W where the podium had been.

Every so often the W would pulsate, the glow increasing to almost blinding intensity. The wattage would then lower to a phlegmmy sort of yellow, and the glow would begin to intensify again.

The crowd gathered around the W, their eyes wide. Some of them reached out, as if trying to touch it.

"FOUR MORE YEARS! FOUR MORE YEARS!"

BOATER-GATE:
Clown Confounded by Colby Conundrum!

★ 38 ★

A couple days later I sat down at Jerry's computer and did a little internet research. It was an unpleasant thing to do, and took up far too much time – but I had become curious about the William Colby quote on the flyer the four-eyed lady had given me. The Twain and Goebbels quotes seemed obvious enough, I was ready to let them slide, but the one from Colby kept burning in my mind: *The Central Intelligence Agency owns everyone of any major significance in the major media...*

There was no shortage of the quote in the internet world, it popped up instantly on hundreds of sites – mainly those, it must be said, with "lefty guerrilla" or the U.S. president-and-Queen-of-England-are-shape-shifting-reptiles points of view. In each case, though, what I was really looking for was conspicuous in its absence – the *where* and *when* that Colby might have said it.

Goddamn internet whack-offs. I was looking for the real goods – when did Bill Colby say this damn thing?

I bounced around dozens of sites, searching for Colby quotables and amassing copious Colby info. Born in Minnesota in 1920, Colby attended public high school in Vermont before enrolling at Princeton University. He was described as an eyeglasses-wearing young man of some five feet, eight inches tall.

Colby joined the U.S. Army in 1941, at the outset of the U.S. involvement in World War II, and in 1943 signed up with the Office of Strategic Services (OSS), the forerunner of the CIA. Colby apparently took part in clandestine missions behind enemy lines in France and

Norway during the war – in one case, leading a raid that destroyed the Tangen railroad bridge in Norway to prevent Nazi troops from redeploying to fight advancing Allied forces in Germany.

After the war, Colby went to Columbia University law school and took a job with the National Labor Relations Board in Washington. Then, before long, he had signed up with the Central Intelligence Agency. He apparently spent much of the 1950s in Italy, leading "covert operations" in support of anti-Communist groups, with the goal of halting a Commie takeover of the Italian government. Much of Colby's work appeared to involve secretly funneling funds to centrist or "left-center" groups to dilute any potential Commie electoral power[1]. Colby was described as being a heavy Roman Catholic.

Internet clowns had worked like nuts, Colby data overflowed, Colby quotes and info piled up. It was very compelling, very riveting and fascinating – but still no *where* and *when* on the *owns everyone* quote.

Colby was appointed CIA station chief in Saigon, Vietnam, in 1959, holding the job until 1962. He then returned to Washington to take over as chief of the CIA's Far East Division. In 1968, Colby helped launch the Accelerated Pacification Campaign, part of which was the PHOENIX project, a "killing campaign" designed to "neutralize" VCI, or Viet Cong Infrastructure. According to the CIA's website, Colby ran PHOENIX in his cover role as director of Civil Operations and Rural Development Support (CORDS) for the U.S. Agency for International Development. Essentially, it appeared, PHOENIX team operatives murdered anyone *suspected* of supporting North Vietnamese activity.[2] Estimates of the number killed during PHOENIX range as high as 60,000 people.[3]

Colby apparently believed PHOENIX was preferable to raw military force, which he felt could be "too crude" an instrument, and often self-defeating, from the standpoint of the United States and its political goals. Critics would later condemn PHOENIX as an organized bloodbath, war crime and crime against humanity perpetrated by obvious psychopaths... In any case, the project failed to perform as advertised, and as the United States' defeat in Vietnam began to gather

---

[1] The Italian Communist Party lost in the 1948 elections and has never returned to government. – ED.
[2] The United States supported the South Vietnamese. – ED.
[3] Colby himself preferred to place the number of those taken out under PHOENIX at 20,587. – ED.

pace, President Richard M. Nixon rewarded Colby for his efforts by appointing him CIA Director in September, 1973[4].

Colby's tenure at the top of America's spy hierarchy notably included the Church and Pike Congressional investigations into CIA illegality and "malfeasance." The hearings resulted in disclosures about CIA interference in foreign countries including Chile, Italy, Iraq, Angola and so on, and attempted skullduggery such as trying to assassinate President Fidel Castro of Cuba. Other Church Committee disclosures included the revelation of a secret and illegal CIA program that had apparently intercepted, opened and photographed more than 200,000 pieces of Americans' mail[5].

The Committee also came out with disclosures about what was called Operation Mockingbird, a "CIA program to manipulate U.S. and foreign media." The Committee reported: "The CIA currently maintains a network of several hundred foreign individuals around the world who provide intelligence for the CIA and at times attempt to influence opinion through the use of covert propaganda. These individuals provide the CIA with direct access to a large number of newspapers and periodicals, scores of press services and news agencies, radio and television stations, commercial book publishers, and other foreign media outlets."

Colby acknowledged the existence of Mockingbird, saying it had the willing collaboration of senior news industry managers. Colby was quoted: "Let's not pick on some reporters. Let's go to the managements. They were witting."

Interesting Bill Colby, fascinating Bill Colby… but still no *give* on the *owns everyone*.

I called up more and more internet sites, culling copious Colby/CIA manipulation/malfeasance info. Carl Bernstein of Watergate scandal fame wrote an article for *Rolling Stone* in 1977 which declared that "more than 400 American journalists" had, over the previous 25 years, secretly carried out assignments for the CIA.

According to the article: "Journalists provided a full range of clandestine services – from simple intelligence gathering to serving as go-betweens with spies in Communist countries. Reporters shared their notebooks with the CIA. Editors shared their staffs. Some of the

---

[4] Colby's only daughter, Catherine, died in April, 1973, after an illness. – ED.
[5] With some Congress members calling for the CIA to be shut down entirely, Colby apparently believed that "partial disclosure" of a carefully-selected set of crimes and misdeeds would increase the agency's chances of survival. – ED.

journalists were Pulitzer Prize winners, distinguished reporters who considered themselves ambassadors-without-portfolio for their country. Most were less exalted: foreign correspondents who found that their association with the Agency helped their work; stringers and freelancers who were as interested it the derring-do of the spy business as in filing articles, and, the smallest category, full-time CIA employees masquerading as journalists abroad. In many instances, CIA documents show, journalists were engaged to perform tasks for the CIA with the consent of the managements of America's leading news organizations..."

The article named executives and journalists at the U.S.A.'s most prestigious clown brands: *The New York Times*, the Columbia Broadcasting System (CBS), the American Broadcasting Company (ABC), the National Broadcasting Company (NBC), *The Washington Post, Newsweek, Time*, the Associated Press, United Press International, Reuters, Hearst Newspapers, Scripps-Howard...

I hit a flurry of alleged Colby quotables: Asked in 1976 whether the CIA ever told its media agents what to write, Colby supposedly replied, "Oh sure, all the time." Asked about the murder of mobster Sam Giancana[6], Colby supposedly said: "We had nothing to do with it."

Internet pages flowed, internet sites yielded interesting media info: In 1985, the ABC network was acquired for $3.5 billion by Capital Cities Communications, a media company whose founding investors included William Casey, who was appointed CIA director under President Ronald Reagan.[7] In 2000, Major Thomas Collins of the U.S. Army Information Service confirmed that members of the Army's 4th Psychological Operations (PSYOPS) Group worked in the news division of the Cable News Network (CNN) as part of an Army program called "Training With Industry."[8] In 2005, "right-wing columnists" Armstrong Williams, Maggie Gallagher, and Michael McManus were revealed as having been paid government money for promoting White House policies – Williams receiving $241,000 through the Education Department for "promoting" the "No Child Left Behind" initiative[9].

---

[6] See assassination of President John F. Kennedy – ED.

[7] The Walt Disney Company acquired Capital Cities/ABC in 1996. – ED.

[8] In response, CNN issued a statement describing the U.S. military personnel in question as "interns," adding that "no government or military propaganda expert has ever worked on news at CNN." – ED.

[9] Williams claimed the money had "not influenced" his views. – ED.

The New York Times reported the existence of a "Pentagon information apparatus" that was set up to disseminate pro-war propaganda in the U.S. news media. The program involved Pentagon officials selecting dozens of former generals and military officers and providing them with false or misleading "talking points" – otherwise known as "propaganda," or "lies" – about the progress of the war and American military "successes." The generals and officers, in most cases knowingly, then conveyed this false or misleading information to the public in their appearances as "independent military analysts" on scores of network television and radio shows and in newspaper columns, according to the report, which was based on thousands of pages of e-mails and other records that the newspaper had sued to obtain from the Defense Department.

The program appeared to be in direct violation of U.S. laws against the government mounting covert propaganda operations against the American public. One retired general who participated described the program as "psyops on steroids." Most of these "military analysts," according to the report, also had lobbying or business links to more than 150 military contractors who were seeking some of the billions being spent on the administration's "war on terror." No hint of these conflicts of interest and gross ethical violations was ever suggested by the broadcasters or publications, who instead advertised the "military analysts" as offering not propaganda and lies, but an objective and expert look at the war situation.

Finally, after too long, I hit a citation for *owns everyone*: A few sites mentioned it as appearing in a book, *Derailing Democracy*[10], by somebody named Dave. I mashed internet links and called up the website of this Dave.

Dave was a member of the community which believed that the United States government lied about literally everything. And there was plenty of good evidence to that effect. Dave had marshaled facts and pieced together various anomalies to present the view that nearly every part of the "official story" about the September 11, 2001, attacks was a lie and/or manipulation designed to deceive the American people. Islamic terrorist hijacker-pilots, armed with box cutters, somehow outsmarting and slipping past the defenses of America's vast intelligence and military apparatus to slam gigantic airliners into the World Trade Center and Pentagon, thereby violating and bloodying

---

[10] Common Courage Press, 2000. – ED.

America in most of its strategic power-orifices? *The Pentagon?* Not a chance of it, said Dave. That was a big, big laugh. The game was really played much, much deeper than that. And what about 7 World Trade Center[11] anyway? No serious explanation had been supplied for why that third building had fallen in Manhattan late in the afternoon on 9/11. And many, many others...

And indeed, it did seem there were a great many baffling oddities about the events of September 11, 2001, that did deserve, at last, an honest investigation. There were simply too many questions and no real answers, and why didn't the authorities get to the bottom of it, finally? Why hadn't there been a serious, criminal probe into what went wrong that day – an investigation you could have reasonable confidence in? Why did the authorities, from the president on down, continue to behave as if they had something to hide?

Dave didn't claim to have found the final "smoking gun" answer to the whole 9/11 who-really-done-it, but his facts and analysis of the available data suggested that high government officials and their mass media / non-government or ex-government allies were involved in major crimes and malfeasance of the worst kind. Dave seemed as confused as anyone, but at least he wasn't taking whatever they were spoon-feeding out there for an answer. I kind of thought of him as a hero. He was trying to find a route through the madness, however mad and hopeless that effort itself may have been...

Well, there was a chance – small and dumb, but a chance – maybe Dave had the real Colby info. I slapped out an email.

---

[11] Apparently refers to the attacks of September 11, 2001, in which alleged Islamic terrorist conspirators allegedly murdered flight crew members and allegedly took over the piloting of two commercial jetliners and crashed the planes into the upper stories of the World Trade Center twin towers in New York City, according to U.S. authorities. The alleged crashes allegedly caused the Twin Towers to weaken and crumble to the ground in a matter of seconds, according to authorities. A total of more than 2,500 people were killed due to the crashes and buildings collapses, according to authorities. That afternoon, a third nearby office building, World Trade Center 7, also allegedly crumbled to the ground in a manner similar to the two other towers, although no plane was seen crashing into WTC 7, according to authorities. On the same day, alleged Islamic terrorists allegedly piloting an allegedly hijacked airliner also allegedly breached the alleged air defenses of the U.S. capital Washington, D.C., and allegedly crashed an airliner into the first floor of the Pentagon U.S. military headquarters, according to authorities. Also on September 11, 2001, alleged civilian passengers aboard a fourth allegedly hijacked plane allegedly attacked the alleged Islamic terrorist hijackers in the cockpit, allegedly causing the plane to crash into a field in Pennsylvania. – ED.

Dear Dave,

    I have been trying to learn the date and source of this quote, which I have run across numerous times now in online articles. In nearly all cases, the quote is simply given, without the year or location where Colby said it. The closest I have come to finding a source is a few articles which have cited your book, "Derailing Democracy"...

By now it was nearly 8 o'clock. I locked up and went down Verdugo to the Banzai Burger. Numerous bum-types meandered outside in the darkness, rummaging through trash bins, pulling the plastic tops off discarded cups, searching for a little taste of sugar-juice. The bums seemed to have very, very sad faces...

    Inside, Banzai Burger was crowded, stinking of grease and fried cat turds. It was the back end of the dinner rush – mainly teenager types, mothers with small children and various derelicts, picking up the evening's slop. Banzai had a deal on – two extra-crispy tacos and a side of Cajun-jalapeño curly fries for 99 cents. Drink extra. I got two orders to go, no drink.

    I stood and waited with the rest of the saps. People seemed to be losing their minds, it looked like blood could start hitting the burnt-orange tiles at any moment. To the left of me, a scruffy guy in a beard and hooded sweater screamed at the counter girl, "YOU CALL THIS KETCHUP!" Enraged, his face turning from red to purple, he bit at his lips and hurled a handful of small ketchup packets at the poor blue-suited girl. A packet caught her in the breast and another got her arm, but most smacked harmlessly into the french-fryer.

    A rent-a-cop in an over-stuffed jacket shuffled over for a look but did nothing, just stood there. The insane beard walked off with his slop...

    A few seconds later, a guy to the right started screaming that they wouldn't take his torn $10 bill. Hunchbacked guy with dirty black hair. The bill was basically torn in half, held together by a thin shred at the bottom. The hunchback waved it threateningly, made like he was going to rip it apart.

    Goddamn nut. People seemed ready to do nearly anything for a bag of slop. The fat rent-a-cop shuffled over for a look but did nothing, just stood there. The poor slob working the cash register took the money. The hunchback walked off with his slop.

Then, on my way back, as I was turning the corner at Verdugo and Blanchard, a guy bumped my shoulder. Short guy and nearly bald, wearing a leather jacket and scarf. Looked about 40. I gave him a glance, kept moving.

"H-how much for a d-dick-suck?"

"Huh?"

I whirled around. He leered up at me expectantly, his eyes like shiny rats.

"I-I-I'll suck you for free…"

I shook my head and walked off, cradling my slop just a bit tighter. Goddamn freaks. I knew I was going through a rough spot, but – had it already come to this? I mean – was there something wrong with *my face?*

I came back in, tore open the slop, hit more Colby buttons. No message from Dave.

In 1975, the South Vietnam regime fell to the North Vietnam Communists, marking the final defeat for the U.S. Vietnam project in which Colby had invested so much of his career. In the meantime, Colby had instituted several significant reforms – such as a ban on CIA assassinations as a "tool of policy," as well as introducing briefings about CIA activities to select members of Congress. But he continued to come under attack from both the Left and the Right over the damaging disclosures of the Congressional committees. The anti-war Left wanted his blood over the war and the astonishing record of CIA malfeasance. The Right wanted him gone over the disclosures to Congress and his alleged "liberalism" and perceived "Christian conscience."

In early 1976, President Gerald Ford replaced Colby as CIA chief with George H.W. Bush. In response to the CIA-journalist program, Bush announced a new policy: "Effective immediately, the CIA will not enter into any paid or contract relationship with any full-time or part-time news correspondent accredited by any U.S. news service, newspaper, periodical, radio or television network or station." However, the first Bush who would go on to be president offered assurances that the CIA would continue to "welcome" the "voluntary" and "unpaid" cooperation of journalists.

Ousted as CIA chief, Colby appeared to confirm the allegations of "liberal leanings" by becoming a supporter of a nuclear arms freeze and reductions in U.S. defense spending. In the 1990s, he allegedly worked to "develop a video game" with a former Soviet KGB counterintelligence chief. Colby also allegedly started "investigating the suicide" of Vincent Foster[12] for a publication called *Strategic Investment*.

Then, amidst all this, Colby allegedly went "rowing at midnight" on April 27, 1996, near his home in Rock Point, Maryland. The authorities would announce that he had died from drowning/hypothermia after allegedly suffering a heart attack and/or stroke and "falling out" of his canoe. His body (minus life jacket) was not found for more than a week. Earlier searches of the area had apparently "failed to detect it."

There it was, the final incarnation – Bill Colby, Midnight Canoeist. The oddity of his demise was indeed strange, and the internet truth-digging squads were nearly unanimous in the verdict – *murder*. They could not seem, however, to agree on a reason for this most suspicious "boat trick hit."

One faction maintained that Colby was taken out because his alleged "investigation" of the Vincent Foster conspiracy was apparently getting too close to powerful Clinton Administration elites. Well, yes, possibly. A separate faction linked Colby to Aldrich Ames, the CIA analyst who was convicted in 1994 and sentenced to life in prison for spying for the Soviet Union.[13] According to this theory, Colby was actually a deep-deep-cover Russian spy who had helped "coordinate" Ames' activities and helped Ames pass several lie-detector tests, and was thus "removed" to protect the reputation of the CIA. Well – hmmm... The CIA website itself noted that some CIA officers had in fact suggested "foolishly or scurrilously" that Colby might have been the famously unknown Soviet mole that legendary Counterintelligence chief James Jesus Angleton had supposedly been hunting for... Colby had, of course, fired Angleton after becoming CIA Director...

A third faction argued Colby was taken out because he was apparently planning to disclose that missing U.S. Prisoners of War from Vietnam had been secretly working as "zombie mules" for a drug-smuggling operation linked to high American officials... Colby, according to this theory, was obviously neck-deep implicated in CIA

---

[12] See President Bill Clinton sex-crimes trial – ED.

[13] It is believed that Ames, who joined the CIA in 1962 and rose through the ranks to become a Soviet intelligence analyst in the CIA's Counterintelligence branch, provided information to his Soviet handlers that led to the exposure of at least 100 secret U.S. intelligence operations and the execution by the Soviets of at least 10 U.S. agents – ED.

Golden Triangle dope-smuggling operations, as based on his Vietnam connections and CIA leadership role... It was also said that Colby, after leaving the CIA, apparently served as "legal counsel" for something called the Nugan Hand Bank, an Australia-based bank linked to narcotics trafficking, gun-running, money-laundering and fraud...

Well, so nothing. Nothing and nothing. Cartoon airplanes that crash into skyscrapers, and dope-running CIA directors. The president's father was a shape-shifting reptile.

And why not?

I had been a goddamn fool. Internet clowns plus CIA was always going to equal ugliness and stupidity and uselessness. I felt soiled and shoddy, exhausted... It was a sad state of affairs – I had become one of *them* – a clown looking for answers on the internet – and it hadn't provided anything of the kind. Of course it hadn't. A person could only take so much of this crap.

It was almost midnight. I shut off the machine and wandered back out. Maybe I was just shaken up, but it seemed there were more scumbags lurking around than usual – everybody a junkie or prostitute of some kind. A group of gang dopes stood across the street, whistling up at some building. They saw me and stopped, as if somehow I hadn't seen it and therefore wouldn't think they were gang twerps. Shit, who the hell knew what they thought...

Near Verdugo, a guy stood frozen on the walk, staring up vaguely at a streetlamp. I didn't know what to make of it until I saw the stream of urine rolling out his pants and over his shoes. He was standing in the little puddle, a look of pure magic and mystery on his face...

A minute later, a guy who was stumbling along a few steps ahead of me dropped something. As I passed, I saw it was an open switchblade. Goddamn freak had just dropped a *switchblade*. He bent down and slowly picked it up...

I should have goddamn kicked him in the face.

As I came up to Happy Bo-Bo-Li Liquors, near the corner, a guy was sitting against a building, beer can crinkled in his hand. His legs were gone – all he had were these dark-colored plastic bundles, wrapped and tied around the area of the knees.

I'd noticed him around before, sitting here or there... A wooden skate-type vehicle was propped against the wall behind him – this was how he got around, using his hands to pull himself along the walk, rolling along on the board. In front of him, he had set a couple of faded, cracked plastic dishes that had once contained cream whip.

He caught me looking and winced up.

"Lil' help, pardner?" he said from beneath a beard of scraggled brown.

"Oh, sure..."

I dug into my pocket, tossed a few coins into one of the buckets.

"Thanks... How about a smoke?"

"O.K."

I handed him two. I was an easy touch.

"Thank you, brother. God will bless you, I know he will..."

"Yes, we can hope..."

A 12-pack of beer cans, a bottle of vodka and a pack of smokes drained me of my wad of $19. To avoid another encounter with the legless bum, I looped around the other side of the block on the way back to the apartment. I kept my head down and pushed forward.

Goddamn it, I didn't want any more freaks. I didn't want any shootings, stabbings, begging cripples, gang goons, wackos trying to wank my weenie. I just wasn't in the mood.

I drank as much as I could as fast as I could, then vomited in the bathroom. I cooked a can of baked beans on the stove and vomited into the kitchen sink.

A couple days later I got an email from Dave.

> Thor,
>
> That Colby quote has been circulating for a long time, long before I used it. I assumed it was legit since I had seen it so many times. However, after getting several inquiries about it over the last few years, I dug around to try to find the original source and had no luck. If I had it to do over again, I would not have used it. It could very well be legit, and the sentiment is certainly true, but I cannot verify it.
>
> Dave

RELIGION: Nutjob Insists: America Must Die, Die!

★ 39 ★

EAT TILL YOU DROP, AMERICA! Get the new butterscotch egg breakfast bacon egg burrito at Taco Station! Sink your teeth into gooey caramel, creamy-crunch peanut butter bacon and healthy double-scoop hot egg patty bacon on a freshly baked tortilla bacon croissant! Add a slice of ham, cornbread, bacon, cinnamon oatmeal bun or spicy sausage for 59 cents! Double-size your healthy egg or bacon order for just 79 cents! Bottomless free bacon with every order of two. Get your morning bacon egg moving at Taco Station! Because it's your country bacon and eggs... and your breakfast healthy bacon egg burritos! EAT! EAT! EAT!

BREAKING: NEW TERROR VIDEO

The theme music blared, ominous and nerve-wracking, yet also triumphant. The clown logo veered and flipped about before vanishing. The film showed a man wandering about through scrub brush and stones, a treeless, yellow-green hill behind him. He had a long red beard and was wearing white sheets, a smaller piece of the white material wound atop his head. Two or three machine guns were slung over each of his shoulders. Crossed about his chest was a pair of copper-green bandoliers filled with silver bullets.

CLOWN: *Ladies and gentlemen, we are now bringing you excerpts of the new terror tape from terrorist mastermind Oomalammah "Nipsy" Van Ghoubelin... It premiered in the last hour on the Arabic television channel Al-Haram, and we are now picking up the feed...*

The man paused and removed a sword three or four feet long from a holder on his waist. He gazed down approvingly at the dull grey metal, touched its sharp edge with his index finger. He looked over at the camera and smiled, his eyes seeming to twinkle. He repositioned the sword in the waist holder and continued on.

The man stepped slowly over a number of boulders and shuffled past several bushes, sheets dragging in the dirt behind him. He came to a stop and looked out over a mountain ridge covered with drab green plants. He removed the sword from the holder once more and pointed it out in front of him. He gazed down admiringly at the dull grey metal. He moved the weapon from side to side and up and down. He cocked his head and smiled, eyes seeming to twinkle.

The shot cut abruptly. The man was suddenly looking directly into the camera, low-lidded brown eyes seeming to twinkle, a yellowish-white light glowing on the wall behind him. He was sitting on the ground in what appeared to be a small, cramped space, possibly a cave. He appeared well-tanned, his beard a tangle of strawberry red. Lines around his eyes crinkled, his mouth opened and shut. No sound came out.

BREAKING: NEW TERROR TAPE TARGETS AMERICA

CLOWN: *Here he is now, ladies and gentlemen, Oomalammah "Nipsy" Van Ghoubelin, speaking from an undisclosed location at an unknown time... Stand by for the interpreter...*

CLOWN: *Deh-deh-deh, deh-deh-deh... In the name of Allah, the compassionate, the merciful... No, no to America. No, no to Israel. No, no to the Devil. No, no to the woman. No, no to the homosexual... Protect the woman, keep her in a bag. Throw the homosexual from the mountain. All praise to Allah, who created the creation for his worship and permitted the one who has been wronged to retaliate against the oppressor in kind... Deh-deh. Deh-deh-deh. Deh... O American people, contrary to the Crusader Mnung's claim, we the sons of light do not hate freedom. Let him explain why we do not destroy Lithuania and Norway? May Allah have mercy. We fight the Crusader and his Zionist pawn because we are free men who do not wish to sleep under oppression but to restore freedom and dignity to our nation. No one but a foolish goat thinks that to toy with the security of another, one may make himself more secure. The heroic strike against Manhattan was a blow to the serpent's head... Allah is great, praise be to Allah... Deh-deh-deh... American people, your foolish Mnung is continuing to distort, deceive, attack Muslim people, pilfer oil and torture Muslim women and children, and hide from you the real causes of your declining civilization. As Mnung remains, the chances of a repeat calamity are only increasing. You are like a helpless child before a crocodile, praise be to Allah... The pretenders who occupy the White House stain your name, noble Americans, with their arrogance, greed and stealing of wealth from Muslims. They rape and pillage the Muslim nation to give oil and contracts to their favored corporations and support the Jew-pig in wars that you are destined to lose in disgrace, Allah permitting... Deh-deh. Deh-deh-deh. Deh... Worship of Allah is the only command. True liberty is obedience to Allah... Better to return to truth than persist in error, American people... I warn – take well your opportunity to reclaim your noble soul. Your security is not in the hands of Mnung, but in your own hands. Every country that does not play with our security has automatically guaranteed its own security... Allah is our guardian and helper, while you have no guardian or helper. All peace upon those who follow the guidance, Allah willing, praise be to Allah... Deh-deh-deh-deh. It may benefit you to reflect, Americans of dignity, as you choose your leader... Protect the woman, keep her in a bag. Throw the homosexual from the mountain... America treats its women like playthings to be posed nude on television and building walls. Allah dictated to the prophet that women must guard their unseen parts, because Allah has guarded them. In America, women are offered like uncovered meat, and they become like soldiers of Satan to tempt the Allah-obeying. America promotes pride and promiscuity in the service of human degradation, and therefore seeks to exterminate Islam... Deh-deh-deh. Deh... Allah willing, the Crusader dog Mnung will be destroyed, the international balance will change, the falsehood will end. The Islamic caliphate will lead the human race to the land of safety and the oasis of happiness... America will be destroyed, Israel will be destroyed, Allah willing... No, no to America. No, no to Israel, No, no...*

CLOWN: *That's quite enough of that, I think... Well, that was the new terror tape from terrorist mastermind Oomalammah "Nipsy" Van Ghoubelin, ladies and gentlemen... If I understand correctly, he appears to be attempting to discourage the American people from voting for President Wolfgang G. Mnung in the upcoming election. It seems he truly does not admire our president... We'll go now to NNN's own Bunny Sylvester in the* Countdown: Election *studio with the early results of our new NNN Insta-Poll... Bunny, what are the American people saying about this new terror tape from the terrorist mastermind?*

CLOWN: *Well, Erlo, if Nipsy had wanted the American people to cast their vote for someone other than Wolfgang Mnung, his plan has backfired... The Insta-Poll results show a positive surge for the president of six to eight points – which if I'm not mistaken, pulls him solidly into* the lead, 51 to 48 percent, with a three percent margin of error... It seems the American people just don't take kindly to terrorist folks telling them what to do on Election Day... Back to you, Erlo...

CLOWN: *Thank you, Bunny... The terror alert is blinking orange, Mr. and Mrs. America, and the experts say it's not if, but when, the next terror strike comes... We are standing by on the ramparts of freedom, and you're watching NNN, the News Now leader, your news peak at the summit of media mountain...*

CLICK. The man sprayed the pretty woman in a bright red coat with some spray, then slugged her in the shoulder. She flew back against the car. Her arm came out and she scratched the freak. His hands flew up, clawing at his eyes. The woman fell to her knees and began to crawl away. The freak staggered after her. The music swirled. The lady crawled. The freak staggered. The freak jumped on her back. He took out a cord, wrapped it around her neck, began to strangle her. She choked, her eyes bulging. She rolled over. He rolled over. He strangled her. The music surged. She choked. The music strained. He strangled her. She choked. He strangled. She choked.

SHAME, SHAME!
Clown Drowns in Human Waste

★ 40 ★

> MAN GETS LIFE FOR ASSAULT ON DAUGHTER
>
> BAY CITY (CNS) – A jury sentenced a 32-year-old Bay City man to life in prison Tuesday for beating his infant daughter nearly to death to "stop her from crying."
>
> The Bay City Municipal Court jury deliberated for 90 minutes before handing down the maximum punishment to Sergio Nechayev, an unemployed computer repairman.
>
> Nachayev's attorney, William Sampson, said his client would appeal.
>
> The jury last week found Nechayev guilty of attempted murder and first-degree sexual assault after prosecutors presented evidence showing that the girl had been hospitalized in April with two broken legs, fractures to three ribs, and a fractured skull and vertebrae.
>
> The girl, who was eight months old at the time, had also received vaginal and anal injuries from sexual assault, and her tongue had been nearly severed.

I called it "The Dump," alternately "The Dungheap," the place where human trash piled up. Skinny Blinn was tossing it in and retiring to South Lake Tahoe. Sernath had called me in to inform me of my promotion to Legal Affairs Reporter.

"It shows this company has great confidence in you, Thor," he had said the big Monday morning, adding: "How was your weekend? Mine was great. My wife was in town, didn't kill her... Won $640 at the tables..."

APPEALS COURT UPHOLDS 55-YEAR SENTENCE FOR DRUG DEALER RE-TRIAL FOR KILLING OF TRANSGENDER TEEN CITY CONTRACTING HEAD CONVICTED OF EXTORTION, BRIBERY EX-FUNERAL DIRECTOR CHARGED WITH ABUSING 29 BABY CORPSES MAN CONVICTED FOR BEHEADING HOUSEKEEPER JUDGE: MURDER SUSPECT COMPETENT FOR TRIAL

I sat on the peeling wood benches of nearly vacant courtrooms, watching the hours roll by in the championship of bureaucracy known as "due process." What I would come to understand was that there could be a lot of rigmarole, a lot of document-filing, a lot appeals and injunctions and delays and reschedulings before they would get down to it: Did the scumbag do it, and how long would they get when they finally got packed away?

The defense counsel would intone in grave seriousness about the accused drive-by shooter scumbag: "Social intolerance and misunderstanding are the perfect partners in the trial before us. Are we to judge the defendant purely on his actions, or his perceived motives? Is he guilty through provocation, or impulse?"

Well, yes, perhaps, certainly, but – mainly, he was *guilty*... They were guilty, most of them – guilty of things like Homicide and Felony Assault with Intent to Cause Great Bodily Harm, and First-Degree Felony Sexual Assault on a Minor Under 12. That was the catch, wasn't it – *most* of them.

"But, oh!" the perps would wail, "I didn't do it! It's a frame-up! I wasn't even *there!*"

Of course not. Of course not... They were rich, they were poor. In a great many of the cases, they were poor black bastards. Most were, of course, without question, "victims" themselves. Victims of an unfair economic system, a systemic lack of opportunity – victims of a bad educational system, bad movies, bad food, bad drugs, bad parents, bad racism, general bad voodoo...

"We do not believe the government has enough evidence to convict," the defense attorneys would explain. "We believe the trial will show that my client cannot be linked to these weapons or these drugs..." "We will present evidence showing that my client was on the influence of drugs when he allegedly broke into his so-called ex-girlfriend's apartment, ejaculated upon her personal belongings and threw Ribsy, her poodle-terrier mix, out the 24th floor window...We will show that my client cannot therefore be guilty as charged, and that what he needs instead is counseling. He voluntarily surrenders for such counseling, Your Honor, if the court will permit..." "My client was acting in *self-defense* when he allegedly shot the three meat inspectors at his sausage factory! These inspectors had been harassing him for months! They had cornered him and were threatening to shut down his livelihood..." "My client wishes to plead guilty and to volunteer for a chemical castration procedure, Your Honor, because he is sincerely regretful for his actions, he recognizes he has done wrong and pleads for the mercy of the court..." "Your Honor, we will present evidence showing that my client suffered from schizophrenia and psychotic delusions and he is now getting professional treatment for his condition..." "Whoever did these things is clearly a monster... I am certain that my client is not this monster, and we intend to show from the facts that he could not have committed these crimes as the police have alleged..." "The charges against my client are based on the false testimony of jailhouse informants who have been promised leniency in exchange for cooperating with police. The police must learn they will not succeed in reducing crime by putting innocent men in jail thanks to the fabrications of guilty men..."

JURY GETS MURDER CASE AGAINST DRUG DEALER 13-YEAR-OLD CHARGED IN BASEBALL BAT KILLING JUDGE RELEASES 5 AFTER DRUG CASE TESTIMONY RULED TAINTED MAN PLEADS NOT GUILTY TO PLOTTING 'JIHAD' GRENADE ATTACK ON BAY SHORES MALL ARSONIST GETS 11 LIFE TERMS FOR HOTEL FIRE THAT KILLED 11 SHERIFF'S DEPT. ORDERED TO PAY MAN $1.6 MILLION AFTER SHOOTING SUV WITH 67 BULLETS

It was a natural progression, the place where the blood-stained pavements I had witnessed in my earlier incarnation as leg-man were transformed into sharp stacks of legal documents and the softly clinking chains and orange jumpsuits that indicated some scumbag had at last been brought "within the system."

The promotion had not resulted in much of a pay-raise, but the perks included having my own little press box in the crumbly gray Superior Court building. At any given time, I kept tabs on 15 to 20 cases taking place within the downtown Court Complex – sitting in the courtrooms, listening to public defenders, chasing after Assistant

D.A.'s and the family members of victims down the long marbled hallways – but many times, simply waiting in an administrative office to pick up copies of documents.

The main message of the courts seemed to be: People were getting too much into each other's *stuff*, and apparently they would not stop. My days were filled with having to look at scumbags and *accused* scumbags, and never did I discover a clue to how they ticked. Some of them seemed squashed with the shame and fright of what had happened, but many seemed *just fine* with it as they stared off at the walls, scratching themselves and licking their lips – this population of *accused* baby-shakers and weenie-waggers, *accused* toe-suckers and girl-torturers, *accused* gang poops and bum-bashers, *accused* fag-beaters and wife-whackers, *accused* shoplifters and drunk drivers, *accused* credit-card fraudsters, forest-fire setters, abortion-clinic bombers, prostitute stranglers, former soldiers gone nuts on one-man crime sprees... And most of all, dopers – dope hounds, dope dealers, dope-lab operators, dope-dupes and dope-dopes, dopes doing nearly anything for dope and blaming the dope when they got caught.

The authorities were apparently waging a War On Drugs, a war whose main results seemed to be more drugs on the streets, more addicts, more violence and death, more police corruption, more destruction in general.

Some liked to say that when and if the authorities ever got around to "legalizing" dope, they'd probably be able to shut down half of all the courtrooms and prisons. I wasn't sure, but in any case, legalization wasn't likely to happen any time soon. Too many "moral majorities" had staked too much political capital on opposing it at all costs, for one thing – "law-and-order voters" had always enjoyed a good Say No To Drugs speech, it was something they could easily understand – and why shouldn't they?

But mainly, illegalization seemed to be just too profitable and, in a way, too important to the local and global economies as we knew and loved them. The drug octopus stretched out in all directions, penetrating every layer of society, charming and enriching the lives of more than a few. "Billions and billions" of dope-money was allegedly floating around out there, according to the authorities – a gigantic pool of untaxed and ready capital that was used by the traffickers not for whores and fast cars but rather, the experts said, for reinvestment in legitimate businesses, including property and construction, hedge funds and the stock market, in a process otherwise known as money-laundering.

In any case, the flow of drugs remained massive and constant – Washington seemed to have real difficulty getting the citizens of places like Afghanistan and Thailand and Latin America to sign up to seriously fight America's Drug War. Some said nobody really wanted it to stop. On the cop side, the Dope War meant steadily increasing budgets, more police surveillance toys, bigger police powers, to say nothing of the huge money that had grown around the prison-industrial complex.

Indeed, tens of thousands of good American people relied on the Dope War for their livelihood – think of all the cops, judges, lawyers, prison guards, probation officers and journalists who would be out of a job if the war suddenly went out of business – talk about an unemployment spike! While no one, it seemed, had ever found much advantage in dealing with the crisis of Demand and seeing the war on to "final victory." And if the War systematically crushed poor neighborhoods and poor scumbags – well, that was nothing but the inevitable "unfortunate" part of the game for those too stupid to know any better…

Well, who knew? I didn't. I didn't know a damn thing. I would crack open the screenless window in my little box, illegally light up a smoke and tap out another Dungheap nugget detailing variations of human pain, shame, torture and stupidity.

>   NEO-NAZI CONVICTED OF HISPANIC ATTACK
>
>   BAY CITY (CNS) – A 19-year-old self-confessed neo-Nazi skinhead was convicted Friday on charges of attempted murder and sexual assault for the nearly fatal beating of a 16-year-old Hispanic boy.
>
>   Henry Tucker David faces 25 years to life in prison during sentencing scheduled for next month.
>
>   The Bay City jury convicted David after more than two days of deliberations.
>
>   During the trial, prosecutors said David beat the teenager, kicking him with steel-toed boots and causing severe head and spinal injuries, before sodomizing him with a plastic pipe while chanting the phrase, "white power."

> Police testified that the teenager was also burned by cigarettes, doused with bleach, and slashed in the chest by an unknown object during the assault.

Despite the rigmarole, it was an efficient and prolific system whose future prospects seemed nearly limitless. Gee whiz, they already didn't have enough prisons – there were so many convicts they were trying to ship them out of state to avoid releasing an armed robber or rape-o early. They claimed they couldn't build the jails fast enough – the Corrections Department had written up a "master plan" that foresaw prison construction stretching 25 years down the road.

And truly, there did seem a lot to correct. They were packing them away for life after "three strikes," seizing their property for running dope, giving them 22.5 years for possessing a kilo of coke, sentencing them to death for gunning down random soda-slurpers in a robbery attempt at the gas station. They were 63-year-old grandmothers like Frances Malorny, confessing to selling heroin, crack, and marijuana from their backyard. They were six-member fraudster-teams pleading guilty to charges of opening more than 1,000 credit card accounts and buying $6.7 million dollars worth of junk that they did not pay for... They were fathers like John McAfee, 35, charged with raping and sodomizing his 11-year-old daughter Opal, who would go on to hang herself in the shower. They were single mothers like Juanita Ramirez, 26, who pleaded no contest to killing her five- and seven-year-old sons by locking them in the trunk of her car while she worked the evening shift at Sav-Mor.

They were "radical eco-terrorists" like the Earth Freedom Front-connected Claude Johnson, sentenced to 35 years to life for bomb attacks on two sport utility vehicle (SUV) dealerships and a logging-truck parking lot adjacent to Bay National Forest. They were people like best buddy-pals Frederick Tanders and Joshua Atzerodt, who admitted in court that they bound, gagged and repeatedly raped 13-year-old Jason Travis, but were not in fact responsible for the youngster's death because bullshit bullshit bullshit...

ARMY RESERVE SOLDIER PLEADS INNOCENT TO SHOTGUN ATTACK MOTHER CHARGED WITH USING INFANT AS WEAPON TO HIT BOYFRIEND DEFROCKED REV. CHOWDER-MILK PLEADS GUILTY, GETS 60 YEARS FOR CHILD SEX ABUSE HUMAN SERVICES CHIEF FINED $10,000 FOR RELEASING

MENTALLY ILL MAN CONVICTED OF KILLING MOTHER, DISFIGURING GIRLFRIEND

You would see the victims limping into court, sad specimens staggering forward on crutches, being pushed in wheelchairs – bad-luck, wrong time-wrong place babies missing fingers and noses, fitted out with colostomy bags due to having been "impaled" by a broomstick, blotchy purple scars across their faces, hands, arms and necks.

They'd painfully take their place in the legal citadel, forced to relive the horror again, or to watch as their tormentor scumbag denied that anything much at all had happened – that young Missy, for example, raped for 16 hours and now with severe spinal discombulations, had... *made it all up*. It seemed there was little that could be said to people like 14-year-old learning-disabled Debbie, beaten and burnt by aerosol cans that had been turned into flamethrowers, forced to drink urine and cigarette butts and eat chili powder by neighborhood pals Bonnie, Hailee, Edward and Dirk. "Unspeakable and wicked," pronounced Judge Marvin R. Hirschberg.

Many victims, of course, did not and could not show up to bear witness, such as 2-year-old Monica Lituya, whose parents allegedly inflicted 64 wounds on her, including cigarette burns and scalded feet, and whose dead body was found nearly emaciated, according to investigators... Or 9-year-old Victor Smythes, who suffocated on his own vomit after his adoptive mother, Rebecca Smythes, wrapped him in duct tape, with only his nose uncovered, as punishment for allegedly "stealing cookies..." Or 1-month-old Margaret "Baby Marge" Parnett, whose mother received five years in prison for overcooking her in a microwave oven (Mother Charlene produced experts who claimed she suffered from epileptic seizures that led to "blackouts of up to 45 minutes," in which she "might not know what she was doing"). Or 3-year-old Jeremy Ovalle, whose adoptive parents, Garry and Grace, received 15 years each for poisoning the boy with an estimated five teaspoons of salt per day and inflicting at least 13 "blunt trauma" injuries to his head...

WOMAN SENTENCED TO 15 YEARS FOR KILLING CANCER-STRICKEN HUSBAND MALL 'JIHAD' SUSPECT SAYS 'FRAMED' BY FBI INFORMANT BAIL DENIED FOR SHOOTING SPREE SUSPECT MAN SENTENCED TO 25 YEARS TO LIFE FOR BEHEADING EX-GIRLFRIEND'S CAT UNDER 3rd STRIKE LAW MOTHER WHO DROWNED SONS RULED INSANE

The guilty ruined it for the innocent, the bad cops ruined it for the good, and it had long been clear that the police did not deserve to be totally trusted on anything. It could not be ignored that cops sometimes lied, sometimes concocted evidence, sometimes hid behind a "code of silence," sometimes coerced confessions and relied on the false statements of "prison snitches" to get their scumbag in jail.

The cops looked out for their own interests, above all – and in their world, depending on what they wanted or thought they could get after catching a particular suspect or perp, the line could be very elastic indeed between whether they would decide to describe the conduct in question as Homicide, Manslaughter or Self-Defense. In such cases, "facts" and "evidence" could be whatever the cops decided they were... Deals were inevitably cut and backs were scratched, and they tended to be cut and scratched behind closed doors... Yes, and one hardly knew what to do with the case of Jacqueline Blake, the FBI Laboratory Biologist who pleaded guilty to submitting falsified DNA analysis reports in more than 100 cases.[14]

FATHER DENIES FORCING SON TO SELL CRACK WOMAN SENTENCED TO DEATH FOR MURDERING HUSBAND WITH OLEANDER, ANTIFREEZE ATTEMPTED MALL 'JIHAD' BOMBER SENTENCED TO 17 YEARS FOUR SENTENCED TO LIFE FOR RAPE, MURDER OF GIRLS IN 'GANG INITIATION RITUAL' JUDGE ORDERS BEATEN COMA BABY'S LIFE SUPPORT TURNED OFF

From time to time there were "happy endings" – people like Colleen Brockman, 52, acquitted by a jury of shooting her husband Oliver, 60, after defense lawyers demonstrated "a pattern of spousal abuse" that had included at least 16 hospital trips by Colleen over 24 years of marriage... Or Kenneth Arnold – the clowns said he looked "overjoyed," but I thought he looked nearly dead.

DNA EVIDENCE FREES MAN AFTER 29 YEARS
BAY CITY (CNS) – A man who spent nearly 29 years in state prison for two rapes was ordered released

---

[14] A subsequent FBI investigation found that "Blake's actions did not affect the outcome in any criminal case in which her test results were presented as evidence," although "her false statements undermined the usefulness of the DNA tests she performed and, in general, the integrity of the FBI's DNA lab," according to an FBI news release. – ED.

Wednesday after he was cleared of the crimes by DNA evidence.

State Attorney General Philip Sneeth ordered Kenneth Arnold freed following a court hearing in Bay City in which the state withdrew the charges.

"Thank you to Jesus for DNA testing," said Arnold in brief comments to reporters outside the court. "I've been in hell, but this feels like heaven."

Arnold, 53, was convicted and sentenced to 75 years in prison almost 29 years ago for two rapes that occurred in South Bay City within 90 minutes of each other on July 14.

Both women testified that Arnold had been their attacker.

Sneeth ordered a review of the case after Arnold, acting as his own lawyer, succeeded in persuading the appeals court to allow DNA tests of samples collected from the two women following the assaults.

According to court documents, certified laboratories concluded the samples did not belong to Arnold.

At the time of Arnold's trial, DNA analysis of evidence was not available.

Weary of the constant stream of murder, drugs, torture and rape, Sernath made a point of asking that I seek out the "offbeat" and "lighter side" of the legal universe as well – for example, the lawsuit filed by Janice Unger, the Bay State University student who was arrested and spent three weeks in jail after airport security guards found three condoms filled with "white powder" in her carry-on luggage. The police claimed "initial tests" had revealed "traces of drugs" inside the condoms, but later tests revealed the 100 percent presence of flour – as Janice had maintained throughout. Janice told investigators that she and her friends had used the condoms "for squeezing" when they got "stressed out" over tests and social difficulties. The city compensated her $270,000 for her time in prison...

Or Walter Gebbington, the middle school health and social studies teacher who sued Bay City Unified School District for "wrongful termination" after he was canned for asking his seventh-grade students to come to the blackboard to draw their "concept of male genitalia" in front of the class. Gebbington, who was seeking $100 million in damages, contended the anatomical-drawing exercise was both "voluntary" and a "good learning method for youths entering puberty and exploring their sexuality..."*

> MOTHER GETS 15 YEARS FOR DAUGHTER'S DEATH
>
> BAY CITY (CNS) – A Bay County judge on Wednesday sentenced a mother who used heroin with her 14-year-old daughter, who died, to 17 years in prison.
>
> A jury in March found Sherron Pratt guilty of reckless behavior leading to the death of her daughter, Cyinda.
>
> Superior Court Judge Malcom Yelvington told Pratt that "instead of seeking treatment for drug addiction, you led your young daughter directly down the path of destruction."
>
> Pratt broke in tears as the sentence was read, saying, "My baby won't come back."
>
> Prosecutors said Pratt and her daughter injected heroin together last April 13 at their apartment in the Six Points area of Bay City. The daughter lost consciousness and was pronounced dead after paramedics were called to the home two days later.

In any case, within weeks I had given up hope of ever running into Chrissy (I knew she rarely went to court, anyways), and within months I was yearning to get back to the clarity and chaos of being a legman. It was less "prestige," maybe, but perhaps overall less confusion, paper-shuffling and sadness. Somebody got popped – that was a one day story on the leg desk. In the courts, it could last for weeks and months, even years.

Teenagers accused of gunning down pizza deliverymen, 19-year-old dopes who beat a "gay man" to death with a pool cue... On and it went, suffering and stupidity, no end in sight. It was no way to live, having to deal on daily basis with the likes of Agahassaan Abedi, sentenced to 25 years for using scissors to to cut off his 2-year-old

---

* Gebbington would go on to lose the case. – ED.

daughter Ayana's clitoris in a charming and insane old-country ritual they called "female circumcision"... or "white supremacist" tough guys like William Leinich, sentenced to 14.5 years for possessing "chemical weapons materials" including sodium cyanide and hydrochloric, nitric and acetic acids, as well as more than 80 pipe bombs, 16 machine guns and more than 300,000 rounds of ammunition... drug-dopes like Alfonse Cibiades, sentenced to life in prison without parole for setting a Pine Ridges apartment fire that killed seven people, including three children, after one of the residents "snitched" him out to police as an alleged drug dealer... mothers like Alceedee Thompson, sentenced to a maximum of 10 years for giving birth to a stillborn daughter while high on methamphetamine. Doctors said said the dead child had enough meth in her system to kill two normal adults...

I wanted out of The Dungheap – I could no longer bear it. Man was the greatest enemy to man, and nobody understood what was happening in the world. Yes, fine. We were a species in permanent trauma, the tragedies of the courtrooms were reflections of a society whose soul was drowning in darkness... There was just a *meanness* in this world, mister... I could not help it, I felt myself going mad – that so many of these things were treated as "normal everyday business," and that the outcome was considered "justice" being seen and being done – this was itself an expression of the madness.

>BARDACH PLEADS GUILTY, FINED $321,000
>
>BAY CITY (CNS) – Former Drugs-Enforcement Agency Regional Director Louis Bardach pleaded guilty Wednesday to two federal ethics violations and was ordered by a judge to pay $321,000 in fines.
>
>Immediately following the guilty plea, Bay City Mayor Ernest J. Favella removed Bardach's name from the city's new Drug Combat Center, which had been named in honor of Bardach, a decorated former Bay City police officer.
>
>In the hearing at Bay City Federal District Court, Bardach pleaded guilty to accepting gifts and loans from Giametti Trucking Inc., a Lakeview-based firm facing a federal grand jury probe for fraud and extortion.

Yes, I wanted a better world, most of us did, but the scope for action seemed severely limited. Blow it up, tear it down, cry another thousand tears... How about: More justice, more peace and quiet, and better parents and more equal schools... and fewer bombs and fewer wars, and more money for everything and – there, that would be a good start... Also, fix global warming.

After a while, I felt only exhausted. It was "just work," a shrug and a sigh – another sausage after another sausage after another.

If others who might commit crimes were to be deterred, all to the good. If the depraved and deranged could not be deterred by the threat of the criminal justice system, it did not matter.

There might have been some other way, but those who had the bright idea hadn't spoken up yet. Until then, the society had a duty to send the message, obvious and ineffectual as it might have seemed: You don't do heroin with your daughter. You don't improperly take money from scumbags when you hold a position of high responsibility. And you certainly, above all else, do not suck the toes of defenseless little boys for "fun."

> MAN GET 20 TO LIFE FOR SUCKING BOYS' TOES
>
> BAY CITY (CNS) – A former Bay City Recreation Department supervisor was sentenced to 20 years to life in prison Friday following his conviction for sucking the toes of more than 30 boys aged 6 to 10 under his care over a three-year period.
>
> Bryan Barry Gordon, 43, wept as Judge Thomas Crain sentenced him to the maximum sentence available under state law for child molestation.
>
> Crain told Gordon: "You were entrusted with the welfare of these boys, but you violated their trust and gave them and their families scars that will last a lifetime. I believe, Mr. Gordon, that you pose a threat to children."
>
> Gordon, who had led an after-school program at Bay City's Citrus Lanes Park for 12 years, had pleaded for leniency, claiming his actions did not constitute sexual misconduct.
>
> "I would never harm these children, your honor," he said in a statement read during the sentencing hearing. "I never felt sexual feelings or desire for them. I

understand, though, that my concept of fun and play was wrong, odd and inappropriate... I feel remorse and sadness for my conduct, which I feel is improper but not criminal."

QUICKSAND! 'No Sense in This Thing,' says Clown Confidant

★ 41 ★

"Just remember, kid," Richie was saying, "I will always worship the quicksand you walk on... Really, kid, really, do not doubt... When you are hungry and tired, and you sit in the bathtub alone of an evening most slow and dreary, with books from the library wet on your chest, a freshly unfrozen burrito decomposing in your innards, realizing you are but another cipher in the horde of completely and utterly unnecessary duplicates infesting this sloppy little platform of pain and suffering and being cold... " He paused to bring his index finger to his nose. "... know that Little Richie is thinking of you."

Richie had resigned from Cities News on Friday and was leaving for the war. We were on the street, heading for the Flite Room and goodbye drinks.

Richie had come dressed in his new war gear. He wore a dark blue bulletproof vest that had PRESS in bright orange letters. He had on a Kevlar helmet with goggles, a backpack dripping with various bungee cords, canteens and bottles, a sleeping bag tucked in at the bottom. He showed me his two-way radio, satellite phone, gloves and knife as we walked along.

"These goggles don't fog, kid... That's a promise, and I'm a promise-keeper. Whatever you do, whatever they say – never tell 'em my goggles fogged..."

"You know I wouldn't think of it, Richie..."

Some guy with greasy long hair and a striped sweatshirt walked by, carrying a chainsaw.

"Where's he going?" Richie turned and shouted. "HEY, YOU'RE UNDER ARREST! HALT, YOU! YOU'RE UNDER ARREST!"

The guy kept going. Didn't even look back.

I had just signed Wayne's get-well-soon card (there had been another surgery, apparently) when the famous tape of the confrontation appeared on the office TV: Richie shouting at mayoral aide Trent Ghassanid. Shaky frames, the audio not quite intelligible, and from a distance of 15 or 20 yards, yet unmistakably – Richie raising his arms and blasting forth with all sorts of mustached froth, waving a pen semi-threateningly – then getting slammed and bent over, his arms twisted behind his back, by three and then four and then nine of the mayor's finest...

The problem, as later deciphered, had involved, at first, the mayor announcing 900 city job cuts and demanding a 10 percent pay cut and other reduced benefits for the employees who were allowed to remain. It was due, the mayor had explained, to the "$320 million budget deficit."

In his prime-time speech, Favella had also announced the reduction of the city's 24-hour bus service to 20 hours, and disclosed plans to sell off and "privatize" the city's entire transport network (buses, subways, street cars), Street Lighting Maintenance Department, Curb Painters Division and Animal Protection Service.

"Our situation requires tough decisions and sacrifices from everyone," the mayor had declared.

Shortly thereafter, it had been discovered that the Mayor's Office had in August leased a $97,000 Range Rover luxury sports utility vehicle with sunroof, secure communications system, and heated seats. Apparently, it was mainly being used for outings involving Favella's wife and teenage children, Grant and Daisy. Richie went digging through the official paper and found that the Mayor's Office had paid exactly $24,998 dollars on a one-year lease for the vehicle – $2 below the limit at which the expense would have to be approved by the City Council.

When finally asked about it at a press conference, the mayor strenuously claimed the vehicle was in fact being used for "undercover police work and the fight against terrorism."

Three days after the Richie blow-up hit the local clown shows and Richie's accreditation was "suspended" by Sernath and Wayne, the mayor issued the following written statement: "I accept responsibility for the actions of my staff and apologize to any members of the community who have been offended by my failure to promptly investigate this matter after questions were raised. My Office has now authorized a full independent inquiry..."

We sat down in the booth. Richie pulled off his helmet to reveal a shaved, shining head. He grinned at me.

"Like it, kid? I've been dreaming of doing it ever since the vice president shot that old man in the face and got away with it. It just... *fits*, don't it?"

"Yes, Richie..."

"This way, when I convert to Islam and they cut my head off on international TV, you'll know who it is. Imagine the look of strangeness and wonder that'll be on my face as they saw away, muttering their prayers as they offer me up as a sacrifice to their god! You'll say, 'Why, it's that old hack Little Richie! His famous two minutes at last!"

"Sure, Richie..."

"Who did the anthrax attacks,* kid? They swore they'd tell us! They swore they'd catch the dirty rascals! They swore they'd get to the bottom of it! They *swore* it!"

"Well, they're working on it. You know, it's a tough case..."

"And mine eyes filled with sand, kid, when the pale horse turned red. Ahoy, and I saw the lion standing alone. Let history show they were in the White House buggering each other and committing treasonous acts..."

"Yes, you may be right."

"It's a Barnum and Bailey world, sweet pea, fake as anything could be..."

Richie explained he had set up tentative freelance gigs with *The Christian Science Monitor, The Knoxville Sun-Reporter, Tampa Daily Digest-Times*, a few others. *The Washington Times* was "very interested," with the editor even wiggling a "possible blog slot" if Richie panned out.

---

* Apparently refers to a series of letters containing deadly anthrax spores that were mailed to a number of U.S. news media outlets and two Democratic Party senators. The letters were mailed over several weeks beginning on September 18, 2001, one week after the September 11, 2001, attacks. Five people were killed and 17 others were infected as a result of the anthrax mailings. The U.S. Federal Bureau of Investigation (FBI) says it has spent years investigating the suspicious mailings. No arrests were ever made in the case, and in 2008, U.S. authorities declared that the suspected perpetrator of the mailings, a U.S. government scientist named Bruce Ivins, had committed suicide with an overdose of acetaminophen. – ED.

"I'll be a two-buck blog-whore, kid, bringing American death and destruction in all its patriotic glory to a needy population of two or three morons... until they cut my head off on international TV..."

"If you're lucky..."

Richie laughed. "Bing-bing newsflash! – you're a slave to a world where what you copy and paste is sold for profit... Bing-bing newsflash! – news is to truth as cancer is to health! Bing-bing! War is to the health of the state, as whole-wheat bran is to the health of the colon! Bing-bing! The more things change, the more they stay insane..."

"Yes..."

"So what's it gonna be, boss? Pacified or crazy? PACIFIED OR CRAZY?"

"A little of both, I hope."

"Oh, it's wings... over the Na-vee," Richie sang, raising his hands in the air and crashing them down to drum the table, "sailing the seven skies above..."

The soldiers, sailors and marines
Are demons at eating pork and beans
Or posing in the dirty magazines
But if there's gonna be
A fightin' jamboree
Oh, it's wings over the na-vee...

I drank heavily, a beer with each whisky sour, the double-shot about every 20 minutes, and dodged out for a smoke every 10-15 minutes. Richie stuck with soda water, downing a total of two in the two hours we were in the bar.

"All this booze will kill you, kid."

"No, it keeps me alive..."

"I don't exclude it, kid. Dance with the devil by the pale moonlight. Comrade wolf knows when to eat, and he eats without listening. It can't rain all the time. Time flies like an arrow, and fruit flies like a banana. Shoot the wounded, arrest the hostage. You're goin' nowhere when you ride on the carousel..."

He touched his nose. "That's how you know. That would be my only advice."

"I appreciate it, Richie..."

Richie put on the helmet, slipped the goggles over his eyes. He was going to leave. I, apparently, was going to stay.

"You got to fuck somebody, kid, but listen to little Richie: the fewer the better... And don't ever let me hear about you fucking somebody over."

"Yes..."

"What they say is: One only understands the things that one tames. Ever hear that, kid? But I've never yet seen a woman beautiful *and* tame. That don't work – now, then, or never. That's how they get you. They get you up a tree and leave you there without a paddle."

"Couldn't have said it better myself."

"You got to remember, kid, there's no sense in this thing. Above all else."

"You mean... the sense of it is that there's no sense."

"You're way too tricky."

"You really going to do it? War is for losers..."

"That's right, kid. Nobody never arrives nowhere. Ain't no reason for nothin'. You can never be strong. You can never be free. You can only have smokes. And I don't even got that."

"Don't get killed..."

"Roads of battle... paths of victory I shall walk... The evenin' dust is rollin'... There's a one-way wind a-blowin' and it's a-blowin' at my back... See you around, kid."

Richie saluted. I helped him lift the backpack on to his shoulders. He stared at me through the goggles.

We shook hands and he walked out.

> POLICE CHIEF'S GRANDDAUGHTER SHOT, KILLED
>
> BAY CITY (CNS) – Bay City Police Chief Nathan O. Nachba's granddaughter was shot to death Tuesday as she sat in a car outside a Burger Century outlet in Bay City's Commerce Avenue section, police said.
>
> Sgt. Major Jake Tallman said Delissa Plager, 22, was shot several times by a gunman who walked up and opened fire on Plager's car in the parking lot of the restaurant in the 8100 block of Park Rd.
>
> Tallman said investigators believe a male passenger was the likely target of the attack at about 1:45 p.m. The passenger, whom Tallman declined to name, was not injured in the attack.

The police spokesman said investigators are probing whether the incident may have been a case of "mistaken identity." He declined to give further details.

"She was in the wrong place at the wrong time," Tallman said of the victim, who was a senior year student in the pre-medical program at Bay State University. "We do not believe she herself was involved in any criminal activity that may have been related to the shooting."

Tallman said there are no suspects in the case so far.

Tallman said Chief Nachba and his family were "devastated" by the death and were "grieving in seclusion."

TEXECUTION:
Klown Konfab as Killer Kroaked!

★ 42 ★

The execution was midnight Friday at the Andersenville State Supermax: Stephen "Tex" Walker, convicted and condemned to die for the slaughter of at least 58 human beings, mostly children and old women, though at least 16 men as well, mainly homeless bums and a few Marines. Sernath was interested in breaking coverage, but only after I had swung a car-pool/hotel share deal with Marty Atrazine, the "Justice Correspondent" for the Santa Costa paper.

Twelve years ago, a cop had pulled over Tex's white Econoline van at 2:47 a.m. on suspicion of failing to come to a complete halt at a stop sign. Tex had used a shotgun to execute patrolman Frank Sheerhan, an 18-year police veteran and father of four, before going to the house of his alleged drug dealer, Carlos "Eddie" Cardone, and executing the six people who were there, including Eddie's nine-year-old daughter (Cardone himself was not home).

Tex then used the house phone to call the police, allegedly saying, "For heaven's sake, come get me, you pigs… I'm tired of all… this."

The subsequent year and a half of searches on Tex's isolated Lakeview County home yielded so much evidence that the authorities could have continued executing him for several decades into the future, if that had been possible. The major finds included: two 13-year-old twins, Kimi and Kai Ponchar, tied spread-eagled to radiators; one (still unidentified) decaying headless corpse in the bathtub; a ribcage in the kitchen sink; the obligatory severed penis, provenance unknown, in a pot of boiled spaghetti, several months old; a head in the freezer, most of the skin torn off and a two-inch hole in the cranium, from which brain matter had apparently been extracted; three more heads in a wheel barrow in the basement; a dozen hands and parts of feet stuffed in plastic buckets; several glass jars of teeth; at least 16 dildoes; several dozen containers of various types of acid and industrial lyme; and at least 15 shallow graves scattered across Tex's acreage, each containing an array of body parts.

Marty and I wound through the golden hills of late morning, heading toward our rendezvous with Tex and the execution chamber.

"Good-looking young guy like you must really get the ladies," said Marty, who was somewhere in his 40s. "*Snatch*, we used to call it... I bet you get a lot of *snatch*, huh?"

"Not really, Marty. It's harder than you might think out there..."

"Ah, modesty. Well, I would recommend that you take advantage of it while you can. I wish I had gone for a few more myself. It comes to an end really fast, let me tell you. Then you're stuck with one... I been with my wife 21 years."

"That's a long time. I'm sure it's not all bad..."

He nodded. "We got two kids, yeah. They're good kids. They get a B average in school. Yeah, sometimes we share something special..."

"See, that's something."

A team of forensic psychologists had determined that Tex's mother, Corrine, had forced him to wear rubber underwear until the age of 11 because of persistent nocturnal wetting problems. Tex's father, a truck driver, had been beaten to death with tire irons in a parking lot, allegedly over a debt.

The psychologists said that in the difficult months after the murder, Tex's mother had apparently started to screw her brother, Vinnie, who had lost a leg, a foot and three fingers when he was shelled by fellow American soldiers in the Korean War. When not screwing Tex's mother, Vinnie had often taken young Tex to bars in the town of Kirven, Texas, according to the psychologists. Tex learned to tell jokes and how to play to darts and pool. He began drinking at an early age.

The investigating psychologists, after hundreds of hours of interviews with Tex, determined that Tex most likely was sexually assaulted at least several times by drunks in the bars. Tex's mother, for her part, would beat him and his uncle for hanging out at the bars. Hospital records showed that Tex was treated for numerous fractures, lacerations and burns before the age of 12. His mother and uncle were also repeatedly treated for injuries, as well as for crabs and chlamydia.

According to the psychologists, Tex's mother told him she tried to abort him but couldn't find a doctor in time. Corrine said Tex's real father was General Dwight D. Eisenhower. She said Tex was born the day that Enrico Fermi died. Corrine went on to convert to the Church of Jesus Christ, Scientist. She suffered severe spinal damage when she was hit by a car while walking on the street. Tex had to take care of her from the age of 14, including changing her diaper.

Marty gunned his Subaru wagon toward the Supermax. We absolutely had to make the 3 p.m. news conference or we could forget about being on-site for what had become popularly known on TV and the internet as "The Texecution." More than 400 clowns from across the U.S.A., as well as dozens of foreign clowns, had formally applied to cover the "state-ordered legal homicide." Because of the overflow, there was to be a drawing to determine which 25 clowns would be able to witness the execution in person, alongside family members of the victims. Unlucky clowns would have to watch the killing on secure closed-circuit television in the prison auditorium.

The Supermax was completely enclosed by 30 foot-high concrete walls, with the special "Death Wing" extending to the southeast. The wing included the Execution Chamber and eight cells housing those next in line to get the lethal skin prick. In addition to Tex, the current occupants included:

★ Mughal "Mugsy" Whyte, who had gunned down six people in a convenience store during a crack-fueled robbery in which he made off with $54 cash and two cartons of cigarettes.

★ Ian "The Sapper" Soham, convicted of raping and strangling 11-year-old Leticia Bailey and 10-year-old Kimberly Muliaga after abducting them from a park where their parents were participating in a softball game. Soham sent pictures of his craftsmanship to Leticia's mother over the girl's cell phone.

★ Francine Koza, 68, convicted for the poisoning murders of five husbands over 26 years.

★ Walter "Evil Eyes" Sheridan, convicted of kidnapping, sexually assaulting and eventually killing at least 14 women aged 24 to 52 that he had kept chained in an underground dungeon in his suburban tract home because, he testified, they had "evil eyes."

★ The allegedly mentally retarded Juan Gonsalves, 39, convicted of abducting, raping, and pouring roach killer down the throat of 9-year-old Christina Gontares, who was left blind and brain-damaged before finally dying six months after the attack.

★ Rashawn "Gumby" Saunders, the Blood Bounty Hounds gang founder, convicted for the gun murders of nine Vietnamese immigrants during the bungled attempted robbery of a car-wash.*

★ Daniel "Kluster Killer" Ignoto, the mortgage banker convicted of killing 19 prostitutes and burying their bodies in "clusters" in the forests surrounding his gated Meringue County mansion.

★ Andrew "Angel of Death" Strassmeir, a registered nurse who had pleaded guilty to using drug cocktails to end the misery of at least 37 mostly severely injured patients, as well as some who were about to be released, in a hospital burn unit over three years.

★ Lawrence "Buddy" Miles, former operator of the child-porn sites lolitatoysnboys.com and babygotcrackd.net, who had somehow successfully traveled to Volgograd to adopt a 4-year-old blond Russian girl named Svetlana, whose body was never found but whose photographs testified to the capacity of the human body to suffer pain.

Supermax spokesman Ben Greenman addressed the clown mob from the podium: "Ladies and gentlemen, the death mixture will include Sodium Pentothal to make Mr. Walker unconscious, Panuronium Bromide to stop his respiration, and finally Potassium Chloride to halt the movement of his heart. Mr. Walker should feel nothing more than that he is going to sleep..."

Clowns shouted: "What's the last meal, Ben? What's he gonna have?"

"Mr. Walker has requested from the prison kitchen 16 bologna, cheese and mustard sandwiches, three bags of Lay's potato chips – barbecue, sour cream n' onion and salt n' vinegar flavors – one container of rainbow sherbet ice cream, one packet of peanut M&M's, and a two-liter bottle of Diet Pepsi..."

"In conclusion, Governor Wattle supports the death penalty because he believes it is Constitutional, that it saves lives, that it punishes murderers, and that it can act as a discouragement to others who would willingly take the lives of others... The governor believes, of course, in the absolute importance of executing only guilty men, and in the case

---

* Saunders had long proclaimed he had "nothing to do" with the killings, but as his scheduled execution drew closer he finally admitted to organizing and encouraging the bloodbath by his gang pals and began to plead for mercy, claiming he had seen the light and had decided to devote his life to helping the poor, stupid and criminal overcome their conditions and join the religion of Christianity. He had gone on to form a number of prison prayer groups and to author several well-received books for children and teenagers explaining the "dangers of gangs." Despite his numerous good works, he was executed as planned. – ED.

of Mr. Walker, there is no doubt, reasonable or otherwise, that he is guilty of terrible crimes... It does not give the governor any joy to put men to death, but he believes it is a solemn duty that he is Constitutionally obligated to carry out..."

Marty's name showed up on list of those allowed to watch them zap Tex live. I was an unhappy clown. I would have to watch the TV.

"Don't worry," said Marty, "I'll give you some good inside poop for your piece."

"Thanks, Marty. I guess I can fake it..."

Tex was never investigated for involvement in the house fire that killed his mother and uncle. He was instead sent to a series of "homes" and "institutions" operated by the state or religious groups.

According to the psychologists, who interviewed many of the workers who looked after Tex during this time, Tex was a somewhat unusual youth who was fascinated by fire and had an odd propensity to "find" dead dogs and cats. When Tex was 18, his friend Joey Poggan apparently slipped off a rock and fell 80 yards to his death in a box canyon below. Tex told investigators he was on the other side of the rock and hadn't seen anything.

At the age of 19, Tex decided to join the U.S. Marines and actually managed to pass the physical and psychological tests. The official military paperwork noted Tex's "slightly higher than average intelligence," but said the young man suffered from a "lack of discipline and stability." The recruiters were hopeful that Tex stood a "good chance of benefitting from the rigors of the Marine environment."

Tex was discharged from the Marines after less than a year due to "bizarre and disruptive behavior," according to the psychologists. Tex had apparently developed a fondness for inspecting the genitalia of his fellow Marine Corpsmen, resulting in a series of fights in which Tex suffered several broken bones and, in one case, internal bleeding. Tex also received a series of punishments from the Marine commandants after being blamed for starting at least six fires in trash cans and dumpsters on the base.

After leaving the Marines, Tex received a large tattoo on his stomach. It showed a frog drinking from a beer bottle. Tattoos of a cobra on his left bicep, and a leopard on his right, soon followed, as did more than a dozen "figure-8" tattoos of varying design on his arms, legs and hands.

Tex lived for at least the next several years with Franklin "Franky" Hogue, a maker of chicken feed in Lakeview County. Hogue was a known alcoholic and a paroled molester of boys as young as three. Hogue was found dead in 1976 with multiple stab wounds and three plastic bags over his head. Tex, who had relocated to Reedsport, Oregon, by the time the body was found, was never questioned in connection with the death.

Tex apparently spent the next few years "wandering," according to the authorities. Investigators found evidence showing he had logged time in Hollywood, Florida, as well as Louisiana, Montana, New Mexico, Vancouver and Salt Lake City. Eventually, though, he returned to Lakeview County and took a series of handyman and driver jobs with the school district and local businesses. Investigators never determined how he acquired the more than $40,000 in cash with which he purchased the farmland property, but burglary or robbery was suspected.

"Listen, Marty," I said as we drove to the Inca Hotel, where would be staying the night, "this thing's gonna get over too late to stop at a bar afterwards. Let's hit a store and get few bottles for the hotel... I'm gonna need something."

"Yeah," said Marty, "a couple bottles, why not... This is my first execution, too. Let's blow the roof off when this thing is over, me and you. I'll have to write a think-piece for Sunday's paper, but I can do it Saturday morning."

"Sounds good, Marty."

"My wife won't care if I have few drinks, not after this thing... Yeah, let's get a bottle or two."

Marty pulled the Subaru into a Safeway. I picked out the largest bottle of Jameson's, while Marty, after some deliberation, grabbed a jug of Equinox Dry. I added a flask of Rossini, the medium-size one, and we agreed on an 18-case of Bud Ice in cans. We threw in a couple large bags of chips and cheese puffs.

Court hearings forced police to admit that Tex was the same "Tex" they had interviewed at least 24 times since 1981 in connection with a variety of homicide and missing persons cases. Police admitted Tex had passed at least three polygraph examinations during this period. Police admitted they never sought a search warrant for Tex's property, nor even requested that Tex submit to a voluntary vehicle search.

Tex responded, during the trial, by saying he had "worked" for the police, as well as the FBI and CIA. Tex said he was part of a "big network," and had enjoyed extensive contacts with government operatives from all the major agencies and even agencies that nobody had ever heard of...

The FBI admitted in court documents that Tex had in fact worked on contract for the Bureau as a "delivery driver" for "not more than 14 months" in 1984-85... but "under no circumstances," said the FBI, had he been "employed" by the Bureau...

Tex said he was innocent, that the whole thing was a "big mistake." Tex said he had lost track of how many people he had killed. Tex said he killed to save the world from nuclear bombs. Tex maintained there had not been a nuclear bomb explosion since he began killing. Tex said, however, that he had been unable to prevent Chernobyl because he had not killed when he should have. Tex said he had been able to prevent a number of earthquakes, however, because he had killed at the right time.

Tex went on to say that actually, he had been a "hit man" for the CIA, and that all his kills had been "targeted hits." Tex said the FBI had ordered him to kill as part of secret mind-control experiments. Tex claimed the CIA had been frying his brain with "rays" since he was in the Marines. Tex said he had been "set up" by the local police force to kill drug dealers, prostitutes and troublemakers whom they wanted to get rid of. Tex claimed he had received experimental drugs from FBI operatives, and had submitted to regular testing of the effects.

Tex said he didn't know why he had killed.

Tex apologized repeatedly to the families of his victims, but said he had been forced to kill in order to save a greater number of lives.

Tex reached an agreement with prosecutors to plead guilty for 58 killings. The cops said they were ready to continue the investigation and might be able to add maybe 20 more homicide charges.

The case came down to the sentencing phase. The defense attorneys said Tex should be allowed to avoid the death penalty "by reason of insanity." The state prosecutors said Tex had attempted to cover up his crimes and dispose of evidence and was "clearly not insane."

Prosecutor David Gilleland declared to the jury: "Ladies and gentlemen, Stephen Walker killed these people because he wanted to kill them. End of story. He covered up his crimes and did not report them to police because he understood that these acts were against the law, and he wanted to escape responsibility and not be held accountable. End of story. Ladies and gentlemen of the jury, it is your responsibility to hold Stephen Walker accountable here, in this courtroom today..."

The verdict came in: Not Insane.

The verdict made Tex angry. He denounced it through his attorneys as "unfair" and "unjust" because, among other things, Lawrence C. Olester, the Green Ripper Slayer, had only received life in Ohio after confessing to more killings (71) over a similar period of time.

For the past five years, Tex's lawyers had been fighting in court to overturn a regulation preventing male prisoners from wearing makeup. The State Equal Opportunity Commission had originally ruled that the Andersenville Supermax authorities were not guilty of "gender identity discrimination" by denying Tex access to eyeliner and lipstick. With that case still pending, Tex succeeded in changing his first name to Stephanie and had his attorneys file another suit to force the state to pay for sex-change surgery.

Tex's court-appointed lawyer, Barbara N. Clempstein, argued that the authorities were obligated to treat Tex's "gender identity crisis like any other medical condition." Clempstein argued that the state's refusal to pay for the operation violated Tex's Eighth Amendment right against cruel and unusual punishment. She brought into court experts who testified to their belief that the sex-change surgery was "medically necessary" for Stephanie Walker because, they said, he/she might try to commit suicide if he/she did not have it.

After an initial setback, the appeal went in Tex's favor, and Tex had accordingly received the mandatory psychotherapy, followed by injections of female hormones and laser hair removal from his chest, legs and pubic area, as well as unrestricted access to lipstick and eye shadow.

This had resulted in, among other things, larger Tex breasts. Prison authorities, however, refused to relent on the issue of male lipstick, and had in fact countersued to block the actual sex-change surgery, saying they could not condone any "elective surgery" that would increase the likelihood that Stephanie would become the target of sexual assaults by other inmates.

The case was still tied up in the district courts when Tex/Stephanie, now age 63, was rolled into the turquoise-tiled execution chamber, buckled to the gurney with eight yellow leather straps.

Justianne Hamandpour had landed Tex's final media interview.

CLOWN: *Tex, what can you possibly say to the families whom you have hurt? To those whose loved ones you have taken because of your* greed and overwhelming, grotesque perversity? What about the people, the people, the children, the little boys and girls, who will have to live with the legacy of your selfish, perverted crimes? Do you have any answer, Tex Walker? Do you have one single thing to say? I'm waiting, Tex Walker! Listen to me, Tex Walker! Do you have anything to say? I'm waiting!

Tex, who had ballooned to 365 pounds, according to prison officials, used one hand to rub his beard, the other to touch his left breast. His hair and beard were completely gray. His eyes were bloodshot, face bloated, mouth toothless. He spoke in a soft, slightly backwoodsy voice.

CLOWN: *Well, Justianne... you look lovely, by the way, I love what you've done with your hair... But you see, Justianne, nature is an interrelated field or continuum, no part of which can be separated from or valued above the rest...*

"I feel so much love," the execution chamber microphone caught Tex saying. "I'm ready for the final blessing..."

I wrote it down. Several hundred of us clowns were looking up at the auditorium screens, chewing nails and biting lips, hanging on each Tex-death phrase. Standing Room Only – clown crews and contingents catching chatterbox Tex/Stephanie on the final death crawl. We chewed gum and sucked breath-mints, sometimes gulping free coffee from the complimentary red, black and blue SUPERMAX® mugs ($8.99 in the prison gift shop) that prison staffers had distributed as we entered.

A team of medics walked up to the gurney and fastened the tubes into his arm. As they worked, Tex/Stephanie began to sing.

Silent night, holy night
All is calm, all is bright
Bound young virgin,
Mother and child

"That's disgusting!" said a clown to the left.

"Can't they make him *stop*?" said a panicked-looking Nathalie Q. Kacchnitz of *The New York Times*.

Several clowns began to boo.

"They've got to be *joking*," said a clearly outraged Bartolo Palaverman of *The Wall Street Journal*.

"This is *appalling*!" shouted Heanus Williams of *It's Tough-Tough Questions Time With Heanus Williams*.

Within 20 minutes, Williams would hit the international airwaves live to denounce the "disturbing spectacle that prison authorities had permitted to take place. Ladies and gentlemen, they allowed Tex Walker to have the last laugh. It was as if he had been allowed to kill again, and again, even in his own death chamber..."

Sleeeep in heavenly peeeeeeeeeeace
Sleeeeeeeeee

It was hard to tell from the TV screens, but Tex's eyes seemed to widen. He fell silent. The auditorium fell silent.

Tex's head rolled to the side, then suddenly jerked up, as if he was about to speak. His face made several contortions, a lengthy grimace. His Adam's apple bobbed up and down, up and down.

Finally he slumped. A doctor in a white smock and facemask came over, checked a few dials. He pulled a green bag over Tex/Stephanie's head.

> NEWSFLASH - URGENT
> ANDERSENVILLE – STEPHEN 'TEX' WALKER PUT TO DEATH FOR MURDERS OF 58

Clowns sat and wrote it up, or went live on TV and radio. Marty called me after about 15 minutes. He told me several family members had broken down tears as Tex sang. He told me Head Warden Orberndorfer had given the signal to the "anonymous executioner" by raising his eyeglasses to his forehead.

"Go ahead and use it if you want," said Marty. "We're all going to put it in."

"Thanks a lot, Marty."

I typed the tidbit into my final edit, then decided to take it out... It was useless. It was all useless. I shipped the piece over the phone.

I thought about the cigarette I would soon be smoking outside, and the booze I would soon be drinking at the hotel.

✪

"Hey, there... cheers," said Marty.

"You bet, Marty..."

I leaned over and we clinked our complimentary SUPERMAX® coffee mugs, which were now filled with Jameson's and hotel ice. Marty sat back on the couch. I was sitting at the table. It was about 3 a.m. I pulled from a beer, had a gulp of the Jameson's. Marty flicked around through the TV channels.

"I still got to write that think-piece for the *Sunday Outlook* section," said Marty. "They want it by eleven."

He was wearing a t-shirt and boxer shorts, shoes and socks off. He set an empty beer can on the table, gobbled a handful of cheese puffs. He got up to pour himself from the Equinox.

"This morning?"

"Yeah... They want to know *what it means*, you know? They won't even give me a minute to relax. They're never satisfied. They wouldn't be satisfied with Hemingway sending it in."

"Listen, I'll write it for you."

"Really?"

"Sure, Marty..."

I grabbed a napkin, scribbled HE'S DEAD and handed it to him.

Marty laughed, threw the napkin to the floor. He punched TV channels.

"Hey, what the heck's this? Says here, *Splooge Storage III*..."

Marty turned up the volume. A guy in a big black mustache reached back and slapped a woman in the face. She was on her knees, a red bow in her hair and her tits hanging out. The camera panned over her red latex boots.

The male seemed angry for some reason. He was a skinny little guy, frog legs and a stick for a neck.

Fuckin' slut... Suck it, you bitch!

The guy pulled her hair, slapped her again.

Oh yes, hit me! she whined. *Hit me! I've been so bad!*

He pulled her hair, smacked her again, the other cheek.

Oh yeah, she said, the slapped spot pinkening. *Oh... that... felt... good...*

She grabbed hold of his penis with both hands, put it in her mouth. They were in a big house somewhere – white leather couches, palm trees visible out the window.

A different guy came up, already naked. He got down on all fours and began to lick her asshole. As he did so, the camera showed a different woman crawling over. She bent apart this guy's cheeks and began to lick *his* bung. A third woman came up and attached her tongue to the second woman's ass...

It seemed assholes had never tasted so good. Pretty soon, everyone was licking assholes, except for those women who had penises in their mouths.

"My God, shit," said Marty, reaching for a corn chip. "Shit, my God..."

The males stood and slammed their penises into the throats of the females. The males seemed to be having difficulty, however, they could not seem to get very hard. Their penises bent backward slackly, or fell toward the floor when they happened to slip out of the mouths dripping with saliva. The penises also appeared small, embarrassingly small – I had really expected much bigger.

Something was badly wrong. We had a right to see bigger cocks than this. Much bigger. We had the right to demand them as big as trombones.

Spare females crawled around, looking for assholes to lick and penises to suckle. The males grabbed the sides of the females' heads and pulled them forward, forcing them to choke and gag upon their penises.

Urf, went the females as they gagged, *urf... urf-urf... urf...*

Their faces turned red, the females were needing air. One by one they succeeded in spitting out the half-hard penis, huffing in a breath, then grabbing for the penis and gulping it back down.

Urf, oh, urf-urf... that's so good! said one, gasping for breath. *Oh, it's so big, big... urf... urf-urf...*

She lied. It was small.

"Jesus, don't tell my wife!" said Marty. He giggled.

"Sure, Marty..."

Marty swirled his index finger around in his glass, had a guzzle of Equinox. His arm jerked out for the bag of cheese puffs.

"My God, I've never seen it like this! Have you?"

"Never, Marty..."

Oh yeah, I love it hard, urf... urf-urf... (GAGGING)... urf...

Five or six guys had surrounded the woman, slapping her face with their barely hard penises.

I love it tough, urf... Oh, fuck yeah... urf-urf... give it to me... I've been such a bad girl, urf... (GAGGING)... urf-urf...

"Lookit there," said Marty, "she's got one tit bigger than the other. I swear she does! Those tits don't look real to me... Do they? What do you think?"

"They look like bowling balls, Marty..."

"Yeah, they do! Bowling balls, ha, that's funny!"

Oh, oh... Yes, I want three big, big men to fuck me... please, please, please give it to me... Oh, oh... urf-urf... urf... (GAGGING)*... urf-urf...*

"Jesus, they're really reaming her!" said Marty, cheese puff crumbs falling from the corners of his mouth and on to his T-shirt front. "Jesus, would you look at that... They've got her in every hole! Goddamn it, the fuck! They're gonna rip her in half!"

A guy groaned and ejaculated into a woman's rectum. A second woman ran over and sucked up the semen as it oozed out of the first woman's anus, taking care to slurp up each bit, sticking her tongue into the anus for good measure. She then took the semen and dripped it into a third woman's mouth. The two women French-kissed, smearing the sperm over their lips and cheeks and finally blowing bubbles with it.

"Ha-ha!" said Marty.

Equinox Club jumped from the jug, into his glass, out on to the table. He filled it back up.

"Jesus, my wife would kill me if she knew I was watching this..."

I woke up about noon and lit a cigarette. The TV was still on.

I like it rough, really rough ... gimme your cock... um, um, I love it... urf-urf...

Marty was passed out in a chair in front of his laptop.

I looked at his screen. He had written a headline: JUSTICE FINALLY ACHIEVED IN WALKER CASE?

I shook him.

"Marty... Hey, Marty... You really should finish your thing..."

DADDY KNOWS WORST: Clown Cowers as Father Flounders!

★ 43 ★

The phone rang. It was my father.

"I just called your mother and apologized for everything, son... I asked her to forgive me."

"Oh, wow."

"She gave me your number, I hope you don't mind... Son, I'm calling to tell you that I've checked into the treatment center... I apologize to you, son. Please forgive me."

"For what?"

His voice sounded thick and crispy. Slow, tired, draped over with a rehearsed, attempted humility.

My father was a big smart man, several years of college at several colleges. Married five times, a real master of the personal three-ring circus. Stuff so funny you could laugh until your guts broke... but my father had never quite seemed to understand the joke.

I had been seventeen the last time I had allowed him to whack me upside the head. I had laughed inappropriately at something his wife had said, or failed to react quickly enough to a demand to toss the kitchen trash, I'm still not sure.

At one point, my father had been heavily into golfing. At one point, he had been heavily into poker. At one point, he had been heavily into cars, owning a red Corvette Stingray, steel blue Trans Am and a mid-size truck. At one point, he had been heavily into motor-boating. At one point, he had been heavily into fishing. At one point, he had been heavily into baking with all-natural ingredients. At one point, he had been very much into marrying teenaged girls. At one point, he had been very heavily into fast-pitch softball. At one point, he had been heavily into painting ceramics. At one point, he had been heavily into plants, soil and greenhouses. At one point, he had been heavily into collecting the records of Bob Dylan.

At one point, he had very heavily been into owning restaurants. He had owned and lost, owned and lost, many restaurants. He had made and lost, made and lost, many restaurant fortunes. It was never because of what he himself had done. It was just that people were always "screwing" him over – "business partners," mainly, as well as cooks and waitresses who shot drugs, stole and got high off cans of whipped cream.

At one point, he told the court that he could not pay more than $150 per month to my mother in child support. He was "barely making it" as it was. My mother cried to the judge, as instructed by her lawyer, said there was no money for new shoes. But it hadn't helped. The judge looked over my father's paperwork, nodded. My father walked out, drove off in his rental car, flew back to Idaho or wherever.

At one point, my father had telephoned our old house, only to be told by Webster that my mother had left him and moved us to my grandmother's – nine or ten months before. Webster was very sad. My father was very sad. Webster gave my father my grandmother's phone number. Webster and my father had held a "good heart-to-heart," according to my father.

After I turned 13, I saw him about once or twice a year. He'd roar up outside our house in his Trans Am, slide out and put a white boot on the front tire. His hair would be freshly permed, a big silver watch on his wrist.

"You playin' baseball?" he'd crack in a whisky-soaked voice.

"Um… no."

"Why the fuck not?"

"Uh, nobody signed us up?"

"Your mom didn't sign you up? Shit. That's why I fucking send her all that money every month."

"I guess she forgot."

"Is your aunt still in jail?"

"No, I think she got out."

"What about Tonto?'

"Still in, I think…"

"Is your aunt living here now?"

"No," I would say, beginning to cry.

"Is your mom dating again?"

"I don't know... Maybe."

He'd laugh. "Shit, must take time to find a rich one..."

I got up and walked around the room, carrying the phone in my hand. A clump of worms slid down the wall, fell to the carpet. I went over and stepped on them. My father went on with his speech.

"As you know, son, I have had many problems..."

Out the window, across the street, I saw a little guy wearing long shorts and a white baseball cap. He came up to an apartment building, pulled the door handle. Locked, apparently. The guy went down the stairs, turned, went to the next place on the block. He went up and pulled. Locked. He went down the stairs...

I heard my father flick a lighter, inhale and exhale from a cigarette.

"I wasn't, uh, I wasn't a good father to you or your brother. I have to tell you that. It's all connected with why I'm here today in the treatment center, son. My parents never taught me how to behave properly... They had many problems, they never dealt with them, and so they transferred them to me. It's the basis of my problems... But it's not their fault, it's mine. I alone am completely responsible. No one else. I have to accept that... We all have problems, son... So here I am. This is what I must do, tell you these things. It's an important part of the healing and treatment process."

The guy went to the next door. Locked. He went down the stairs, up the next set. He pulled. It opened. He went in.

"Gayle had to go to the hospital, son... She stayed the night... She told them I hit her."

"Did you?"

I found a pack of smokes, lit one.

Gayle was wife number five. The few times I had met her, she seemed to have a wine glass permanently attached to her hand. Her background was in Utah or somewhere like that, and she had worked for many years officially selling alcohol for the state of Idaho. One of her daughters was a stripper whose six-month-old son, Chase, had been taken away by the child-welfare people after she passed out and collapsed on to the floor of a bus. The police found meth and crack in her pockets and took her to jail. My father and Gayle had failed in an attempt to get custody of the kid – it was apparently living with the parents of the father, who was in jail for a number of criminal offenses.

Gayle's other daughter was a stripper who had gone on to receive a mail-order pharmacology degree. She allegedly now worked filling prescriptions at Rite-Mart. One of her former boyfriends had been arrested on suspicion of murdering a prostitute. He had denied any involvement. She had denied any involvement. She had never been indicted. This daughter was the "good one" – never caught for anything except "stealing" from my father and his wife and crashing their car.

"I remember being angry with Gayle, son, very angry, but I do not recall everything that she told the police. I apparently broke the window and cut my hand... I do understand that I have a problem with my anger, especially if I have been drinking."

"O.K..."

"I was drinking too much, and she made me angry by not bringing the right food I had asked for at Taco Town. I spent two days in jail, son."

"That's not so bad."

"She hasn't dropped the charges yet. She has said she might if I complete the treatment program... We are trying to work it out. We love each other. I don't know if we will. It's slow and hard, but we are trying."

"That's good."

My father's wife number four had been the "intellectual" – Bonnie, with the twin masters from the University of Minnetonka and Oxford. She had read texts in the original Greek and knew all about X-ray telescopes, and despite my dad having a restaurant, she never seemed to eat food. From what I could gather, she had been fond of sunsets and twisting pine needles into Christmas ornaments, as well as booze and flip-outs. It was another perfect match, my father had claimed, and Bonnie had run off with a bricklayer after two and a half years.

Wife number three, Tammy, had married my father a year or two after she graduated from high school, where she had been head cheerleader. "My teen bride," my father had enjoyed telling anybody who would listen. They had met at a car rally in Idaho. Tammy liked to drink and dance on tables, and her mother had accused my father of various crimes and sued for control of the two restaurants he'd had at the time (he had apparently borrowed money from her). She ended up getting one of them.

Wife number two, Annie, was a blond who'd had two daughters by two different men. One of the men had died from an "overdose," the other was in prison. My father had adopted both daughters, and after the divorce (Annie had run off with a drummer), he hadn't seen them for 15 years.

Number one had been my mother – they'd met at a dance at my father's Catholic high school.

"Son, what's going on – where are you working? Are you still at the phone company?"

"No. I told you the last time – I work for Cities News Services."

"Oh, that's right. It's the news? Son, you should, for your own future's sake –"

"My future?"

My father's lighter flicked.

"I know. I'm sorry, son, I, I'm sorry... My back has been hurting me. They don't let me have anything for it right now. It's painful, but I can make it..."

"O.K."

"I'd like to help you, son, but I'm $85,000 in debt..."

"I don't need any help."

"Every month the creditors keep asking for more... I don't have it..." He tried to laugh. "I can't even buy a used car right now. As soon as I get out of here, I'll have to declare bankruptcy. That's a good law, son. Those a-holes will have to stop. Bankruptcy gives you a chance to rest up and make a fresh start."

I kept watching the door. The little guy never came out.

I saw what looked like a woman's bra laying in the gutter. It was tan in color, dark where it had gotten wet from the gutter scum.

I lit another smoke.

Out the window to the right, something was hunched over, man or woman, it wasn't clear, digging through a trash bin. It threw plastic wrap and cans, milk cartons, on to the cement. An old man walked by slowly, limping on a crutch.

A worm fell from the ceiling on to my wrist. I flicked him on to the coffee table, picked up the lighter and smashed the greasy sucker with the flat end.

"Son, I do believe that everything happens for a reason. You and me and your brother, your mother... I really do believe that."

"What's the reason?"

"I'm sorry?"

"What's the reason?"

"Well... God's will, I guess you could call it..."

"God's will?"

"Yes, I think so. Otherwise, it... it... it wouldn't be. Do you see? Maybe you'll understand in time, son. We all need time... Well, that's all for now. I've got to get back, there's a meeting almost every hour here... I'm proud of you, son... I'll try to call again. Goodbye."

STUDY: AMERICANS MORE MENTALLY ILL
By Nelson M. Nabytek

BOSTON (AIP) – A new study published in The Journal of the American Medical Foundation has found there is more mental illness and insanity in the United States than in other developed societies.

The study, led by Dr. Harold Maucher of the Harvard-A.L. Sloney Medical School, found evidence showing that 32.8 percent of people in the United States suffer from medically-diagnoseable mental problems and personality disorders, including schizophrenia, depression and bipolar mania.

This is contrasted against 6.3 percent in Denmark, 8.2 percent in Italy, 10.9 percent in France, 13.7 percent in Canada, 21.6 percent in Germany and 28.9 percent in Britain.

In published comments accompanying the study, Maucher said "concerns for the future well-being of the world are understandable considering that nearly one-third of the people in the most powerful nation have genuine mental problems."

The study cites statistics showing that:

★ One percent of the American population holds nearly 50 percent of the country's wealth, while one in every five American adults lives in poverty. This is contrasted to Italy, one of the world's biggest and wealthiest economies, where just one adult in 15 lives in poverty.

★ The United States spent $581 billion in known military expenditures last year (not counting the costs of the nation's numerous wars themselves) – more than the combined total military spending of the next 32 most powerful nations. Wars and the military-industrial establishment have become a cornerstone of the U.S. economy, with their influence affecting the structure of society and the activity of people and businesses in every state of the nation, according to the study.

★ The United States accounts for less than five percent of the world's population, yet is responsible for 25 percent of the world's prison inmates.

★ There are an average of 2.4 murder-suicides each day in the United States – by far the highest rate of any developed country. This, according to the study, is a "clear indication of a society that is increasingly dysfunctional and brutal."

★ American workers are given, on average, just 12 days of vacation per year, compared to 39 days in France, 27 in Germany, and 21 in Canada.

The study said evidence indicates American insanity is due in part to a gene pool "fouled" by the heavy early migration of criminals and Puritans, the latter of whom were described as "mentally-disturbed religious fanatics whose influence is still felt in myriad ways."

"Americans live in a society dominated by giant multinational corporations, in a system that subordinates all human needs to the accumulation of personal wealth," the report said.

"An almost unrestrained admiration for greed infuses American culture. At the same time, the average American works more but is paid less than his cohorts in other developed nations. Despite the average American's high rate of labor productivity, wage growth has remained depressed for decades. The majority of ordinary Americans thus find themselves continually grasping for a level of material success that is beyond their rational means. The result is an ever-more unstable society, with growing numbers of Americans being diagnosed with mental illness or resorting to alcohol and drug abuse, which have their own associated pathologies and negative societal impacts."

The study added: "In tune with an increasingly mentally-ill society, America's leaders are demonstrably the most war-mongering on the planet. They appear bent on a course of foreign policy blundering and fiscal mismanagement that is almost certain to lead to bankruptcy and the irreversible decline, if not total impoverishment, of the nation and its people. The

U.S. population, crippled by its mental illness and made impotent by conglomerate control of the mass media, appears incapable of offering any meaningful resistance when their politicans nonsensically announce the start of another overseas war in the 'interests of peace and free markets,' but which only serves to further endanger the future livelihood of the average American citizen."

PECULIAR: Drunken Genius Writer Invades Police Party!

★ 44 ★

I made a coffee, removed the last beer from the fridge. I drank the beer first, then the cooled coffee. I finished the coffee, went down the block and got another six of the beer.

I took off my shoes, sat on the couch. I put *Order of the Leech* on the stereo, picked up the paperback and tried another time with *Sister Carrie*.

"Half the undoing of the unsophisticated and natural mind is accomplished by forces wholly superhuman," the author had written.

Order of the Leech sawed back and forth, cruel and savage, bitter. Over and over, the musicians worked to build a clear, wide avenue, only to savagely hack it off, leaving the outline of a terrible and disturbing memory.

Sister Carrie chimed in: "A woman should some day write the complete philosophy of clothes…"

The complete? Oh, yes indeed.

Order of the Leech left another pile of chopped thumbs on the floor.

Sister Carrie was having problems. I flipped to the last page: "It is when the feet weary and hope seems vain that the heartaches and the longings arise. Know, then, that for you is neither surfeit nor content. In your rocking-chair, by your window dreaming, shall you long, alone. In your rocking-chair, by your window, shall you dream such happiness as you may never feel."

Yes, completely. Well, if it didn't totally explain the birth of country and the blues…

Pretty soon all the drinks were gone. I tossed the book, locked up and went down to Verdugo. I passed an old woman sitting on the ground, wrapped in a dirty pink blanket. Her feet were tied with string and newspapers. She was singing.

The judge don't wear no underwear, the doctor don't have no nurse... The judge don't wear...

I threw a quarter in her bucket.

I decided to head over to Jackson Square Park, where the much-promoted police festival, We're Winning The War Against Crime, had gotten under way. I sauntered in under the sunlight, a thousand red and white balloons wafting through the skies.

A couple dozen people were standing in the main square, waiting in lines for free hot dogs and ice cream. The police and city government had set up stalls on all sides: LEARN TO LOOK FOR SUSPICIOUS BEHAVIOR SAFETY IS SECURITY BE YOUR OWN ANTI-DRUG. On the southeast corner, cops were teaching kids judo, gently flipping youngsters on to foam mats. Kids posed for free pictures with Deputy Ruff-Ruff and the Firefighter Fanatic. A clown in makeup and a pouffy white and blue costume walked around on stilts, juggling basketballs and tossing them into a hoop as kids shrieked...

Over on the north, packs of teenagers gawked in front of the U.S. military booth, where a buzz-cut Marine was doing one-arm pull-ups with his shirt off. JOIN THE ARMY OF FREEDOM. I stood there a few minutes, watching a number of boys take their turns. A couple squeezed off one or two, but most couldn't make one. Then a skinny girl jumped up and did twelve without a problem. The Marine raised her arm and handed her a yellow and red T-shirt.

An armored cop van sat off to the side, canvas banner fluttering: AMNESTY. TURN IN GUNS HERE. NO QUESTIONS ASKED. Two cops sat at a table beneath the banner, laughing and playing cards.

At the end of the square, several sets of bleachers had been erected. I helped myself to a free MacBeefy's strawberry syrup drink and took a seat.

A high school marching band paraded past, piping away on "Low Rider." Overweight teens with multiple chins and horrible haircuts sat like rows of ducks, chomping through bags of chips and hot dogs.

Delegations of high honchos and retired flatfoots walked by, many wearing ancient cop or military uniforms. Another high school band went past, piping away monstrously on "Heard It Through the Grapevine." A full-dress delegation bearing a banner reading AFRICAN-AMERICAN AND LATINO COPS FOR PEACE & TRANQUILITY strutted by, flashing peace signs. It was followed by about 20 cops representing the CHRISTIAN, JEWISH AND ISLAMIC LAW OFFICERS FOR DRUG-FREE YOUTH. Kids scrambled down from the stands as an enthusiastic officer from the GAY AND TRANSGENDERED POLICE FOR PEACE ON OUR STREETS did cartwheels and tossed handfuls of foil-covered chocolate coins.

I sat there and called Jerry, but got no answer.

I was thirstier than ever. I walked to a market across the street and got a 40-ouncer in a bag. I meandered about on the boulevard, taking long quaffs.

On the stairs leading to the Barnett Avenue Station, I noticed a guy with his thing sticking out of his jeans. He was in the corner, between a phone booth and the newspaper stand, jerking himself off. Guy with a leather jacket and paisley yellow bandanna wrapped around his head, pleased as all punch at the splendor of riches. Commuters walked by and lowered their eyes, some of their faces wrenched in fright from the horror.

I thought briefly about going down there and throwing my bottle at his head. Instead, I turned down the alley to take a piss, stepping through weeds and trash and cardboard boxes up to my knees. I crunched over paper and various broken objects, kept walking. At one point, a hairy mass raised up and pawed at my ankle.

"Hey, I'm sleepin' here!"

I kicked free, spilling beer on my shoes and shorts.

"Oh, sorry..."

At the other end of the block, a guy in a white t-shirt was sitting on his haunches, one arm jutting out, staring at the street. I came up from behind, passing on his right. It was then that I noticed the hypodermic needle sticking out of the crook of his arm. It was drooping down out of the arm, hanging, pulling a little skin with it. He squatted there, blissed to high hell. I thumped his knee and he fell to the ground, saying nothing, the needle still in his arm...

Music boomed from the park. I headed back, stepping over a curb littered with smashed plastic and cassette tape ribbon. Under a giant magnolia tree, a white-haired man in glasses was bent over, hands on his knees, watching feces exit the asshole of a little red wolf-dog. The dog finished his business, scratched his feet excitedly against the grass. The old man beamed, delightfully thrilled.

I pushed through the throng, saw Bo Diddley on the stage.

"Good Lord made us, didn't nobody make theyselves," said Bo. The band launched into "Road Runner."

I walked along the edge of the crowd, pushing down toward the stage. Bo Diddley stroked his guitar, ju-ju noises floating out of the speakers. Bo was wearing a black cowboy hat, a yellow skull dangling from a chain around his neck. Members of Bo Diddley's band wore long black shirts, white carnations and yellow shoes. From the bass player's neck swung beads and a black crucifix, five or six inches long.

A dog in a choke-chain collar walked up and sniffed my knee. I lit a smoke. A guy with a tan bandage around his head came up and offered to trade me a food stamp dollar for a smoke. He was missing several teeth. I gave him two, put the food buck in my back pocket.

Bo Diddley said, "I don't feel so good, but I do feel like a boogie..."

I made my way out of the crowd, exited the square, crawled into a small stand of bushes. I vomited, several heaves worth, then rolled over and lay there on the leaves. I could feel bits of spider web floating down on to my face.

I don't know how long I stayed there. I may have even dozed off for a while.

When I finally rolled out from under, the sun had begun to set and the park was much more crowded. Throngs of gang bwoys and bitches walked around in bad clothes.

A rapper and his obese sidekick had taken the stage. The pipsqueak jumped around in gigantic basketball shoes, swayed back and forth, tried to roar threateningly into the mic. The obese, goateed sidekick issued various noises from his computers, the beat thudding and squeaking along.

Hell no, won't give my blood for oil
There's already war on this here soil
Jack the po-lice with my .22 clip-clip
His blood on the wall
It go a-drip-drip-a-drip

It seemed like a trap. This would be good place for the police to drop a bomb and set everyone's hair on fire. They were probably already photographing everybody.

I clawed my way out of there, went across the street to the Golden Pump, started having a few. On the third one, I found myself wondering what it was *exactly* that Gene Keaks had said about Lincoln and Kennedy... That Kennedy was killed while being driven in a Lincoln... that Lincoln's secretary was called Kennedy, something like this.

It seemed of major importance. What was it – *exactly?* I got out the phone and dialed. Gene's answering service picked up.

I dialed Jerry again, but got nothing. Probably left his phone at home, I figured. I called information and got Candace and Heather's number. Candace picked up.

"Candace? Hi – i-i-i-i-s, it's – ah, is H-H-Heather there?"

"*Heather?* Get lost, Thor... I have no idea where Jerry is, either."

"I just –"

"*I'm fucking busy!*" She hung up.

I dialed Jerry again, Gene again, my brother, Jerry again, Chrissy, my brother again... No pick-ups.

I walked the 10 or so blocks up to the Ding-A-Ling, took a seat at the bar, ordered a beer and a shot. The corner television rolled footage of landscapes several feet under water, submerged cars, floating refrigerators, water-logged dogs and cats, cops waving guns, people weeping...

BREAKING: FLOODS RAVAGE AMERICA'S HEARTLAND

CLOWN: *It seems these poor people have lost everything, Brian... There's no sanitation or water supplies in the Superdome, and the hallways are full of, um, well, the police are calling it human waste... We've heard reports of rape and assaults, gangs roaming about on rafts, attacking people, prisoners escaping because the guards have run off, sharks in the floodwaters because the aquariums have spilled over... The government appears helpless at the moment to do anything, to help these people, though officials have assured us they are working as hard as they can, it should only be a matter of hours before help arrives...*

BREAKING: AMERICAN HEARTLAND DROWNING

A guy wearing a brown plaid cap and plastic white jacket walked up. He clapped me on the back of the shoulders.

"Hey... You lookin' for some *pussy*, man?"

"No, I – just – I –"

He grinned, smacked me on the back. He leaned in close, whiskers an inch or so from my face. He smelled like wine and cologne. He winked.

"I said... are you lookin' for some *pussy*, man?"

"No, I – I mean, I –"

He rocked back on his heels, raised his arms, pointing his hands at himself.

"How you want it, man? Fifteen about right? Sixteen? You know what? I can do that..."

"Uh, I –"

"Fourteen? Huh? What? *Thirteen*?"

He shook his head, grinned, pointed a finger.

"Aw, you... Then *I'm* takin' a risk, see? That'll cost extra. You got it or what? Or *what*, man?"

"I just, uh – I just, uh –"

"C'mon, somethin' wrong, man? All I asked was if you wanted some *pussy*... You got a problem with that? Or *what*?"

"No, I, you know – I just – I –"

"You lookin' to get high? Is that it? You wanna get *high*, man?"

"No, I – I just – I was –"

"So what you *want* then, man? I'm gettin' tired now. Just *tell* me. Come on, you can do it, I know you can... Just *tell* me what you *want*."

"I just, I – I – you know, I –"

He grinned, pointed his finger.

"Yeah, I know... You *know* I know..."

He grinned and walked off.

After a while, the president appeared on the television. He was decked out in a space shuttle suit, complete with helmet, visor down.

MNUNG: AMERICA IS STRONG

The president gestured, gloved hands moving about in circular motions. The barkeep hit the remote, but still no noise came out. The barman climbed a stool. He pressed the volume button on the TV, but still nothing.

CLOWN: *There must be some problem with the transmission... Can you hear me, Washington? Stand by, ladies and gentlemen... There appears to be a problem with the presidential feed...*

"What the hell is this crap?" a guy said. He walked out.

MNUNG: AMERICA IS STRONG

I had another two or three, stumbled out. I had the phone in my hand. It was Sernath's voice in my ear.

"Thor, you sound drunk –"

"Fuck... you!"

"O.K, I'll let it pass, this time... But listen, either go home and sober up, or get your rear end into another bar. Right now! Stop wasting the company's money calling me names..."

"Fuck... you!"

"O.K., this is your last chance... Everybody's got a right to get drunk from time to time... You work hard, you're a good man. Wish I could be out there with you telling everyone how much and where to pay it. O.K.? Have one for me... *But get off this goddamn phone right now!"*

I clicked off, tears running down my cheeks. Lights whirled, cars screamed past. There was a tremendous roar as dozens of motorcyclists weaved through the intersection. The motorcyclists were wearing colorful monkey suits, shiny colorful leather jumpsuits. They gunned their motors, doing little wheelies as they threaded their way through cars lined up at the light.

I found a store, bought a bottle of King Saiga Vodka for $6.95. I walked back out and entered Francis Perkins Park through the gate at Longfellow. I stood under a tree, watching a boys' flag football practice. The coach blew his whistle and shouted, "That's twenty-five!" The boys fell down as one and began grinding out push-ups.

Clouds mottled the sky, it started to drizzle. I took the long way through the park, under the trees along the bicycle paths, finally cutting through the Cactus Garden.

At last I hit Chandler, the car headlights a fantastic blur. I stood for I don't know how long under a music store awning across from the Monarch Theatre. People came, went. Cars drove up, stopped, drove away.

I crossed the street and stood on the walk just out of range of the spotlights. At one point, a beautiful blond in a white dress walked out of the theatre, leading a boy with Down's Syndrome to a silver Volvo. They got in the back seat and the car pulled away.

I finished the Saiga, set the bottle on the sidewalk. I went into a store, put nine dollars on the counter, walked out twisting the cap on another bottle.

The sky was gray and I was laying on the wet grass. The sock on my right foot was soaked.

Chrissy threw my shoe. It landed on the sidewalk with a clunk. Blue and orange lights circled in mish-mash patterns on top of a cop car. Chrissy walked away from the cops.

"Thor, the taxi's here... Don't come back here, O.K.? Don't make me make them arrest you..."

I got up, spun dizzy, grabbed for the shoe.

I staggered into the street. One cop took me by the arm, leaned me against the car. The other had a camera. He snapped my picture.

The cop led me to the taxi. He opened the door and I got in.

"Bless you," said the taxi man. "She nice lady, your friend. The police told me I tell you they give the people in jail only one condom for every one day. They make sure that I say you..."

He drove me down the hill.

POPE: ISLAM IN 'GUTTER,' MUSLIMS 'FAGGOTS'

VATICAN CITY (AIP) – Pope Bartolomiew Agnew Funicello XIX on Sunday called Muslims "evil faggot terrorists who try to spread by the sword the insane, gutter religion they preach."

In his weekly lecture in St. Peter's Basilica, the 76-year-old head of the Roman Catholic Church spoke favorably of Islam's repression of women, but said that when one studies the Islamic faith, "one finds only an unreasoning, blasphemous, hypocritcal hierarchy unworthy of even dogs. It is an unholy form of madness and pestilence that our forbears rightly sought to exterminate."

The pontiff concluded: "We must adhere ardently to our supreme values of faith and intellectual rigor as divinely-created beings endowed with the ethos of the Creator... Not to act reasonably, with logos, is inhuman and contrary to the nature of God."

Reacting to the pope's statement, more than 1,000 Islamic clerics and scholars, meeting in Lahore, Pakistan, burned an effigy of the pontiff and warned in a statement that "Bartolomiew and all infidels, Americans and Zionists face severe consequences such as those suffered by the infidel Theo van Gogh and Danish cartoonists for making insulting remarks against the Prophet and Allah."

The Muslim Association of Obedient Esteemed Islamic Scholars added in its final communique: "The pope should be removed from his position and immediately put on trial for encouraging war and fanning hostility among peaceful faiths... No Muslim, under any circumstances, can tolerate an insult to the Prophet Muhummad. Western people should be prepared to face the ultimate punishment for transgressing against the one true religion."

SHE TALKS TO ANGELS: Funeral for All-American Sweetheart

"I SAID TURN OFF THE LIGHTS!"

I flipped them back off, went into the kitchen, opened another beer.

Jerry had been the last 25 minutes in front of the bathroom mirror, hair dryer blowing in his face. He seemed to like it that way, blowing the hair dryer in his face with the lights off in front of the bathroom mirror.

He came out after about 10 more minutes. He sat on the couch in the near-darkness, began picking and scratching at his guitar. He had the thing wired into his amp, notched over to full volume. He howled it out like his balls were being murdered, the guitar making horrible squeaking and scraping noises.

Let the good times roll
Let them knock you around
Let the good times roll
Let them make you a clown...

The fall had come, the chestnuts were dropping. We had got back from Heather's funeral earlier in the afternoon. I didn't bother to see the body, wasn't too interested in it anymore. Jerry said they had put her in a wig, tried to make her like she looked before. He said it hadn't worked.

The pre-service song selection had included "With or Without You," "Imagine," "Yesterday," "Wish You Were Here" and "Amazing Grace." A selection of framed photos had been placed on the table – Heather graduating high school... girl Heather dressed as a pirate for Halloween... Heather in front of Big Ben... Heather at the pyramids... Heather laying on top of a limousine... Heather learning to scuba dive... Heather in a hospital gown with all her hair gone, smiling sweetly and looking beautiful...

The preacher said Heather had been a nice girl. She'd had some difficult times, of course, but she had believed in world peace. She had liked to have fun. She could be smart and knowledgeable. She had talent, she was going to school and thinking about a possible career as a publicist. She had loved the children, had planned on having her own kids. She had wanted her own little house on the beach. She had liked to play tennis. She had taken guitar lessons. She loved peanut butter on toast, with sunflower seeds sprinkled on top. She had liked crispy rice squares. She had liked filet mignon, rare. She had been a fun-loving girl with a good heart...

Candace and her mother bawled. Mommy squeezed the hand of her boyfriend, a muscular puffy-haired fellow who apparently worked as a dog acupuncturist. They had met when Arnie, the chihuahua long hair, had come down with serious back pain. It was a weekly treatment, then twice a week, then much more. The fellow had done wonders with the dog, Jerry quoted Candace as saying.

Candace and Heather's father had brought along his personal masseuse/assistant, a tall brunette in lip gloss and a black pantsuit. She had apparently played basketball at UCLA about 10 years ago. She had been assisting Phil with his whole-body rejuvenation, wrinkle-treatment, prostate massage, hair restoration and lip implants. She had done wonders for Phil's back, according to Jerry, quoting Candace.

The preacher told a story about Jesus on the cross.

"If Jesus said He would remember the thief, then surely He will not forget about our Heather. We can take comfort in knowing that her destiny is the most good place of all the most good places..."

Candace and her mother bawled. I didn't pay much attention to the rest.

Afterwards, Chrissy had swept up soundlessly from behind and touched my shoulder. Her cheeks glowed with pinkness, mouth red and full, eyes a bright blue-green. Her hair tumbled well past her collar, long and slightly tousled. If there was a flaw, and there might not have been, it might've only been the smallest smudge of lipstick on one of her front teeth. In any case, it was only the smallest of smudges.

"Thor, hi..."

"Chrissy, I, uh –"

She brought a finger to her lips. "No talking. I just wanted to say 'hi.'"

"Sure..."

I stood there. She turned and walked off with some guy who looked like a grizzly bear, but more hairy.

Well, it was all over. So long, sweethearts. We'll see you next time.

✪

Let them leave you up in the air
 Let them brush your rock 'n roll hair
 Let the good times roll
 Oooh let the good times ro-o-lllll
 Let the good times roll...

Jerry got up and hopped around, screaming and scratching it out. I came back in with another beer. He stopped and looked at me.

"Don't stop. You're making a good point there, Jerry."

"No, it's all crap," he said. "It's meaningless."

"That's true, too..."

He tossed down the guitar, walked into the bathroom. He turned on the hair dryer.

Over the racket, I heard the ding of the doorbell. Well, who knew?

I walked down and took a peep through the hole. I didn't recognize Scotty at first – he had grown a short blond-brown beard, and there was a ponytail coming out from underneath a white tennis cap. Two gold hoop earrings in the right earlobe. Also, he seemed a good twenty-five pounds heavier – big bulging gut and lousy breasts sagging in a light green T-shirt. Double-chin and the works. Maybe thirty-five pounds.

He was holding a big cardboard box. Inside I saw bottles, packages of food. Booze bottles. He hit the bell again.

"Let me in, man," he said, looking over his shoulder at the street. "C'mon, this neighborhood sucks..."

I opened the door. Scotty grinned, walked past me and set the box on the bench inside.

"C'mon, help me unload, man. I brought a bunch of stuff for you guys..."

"Goddamn, Scotty..."

We went out to the street. Scotty unlocked the back of his Malibu Rover and I helped him carry in three or four more boxes. It was bottles of booze mainly – Chivas Regal in purple sacks, whisky and bourbon, several brands of vodka, six or seven bottles of wine, about a case and a half of Tecate in cans, along with food – club sandwiches wrapped in paper, peanuts, crackers and olives, tortilla chips, a chocolate cake, a cherry pie, several packs of Dunhill cigarettes...

"Damn, Scotty – where'd you get it?"

"I got a buddy who works at the Truman Gardens... They were going to throw it away after this big party or some shit..."

"The hell they were. It looks unopened..."

"No, hell, man. Rich shit-fuckers bought it for their party, they don't care..." He shrugged. "My friend threw in a couple freebies, they got tons of it."

He threw his arm over my shoulder as we walked in.

"Haven't seen you around, man, since you got the promotion to the court job. I been missing you, man! It's not the same with Richie and you gone."

"That's cool, Scotty..."

Scotty sat down on the futon and cracked open a bottle of Johnny Walker Green Label. We each had a good slug. Jerry and I lit some of the Dunhills, menthol and normal. Scotty got up and opened another window, turned on a light. He took off his hat and untied his ponytail, letting his hair fall down his back.

"I know you guys don't really like me, but it's cool," said Scotty. "I think you guys are all right..."

"The fuck... what do you mean?"

"Shit, remember that time I called you? To ask you about some news shit? Well, you didn't hang up your phone right. You thought it was hung up, but it wasn't... I could hear you guys talking... You called me a *dick*... Said I was full of shit, all this type of shit... I heard you, Thor, tell Jerry I was this total *asshole* guy who couldn't write worth a shit... That I was this huge *asshole* guy, an awful shitty writer, a massive dickhead who didn't know shit about nothin'..."

We sat there quietly.

It was strange. I didn't remember Scotty ever calling, but I couldn't totally exclude it. Jerry wasn't sure...

"You crazy fuckhead!" I said. "That didn't happen!"

Scotty laughed. We all laughed. We clinked glasses and gulped.

We began opening the bottles and packs of food, whatever seemed good at the moment. It was all excellent stuff. I lined up three glasses in front of me – whisky, vodka, and one for an orange-flavored liqueur – mixing them all with beer slugs.

"Goddamn it," said Scotty, "what is that *crap* on your ceiling?"

Worms, we said.

Jerry grabbed the broom and knocked down a few on Scotty's head.

"Ah shit, shit!" Scotty exclaimed, brushing them from his arms to floor. Jerry and I laughed.

"Look at this place!" Scotty roared. "You guys live like pigs!"

We laughed and had shots. Jerry and I told Scotty a brief story about Heather and the funeral. This led to a story from Scotty about going back to Connecticut and his father telling him he had bone cancer. His father was nearly dead, apparently, bed-ridden all that jazz. Scotty had already figured out how many times he'd still have to see him – "probably no more than nine." We all hung our heads for a minute, thinking about that. Scotty talked about various people he knew who had died – suicides and car crashes, mainly. Jerry talked about a few he had known.

Well, I said, everything was sure sad, but the world was definitely going to be a worse and sadder place with Heather gone. Now, I said, we're stuck only with Candace.

Scotty didn't understand, but Jerry laughed.

We drank and ate and laughed like hell. Jerry started putting on albums – the Dead Kennedys and Corpse By Day, Velvet Underground's *Loaded*, the Pooh Sticks, *Zen Arcade*, Social D, *Screaming For Vengeance*, the Cult and *Kill 'Em All*…

At one point, we listened to "Spirit of the Radio" six times in a row, Scotty clicking it back on each time it ended. Here it was, no doubt, finally – the greatest song of all time. Question answered, none others need apply! We all swore it, over and over.

Scotty had brought several joints, we each had a bite. I cut out pieces of pie while Jerry mixed fresh cocktails. Scotty began throwing peanuts off the wall, off the ceiling, knocking down large clumps of worms. Once, I started lighting another cig with one already smoking in my mouth. Pretty soon, me and Jerry were smoking three smokes in our mouths each.

It was funny – oh *goddamn* it was funny.

"It won't be long before everyone is gone," said Jerry.

"I suppose I'll wind up dead and broken-hearted," I said.

"Bitches and money," said Scotty. "It starts and ends there. The rest is a bunch of junk."

"Asshole!" screamed Jerry.

We laughed. I went off to the bathroom to vomit for a while, then felt immediately better. As I stumbled back in, Scotty hit the side of my arm with a piece of chocolate crème cake. Jerry caught a piece of cherry pie in his neck, before nailing Scotty above the eye with a tinfoil cheese thing.

Before long, six or seven pickle slices were stuck to the wall.

Jesus, it was fun, we laughed so much. I poured myself three more.

At some point, Scotty fired up the internet and began clicking through various pictures that U.S. soldiers had taken in the war zone. They included shots of soldiers kicking the decapitated heads of "insurgents" like soccer balls, shots of heads blasted open against windshields, a few rather humorous shots of a body laying in the sand one place, its head laying a few feet behind and to the side...

We sat back as Scotty scrolled through the shots, laughing frequently. Goddamn stupid troops. They had been suckers. They had signed up to fight in Uncle Sam's gang, and they had believed, and they had known nothing. Just shout the word "freedom" and watch the Americans begin the killing, and the dying... They were already the forgotten heroes of a war that would be soon forgotten, except for the many years of movies about the mess that we'd soon have to start sitting though, and the ex-military homeless who would soon be littering the streets like old burger wrappers, and the dozens of massacres and shooting rampages they would inflict on their spouses, children, girlfriends and innocent bystanders after returning to the homeland. The scores of stabbings, beatings, strangulations and bathtub drownings, drunken suicidal onslaughts and terror sprees as the stress and crimes and bloody trauma finally boiled over...

Scotty clicked over to a different place that had hundreds of new pictures of U.S. troops torturing prisoners. America might be a lot of things, but never would she run short of dingbats ready and willing to twist the screws on helpless Arabs.

Here was our September 11 "payback," in full-color, hi-def brilliance. The soldiers seemed to especially enjoy bringing dogs around to frighten the Muslims. The naked prisoners appeared horribly terrified. Most of the Muslims had their hands tied behind their backs, sometimes wearing bags or underwear over their heads. The dogs appeared very angry, very upset. Another shot had a Muslim laying on his stomach, a bag over his head and blood streaming out a wound on his leg. A U.S. soldier was on top, pressing his knee into the guy's back.

U.S. Military Field Manual: Proper Use of Dogs and Feces on Muslims, Vol. 1.

    Section 2.a.(i) – Once the soldier has stripped the target Muslim nude and secured him and/or her, the soldier is advised to bring in one (1) muscled and hungry attack canine (breed undetermined). The soldier is advised to let the Muslim squirm amidst his own blood and feces while being threatened by the vicious canine. The soldier is advised to take photographs of ensuing interrogation.

Section 2.a.(ii) – Soldier is advised to take one (1) pair of used underwear, preferably from menstruating American woman or European-based homosexual male, and place over head of bound and gagged Muslim. Underwear should be lightly stained with bodily excretions, as this causes maximum deep dark shame and humiliation for target Muslim. After securing underwear to head of Muslim, soldier is advised to bring in attack canine to threaten Muslim. Soldier is advised to take photographs during subsequent interrogation, informing Muslim that photographs will be released to media and/or his/her family unless desired information is promptly provided to interrogator(s)...

"Oh, shit! Oh, shit!"

"Oh, God! Oh, God!"

Pretty soon, Scotty found a stack of mail that contained Jerry's credit card bills. He tore open the envelopes and we laughed at the amounts - $3,104.23, $503.14... Oh, it was funny. Oh, it was a blast. We burned the bills and the rest of the mail in the sink, lifting all the windows high as the smoke poured out.

LIFE'S PEACHY!
Clown Gets Raise as Riot Rages

★ 46 ★

Yes, I've seen the tape, the mayor was saying on the TV. *My initial reaction is that it appears our officers acted properly, that procedures were appropriately followed, that our personnel were defending themselves within the limits of the law... It does not appear that they used excessive force against this obese African-American man – and I would go so far as to say the officers showed remarkable restraint and indeed, professional acumen, despite this troubled young African-American man's belligerent, threatening and combative behavior... Of course, there will be a thorough official investigation to determine what exactly transpired and the level of illegal drugs in this young African-American man's system... We will examine carefully all the factors that may have led to this incident. And we will, appropriately, go where the inquiry leads... Citizens can rest assured that their skilled officers of the law will leave no stone unturned in the search to discover the truth...*

"All right, that's enough." Sernath grabbed the remote and hit the mute. "That fuckhead Favella. I knew he would fuck this up."

He handed me the Evaluation.

```
OVERALL RATING: VERY GOOD
   Thor is a talented writer and
skilled reporter whose work has
frequently exceeded expectations... Thor
deals courteously and professionally
with his sources and generally gets
along well with Co-Workers and
Supervisors... His 100 percent Attendance
```

>   record is noted, as is his one citation
>   for violation of the Condor Plaza
>   Building No-Smoking Policy. Thor is
>   urged to take advantage of the
>   Company's Smoking Cessation Benefit.
>   1.87% Salary Enhancement *RECOMMENDED*

Sernath brought his hands together. "Sorry, we can't give you a COLA this year. That's straight from headquarters. Not in this economy. Nothing I can do about it…"

"How about a 7-UP or a Sprite, then? Hell, I'll take a Dr. Pepper…"

"No, it's a C-O-L-A. It means, Cost, C, Of, O, Living, L, Adjustment, A…"

"Sure, boss. It was just a joke."

He smiled. "Yeah, the funny guy. You're lucky I'm in a good mood."

We laughed. The TV showed the leaked security-tape film again – 380-pound LeRoy Zebrack getting sprayed, stunned and whacked by cops outside a Six Points MacBeefy's. A careful count showed that the police – five white officers, one black – had struck him 45 times with metal nightsticks. Even after they finally got him handcuffed, one officer – one of the whites – couldn't seem to resist zapping him three more times with pepper spray.

The people who kept track of such things had already said LeRoy was the 22nd male to die in a violent confrontation with Bay City police since 1998. The coroner would go on to muddle things somewhat by reporting that LeRoy suffered from an enlarged heart, obesity, and had "intoxicating levels" of cocaine, PCP and methanol in his blood – which perhaps played a role in LeRoy's unpleasant boo-hoo act in the restaurant that had resulted in a call to the police and his subsequent neutralization.

The TV cut to protesting crowds, shouts and angry faces, signs waving illegally upon sticks and metal poles: STOP BCPD RACIST TERROR / JAIL THE COPS / SHOOT BACK / POLICE ARE KILLING US. Sernath hit the volume.

CLOWN: *The mayor has just issued an appeal to citizens not to take the law into their own hands. Violence is no way to address complaints, in fact it is counterproductive. The mayor has promised to meet with community groups tomorrow morning to listen to concerns –*

The Nath hit the mute.

"Don't worry, you won't get a call. The desk will handle it. If I was you, I'd go home and lock the doors. Or get out of town, if you can."

"Not a chance, boss. I'd rather go down with the ship."

The Nath laughed. He stood and picked up his coat.

"I'm out of here. Lynn's picking me up. We're going to spend the night at the Sunspot Casino out in Lakeview."

"Cool," I said.

We shook hands.

"Nice work. Keep it up and you'll go places."

"Where?"

The Nath laughed. "Some place else."

One of my teeth, a lower molar on the right side, broke apart as I crunched on a chip during a solitary dinner at La Cantina Fiesta. I spat it out on to my plate, brown-black pieces of tooth mixed with tortilla chip and red salsa bits... The spot began to pulsate, there was pain every time I opened my mouth. Contact with the air seemed to make it worse.

I dropped the fork. I could forget about eating. It made sense, I guessed, I hadn't really brushed my teeth on a regular basis for several years. Perhaps, I thought, I hadn't really brushed them at all since the Chrissy days.

I came out to find the streets reeking of smoke. Cop cars, fire trucks and ambulances whizzed down Commerce. At least two helicopters seemed to be in action overhead. I walked a few blocks in the direction of the trouble, just sort of curious, then thought better of it.

My tooth hurt, my jaw throbbed. I saw a place called Ignacio's, went in and ordered a beer and a shot. I downed them both in about three minutes and ordered another round.

BREAKING: MAYOR URGES PEACE, RESTORATION OF LAW AND ORDER

Sirens screamed past the doorway, one about every three or four minutes. Pretty soon the place had filled up. The key was put in the lock and the door slammed shut.

The barman jumped on top of the counter: "Nobody else comes in here, only out, O.K.? If you stay, you can have two for one. But if they come in here, we all have to fight together."

The place erupted in cheers.

CLOWN: *To the folks watching at home, if you've got a fire or other emergency, the police and fire people are telling us it may be some time before they can reach you because of the, uh – well, I don't want to call it* rioting, *but the, uh – the looting and disturbances in Pine Ridges and downtown that we are now bringing you live… So hang in there while the authorities try to bring this situation under control…*

"Shit, I hope the cops kick their ass," said a weasel-necked guy two or three chairs down the bar. "I am goddamn *tired* of this bullshit!"

"Shit, I hope they burn it down," I said. "Yeah, man. I want to wake up tomorrow and see it all gone. The whole goddamn place. Every inch. A big, burning piece of ash…"

I took two long drinks off the beer, two quick sips from the scotch, another from the beer. I glanced at the television, then at the rows of bottles lined up in front of the bar mirror. There were a lot more laughs and fun inside those bottles than the television or these clowns would ever deliver.

"Hey, you hear this guy? He want to burn it all down!"

A guy with shaggy brown hair hanging down to his collar ran up. I stared off.

"Did I hear you say that YOU HOPE THEY BURN IT DOWN?"

"You bet," I said. "The whole goddamn place. Every inch. Why not? What else do you got?"

The clown bored me. I glanced again at the row of bottles. What a gorgeous sight. There were a lot of laughs and tears, beautiful thoughts and little devils writhing around in those bottles, just waiting to get out. It would all be pretty funny before anybody knew.

The guy stood there. I finally looked over at him. He looked at me. He was unshaven, black speckles across his mug. Skin hanging down. Cloudy brown eyes. Dank, unwashed hair over his ears. More skinny than wiry. MY OTHER CAR IS MY BEST FRIEND'S WIFE, his t-shirt said.

The fucker bored me. If he took a swing, so what.

A few of the others looked our way, then looked off. Nobody seemed much interested.

They were right – the TV was so much more fascinating.

I finished my round and ordered another. The fuck continued to stare at me, fists clenched.

"Hey, no trouble," said the barman, finally noticing the stand-off. He smacked his palms on the bar and tried to look threatening. "O.K.? O.K.? Take it outside if you want. Not in here."

"No problem," I said.

The guy walked off, went down and huddled next to his buddy on stools at the end of the bar. The buddy stared at me.

He bored me. I looked away.

Well, most people didn't know what to do. I didn't either. Oh, well.

CLOWN: *We are getting word now of at least three casualties in a shooting... The police are on the scene, more details on that as we get them... And the Fire Department is now saying they are battling seven separate fires... Police and fire reinforcements are being called in from Santa Costa and Meringue Counties... Governor Wattle has been awakened at the Governor's Mansion and he is reportedly considering a deployment of the National Guard...*

TV helicopter footage showed a warehouse on fire, flames coming out the window of a car, a small whirlwind of paper. The producers cut to a new feed of punks throwing a newspaper rack against a bank window. The rack bounced harmlessly off the glass, slid along the pavement, rattled to a stop. A different feed showed shop windows smashed open, fires raging inside, hoodlums running past carrying bean bags and toasters, teenagers running up and grabbing radios and electric blenders, riding off on bicycles...

WOULD-BE STEWARDESS GETS HEIGHT OPERATION
By Annabel Clonge-Smythe
Smith-Jones News Service

NEWTON, Kentucky - A 16-year-old Kentucky girl who was too short to become a stewardess has had an operation on both of her legs in a bid to gain a few inches and fulfill her dreams, her family announced Wednesday.

Emma Richards stopped growing when she was four feet, nine inches tall, well below the five feet, three inches minimum required to be a stewardess on commercial airline flights.

In January, she underwent a six-hour operation during which her femurs were broken and metal plates inserted, with the aim of enabling Emma to reach the minimum height requirement.

However, after spending four months in bed, Emma had gained only five inches – still less than her target.

"Emma didn't want to be four feet, nine inches – she wanted to be a stewardess," her mother, Irene Richards, said. "She knows what she wants from life. That's the whole point of the operation."

Since January, Emma has caught an infection and broken her legs twice because of her fragile bones. She is currently undergoing traction in a hospital in Newton, western Kentucky.

"We knew there were risks, but Emma is strong and has coped well," said her mother. "She had sessions with a psychologist before having the operation."

SHE'S THE BOMB:
Clown Cuddles with Court Cutie!

★ 47 ★

Cathy Fong was wearing a green-and-white striped stocking cap on her head. She had several fading purple hickeys on her neck.

"Looks like you got some love bites there..."

Fong tried to laugh. "No, I don't! It's just my skin. I have bad skin!"

I had met Fong at Bay Federal District Court – another fringe benefit of the job, you could suppose. Fong was a part-time Court Assistant – that is, she put court documents in their right places, made copies of court documents for people who wanted them, and sometimes answered the phone in the court's main office... She was good to know, I figured she might be able to help out if I needed some hard-to-get court record or something. But I had never needed any of that. All the records I needed had been very easy to obtain.

According to her internet page, Fong was pursuing a master's degree in Biopsychology at Bay State Technical University. She had told me to look at this internet page before we went out.

IT'S ME – CATHY FONG! Age: 20. Interests: cats, dancing, fun & positive people!, Red Hot Chili Peppers, massage, pronoia, soul, techno, jazz, emo, math rock, road trips, vegetarians, Freddie Prinz, Justin Timberlake!, Keanu Reeves, biopsychology...

Fong's ass hung low but it shook and wobbled, it seemed happy flab. She seemed to lose almost half her height when she took off her high heels.

"I'm sorry, it stinks over there... That's where the cat knocked over the bong." Fong laughed.

"Cathy Fong's bong. You got any pot, Fong?"

"Oh, sure..."

"You got anything to drink? That's what I really want. You look like you might have wine..."

She had half a box of some Australian red, cold from the fridge. She gave me the wine and a glass, then came out with the loaded bong. A fat fluffy cat, with white, orange and black tufts, walked in and jumped on the chair.

"This is Clooney," she said. "He farts, so if you smell something funny, it's not me!" Fong laughed.

"I'm allergic to cats."

"Are you?"

"Yeah... I'll be all right, as long as he doesn't sit on my face."

Fong laughed again and stoked the flame. We each had several long inhales. In between, Fong explained how she was "mostly a vegetarian," yet had remained "fat." She had thought becoming mostly a vegetarian would make her thin. But she couldn't keep off the chicken.

"It's because of the hormones they give the chicken. I heard that, I read that... I love chicken, I would eat it every day if I could... That's why everybody's fat, because all the chicken meat is white and squishy from the hormones... We're fat like the chickens! You have to look hard to find dark meat anymore, because they don't let the chickens run around. That's where the dark meat comes from."

"You're not fat, Fong. I like a little meat on the bones..."

"Come on, don't call me Fong! I told you I hate that! It's Cathy, O.K.?"

"All right, Cathy..."

Her room had six or seven posters of Keanu Reeves on the walls, gigantic movie advertising posters as well as action shots from different movies. She had a small microwave, a large television, school books, paperbacks by Patricia Cornwell, Martin Cruz Smith, J.R.R. Tolkien and Dan Brown... A note stuck on her refrigerator said: GET YOGURT!!!!

She came up and we kissed. She tasted something like peppermint and warm apple sauce. I rubbed her arms, brought my hands down and squeezed her hips. She backed away, pulled off her dark blue tank top. She undid the button and stepped out of her grayish jeans skirt... She had a tattoo of a space alien on her left shoulder, something that looked like a heart with wings on her lower back. Big brown nipples on darkly freckled breasts. Fong had what looked like a dragonfly, gold with a bit of diamond, pierced into her navel.

"Here's how I'm fat," said Fong. "Look, the Pencil Test."

She lifted a boob and put a pencil under. The boob flopped down. The pencil stayed in place, stuck between the boob and the rest of her body.

"And... ?"

"If I wasn't fat, the pencil would fall down! That's how you know!"

"Heck no... You've just got great boobs, Cathy Fong."

I drained the glass of cold Australian, gagged for a second, poured another full glass and drained half of it. I shook the box. Almost empty.

We had met up earlier at Rock Candide, where we had a couple drinks and shared a plate of fried tortilla strips with sides of sour cream and salsa. I was sort of liking Fong's massive brown lips, her hair pulled back in a ponytail beneath the stocking cap, the dimple when she grinned...

"I believe in *pronoia*," she had said, sitting across from me at the table.

"Sure you do, Cathy... What's that?"

"It's like the opposite of paranoia? Like, if you're paranoid, you think everything bad is going to happen. But with pronoia, you're thinking that everything good is going to happen... You know?"

"Does it really exist? Or is it just something you say to be so sweet and entertaining?"

"Oh, I don't know! To be honest... Oh! I never really thought about it. O.K., yes... I think it exists." She smiled.

"You're cute, Cathy. Really cute... And I mean that."

"Oh... Do you really?"

"Yes, absolutely. As much as I've ever meant anything."

The waiter swung by, I ordered two beers.

"I can't!" said Fong. "I'm not 21 yet!"

"Don't worry," I told the waiter, "they're for me."

Goddamn fool would only let me have one at a time.

Behind Fong, I noticed a guy setting down a steak knife on his plate. The knife's razor teeth caught the light, sending off silver flashes. The guy eyed me – weird burly skinhead guy. The guy seemed to mumble something to himself, moved his neck and shoulders in a strange way.

My guts spasmed, I took a beer slug. I didn't like anything about it. What was to stop him from coming over and stabbing me – from coming over and trying to cut off Fong's head as she sat there?

I drained the last of the beer.

"Let's go, Fong. C'mon, let's *do* something..."

"O.K., but don't call me Fong! I hate that! My name's Cathy."

"O.K., Cathy..."

I paid and we got up and took a little walk around the books section. Most of the bestsellers seemed very dull, very uplifting. *The New York Times* #1 Bestseller: STONED OUT OF MY GOURD: *One Man's Stunning Real-Life Victory Over Drug and Alcohol Addiction.* In the Fiction Section stood a large cardboard cut-out display for *Sex, Diamonds and a Cinnamon Latte.* It featured a short-haired blond in a polka-dot pink dress and the blurb: *A confused young girl's quest for love, life-ness and the perfect lipstick. The brilliant debut novel the critics are raving about!*

The magazines seemed so much shorter and more interesting: *The National Star*: BARBRA HELPLESS AS BODY BALLOONS! *Global Inquirer*: MADONNA: RUSSIAN MAFIA TRYING TO KILL MY BABIES! *Cosmopolitan*: WHAT TO DO WHEN IT'S HIS SPERM ON YOUR BREATH?! *Weekly World Eye*: PARIS IN PLASTIC SURGERY NIGHTMARE! *Music Monkey*: THE TOP 50 RAP-ROCK ALBUMS OF ALL TIME! *Maxximumm*: HOT BABES! DON'T QUESTION, JUST LAP IT UP!

We sat down next to each other on one of the couches. Fong started complaining about how she only got $10.48 an hour.

"$10.48? Fong, shit. I'm stuck at $9.31..."

"Oh, you're funny!"

"It's no joke..."

I told Fong the story of the homeless woman who was on trial for drowning her baby in a bucket of vomit. The lady had been "drinking gin" somewhere, then came back to the shelter and vomited into a mop bucket that was already filled with soapy water. She claimed during the trial that she had lain down with the baby on her chest, only to wake up to find the baby dead with its head in the bucket of puke water. She was holding the girl by her ankles – "I remembered she was going to fall off me," the lady had said.

"The prosecutor wants a minimum 25 years."

"They should give her life!" said Fong.

"Nah, they should set her free and forget about it... Everyone should forget about it."

"Well, maybe... but only if they tied her tubes so she couldn't have any more babies."

"Sure, Cathy..."

A whiny piano song by Norah Jones played on Fong's computer. I took off my shirt and started to give Fong a massage. I pulled back the comforter. Fong had many pimples on her ass, bright red ones, as well as bigger ones that were more purple in color. The lower back tattoo was indeed a heart with wings – a halo floating above the heart, a devil's tail twisting out below. Fluffy white angel wings on both sides... I squeezed the oil, letting it pour off her sides, using circular hand motions to rub it in from her shoulders to her thighs. Her skin shined, a dark gold in the lamp light. She rolled over and I looked down at her small, thick cunt – dark thick lips, the clit hood pierced with a little gold ring. The pubic patch appeared to have been the recipient of some care and dedication, the hairs styled to fan out in a neat diamond shape...

The thought kind of bored me, but I kneeled down and began lapping at her opening anyhow. Upon closer inspection, the gold ring appeared to be encrusted with a small amber bauble. I wasn't sure what do with it. I flicked it back and forth with my tongue several times. I put it in my mouth, gently pulled. Fong seemed to enjoy it.

Then it was her turn. She closed her eyes, her brow hardened in concentration.

Fong lacked touch, it was even a bit painful the way she did it – too fast, first of all, and also strangling it too much with her hand. Altogether too much straining back and forth – too much "show," not enough soul. Poor Fong.

Eventually I put an end to it and got on her on all fours, the heart wings tattoo staring up at me. I squeezed out a palm-full of oil, started to loosen up her butthole with the thumb of my left hand as I slipped in and out of her pussy. She never broke rhythm. I leaned forward, grabbed both boobs, then leaned back and pushed her down just a bit. My cock sprang out and up and I sodomized her. It seemed to slide in with a slight hiss.

"Oh, oh," she whispered. "Yeah... oh, yeah."

I could not come. I stroked and stroked away, but nothing. I rolled her on to her back and switched to her pussy.

Finally, a picture of Chrissy's bunghole exploded in my mind. I popped it out on to Fong's stomach.

✪

"That was cool," she said in the morning. "I love anal sex…"

"Do you?"

"Well, not everyday!" Fong laughed. "But yeah, I mean, if the guy's into it… Not, like, that there's been so many!"

"Do you have any aspirin?" I said.

"Yeah… You want coffee?"

"That'd be great, Cathy."

She brought it, and we sat there.

It wasn't long before Fong started talking again about the riots, which, according to the final official tally, had left 51 people dead and 133 injured over four days of fires, looting, drivers being pulled from their cars, and finally a city-wide curfew. Fong was still "pissed off." She "honestly" thought we "should blow up the roads so they can't get out of their jungle." She knew it was racist to say that, but look what they did. It was our town, too.

"Now hold on, Cathy. They could say they same thing about Japs like you. Just blow up the roads and throw them in camps if you start causing too much trouble…"

"I'm not Jap! I'm Korean…"

Fong said that actually, truly, honestly, she wasn't racist, but her father was. Her dad once heard somebody call them "jungle bunnies," and he thought it was amazingly funny, so that's what he calls them. But he can't talk English right, so he says it like "jungo buddies." Fong laughed.

"Does he go, 'Ye-yin-yah-yan-yin-yin-yih-yan-yan-yah-yin' when he says it?" I said, squinching my face and rattling my jaw up and down.

"Oh, *fuck you…*"

Fong looked off. Then she turned back and laughed.

"Actually, he does talk like that!"

I took two more aspirin and lit us both cigarettes.

"I don't really mind blacks so much," she said, "but I *am* racist when it comes to Chinese."

"Oh, yeah?"

"Yeah, I admit that. My dad probably made me that way. Chinese are the rudest people. They spit on the floor and throw bones."

"Chinks do? I've never seen it."

"Not here so much. But in China, in Asia..."

"Well, if you say so..."

Fong sat naked on the comforter and started painting her nails. The aspirin had a nice effect. I ran my finger along her calf and knee for a minute or two, then lay her back down. Fong giggled. I climbed on and stuck it in. The basic this time, no funny business. I went about ten minutes, until a sweat broke... We lay there, saying little. I watched the clock until 15 minutes went by. I rolled over and said I had to go.

"Oh, really?" said Fong. She sat up. "I thought we could go get brunch... C'mon, let's go! Let's take a shower and we can go over to Juneau's."

"I can't, Cathy... I've got to get to work later."

"On Saturday?"

"Yeah... This guy is going on trial. He smacked his daughter in the head with a coffee pot when he was having an argument with the mother. She's in a coma with brain damage. It's a big case, I got to write the preview for Monday morning..."

"Oh..."

As I started to dress, Fong asked if she could take my picture on her phone. I said O.K. I stood there and she snapped it. I thought she was done, but when I sat down to put on my socks she leaned forward and snapped another, this one of my limp cock.

"Now, Cathy... You're going to put this on the internet, is that it?"

Fong giggled. "No, I won't! I don't do that... I'm sorry... I'll delete it."

"It's all right... I don't give a damn what you do."

Fong walked me to the door, the comforter over her shoulders. We stood with the door open, bright sun slicing across the balcony on to our faces.

"Let's go see a movie tomorrow! Or sometime this week..."

"Sure, maybe. Only thing is, I might have to work at night..."

"Night court! You don't go to night court!"

"Yeah, sure. Listen, it was real great hanging out. Take care, Cathy. Good luck with your cat and everything. I'll see you in court..."

Fong laughed. She dropped the blanket and hugged me, pulled me forward and stuck her tongue in my mouth. I let her go at it for 15 or 20 seconds. We both could have used a good tooth brushing.

"Cathy Fong, you're the bomb..."
"Come to my office! I work Tuesday, Wednesday and Thursday."
"I know, Cathy..."
"I'll send you an email!"
"You bet..."

I went slowly down the stairs. Cathy Fong's door slammed. A cat, not Clooney, jumped out of a bush and leaped across the sidewalk in front of me.

PRESIDENT ORDERS RE-INVASION, FIRES GENERALS
By Thomas N. De Toode, Jr.
Washington Post Staff Writer

WASHINGTON – Amid escalating violence and continuing slaughter, President Wolfgang G. Mnung announced Thursday that he has ordered the re-invasion of the country already occupied by more than 150,000 U.S. troops.

In a nationally-televised speech from the Oval Office, the president, clad in a set of dreadlocks and a yellow leather codpiece, also announced he had relieved from duty all generals responsible for the war effort thus far.

Mnung further warned all neighboring regional countries that they risk being bombed by U.S. forces and invaded unless they halt their "meddling" in the affairs of a "sovereign nation where America is trying to implant democracy and free markets."

"Make no mistake," the president said, reading from prepared remarks, "the blame for this situation lies with the troublemakers and terrorists who are resisting our generosity and reverting to age-old tribal blood-feuds and an irrational fear of modernity and progress. We have given the gift of freedom, but a gift must also be received."

The president continued: "We must honor the valiant American soldiers who have been killed by continuing to kill the terrorists and insurgents who have killed them, until victory is achieved and killing is no longer necessary. Because failure and defeat are not an option. In America, as we know, winning is not everything – it is the only thing."

The president's speech came as butchery and bombings around the country claimed the lives of another 160 local police and civilians. The U.S. military reported the deaths of 11 American soldiers, including three who were castrated and hung from a bridge as thousands of onlookers cheered.

U.S. F-16 Warhawk fighter-bomber aircraft later bombed the bridge in what officials described as a successful operation against "terrorist provocateurs."

Earlier Thursday, the Congressional Budget Office reported that the war effort has so far cost American taxpayers more than $1.3 trillion. The office reported, however, that its investigators were unable to "reliably account" for nearly half of this total amount, and were thus unable to say whether it had been spent for its intended purposes.

NEW GAL PAL CLAIMS:
Better Living Thru Therapy!

★ 48 ★

It was warm and sunny the day Joyce and Jerry showed up to move Jerry out. They drove up in a white rental van.

Joyce, according to Jerry, had a "degree in brain surgery" and was enrolled in a work-experience program at Bay City Medical University. What they did there, apparently, was experimental surgeries on rats. According to Jerry, Joyce's job was to knock out the mouse, lock him into a contraption, then use a laser and scalpel to remove the top of his skull. Later, other experts would come in to work on the brain.

Jerry had met Joyce at a Narcotics Anonymous meeting. Shortly thereafter, Jerry had also joined Alcoholics Anonymous.

"You should go too," he had said to me.

"Forget it, not a chance…"

"O.K., but you're only fooling yourself… I feel for you, bro. I know how it is to be lost in your pain. You just need to know there's a way out. People are there for you."

"Thanks for caring so much."

"I am sincerely trying to help you."

Joyce was a big girl, nearly six feet tall, four or five inches taller than Jerry. She wore a purple sweater, her bulky thighs covered with loose blue jeans. She was light-haired and full-faced, with a look to her eyes that seemed to combine wholesomeness and insanity.

After his first date with her, Jerry told me she had been a practicing lesbian for several years. But the lesbianism was several years in the past now.

After the second date, he told me that she believed I was a big part of his problems.

"You're not the cause, but more of a symptom that reinforces all the reasons why I'm unhappy..."

"You think so?"

Jerry shrugged. "There might be something to it... I don't want to dog you, bro, we've been through too much... Her thing was, she said I can't ever be my *real* self around you, around people like you... To be honest, I see what she means. I don't want to be harsh on you, man, it's not *you* – you know? I'm in charge of who my friends are. Do you see what I mean?"

"No. Yeah. No. Yeah. Absolutely not. Sounds like crap, bro. C'mon, wake up! What is all this?"

"Listen to me, bro – I smoked heroin with Candace. I smoked heroin with the girl that killed my baby. Think about *that*."

"Shit... I don't want to think about it. That sucks, man."

"Think about that... I murdered my *baby*, man. Or at least I let Candace murder it. It's nearly the same thing, bro. It's something I'll always have to live with. I can be forgiven, but I don't know if I'll ever be able to forgive myself... You know what I mean? There's no excuse for people who kill babies as a birth-control method for their personal convenience. There was a *baby* moving around in there, man! My baby. And she sucked its brain out and they threw it in the trash."

"I'm sorry, man..."

"Who knows what it would have become? Even if it had lived a shitty life, it still would have been worth it. Just to be like me and you, talking, that's worth everything, isn't it? Could have been a guy like me and you. Why would she want to take that away?"

"It hurts, Jerry, I know it hurts... I don't have an answer..."

"I mean, doesn't it feel great to be alive? Even if it feels bad sometimes, doesn't it feel great?"

"Yeah, it feels all right, Jerry."

Jerry had cut his hair short and grown out his goatee. He had kept the earrings, but got rid of the contact lenses. He wore glasses everywhere now.

The latest thing was Joyce had converted him to Christianity. They went several times per week to a church where the priests and other high honchos were nearly all homosexuals and lesbians. They held barbecues and ping-pong nights. Church of the New Christ Savior Risen, it was called.

"You did *what*?" I remember saying.

"See, that's part of the problem," said Jerry. "No one ever listens to what Jesus really says. Jesus offers the way out, bro... He says we don't *need* all this craziness, this garbage. We don't need to destroy ourselves. He says 'Let it be, because I am the truth and the light.' He doesn't lay all these trips on you – that's not Jesus. That's other churches and people that abuse him. Jesus just shows... how easy it is to be a good person, to cast your troubles away and try to help others, to forgive and go on... That's why, like – I forgive you, Thor... I apologize to you, and I forgive you."

"Well, shit... I forgive you, too, pal."

"You don't really mean it. You're just saying it. Or do you?"

"Sure, I mean it. I don't hold anything against you... You're my best pal."

He came forward and we had a hug.

"This world's coming to an end," said Jerry. "I want you to be ready, bro. Nobody knows how or when, but we know it's coming. This whole place is gonna go up in flames, man. It'll be a question of who's ready and who's not. I hope you'll be ready."

"I'm ready, Jerry. I'm waiting for it like everybody else. Don't worry about me. I'll be just fine."

It took about 45 minutes for the three of us to load Jerry's things into the van. Joyce seemed very bothered by the worms in the apartment, she recommended that I move out and that the city health authorities be called in. She offered to call them herself. She claimed to be worried about my health.

"It's all right, Joyce," I said. "They're not really bothering anybody..."

When we were done, I offered to take them out for a drink and a hot dog. They agreed, but added they only had "about an hour."

I climbed into a crawl space in the back of the van, and Joyce drove us the mile or so to The Hacienda. I ordered a pitcher of beer and three shots of tequila, despite their protestations. They insisted that they would not and could not drink, under any circumstances – and they did not. Joyce had a green tea. Jerry had an O'Doul's non-alcoholic, then settled for a tea himself.

I drank their shots and the beer pitcher. I went out for a smoke, came back and ordered another pitcher and two more tequila shots.

"We said we don't drink..."

"Don't worry... they're for me."

We sat there.

Jerry went off to the toilet and Joyce asked, "So what are you going to do, Thor?"

"Not much." I took a slurp, raised my glass. "You're looking at it. Continue until victory."

"What do you call 'Victory'?"

"I'll know it when I see it."

I slugged a tequila, gulped beer.

"Maybe there is no victory, Joyce…" I took more drinks. "Maybe this is the victory right here. Bottoms up, baby…"

She looked at me, shook her head. She sipped tea, smiled sadly.

"Living healthily is the only victory," she said.

"Joyce," I said, "do you know what they used to call *syphilis?*"

"Oh, come on… What's that supposed to mean? You're projecting…"

"They called it the Frenchman's disease. Except in France, where they called it the Italian disease…"

"Boy, you've really got a problem…"

"Hey, Joyce – when did the fly fly?"

"*What?*"

"When the spider spied her…"

"You're crazy…"

"Hey, Joyce, listen… what weighs more – 100 pounds of iron, or 100 pounds of feathers?"

She looked off.

"Joyce, I'm waiting…"

Jerry came back.

"C'mon, I don't want you guys to fight. You're important people to me… Can't I even leave you alone for a second?"

"We're not fighting…"

Joyce stood up. She had started crying.

"We're gonna go, Thor," Jerry said.

"O.K., man. Let's get together real soon…"

"Yeah… You should go to a meeting, Thor."

"Sure, man…"

I licked the bottom of the tequila glass. I sat there and downed the last of the beer from the pitcher.

U.S. STUDENTS: TOO MUCH MEDIA FREEDOM
By Sandra Gibbering
Shanft-Micro Newspapers

CLEVELAND – Nearly 40 percent of American high school students say the news media ought to be more restricted, and that the government should be able to approve newspaper, television and radio stories before publication or broadcast, according to a new survey.

The survey of 115,114 tenth, eleventh and twelfth graders found that 39 percent believe newspapers and broadcasters should need "government approval" of stories before publication or airing.

Thirty-seven percent of the students say they believe news media should be able to transmit stories "freely," while 23 percent had "no opinion."

The survey was commissioned by the Thomas R. Erdelyi Foundation and was conducted by the Sociology Department of the University of Southern Utah (USU).

VICTORY! Clown Wanders Through Death, Misery

★ 49 ★

The guy in line ahead of me paid the $1.48 charge with a combination of pennies, nickels and stamps, then put his empty wallet in his front pocket for safekeeping. He looked around nervously, as if to see if someone was watching.

Well, he was right. You could never tell anymore. But it was only me.

The guy pulled the cap lower over his eyes, yanked up his pants by the belt. He grabbed his milk, bread loaf, and three oranges and hobbled out.

Times were tough, that was for sure. Times were getting tougher, of that there could be no doubt.

Beardsley Blunkett was waiting in the darkness in front of the place when I got back. Beardsley had sprung for tickets to see Sand People, Spikenard and Carriage of Sorrows at The Gecko – he had driven up, his big night out in the city. Beardsley still lived with his parents. He did something in an insurance office.

Beardsley appeared to be going to seed, rapidly – he had shaved off his beard, once so massive and defiant, with a number of critters living inside, to get the job, and he was even fatter than before. His arms had gone all puffy, with a series of red welts stretching down to his wrists. It was apparently an "allergic reaction" of some kind. He told a long story about it. I didn't really pay much attention.

We had a few from the bag I had brought, then Beardsley took one out and lit it. He was a freak for the pot, always had been. Not so much the pot, it seemed, but rather the growing of it, the techniques and so forth. He seemed to almost prefer the growing to the smoking – he could talk about the work of cultivation for hours, the beauty of the flowers. He grew it in various places in his parents house – up on the roof, mainly. He claimed they didn't know.

I had a puff or two. It seemed fair to horseshit, but I couldn't really be sure.

"Hey Thor, man... What's all that... *stuff* on your windows?"

"Worms, Beardsley..."

"*Worms?* They're everywhere. They're... all over the ceiling..."

"Sure, Beardsley... If they fall on you, just flick 'em off. They won't bite..."

"They're like... on every inch..."

"Sure, Beardsley."

Beardsley took a disc out of his backpack. It was the new Hindu Zoo, he said. He put it in Jerry's old player. I opened a fresh bottle. The record twanged, banged and moaned.

"You like it?"

"It's all right, Beardsley..."

"I like it. I think it's cool..."

The tunes rattled and clanked. A clump of worms fell on Beardsley's shoulder. He slapped them away.

"Come on, Thor... That's *disgusting*, man..."

"Yeah..."

Beardsley was too worked up. I told him to drink faster.

Worms fell and slid, the music clattered and droned. Beardsley started talking about this "hot chick" who had started working in his office. She sat several desks away, looking hot the whole day. He was jacking off to her all the time, he explained. She was hot, very hot. She wore these short tight hot skirts. Every guy in the office was jacking off to her.

One day, Beardsley said, he had to stay late at the office. He realized that no one was around. He got up and walked over to her desk.

"I leaned down and I sniffed her chair, man... I did!"

"Did you smell cunt?"

"Yes, I did... I think I actually did!"

"The fuck you did," I said, "that's a fucking lie!"

I got up to take a piss. I returned to find that Beardsley had flipped on the television. A pro-football show – *Jack-Hammers*, they called it. The film showed players flying through the air and smashing into each other at incredible speeds. A guy screamed through the air like a missile and smacked into some other guy, whose helmet flew off. The ball bounced away. Job well done. The guy lay groggily on the fake grass, looking half dead. A few players jogged over to help him up.

CLOWNS: *No fear, no fear... but then he got... JACK-HAMMERED!*
Clowns giggled.

The show cut to another play. A guy ran out for a flip-pass on the side. Right as he was about to grab it, he was hit smack in the gut by a guy flying like a torpedo. The torpedo got up and jogged off. The guy who was hit flopped around in agony on the turf. He finally struggled to his feet. The clowns giggled.

CLOWNS: *No fear, no fear... but then he got... JACK-HAMMERED!*

The film showed the next guy leaping into the air in slow-motion, ready for the catch. The bomb came in, right on target, just inches from his fingers...

CLOWNS: *No fear, no fear...*

"Turn off the TV, Beardsley..."

"Aw, you don't like it? It's a cool show..."

I sucked from the whisky with ice cubes, had a knock of the beer. A clump of worms fell from the wall into the corner.

"Fuck John Elway," I heard myself saying. "All right, Beardsley? Just fuck him... I don't care how good he supposedly was. He sucked. He totally sucked..."

"Aw, man... that's gnarly..."

"Fuck Tom Brady too, O.K.? Yeah... He totally, really sucks. And fuck Joe Montana while were at it... He totally stank..."

"Aw, man. They won four Super Bowls..."

"No, they sucked. Only four? That's not enough. Gimme a break, man. They were awful, absolutely terrible. Nobody was worse. Troy Aikman, too. Chipmunk-faced redneck, he didn't even know which end of the ball was up..."

"Aw, man. Man, man. Don't do this..."

It was finally time to go. I locked up and we went around the corner to Verdugo, up toward the bus stop. Off to the side, I saw Mr. Goodbar. He was passed out in the shadow of a chain-link fence, laying next to a couple bottles and torn strips of cardboard.

"Goddamn Goodbar," I said.

"Huh?" said Beardsley.

"Nothing, Beardsley..."

⭐

After the show, we decided to head down to Tommy Bong's. We cut through on Sycamore, trying to get back to Coronado.

"Wasn't it great? Don't you think?"

"It was all right, barely. No, I don't know, Beardsley... They didn't murder rock n' roll, if that's what you mean. They were soft, man. I wasn't worried for a second..."

"That's asking for a lot, man... Murder rock n' roll?"

"It was the least they could do..."

"You think so?"

"Of course, Beardsley..."

We were about to cross over when we heard a shout. Several guys were running down the walk towards us.

"GET HIM! GET HIM!"

I wasn't really interested and started to move to the side. Beardsley, however, stepped in, stuck out his ass and threw a body block. The guy tried to dodge around, but it was too late. He swung his arm crazily and crashed into Beardsley. They both went smacking to the ground.

The other guy was already up on his knees, trying to squirm away. I ran over and jumped on him, throwing him on to his back. I wrestled him down and sat on his chest, my knees holding down his arms.

After a few seconds of chaos, I noticed that Beardsley had caught it near his left eye. Blood was pouring down his face.

"You all right, Beardsley?"

He grunted, shook his head, wiped at the blood.

"Get off me, man, fuck!" said the guy. He writhed beneath me, trying to free his arms. *"Get the fuck off me, asshole!"*

The two guys who had been chasing behind showed up. They explained something about how they had caught the guy breaking into a car.

"LIAR! Get off me, motherfucker!"

He squirmed beneath me a little more, then hit me in the eyes and nose with a gob of spit. My head jerked back, stunned and blinking.

Beardsley ran over and kicked the guy in the side of the head. He was about to do it again when I screamed.

"STOP IT! FUCK, STOP IT!"

The guy writhed, rolled his head.

"What are you gonna do," he rasped, "kill me?"

I looked over at Beardsley. "Should I? Should I just go ahead and kill him?"

"Don't," the guy whined, starting to cry. "Don't kill me, man... please."

Beardsley was bending down, picking up pieces of his broken glasses, while at the same time holding his shirt to his face to catch the blood. He shrugged.

"Yeah, why not..."

"No, don't," said one of the guys whose car had been broken into. "I already called the cops..."

"All right... Anybody got a napkin?"

Nobody did. I wiped away the spit with my shirt.

Four cop cars arrived a minute or two later. For a while, it looked like they might arrest me. A pair of the cops leaned me up against a tree and patted me down.

"Listen," I said, "I'm with the media..."

"Yeah?"

"Yeah..."

I took out my press badge.

Everything eventually got sorted out. They handcuffed the bad boy and put him in the back of a police car. No charges would be filed against Beardsley and I. The car drove off. Two other cops went down the block to investigate the car break-in, while another flatfoot set up Beardsley with a bandage from a first-aid kit.

We shook hands with the cops and walked off. I was shaking pretty hard. I was looking forward to getting into Tommy Bong's and drinking it off. It took Beardsley ten or fifteen minutes to calm down. He was worried now that they were going to break into his car back at my pad.

"How do you live in this fuckin' place?" he said. "I couldn't do it."

"I don't know, Beardsley... I got to do something... You got any ideas?"

✪

Bong's kicked us out at 2:30 on the spot. We wandered down Verdugo ten or twelve blocks until Sweet-O Donuts appeared on the right. Beardsley sprang for two coffees and a tray of cakes – two vanilla crèmes, two bearclaws.

Beardsley talked about how his mother was going in for surgery next week. She was going to get her stomach "stapled" or something. The doctors said it could save her life. She needed to lose at least 140 pounds, according to Beardsley.

"You think it'll work?"

"It's got to," said Beardsley. "It's the only hope."

I had the vanilla crème, some of the coffee, then the bearclaw. I was standing in line for a pair of rainbow sprinkles when the boom went off.

It seemed to last several seconds, making the Sweet-O windows vibrate and hum.

Half of us jumped. The other half ducked. There was a squeal of tires, then nothing.

Finally someone went out, the door shaking the chime.

I forgot about the sprinkles. I grabbed Beardsley and we went out to the corner for a look.

The guy was laying in the middle of the intersection. The white Chrysler Cutlass Supreme 10 or so yards ahead of him. Driver's door open, headlights on, engine still running.

Both his arms were thrown to the right. His bandanna had been knocked off, a pool of blood and brains off to the side of his head. We watched as the pool overfilled and a stream of the stuff, mainly red but also some orange and pink, started running down the pavement toward the curb.

"Is that brains?" said Beardsley.

"Goddamn it," I said.

The guy had been wearing some kind of snakeskin slippers on his feet, in the pattern of the rattlesnake. One of them had been knocked half off his foot.

"He must've got out... tried to go after them," said Beardsley.

"Yeah... and then his brain fell out."

I heard water running in the gutter at my feet. I watched as some of the blood and brains made it down. The stuff mixed in with the water, swirled briefly, traveled on its way.

I thought about dialing the office – sudden death in the middle of the street.

I got out the phone, then put it back in my pocket.

I just wasn't in the mood. Clowns would have to wait.

Both sides of the block started to fill up with the concerned and curious. The first cop car arrived. The flatfoot got out, had a look, went back to his rig and called it in. He put the radio down and walked toward us on the curb.

"Get outta here, ya sickos... There's nothin' more to see..."

Young girls wearing sparkly, pastel-colored hooded sweatshirts had arrived from somewhere. They came up to the edge of the curb, arms full of flowers.

They were sad, sad, sad. They cried out, words in Spanish. Scumbag's original fan club, apparently.

Tears shined on their smooth faces, reflecting blinking cop light. They tore off rose petals and threw them into the street. Some of the petals floated down to the gutter, hit water, traveled on.

A helicopter fluttered low, blowing air, shooting a light. Seconds later, five or six more cop cars roared up. Cops jumped out and began setting up a perimeter tape. A pack of four cops began moving through the crowd. That was the signal for most of the loogies to exit.

As a cop examined my press badge, an orange *COP PARTY* van drove up, escorted by a black and white. The *COP PARTY* clown crew clomped out and trained their clown cams on Stiffy the Scumbag.

They'd love it out in Nebraska. They'd gobble it right up.

I lit a smoke.

"Let's go, Beardsley..."

✪

We continued down Verdugo a ways, then went north up Pickwick. The edges of the sky had begun to turn light blue and purple. We were waiting outside the Clipper Inn Lounge by 5:35.

"You still want more?" said Beardsley. "I can't believe that..."

"Nightcap. One for the road, Beardsley. You can do it."

As the magic moment approached, more and more early risers began to arrive. About 15 of us were waiting to go in by the time the clock hit 5:50. Mainly guys, along with a few hardcore haggard bags. It was always mostly guys.

"HAAA! Heh-heh!" a guy screamed to another guy down by the bus bench. "He been suckin' dat devil's dick!"

Somebody was passed out on the bench. The screamer slapped his thighs, whooped, kicked at the guy.

"Heh-heh! HAAA! He been suckin' dat devil's dick! Heh-heh! HAAAA!"

The barkeep pulled the door at 5:57. I spent the last of my wad on beers and shots. Nothing much but a buck and change left.

It was all right. I remembered a third of the whisky was still waiting in the bottle back at the place.

We sat in one of the red leather plastic booths. An orange glass candle holder was screwed to the center of the table. There was no candle inside, just trash – candy bar wrappers, Q-tips, bottle caps and crumpled cigarette packs mainly, some of it burnt.

A mural of a green dragon with smoke shooting out of its nostrils had been painted on the wall to our right. Graffiti had been scrawled over most of it.

Somebody ran over and put "Night Fever" on the jukebox. In the booth next to us, I saw a guy drink down his bottle in one gulp.

He walked back up to the bar, turned to us and said, "Hey, let's bet!"

He took the fresh bottle from the barkeep, chugged it down, set it on the bar. He had a strip of dirty dark brown hair running long down the back of his neck like a rat's tail. Sideburns, a pair of silver-stud earrings, a black flower or some damn thing tattooed on his neck. He reached into his pocket and took out a quarter.

"Heads you buy our table... tails we buy yours."

"You got four guys," said Beardsley.

"C'mon, it's a bet!"

"All right," I said.

We went over to the bartender for the flip. He walked under the light and tossed it.

Tails.

The guy took out his wad and paid us a new round – beers. We shook hands.

Five minutes later he was back. He tossed the coin, caught it.

"O.K., let's go..."

"All right, sure."

We got up and went over. The barkeep tossed. Tails. The guy paid another two beers, another for himself. Beardsley slapped me five.

The guy was in back in less than a minute.

"Nah, that's it, I'm broke," I said. "Can't go, man. Honest, I got nothing. A bet's a bet, that's it, sorry..."

The weirdo jumped forward, swung his arm and smacked me on the back, between the shoulder blades.

"No, man! Come on, let's go! You *owe* us..."

Goddamn drunks. I wasn't in the mood any more.

I shot up, my thighs smacking the table edge. Bottles and glasses crashed into each other.

"Hands off, fuckhead! I don't owe *shit!*"

The freak froze for a second, then waddled over to the other side, mumbling something at his buddies.

His buddies looked over hatefully.

"That's *bogus*, man" one of them said.

"That's *bull*," said another.

"You didn't have money?" Beardsley whispered. "No money at all?"

I shrugged, took a long pull. Good and cold. I took another.

Beardsley stood. "I'm leaving, man…"

"Where ya goin', Beardsley?"

"I'm gonna drive home."

"Oh, yeah?"

"Come with me, man. Don't stay here. Those guys, they might, they, look at them…"

"They won't do a damn thing, Beardsley…"

"I'm serious. Come on, let's go, man…"

"Quit your damn worrying."

I glanced at the table. Beardsley had two full beers and a half left, along with the shot.

No problem, I could handle it for him.

All right, Beardsley, we'll see you later. Chomp-chomp, kid.

Beardsley turned and walked out.

★ THE END ★

About the Author
Thor Garcia was born in Long Beach, California. He has worked as a journalist in Los Angeles, San Francisco, New York City and Prague, Czech Republic. His other books include the story collection TUND (Litteraria Pragensia, 2011).

www.ingramcontent.com/pod-product-compliance
Lightning Source LLC
LaVergne TN
LVHW041616060526
838200LV00040B/1306